By the same author

Arturo's Island (1959)

HISTORY | A NOVEL

10.95

HISTORY

A NOVEL

Elsa Morante

TRANSLATED FROM THE ITALIAN BY WILLIAM WEAVER

Alfred A. Knopf, New York, 1977

THIS IS A BORZOI BOOK

PUBLISHED BY ALFRED A. KNOPF, INC.

Translation Copyright © 1977 by Alfred A. Knopf, Inc.

All rights reserved under International and Pan-American Copyright Conventions.

Published in the United States by Alfred A. Knopf, Inc., New York, and simultaneously

in Canada by Random House of Canada Limited, Toronto. Distributed by Random

House, Inc., New York. Originally published in Italy as *La Storia: Romanzo*

by Giulio Einaudi Editore, S.P.A., Turin.

Copyright © 1974 by Elsa Morante and Giulio Einaudi editore s.p.a., Torino

Library of Congress Cataloging in Publication Data

Morante, Elsa [date]   History: a novel

Translation of La storia: romanzo

1. World War, 1939–1945—Italy—Rome (City)—Fiction.

I. Title.

PZ3.M7953Hi3   [PQ4829.0615]   853'.9'12   76–45755

ISBN 0–394–49802–X

A limited edition of this book has been privately printed.

Manufactured in the United States of America

First American Trade Edition

Por el analfabeto a quien escribo

There is no word in the human language capable
of consoling the guinea pigs who do not know
the reason for their death.

(*A survivor of Hiroshima*)

. . . thou hast hid these things from the wise and prudent,
and hast revealed them unto babes . . .
for so it seemed good in thy sight.

Luke 10 : 21

Contents

• • • • • • • 19 - -

". . . procure me a catalogue, a pamphlet,
because out here, Mother, news of the
great world does not arrive . . ."

(from Siberian Letters)

. 1900–1905
The latest scientific discoveries concerning the structure of matter mark
the beginning of the atomic century.

1906–1913
Nothing very new, in the great world. Like all the centuries and the
millennia that have preceded it on earth, the new century also observes the
well-known, immobile principle of historical dynamics: power to some,
servitude to the others. And on this rule are based, in agreement, both the
internal order of society (at present dominated by the "Powerful," known
as the capitalists) and the international order (known as imperialism)
dominated by certain Nations also known as "Powers," which have virtually
divided the entire surface of the globe into their respective properties, or
Empires. Among them, the latest arrival is Italy, which aspires to the rank
of Great Power, and to reach it has already taken armed possession of some
foreign countries—weaker than she—forming a little colonial property, but
not yet an Empire.

Though always in menacing and armed competition among themselves,
the Powers from time to time join in blocs, for common defense of their
interests (which are also, on the domestic side, the interest of the "powerful." For the others, those in servitude, who have no share of the gain but
still must serve, such interests are presented in terms of ideal abstractions,
varying with the variations of advertising methods. In these first decades
of the century, the favorite term is Fatherland).

At present, supremacy in Europe is disputed by two blocs: the Triple
Entente of France, Great Britain, and czarist Russia; and the Triple
Alliance of Germany, Austria-Hungary, and Italy (Italy will later shift to the
Entente).

At the center of all social and political movements are the big industries, promoted, for some time now, with their enormous and increasing
development, to systems of mass industry (reducing the worker to "a simple
accessory of the machine"). The industries need the masses as workers and,
conversely, as consumers. And since labor in industry is always at the service
of the Powerful and the Powers, among its products prime importance is
naturally given to arms (the armament race), which in a mass-consumption
economy, find their outlet in mass warfare.

1914

Outbreak of the First World War, between the two opposing blocs of Powers, later joined by other allies or satellites. The new (or perfected) products of the armament industry go into action, among them tanks and gases.

1915–1917

Though most of the country's citizens are opposed to the war (and are therefore called defeatists), the King, the nationalists, and the various powerful interests prevail. Italy enters the war on the side of the Entente. Among others, the United States, a Super-Power, also sides with the Entente.

In Russia, end of the war against the great Powers, following the Marxist revolution for international social-communism, led by Lenin and Trotsky ("Workers have no Fatherland" "Make war on war" "Transform the imperialist war into civil war").

1918

The First World War ends with the victory of the Entente and its present allies (twenty-seven victorious nations, including the Japanese Empire). Ten million dead.

1919–1920

Representing the victorious Powers and their allies, seventy people are seated at the peace table, to establish among themselves the new division of the world and to draw the new map of Europe. With the end and dismemberment of the defeated Central Empires, the ownership of their colonies is transferred to the victorious Powers, and new independent European states are defined on the basis of nationality (Albania, Yugoslavia, Czechoslovakia, and Poland). Among other things, Germany is obliged to cede the Danzig corridor (valuable as an access to the sea for Poland), cutting its national territory in two.

The peace terms are contested as being unsatisfactory and temporary by some of the parties, among them Italy (the mutilated peace); and they prove unbearable for the peoples of the defeated countries, condemned to hunger and desperation (punitive peace).

Absent from the peace table is Russia, now surrounded and reduced to an international battlefield with the military intervention of the major Powers (France, Great Britain, Japan, and the United States) in the civil war against the Red Army. In this crucial test, and amid massacres, epidemics, and poverty, the Comintern (the Communist International) is founded in Moscow. It summons all the world's proletariat, with no distinction of race, language, or nationality, to the common goal of revolutionary unity, striving towards the International Republic of the proletariat.

1922
After years of civil war in Russia, ending with the victory of the revolutionaries, the new state, the USSR, has been formed. It is to represent the symbol of hope for all the "wretched of the earth," who from the war—lost or won—have gained nothing but a worsening of their trials; whereas it is to represent the famous "Specter of Communism," now menacing Europe, for the Powers and for the landowners and industrialists, for whom the war has been, mostly, a great speculation.

In Italy (headquarters of one of their most sordid branches) they join their servants and some ill-assorted objectors to the mutilated peace in a desperate fight to save their own interests. And they are not long in finding a champion and suitable instrument in Benito Mussolini, a mediocre opportunist, a "compound of all the flotsam" of the worst Italy. After having tried to launch his career under the banner of socialism, he has found it more advantageous to shift to the opposite side of the Powerful established figures (property owners, the King, and later also the Pope). With a platform consisting only of a guaranteed anti-Communism, truculent and vulgar, he has founded his fasci, a collection of vassals and assassins of the bourgeois revolution. And in such company, he defends his employers' interests with the terrorist violence of poor action squads of bewildered mercenaries. The King of Italy (a man with no title to distinction except the inherited title of king) gladly turns over the government of the country to Mussolini.

1924–1925
In Russia, death of Lenin. Under his successor, who has taken the name of Stalin (steel), the internal requirements of the country (collectivization, industrialization, defense against the Powers who have made a coalition in anti-Communism, etc.) cause an inevitable shelving of the ideals of the Comintern and of Trotsky (permanent revolution) in favor of Stalin's thesis (socialism in a single country). The dictatorship of the proletariat, predicted by Marx, after being reduced to the hierarchic dictatorship of a party, will eventually be degraded to the personal dictatorship of Stalin alone.

In Italy: totalitarian dictatorship of the Fascist Mussolini, who in the meanwhile has conceived a style of demagogy meant to strengthen his power at its roots. It is especially effective with the middle classes, who (through their pathetic ineptitude for true ideals) seek in his false ideals a justification of their own mediocrity: this demagogy consists of the appeal to

5

the glorious race of the Italians, legitimate heirs of history's greatest Power, the Imperial Rome of the Caesars. Thanks to this, and to other similar national directives, Mussolini will be exalted as a "mass idol" and will assume the title of Duce.

1927–1929

In China, the guerrilla war of the Communist revolutionaries begins, led by Mao Tse-tung, against the nationalist central government.

In the USSR, defeat of the opposition. Trotsky is expelled from the Party, and then from the Soviet Union.

In Rome, the Lateran Treaty between the Papacy and Fascism.

1933

In a situation analogous to Italy's, in Germany the established Powerful men turn over the government of the country to the founder of German fascism (Nazism), Adolf Hitler, a poor maniac, viciously obsessed by death ("The aim is the elimination of living forces"), who in turn is exalted to mass idol, with the title of Führer, adopting as his Super-Power formula the superiority of the German race over all human races. In consequence, the already-conceived program of the great Reich requires total subjugation and extermination of all the inferior races, beginning with the Jews. Systematic persecution of the Jews begins in Germany.

1934–1936

The Long March of Mao Tse-tung across China (7,500 miles) to elude the preponderant forces of the nationalist government (Kuomintang). Of the 130,000 men of the Red Army, 30,000 survive.

In the USSR, Stalin (also, by now, "mass idol") begins the "Great Purge," with the progressive liquidation of the old revolutionaries of the Party and the Army.

In accordance with the Duce's imperial formula, Italy employs armed violence to seize Abyssinia (an independent African state), and is promoted to the rank of Empire.

Civil war in Spain, provoked by the Catholic-Fascist Franco (called the Generalissimo and El Caudillo) for the benefit of the usual powerful forces, under the threat of the "Specter." After three years of devastation and massacre (among other things, in Europe for the first time whole cities, with their inhabitants, are destroyed from the air), the Fascists (Falangists) prevail, thanks to the solid assistance of the Duce and the Führer and the connivance of all the world Powers.

Führer and Duce form the Rome-Berlin Axis consolidated later in the military treaty known as the Pact of Steel.

1937

Having signed an anti-Comintern pact with the Axis countries, Imperial Japan invades China, where the civil war is temporarily halted so that both sides can make common cause against the invader.

In the USSR (politically isolated in a world of interests hostile to Communism), Stalin intensifies his system of terror at home, while in his foreign relations with the Powers increasingly adopts an objective Realpolitik strategy.

1938

In the USSR, the Stalin system of terror is extended from the higher echelons of the bureaucracy to the masses of the people (millions and millions of arrests, deportations to labor camps, indiscriminate and arbitrary death sentences in a convulsive multiplication, etc.). Still, the earth's oppressed multitudes—for that matter, ill-informed and deliberately deceived—still look to the USSR as the only homeland of their hope (hope difficult to give up, when there are no others).

Munich agreement between the Axis leaders and the Western democracies.

In Germany, after the bloody night known as the Kristallnacht, German citizens are virtually authorized to carry out unhindered genocide of the Jews.

Following the dictates of its ally Germany, Italy proclaims her own racial laws.

1939

Despite the conciliatory pledges given recently in Munich to the Western Powers, Hitler is determined to carry out his program, which demands first of all the satisfaction of German imperial claims against the punitive peace of twenty years earlier. So, after the annexation of Austria, the Führer proceeds to the invasion of Czechoslovakia (immediately imitated by the Duce, who annexes Albania) and then begins diplomatic negotiations with the Soviet Power of Stalin.

The result of the negotiations is a non-aggression pact between Nazi Germany and the Soviet Union—which allows the two parties to carry out double aggression on Poland, dividing the country between themselves. Hitler's immediate action against western Poland provokes response from the West; France and Britain declare war on Germany, initiating the Second World War.

This will be supplied by the tireless, incessant activity of the war industries, which, putting millions of human organisms to the machine, are

7

already turning out new products (among the first, super-tanks and super–armored cars known as Panzers, as well as fighter planes and long-range bomber planes, etc.).

Meanwhile, carrying out his own strategic plans (which already foresee an inevitable clash with Imperial Germany), Stalin, after the agreed invasion of Poland from the East, has proceeded to subdue the Baltic States by force, responding to Finland's incredible resistance, which will finally be quelled by Soviet arms. The Soviet industries also, in a totalitarian commitment, go into mass war-production, concentrating especially on new techniques of rocketry for carrying higher quantities of explosive, etc.

SPRING–SUMMER 1940

The first phase of the Second World War is marked by the Führer's rapid advance. Having occupied Denmark, Norway, the Netherlands, Belgium, and Luxemburg, he overwhelms France and reaches the gates of Paris. Convinced of the imminent victory, the Duce, who has remained more or less neutral till now, decides, at the last minute, to live up to his part of the Pact of Steel ("a few thousand dead will be worth it, for a seat at the peace table"); and he makes his declaration of war against Great Britain and France, four days before the Germans enter Paris. But neither Hitler's triumphant successes nor his peace overtures succeed in achieving the withdrawal of Great Britain, which instead engages in a desperate resistance. Elsewhere, Italian intervention causes the opening of a new front in the Mediterranean and in Africa. The Blitzkrieg, or lightning-war, of the Axis is extended and prolonged beyond all expectation.

Air war of Hitler against England, with uninterrupted bombings and total destruction of roads, harbors, installations, and entire inhabited cities. A new verb is invented: to coventrize, from the English city of Coventry, pulverized by the German air raids. The terroristic battle, continued without pause for weeks and months with the intention of breaking down British resistance (in view of a possible, decisive landing), does not, however, achieve the desired effect.

The action in progress in the West, meanwhile, does not distract the Führer from other secret projects of his own for an imminent action in the East against the Soviet Union (foreseen in the historic plan of the Great Reich, which calls for the extermination of the inferior Slavic race and the erasing from the earth of the Bolshevik Specter). But here again the Führer underestimates his adversary's resources, as well as the operation's risks.

Tripartite Pact: Germany-Italy-Japan, with the aim of establishing a "new order" (Imperial-Fascist) in Eurasia. The pact is signed also by Hungary, Rumania, Bulgaria, Slovakia, and Yugoslavia.

AUTUMN–WINTER 1940

Sudden Italian aggression against Greece, announced by those responsible as "an easy stroll." The ill-advised undertaking proves, instead, disastrous for the Italians. Driven back by the Greeks, in a disorderly rout, without supplies, they are overtaken by winter in the mountains of Epirus.

The Italian fleet suffers severe losses in the Mediterranean.

In North Africa, the Italians have difficulty defending their garrisons, threatened by the desert army of the British . . .

One January afternoon in the year
1941
a German soldier was out walking
in the San Lorenzo district in Rome.
He knew precisely 4 words of Italian
and of the world he knew little or nothing.
His first name was Gunther.
His surname is unknown.

1 One January afternoon in the year 1941, a German soldier was out walking, enjoying an afternoon's liberty, when he found himself wandering alone, through the San Lorenzo district of Rome. It was about two o'clock in the afternoon, and as usual at that hour there were very few people in the streets. None of the passersby looked at the soldier in any case, because the Germans, even if they were the Italians' comrades in the current world war, were not popular in certain working-class areas. Nor was the soldier in any way distinct from the others of the series: tall, blondish, with the usual excessive discipline in his bearing and, especially in the position of his cap, a provocative assertion of conformity.

Naturally, if anyone chose to observe him, he showed some individual characteristics. For example, in contrast with his martial stride, he had a desperate expression in his eyes. His face betrayed an incredible immaturity, although he was six feet tall, more or less. And his uniform—a really comical thing for a soldier of the Reich, particularly in those early days of the war—though new and fitting his thin body tightly, was short at the waist and in the sleeves, exposing his thick wrists, rough and innocent, like a worker's or peasant's.

He had, as it happened, grown suddenly, unseasonably, all during the last summer and autumn; and so, in his body's haste to reach maturity, his face, through lack of time, had remained the same as before. It seemed to accuse him of not having the minimum age requirement even for his very low rank. He was a simple recruit called up in the latest draft. And until the time of his summons to his military duties, he had always lived with his brothers and his widowed mother in his native home in Bavaria, near Munich.

His legal residence, to be specific, was the rural village of Dachau, which later, at the war's end, was to become famous for the camp on its outskirts devoted "to labor and to biological experiments." But at the time when the boy was growing up in the village, that insane slaughter-machine was still in its initial and secret testing phase. In the vicinity, and even abroad, it was actually praised as a kind of model reformatory for deviants . . . In those days, its inhabitants numbered perhaps five or six thousand; but the camp was to become more populous each year. At the end, in 1945, the total number of its corpses was 66,428.

However, just as the soldier's personal explorations could not extend (obviously) to the unheard-of future, so also towards the past, and even within the present itself, they had thus far remained very vague, few, and limited. For him, that little maternal hamlet in Bavaria signified the only clear, domestic spot in the tangled dance of fate. Beyond there, until he became a warrior, he had visited only the nearby city of Munich, where he went to do some jobs as an electrician and where, rather recently, he had learned to make love, thanks to an elderly prostitute.

The winter day in Rome was cloudy, with a sirocco wind. Yesterday had been Epiphany, "the holiday that ends the holidays," and only a few days earlier the soldier had ended his Christmas leave, spent at home with the family.

His Christian name was Gunther. His surname is unknown.

They had unloaded him in Rome that very morning, for a brief preparatory stage along his journey towards a final destination, knowledge of which was reserved for the General Staff, but kept from the troops. Privately, his companions in his unit guessed that the mysterious destination was Africa, where apparently there were plans to set up some garrisons to defend the colonial possessions of their ally Italy. This news had thrilled him from the beginning with its prospects of genuine exotic adventure.

AFRICA! For someone who is barely grown, whose journeys have all been by bicycle or bus to Munich, this is a magic name!

AFRICA! AFRICA!!
. . . More than a thousand suns and ten thousand drums
zanz tamtam baobab ibar!
A thousand drums and ten thousand suns
on the breadfruit and the cocoa trees!
Red orange green red
the monkeys play football with coconuts
Here comes the head Witch Doctor Mbunumnu Rubumbu
under a parasol of parrot's feathers!!!
Here is the white marauder riding a water buffalo
who combs the mountains of the Dragon and of Atlas
zanz tamtam baobab ibar
in the tunnels of the river forests
where the anteaters jump in droves!
I have a gold-bearing and diamond-bearing hut
and an ostrich has nested on my roof
I go dancing with the headhunters
I have bewitched a rattlesnake.
Red orange green red
I sleep in a hammock in the Ruwenzori
In the zone of the thousand hills
I catch lions and tigers like hares
I ride in a canoe on the hippopotamus' river
a thousand drums and ten thousand suns!
I catch crocodiles like lizards

in Lake Ngami
and in the
Limpopo.

. . . This stop, here in Italy, was his first foreign experience; and it could already serve as a foretaste of curiosity and excitement. But even before arriving, as he crossed the German border, he had been gripped by a ghastly, lonely melancholy, proof of his still adolescent character, filled with contradictions. To some extent, in fact, he was impatient for adventure; but to some extent, also, unknown to himself, he remained a mamma's boy. At times he vowed he would perform superheroic acts, in honor of his Führer; and at the same time, he suspected the war was a vague algebra, thought up by the General Staff, which had nothing to do with him. At times he felt ready for any bloodthirsty brutality; at other times, during the journey, he brooded constantly, in bitter compassion, about his prostitute in Munich, thinking how she wouldn't find many customers these days, because she was old.

As his journey proceeded towards the South, this sad mood prevailed over every other feeling, until he became blind to landscapes, people, to any sight or novelty: "Here I am," he said to himself, "being carried bodily, like a cat in a sack, towards the Black Continent!" Not *Africa*, he thought this time, but actually *Schwarzer Erdteil, Black Continent*: seeing the image of a black tarpaulin already stretched out above him to infinity, isolating him even from his present companions. And his mother, his brothers, the climbing vines on the wall of the house, the stove in the hall, were a vortex that spun away, beyond that black curtain, like a galaxy in flight through the universes.

This was his state when he reached the city of Rome and used his afternoon pass to venture, at random, into the streets near the barracks where his unit had been installed for their stay. And he happened into the San Lorenzo district, not through any choice, but like an accused man encircled by guards, who doesn't know what to do with his last mockery of freedom, useless as a rag. He knew a total of 4 words in Italian, and of Rome he knew only the bits of information taught in school. So he could easily assume that the old, decrepit apartment blocks of San Lorenzo were no doubt the ancient monumental architectures of the Eternal City! And when, beyond the wall of the enormous Verano cemetery, he glimpsed the ugly tombs inside, he may have imagined they were the historical graves of Caesars and Popes. This thought, however, did not lead him to stop and examine them. By now, Capitolines and Colosseums were piles of rubbish. History was a curse. And so was geography.

To tell the truth, the only thing he was looking for at that moment, instinctively, in the streets of Rome, was a brothel. Not so much because of any urgent, irresistible desire, but rather because he felt too alone. It seemed to him that only inside a woman's body, plunging into that warm and friendly nest, would he feel less alone. But for a foreigner in his position, oppressed by that grim and sullen mood, there was slight hope of finding such a refuge thereabouts, at that hour and with no guide. Nor could he count on a lucky encounter in the street; for though he had developed into a handsome youth almost without knowing it, Private Gunther was still fairly inexperienced and, basically, also shy.

Every now and then he released his tension by kicking the stones he came upon, perhaps distracting himself, for a moment, by pretending in his imagination to be the famous Andreas Kupfer, or some other personal football idol of his; but he immediately remembered his uniform, a fighter for the Reich. And he resumed his decorum, with a shrug that shifted his cap slightly.

The only lair that turned up, in his wretched search, was a half-basement, down a few steps, which bore the sign: "Remo's—Wine and Food"; and remembering that at noon, lacking appetite, he had given his rations to a companion, he promptly felt the need to eat and descended into that interior, lured by the promise of some consolation, however meager. He knew he was in an allied country: and in that welcoming cellar he expected—not of course the ceremonies due a general—but a cordial and friendly reception, at least. Instead, both the proprietor and the waiter greeted him with a distrustful, listless chill and with some hostile glances that promptly cured his hunger. So instead of sitting down to eat, he remained standing at the counter and threateningly ordered wine; and he was served it, after some resistance from the two men and some private confabulation between them in the room behind the shop.

He was no drinker; and in any case, to wine he preferred beer, a taste familiar to him since childhood. But as a show of protest against the waiter and the proprietor, his manner became more and more menacing as he made them serve him five quarter-liters, one after another, which he drained, downing the wine in great gulps, like a Sardinian bandit. Then he violently flung on the counter almost all the scant money he had in his pocket; while his anger tempted him to knock over the counter and the tables and to behave not like an ally but like an invader and a murderer. However, a slight nausea was rising from his stomach, and it dissuaded him from any action. With a still fairly martial tread, he climbed out into the air again.

The wine had descended to his legs and risen to his head. And in the street's putrid sirocco, which swelled his heart at every breath, he was seized by an impossible longing to be at home, curled in his too-short bed, between the cold and swampy odor of the countryside and the smell of the cabbage his mother was boiling in the kitchen. However, thanks to the wine, this enormous homesickness, instead of tormenting him, made him jolly. For somebody strolling around drunk, any miracle, at least for a few minutes, is possible. A helicopter could land before him, ready to return at once to Bavaria, or a radio message could come to him through the air, announcing an extension of his leave until Easter.

He took a few more steps on the sidewalk, then turned at random, and coming to a doorway, he stopped on its threshold, with the carefree notion of huddling up in there and sleeping, perhaps on a step or in the area beneath the stairs, as masked revelers do during Carnival, when you act as you please and nobody pays any attention. He had forgotten his uniform; a comical interregnum had taken over the world, and the total whim of childhood now usurped the military law of the Reich! This law is a farce, and Gunther doesn't give a damn about it. At that moment, the first female creature who happened to come into that doorway (we don't mean just an ordinary girl or some little neighborhood whore, but any female animal: a mare, a cow, a she-ass!), if she looked at him with a barely human eye—he would have been capable of embracing her violently, or perhaps flinging himself at her feet like a lover, calling her: meine Mutter! And when, a few instants later, he saw a woman arriving from the corner, a tenant of the building, a humble-looking but decent little thing, coming home just at that moment, laden with shopping bags and purse, he didn't hesitate to shout at her: "Signorina! Signorina!" (this was one of the 4 Italian words he knew). And with a leap he appeared before her, although he himself didn't know what to demand.

She, however, seeing him confront her, stared at him with an absolutely inhuman gaze, as if confronted by the true and recognizable face of horror.

2 The woman, an elementary-school teacher by profession, was named Ida Mancuso, née Ramundo, a widow. To tell the truth, her parents had meant her first name to be Aida. But because of an error by the clerk, she had been inscribed in the registry as Ida, called Iduzza by her father, a Calabrian.

Her age was thirty-seven, and she certainly made no effort to seem younger. Her rather undernourished body, shapeless, the bosom withered,

17

the lower part awkwardly fattened, was covered more or less by an old woman's brown overcoat, with a worn fur collar and a grayish lining whose tattered edges could be seen hanging from the cuffs of the sleeves. She also wore a hat, held fast with a couple of straight pins, complemented by the little black veil of her long-standing widowhood; her legal status of *Signora*, indicated by the veil, was further proved by the wedding ring (of steel, replacing the gold one long since donated to the Fatherland for the Abyssinian enterprise) on her left hand. Her coal-black, curly hair was beginning to gray; but age had left strangely intact her round face which, with its protruding lips, seemed the face of a worn little girl.

And in fact, Ida had remained basically a little girl, because her chief attitude towards the world had always been and still was (consciously or not) one of frightened awe. The only people who had never frightened her, really, had been her father, her husband, and later, perhaps, her little pupils. All the rest of the world was a menacing insecurity, which, unconsciously for her, was deeply rooted in some tribal prehistory. And in her great dark almond eyes there was the passive sweetness of a very profound and incurable barbarism, which resembled foreknowledge.

Foreknowledge, actually, is not the best word, because knowledge had nothing to do with it. Rather, the strangeness of those eyes recalled the mysterious idiocy of animals, who, not with their mind, but with a sense in their vulnerable bodies, "know" the past and the future of every destiny. I would call that sense—which is common in them, a part of the other bodily senses—the *sense of the sacred*: meaning by *sacred*, in their case, the universal power that can devour them and annihilate them, for their guilt in being born.

Ida was born in 1903, under the sign of Capricorn, which favors industry, the arts, and prophecy, but also, in some cases, madness and foolishness. As far as intelligence went, she was mediocre; but she was a docile student, diligent in her work, and she was promoted each year. She had no brothers or sisters; and her parents both taught in the same elementary school in Cosenza, where they had met for the first time. Her father, Giuseppe Ramundo, came from a peasant family, in the deep Calabrian south. And her mother, whose name was Nora Almagià, came from Padua, of a shopkeeping, petty bourgeois family. She had ended up in Cosenza, an old maid of thirty, and alone, as the result of a competition for a teaching post. In Giuseppe's eyes, she—in her manners, her intellect, and her figure —stood for something superior and delicate.

Giuseppe, eight years younger than his wife, was a tall and corpulent man, with red stubby hands and a broad flushed face, immediately likable. In a childhood accident, a hoe had wounded his ankle, leaving him slightly lame for the rest of his life. And his limping gait accentuated the sense of trusting ingenuousness he naturally emanated. Since he was no good for certain farm jobs, his family, poor sharecroppers, had contrived for him to study, sending him first to the priests for lessons, with some help from the landowner. His experience of priests and landowners had not extinguished, but had rather fanned, it seems, a secret passion of his. Somewhere, somehow, he had dug up texts by Proudhon, Bakunin, Malatesta, and other anarchists. And on these he had based a personal creed, ignorant but stubborn, and destined to remain a kind of private heresy. In fact, he was forbidden to profess it, even within the walls of his own home.

Nora Ramundo née Almagià was, as her maiden name indicates, Jewish (indeed, her relatives still lived, as they had for several generations, in the little ghetto of Padua); however, she didn't want anyone to know, and she had confided only in her husband and in her daughter, under a solemn oath of secrecy. In official and business matters, she used to camouflage her family name, transforming it from *Almagià* into *Almagía*, convinced that by changing the accent she was fabricating an immunity for herself! In any case, in those days, obscure *racial* backgrounds were not yet really being explored or recorded. That poor *Almagià* (or *Almagía*, whichever it was) down South was accepted by all, I believe, as an ordinary Venetian surname, innocuous and meaningless; and by now, for that matter, people didn't even remember it. Nora, to everybody, was Signora Ramundo, considered obviously a Catholic like her husband.

Nora had no special qualities, mental or physical. And yet, without being beautiful, she was certainly pretty. From her prolonged spinsterhood she had retained a chaste and puritanical reserve (even in her intimacy with her husband she had certain childlike modesties) which was held in great esteem in that region of the South. And the Venetian grace of her manners made her girl students love her. She was subdued in her behavior, and shy by nature, especially among strangers. However, her introverted character nurtured some tormenting flames, which could be seen burning in her gypsy eyes. There were, for example, some unconfessed excesses of youthful sentimentality . . . But most of all, there were suppressed ferments, which became outright manias in her. Then, gnawing at her nerves, they erupted, within the walls of the house, in rash and oppressive forms.

These outbursts of hers had a single, natural target, the closest one: Giuseppe, her husband. She would turn on him at times, worse than a witch, upbraiding him for his birth, his village, his relatives, slandering him horribly with obvious falsehoods, and even shouting at him: "Sign of God's wrath! Walk on the path!", a dialect verse, referring to his lamed foot. Suddenly, then, she would be exhausted and would lie there, drained, like a rag doll. And she would start stammering in a faint voice: ". . . what did I say? . . . I didn't mean that . . . that wasn't what I meant, poor me . . . Oh my God . . . my God . . ." her face livid, her hands clutching the curly hair of her aching head. Then Giuseppe, moved to pity, would try to soothe her saying: "Ah, what does it matter? It's nothing. It's all over. You're a loony, that's what you are, a little silly thing . . ." while she would look at him, dazed, her eyes speaking of infinite love.

A little later, she would remember these scenes of hers as a frightful dream, of a split personality. It was not she, but a kind of leechlike creature, her enemy, who clung to her, inside, forcing her to play a mad and incomprehensible role. She wanted to die. But rather than reveal her remorse, she was capable of maintaining, for the rest of the day, a grim and acid silence, almost accusatory.

Another characteristic of hers was certain exaggerated, solemn rhetorical turns of speech, handed down to her perhaps from the ancient patriarchs. These Biblical expressions, however, were mingled with the usual phrases and cadences she had absorbed from the Veneto region, which, in these surroundings, sounded like a comical little song.

As for her Jewish secret, she had explained to her daughter, from early childhood, that the Jews are a people destined, since time began, to suffer the vindictive hatred of all other peoples; and that even during apparent periods of truce, persecution will always dog them, eternally recurring, as their prescribed destiny. For these reasons, she herself had insisted on having Iduzza baptized a Catholic, like her father. Who, though recalcitrant, had agreed for Iduzza's sake: submitting even, during the ceremony, to making in great haste a huge, sloppy Sign of the Cross, in front of everybody. In private, however, on the subject of God, he was accustomed to quote the saying: *The God hypothesis is useless,*" adding in solemn tones the signature of the Author: "FAURE!", as he never failed to do with all his quotations.

Besides the main secret, Nora's, other secrets existed in the family; and one was that Giuseppe was addicted to drink.

It was, as far as I know, the only sin of that guileless atheist. A man so steadfast in his affections that, for all his adult life, as earlier in his youth, he regularly sent a large part of his salary to his parents and his brothers, poorer than he. Political motives aside, his instinct, I believe, was to embrace the whole world. But more than the whole world he loved Iduzza and Noruzza, for whom he was even capable of composing madrigals. To Nora, when they were engaged, he used to say; "My Eastern star!" and to Iduzza (originally meant to be *Aida*) he would often sing (N.B. both he and Nora had been constant spectators at the performances of the barnstorming opera troupe):

"Celeste Aida forma divina . . ."

But his drinking bouts (Nora's cross) were something he couldn't forego, even if, out of respect for his position as teacher, he renounced visiting taverns, devoting himself to his wine at home, in the evening, especially on Saturdays. And since he was still a young man under thirty, on such occasions he would naturally and heedlessly expound his clandestine ideals.

The first signal of his free speech was a certain restlessness of his huge hands, which began to shift or knock over his glass, as his dark brown eyes became troubled and pensive. Then he would start to shake his head, saying: *betrayal! betrayal!*, meaning that he himself, since he had become an employee of the State, was behaving like a traitor towards his comrades and brothers. A teacher, if he was honest, facing those poor little creatures in the school, should preach anarchy, total rejection of the established order, of the society that raised them to be exploited or used as cannon-fodder . . . At this point, the worried Nora would run to close the doors and windows, to muffle these subversive notions from the ears of neighbors or passersby. And, for his part, he would stand squarely in the center of the room and start quoting in a full voice, louder and louder, holding up one finger:

". . . the State is the authority, the rule and the organized force of the propertied and self-styled enlightened classes over the masses. It guarantees always what it finds: to the former, freedom based on ownership; to the latter, servitude, fatal consequence of their poverty. BAKUNIN!"

". . . Anarchy, nowadays, means attack, war on all authority, on all power, on all government. In the society of the future, anarchy will be defense, the obstacle opposed to the reestablishment of any authority, any power, any government. CAFIERO!"

At this point Nora would begin to plead: "Ssssh . . . sssh . . ." lurching from one wall to another, like a possessed creature. Even when the doors and windows were closed, she was convinced that certain words and certain names, uttered in the house of the two schoolteachers, would create a universal scandal: as if around their poor, closed, barred rooms there were an enormous crowd of listening witnesses. In reality, though she was as much an atheist as her husband was, she lived as if subject to a vindictive jailer-God, who spied on her.

"Freedoms are not granted. They are seized. KROPOTKIN!"

"Ah, what a cross! Quiet, I tell you. You want to plunge this household into the abyss of shame and dishonor! You want to drag this family in the mire!"

"What mire, Noruzza sweetheart? The mire is on the white hands of landowners and bankers! Mire is our rotten society! Anarchy isn't mire! Anarchy is the honor of the world, the true and holy name of the only new history, immense, *implacable* Revolution!!"

"Ah! I curse the day, the hour, the minute when I won that competition! I curse my infernal destiny, that brought me down among these Southerners, all of them highway bandits, the lowest scum of the earth, infamous creatures, worthy of hanging, one and all!!"

"You want us hanged, Norù? Hanged, light of my life?!"

In his amazement, Giuseppe sank back into a chair. But half-sprawled, he would irresistibly be inspired to sing once more, his eyes on the ceiling, like a wagon-driver singing to the moon:

"Dynamite the churches, blast the palaces,
  Death to the hated bourgeoisie! . . ."

". . . Aaaaaha! Be quiet! Murderer! Be quiet, criminal! Or I'll throw myself out of the window!"

To make sure the neighbors couldn't hear her, Nora was careful to keep her voice low, but the effort made her veins swell, as if she were choking. Finally, strangled and exhausted, she would fling herself on the little sofa, and then Giuseppe, concerned, would go to her and apologize, kissing her hands, as if she were a great lady, those thin hands, already aged, and chapped from housework and chilblains. And after a moment, she would be smiling at him, consoled, her ancestral anguish temporarily allayed.

From her little colored chair (bought by her father specially to suit her size), Iduzza would follow these quarrels, eyes wide, naturally not understanding anything of them. From birth, she never had the slightest tendency towards subversion, to be sure; but if she could have expressed an opinion, she would have said that, between the two litigants, the more subversive was her mother! In any case, all she could understand was that her parents disagreed on certain questions; nor, luckily, was she overly frightened by their scenes, since she was used to them. Still, as soon as she saw peace return between them, she would smile a little smile of contentment.

For her, those evenings of drinking were also holiday evenings, because once her father was in his cups, after having waved his flags of revolt, he would give free rein to his natural good humor, and recall his background as a peasant, ancient relative of animals and plants. He would imitate the sounds of every animal: from *ucedduzzi*, the smallest of birds, to *leuni*, lions. And at her request, he would repeat Calabrian songs and fables as often as ten times, making them comic when they were tragic, because like all children, she enjoyed laughing, and her wanton laughter was music in the family. At a certain moment, Nora, too, defeated, would join in the performance, her ingenuous and slightly off-pitch voice producing a small repertory of her own—limited, actually, as far as I know, to a total of two numbers. One was the famous salon song, *Ideale*:

"I followed you like Peace's rainbow
Through the pathways of heaven . . ."

etc., etc. The other was a song in Venetian dialect, which went:

"Look at the sky serene with all the stars,
What a fine night this is for stealing girls
Those who steal girls are not called thieves
They're called young lovers . . ."

Then, around ten, Nora would finish tidying up the kitchen, and Giuseppe would put Iduzza to bed, accompanying her, like a mother, with certain lullabies almost Oriental in sound, which his mother and his grandmother had sung to him:

"O come, sleep, from the mountain
The wolf is eating the sheep . . .
O nní o nnà
Go to sleepy
Sleep
    sleep
        sleep . . . sleep . . . slee . . ."

Another lullaby, which Iduzza liked very much, was then handed down to the next generation. It was in proper Italian, and I have no idea where Giuseppe came across it:

"Sleep, little eyes, sleep, little eyes,
For tomorrow we're going to Reggio.
There a golden mirror we'll buy,
All painted with roses and flowers.
Sleep, little hands, sleep, little hands,
For tomorrow we're going to Reggio.
There we'll buy a little loom
With a shuttle of finest silver.
Sleep, little feet, sleep, little feet,

For tomorrow we're going to Reggio
There we'll buy some little shoes
To dance on the feast of Saint Ida . . ."

Iduzza forgot all fear at her father's side. To her, he seemed a kind of warm baby-carriage, radiant and limping, more impregnable than a tank, as he gaily took her out riding, safe from the terrors of the world, accompanying her everywhere, and never allowing her to be sent out alone into the streets, where every door, window, or alien encounter threatened her with harm. In the winter, perhaps for economy, he wore a kind of shepherd cloak, broad and rather long, and in bad weather he would protect her from the rain, holding her close, under his mantle.

I don't know Calabria well. And I can draw only a vague picture of Iduzza's Cosenza, from the few reminiscences of the dead. Already at that time, I believe, modern buildings were spreading out from the medieval city that girds the hill. In one of these buildings, in fact, humble and ordinary, there was the Ramundos' cramped apartment. I know a river runs through the city, and the sea is just beyond the mountain. The advent of the atomic age, which marked the beginning of the century, surely was not felt in those regions; nor was the industrial development of the Great Powers, except through emigrants' tales. The region's economy was based on agriculture, progressively declining because of the impoverished soil. The ruling castes were the clergy and the landowners; and for the lowest castes, I suppose there, as elsewhere, the habitual daily sustenance was the onion . . . I know for certain, in any case, that Giuseppe, as a student preparing for his teacher's certificate, went for years without ever knowing the taste of hot food, nourishing himself chiefly on bread and dried figs.

.   .   .

Towards the age of five, for a whole summer Iduzza was subject to attacks of an unnamed disease, which distressed her parents as if it were some genetic defect. In the midst of her games and her childish prattle, she would suddenly fall silent, turn pale, with the impression that the world was spinning and dissolving around her. In reply to her parents' questions, she would utter only a little animal lament, but it was obvious she had already stopped hearing their voices; and a moment later she would put her hands to her head and throat, in a gesture of defense, while her mouth trembled in an incomprehensible murmuring, as if she were having a frightened dialogue with a shadow. Her breathing became shallow and feverish, and here, she would hurl herself violently to the ground, writhing and shaking in convulsive turmoil, her eyes open, but empty in a total blindness. From some subterranean source, a brutal electric current seemed to assail her little body, which at the same time was made invulnerable, never suffering wounds or shocks. This would last for a couple of minutes at most, until her movements slackened and diminished, and her body settled again in sweet, seemly repose. Her eyes would swim in a dreamy awakening, and her lips would relax gently, without wholly parting, only curling a little at the corners. The child seemed to be smiling in gratitude for having come home again, to the double protection of her perennial guardian angels who bent their heads over her, at either side: one here, round and rumpled like a sheepdog's; and the other, there, a curly little nanny-goat's poll.

But that smile, really, was only a physical illusion, produced by her muscles' natural distension after their harsh tautness. A few more instants would pass before Iduzza really recognized her domestic haven; and at that same moment, no notion remained in her of the frightful exile and return, as if they were events expelled from her memory. She could report only that she had suffered a great dizziness, and then had heard something like the sound of water, and footsteps and confused noises which seemed to come from far away. And in the hours that followed she would look tired, but more carefree and heedless than usual, as if, unknown to her, she had been released from a burden beyond her strength. For her own part, even later, she believed she had suffered a common fainting-spell, without realizing the theatrical phenomena that had accompanied it. And her parents preferred to leave her in this ignorance, warning her, however, never to tell anyone how she was subject to certain attacks, so as not to compromise her future as a young lady. Thus, in the family, there was now another scandal to keep hidden from the world.

Ancient folk culture, still rooted in the Calabrian earth and especially among the peasants, put a religious stigma on certain inexplicable maladies, attributing their recurrent attacks to the invasion of sacred spirits, or lower beings, who in this case could be exorcised only through ritual recitations in church. The invading spirit, who most often selected a woman, could also transmit unusual powers, such as the gift of healing or of prophecy. But the invasion, basically, was felt as an immense and guiltless trial, the unconscious selection of an isolated creature who would sum up the collective tragedy.

Naturally, Professor Ramundo, with his social advancement, had gone beyond the magic circle of peasant culture; and moreover, in accord with his philosophical-political ideas, he was a positivist. For him, certain unhealthy phenomena could derive only from the malfunctions or infirmities of the body. On this score, he was openly dismayed by the suspicion that he himself, in his very seed, might perhaps have tainted his daughter's blood, through his abuse of alcohol. But Nora, as soon as she saw him worried, immediately did her best to console him, and said, reassuringly, "No, no, don't torture yourself with crazy ideas. Look at the Palmieris. They've always drunk, back to the grandfather and great-grandfather! And the Mascaros, who give their babies wine instead of milk! You can see for yourself! They're all the picture of health!"

In previous years the family would move, in the warmer months, down towards the tip of Calabria, to the paternal home; but that summer, they didn't leave their stifling little Cosenza apartment, for fear Iduzza might be attacked by her illness in the country, in the presence of grandparents, aunts, uncles, cousins. And perhaps the city's dog-day heat, to which Iduzza was not accustomed, increased the frequency of her attacks.

Country holidays stopped completely after that anyway, when as a consequence of that winter's earthquake, which destroyed Reggio and laid waste the plains, the grandparents went to live with another son, in a hovel in the Aspromonte mountains where there was too little room to permit any guests.

From past vacations, Ida remembered most of all certain dolls made of bread, which her grandmother baked for her in the oven and she rocked as if they were babies, desperately refusing to eat them. She wanted them beside her even in her bed, from which they were furtively removed at night while she slept.

There also remained in her memory a very loud cry repeated by the swordfish fishermen over the cliffs, and in her mind it sounded like this: "FA-ALEUU!"

Towards the end of that summer, after yet another of Iduzza's attacks, Giuseppe made up his mind, loaded himself and the child on a little donkey he had borrowed, and took her to a hospital outside Cosenza, where there was a doctor, a friend from his parts, who now lived at Montalto but had studied modern medicine in the North. Under the fingers of the doctor who examined her, shy as she was, Ida laughed when it tickled, making the sound of someone ringing a little bell. And when the examination was over, she was told to thank the doctor, and she blushed all over, saying thank you, then hiding immediately behind her father. The doctor pronounced her healthy. Having already learned privately from Giuseppe that during those attacks she didn't hurt herself or shout or bite her tongue or reveal other disturbing symptoms, he assured the father there was no reason to worry about her. Those attacks of hers, he explained, were almost certainly temporary manifestations of precocious hysteria, which would disappear of themselves as she grew up. Meanwhile, to avoid them, especially since the schools were about to reopen (from her earliest years Iduzza had attended the classes of her mother, who didn't know where to leave her otherwise), he prescribed a soothing syrup for her, to be taken every morning when she woke up.

Ida and Giuseppe made the return journey, merry and lively, the father singing the usual songs of his repertory, in which Ida joined from time to time with her off-pitch little voice.

And after that day, subsequent events confirmed the doctor's predictions. The simple soothing-syrup cure, obediently followed by Iduzza, proved its daily efficacy, with no negative result except perhaps a slight somnolence and dulling of the senses, which the child was able to overcome. And from then on, after the single invasion of that summer, the strange illness never returned, at least not in its original severe form. It did, at times, reappear somehow, but reduced to what had formerly been only its first signal, a kind of dizzying arrest of all sensation, visible on the child's face with a mistlike veil of pallor. To tell the truth, these spells passed so rapidly that they eluded the notice of all present, and even Iduzza's own awareness. However, unlike the previous paroxysms, these imperceptible hints left in her a shadow of sad uneasiness, like an obscure sense of transgression.

These lingering signs of her illness became rarer and weaker as time passed. They attacked her again, with considerable frequency, when she was about eleven; but later, when she had passed the stage of puberty, they disappeared altogether, as the doctor had promised. Finally Ida could stop taking the medicine, and regain her natural little-girl's humor.

Perhaps it was also the stopping of the treatment that provoked a simultaneous transformation in the chemistry of her sleep. In fact, that was the period when her nighttime dreams began their luxuriant burgeoning, which was to complement her daytime life, with pauses and recurrences, to the end, entwining around her days more like a parasite or prison-guard than a companion. Still mingled with the flavors of childhood, those first dreams already put down the roots of sorrow in her, although they themselves were not particularly sorrowful. In one, which returned at intervals with several variations, she saw herself running in a place gloomy with soot or with smoke (factory, or city, or slum), clutching to her bosom a little doll, naked and all a vermilion color, as if it had been dipped in red paint.

·   ·   ·

The First World War spared Giuseppe, thanks to his bad leg; but the perils of his defeatism hovered like bogeys around Nora, so Iduzza also learned to fear certain subjects of her father's (even when they were barely hinted at, within the family, in a low conspiratorial tone!). In fact, since the time of the war in Libya, there had been arrests and prison sentences in the very city of Cosenza for defeatists like him! And here he was now, standing up again, raising his finger:

". . . The refusal to obey will become more and more frequent; and at last only the memory of war and armies as they are today will remain. And these times are near. TOLSTOY!"

". . . The people are always the beast that needs a muzzle, that must be treated with colonization and war and denied all rights. PROUDHON!"

Iduzza, for her part, didn't even dare judge the decrees of the Powers That Be, which to her appeared mysterious Beings, beyond her reason, but which possessed, however, the capacity to carry off her father, with policemen . . . At the first hint of certain subjects which frightened her mother, she would cling to Giuseppe, trembling. And Giuseppe, rather than upset her, would be persuaded to avoid such dangerous talk, even at home. From then on, he spent his evenings going over her lessons with his beloved daughter, though he was a bit more drunk than usual.

The post-war was a period of hunger and epidemics. However, as often happens, the war, which for most people had been a total disaster, for others had been a financial success (and they hadn't supported it for nothing). It was now, in fact, that these men began to finance the *black squads*, in the defense of their own endangered interests.

In the industrial cities, this danger came mostly from the workers; but in Calabria (as elsewhere in the South) those whose fortunes were most threatened were the landowners, who, among other things, were largely usurpers, having appropriated in the past, with various methods, lands belonging to the State. These were fields and forests which they often left abandoned and untilled. And this was the period of the "occupations of the land" by the peasants and farm laborers. Illusory occupation: because when they had fertilized and cultivated the lands, the occupiers, in the name of the law, were driven off.

Many were killed. And as for the subjugated ones, who worked for the landowners, the pay (according to the latest *labor agreements*, achieved after long social struggles) was this, for example:

for a working day of sixteen hours, three quarters of a liter of olive oil (half that amount for the women).

Giuseppe's relatives (down in the province of Reggio) were tenant farmers, who also worked out by the day as laborers. In August 1919, a sister of his, with her husband and their two sons, died of Spanish fever. The epidemic, in certain areas, has left a frightful memory. There were no doctors, no medicines, no food. It was during the worst summer heat. The deaths outnumbered those of the war. And the corpses remained unburied for days, since there wasn't enough wood for the coffins.

In this period, Giuseppe sent his relatives his entire salary (which in the present public difficulties was not always paid to him regularly). And, in the inflation of that time, the three had to manage on what Nora made. But Nora, who in some family emergencies was as brave as a lioness and frugal as an ant, managed to support the family without too much hardship.

Less than two years after the war's end, Ida duly received her teacher's certificate. And during the vacation of that same summer, though she had no dowry, she found a fiancé.

The fiancé, Alfio Mancuso, was from Messina, where he had lost all his relatives in the 1908 earthquake. He himself, who had been about ten at the time, was saved by a miracle of good luck. And despite his deep-seated love for his family, and especially for his mother, he did not bemoan that past disaster in later years so much as he boasted of his luck, which on that occasion had come to his aid and which had continued to stand by him. The miracle (enriched, in Alfio's telling, each time with new details and variations) was, briefly, as follows:

In the winter of 1908, little Alfio was working as an apprentice at a small boatyard, for an old man who repaired boats. Both the boy and the old man used to sleep in the yard itself, where the master had a cot, and the youth would make his bed on the ground, on a pile of shavings, wrapped in an old woolen horse-blanket.

Now, on that evening, while the old man, as was his habit, lingered over his own work (in the company of a few glasses), the apprentice, on the other hand, was already settling himself for the night in his horse-blanket, when, after some chance blunder, the old man shouted at him, as he always did on such occasions:

"Eeeeei! rapa babba!!" (which means: *stupid as a turnip!*)

Usually the apprentice took such insults without answering; but this time, maddened, he had answered:

"Turnip yourself!"

And, taking (extreme foresight) his horse-blanket, he had promptly run outside, for fear of his master, who in fact began running after him, ready to beat him, armed with a length of rope folded double.

Now, on the terrain where this pursuit was taking place, there were, at equal distance, a palm tree and a pole. After a moment's hesitation between the two (note this!) Alfio chose the palm tree, and a moment later he was already occupying the top, determined to stay there forever, like a monkey, rather than surrender to the old man, who finally became fed up with waiting under the tree and went back to the yard.

To make a long story short, hours and hours went by—until dawn!— and the blanketed Alfio was still lodged in that palm tree when the earthquake came, razing Messina and the boatyard to the ground, and knocking down the pole; whereas the palm tree, after having its crown shake in a great gust, with Alfio Mancuso perched in there, remained safe and standing.

Was there also some prodigious quality in that horse-blanket (formerly the property of a groom by the name of Cicciuzzo Belladonna)? In any case, at that very moment Alfio determined to name his first son Antonio (after his father) Cicciuzzo (that is to say, Francesco); and his daughter Maria (after his mother) and, as a second name, Palma. (Since boyhood, creating a family had always been his main ambition.)

Among the other signs of his good luck he also counted the end of the war, whose date coincided with his draft summons. Some red tape involving his military discharge had taken him to Rome, where he had found employment as a salesman for a firm. And in his subsequent business travels, he had passed through Cosenza and met his first love there.

Between Alfio and his future father-in-law a great friendship sprang up at once. And Ida quickly became fond of her suitor, who had various qualities which she found resembled her father's, with the difference that Alfio wasn't interested in politics and wasn't a drunkard. Both men, in appearance and behavior, were like big country dogs, and always ready to celebrate any good turn in life, even if it was only a breath of wind in the summer heat. Both had maternal qualities, as well as paternal: far more than Nora, whose proud, nervous, introverted character had always frightened Iduzza a little. Both men acted as her guardians against all violence from outside; and with their instinctive good humor and their innocent love of fun, for her, not naturally very sociable, they provided a substitute for the company of friends her own age.

The wedding was held in church, out of the usual respect for public opinion and also for the groom, who, personally indifferent to religions, was never to know, not even he, the secret of Nora Almagía. Because of their common poverty, the bride, instead of a white dress, wore a dark blue woolen suit, with the skirt tucked at the waist, and a fitted jacket. But she had dainty white leather shoes, a white blouse with embroidered lapels under her jacket, and, on her head, a little tarlatan veil with an orange-blossom crown. Her purse, a present from Nora (who every month, no matter what, always laid aside a few lire against such exceptional events) was of silver mesh. In all her life, before and afterwards, Iduzza was never so elegant and brand-new as on that day; and she felt an enormous responsibility, taking care in church, and also during the subsequent train journey, not to stain her shoes or wrinkle her slip.

The wedding journey (except for a couple of hours' layover in Naples) consisted of the trip to Rome, the couple's new residence, where

Alfio had already prepared their cheap two-room apartment in the San Lorenzo quarter. Iduzza was a virgin not only in her body, but also in her thoughts. She had never seen an adult naked, because her parents never undressed in her presence; and she was extremely modest also about her own body, even when she was alone. Nora had informed her only that to procreate babies the man's body had to enter the woman's. It's a necessary operation, to which you have to submit dutifully, and it doesn't hurt too much. And Ida desired ardently to have a baby.

That evening, after their arrival in Rome, while the husband undressed in the bedroom, Iduzza undressed in the adjacent sitting room. And when she went into the bedroom, shy and embarrassed, in her new nightgown, she promptly burst into irresistible laughter, seeing Alfio also in a long nightshirt, which shrouded his virile, corpulent figure to his feet, making him (with his florid and innocent face) look like an infant in its baptismal dress.

He flushed and stammered, uncertainly: "Why are you laughing?"

Her great hilarity prevented her from speaking, while she also became covered with blushes. Finally she managed to blurt out: "It's . . . the . . . night . . . shirt . . ." and she exploded in laughter again.

The reason for her hilarity, actually, was not Alfio's comic (and also pathetic) appearance, but the very idea of the shirt. Her father, in fact, following the custom of his peasant relatives, used to go to bed in his underwear (wool shirt, socks, and long drawers). She had never imagined that males wore nightshirts, convinced that such garments, like slips, belonged to women, or to priests.

A little later, they turned off the light: and in the darkness, beneath the sheets, she held her breath, dismayed, feeling her husband raise her long gown up above her thighs and seek her denuded flesh with other flesh, moist and burning. Though she had been expecting it, she felt it was terrible that a man whom she had unconsciously compared to her father Giuseppe should inflict such atrocious torment on her. But she lay still, and let him have his way, overcoming the terror that threatened her, such was her trust in him. And so from then on, every evening, she let him have her, sweet and willing, like an untamed child who docilely allows his mother to feed him. Then, as time went on, she became accustomed to that great evening ritual, necessary nutrition of their marriage. And he, for that matter, despite his natural youthful ardor, so respected his wife that they never saw each other naked, and made love always in the dark.

Iduzza didn't understand sexual pleasure, which remained a mystery to her always. Sometimes, she was moved to a kind of tender indulgence towards her husband, feeling him panting on top of her, overcome and made savage by that raving mystery. And at his last, very loud cry, as if at an invoked execution, merciless and ineluctable, she would pityingly stroke his thick curly hair, a boy's still, all damp with sweat.

Four years of marriage, nevertheless, went by before the promised baby arrived. In this period, since she would be so often alone and idle during his salesman's travels, Alfio urged her to apply for a teaching position in Rome. He himself, possessing a certain simple instinct for intrigue, helped her win the competition, through an acquaintance of his at the Ministry whom he rewarded with some commercial favor. And this was, perhaps, Alfio's only important success: in fact, though he combed cities and provinces (always setting forth with the bold, adventurous mien of the famous "brave little tailor" of the fairy tale), Alfio Mancuso was never much of a businessman, poor and vagabond.

And so Ida began her teaching career, which was to end only after nearly twenty-five years. Where Alfio could not help her, however, was in gaining an assignment to a convenient school. Ida found a position not in a school in her own San Lorenzo neighborhood, but quite far away, towards Garbatella (where, after some years, the building was demolished and the school transferred to the Testaccio quarter). All along the way, her heart would pound with fear, in the midst of the alien crowd on the tramways, crushing her and shoving her, in a struggle where she always gave in and remained behind. But the moment she entered the classroom, that special smell of dirty children, lice, and snot, promptly consoled her with its fraternal, helpless sweetness, sheltered from adult violence.

Before the beginning of this career of hers, one rainy autumn afternoon, when Iduzza had been married only a few months, she was startled, up on the top floor, by a loud racket of singing, shouts, and gunfire in the neighborhood streets below. In fact, these were the days of the Fascist "revolution," and on that particular day (30 October 1922) the famous "march on Rome" was taking place. One of the black columns on the march, entering the city by the San Lorenzo gate, had encountered open hostility in that Red, working-class district. And the Fascists had immediately set about taking revenge, beating up the inhabitants and killing some of the rebels on the spot. There were thirteen dead in San Lorenzo. But it was, actually, a chance episode in the course of that easy Roman march, with which Fascism marked its official assumption of power.

At that time of day Iduzza was alone in the house, and like the other neighbor-women, she ran to shut the windows, terrified at the thought of Alfio, out on his rounds with his samples of paints, varnishes, and shoe polish. She supposed this was the outbreak of the famous universal revolution constantly announced by her father . . . Alfio, however, came home punctually that evening, safe and sound, thank goodness, and cheerful as usual. And at supper, discussing the events with Iduzza, he declared to her that the things Don Giuseppe, her father, always said were surely right, sacrosanct; but, in practice, now, what with strikes, incidents, and delays, getting on with the job properly had become a problem for businessmen and merchants like himself! From now on, Italy would have a strong government at last, to restore order and peace among the people.

The boy-groom could say no more than this on the subject; and the girl-bride, seeing him serene and content, didn't bother to ask more. The dead, shot in the street that afternoon, had already been hastily buried in the nearby Verano cemetery.

. . .

Two or three years after that, with the abolition of freedom of the press, of opposition and the right to strike, the setting up of the *Special Tribunals*, the restoration of the death-penalty, etc., etc., Fascism had established a definitive dictatorship.

In 1925, Ida became pregnant, and gave birth in May of '26. The birth, dangerous and difficult, tortured her fiercely for a whole day and a night, leaving her almost drained of blood. However, she brought forth a handsome little boy-child, dark-haired and feisty.

Alfio boasted of him, announcing to everyone: "I've got a boy who's something special, weighing nine pounds, with a healthy little face like a bright red apple!"

After that first child, no more were born of his marriage. As had long been decided, they gave him the name of his paternal grandfather Antonio; but from the beginning they usually called him Nino, or even more often, Ninnuzzu and Ninnarieddu. Every summer, Ida would go back to Cosenza for a little while with the baby, to whom the grandfather would sing the lullabies familiar to her, and especially that "tomorrow we're going to Reggio," with the variation:

". . . we'll buy some little shoes
To dance on the feast of Saint Ninnuzzu."

The summer visits of Iduzza and Ninnarieddu gave Giuseppe Ramundo back his puppylike gaiety, which had seemed eternal in him, but which, instead, had become more and more subdued these last years. His good nature enabled him to resign himself to Iduzza's absence, which at heart, especially in the beginning, he had felt as a theft. But this repressed suffering of his was exacerbated by the advent of the Fascist "revolution," which had aged him worse than an illness. To see that grim parody triumph in the place of the other REVOLUTION he had dreamed of (and, at the end, it had seemed imminent) for him was like chewing every day a disgusting gruel, which turned his stomach. The occupied lands, which still resisted in 1922, had been taken away from the peasants with definitive violence, and given back to the contented landowners. And in the squads reclaiming the proprietors' rights, there were (and this was the worst of it) many boys, deprived and homeless as the others, brutalized by propaganda or money, led to assault their poor equals. For Giuseppe it was like acting out a play, in a dream. The people he found most odious in the city (who, in recent years, had kept their heads down a bit, out of fear) now strode around provocatively, sticking out their bellies, sovereigns restored to power, treated deferentially by everybody, among the walls papered with their manifestos . . .

At school, at home, and with his local acquaintances, Professor Ramundo still imposed an artificial conformity on himself, partly so as not to increase Nora's anxieties and worsen her declining health. However, to make up for it, he had taken to spending much of his time in a secluded little place where he could give some vent to his ideas. It was a tavern of the lowest order, with three or four tables and a barrel of new wine. The owner, an old acquaintance of Giuseppe's, was an anarchist. And he and Giuseppe shared youthful memories.

I have been unable to discover the exact location of that tavern. However, somebody once told me that to reach it you had to take a suburban tram, if not the funicular up the side of the mountain. And I have always imagined that in the place's dark, cool interior, the smell of new wine mingled with the country smells of lime and wood, and perhaps also with the tang of the sea, beyond the coastal range. Unfortunately, I know that area only on the map, and perhaps grandfather Ramundo's tavern now no longer exists. Its few customers, from what I've heard, were farm laborers, migrant shepherds, and an occasional fisherman from the coast. They conversed in their ancient dialects, with their Greek and Arab sounds. And in private, with these drinking friends whom he called, filled with emotion, *my disenfranchised companions* or *my brothers*, Giuseppe would regain his boisterous gaiety and would vaunt his youthful ideals, all the more exciting now, however, since they really were dangerous secrets. Finally he could unburden himself, declaiming some verses he considered peerless, which he had never been able to teach the children in school:

". . . In radiant glory we may fall,
The future's path to clear!
Our blood we'll shed at mankind's call,
For Anarchy so dear! . . .

". . . Outcast and spurned by all the world,
Like slaves made but to serve,
Our heads erect, our flags unfurled,
We'll gain what we deserve!"

But the climax of those meetings came when, after making sure that
no one outside could hear them, the men gathered there would sing in a
low chorus:

"Our Revolution's on its way,
Our black flag will win the day
For An-ar-chy!!"

They were, to tell the truth, poor Sunday anarchists, and this was the
beginning and end of their subversive activities. However, some reports
finally reached Cosenza. One day the tavern-keeper was sent off to en-
forced residence elsewhere; the tavern had to close down, and Giuseppe,
without any specific explanation, indeed with some pretense of respect, was
pensioned off at the age of fifty-four.

At home, with his wife, he pretended to give credence to this show of
respect, deceiving himself with his own reasoning, as children deceive
themselves with fairy tales. Nor, obviously, did he ever speak of his secret
tavern or of the fate of his friend its proprietor, which tormented him
constantly, especially since he felt responsible, at least in part. And since he
really had no other confidant but Nora, he could speak of these things with
no one.

In his personal misfortune, his worst regret was not the harm he had
suffered, or even his forced inactivity (for him, teaching had been a great
pleasure). Those disasters, and maybe even the threat of confinement or
prison, came to him from the Fascists, his natural enemies. But it was the
thought that among the friends of his little table, whom he called brothers,
a spy, a traitor had been concealed: this suspicion, more than anything
else, cast him into melancholy. For some hours he could find distraction by
making wooden toys to give to his grandson Ninnuzzu when he came in
the summer. Moreover, mostly to console Nora, he had bought a radio, so
in the evening they could listen together to operas, which they both had
loved since the days when they used to go and see the traveling company.
But the moment they heard the voice of the news broadcast, which made
him almost rave, he would force her, even rudely, to turn off the set.

For her part, as her nerves gave way completely, Nora grew more cross
and quarrelsome, even persecutive. In some moments of exasperation, she

actually shouted at him that they had dismissed him from his position for professional incompetence! But in reply to this slander he merely teased her (to make her smile again), without attaching much importance to it.

Often, in his pity at seeing her so worn and saddened, he would suggest they go together to visit his relatives, down in Aspromonte. And he would announce this plan as a fantastic journey, in the tone of a rich husband promising his wife a splendid cruise. But, in reality, he was too enfeebled, and no longer had the physical strength to set out. Lately he had taken on a purplish color and an unhealthy, obese heaviness.

He never went to taverns now, and even at home he avoided drinking excessively, out of consideration for Nora; but in some private lair he still had to slake his thirst for alcohol, which had become sick. Every day, some Cosenza citizen would come upon him in the streets, limping along in his old cloak, always by himself, with drunken eyes, staggering now and then and leaning against the wall. He was killed by cirrhosis of the liver, in 1936.

Not long afterwards, in Rome, the still-young Alfio followed his elderly friend in the destiny of death. He had set out for Ethiopia—recently subjugated by Italy—with some business plans so gradiose that he expected to distribute his merchandise throughout the whole Empire. But three weeks later he was back in Rome, unrecognizably thin, with a constant, piercing nausea that kept him from eating and gave him a fever. At first they thought it was some African disease, but instead the examinations showed it was cancer, which had perhaps been developing inside him for a long time without his knowledge, only to attack him then suddenly with precipitous virulence, as it sometimes does in young and sturdy bodies.

He was not told of his death-sentence: they led him to believe he had been operated on for an ulcer, and was on the road to recovery. In reality, they had cut him open in an attempt to operate, but had promptly sewn him up again, because there was nothing to be done. At the end, he had become a skeleton; and when he got up from his hospital bed briefly, he looked so tall and thin that he seemed much younger, an adolescent.

Once Ida found him sobbing and shouting: "No! Nooo! I don't want to die!" with an enormous violence, incredible in his weak condition. Apparently, a nun, to prepare him for a holy death, had hinted at the truth. But his desire to live was so great that it was easy to deceive him once more with reassuring lies.

Another time (it was towards the end; in fact, he was already being given oxygen through a rubber tube), while he lay in a daze under the effect of the drugs, Ida heard him saying, as if speaking to himself:

"Mammuzza mia, this death, it's too narrow. How can I get through? I'm too fat, I am."

Finally, one morning he seemed to recover slightly, and in a faint musical voice, half-whimsical, half-homesick, he declared that he wanted to be buried in Messina. So the little money he left as inheritance was all spent on satisfying his last wish.

His dying had taken less than two months, and morphine had eased it for him.

From his African expedition he had brought Nino some Ethiopian thalers and, as a trophy, a black mask Ida didn't even want to look at. Nino would put it over his face, to frighten the rival neighborhood gangs, singing, as he attacked, the popular song of the time:

"Little black face,
Fair Abyssinian maid,
Maramba burumba bambuti mbú!"

until he traded the mask for a water pistol.

Ida never dared utter the word *cancer*, which for her evoked something fantastic, sacral, unnamable, like the presence of certain demons for savages. In its place she used the definition *disease of our time*, which she had learned there in the neighborhood. If someone asked her what her husband had died of, she would answer, *"the disease of our time,"* in a thin and trembling voice, since that little exorcism of hers was not strong enough to dispel the horrors from her memory.

After losing Giuseppe and Alfio one after the other, she found herself definitively exposed to fear; hers was the typical case of someone who had always remained a child, and was now fatherless. Still she devoted herself with conscious precision to her duties as teacher and mother; and the only sign of the violence she, a little girl, underwent from certain everyday practices of the adult world was an imperceptible but constant trembling of her hands, which were stubby and short, and never really properly washed.

The Italian invasion of Abyssinia, which promoted Italy from Kingdom to Empire, had remained, for our little schoolteacher in mourning, an event as remote as the Punic wars. *Abyssinia*, to her, meant a land where Alfio, if he had been luckier, could apparently have become rich, dealing in special oils, paints, and even shoe polish (though it seemed to her, from her readings in school, that the Africans, thanks to the climate, go around barefoot). In the classroom where she taught, in the center of the wall, just above her desk, next to the Crucifix, there were enlarged framed photographs of the Founder of the Empire and its King-Emperor. The former wore on his head a fez with a rich hanging fringe, and an eagle on the front. Under such headgear, his face, in a display so impudent it was downright ingenuous, wanted to imitate the classical mien of the Condottiere. But in reality, with the exaggerated jut of the chin, the artificially clenched jaws, and the mechanical dilation of eye-sockets and pupils, it resembled more a vaudeville clown playing a sergeant scaring recruits. And as for the King-Emperor, his insignificant features expressed only the narrow-mindedness of a provincial bourgeois, born old and with an inherited income. However, in Iduzza's eyes, the images of the two figures (no less, you might say, than the Crucifix, which to her meant only the power of the Church) represented the absolute symbol of Authority, that occult and awe-inspiring abstraction which makes laws. In those days, on instructions from higher up, she wrote on the blackboard in large letters, for her third-grade students to copy as a penmanship exercise:

"Copy out three times in your good notebooks the following words of the Duce:

Hold high, O Legionaries, your banners, your steel, and your hearts, to hail, after fifteen centuries, the reappearance of the Empire on the fatal hills of Rome!

Mussolini"

For his part, meanwhile, the recent Founder of the Empire, taking this great step in his career, had actually put his foot in the trap that was to doom him to the final scandal, to his downfall and death. This step, in fact, led precisely to where he was being awaited by the other Founder of the Great Reich, his present accomplice and his preordained master.

Between the two ill-starred counterfeiters, different by nature, there were yet some inevitable resemblances. But of these, the most interior and painful was a point of fundamental weakness: both men, inwardly, were failures and serfs, and sick with a vindictive sense of inferiority.

It is known that such a feeling gnaws at its victims with the ferocity of a tireless rodent, and often compensates them with dreams. Mussolini and Hitler, in their way, were two dreamers; but here is where their inherent difference lies. The dream-vision of the Italian Duce (corresponding to his physical desire for life) was a histrionic festival, where among banners and triumphs, he, a scheming vassal, would play the part of certain beatified ancient vassals (Caesars, Augustuses, and so on . . .) before a living crowd humbled to the rank of puppets. Whereas the other (tainted by a monotonous, vicious necrophilia and horrid terrors) was the half-conscious minion of a still formless dream. In it, every living creature (including himself) was the object of torment, to be degraded even to putrefaction. And at the end—in the Grand Finale—all the peoples of the earth (including the Germans) would rot in unseemly piles of corpses.

We know that our dream factory often has its foundations in debris of our waking hours or our past. But in the case of Mussolini, the product was fairly obvious in its superficiality; whereas in the case of Hitler, it was a teeming of infections, clustered around who knows what roots of his disturbed memory. Searching his biography, that of an envious little philistine, one could unearth some of these roots without much difficulty . . . But this is enough for now. Perhaps the Fascist Mussolini didn't realize at the time of the Ethiopian venture, supported by Hitler the Nazi (and then followed immediately by another common venture in Spain), that he had irrevocably yoked his own carnival chariot to the other's funeral hearse. One of the first effects of his servitude was that the national slogan, *Romanity*, of his own coinage, had to be replaced with a foreign one, of another's coinage: *race*. And so it was that in the first months of 1938, in Italy too, the newspapers, the local clubs, the radio, began the preparatory campaign against the Jews.

·   ·   ·

Giuseppe Ramundo, at the time of his death, was fifty-eight; and Nora, sixty-six when she was widowed, was already retired. She never went to visit her husband's grave, prevented by a kind of sacred terror of burial-places; but still it is certain that her deepest bond, which made her stay in the city of Cosenza, was his nearness, since he dwelt there still, in that cemetery.

She would never leave the old house, which had become her lair. She went out only rarely, in the early morning to buy food, or on the days when she had to draw her pension or send the usual money-order to Giuseppe's ancient parents. To them, as also to Ida, she wrote long letters, which the illiterate old couple had to have read to them. But in her letters she took care never to refer, even in the most indirect and reticent way, to her own pressing terrors for the future: by now she suspected censorship and informers everywhere. And in those frequent and endless communications of hers, she did nothing but repeat the same notion in every possible variation:

"How strange and unnatural destiny is. I married a man eight years younger than myself, and according to the law of nature I should have been the first to die, with Him at my side. Instead, it was my destiny to witness His death."

In speaking of Giuseppe, she always wrote Him, with a capital letter. Her style was prolix, repetitive, but with a certain academic nobility; and her handwriting was elongated, fine, even elegant. (However, in her final decline, her letters grew shorter and shorter. Her style became amputated and disjointed; and her written words, all shaky and twisted, groped across the page, uncertain of their direction.)

Besides this correspondence, which occupied her like a mania, her usual pastimes were reading illustrated magazines or love stories or listening to the radio. For some time now, the tales of racial persecution in Germany had alarmed her, like a precise signal confirming her old forebodings. But when, towards spring of 1938, Italy also intoned the official chorus of anti-Semitic propaganda, she saw the thunderous magnitude of destiny advancing towards her door, growing more enormous day by day. The news broadcasts, with their pompous and menacing voices, already seemed to be physically invading her little rooms, sowing panic; but to be prepared, she felt more and more obliged to listen to the news. And she spent her days and evenings on guard, alert to the news-broadcast schedules, like a little, wounded fox that has gone to earth and strains to hear the barking of the pack.

Some minor Fascist officials arrived from Catanzaro one day and spread the unofficial word of an imminent census of all Italian Jews, each of whom would be required to report himself. And after that moment, Nora no longer turned on the radio, in her terror of hearing the official announcement of the government's order, with a time-limit for reporting.

It was the beginning of summer. Already the previous winter, Nora, now sixty-eight, had begun to suffer a worsening of her ailments, due to the arteriosclerosis that had been undermining her for some time. With other people, too, her behavior (which had been shy before, but always tempered by an inner sweetness) had become angry and harsh. She no longer spoke if someone greeted her, not even when it was a former student, now grown up, perhaps one who had until then remained dear to her. On certain nights, she had raving fits, when she tore her gown with her fingernails. One night, she fell out of bed in her sleep, and she found herself lying on the floor, her head aching and buzzing. She often would wheel around, frowning and furious on the slightest pretext, sensing mysterious insults even in innocent gestures or words.

Of all the possible measures threatened against the Jews, the one that most immediately frightened her was the predicted obligation to report oneself for the census! All imaginable forms of near and future persecutions, even the most wicked and disastrous, were confused in her mind like wavering phantoms, among which the terrible spotlight of that single decree froze her in its beam! At the thought of having to declare publicly her fatal secret, which she had always hidden as something infamous, she promptly said to herself: it's impossible. Since she never saw the newspapers or listened to the radio anymore, she suspected the famous decree was by now promulgated and already in effect (whereas, in reality, no racial decree had so far been issued); and indeed, she became convinced, in her isolation, that the time-limit for reporting oneself was already up. She was careful, all the same, not to make inquiries or, worse, present herself at City Hall. As each new day dawned, she repeated: it's impossible, spending the hours then in this constant fear, until the city offices' closing-time, only to find herself, the next day, with the same obsessive problem. In her rooted conviction that she was already late, and hence subject to all sorts of unknown sanctions, she began to fear the calendar, dates, the sun's daily rising. And though the days went by without any suspect sign, she lived every moment from then on in the expectation of some forthcoming, terrible event. She expected to be summoned to the city offices to explain her transgression, then publicly given the lie, charged with perjury. Or else someone from City Hall or Police Headquarters would come looking for her; she might even be arrested.

She no longer left the house, not even for her daily needs, which she asked the concierge's wife to buy for her. One morning, however, when the woman showed up at the door for her list, Nora drove her off with bestial cries, hurling a cup she had in her hand. But people suspected nothing and had always esteemed her, so they forgave her these shrewish moods, attributing them to grief for her husband.

She began to suffer hallucinations. Her blood, rising with effort to her brain, would pound and roar in her hardened arteries, and she would think she heard violent blows in the street, hammering at the front door, footsteps or heavy breathing on the stairs. At evening, if she suddenly turned on the electric light, her failing eyesight transformed the furniture and its shadows into the motionless shapes of informers or armed police who had come to take her by surprise and arrest her. And one night when, for the second time, she happened to fall out of bed in her sleep, she imagined one of these men, having entered by stealth, had thrown her to the ground, and was still roaming about the house.

She thought of leaving Cosenza, of moving somewhere else. But where? And to whom? Padua, with her few Jewish relatives, was impossible. At her daughter's in Rome, or at her in-laws', down in the country below Reggio, her alien presence would be more noticeable than ever, would be recorded, and would compromise the others too. And besides, how could she impose the intrusion of a neurasthenic, haunted old woman on those who already had so many worries and torments of their own? She had never asked anything of anyone; she had been independent, since her girlhood. She always remembered two verses heard in the Ghetto, from an aged rabbi:

Unhappy the man who needs other men!
Happy the man who needs only God.

Why not leave then for some other city or anonymous town, where no one knew her? But, in any place, she would have to report her presence, produce her papers. She pondered escaping to a foreign country, where there were no racial laws. But she had never been abroad, had no passport; and acquiring a passport meant, again, questions at the registry office, the police, the frontiers: all places and rooms denied her, menacing, as if to an outlaw.

She was not poor, as perhaps everyone believed. Through those years (precisely to guarantee her own future independence, in the case of illness or other unforeseen eventualities) she had habitually put aside, little by little, some savings which now amounted to three thousand lire. This sum, in three one-thousand bills, was sewn into a handkerchief which at night she kept under her pillow and the rest of the time always on her person, pinned inside a stocking.

In her inexperienced mind, which was already clouding over, she assumed that, with such a sum, she could pay for any foreign journey, even an exotic one! At certain moments, like a young girl, she would daydream about metropolises that, as a spinster, in her Bovaresque dreams, she had longed for as sublime destinations: London, Paris! But suddenly she would remember that she was alone now; and how could a lone old woman find her way amid those cosmopolitan and tumultuous throngs?! If only Giuseppe were with her, then traveling would indeed still be beautiful! But Giuseppe no longer existed, he was not to be found here or anywhere. Perhaps even his body, so big and heavy, had now dissolved into the earth. There was no longer anyone on earth to reassure her in her terrors, as he used to do, saying to her: "How silly you are! You crazy little thing!"

Though she continued proposing various plans to herself, examining all the continents and countries, for her, in the entire globe, there was no place. And yet, as the days went by, the necessity, the urgency of escape were impressed on her feverish brain.

In the course of the last months, she had heard, perhaps over the radio, talk of Jewish emigrations from all Europe to Palestine. She knew absolutely nothing about Zionism, if she even knew the word. And of Palestine she knew only that it was the Biblical homeland of the Hebrews and that its capital was Jerusalem. But still, she came to the conclusion that the only place where she could be received, as a fugitive Jew among a people of Jews, was Palestine.

And as the summer heat was already advancing, one evening she suddenly decided to flee, then and there, even without a passport. She could cross the border illegally, or else she would stow away in the hold of a ship, as she had heard about in tales of illegal emigrants.

She took no baggage with her, not even a change of linen. She had on her, as always, her three thousand lire hidden inside the stocking. And at the last minute, noticing one of those old Calabrian cloaks Giuseppe used to wear in winter still hanging from a hook in the hall, she took it along, folded over her arm, with the thought of protecting herself if perhaps she went to a cold climate.

It is certain she was already delirious. But still she must have reasoned that to go from Cosenza to Jerusalem overland was not a good idea, because she headed for the sea, choosing the alternative of a ship as the only solution. Some people vaguely recall having seen her, in her little summer dress of black artificial silk with a blue pattern, on the last evening train heading for the beach at Paola. And in fact it is there, in that area, that she was found. Perhaps she wandered for a while along that beach without ports, searching for some freighter flying an Asiatic flag, more lost and confused than a five-year-old boy who runs away to sign on as a cabin boy and see the world.

In any event, though such endurance seems incredible in her condition, we have to believe that, from the station where she arrived, she covered a long distance on foot. In fact, the specific spot where they found her on the sand is several miles away from the Paola beach, towards Fuscaldo. Along that stretch of the coastline, beyond the railroad track, there are hilly fields of corn whose swaying expanse in the darkness, to her crazed eyes, may have created the effect of the sea opening out ahead.

It was a beautiful moonless night, calm and starry. Perhaps she was reminded of that one little song from her parts that she could sing:

what a fine night this is for stealing girls.

But even in that serene and tepid air, at a certain point in her walk, she felt cold. And she covered herself with that man's cloak she had brought along, taking care to fasten the buckle at the throat. It was an old mantle of dark brown country wool, which had been the right length for Giuseppe, but was too long for her, falling to her feet. A local man seeing her go by in the distance, cloaked in that way, could have taken her for the *monacheddu*, the little domestic brigand disguised as a monk, who roams about at night, they say, entering houses by dropping down the chimney. Apparently, however, nobody encountered her, naturally enough, on that isolated shore, seldom visited, especially at night.

The first to find her were some boatmen coming in at dawn from their fishing; and immediately they thought she was a suicide, brought ashore by the sea's currents. But the position of the drowned woman and the condition of her body did not agree with that hasty conclusion.

She was lying below the waterline, on sand still wet from the recent tide, in a relaxed and natural attitude, like someone surprised by death in a state of unconsciousness or in sleep. Her head was on the sand, which the light flux had made even and clean, without seaweed or flotsam; and the rest of her body was on the great man's cloak, held at the collar by the buckle and spread out at her sides, open, all soaked with water. The little artificial silk dress, damp and smoothed by the water, clung decorously to her thin body, which seemed unharmed, not swollen or abused as bodies washed in by the tide usually look. And the tiny blue carnations printed on the silk appeared new, brightened by the water, against the dark background of the cloak.

The sea's only violence had been to tear off her little shoes and undo her hair which, despite her age, had remained long and abundant, and only partly graying, so that now, wet, it seemed black again, and had fallen all down one side, almost gracefully. The current had not even slipped from her emaciated hand the little gold wedding ring, whose slight, precious gleam was distinct in the day's advancing light.

This was all the gold she possessed. In spite of her patriotic comformity (unlike her timid daughter Ida), she had not wanted to part with it even when the government had invited the people to "give gold to the Fatherland" to aid the Abyssinian conquest.

On her wrist, not yet spotted with rust, there remained her cheap little metal watch, stopped at four o'clock.

The examination of the body confirmed beyond a doubt her death by drowning; but she had left no sign or farewell message that indicated any suicidal intention. They found on her, hidden in the usual place beneath her stocking, her secret treasure in banknotes, still recognizable, though reduced by the water to a valueless pulp. Knowing Nora's character, we can be sure that if she had meant to do away with herself, she would first have taken care, wherever she was, to save from destruction that capital, so huge for her, accumulated with such perseverance.

Moreover, if she had really abandoned herself to the great mass of the sea, deliberately seeking death, we can suppose that the cloak's weight, increased by the water, would have dragged her to the bottom.

The case was closed, with the verdict: *accidental death by drowning.*

And this, in my opinion, is the most logical explanation. I believe that death caught her unawares, perhaps when she had fallen into one of those spells she had been prone to for some time.

At that part of the coast, and in that season, the tides are light, especially at the new moon. In her futile, haunted, and almost blind journey in the darkness of the night, she must have lost all sense of direction and even all sensory signals. And inadvertently she must have advanced too far on the strip washed by the tide, perhaps confused between the ocean of corn and the windless sea, or perhaps in some deranged move towards the ghost outline of a ship. There she fell, and the tide, already turning, covered her, just enough to drown her, but without assaulting her or striking her, and with no other sound save its own sucking imperceptible in the calm air. Meanwhile, the water-logged mantle, its edges buried under layers of sand, held her body on the damp slope, restraining it, lifeless, on the beach until the first hours of daylight.

I know Nora only from a photograph taken in the days of her engagement. She is standing against the background of a paper landscape, unfolding a fan, which covers the front of her blouse, and her pensive but formal pose betrays her grave yet sentimental nature. She is tiny and slim, with a woolen skirt, almost straight, pleated, tight-fitting at the waist, and a white muslin blouse with starched cuffs, buttoned up to the throat. With her free arm she is leaning, with almost histrionic abandon, on a little console, typical of middle-class photographers at the end of the century. Her hair is combed tight over her forehead and loose on top of her head in a gentle circle, like a geisha's. Her eyes are deeply fervent, behind a veil of melancholy. And the rest of the face is delicately made but ordinary.

On the photograph's lower margin, a yellowed white, printed on thick cardboard as they were then, in addition to the ornate printed legend customary at the time (*Format*, etc.) the dedication is still legible, in her gentle, diligent, and fine hand:

> *For You, beloved Giuseppe!*
> *from your*
> *Eleonora*

In the lower left-hand corner there is the date: *20 May 1902;* and a bit farther down, on the right, in the same little hand, there follows the sentiment:

> *With You forever*
> *as long as I live and beyond.*

3 ARTICLE 1: THE MARRIAGE OF AN ITALIAN CITIZEN OF ARYAN RACE TO A PERSON OF AN-OTHER RACE IS FORBIDDEN.

·   ·   ·

ARTICLE 8. BY LAW:

A) THE JEWISH RACE INCLUDES ANYONE BORN OF PARENTS BOTH BELONGING TO THE JEWISH RACE, EVEN IF THEY ARE OF A RELIGION OTHER THAN THE JEWISH RELIGION; . . . . .

·   ·   ·

D)

·   ·   ·

ANYONE BORN OF PARENTS OF ITALIAN NATIONAL-ITY, OF WHOM ONLY ONE JEWISH, SHALL NOT BE CON-SIDERED OF THE JEWISH RACE IF, ON THE DATE OF 1 OCTOBER 1938–XVI, HE WAS OF A RELIGION OTHER THAN THE JEWISH.

·   ·   ·

ARTICLE 9. MEMBERSHIP IN THE JEWISH RACE MUST BE REPORTED AND RECORDED IN THE LEGAL STATUS REGISTRIES AND THE CENSUS.

·   ·   ·

ARTICLE 19. IN APPLICATION OF ARTICLE 9, ALL THOSE TO WHOM ARTICLE 8 APPLIES MUST REPORT THEIR STATUS TO THE REGISTRY IN THE CITY OR TOWN OF THEIR LEGAL RESIDENCE . . . . .

·   ·   ·

So read the Italian racial law, proclaimed in the autumn of 1938. With it, moreover, all citizens said to be "of Jewish race" were excluded from the management of businesses, properties, possessions, were forbidden to attend schools of any kind, and were banned from all professions and employment in general, beginning, obviously, with the teaching profession.

These decrees were dated 17 November 1938. A few days before, throughout the Reich, after years of discrimination and persecution, the plan for the genocide of the Jews had been initiated. Against them, all the Germans had been given free rein to destroy and murder. In the course of several nights, many Jews were slaughtered, thousands carried off to the Lagers, their houses, stores, synagogues, burned and devastated.

Nora, with her death, had eluded by a few months the Italian racial decrees, which now stigmatized her irremediably as a Jew. However, her foresight, which thirty-five years earlier had led her to have Iduzza baptized a Catholic, now saved the latter from losing her post as schoolteacher and from the other punitive provisions, according to paragraph D) of *Art. 8.* On this score, *Art. 19* decreed the obligatory steps to be taken by those concerned. And so it was that Iduzza, as timid and stunned as if she were on trial at the Palace of Justice, presented herself at the City Offices in Rome.

She had duly provided herself with all the required documents: both those on her Jewish maternal side and those on her Aryan paternal side, including her baptismal certificate, as well as Giuseppe's, and those of her Calabrian grandparents (also in their graves now). Not a thing was lacking. And since she was ashamed even to open her mouth, along with this dossier, she also handed the clerk a page from a notebook where, in her own hand, she had written out her personal data. But a kind of repugnance, tantamount to a final little tribute, had made her omit any accent on her mother's maiden name.

"*Almàgia* or ALMAGIA?" the clerk inquired, examining her with an inquisitorial eye, authoritative and threatening.

She flushed, worse than a pupil caught copying an answer. "Almagià," she murmured hastily, "my mother was Jewish!"

The clerk sought no further information. And so, for the moment, the matter was settled.

In any case, Authority, in its secret coffers, from that day on retained the knowledge that Ida Mancuso, née Ramundo, schoolteacher, was a halfbreed, though for everyone else, still, she was an ordinary Aryan . . . In Italy, an *Aryan!* After a certain time, however, through private sources of hers, Ida learned that the laws were different in the Reich . . . And she began to suspect that any day a possible amendment of the national decrees might occur, involving not only her alone, but perhaps also her son Nino! Like her husband Alfio, Ninnuzzu, too, had always been unaware, and could never have dreamed, that there were Jews among his own relatives. He grew up carefree, heedless of everything, and a fanatical admirer of the Blackshirts.

Meanwhile, the Mussolini-Hitler bond became tighter and tighter until, in the following spring of 1939, the two formed a military alliance with their *Pact of Steel.* And without further ado, as Benito had colonized the Ethiopians, Adolf set forth to colonize the people of Europe, under the empire of the supreme German race, as he had promised. Still, at the outburst of the World War that shortly followed, the Italian partner, in spite of the pact, preferred to remain to one side, insecure, temporizing. And only the sensational winnings of his partner (who in the course of one moon, having devoured all Europe, was already at his goal, Paris) and a wish to guarantee his own share of glory made him enter the war at Adolf's side. It was the month of June 1940; and Ninnuzzu, then fourteen, welcomed the news with pleasure, though irked at the delay. In fact, he had become fed up waiting for his Duce to decide on this new, grand action.

Of all the rush of world events, Iduzza followed nothing, except the announcements of resounding Hitlerian victories which reechoed in the house through Nino's voice.

In the days of Italy's entry into the war, she happened to hear various opinions of the matter. Called one afternoon by the Principal of the High School, because of certain unjustified absences of her son Nino, she found the official in a state of radiant euphoria at the Duce's prompt decision. "We are," the personage declared to her with great pomp, "for peace with victory, at the least possible cost! And today, when the Blitzkrieg of the Axis is about to achieve its goal of peace, we hail the foresight of our Leader, who has won for our Fatherland the fruits of success with the greatest economy. In a single move, saving even the price of tires, here we are at the finish-line, alongside the winner!!" This authoritative speech impressed Ida, who didn't reply.

As far as she could understand, her fellow teachers at the elementary school, whose talk she overheard in the corridors, thought, more or less, like the Principal of the High School. Only an elderly charwoman (called Barbetta—the Beard—by the children because of a senile wisp that grew on her chin) had been caught by Ida as, to ward off evil, she was touching all the doors and murmuring, as she went along, that this action against the French was a "stab in the back" and that certain *lucky* actions sooner or later always bring bad luck.

On the other hand, that same morning, at her appearance in the school, the doorkeeper, marching through the vestibule like a conqueror, had greeted her with this sentence: "Signora Mancuso, when do we enter Paris?" But then, as she was going home later, she heard the baker's apprentice, in the door of the tavern, frowning, confide to the proprietor: "If you ask me, the Rome-Berlin Axis is all wrong. You see what happens? Those Berliners pull some shitty trick, and we, here, from Rome, go and lend them a hand!!" Among such divergent opinions, poor Iduzza didn't dare formulate any view on her own.

To the many mysteries of Authority which frightened her there had now been added the word *Aryans*, which she had never known before. Actually, in this case, that word had no logical meaning; and the Authorities could have replaced it, at will, and with the same public efficacy, with *Pachyderms* or *Ruminants*, or any word whatsoever. But to Iduzza's mind, it became all the more authoritative because it was arcane.

Not even from her mother had she ever heard this denomination "Aryans"; in fact the denomination of *Jews* itself for little Iduzza in the house down in Cosenza had remained an object of great mystery. Except by Nora in her secret councils, it was never uttered in vain in the Ramundo home! I have learned that once, in one of his great anarchist perorations, Giuseppe happened to proclaim, in a thundering voice: "The day will come when masters and proletarians, black and white, male and female, *Jews* and Christians, will be all equal, in the sole honor of being part of humanity!!" But at that shouted word *Jews*, Nora let out a cry of fright and blanched as if seized by a serious illness; whereupon Giuseppe, all repentant, came to her and repeated, this time in a very low voice: ". . . I said, *Jews and Christians* . . ." As if by whispering the word very softly, after having shouted it very loud, he were repairing the disaster!

In any case, now, Ida learned that the Jews were different not only because they were Jews, but also because they were *non-Aryans*. And who were the *Aryans*? To Iduzza this term used by the Authorities suggested something ancient and lofty, on the order of *Baron* or *Count*. And in her concept the Jews were opposed to the *Aryans* much as the plebeians to the patricians (she had studied history!). However, obviously, the non-Aryans, for the Authorities, were the most plebeian of the plebeians! For example, the baker's apprentice, plebeian by class, compared to a Jew was as good as a patrician, because he was Aryan! And if, in the social order, the plebeians were already like scabies, the plebeians of the plebeians must have been leprosy!

It was as if Nora's obsessions, swarming in disorder after her death, had returned to nest inside her daughter. After reporting to the registry, Ida had resumed her former life. She lived just like an Aryan among other Aryans, no one seemed to doubt her total Aryan-ness, and on the rare occasions when she had to show her documents (for example, at the Bursar's office), though her heart was pounding in her breast, her mother's maiden name went completely unnoticed. Her racial secret seemed buried, once and for all, in the files of the Registry; but she, knowing it lay recorded in those mysterious tombs, was still afraid some news of it might filter to the outside, branding her—but especially Nino!—with the mark of the outcast and the impure. Moreover, particularly at school, where she, a clandestine half-Jew, enjoyed the rights and functions due *Aryans*, she felt guilty, a usurper, a counterfeiter.

Also on the rounds of her daily shopping, she had the feeling she was begging, like an orphaned stray puppy, in other people's territory. Then one day, she who, before the racial laws, had never encountered another Jew except Nora, began to follow an incongruous trail of her own, preferring the confines of the Roman Ghetto, the stands and shops of some little Jews who, at that time, were still allowed to continue their humble trade as before.

At first her shyness led her to trade only with certain old people, with half-spent eyes and sealed lips. But chance gradually brought her some less taciturn acquaintances, usually some neighborhood woman, who, encouraged perhaps by Ida's Semitic eyes, would chat with her in passing.

Here she derived her chief historical and political news, since with Aryans she avoided certain subjects, and for one reason or another, she also made slight use of the common sources of information. The family radio, already owned when Alfio was alive, had stopped working over a year ago, so Ninnarieddu, one fine day, had demolished it completely, taking it apart and using the pieces for various constructions of his own (nor did she have the money to buy another). And as for the newspapers, she wasn't in the habit of reading them, and in her home only sports papers appeared, or illustrated film magazines, for Nino's exclusive consumption. The very sight of newspapers had always aroused in her an innate alienation and aversion; and, more recently, she became alarmed at a mere glimpse of the front-page headlines, so thick and black. Passing the newsstands, or on the tram, every day she would happen to glance at them, with distrust, to see if by any chance they denounced, among the Jews' many misdeeds, also her own, with the infamous surname: ALMAGIÀ . . .

Not distant from her school, the Ghetto was a small, ancient quarter, segregated—until the last century—by high walls and gates that were locked in the evening, and subject in those days to fevers, because of the vapors and muck of the nearby Tiber, which did not then have embankments. Since the old quarter had been made more hygienic and its walls torn down, its population had done nothing but multiply; and now, in those same few narrow streets and those two little squares, thousands of people contrived somehow to live. There were many hundreds of infants and youngsters, mostly with mops of curls and lively eyes; and at the beginning of the war, before the famine began, numerous cats still roamed around, resident among the ruins of the ancient Theater of Marcellus, a stone's throw away. The inhabitants, for the most part, were peddlers or rag-men, the only trades allowed the Jews in past centuries, though soon, in the course of the war, these would also be forbidden by the new Fascist laws. A few of these little merchants had, at most, a room or two on the street, to use as a shop or a storehouse. And these, more or less, were all the resources of the small village, where the racial decrees of 1938, still in force, had not been able to affect their lot much.

In certain families of the quarter, the news of those decrees had hardly been noticed, as if they were things concerning the few rich Jewish ladies and gentlemen who lived scattered through the bourgeois residential districts of the city. And as for the various other threats, which circulated darkly, the information Ida gathered about them there was incomplete and confused, like prison grapevine news. In general, among her acquaintances in the little shops, there reigned an ingenuous and trusting incredulity. If she, as an Aryan, gave some faint little hint of knowledge, those poor busy little women, for the most part, responded with an evasive heedlessness or else a reticent resignation. So much of the news was invented for propaganda. And besides, in Italy, certain things could never happen. They trusted in the important friendships (or also in the Fascist merits) of the heads of the Community or of the Rabbi; in Mussolini's benevolence towards the Jews; and even in the protection of the Pope (whereas Popes, in reality, over the centuries, had been among their worst enemies). If some one of them seemed more skeptical, they didn't want to believe him . . . But, to tell the truth, in their position, they had no other defense.

Among them, now and then, there was an aged spinster by the name of Vilma, whom they treated, in those parts, like an imbecile. The muscles of her body and of her face were always restless, while her gaze, on the contrary, was ecstatic, too luminous.

She had been orphaned very young, and, unable to do anything else, she adapted herself to heavy jobs, like a laborer. She ran around all day long, tirelessly, in Trastevere and in Campo dei Fiori, where she also begged for leftovers, not for herself, but for the cats in the Theater of Marcellus. Perhaps the only holiday in her life was when, towards evening, she would sit there on a ruin, in the midst of the cats, scattering half-rotten fishheads and bloodstained offal on the ground for them. Then her always feverish face would become calm and radiant, as in Paradise. (However, with the progress of the war, these blissful encounters of hers were to become only a memory.)

For some time, Vilma brought back to the Ghetto from her daily laboring rounds strange, unheard-of information, which the other women rejected as fantasies of her brain. And in fact, her imagination was always toiling, like a convict, in Vilma's head; however, later, certain *fantasies* of hers were to prove far less fantastic than the truth.

She insisted that the person who kept her so informed was a *Nun* (she went to work in a convent, among other places . . .); or else a *Signora* who, in secret, listened to some forbidden radio broadcasts, but Vilma was not to say the lady's name. In any case, she tried hard to convince them her information was genuine; and every day she would repeat the news, through the quarter, in a hoarse, urgent voice, as if she were pleading. But realizing that no one listened to her or believed her, she would burst into

51

an anguished laughter like whooping cough. The only one, perhaps, who did listen to her, with terrible seriousness, was Iduzza, because in her eyes Vilma, in her appearance and her behavior, resembled a kind of prophetess.

At present, in her messages, as obsessive as they were futile, she harped constantly on the warning to *save the children at least*, declaring she had learned confidentially from the *Nun* that in the imminent future's history a new slaughter was written, worse than Herod's. As soon as the Germans occupied a country, the first thing they did was herd all the Jews, without exception, into one place, and from there, drag them off, beyond the borders, nobody knew where, in "the night and in the fog." Most collapsed or died on the journey. And all of them, the dead and the living, were thrown on top of one another into huge pits, which their companions or relatives were forced to dig in their presence. The only ones allowed to survive were the stronger adults, sentenced to work like slaves for the war. And the children were all slaughtered, from first to last, and thrown into the common ditches along the road.

One day, listening to this talk of Vilma's, in addition to Iduzza, there was also an elderly little woman, humbly dressed, but wearing a hat on her head. Unlike the woman who kept the shop, this stranger gravely agreed with Vilma's insane, hoarse lamentations. In fact (in a low voice, for fear of informers), she spoke up, insisting she herself had heard, from a Carabiniere sergeant, that according to the Germans' laws, the Jews were vermin and were all to be exterminated. After the Axis victory, which was now certain and near, Italy would also become territory of the Reich, and subject to the same, definitive law. Over St. Peter's, instead of the Christian cross, they would put the swastika; and even baptized Christians, if they were not to be included in the blacklist, would have to prove their Aryan blood, FOR FOUR GENERATIONS!

There was ample reason, she added, why all the young Jews of good families who had the money had emigrated from Europe, some to America, some to Australia, while they were still in time. But by now, with money or without, all the frontiers were closed; it was too late.

"Who's in is in, and who's out is out."

At this point, in an unsteady voice, like a fugitive from justice afraid of leaving clues, Iduzza managed to ask her the exact meaning of FOR FOUR GENERATIONS. And the little woman, with the smugness of a scientist or mathematician, and not without elaborating and repeating when she deemed it necessary, explained:

"that in the German law, blood was calculated by heads, quotas, and dozens. Fourth *generation* means: *great-grandfathers*. And to calculate the heads, you only have to count great-grandparents and grandparents, which come to a total of:

"8 great-grandparents + 4 grandparents = 12 heads

"namely, one dozen.

"Now, in this dozen heads, each head, if Aryan, counts as an Aryan quota: one point in the person's favor. If, instead, it's Jewish, it counts as a Jewish quota: one point against. And in the final calculation, the result must be at least two-thirds plus one! A third of a dozen = 4; two-thirds = 8 + 1 = 9. Anyone appearing to be judged must present a minimum of 9 Aryan points. If he has less, even half a point less, he is considered of Jewish blood."

At home, alone, Ida plunged into a complicated calculation. For herself, really, the solution was simple: born of an Aryan and a mother whose family had been Jewish for many generations, she had only six points out of twelve, and the result was therefore negative. But her main concern, namely Nino, proved more abstruse, and here the sum, as she computed it again and again, became muddled in her brain. She was then inspired to take a sheet of paper and draw a family tree for Nino, in which a J marked his Jewish grandparents and great-grandparents, and an A, the Aryans (an X stood for the names that, for the moment, had escaped her memory):

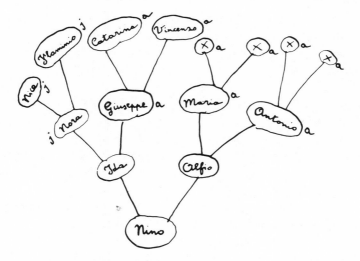

And the count came out propitiously. Nino, if only by a slight margin, fell within the obligatory number of points: nine out of twelve. Aryan!

This result, however, wasn't enough to give her peace, not even about her son's position. The real terms of the law, in the future and also in the present, remained too variable and obscure to her. She recalled, for example, having heard in Calabria from an American emigrant that dark blood always wins out over pale blood. A single drop of black blood is enough to determine that a man isn't white, but a black halfbreed.

4. And so, it's finally clear why the poor woman, on a January day in 1941, greeted the encounter with that humble soldier at San Lorenzo like a nightmare vision. The fears besieging her prevented her from seeing anything of him except a German army uniform. And on meeting, at the very door of her home, that uniform which seemed stationed there, waiting for her, she thought she had arrived at the terrible rendezvous preordained for her since the beginning of the world.

He must be an agent of the Racial Committee, perhaps a Corporal, or a Captain, of the SS, come to identify her. For her, he had no features of his own. He was a copy of the thousands of similar faces that multiplied to infinity the sole, incomprehensible face of her persecution.

The soldier was offended, feeling the unknown lady's evident and extraordinary disgust was an injustice. He wasn't accustomed to inspiring disgust in women, and furthermore he knew (despite his earlier little disappointments) he was in an allied, not an enemy country. However, in his mortification, instead of giving up, he insisted. When the family cat, through some absurd ill-humor, crouches in his private hiding-places, the children persist in hunting him.

For that matter, she didn't even try to move aside. Her only act was to hide in one of her shopping bags—like threatening documents of her own guilt—some school copybook she was holding. She did not see him so much as, in a splitting of her personality, she saw herself, stripped now of every disguise, down to her private, half-Jewish heart, there before him.

If she could have seen him, truly, she would perhaps have realized he stood before her as a beggar rather than an assassin. As if acting the role of the pilgrim, deliberately to move her to pity, he had placed his tilted cheek against his palm. And his bass voice, already mature, but fresh and new, with a certain greenness of growth in it, repeated twice the cheerful but stubborn plea:

"Schlafen . . . Schlafen . . ."

To her, totally ignorant of the German language, the incomprehensible word, with its mysterious pantomime, sounded like some formula of investigation or accusation. And in Italian she attempted a vague answer, which was reduced to an almost tearful grimace. But for the soldier, the wine had transformed all the terrestrial Babel into a circus. Resolutely, on a gallant-bandit impulse, he took the bundles and shopping bags from her hands; and with a trapeze-artist's leap, he preceded her forthwith up the stairs. At each landing, he stopped to wait for her, like a son who, coming home with his slow mother, acts as scout. And she followed him, stumbling at every step, like a petty thief dragging himself behind the bearers of his cross.

Her worst anxiety, during that climb, was the thought that Nino, today of all days, by some rare chance might be at home in the afternoon. For the first time since she had become a mother, she hoped her little street ruffian would stay out all day and all night. And she swore to herself desperately that, if the German asked about her son, she would deny not only his presence, but even his existence.

On the sixth landing, they had arrived. And when, bathed in icy sweat, she had trouble dealing with the lock, the German put the bags on the floor and promptly lent her a hand, like someone coming into his own home. For the first time since she had borne him, she was relieved to discover Ninnarieddu was out.

The interior consisted of two rooms in all, plus lavatory and kitchen; and it displayed, besides its untidiness, the coupled desolation of poverty and the lower middle class. But the immediate effect of that place on the young soldier was a savage homesickness and melancholy, because of some slight affinities with his maternal house in Bavaria. His desire to play vanished like the smoke of a Bengal light; and his drunkenness, not yet worn off, became a feverish bitterness in his body. Plunging into total silence, he began to march among the considerable clutter of the room with the tough look of a stray starving wolf, seeking something to appease his hunger in an alien lair.

In Ida's eyes, this look corresponded exactly to his police duties. Preparing herself for a general search, she remembered the paper with Nino's family tree, which she had put in a drawer among other important documents; and she wondered if those enigmatic marks would not be obvious clues for him.

He came to a halt at an enlarged photograph, which occupied the place of honor on the wall, framed like an important oil painting. It portrayed (at about half life-size) a little hoodlum of perhaps fifteen or sixteen, wrapped in a sumptuous camel's-hair coat, which he wore as if it were a flag. Between the fingers of his right hand you could vaguely discern a cigarette's whiteness; and his left foot rested on the running-board of a custom-built sports car (parked there at random by some unknown owner), with the masterful attitude of tiger-hunters, in the great forests.

In the background, the buildings of a city street were visible, with their signs. But the excessive enlargement, blown up from what had been originally the cheap product of a street photographer, had made the whole scene somewhat faint and blurred.

Having examined the picture thoroughly, the soldier connected it, in his own supposition, with the family cult of the dead. And pointing his finger at the subject of the photograph, he asked Ida with the gravity of an investigator:

"Tot?" (dead?)

The question, naturally, was incomprehensible to her. However, the only defense her terror counseled her today was to answer always *no* to whatever inquiry, like illiterates under police interrogation. And she didn't know that, this time, contrary to all her intentions, she was giving information to the enemy.

"No! no!" she answered, in a doll's little voice, her eyes amazed and fierce. And, in fact, that was truly not the memorial of a dead person, but a recent photo of her son Ninnuzzu, which he had had enlarged and framed, on his own initiative. In fact, among bitter quarrels, she was still paying the instalments on that camel's-hair coat which Nino, last autumn, had ordered without authorization.

For that matter, the house itself betrayed hopelessly, and in a loud voice, that fugitive inhabitant she wanted to conceal! The room, which the German had boldly invaded from the hall, was a kind of living-room-study, and at night it served also for sleeping, as was obvious from a daybed, still unmade and consisting simply of some elementary springs without legs, and a lumpy mattress. Around this daybed, like a dog's pallet (the pillow askew, stained and greasy with brilliantine, sheets and blankets all rumpled and tangled) there lay, hurled on the floor the previous evening, an artificial silk counterpane and some hard cushions (which in the daytime camouflaged the bed); and among these, further, were to be found: a sports magazine; a pajama top, pale blue, of a still fairly small size; and a medium-size sock, dirty, with a hole, in a loud plaid pattern . . .

On the wall, over the bed, in the place of holy pictures, there were various photographs, cut out of magazines and held by thumbtacks, of movie actresses in bathing suits or evening dress: the most spectacular had been marked with great scrolls in red pencil, so emphatic they seemed the trumpet signals of an assault, or the cries of an amorous cat out hunting. On the same wall, but to one side, and also attached with thumbtacks, there was also a copy of a poster showing a Roman eagle clutching the British Isles in its talons.

On a chair, there was a football! And on the little table, among unbound schoolbooks (horribly mauled and debased until they seemed rats' leftovers), there were piles of other sports papers, magazines, and cheap adventure serials; a thriller showing a half-naked lady on the cover, screaming, threatened by a huge, apelike hand; and an album with illustrations of redskins. And further: a Young Fascist's fez; a wind-up phonograph with a few scattered records; and a complicated, vague structure, in which you could recognize, among other things, the parts of a small motor.

Beside the sofa, on a rickety easy chair, set against the wall, beneath a printed view with the legend *Grand Hôtel des îles Borromées*, there were piled up some parts of flotsam of vehicles, a deflated tire prominent among them, a mileage gauge, and some handlebars. On the arm of the chair rested a jersey with a team's colors. And in the corner, propped against the wall, was a real musket.

Amid such an eloquent array, the soldier's fantastic movements were converted, for Ida, into the precise movements of a fatal machine which was printing also Nino's name beside her own in the blacklist of Jews and their hybrids. As the minutes passed, her own misconceptions were acquiring an obsessive power over her, reducing her to the native, ingenuous terror of a prerational age. Standing motionless, her coat still on and her little mourning hat on her head, she was no longer a lady of San Lorenzo, but a desperate Asiatic migratory bird, with brown feathers and black crest, overwhelmed in its temporary clump of bushes by a horrendous Occidental deluge.

And in the meanwhile, the German's drunken thoughts did not concern races or religions or nations, but only ages. He was mad with envy and, to himself, he argued and silently stammered: "God-damn-it, the luck-y ones are still un-der the draft age—and—and—they can enjoy their be-long-ings at home—with their mothers! and the foot-ball! and screw-ing and every-thing—everything! as if the war was on the moon or the plan-et Mars . . . grow-ing up is the worst luck . . . Where am I any-way? What am I do-ing here? How did I get here? . . ." At this point, remembering he still hadn't introduced himself to his hostess, he went and stood squarely facing her; and without even looking at her, his mouth cross, he declared:

"Mein Name ist Gunther!"

Then he remained there, in a discontented attitude, expecting this propitiatory introduction to produce an effect denied him in advance. The lady's huge eyes, hostile and dazed, merely blinked briefly, suspiciously at those German sounds, whose only meaning for her was a sibylline threat. Then the soldier's gaze darkened, though he allowed a hint of lively warmth to show in his eyes, as he felt an incurable affection. And remaining there, half-seated on the edge of the cluttered table, with a kind of reluctance (which betrayed a jealous privacy) he produced a little piece of pasteboard from his pocket and held it under Ida's eyes.

She took a frozen, sidelong glance at it, expecting an SS identity card with a swastika, or perhaps a Wanted photograph of Ninnuzzu Mancuso, with a yellow star. But instead it was a snapshot of a family group, in which she could vaguely discern, against a background of little houses and canebrakes, the heavy, radiant figure of a middle-aged German woman surrounded by five or six half-grown boys. Among them, the soldier, with a faint smile, pointed out one (himself), more grown than the others, dressed in a windbreaker and a cyclist's cap. Then, as the lady's eyes wandered over that anonymous group with dark apathy, he moved his finger to point out the landscape and sky in the background, informing her:

"Dachau."

His tone of voice, in uttering that name, was the same that a three-month-old kitten might have, claiming its basket. And for that matter, the name meant nothing to Ida, who had never heard it before, unless by chance, without remembering it . . . However, at that innocuous and indifferent name, the wild, transitory migrant, now identified with her heart, leaped inside her. And fluttering horribly in the distorted space of the little room, it began to slam, in chirping tumult, against the walls that had no exit.

Ida's body had remained inert, like her consciousness, with no movement but a throb of the muscles and a defenseless gaze of extreme repulsion, as if she were facing a monster. And at that same moment, the soldier's eyes, their dark-blue, sea color, approaching violet (an unusual color on the continent; it is more often encountered in the Mediterranean islands) filled with an innocence almost frightening in its timeless antiquity: contemporary with the Earthly Paradise! To those eyes her gaze seemed the definitive insult. And instantaneously a tempest of anger clouded them. And yet through this clouding there filtered a childish questioning, which no longer expected the sweetness of an answer, but wanted one all the same.

It was at this point that Ida, without thinking, began to shout: "No! No! No!" in the hysterical voice of an immature girl. In reality, with this *no* of hers, she was not addressing him or the outside world, but another secret threat she sensed from some interior point or nerve, suddenly rising within her from her childhood years, something of which she thought herself healed. As if returning to that age, backwards, through foreshortened time, she promptly recognized the great dizziness, the strange echoes of voices and torrents which, when she was little, had announced her spells. Now her cry was against that snare, which would steal her from safeguarding the house, and Nino!!

However, this new, inexplicable reaction of hers (*no*, the only answer she had given this day) acted on the soldier's confused wrath like a signal of revolt against an immense transgression. Unexpectedly, the bitter tenderness that had humiliated him with its torture since that morning was unleashed in him, with a fierce determination! ". . . fare amore! . . . FARE AMORE! . . ." he shouted, repeating in a boyish outburst another two of the 4 Italian words that, in his foresight, he had made them teach him at the frontier. And without even taking off his uniform, caring nothing that she was old, he hurled himself on top of her, throwing her on that disheveled daybed, and raping her with rage as if he wanted to murder her.

He felt her writhe horribly, but, unaware of her illness, he thought she was struggling against him, and he became the more obstinate for this reason, like all drunken soldiery. In reality, she had lost consciousness, in a temporary absence from him and from the situation, but he didn't realize this. And he was so charged with stern, repressed tensions that, at the moment of orgasm, he emitted a great scream above her. Then, in the following moment, he peeped at her in time to see her face, filled with amazement, relax in a smile of ineffable humility and sweetness.

"Carina carina," he started saying to her (this was the fourth and last Italian word he had learned). And at the same time he began kissing her, with little kisses full of sweetness, on the dazed face that seemed to look at him and continued smiling at him with a kind of gratitude. Meanwhile, she was gradually coming to, abandoned beneath him. And in the state of relaxation and calm that always passed between the spell and consciousness, she felt him again penetrating her, but slowly this time, with a heart-rending and possessive movement, as if they were already kin and accustomed to each other. She found again that sense of fulfillment and repose she had known as a girl, at the end of an attack, when she was received once more by the affectionate room of her father and her mother; but that childish experience of hers was extended today, through her half-waking state, into the blissful sensation of returning to her own, complete body. That other body, greedy, harsh, and warm, which explored her in the center of her maternal sweetness was, at once, all the hundred thousand fevers and coolnesses and adolescent hungers that flowed together from their jealous lands to fill to the brim her girlish river. It was all the hundred thousand young male animals, terrestrial and vulnerable, in a mad and merry dance, which struck into her lungs and to the roots of her hair, calling her in every language. Then it slumped down, becoming once more a sole imploring flesh, dissolving within her womb in a sweet, warm, ingenuous surrender, which made her smile, moved, like the only gift of a poor man, or a child.

It wasn't, for her, not even this time, a true erotic pleasure. It was an extraordinary happiness without orgasm, as sometimes happens in dreams, before puberty.

The soldier, this time, in sating himself, let out a little moan, among light kisses, and letting his whole body sink on her, he promptly fell asleep.

59

Regaining consciousness, she felt his weight on her body, the rough uniform and the belt buckle pressing on her naked belly. And she found herself with her legs still apart, and his sex, now poor, helpless, and as if cut off, resting gently against her own. The boy slept serenely, snoring; but as she moved to free herself, he clutched her instinctively against himself; and his features, even in his sleep, assumed a grimace of possession and jealousy, like a real lover.

She was so weakened that in separating from him she had the impression she was performing a mortal labor; but finally she managed to free herself, and she sank to the floor on her knees, among the pillows scattered beside the cot. She straightened up her clothes as best she could; but the effort produced in her a nausea that made her heart turn over; and she remained there, where she was, on her knees beside the daybed with the sleeping German. As always, when she came to, only the shadow of a recollection was left her from her illness, no more than the initial sensation of a confused theft, an instant's duration. In her memory, actually, there was a total blank, from the moment the boy had started kissing her face, whispering *carina carina*, to the other moment, earlier, when he had showed her the photograph.

However, the whole previous period, not just the frightened hour before her attack, but the entire past, in retrospect, also presented itself to her recollection as a point of arrival, still confused in an immense remoteness. She had set sail from the crowded and vociferating continent of her memory, on a boat that in this interval had gone around the world, and now, returning to its port of departure, found it silent and calm again. There were no more shouting crowds, no lynching. The familiar objects, stripped of all emotion, were no longer instruments, but creatures, vegetable or aquatic, algae, coral, starfish, which breathed in the sea's repose, belonging to no one.

Even the sleep of her aggressor, stretched out there before her, seemed to rest on the leprosy of all experiences—violence, fear—like a healing. In moving her eyes (cleared by the recent spell as if by a bath of luminous transparency), she saw on the ground, at some distance from each other, her run-down shoes, which she had lost, along with her hat, while writhing unconsciously in the German's arms. But not bothering to pick them up, seated, inert, on her bare heels, she fixed her widened eyes again on the sleeper, with the stupid look of the maiden in fairy tales, staring at the dragon which a magic potion has made harmless.

Now that his lover had escaped him, the boy had embraced the pillow and was hugging it tight, stubborn in his possessive jealousy of a moment before. However, his face had meanwhile taken on another expression, intent and grave; and Ida, almost without realizing it, immediately read there the subject and the plot of his dream, if not the details. The dream was suited to a boy of the age, roughly, of eight. There were important matters under discussion: the sale of bicycles or accessories, where he had to deal with an untrustworthy character, no doubt an eccentric sort, a Levantine smuggler perhaps, or a Chicago gangster, or a Malayan pirate . . .

This character was trying to cheat: and consequently the sleeper's lips, of a parched pink, wild and a bit chapped, protruded in an ill-concealed pout. His eyelids hardened, fluttering the gilded lashes, so short they seemed dust. And his brow furrowed in concentration, below the clumps of hair, darker than his lashes, smooth, suggesting a cool, damp softness, like the coat of a little brown kitten just bathed by its mother.

It would have been easy, now, to kill him, following the example of Judith in the Bible; but Ida, by nature, couldn't conceive such an idea, not even as a fantasy. Her mind, distracted by its reading of the dream, was darkened by the thought that perhaps the intruder would go on sleeping until late in the evening, and Nino, coming home, might surprise him, still here. Nino, however, with his political ideas, might even be proud of this visit, and would hail the German, his mother's rapist, as a companion . . .

Instead, as suddenly as he had fallen asleep, the German woke abruptly, as if at a trumpet's brutal blare. And immediately he looked at the watch on his wrist: he had slept barely a few minutes, still he didn't have much time to get back to the transit camp for roll call. He stretched: not with the arrogant bliss of boys when they release themselves from sleep, but rather with the disgust of an anguish and a curse, as if he had discovered again the chains of prison attached to his limbs. The twilight shadows were beginning; and Ida, having risen, with her barefoot and trembling body, approached the light socket, to insert the plug. The wires were loose, and the light of the bulb flickered. Then Gunther, who in Germany was an electrician by trade, took from his pocket a special clasp-knife (the envy of the whole army, a multiple tool which, in addition to the blade, hid a razor, a file, and a screwdriver in the handle); masterfully he repaired the plug.

It was clear, from his eager promptness, full of commitment, that this operation had a double value to him. First: it gave him an opportunity, slight as it was, to exert himself for the victim of his crime, which now, as his drunkenness was wearing off, began to alarm him and assail him with remorse. And second: it was an excuse for him to linger a while longer in the tiny room that today (though unwillingly) had received him again in a human space. When he left here, only a final Africa awaited him; now it was absolutely no longer identified with the interesting and colorful Africa of films or books, but with a kind of deformed crater, in the midst of a wasteland of wretched boredom.

Meanwhile, huddled in the shadow of the wall, Ida observed his little job with mute admiration, because in her (as in certain primitive peoples) there remained a timid, unconfessed distrust of electricity and its phenomena.

When he had finished fixing the light, he still remained seated, where he had put himself, on the edge of the cot; and, to broach a dialogue, pointing his forefinger at his person, he was about to boast,

". . . nach Afrika . . ." but he remembered this was a military secret, and kept his mouth closed.

For perhaps a minute more he lingered, sitting there, his torso bent forward, his arms lying across his knees, like an emigrant or a life-prisoner, already herded onto the departing vessel. With no further object to look at, his lonely eyes seemed drawn to the bulb, which now shone steadily at the head of the daybed (it was the same one that Ninnuzzu kept burning at night to read his picture magazines in bed). His eyes expressed a kind of dazed curiosity, but in reality they were empty. In the electric light, their dark blue center seemed almost black, while the surrounding white was no longer bloodshot or clouded by wine, but milky, tinged with pale blue.

Spontaneously, the boy raised his eyes towards Ida. And she met his tormented gaze, of an infinite ignorance and of a total awareness: both lost, the one and the other, in begging a single, impossible charity, vague also for him who asked it.

As he was about to go, it occurred to him to leave her a souvenir, according to a custom observed in his farewells to other girls. However, not knowing what to give her, he rummaged in his pockets, then found his famous knife; and though it meant a great sacrifice for him, he placed it in her palm, without further explanation.

In exchange, he also wanted a souvenir to take away. And he turned his puzzled gaze around the room, without discovering anything there; when his eyes fell on a little bunch of flowers, trampled-looking and almost greasy (an offering of her poor pupils), which nobody had bothered to put in water since morning and which lay on a shelf, half-withered. Then he detached a little reddish flower and gravely placing it among some papers in his wallet, he said:

"Mein ganzes Leben lang!" (*For all my life!*)

For him, naturally, it was only a phrase. And he said it with the usual bragging and traitorous tone of all boys when they say it to their girls. It's a phrase that makes an effect, to be used for that purpose; but naturally it isn't valid, since nobody can really believe he will preserve a souvenir for that whole indescribable eternity which is life! He didn't know, on the other hand, that for him the eternity would be reduced to a few hours. His stay in Rome ended that same evening. Less than three days later, the air convoy in which he had just been embarked (from Sicily towards some southern or southeastern direction) was attacked over the Mediterranean. And he was among the dead.

. . . . . . **1941**

JANUARY

Continuation of the disastrous winter campaign of the Italian troops sent to invade Greece.

In North Africa, the Italians are attacked by the British and abandon their colonies of Cyrenaica and Marmarica.

FEBRUARY–MAY

Following the landing of German armored troops in North Africa, the Italo-German forces reoccupy Cyrenaica and Marmarica.

The Germans intervene in Greece, to prevent the complete rout of the Italian expedition. For this enterprise the collaboration of Bulgaria and Yugoslavia is asked. Yugoslavia refuses, and Germany reacts by occupying and devastating its territory, with punitive bombardments of Belgrade. Greece, after its long resistance, is quickly forced to surrender and is subjugated by the Italo-Germans.

Non-aggression pact and mutual concessions between Imperial Japan and the Soviet Union.

In East Africa, victorious offensive of the British armies which occupy the three capitals of the Italian Colonial Empire (Mogadishu, Asmara, Addis Ababa) and, in collaboration with the Ethiopian partisans, restore the emperor of Ethiopia, Haile Selassie, to his throne.

JUNE

Germany unleashes its great Operation Barbarossa against the Soviets, guaranteeing its triumphant conclusion before winter ("Stalin's Russia will be wiped off the map in eight weeks"). Italy decides to participate in the venture. At Verona, Mussolini reviews one of the divisions setting off for the new front.

JULY

Japan occupies Indochina, formerly a French possession.

In Yugoslavia, the resistance struggle against the Nazi-Fascist occupation begins.

German forces advance triumphantly across Soviet territory.

SEPTEMBER

The German government decrees that all Jews above the age of six are required to wear a yellow Star of David on their chests.

OCTOBER

Mahatma Gandhi of India urges recourse to passive resistance (which he has already declared among his own people) for all peoples subject to the British Colonial Empire.

In Poland, the obligatory segregation of the Jewish population, already established with the Nazi occupation, is followed by the decree of the death penalty for any Jew caught outside the ghetto.

The victorious advance of the Panzerdivisionen and the German infantry continues in Soviet territory. In the four months since the beginning of the Operation, three million Russians are already out of combat (by the Führer's order, the fate of prisoners of war, as of other subhumans, is extermination. All international war conventions are considered void).

NOVEMBER

Meeting of the Führer with Himmler, head of the SS and of the Gestapo (secret police) for the final solution of the Jewish problem, according to the plan already initiated, which provides for the deportation of all living Jews to extermination camps. Plants and equipment for mass liquidation of the deported are already operating in various Lagers, and some of the most important industrial firms of the Reich collaborate in their technical installation.

In Russia, the armies of the Reich continue their victorious advance, besieging Leningrad and heading towards Moscow.

DECEMBER

Leningrad does not surrender. Farther south, driven back by a Russian counterattack, the Germans interrupt their march on Moscow, executing a difficult withdrawal through the mud and ice of the winter.

In North Africa, the Italo-Germans are forced to withdraw from Cyrenaica.

In East Africa, the surrender of the last garrisons to the British forces marks the end of the Italian Colonial Empire.

With the "Night and Fog" decree, the Führer orders his troops in all occupied countries to capture and suppress without a trace anyone who represents a danger for "German security." The executions, entrusted to special units of the SS and the SD, amount to about one million in Europe.

In the Pacific, the Japanese suddenly attack the American fleet, stationed at Pearl Harbor. War between the United States and Japan, extended to the other Tripartite Powers (Italy and Germany). This further extension of the world conflict will increase to forty-three the number of belligerent nations . . .

Three hundred rejoicing heralds, banners flying,
run through the cities, with drums and trumpets.
All bells peal.
The Gloria is intoned
by the organ in the cathedral.
Messengers have set forth on plumed horses
to carry the news in all seven directions.
From kingdoms and principalities the caravans move off
bearing as gift the treasures of the forty escutcheons
in coffers of aromatic wood.
All gates are flung open. On the thresholds pilgrims make
      greeting with hands pressed together.
Camels, asses, and goats bend their knees.
And on all lips a single song!
Everywhere banquets, balls, and fires of rejoicing!
For today the queen
has brought into the world an heir to the throne!

1 Ida never came to learn the fate of her aggressor. She never even knew his name, nor did she try to know it. The fact that, after his exploit, he sent no further word and vanished as he had appeared, for her, was a certain and natural conclusion, preordained. But still, from the very night after her encounter with him, she began to fear his return. When he had left, in her somnolent state and with mechanical movements, she fixed supper for herself and for Nino, who, however, was late as usual in coming home. In the days of her childhood, the attacks of her illness always left her with a voracious appetite; but this time, instead, while she reluctantly chewed a bit of food, she dozed off on her chair in the kitchen. Around nine, she was wakened by the great ringing of the bell in the hall, as Nino returned; and as soon as she had opened the door for him, she went to bed, falling at once into a dreamless lethargy. She slept in this way for a few hours; then, in the middle of the night, she woke with a start, feeling that the German, taller and bigger than life, was bending over her in the darkness, ready to assault her again, whispering unknown words into her ear, hissing and meaningless, the kind you use with babies or with pets. She turned on the light. The alarm said four o'clock; and the events of the previous day ran once more through her absolutely lucid mind in a rapid clash of sharp shadows, like a film in black and white. Beyond the closed door of her room there was that other room, where Nino was now sleeping! Remembering she hadn't remade his bed, she shuddered in shame and dismay; and feverishly turning off the light, to take refuge in the darkness, she huddled under the covers.

She was wakened at six by the sound of the alarm clock. And that morning, and the following ones, she held her classes with the insistent sensation that she had a visible halo around her body, like a second body of hers (at times icy, at times searing) which she had constantly to shift. She didn't feel the same Ida as before, but rather an adventuress, leading a double life. And it seemed to her that her limbs projected the dishonor of her rape onto her pupils and onto everybody, and that on her face, as on soft wax, the marks of those kisses were imprinted. In her whole life, she had never approached any man but Alfio, not even in thought; and now her adventure seemed written everywhere, like a sensational adultery.

In the street, if she barely glimpsed a German soldier in the distance, she immediately thought she recognized that one (from a certain gait, a certain tilt of the head, or a position of the arms) and she would turn the corner, her heart pounding. And this new fear had temporarily driven out her other fear, of Nazi persecutions. Also the unexpected return of her illness, after she had been cured for so many years, didn't worry her. At heart she was convinced (and, in fact, she wasn't mistaken) that the attack wouldn't be repeated. She wondered at first if she should consult the pharmacist for some special sedative, no longer recalling the name of the one used before in Calabria; but then she gave up the idea, suspecting that the pharmacist might guess not only her old illness, but worse, also the circumstances of this belated relapse.

Every day, on coming home, she would peep around the corner towards the door of the building, in the fear of seeing him again, waiting there, as if by appointment. Then, running through the entrance, she would begin to suspect that, knowing her schedule, he had already preceded her to the landing, where she would find him ready, outside the door there, acting as if he wanted to give her a surprise. She pricked up her ears to hear his breathing; she almost thought she could catch his smell, and without strength, she dragged herself up the steps, growing steadily paler as she came closer to the seventh floor. Having opened the door, casting a sidelong look, she thought she glimpsed his cap on the rack, where he had put it that day, on entering.

During her afternoons in the house, she expected a new invasion of his at any moment. And this anxiety gripped her especially when she was alone, as if Nino's presence were a safeguard against danger. Every now and then, she would go into the hall and listen, her ear to the door, afraid of hearing again that firm tread which had remained in her ears, recognizable among all the footsteps of the earth. As much as possible she avoided staying in the living-room-study; and when she made up the daybed she was hindered by a terrible heaviness in her arms and legs, which nearly made her faint.

At night, during this period, she didn't dream; or at least, on waking, she didn't recall having dreamed. Often, however, she would be roused from sleep, as on that first night, with the sensation that he was near her, a weight so hot it almost burned her. And that he was kissing her, wetting her face with saliva, and meanwhile he was muttering in her ear no longer tender little words but incomprehensible reproaches, in threatening German.

She had never felt at ease in her own body, to such a degree that she didn't look at it even when she bathed. Her body had grown up with her like an outsider; and not even in her girlhood had it ever been beautiful, with its thick ankles, frail shoulders, and the prematurely withered bosom. Her single pregnancy, like an illness, had been enough to make her misshapen forever; and afterwards, in her widowhood, she had never thought that someone might use her body again as a woman's, to make love. With this excessive weight on its hips, and the wasting of its limbs, it had become for her only a toilsome burden.

Now, after that notorious afternoon, in the company of her body she felt more alone. And while she dressed in the still-dark dawns, when she had to perform certain intimate acts, such as fastening her corset or straightening her stockings, she would irresistibly start crying.

That very first day she had hastily hidden the knife he had left her, at the bottom of a chest in the hall, full of scraps and rubbish. And she had never dared look at it again, or shift those scraps, or open the chest. But every time she passed it, she felt a thump in her blood, trembling like a timid witness who knows the hiding-place of some criminal loot.

Gradually, however, as the days went by, she became persuaded her fear of encountering the soldier again was absurd. By now he was surely at some distant front, raping other women or shooting Jews. But, for her, his menace had waned. Between that stranger and Ida Ramundo no relationship existed any more, neither present nor future.

Except for herself, no one knew anything of their fleeting relationship; and not even Nino had any suspicions. So now she had only to expel it from her memory, continuing her usual life.

She began all her days by waking at six, then going into the kitchen and, with the electric light on, preparing their breakfast and Nino's noonday meal. Then she would dress and, having waked Nino, always rushing and breathless, she would go to her school, two tram-rides away from the house. On coming out after her classes, her cheeks flushed and her throat hoarse, she would bustle about the neighborhood of the school, to do her shopping before the stores' afternoon closing (since, in fear of the wartime blackout, she avoided going out after dark); and on the way home, three times a week, she would get off, with her shopping bags, at Castro Pretorio, where she gave private lessons. Finally, she came home; and after eating Nino's leftovers, she would straighten up the rooms, correct her pupils' homework, prepare supper; and then her nightly waiting for Ninnarieddu would commence.

Perhaps a week had gone by when the series of her dreamless nights was disrupted, and she dreamed. She was apparently coming home, carrying, through theft or error, not one of her shopping-bags but instead a basket of the kind used in Calabria for the vintage. From the basket a green plant sprouted and, in an instant, it ramified through the room, and outside the house, over all the walls of the courtyard. And it rose to become a forest of fabulous plants, foliage, bougainvilleas, gigantic campanulas with Oriental and tropical colors, grapes and oranges as big as melons. Inside the forest, some little wild animals played, like squirrels, all with tiny blue eyes, peeping out in merry curiosity, and now and then they darted through the air, as if they had wings. Meanwhile, a crowd of people had started looking out of all the windows, but she herself was absent, God knows where; however, it was known she was the defendant. This dream followed her for a few more minutes, after she had waked; then it vanished.

By the end of January, she had already relegated to the depths of her memory that post-Epiphany afternoon, pressing it down among the other remnants and shreds of her past life, all of which, if she remembered them, hurt her.

But among the many terrors and dangers, possible and impossible, consequent to her famous adventure, there was one, possible, which had never occurred to her: was it an unconscious defense, perhaps, supported by her matrimonial experience, which, in all those years of love, had given her only one child?

Since puberty, her body had been subject to certain irregularities of rhythm. The uterus, with its menstruations, was, in her, like an anomalous wound that at times exhausted her with violent hemorrhages, and at other times seemed to arrest its natural flow, gnawing at her from inside, worse than an ulcer. From the age of eleven (her puberty had come early), Ida had meekly grown accustomed to such obscure caprices; and now amid her doubts and ailments, a number of weeks passed before she recognized this supreme and unthought-of scandal: that her indecent relations with an anonymous German had left her pregnant.

.   .   .

The idea of somehow procuring an abortion never even entered her imagination. The only defense she managed to think of was to hide her condition from everyone as long as she could. The other problems, then, which threatened her from the imminent future, were absolutely inconceivable to her; and she could only thrust them from her mind. This was easier for her in her new physical state, which daily made her perceptions more blurred, detaching her from her outer motives for anguish, and lowering her into an almost thoughtless passivity. Nobody bothered to ask her about the occasional nausea (not serious) that afflicted her, and for which, when necessary, it was not hard for her to invent excuses. At that time, among current illnesses, colitis was fashionable, even in proletarian neighborhoods; and to explain certain little indispositions, she invented the story that she suffered from a form of colitis. This nausea came over her suddenly, at the sight of the most commonplace objects: a doorknob, for example, or a tram-track. Abruptly, such objects seemed to become embodied in her own being, fermenting there in a yeast of bitterness. From the past then, she was stirred by memories of the time when she was carrying Nino. And at the moment she was forced to bend over and vomit, it seemed to her that the past and the future and her senses and all the objects of the world were turning in a single wheel, in a disintegration that was also a liberation.

Her only raving, during that season, was in her dreams, which had resumed visiting her, fairly often, with their old violence. She finds herself running here and there, completely naked, through a square that seems deserted, but yet resounds, on all sides, with insults and laughter . . . She is imprisoned in a kind of kennel, and from her little barred window she can see tall young girls go by, dressed in many colors, like certain grand wet-nurses, who carry beautiful infants, laughing, in their arms. The young women know her, but they look away so as not to see her; and also the infants are not laughing for her. She was mistaken, to believe that . . .

She is walking with her father, who shelters her beneath his cloak; but then the cloak flies off, as if on its own, without her father any more. And she finds herself a tiny girl again, alone, on some mountain paths, with little trickles of blood from her vagina. The whole path behind her is marked by the spoor of her blood. To worsen the looming scandal, the familiar whistle of Ninnarieddu is heard from below; and like a fool, instead of running off, she stops on the path to play with a nanny-goat . . . How could she have failed to see the goat is howling, in labor, about to give birth! And meanwhile, nearby, all ready, there is the *sergeant-major* of the electric slaughterhouses . . .

. . . Lots of little Polish children, in rags, are playing, rolling some tiny golden rings. Blessed rings, and they don't know it. This game is forbidden, in Poland. Punished by death!!! . . .

Such dreams, even the most futile ones, left her in a state of grievous distress; but then, in the course of the morning, she would forget them.

Now, every day she had to make a great effort to get up; and in the succession of her hours there was no act, however simple, that wasn't toilsome for her. But this struggle, while it reminded her constantly of her condition, sustained her, like a kind of drunkenness. She ran from one tram to another, and from one neighborhood to another, always with her shopping-bags and her little hat, its veil askew, and a furrow above her eyebrows. Once she had reached the school, she proceeded as usual with everything: roll call, general inspection of ears and fingernails for the daily hygienic check . . . And even to these tasks, as to the others of her teaching, she applied herself with extreme gravity and concentration as usual, as if they were matters of the most serious importance. From habit, she never sat behind the desk, but moved along the rows, with eyes that, in this duty, were never still, beneath her frowning brows.

"Write in your copybooks: *Dictation*

"*The hero-ic Ital-i-an ar-my has* (third person singular of the verb 'to have') *car-ried the glo-ri-ous ban-ners of Rome be-yond the moun-tains and be-yond the seas to fight for the great-ness of the Fa-ther-land* (capital *F*) *and to de-fend its* (capitalize again!) *Em-pire un-til the fi-nal vic-to-ry* . . .

"Annarumi! Stop trying to copy from Mattei! I see you!"

"But, teacher. I'm not copying."

"Oh, yes, you are. I saw you. Yes, yes. And if you try it again, I'll give you an F."

". . . . ."

". . . . ."

"But what if I don't copy?"

"Then I'll forgive you."

. . . "And what's our homework for tomorrow, teacher?" "What's our assignment?" . . . "What's the assignment for tomorrow?" "Signora Ramundo, what's our homework for tomorrow?"

"For tomorrow: Composition: theme: *A thought about swallows.* Problem: *Luigino is three years old. His brother is twice his age, and his sister one third. How old is his brother? How old is his sister? And how many months old is Luigino?* Penmanship: write three times in your fair copybook: *Vittorio and Elena are the names of our August Sovereigns . . .*"

At evening, in the kitchen, with supper prepared, she waited as usual for Ninnarieddu, who, even when he came home before the door to the building was closed, rarely went to bed after dinner. Far more often, he devoured the supper in haste, without even sitting down, leaning out of the window every now and then to give a whistle to his friends impatiently waiting in the courtyard below. And then he would ask for money for the movies. And she would doggedly deny it to him, until he would stalk around the room angrily, like a true exploiter of women, and finally would take it from her, by force or with threats of running away from home forever. Many evenings, this first quarrel would be followed by a second, because he would insistently demand the doorkey for the double-lock at night, as well as the key to the front door downstairs, while she stubbornly refused them to him, shaking her head as she repeated No, No, No, because he wasn't old enough yet; and on this point she would not give way. She would throw herself out of the window first. He was the one who, in the end, distracted by more and more desperate calls from below, and also impatient to get to the movies, gave in to the inevitable. And he dashed off, grumbling his protests along the stairs, like a noctambulist cat driven off by a broom.

In the past, she had refused to go to bed until she had seen him come home; and in the long vigil, she would usually doze in the kitchen. But now, brutalized by weariness, she couldn't resist her desire to lie down, remaining alert, all the same, during her sleep, until she was called, from the street, by the whistle of her escaped chaffinch. Then, crossly, she would go downstairs to open the door for him, a pair of shapeless slippers on her feet, her flowered flannelette bathrobe over her nightgown, and her black hair, barely streaked with gray, disheveled, down her back, curly and full as an Ethiopian's. With the impetuosity of a charger demolishing an obstacle, he would enter the building, still excited by the movie. All the fire of his thoughts was directed towards those stars of universal beauty, those amazing stories. And preceding Ida up the stairs, unable to adapt his pace to her slowness, he would vary the climb with impatient fancies. He would linger a moment to kick at a step, or would jump up three or four at once; then, higher, he would stretch out full length on a landing, with a yawn, then suddenly rush up a whole flight as if he were soaring to heaven. But he always arrived at the door of the house with a considerable lead; and from there, astride the railing, leaning a bit into the stairwell and glancing at Ida, clumping up the stairs, he would say to her, in a tormented tone: "Ah, mà, come on. Let's go. Shift into high. Give it some gas!"

In the end, her resistance exhausted, and afraid also that, seeing her in her nightclothes, he might recognize her swollen belly, she resigned herself and granted him the famous right to the keys. And that evening for him was a celebration, like male initiation among tribes. He flew out of the house, without saying goodnight, his curls looking like so many little bells.

Even as her pregnancy advanced, it was not hard for Ida to hide it. Her body, already ill-made and out of proportion from the waist to below the pelvis, showed only slightly the new change, which remained limited. Certainly the hidden, undernourished little creature could not weigh much, demanding so little room.

Even though rationing was still a few months off, many items of food were already beginning to grow scarce, and prices were rising. Nino, still a growing boy, had an unruly and insatiable hunger; and his share, inevitably, was achieved at the expense of the portions of Ida and the other invisible being who asked nothing. He already made himself felt, true, moving now and then in his hiding-place; but the little blows he gave seemed more information than protest: "I inform you that I am here and, in spite of everything, I'm coping, and I'm alive. In fact, I'm already feeling the urge to enjoy myself a bit."

There was a shortage of gas in the houses, and people had to wait in long lines to win two shovelfuls of coal. Ida could no longer, as she had in the past, complete her shopping in the morning; and sometimes darkness overtook her still out in the streets, plunged into the wartime blackout. If from some window a thread of light happened to shine, curses would immediately rise from the streets: "Murderers! Criminals! Put out the liiiight!" From the taverns' blacked-out doorways, radios could be heard at full volume, or choruses of young men would release their energies, singing popular songs and playing the guitar, like village boys. At certain lonely intersections, Ida, with her load of potatoes and coal, would hesitate, aghast, in her ancient panic fear of the dark. And immediately the little individual inside her would answer her with lively kicks perhaps meant to encourage her: "What are you scared of? You're not alone. After all, you've got somebody with you."

Unlike other mothers, she never reflected on the enigma of whether the infant was a boy or a girl. In her situation, even this curiosity would have seemed a greedy whim, something to be ashamed of. She was allowed only indifference, which she could use as white magic against destiny.

With the warm season, which forced her to leave off her wool coat, she tried to draw her corset tighter. As a rule, she would leave it rather loose, to alleviate its torment, even if her schoolmistress decorum obliged her always to wear it. In these last few months, her arms and legs had grown thin as an old woman's, her cheeks were flushed but emaciated, even in their round shape; and in the classroom, when she wrote on the blackboard, certain letters came out crooked. Summer arrived early and sultry, her flesh was all sweaty day and night. But she reached the end of the term without anyone's having caught on to anything.

Towards the end of June, Germany attacked the Soviet Union. At the beginning of July, German officials were assigned to organize the total evacuation of the Jews from all occupied countries (which now comprised all Europe) in view of the *final solution*.

The women who kept the little shops in the Ghetto, where Ida stopped off on her rounds, had become more taciturn and reticent, and they went on with their humble everyday trade as if European events didn't concern them. At intervals she still ran into Vilma, dejected because collecting scraps was becoming daily more difficult, and also, more and more of her cats in the ancient ruins were failing to show up at roll call. She knew them individually, and would ask around the quarter in a wretched, disconsolate voice: "Hasn't anyone seen Gimp? Or Casanova? And the tom with only one eye? And Fiorello? And the orange one with mange? And the white one, about to have kittens, who used to hang out at the baker's?!" The people questioned would laugh in her face; but she could still be heard calling, incurably, among the ruins of the Theater of Marcellus: "Casanooova!!! Whiskers!! Chubby!"

From her private informers, the *Signora* and the *Nun*, Vilma always had some new revelation, which she would report with her lunatic gesticulations, in a low voice. She told, for example, how in all of conquered

Europe, these days, in houses where they still suspected the concealed presence of some Jew, the windows and doors were walled up, then the houses were pulverized with some special gases called *cyclones*. And in the countryside and the forests of Poland, from all the trees hung men, women, and children, even tiny babies: not only Jews, but gypsies, and Communists, and *Polandese*, and *fighters* . . . Their bodies were falling to pieces, with foxes and wolves quarreling over them. And in all the stations where the trains passed, you could see skeletons at work on the tracks, skeletons *that had only their eyes* . . . Similar reports, as always, were received as fantastic products of Vilma's mind; and so they were, in part, although, here too, afterwards, historical results were to surpass them by far. In fact, no living imagination could, on its own, conceive the aberrant and complicated monsters produced by its opposite: namely, by the total lack of imagination, which is the property of certain mortuary mechanisms.

Not only the strange news from the *Signora* and the *Nun*, but also the more or less semiofficial news from the prison grapevine continued, there in the Ghetto, to encounter a kind of stubborn passivity. For that matter, nobody, in the Ghetto or elsewhere, had as yet learned the true meaning of certain official terms, such as *evacuation, internment, extraordinary pacification action, final solution,* and so on. The world's technological-bureaucratic organization was still in a primitive phase: that is, it had not yet contaminated, irremediably, the people's consciousness. Most people, in a sense, still lived in prehistory. And so the simple ignorance of some very humble Jewish women should not be too amazing.

Only one of them, one day, Signora Sonnino, who had a little stand of cheap clothing accessories near the café at the bridge, on hearing the Führer's voice from inside there, as he was ranting over the radio, observed pensively:

"Those characters want to turn everything into arithmetic: add, subtract, multiply, until the numbers come out zero!!!"

And thus meditating, she shook her little head, thin and alert as a lizard's, though she went on counting the buttons she was selling Ida: as if this arithmetic concerned her more closely than that other.

By now, all the people in general, Aryans and Jews, poor and rich, considered the Nazi-Fascists' victory a certainty, especially after their recent progress in Russia and Africa.

But inside Iduzza's brain, at present, all the talk she listened to made a dull noise, like printed letters set before an illiterate. At home in the evening, in the dim votive light of the darkened bulbs, the Fascist Ninnarieddu would sing, with his still-untuned childish tenor:

"Colonel, I don't want bread;
I want bullets for my gun!!"

But every now and then he would vary it:

"Colonel, I don't want bread:
I want real coffee with my steak!"

in a loud voice, and with the windows open, on purpose, to act big and heedless, defying the police informers. Ida, however, no longer had the willpower to get up and close the windows, as she used to do. By now, she let him go on.

Every so often, at night, the air-raid alarm sirens would resound through the city; but the people of San Lorenzo paid little attention to them, convinced that Rome would never be hit, thanks to the protection of the Pope, who in fact was nicknamed *the Capital's ack-ack*. The first times, Ida, in agitation, had tried to waken Nino; but he would wriggle down in his cot, grumbling: "Who is it? . . . who is it? I'm asleep!" and one night, half-asleep, he mumbled something about a band with a saxophone and drums.

The next day he asked if there had been an alarm, complaining that Ida had spoiled his dream. And he told her, definitively, not to disturb him again when the siren went:

"What do we care about the siren, anyway? Say, mà, can't you see nothing ever happens here? English bombs! Yeah, made out of paper!!"

Later she also stopped getting up at the sound of the alarm, barely shifting, half-awake, beneath the sweat-damp sheets, amid the scream of the sirens and the firing of the anti-aircraft in the distance.

One night, shortly before an alarm, she dreamed she was looking for a hospital, to give birth. But all rejected her as a Jew, saying she should go to the Jewish hospital, and pointing out a very white cement building, all walled up, with no windows or doors. A little later, she found herself inside the building. It was an immense factory, illuminated by the beams of blinding spotlights; and around her there was no one, only gigantic machines, complicated and cogged, which rotated with terrible din. When, suddenly, it turns out that this racket comes from skyrockets for New Year's Eve. We are on a beach. With her there are lots of little kids, and among them there is even Alfio, also a kid. All, with their shrill voices, protest because, down here, they can't see the fireworks: they need a platform, a balcony! It's already midnight, and we're disappointed . . . but all at once the sea before us is marvelously illuminated by huge, countless clusters of light, green and orange and pomegranate red, against the blue of the water at night. And the kids, pleased, say: "Here we can see better than up above, because the whole city is reflected in the sea, even the skyscrapers and the mountain peaks."

Towards the end, almost every day, on the pretext of having to buy some little article, but actually without any specific motivation, Ida, on leaving school, would set off for the Jewish quarter. She felt drawn there by a summons of sweetness, like the stable's smell for a calf, or a souk's for an Arab woman; and also by an impulse of obsessive necessity, like a planet gravitating around a star. From Testaccio, where her school was located, in a few minutes she would reach the little settlement behind the Synagogue; but even after the beginning of summer vacation, despite the distance from San Lorenzo, every so often she would follow her familiar summons. And so it was that one afternoon, in the dead of summer, she happened into a food shop only a few hours after the proprietress, in a little room next to the shop, had given birth to an infant. In the shop, the midwife, a Neapolitan Jewess, was still bustling around. Her thick eyebrows, her sturdy, arched nose, her heavy feet and her stride, and even the way she wore her white cotton cap over her curly gray hair, made her resemble an engraving of the prophet Ezekiel.

Ida mustered her courage; and taking this woman aside for a moment, she asked her address in a faint voice, claiming she wanted it for a relative who would soon need her. Saying this, she became all red in the face, as if accusing herself of something indecent. But Ezekiel, since Iduzza was totally unknown to her, took her question as something licit and natural. In fact, she congratulated Ida's relative. And promptly she gave her a printed card, with her name, address, and telephone number. She was also named Ida; Di Capua was her last name. She lived in the neighborhood of the Lateran, the San Giovanni district.

As the summer ripened, among the many imminent problems now besieging Ida, the most serious for her was Nino, who still suspected nothing. Terrified, she saw the day approach when she would necessarily have to give him some explanation, she didn't know how. Vaguely, she thought of going off alone, to have the baby in some other city, then coming back with it, pretending it had been entrusted to her by some deceased relative . . . But Nino knew very well she had no relatives; and, still less, such a close one that she would accept the burden of a baby in times like these! Nino was not the type to be taken in by certain tales. So here too, Ida's only refuge was to withdraw in the face of the impossible, letting destiny act.

The infant somehow came to her assistance, anticipating its birth by several weeks. Foreseen for the autumn, it occurred instead at the end of

August, while Nino was off at a Young Fascists' summer camp. On the 28th of August, when she felt the first labor pains, Ida was alone in the house; and, seized with panic, not even announcing her arrival by a phone call, she took a tram towards the midwife's address.

As she climbed the woman's long stairs, her pains increased, until they became terrible. Ezekiel in person answered the door; and no longer capable of giving explanations, Ida, the moment she was inside, flung herself on a bed, crying: "Signora! Signora! Help!"

And she began to writhe and scream, while Ezekiel, practiced and soothing, was freeing her of her clothes. But Ida, even in her spasms, was terrified at the thought of revealing her nakedness; and she began groping to cover herself with the sheet. When the other woman then started undoing the corset, Ida clung to her desperately to prevent it: because there, under the corset, fastened with a pin, she had a sewn-up little sock containing her savings. In fact, despite the difficulties of the war, she hadn't abandoned her habit of putting aside a bit of her salary every month. In her distrust of the morrow, and in the certainty, alone as she was, of being unable to count on anyone's help at any twist of fate, she kept in that stocking her whole independence, her dignity, her treasure. In all it came to a few hundred lire; but to her it seemed a great sum.

Understanding, after some difficulty, the reason for her frantic resistance, Ezekiel found a way of convincing her, nonetheless, to allow the corset to be removed; and to reassure Ida, she placed it under the very mattress where Ida lay, the stocking still fastened to it.

The birth was not long or difficult. That unknown creature seemed to be trying to come into the world with his own strength, without costing others too much suffering. And when, emitting the final scream, the mother lay free at last, submerged in her own sweat as in a salty sea, the midwife announced:

"It's a little man!"

He was, indeed, a little man; that is to say a male, but very little, in truth. The infant was so small he could fit comfortably in the midwife's two hands, as in a basket. And after having proved himself by the heroic enterprise of coming into the world on his own, he hadn't even the voice to cry. He announced his presence with a whimper so faint he seemed a little lamb, born last and forgotten in the straw. Still, for all his tiny size, he was complete, and even pretty, well-made, as far as they could tell. And he meant to survive: in fact, at the right moment, he sought his mother's breasts eagerly, on his own initiative.

And through the mysterious workings of her maternal organs, she never lacked the necessary milk. Obviously, what little she had eaten had been divided entirely between the hidden little one and her milk supply. As for herself, the delivery left her so scrawny she looked like a stray bitch who had whelped at a street corner.

The infant's hair—all in little tufts, like plumes—was black. But as soon as he allowed a glimpse of his eyes, even in the two little slivers he barely revealed, Ida immediately recognized that blue color of her scandal. The eyes were not long then in opening wide, and proved so big in the tiny face that they seemed already spellbound by the spectacle they beheld. And beyond any doubt, their color—even in its first milky haze—reproduced perfectly that other blue, which seemed born not from the earth but from the sea.

On the other hand, you couldn't yet tell where he got his features. You could discern now only their delicate and pretty form. The mouth perhaps, with its soft, protruding lips, also recalled slightly that other mouth.

Until she was able to move, Ida stayed with Ezekiel, who left her the bed and settled herself on a mattress on the kitchen floor. The apartment, in fact, where the midwife lived alone, consisted entirely of the kitchen and the bedroom. Here there was a big Neapolitan bed, of painted iron; and from a window on to the street you could glimpse, obliquely, the Lateran Basilica, crowned by the fifteen immense statues of Christ, the Saint Johns, and the Doctors of the Church.

The midwife was very pleased and proud of her private lodging. And seeing her here at home—with a long cotton robe that looked like a tunic —it was harder than ever to tell whether she was a woman or an old man. Her voice wasn't a woman's either, but an old man's. It sounded like one of those bass voices that, in operas, sing the parts of aged kings, or of hermits.

The second day, she reminded Iduzza that the baby had to be given a name; and Ida answered that she had already decided to call him Giuseppe, after his maternal grandfather, her own father. Ezekiel, however, kept saying that a single name wasn't enough; a second name was needed, and a third. But Iduzza hadn't thought about these other two names. And the midwife, after pondering the question, suggested she call him Felice, or "happy," as a second name, to bring him luck; and as third name, Angiolino, because he was so small, and had blue eyes, and was good as a little angel, and didn't make much noise.

The names having been settled, the midwife offered to go herself to the Registry, for the necessary declaration. Iduzza was at first recalcitrant, for the imaginable reason; but after thinking it over, finding herself faced with the choice of having to declare her own dishonor either to a civil servant of the City or to the midwife, she preferred to reveal it to the midwife. And without giving any spoken explanation, she wrote out for her in printed letters, in a trembling hand:

GIUSEPPE FELICE ANGIOLINO
BORN IN ROME 28 AUGUST 1941
MOTHER: WIDOW IDA MANCUSO, BORN RAMUNDO
FATHER: UNKNOWN

Each day, Ezekiel appeared at meal hours to do the cooking; but the rest of the time, she was always out on her professional rounds. And Ida would lie for the whole day in that enormous bed, with its clean sheets; in it, Giuseppe was too small not to feel lost among the huge people of the world. Most of the time, both slept. The dog-days weighed on the city; but even the great sweat in which she lay drenched gave Ida a sense of abandonment and of passivity, like a warm and briny sea in which her body was unraveled. And she would have liked to die in that bed along with her child, both leaving the earth, as if in a boat.

On the fourth day, she decided to go home; Ezekiel offered to accompany her, but Ida wouldn't hear of it, already aghast at the thought the woman might turn up sometime in her neighborhood. In fact, anyone who knew her secrets became, for her, a disturbing figure, whom she was careful to avoid, like desert animals when they try to cover their trail against the enemy's scent.

So she prepared to leave by herself, prudently waiting till dark. At the settling of their accounts, Ezekiel made Ida pay for her food; but for the rest (seeing that swollen and wretched body, which, with what clothed it—despite the famous stocking—betrayed poverty) she wanted nothing. She herself supplied a broad rag, faded but clean, in which Giuseppe, sleeping blissfully, was wrapped up so that only his nose stuck out. And laden with this bundle, besides her shopping-bag, Ida took the tram again for San Lorenzo. As on every evening, because of the blackout, the street lamps were extinguished, and on the trams the little masked bulbs cast a dim bluish glow.

The darkness, however, was in her favor on this occasion: coming home like a criminal returning to the scene of his crime, she managed to avoid anyone's noticing her. Her bedroom was at the corner of the building, and its one window looked down on the street; so from there Giuseppe's rare crying could hardly give him away to the neighbors, whom Ida wanted to leave in ignorance as long as possible. She settled her tiny son beside her own double bed in a little iron cot with sides, which had belonged to Nino in the days of his early infancy, and which afterwards had served to hold blankets, boxes, old books, and every sort of junk. And there, Giuseppe, like an outlaw whose hiding-place no one must know, spent the whole day, sleeping and resting.

Nino's absence was to last until mid-September, the schools were closed, and in this period she had no private lessons; so Ida stayed in the house most of the time, going out only for the necessary shopping, towards nightfall. Among her other concerns, she wondered if she should have the infant baptized, the better to protect him from the famous list of the impure; but the idea of taking him inside a church was too repugnant to her, like a final betrayal of the poor quarter of Jewish pariahs. And she decided to leave him, for the present, without a religion: "Anyway," she said to herself, "he's different from Nino; he has only half a family tree. How could his Aryan half be proved? The Authorities would declare him even less Aryan than me. And besides he's so tiny, that whatever happens, wherever they may send me, I'll always take him with me, even if we have to die together."

The fifteenth of September, for her, was a critical day, since that was approximately the date of Nino's expected return, and hence the moment of the fatal explanation, which she had always postponed. Into her mind, at intervals, came that sole, miserable pretext she could invent: the imaginary relative. And she began to ponder it, but reluctantly, without conviction; it immediately gave her palpitations, along with a disgusted indolence. Expecting Nino's return any moment, that day she went out earlier than usual for her daily shopping. But it was precisely during this interval that Nino came home; and now master of the keys, he entered the house freely in her absence.

From beyond the door, while she was fussing with her shopping-bags and the lock, she heard a stirring inside the rooms. And, coming into the hall, she saw the knapsack on the floor. Then Nino promptly appeared, still wearing his uniform pants, but with his chest bare (since, on first arriving, he had quickly taken off his shirt, in the great heat). He was all tanned, and an extraordinary liveliness shone in his eyes. With a thrilled voice, in irresistible surprise, he said:

"Hey, mà! Who's that?"

And he led her straight into the bedroom, where with little peals of rejoicing laughter, which already seemed a dialogue, he bent over the cot. And there was Giuseppe, who looked at him as if he recognized him already. His gaze, till then dreamy, misted in infancy, seemed to express in this moment the first thought of his life: a thought of supreme festive understanding. So that even his little arms and his tiny legs accompanied it, hinting at a minimal, primitive waving.

"Who is it, mà? Who's he?!" Nino repeated, more and more wild with amusement.

In a dizzying urgency, Ida felt the old story of the relative rising in her throat; but this cursed pretext refused to reach her lips. And the only explanation that came to her, absurdly, in a stammer, was:

"He . . . he . . . was found in the street!"

"And who found him?" Nino asked further, immediately excited by such a formidable event. But barely for an instant: when he had hardly noticed, you might say, the distraught flush on his mother's face, already he no longer believed the story. His gaze, aware, downright cynical, went from his mother's inflamed face to her body, as if in sudden recollection of a sign which, at the time, he hadn't perceived. And for ten seconds his thoughts were amused at the comical idea: his mother had a lover. "Who can ever have taken her, old as she is?" he wondered, uncertainly. "It must have been," he decided privately, "a passing thing, just once . . ." From his gaze, meanwhile, Ida had already realized he saw through her; but in the end he cared little about the source of this unexpected present: what mattered to him was to make sure of it, forever. And letting all further inquiry lapse into indifference, he asked anxiously:

"We're going to keep him now, though, aren't we? We'll keep him here with us!"

"Yes . . ."

"What's his name?" he asked, radiant with contentment.

"Giuseppe."

"Hey, Peppe! Hey, Peppiniello! Oh! Hey!" he began to exclaim, acting crazy in front of the baby. While the latter, in response, continued his tiny, beginner's kicks, in the happiness and gratitude of knowing life, starting today.

"Say, mà, how about it? Can I hold him a while?" the delirious Nino proposed at this point, his hands already over the crib.

"No! no! nooo!!! You'll drop him!"

"Aaah, I can lift weights with both hands, and you think I can't hold him!" Nino turned, with contempt. But he had already given up his project, shifting, in the turbulence of his thoughts, to quite a different question to be resolved, now that the moment was propitious. And he demanded, without delay:

"Say, mà! Now that Giuseppe's here, we can have a dog, too, here in the house!"

This was one of the eternal quarrels between him and his mother. Because he was dying to own a dog, and she, for any number of reasons, wouldn't hear of it. But today, in her position of horrible inferiority, she could only give in to the blackmail: "Well . . . um . . . um" was her first, inarticulate reply, already condemned to resignation.

However, with vehemence, she added: "You want to plunge this house into ruination!!!"

In her quarrels with Ninnarieddu, she unconsciously imitated certain of Nora's Biblical invectives, but uttered by her, with her incongruous twelve-year-old's face, they seemed positively comical, rather than offensive. This time, too, from Nino's eager look, it was already clear he was anticipating her unconditional surrender . . .

". . . do as you like! Oh God! . . . I've known for ages it would end like this . . ."

"Great, mà! Then I'll bring him home! There's one who always waits for me outside the tobacco shop!!" Ninnarieddu shouted, beside himself. Then he remained silent for a little while, cherishing canine visions which made him obviously, blissfully happy. And here Ida, already disconsolate at heart for having given in to this new calamity, wanted perhaps, in her turn, to extract at least some advantage from the situation. And she said, with effort:

"Listen, Nino . . . now I must say something . . . it's something very serious . . . Mind you: don't tell anyone about . . . about this baby. For the present, it's better to keep it a secret that . . . that he's here . . . But if people should find out somehow, and anybody asks you, the only thing to do is tell them he's a nephew, left all alone in the world, without any other relatives . . . and so he's been entrusted to us . . ."

In the space of a rapid glance, Nino radiated arrogance, compassion, supremacy, and freedom. He shrugged one shoulder with a grimace, and replied, planting his feet in the pose of a barricadiero:

"If they ask ME anything, I'll say: *what the shit do you care?*"

At that same moment, from the crib a whimper was heard, which immediately made him laugh. Fickle, the happy images of a moment before returned to joke in his eyes. And changing the subject, hands in his pockets, he suggested to his mother:

"And now, to celebrate Giuseppe's being here, how about some money for a pack of Nazionali?"

"I knew you'd take advantage of this, too! You're an exploiter! And an opportunist and a profiteer! Now, to celebrate Giuseppe, you want to set him an example of vice. You're not even sixteen yet! Is that any age to be smoking?"

"If you don't smoke at sixteen, when are you supposed to smoke? At ninety?" he rebutted, with bullying impatience. Then suddenly, as if following an inspiration, he went on:

"And how about an ice cream cone, too? No, let's make it a couple: one for me and one for you."

"Why, Nino . . . What are you thinking of? You think I've become a millionairess today? You want us to be completely ruined!! . . . And besides, these ersatz ice creams . . . there's no telling what they're made of . . ."

"There's the dairy, next to the tobacco shop; they make great ones."

"Ice cream *or* cigarettes. Here: I'm not giving you more than two lire."

"Cigarettes, plus the cones, plus the *Corriere dello Sport* and the *Gazzetta* (did you forget today's Monday?): that takes five lire, not two! Come on, mà, don't give me the same old whine! Five lousy lire won't ruin you. Come on, cough it up, will you?! You're getting to be worse than a Jew!"

This last remark, for Nino, was an ordinary slang expression, with no real meaning. In fact, Ninnuzzu hadn't the slightest interest in the Jews and their present vicissitudes. He was about as ignorant of them as if they had been the Cimbri or the Phoenicians. So Ida's inevitable, slight shudder was invisible to his eyes. But still, Ida, to release her tension, attacked him on another topic (by now rancid, to tell the truth) of their family brawls:

"Ah, how many times have I told you how it disgusts me to hear you speak such low dialect, and these bad words, worthy of a house of ill-fame! Who would ever think, hearing you speak, worse than a jackass, that instead you . . . you are the son of a teacher, and are attending the classical High School!!! You're not an ignorant peasant, after all! You've studied good Italian . . ."

"Madame, allow me the pleasure of repeating my request: give me a dubloon."

"You're a hoodlum . . . I can't bear you! When I have to see you, I see red!"

Nino, now fuming with impatience, had started whistling "Deutschland, Deutschland": "Well, fork over the cash!" he interrupted her.

"Money . . . that's all you think of! Always money!"

"And without money, where's the party?!"

Determined to go out, and intolerant of further delays, he considered the restricted and enclosed space of the house an injustice. And he began to pace back and forth in the room as if inside a prison, kicking a slipper, a rag, an empty basin, and any other object that came within range of his feet: "The dough, mà!" he concluded, worse than a bandit, facing his mother.

"You'll end up a thief and a murderer!"

"I'll end up Chief of the Black Brigades. As soon as I'm old enough,

I'm going off to fight FOR THE FATHERLAND AND FOR THE DUCE!"

The excess of defiance in his voice as he uttered these capitals, betrayed a blasphemous intention. You could sense that, in his boyish demands, Fatherlands and Duces, and the whole theater of the world, were reduced to a farce, which had value only because it agreed with his rage to live. Again, his eyes suggested his mysterious adulthood, ready for any scandal and every wickedness; then suddenly, in rapid contradiction, a radiant innocence appeared and transfigured his gaze. At that moment, in fact, his mother had taken her mangy little change-purse from her shopping bag and was handing him the famous *dough*. And he, grasping it, flew without delay towards the door, prompt as a flag-bearer dashing onto the field of victory.

"What are you doing?" his mother stopped him. "Aren't you going to put some clothes on? Are you going out naked?"

"What's wrong? Don't I look good?" he replied, though giving in to necessity. And as he ran back towards the chair, where he had flung his shirt, he didn't fail to pause at the wardrobe mirror, to give himself a satisfied look. His slender tanned body still betrayed his childishness, in the grace of his nape and the still-thin back with protruding shoulder blades; but his arms, on the contrary, were already developing their virile muscles, which he measured at the mirror, displaying them to himself with insatiable self-assertion. Then, running, he started to put his black shirt on again, but finding it sweaty and hot, he slipped on instead a little white cotton jersey over his uniform pants, careless of this contamination, in his haste to run downstairs! And he vanished.

Iduzza was already prepared (even with some relief) not to see him reappear, perhaps, till late evening, now that he must have flown off with her five lire towards his usual band, like a bee to a sunflower! But less than twenty minutes had gone by when a certain confusion at the front door announced his return. And even before him, there came into the room a little brown dog, held on a leash, jumping in a paroxysm of happiness. It was an animal of slight dimensions, round, with crooked legs and a curled-up tail. It had a big head, with one ear more erect than the other. Altogether, it was a typical homeless dog (or *dog of others*, as the Slavs say).

"What? What? Today? Already! We weren't talking about today! *Not at once! Not* today!" Ida stammered, almost voiceless in her desperation.

"When then? I told you, he always waits for me by the tobacco shop. And he was there now, waiting for me! For this whole month I've been away, he's gone there to look for me every day! And he comes when I call his name, too! Blitz! Blitz! You see? He knows his name! Ah!"

Meanwhile, Giuseppe, who had taken advantage of Nino's absence to have a little nap, reopened his eyes. And he proved not only unafraid but even transported, serenely ecstatic at the sight of this first examplar of dog, indeed of fauna, that had appeared to him from all Creation.

"Giuseppe! You see who's here? Blitz, say something to Giuseppe! The party's in his honor! Hey, Blitz, did you hear me? Say something!"

"Oof! oof!" Blitz said.

"uuuuuuhin . . ." Giuseppe said.

It was Nino's triumph. His laughter, fresh and overwhelming as a skyrocket, flung him to the floor, in a riot of leaps and somersaults with Blitz. Until he went and sat on the edge of the bed, to rest blissfully, taking a humble, crushed cigarette from the rear pocket of his pants.

"I could only buy two Nazionali," he said, hardly concealing a certain regret, while still puffing on his cigarette with a depraved air, "because I didn't have enough money for a whole pack. I went without the ice cream cones, too. They would of melted on the stairs anyway." (For himself, actually, he had bought a cone, a small one, and consumed it on the spot. But he skipped this point, which didn't concern Ida.) "With the rest, I paid for his collar and leash," he explained proudly.

And he bent over Blitz (who had settled at his feet meanwhile) to take off the leash. "It's real leather, not fake," he boasted. "It's de luxe."

"Then, goodness only knows HOW MUCH it cost . . ."

"Oh, it's not new. I bought it second-hand, from the news-vendor, who gave me a bargain. It belonged to his puppy, who's grown up now and stays in the country, at Tivoli. Don't you remember that little dog that used to piss on the newspapers sometimes? What? You don't remember? I showed him to you a hundred thousand times! A purebred! An Alsatian! And here, on the collar-plate, there's still his name: WOLF. But now I'll scratch it out with a nail, otherwise you can tell right off it's second-hand. Blitz doesn't belong to that breed, after all."

"And what breed is he?"

"He's a bastard."

The casual word shocked Ida, who blushed at once; and she gave an involuntary look towards the crib, as if the infant might have understood. In his turn, then, Nino conceived the thought: "Yeah! Giuseppe's a bastard, too. In this house, there are two bastards," he deduced, highly amused by his discovery.

But in the meanwhile, having put his hand in his pocket to look for the nail, he found a final purchase, which he had nearly forgot. "Hey, Blitz!" he cried, "I forgot! I found your supper for you, too! Go on, eat up!" And taking out a revolting package of tripe, he dropped it on the floor in front of the dog, who, with the skill of a magician, made it vanish immediately.

Nino watched him, with pride: "Blitz's breed," he resumed, smiling at another invention of his that charmed him, "is also called the *starred breed*. Blitz! show them the nice star you have!"

And Blitz promptly rolled over on his back, his paws in the air. Below, as above, tail included, he was all a uniform dark brown color: except in the center of his belly, where he had a little white patch, crooked, more or less stellar in shape. This was his sole beauty and distinction, visible, however, only when he rolled over. And he was so delighted to display it that he would have remained still, as if ecstatic, in that position, but Nino straightened him up, tickling him with one foot.

Iduzza didn't observe the performance; she was still dazed by that word *bastard*. Her mortified eyes, which hadn't even glanced at Blitz's star, fell on the greasy tripe wrapping, empty on the floor. This sight offered to sinner Ida another object of diversion, of release . . .

"And now?" she rose up, with dramatic bitterness, "there's another mouth to feed, here in the house! . . . And who's going to give us a ration card for him? . . ."

Nino became glum, and didn't answer her at all. Instead, he turned to the dog; and with his face close to Blitz's, he said to him, in intimate privacy:

"Don't pay any attention to what she says. I'll take care of you; me and my friends, we won't let you starve, you can count on that. How did you eat till now? You can tell the whole world, we don't need anybody else's shit!"

"Aaah," Iduzza intervened again, with a condemned sigh, "now you're even going to teach the dog your foul, vulgar speech. And you'll be all ready to teach it to your brother . . ."

At this last fatal word which had escaped her lips, she staggered as if clubbed. And aghast, with the movements of a poor animal, she turned to pick up that greasy paper from the floor, no longer daring to address Ninnarieddu.

But the word seemed so natural to him that he didn't even notice it. Instead, he replied, spirited and glowing:

"We live in Rome, and we talk Roman! When we're in Paris (where I plan to go soon, now that Paris is ours!) we'll talk Parisian! And when we're in Hong Kong, on our next cruise, we'll talk Konguese. You can be sure I'm not going to stay here in Rome! I'm going to cover the whole world like it was a neighborhood, and in airplanes and racing cars, not on foot! I'll cross the Atlantic and Pacific, and I'll take Blitz along with me! And we'll go around the world, nonstop! We'll go to Chicago, Hollywood, and Greenland, and on to the steppes and play the balalaika! We'll go to London, to Saint-Moritz, and to Mozambique! We'll go to Honolulu and on the Yellow River and . . . and . . . And I'll take Giuseppe along with me, too! Hey, hey, Giuseppe, I'm taking you, too!"

Giuseppe had fallen asleep again, hearing nothing of this grandiose program. And in the ensuing silence, between Ninnarieddu and Ida, who still had her back turned to him, there was an unspoken, final dialogue, perhaps unformulated even in their thoughts, but expressed by their persons with eloquent clarity.

In her dress of artificial silk, rotted by sweat, Ida's back was thin and hunched like a little old woman's: it said to Nino:

"Are you going to take me?"

And Nino's set, sulky expression, with his darting eyes and his harsh, violent mouth, answered:

"No. I'm leaving you here."

2 Giuseppe, precocious in his birth, proved from the beginning precocious in everything. At the usual natural stages which mark every infant's advance along the itinerary of experience, he always arrived ahead of time, but so far ahead (at least for those days) that I myself could hardly believe it, if I had not shared, in some ways, his fate. It seemed that his tiny forces were all directed, in a great urgent fervor, towards the spectacle of the world in which he had just appeared.

A few days after the discovery of his existence, Ninnuzzu couldn't resist the temptation to reveal it to two or three of his best friends, boasting to them that at home he had a little brother who was a champion: so tiny he was actually comical, but with huge eyes that could talk with people. And that same morning, taking advantage of Ida's absence, he led those friends up to the house to introduce them. Five of them climbed the steps, counting Blitz, who now followed Nino everywhere, as if he were half of his soul.

On the stairs, one of the friends, a middle-class boy, expressed his puzzlement about this brother Nino had announced, since it was known that his mother had been a widow for many years. But, with contempt for the other's lack of intelligence, Nino answered: "So what? You think only husbands can make babies?!" with such absolutist naturalness that they all laughed, in chorus, at that ignorant (or malicious?) boy, shaming him.

In any case, while they were still on the stairs, Nino lowered his voice to warn them this brother was an outlaw, and they shouldn't mention him to anyone, otherwise his mother would raise hell, because she was afraid people would think she was a tramp. At which, his friends, like conspirators, swore to keep the secret.

Once they were in the bedroom, they were somewhat disappointed; for Giuseppe at that moment was sleeping, and asleep like that, apart from his tiny size which was authentically pigmy, he showed nothing extraordinary; on the contrary. His eyelids, like all infants', were still wrinkled; but suddenly he opened them. And on seeing those great widened eyes in his face as small as a fist, greeting the five visitors as if they were a sole marvel, all were exhilarated. Then, rejoicing in the company, Giuseppe, for the first time in his life, smiled.

A little later, the visitors ran off, afraid of being caught by the mother. But Nino impatiently awaited her return on purpose to announce to her the sensational news: "You know what? Giuseppe smiled!" She remained skeptical: Giuseppe, she said, isn't old enough to smile yet; babies don't learn to smile until they're a month and a half, or two months old, at least. "Come and see!" Nino insisted, and he dragged her into the bedroom, plotting some thrilling trick that would induce his brother to repeat his exploit. But there was no need, because just seeing him, Giuseppe, as if by appointment, smiled for a second time. And afterwards whenever he saw Nino, even if he had been crying until then, he would promptly repeat that fraternal little smile, which was soon transformed into real laughter of welcome and content.

By now the schools had been open again for some while, and from early morning the house was left deserted. Blitz himself, in fact, madly in love with Nino as he was, wasn't satisfied just to follow him and his bands always, wherever they went; he even waited for him outside the gates, while he was at school or at pre-military training. So Nino fitted him out also with a muzzle, afraid that the dog-catcher, coming by, might arrest him for being nobody's dog. And he had someone engrave on his collar: BLITZ—*Owner: Nino Mancuso*, with the complete address.

Sometimes, on the (rather frequent) mornings when he played hookey, Nino, happening to pass near the house, would turn up again with some schoolmate at Giuseppe's crib (also for the pleasure of breaking the maternal veto). These were rapid visits, because those boys, and especially Nino, were in too great a hurry to run towards the attractions of their illicit holiday; but they were always celebrations, made all the more fascinating by the infraction and by mystery. The season was still mild, and Giuseppe, in his crib, was completely naked; however, modesty didn't exist for him. His only feeling was the desire to convey to his visitors his pleasure in receiving them. It was infinite, as if every time, he had the renewed illusion that this very brief festivity would last forever. And in his almost crazy need to express that infinite pleasure with his scarce means, Giuseppe would multiply all at the same time his timid kicks, his enchanted looks, his whimpers, smiles, and laughs; he was rewarded by a devilish display of greetings, wisecracks, and some compliments of little kisses. On these occasions, Nino never failed to reveal, with pride and glory, his brother's various specialties: pointing out, for example, that, although small, he was already a true male, complete with prick and everything. And that he hardly ever cried, but he already made special sounds, different from one another, all perfectly understood by Blitz. And that on his hands and his feet he had all twenty nails, imperceptible perhaps, but in perfect order, and his mother already had to cut them, etc., etc. Then, as suddenly as they had arrived, the visitors would rush off, together, recalled in vain by Giuseppe's exceptional crying, which followed them down the stairs and died away, solitary and disconsolate.

At first, as soon as her class was over, Ida had to hurry home, breathless and always late, to nurse him. But he soon learned to manage on his own, with a bottle full of artificial milk, which she left him during her longer absences. And, true to his private determination not to die, he would suck for all he was worth. He didn't grow much; however, he had filled out a bit, and there were some little rings of fat on his arms and thighs. And despite his segregation, he had taken on a pink coloring which enhanced his eyes. These, in the center of the iris, were of a darker blue, like a starry night's; whereas, all around, they were the light color of air. His gaze, always intent and eloquent, as if in a universal dialogue, was a joy to see. His toothless mouth, with protruding lips, sought kisses with the same eager demand that it sought milk. And his head was black; but not curly like Nino's; with smooth clumps, moist and shiny, like certain migrant ducks known to hunters by the name of *morette*, "little blacks." Among his many clumps, already, there was a bolder one, right in the center of his head; it was always erect, like an exclamation point, nor could any combing keep it down.

Very soon he learned the names of the family: Ida was *mà*; Nino was *ino* or else *aiè* (Ninnarieddu) and Blitz was *i*.

For Blitz, meanwhile, an almost tragic dilemma had begun. As time passed, he and Giuseppe understood each other better and better, conversing and playing together on the floor with immense amusement, and so he found himself madly in love also with Giuseppe, as well as Nino. But Nino was always out, and Giuseppe always at home: thus it was impossible for him to live constantly in the company of both his loves, as he would have wished. And in consequence, with either one, he was always tortured by regret: and if he was with one, the mere mention of the other's name or a smell that recalled him was enough for his homesickness to stream behind him, like a banner against the wind. At times, while he was on sentry duty outside Nino's school, suddenly, as if at a message brought him by a cloud, he would begin to sniff the sky with a mournful whimper, recalling the incarcerated Giuseppe. For a few minutes, a dissension would rend him, drawing him in two opposite directions at the same time; but finally, having overcome his hesitation, he would dash towards the San Lorenzo house, his long nose cleaving the wind like a prow. But at his destination, unfortunately, he found the door barred; and all his cries, mortified by the muzzle, passionately calling Giuseppe, were in vain; for Giuseppe, though hearing him and suffering in his solitary room, longing to let him in, was unable to do so. Then, resigning himself to his destiny of waiting outside doors, Blitz would stretch out there on the ground, where, at times, in his boundless patience, he would doze off. And perhaps he had a dream of love, which brought him a reminiscence of Nino: it's a fact that, a moment later, he would stir from his sleep and hop down the steps with desperate whimpers, to retrace his way to the school.

Nino wasn't jealous of that double love, not considering it a betrayal, but rather a flattery, because the value he himself attached almost equally to Giuseppe and to Blitz was asserted also by the two of them with genuine enthusiasm. Indeed, if he had to go to the movies, for example, or a Fascist rally or any place where the dog might be in his way, he himself would generously urge Blitz on such days to stay at home and keep Giuseppe company. Those were unforgettable strokes of luck for Giuseppe; and perhaps it was in those primitive duets with Blitz that he learned the language of dogs. A knowledge that, with his understanding of other animals' languages, was to remain a valid attainment of his for as long as he lived.

However, apart from these lucky occasions, Giuseppe never had any company. After the early days, when the novelty had worn off, Nino's visits with his friends and accomplices grew infrequent, until they stopped altogether. And no other people ever came to the house. Ida had no relatives or friends; she had never received visits. Still less did she receive any now, when she had to hide the scandal.

The people she encountered in the neighborhood were all aliens for her; and among them, as among her other acquaintances in Rome, nobody yet seemed to have discovered her secret. Unknown to her, really, through Nino's exuberance, within the very building at least a couple of boys knew of it; but they, faithful to their promise to him, had kept quiet about it even at home (all the more gladly because this guarding of such a mystery, not shared with adults, was a double pleasure).

It is certain, however, that in the whole circle of Nino's friends, the news of the secret, as was inevitable, later began to spread all too widely;

but, for the present, it didn't go beyond that circle or band. It must be added that, in reality, as the war continued, people had other things to think about and had become less curious. And besides, in Rome, and in the San Lorenzo district, the birth of a poor little bastard (though the child of a schoolteacher) would never have been, even in those ancient times, such a sensational piece of news that it should be put up on posters or proclaimed with the roll of drums!

In conclusion, Giuseppe continued to grow (after a manner of speaking) just like a bandit whose refuge was known only to various kids of every sort and of different neighborhoods, in a network of complicity whose strands extended through Rome's length and breadth. Perhaps also among the dogs of Rome the secret began to spread, since Blitz, during his waits for Nino, also conversed with passing dogs and strays; and once, in one of those nostalgic dashes of his to the San Lorenzo house, he arrived there in the company of another dog, bastard like himself, but much thinner and more ascetic looking, resembling Mahatma Gandhi. Still, as usual, nobody could open the door that time either, and the two went off together, but then took different directions, losing sight of each other, after that single meeting, forever.

. . . . 1942

JANUARY–FEBRUARY

"Wannsee Conference" for racial planning (decimation of the inferior races through forced labor and inanition, separation of the sexes, special treatment, etc.).

In the Pacific and throughout the Far East, great successes of the Japanese; already masters of Indochina and a large part of China, they advance rapidly until they are threatening British possessions in India.

The Nationalist leader Chiang Kai-shek is named commander of the Allied troops in China, where the war against the Japanese invader has been going on since 1937.

Arduous defense action of the CSIR (Italian Expeditionary Corps in Russia), without adequate arms and without equipment suited to the winter campaign.

Special appropriations for war industry in the United States (plans for 35,000 heavy artillery, 75,000 tanks, and 125,000 planes).

In North Africa, the Italo-Germans reoccupy Bengazi, capital of Cyrenaica.

MARCH–JUNE

In the Nazi concentration camp at Belsen, the "death chamber" is put into operation.

At a meeting of the Reichstag in Berlin, Hitler (who has already assumed personal command of the army) receives official confirmation of absolute power, with the right to decide the life and death of every German citizen.

The great offensive of the British Air Force begins, adopting the tactic (already applied by Germany) of area bombing, night attacks without specific targets, releasing tons of explosive and incendiary bombs, saturating built-up civilian areas. Reprisal counteroffensive by the Germans.

In the Pacific, the US Fleet defeats the Japanese in two battles.

In North Africa, the Italo-German forces, counterattacking, regain, at the cost of enormous casualties, the previously lost territory, advancing as far as El Alamein, in Egypt.

JULY–AUGUST

Among the latest products of the international war industry, tests are being made of the four-engine bombers, Flying Fortresses and Liberators, made in the United States, where, however, there is at present a reluctance, for humanitarian reasons, to engage in area bombing, or the indiscriminate bombardment of centers of civilian habitation.

To reinforce the German troops engaged on the Don, Italy sends another Expeditionary Corps to Russia (ARMIR), composed of the country's finest men (largely Alpine troops), but pitifully lacking the means not only for fighting or for armed defense, but even for elementary survival.

On the Volga, the Germans besiege the city of Stalingrad, where there is house-to-house fighting among the ruins.

After the British again arrest Mahatma Gandhi and members of the Congress Party, there are riots and bloody repressions in India.

Unsuccessful landing of the Allies at Dieppe, on the Channel. Almost all men engaged are killed.

SEPTEMBER–OCTOBER

On the Volga, despite the desperate resistance of the Soviets, the Germans occupy the ruins of Stalingrad.

In North Africa, the British resume the offensive, overwhelming the Italo-Germans, who, after the defeat at El Alamein, withdraw towards Tripoli, while the Americans prepare a landing to their rear.

NOVEMBER–DECEMBER

In Russia, a great Soviet offensive breaks through all along the front. The Soviets move to attack the Germans, trapped in Stalingrad.

In North Africa, the British reoccupy Bengazi, capital of Cyrenaica.

In Europe, the air war is intensified, with the total destruction of illustrious cities and monuments, and the slaughter of the civilian population. In news reports the term carpet bombing recurs regularly. Now the Americans also participate in these operations, with the recent products of their war industry (Liberators, Flying Fortresses, etc.).

In Greece, where, among the consequences of the war and the occupation, the number of deaths from starvation runs to hundreds of thousands, some groups attempt organized resistance against the Axis.

In Italy, repeated air raids on the cities of Genoa, Naples, Turin, and other smaller centers. Sixteen hundred tons of explosive are estimated to have been dropped on Northern Italy during the autumn.

In the United States, on the 2nd of December, the Chicago laboratory puts into operation the first nuclear reactor, achieving a chain reaction (fission of the uranium isotope U-235) . . .

Ring a round the roses
castle all around,
castle and palace,
the sun is in the sack.
Come out, come out, sun,
your Mamma's calling you,
and throw us sandwiches
to give to the boys
and throw us cookies
to give to the children
and throw us fritters
to give to old maids.
  I've had a hat made with flowers on it.
"And when will you wear it?"
When I become engaged.
I've had a smart hat made.
"And when will you wear it?"
When I marry.
And I'll drive out with two coaches.
"Good morning, Knight."
And I'll go out with two flags.
"Good morning, Knight."
And tra-la-la tra-la-lee,
Sugar cream and tee-hee-hee.

(Traditional children's song)

1 The first winter of his life, like the first autumn that preceded it, Giuseppe spent in total isolation, although his world had gradually extended from the bedroom to the rest of the apartment. During bad weather, all the windows were closed; but even with the windows open, his little voice would have in any case been lost in the noises of the street and the voices from the courtyard. The courtyard was immense, since the block of apartments had many separate entrances, from Entrance A to Entrance E. Ida's was apartment number nineteen of Entrance D, and since it was on the top floor, it had no immediate neighbors. Besides hers, in fact, there was only one other door on that landing, farther up, leading to the water tanks. And for Ida, in her situation, this was a stroke of luck.

The rooms of Apartment 19 Entrance D were, for Giuseppe, all the known world; and indeed, the existence of another, outside world must have been, for him, as vague as a nebula, since he was still too little to reach the windows and, from below, he could see only air. Unbaptized, uncircumcised as he was, no parish had bothered to rescue him; and the state of war, with the mounting confusion of orders, favored his banishment from creation.

In his precociousness, he had soon learned to move around the house on his hands and knees, imitating Blitz, who was perhaps his instructor. The front door, for him, was the extreme barrier of the universe, like the Pillars of Hercules for ancient explorers.

Now he was no longer naked, but bundled up against the cold in various woolen rags that made him look a bit rounder, like puppies in their coat. The shape of his face was now becoming clearly defined. His nose began to assume a straight and delicate line; and his features, pure though minute, recalled certain little Asiatic sculptures. Decidedly, he didn't resemble any of his relatives: except for the eyes, almost twins of those distant eyes. Twins, however, in their form and color, not in their gaze. The other gaze, in fact, had seemed terrible, desperate, and almost frightened; while this one, on the contrary, was trusting and festive.

A merrier baby than he had never been seen. Everything he glimpsed around him roused his interest and stirred him to joy. He looked with delight at the threads of rain outside the window, as if they were confetti and multicolored streamers. And if, as happens, the sunlight reached the ceiling indirectly and cast the shadows of the street's morning bustle, he would stare at it fascinated, refusing to abandon it, as if he were watching an extraordinary display of Chinese acrobats, given especially for him. You would have said, to tell the truth, from his laughter, from the constant brightening of his little face, that he didn't see things only in their usual aspects, but as multiple images of other things, varying to infinity. Otherwise, there was no explaining why the wretched, monotonous scene the house offered every day could afford him such diverse, inexhaustible amusement.

The color of a rag, of a scrap of paper, suggesting to him the resonance of all prisms and scales of light, was enough to transport him to awed laughter. One of the first words he learned was *ttars* (stars). However, he also called the lightbulbs in the house ttars, and the derelict flowers Ida brought from school, the hanging clusters of onions, even the door knobs, and later also swallows. Then when he learned the word *wallows* (swallows) he called wallows also his underpants hanging out on a line to dry. And in recognizing a new ttar (which was perhaps a fly on the wall) or a new wallow, he burst out each day in a magnificence of laughter, filled with contentment and welcome, as if he were meeting a member of the family.

Even the things that, in general, arouse aversion or repugnance, in him inspired only attention and a transparent wonder, like the others. In his endless journeys of exploration, crawling on all fours around the Urals and the Amazon and the Australian archipelagoes which the furniture of the house was to him, sometimes he no longer knew where he was. And he would be found under the sink in the kitchen, ecstatically observing a patrol of cockroaches as if they were wild colts on the prairie. He even recognized a ttar in a gob of spit.

But nothing had the power to make him rejoice as much as Nino's presence. It seemed that, in his opinion, Nino concentrated in himself the total festivity of the world, which everywhere else was to be found scattered and divided. For in Giuseppe's eyes, Nino represented by himself all the myriad colors, and the glow of fireworks, and every species of fantastic and lovable animal, and carnival shows. Mysteriously, he could sense Nino's arrival from the moment when he began the ascent of the stairs! And he would hurry immediately, as fast as he could with his method, towards the entrance, repeating ino ino, in an almost dramatic rejoicing of all his limbs. At times, even, when Nino came home late at night, he, sleeping, would stir slightly at the sound of the key, and with a trusting little smile he would murmur in a faint voice: ino.

The spring of the year 1942, meanwhile, was advancing towards summer. In place of the many pieces of wool, which made him look like a bundle of rags, Ida dressed Giuseppe in some very ancient shorts and little shirts formerly belonging to his brother, and ill-suited to him. The shorts, on him, turned into long pants. The shirts, taken in as best they could be at the sides, but not shortened, reached almost to his ankles. And for his feet, thanks to their tiny size, his infant's bootees still sufficed. Dressed in this fashion, he looked like an Indian.

All he knew of spring was the wallows that crisscrossed at the windows by the thousands from morning till evening, the multiplied and brightening stars, some remote clumps of geraniums, and the human voices that echoed in the courtyard, free and resounding, through the open windows. His vocabulary was enriched every day. The light, and the sky, and also the windows, he called *tun* (sun). The outside world, from the front door on, since it had always been forbidden, prohibited to him by his mother, he called *no*. The night, but also the furniture (since he passed beneath it) were called *ark* (dark). All voices, and sounds, *oice* (voice). Rain, *ain*, and also water, etc., etc.

With the coming of good weather, as can be imagined, Nino played hooky from school more and more often, even if his visits to Giuseppe in the company of his friends were now only a distant memory. But one marvelously bright morning, he appeared unexpectedly at home, lively and whistling, in the company of Blitz alone; and as Giuseppe popped up from beneath some piece of *ark*, coming towards him as usual, Nino announced to him, peremptorily:

"Hey, kid, let's go! We're off to have some fun!"

And having said this, he immediately went into action, hoisted Giuseppe astride his shoulders, and flew down the steps like the thief Mercury, while Giuseppe, in the divine tragedy of this infraction, murmured in a kind of exultant chant: "no . . . no . . . no . . . " His little hands were closed calmly inside his brother's; his feet, swaying in their race, hung over Nino's chest, so they could sense the violence of his breathing, in thrilled freedom, against the maternal laws! And Blitz followed, overcome by his double amorous happiness to such a degree that, forgetting how to walk, he tumbled down the steps like an idiot. The three came out into the courtyard, crossed the passage to the street; and no one, as they went by, stepped forward to ask Nino: "Who's the kid you're carrying?" as if, by a miracle, that little group had become invisible.

And so Giuseppe, confined since birth, made his first excursion into the world, exactly like Buddha. Buddha, however, left the gleaming garden of the King his father to encounter, just outside, the abstruse phenomena of disease, old age, and death; while in Giuseppe's case, on the contrary, you could say the world opened out, that day, like the true gleaming garden. Even if disease, old age, and death happened to place their simulacra along his way, he didn't notice them. Close, immediately beneath his eyes, the first thing he saw, during the outing, was his brother's black curls, dancing in the spring wind. And all the surrounding world, in his eyes, danced to the rhythm of those curls. It would be absurd to note here the few streets where they went, in the San Lorenzo district, and the people who moved around them. That world and those people, poor, anxious, and deformed by the grimace of the war, unfolded before Giuseppe's eyes like a multiple and unique phantasmagoria, to which not even a description of the Alhambra in Granada, or the gardens of Shiraz or perhaps even Eden could compare. All along the way, Giuseppe did nothing but laugh, exclaiming or murmuring, his little voice tinged by an extraordinary emotion: "Wallows, wallows . . . ttars . . . tun . . . wallows . . . ain . . . oice . . ." And when they finally stopped at a patch of mangy grass, where two scrawny city trees had put down their roots, and they sat on that grass to rest, Giuseppe's happiness, in the face of this sublime beauty, became almost fear; and he clung to his brother's windbreaker with both hands.

It was the first time in his life he had seen a field; and every blade of grass seemed to him illuminated from within, as if it contained a thread of green light. And so the leaves of the trees were hundreds of lightbulbs, where not only the green glowed, and not only the seven colors of the spectrum, but also other, unknown colors. The blocks of cheap housing around the little square, in the morning's open light, also seemed to kindle their colors through an inner splendor, which gilded and silvered them like the tallest castles. The few pots of geraniums and of basil at the windows were minuscule constellations, illuminating the air; and the people, dressed in colors, were moved around through the square by the same rhythmic and grandiose wind that moves the celestial circles, with their clouds, their suns, and their moons.

A flag was flapping over a doorway. A cabbage-white butterfly had lighted on a daisy . . . Giuseppe whispered:

"Wallow . . ."

"No, that's not a swallow! It's an insect! A butterfly. Say: BUTTERFLY."

Giuseppe smiled hesitantly, revealing his first baby teeth, just sprouting. But he couldn't say it. His smile trembled.

"Come on, try! Say: BUTTERFLY! Hey, are you an idiot or something?! Now what're you doing? Crying?! If you cry, I won't take you out with me any more!"

"Wallow."

"No, not wallow! It's a butterfly, I told you! Now, what's my name?"

"Ino."

"And him, this animal here with the collar, what's his name?"

"I."

"Right! That's my kid brother!! Now then, what's this?"

"Ty."

"Ty hell! BUTTERFLY! Hey, stupid! And this is a *tree*. Say: TREE. And that thing over there is a bicycle. Say: BICYCLE. Say: *Piazza dei Sanniti!*"

"Ty. Ty. Ty!" Giuseppe exclaimed, deliberately this time, playing the clown. And he laughed whole-heartedly at himself, just like a clown. Nino laughed too, and even Blitz: all together like clowns.

"Okay, cut the joking. This is serious. You see that thing waving. That's the flag. Say: FLAG."

"Lag."

"Good. Tricolored flag."

"Aikor lag."

"Good for you! Now shout: eia eia alalà!"

"Lallà."

"Great. And you? What's your name? High time you learned your own name. You know all the names in the world, and you still don't know your own. What's your name?"

". . . . ."

"GIUSEPPE! Say it after me: GIUSEPPE!"

Then his little brother concentrated, in a supreme effort of search and conquest. And heaving a sigh, with a pensive face, he said:

"Useppe."

"Jeezus!! You're an ace, you are! You even got the *ess* right! Useppe! I like that. I like it better than Giuseppe. You want to know something? As far as I'm concerned, I'm going to call you Useppe from now on. Climb aboard. We're leaving."

And with Giuseppe once more astride Nino's shoulders, they hastily started along the road back. The return was even happier than the outward journey: for the world, having lost its first tragic emotion, had become more familiar. In that dash of Nino's, it was like a merry-go-round, a fair; in it, to perform the wonder of wonders, there appeared, in succession: two or three dogs, a donkey, various vehicles, a cat, etc.

"I . . . i . . ." shouted Giuseppe (or rather Useppe), recognizing Blitz in all the four-legged animals that passed, straying or hauling, and perhaps also in the wheeled vehicles. Whereupon Ninnuzzu seized the opportunity to enrich his vocabulary still further with the words *automobile* (momobile) and *horse* (oss); until, fed up for today with acting as teacher, he left him to the creations of his fancy.

On their second excursion, which followed a few days later, they went to see the trains at the Tiburtina Station: not only the part on the square, the area open to passengers (momobiles . . . ark) but also the more special area reserved for freight cars, reached from a back street. Access to this area, for the ordinary public, was forbidden by a fence; but Ninnuzzu, who had some acquaintances on the inside, pushed open the gate and entered freely, as if in an old fief of his. And, in fact, since his childhood, that corner of the San Lorenzo district had been a kind of preserve for him and for his street friends.

At the present moment there was no one inside (except for an elderly little man in coveralls, who waved familiarly to Ninnuzzu from the distance). And the only visible traveler, on any of the few trains waiting there, was a calf, looking down from the open platform of a car. It stood there calmly, tied to an iron bar, barely sticking out its helpless head (its two little horns, still tender, had been torn out); and from its neck, on a string, hung a tiny medal, like a tag, on which the last stage of his journey perhaps was written. None of that information had been given the traveler; but in his broad, moist eyes you could sense a dark foreknowledge.

The only one who seemed to take an interest in him was Blitz, who on sighting him, gave out a soft, drawling whimper; but then, over the head of his brother, who held him hoisted on his shoulders, Giuseppe was also observing the calf. And perhaps between the child's eyes and the animal's there was some unforeseen exchange, subterranean and imperceptible. All of a sudden, Giuseppe's gaze underwent a curious change, never seen before, which, however, nobody noticed. A kind of sadness or suspicion crossed his eyes, as if a little dark curtain had been drawn down; and he kept looking back towards the freight car, above his brother's shoulders, as Ninnuzzu now, with Blitz, was striding towards the exit.

"Oss . . . oss . . ." he managed to say, with a quavering mouth; but he said it so softly that perhaps Ninnuzzu didn't even hear him, nor did he bother to correct him. And here the minuscule adventure ended. Its duration had been infinitesimal. And already the three were coming out into the square again, where another unexpected adventure quickly dispelled the shadow of the first.

A vendor of colored balloons happened to be going by; and amused at his novice brother's rejoicing, the generous Nino spent almost his entire wealth to buy him one, a red one. Then they resumed their way home, no longer three, but four, if you count the balloon, whose string Giuseppe was holding with real anxiety . . . when all of a sudden, perhaps two hundred yards farther on, his fingers accidentally relaxed, and the balloon escaped him, into the air.

It seemed a tragedy; instead, it was the opposite. In fact, Giuseppe welcomed the event with a laugh of surprise and joy. And, his head back, his eyes upraised, for the first time in his life he said the following words, which no one had taught him:

"Fly away! Fly away!"

Similar excursions of the trio were repeated various other times, all through the month of May; and inevitably the news of that droll trio rollicking around the neighborhood soon reached Ida's ears. Now, after a first jolt, she felt refreshed by it, as if by a providential solution. But out of inertia, she adopted a course of non-intervention and didn't mention anything to Nino . . . So those childish flights proceeded in a double intrigue: since for Nino their chief fascination lay in their illicitness, Ida involuntarily favored their success by her silence.

However, this new development was certainly another knot in Ida's already confused skein. Even more than before, when she went out of the house, she would hurry, like a street cat with its ears down, cutting corners to avoid the neighbors and their indiscreet questions. Which, in fact, were always spared her; however, this general silence was inexplicable to her and in her suspicions became a threat, postponed from day to day.

The fact was that the scandal of her maternity, which she thought still a secret, was no longer a secret at all around those parts (Nino's comrades, obviously, had kept their word only up to a certain point); but then, for those Roman proletarians, it wasn't even a scandal. Nobody felt like stoning that poor little schoolteacher, who was always seen bustling about, alone and occupied, in her run-over shoes; and if some neighbor woman, encountering her by chance, mentioned the baby, it wasn't out of malice, but rather as a compliment. Still she would blush as if they had accused her of illegal prostitution.

These encounters with the neighbor women occurred, for the most part, while she was standing in line outside the food stores, which were always the least supplied, and in general they sold ersatz products, instead of the genuine article. The legal rations were being reduced, month by month, to a ridiculous inadequacy, whereas Nino's hunger so ravaged him that he was almost transformed into a cannibal, ready to eat his mother. The only citizens good at filling themselves were the well-off, who could take advantage of the black market; but this was not Ida's case. And then her private war for survival began, which was later to develop, growing more and more ferocious.

The greatest part of her time, outside the school, was spent hunting provisions; and at the same time she begged for private lessons, willing to accept, as payment, a packet of dried milk or a can of tomato paste, etc. These hunting days of hers, reducing her to a condition of primitive struggle, distracted her from all the other daily anxieties inherited from her mother.

Now Giuseppe, too, wanted to eat. His mother's breasts, after the first months, had exhausted their milk, and he, weaned early, that winter had already become used to more virile foods. She prepared him some makeshift gruels, boiling up in a special little pot anything edible she could scrape together; and he, full of trust, fed on these gruels, growing as best he could. It seemed that most of all he wanted to increase his height a bit; but the little he gained in length, he lost in breadth; and he looked fairly skinny, though harmoniously built. His face, however, remained round, with an expression of good health due to his merry disposition. His skin, almost ignorant of the sun, had by nature a tanned Calabrian hue. And his eyes, which had never yet seen the sea, or the river, or even a pool, seemed nevertheless to draw their color from unknown marine depths, like the eyes of fishermen or of sailors.

At night, retiring with him in the larger room, Ida would gaze spell-bound at the sleep of those little eyes, so blissful they seemed unaware of dreams. For herself, on the other hand, even more than the insomnia which had been bothering her for some time, she feared the dreams which had taken to visiting her with an unwonted profusion, flinging her among absurd events, like Alice in Wonderland. Her sleep seemed to have be-come her real wakefulness, and perhaps her present long spells of insomnia unconsciously wanted to delay this chimerical vigil. As soon as she fell asleep, as if at the collapse of a partition, her nighttime labyrinthine jour-ney would begin, without pauses or gaps. Here she is, in a no-man's-land, a kind of suburb, with some temporary constructions. She is the only one wearing clothes in the midst of a crowd of naked people, all standing, their bodies huddled one against the other with no breathing space. And she is ashamed of being dressed, though no one seems to notice her. All those people look dazed, with chalky, staring faces, absent eyes, and without voice, as if every means of communication among them had vanished. She is weeping, so her very loud sobbing is the only sound present; but, pre-cisely because it is the only one, she seems to be laughing . . .

. . . But now the laughter no longer comes from her; in fact, some-body, hidden, is laughing at her, as she stands alone, erect, like a marion-ette, among some piles of beams and rubble. Nobody can be seen, but beneath those piles a din is heard like thousands of chewing teeth, and under it, the whimpering of a child, whom she can't help, no matter how hard she tries, because her movements are rigid as if her whole body were made of wood. Finally, the laughter becomes confused with the barking of a dog, perhaps it's Blitz, who is scratching desperately to free Ninnarieddu and Giuseppe. But at this point she finds she has fallen into some under-ground room, where a deafening music reechoes, horribly comical, forcing her to dance. And in the dance she has to show her legs, but she tries to cover them, knowing she has some terrible scars that disfigure her thigh and calf, and for which she will be punished unto the seventh genera-tion . . .

In these dreams of Iduzza's, personalities of international fame were encountered (Hitler with his little moustache, the Pope with his eye-glasses, or the Emperor of Ethiopia with his open umbrella) in a promis-cuous social reel with her own dead: her mother all dignified in a little violet hat, her father hurrying along with a briefcase, and Alfio setting off with an enormous valise. All of them mingled with barely glimpsed figures from the past: a character known as *Fischettu* and another called *Monumentu*. And amid such a throng, with a crazy and absurd frequency, a present tenant of Entrance B returned, God knows why, a man called *Il Messaggero*, because, in former days, he had worked as a printer for that newspaper. He was an elderly man with Parkinson's disease, who appeared now and then in the courtyard, supported by his wife or by his daughters. He walked in fits and starts, dazed and expressionless as a dummy, and in reality, when Ida did meet him, she compassionately avoided looking at him; while the dream, on the contrary, photographed him in full light, with scientific precision . . . And pupils, colleagues, and superiors from the school, familiar faces or others almost unknown, frozen in her memory, peopled Iduzza's nights in myriads. The only person absent was her German lover: neither then nor afterwards did he ever appear in the dreams of his lover.

.   .   .

More and more often, as the months passed, the air-raid alarm sirens were heard at night, usually followed, a little later, by the roar of planes through the sky. But these were transient planes, heading elsewhere; and the news of other Italian cities' being bombed did not shake the Romans from their trusting passivity. Convinced that Rome was a holy and untouchable city, most of them allowed the alarms and the racket to go by without moving from their beds. And so also Ida had long since fallen in with this habit; except that the alarms, in her house, created a certain fuss all the same.

The chief guilt for this belonged to Blitz, who was always excited at the sound of the sirens; and from the living-room-study where he was shut up, he would begin a feverish, steady appeal to the family, and particularly to his master Ninnarieddu, not yet home . . . Only after the all-clear had sounded would he finally calm down, resuming the silent wait for his Ninnarieddu . . . But in the meanwhile, also Giuseppe would have waked up. And having perhaps mistaken the voices of the sirens for cocks' crowing or some other signal of daybreak, and confusing Blitz's nocturnal waking with a morning waking, he would assume it was already time to get up, persisting in this illusion.

Then Ida, half rising from the sheets, to lure him back to sleep would sing the famous lullaby sung to her in the past by her father and then to Ninnarieddu, with the variation adopted for the occasion:

". . . there we'll buy some little shoes
To dance on the feast of San Giuseppino."

111

The San Giuseppino lullaby, however, did not always suffice to send Giuseppe back to sleep. On some evenings, when the last verse was over, he would ask her, insatiably, to sing him the whole song again from the beginning; and after that, perhaps, he might ask for others, prompting her himself: "Mà, *obbinge*" (the song of the orange) or else: "Mà, *sip*" (the song of the ship). It was a little Calabrian repertory, very ancient, handed down to her by her father. And in spite of her weariness, she would enjoy this little theater, where she could perform like a real and admired singer, postponing, at the same time, the hour of her nightly dreams. Sitting in the middle of the bed, her hair undone for the night, she would repeat meekly, by request:

". . . Orange of my garden . . ."
"And the ship turns, and the ship veers . . ."

She was, by nature, so completely tone-deaf that she could make no difference in notes, between one tune and the other. She set them all to the same music, a kind of shrill and childish chant, with strident cadences. And for this reason, she no longer dared sing in Ninnarieddu's presence. Now that he was grown and a fairly good singer in his own right, he wouldn't even listen to her, but would interrupt her immediately, with shushing, sarcasm, or whistling, if she accidentally hinted at some song while doing her housework.

Giuseppe, on the other hand, still ignorant and simple, didn't criticize her for her unstrung throat. And for that matter, any music, to Giuseppe, was a pleasure: even the tormenting notes of the radio in the courtyard, or the clanging of the tram. Any vulgar music, in his little ears, developed in fugues and variations of unknown freshness, precedent to all experience. And even simple isolated sounds (like colors) echoed in him through all their harmonics, as his ecstatic attention perceived even their intimate murmurings . . . And then when his brother Nino (with his new voice, now acquiring timbre) walked around the house singing his cheap and common songs, Giuseppe, spellbound, panted after his every step: as his namesake Peppe, in the famous tale, ran after the royal band!

But even more than by notes, perhaps, Giuseppe was bewitched by words. Obviously words, for him, had a sure value, as if they were one with objects. He had only casually to hear the word *dog*, to laugh heartily, as if suddenly the familiar and comical presence of Blitz were there, before him, tail wagging. And at times it even happened that from a word he could already receive a presentiment of the thing denoted, even if it was unknown to him, so that he then recognized it at first meeting. One day, seeing the printed drawing of a ship for the first time in his life, he exclaimed, in a tremble of discovery: "Sip! sip!"

Thanks to his outings with his brother, the family of things had become enriched for him, developing in new, natural ramifications. Articles of furniture and domestic objects became for him houses, trains. Towels, rags, even clouds were *lags* (flags). The lights of the stars were grass, and the stars themselves were ants around a crumb (the moon).

He stretched out his hand towards the print of the *Hôtel des îles Borromées* and to the others that decorated the living room, saying, dreamily: "Square . . . people . . ." and he had learned to recognize his brother in the great portrait hanging on the wall, before which he would name Ino in a low voice, with puzzlement and ecstasy, like Dante contemplating the figures carved in the rock.

Now, if asked his name, he would answer gravely: "Useppe." In front of a mirror, seeing himself, he would say: "Useppe." And finally, not only his brother but also his mother became used to calling him by this inedited name. Which then remained his for everybody, always. And I, too, from now on will call him Useppe, because this is the name by which I always knew him.

.   .   .

Since the schools had closed, his excursions with Nino had ended, because Nino now slept every morning till past noon, having been out late at night. However, his mother had made up her mind to take him sometimes (choosing the proper hours) to a poor, lonely little park, not too far away. She would take him in her arms, trying to hide her face against his little body: frightened, as if along the way there were a risk of encountering the bogey-man. And after reaching the park, while he played on the ground, she remained alert, sitting on the edge of the bench, ready to go off in fright if anyone approached her.

But these outings took place, for the most part, at siesta time, when the heat drove all living creatures indoors; and only once did an intruder, a woman, come surprisingly to sit beside her on the bench. She was a little old thing, so shrunken and wrinkled she seemed by now destined to terrestrial immortality, like the papyri in the sands. And she looked like a beggar, but she must have worked somehow at the fish market, to judge by the pungent odor of dried fish which emanated not only from her shopping-bag, but also from the many skirts she wore, gypsy-style, one over the other; they seemed steeped in it, even underneath, in every fold. She stared at the child, and asked Ida: "Is he yours?"

And while Ida looked at her sullenly, without answering, she re-

113

marked, on her own, with a cruel compassion: "Poor little thing. He's too much alive, small as he is. He won't stay long in this world."

Then, addressing him, she asked: "What's your name?"

With his trusting little smile, he answered her: "Useppe."

"Ah, Peppino. I had a little baby, too, just like you, little like you, and her name, too, was Pina. She had lively eyes like yours, only hers were black."

And taking a walnut that stank of dried fish from beneath her skirt, she made him a present of it. Then her decrepit shoulders shuddered as she said: "It's chilly, here in the shade." (It was July, with a temperature of ninety-nine degrees.) And like a lizard seeking the sunshine, she went off, trotting, as she had come.

Another time, in that same little park, while Useppe was sitting as usual on the dusty gravel, the color of a boy's jersey made him think he recognized his brother walking along the opposite sidewalk. Then, as if lifted in a flame of exultation, shouting "ino! ino!" he promptly stood up towards that vision and took a few steps by himself! And as Ida rushed over to help him, afraid he would fall, he realized his mistake meanwhile and displayed an amazed, bitter face to her, like a pilgrim in the desert who had followed a mirage: without even noticing, under the impact of his double emotion, that in that moment, with nobody helping him, he had taken the first steps of his life.

From then on, day after day, almost entirely by himself, he learned to walk. And his explorations of the house took on a new, intoxicating dimension. He often banged against the furniture, or fell; but he never cried, even though he not infrequently hurt himself, so that his body, like a hero's, bore the wounds of his feats. When he fell, he would lie silent for a while on the floor; then he would grumble slightly and pull himself up again; and a moment later he would be laughing, happy as a fledgling sparrow unfolding its wings.

Ninnarieddu gave him a tiny red-and-yellow ball, explaining to him that these were the colors of the *Roma* (the football team) and that consequently the ball was also named Roma. That was the only toy he possessed, besides the walnut the old woman had given him, which he himself from the very beginning had jealously excluded from the category of foodstuffs, considering it a distinguished and special walnut. In the house they called it *Lazio*, so that it wouldn't be confused with the ball *Roma*; and Useppe, with *Roma*, and *Lazio*, held genuine tournaments, in which Blitz often joined and, on the luckiest days, also Nino.

To tell the truth, Nino had become more of a vagabond than ever; and during the few hours he spent at home, mostly he slept, so blissfully that not even those constant family tournaments could trouble his sleep.

His nights, according to his own declaration, were all employed in a kind of patrol duty, undertaken by the Young Fascist musketeers, hand-picked and volunteers, like him, to check the wartime regulations, and especially the blackout. Every time a forbidden glow filtered from some window or crack, they would shout in chorus from the street the menacing warning: "Light! Liiight!" And in this connection, he told of his amusement in shouting, instead of *Luce*, "Duce! Duceee!" deliberately, enjoying the rhyme, while standing under the windows (carefully blacked-out, to tell the truth) of his Greek teacher, suspected of anti-Fascism.

This was the most innocuous of the various exploits, half-comical, half-brigandish, that he boasted of then: which could, however, also be part fiction. Genuine, certainly, was his delight in roaming around on those nights of darkness, perhaps alone, with no aim or plan: especially during the alarms, when restrictions and prudence drove everyone inside. Then, the deserted city appealed to him, like an arena, where he was the toreador, excited by the roars of the sirens and the planes, as he flouted the general rule. As if it were all a game, he amused himself in eluding, with his agility, the surveillance of the armed patrols, which he sometimes challenged, whistling songs at intersections. And if he tired of running around, he would go and sit on a column or on the steps of a monument to smoke a cigarette and hold up the lighted tip towards the sky, deliberately, as the aerial squadrons passed, insulting in a loud voice those invisible pilots with the dirtiest Roman obscenities, and concluding: "And now shoot me! Bomb me! Go on, shoot!"

Actually, he now felt a kind of inner rage, and he began to grow impatient at merely drilling during the day with the squads and platoons of kids. He would really have liked it if one of those night pilots, as in an adventure comic, had responded to the provocation of his lighted cigarette, landing with his parachute there before him, to engage in hand-to-hand combat. Or if the suspended menace of those nights had become flesh, turning into a raging bull, against which he could prove his daring and his invulnerable unconcern. Leaping around the beast, running beneath his hoofs, and flying over him, and pricking him on all sides; and giving him no rest, darting in front of him, then reappearing at both sides almost simultaneously until he was multiplied in the animal's pupils, crazing him, as if not one Nino were against him, but a hundred. And in this whirl of his madness, pierce his chest; and over his bleeding and agonizing carcass, become single again: I, Ninnarieddu, the Invincible, the Ace of the Corrida!

This, naturally, is only a partial reconstruction of the mysterious wanderings of Ninnarieddu on those nights; nor can I give any further information. It is a fact that occasionally—and not always, as he claimed at home—he really was on duty or on patrol through the streets of the city, with his group of companions in uniform. This, in fact, as far as I know, was a special service of order and honor that was assigned in turn, a special occasion. And it was precisely on one of these special occasions that the musketeer Ninnarieddu conceived and carried out a personal, historic, private exploit. Which, perforce, at the time, he kept concealed; and it remained, indeed, a mystery of Rome!

It seems that, for a series of nights, his squad was charged with guarding the zone around the Victor Emmanuel Monument, in the vicinity of Palazzo Venezia itself, where in a room known as the *Sala del Mappamondo*, or Hall of the Globe, the Duce had his office. Before the war, the Duce's large window over the square was always seen alight, to make the people believe that the Duce (called also *The Sleepless One*) was up there working, incessantly, like a perpetual Vestal who, while all sleep at night, never slept. However, since the outbreak of the war, with the blackout regulations, that window also was dark. Everything was black, in the night, around those streets. The black darkness teemed with black policemen, and Ninnarieddu himself wore black shirt, black trousers, black cap, etc. Now on one of those nights, God only knows how, Nino managed to slip off alone behind those historical palaces, like a bandit dashing to the center of the world, carrying, now hidden, a can of black paint and a brush! And, stealthily, in great haste, he wrote on the wall in big letters the following words:

VIVA STALIN.

Not because he liked Stalin, who, on the contrary, at that period, seemed the chief enemy. But just for the hell of it, for a laugh. He would have amused himself by writing VIVA HITLER on the walls of the Kremlin.

Then, having performed his feat, he promptly cleared out, pleased to imagine the wall in the first light of dawn and the effect created there by his prominent, personal work of art.

.   .   .

The winter of 1942–43 (third winter of the war in Rome) was squalid and ravenous. Ida pursued her usual occupations in a state of torpor, due in part to scant nourishment, and in part to some sleeping pills she had started taking nightly after the last summer. In their composition, they were not very different from the medicines that had helped her, in the past, with her childhood spells; now, however, they served to provide her some rest in her unnerving nights. Thanks to these medicines, taken after supper every evening, she now descended, almost the moment she went to bed, into a long sleep, apparently empty of dreams.

Actually, I believe, she did dream; but the dreamed events occurred in a sealed compartment of her imagination, inaccessible to her consciousness. And this virtual splitting of her personality continued during her waking hours, through the whole next day, as that state of torpor dragged on beyond the night. There was an absent Iduzza, dazed, who witnessed the toil of another Iduzza: this one sprang up at the sound of the alarm clock, went here and there for classes, private lessons, lines outside shops, trams, and through neighborhoods, according to some preestablished rule . . . However, the second Iduzza, though it was she who acted, was, of the two, the more spectral: as if she, rather than the other, belonged to the sly world of those nighttime dreams that escaped her, but perhaps did not cease wounding her.

Since Useppe's birth, for fear of running into old Ezekiel (now aware of her scandalous secret) she had considerably lessened her own visits to the Ghetto. She went only in certain extreme economic situations, for the purpose of selling, over there, some family object, second-hand. But her visits were rapid and almost clandestine, the more so since, recently, the Jews had been forbidden to practice even their ancient trade of junk-dealing, and it was best to exercise it in secret. She never happened, on those quick trips, to encounter Vilma, or to exchange chatter or information. Iduzza's only source of political news was cut off.

And so the most recent war news (barely mentioned by her reticent colleagues at school) reached her mainly through Nino's propaganda. In Africa, in Russia, the Nazi-Fascists were withdrawing disastrously. However, these retreats, according to Nino's reports, were only a trick, planned by the Reich's Commanders to guarantee the great success of the final surprise: the secret Weapon!! This, which Ninnuzzu called Weapon X, or Z, or H, according to his whim of the day, was meanwhile being perfected in the underground factories of Silesia or the Ruhr, and soon (perhaps no later than next spring) it would be ready. Announced by the general alarm of all sirens, in one moment it would end the war, with the definitive victory of the Reich and the advent of its dominion over all nations.

What this sublime machine consisted of, how it acted, was, indeed, a secret reserved for the Leaders alone: though Ninnarieddu, by his tone, hinted he was also in on it, keeping it hidden there beneath his clump of curls, without, naturally, giving any clue to it at home, since it was a military secret.

But on certain days of boredom, he deigned to communicate triumphantly that the Reich's High Command had given the enemy countries an ultimatum: either total unconditional surrender, or else within twenty-four hours the explosion of Weapon X. The populace, however, was to know nothing, until X hour; it was to be a surprise. And here, to imitate the imminent explosion, Ninnuzzu would use his lips to produce those indecent, perversely comical noises which have different names according to the various regions, though boys of all regions seem intoxicated by them.

Really, he was not eager for the war to end, but rather for it to begin also for him. It seemed unfair to him to be still deprived of this exceptional, formidable opportunity, excluded like a mongrel, assigned to the beardless category.

And especially since, now, he was no longer beardless: indeed, he made a great show of shaving every day, using, for the operation, a real barber's razor, with a long steel blade, which was precisely that famous clasp knife, of multiple uses, left to Ida by the soldier Gunther.

Ninnuzzu had discovered it some time ago in the chest, when he was searching the house one day for objects, scraps of metal or other material to offer to the Fatherland (according to the Regime's appeal to the population, to assist in the manufacture of armaments). And perhaps believing it nobody's property, something that had somehow turned up there, he had taken possession of it, without reporting to his mother. But instead of donating it to the government, he had kept it for himself.

It happened that one morning, as he was shaving, Ida glimpsed that flashing razor in his hands, and in an instantaneous recollection she seemed to recognize it. She felt herself turn pale; but she avoided inquiring into this disturbing reappearance and forgot it promptly, like her dreams.

That knife then accompanied Ninnuzzu for many months afterwards, in his subsequent adventures, until one day it was stolen from him, or was lost.

. . . . 1943

JANUARY–FEBRUARY

In Russia the collapse of the Don front marks the ruinous end of the Italian expeditionary corps, overwhelmed by Soviet troops. Forced by the Nazi-Fascist leaders to an impossible stand, and then abandoned in confusion, without orders, equipment, or leadership, the soldiers of the CSIR and the ARMIR are dispersed and die, unburied, on the frozen steppe.

On the Baltic, after seventeen months of siege, the Red Army liberates Leningrad. The number of civilians who die during the siege is 630,000.

At Stalingrad, definitive surrender of the Germans remaining in the city, surrounded by the Russian forces and reduced to a depository of corpses. (1446 hours, 2 February: In Stalingrad no further sign of fighting.)

In North Africa, the Italian colonies of Tripolitania and Cyrenaica, abandoned by the Italo-Germans, are placed under Allied military administration.

The Yugoslav resistance against the Axis occupying forces spreads to Greece and Albania.

From the United States, a news bulletin declares that, among the workers in the war industries, there are more than four million women.

In Germany, a decree is issued, drafting all male Germans between 16 and 65 years of age and all females between 17 and 45, for labor in defense of the country.

MARCH–JUNE

In Italy, for the first time during the Fascist period, there is a workers' strike. The strike, called by the workers at the Fiat plant in Turin, spreads to other industries in the North. The organization of clandestine parties, opposed to the regime, is intensified, with the Communist Party particularly active.

In Warsaw, at the end of a desperate revolt by the surviving prisoners of the ghetto, the Nazi occupiers set fire to the quarter and raze it to the ground.

Conclusion of the war in Africa, with the final surrender of the Axis to the Allies, opening the way to Italy.

American naval strategy prevails in the Pacific, and the Japanese suffer a series of defeats.

To show that the USSR is renouncing plans for world revolution, and to favor the coalition with the Western Powers, Stalin dissolves the Comintern.

JULY–AUGUST

New defeats of the Panzerdivisionen on the Soviet front, and landing of Allied forces in Sicily, which is rapidly occupied. In Rome, the Fascist chiefs plot to dismiss the Duce, with the idea of dealing with the Allies and saving their own interests. A similar plan on the part of the King, to save his crown. Meeting of the Fascist Grand Council, where, for the first time in the history of this institution, there is a majority vote against the Duce. Receiving him at Villa Savoia, the King informs the Duce of his dismissal and has the Carabinieri arrest him as he leaves. After various moves, the prisoner is taken, under heavy escort, to an isolated locality of the Gran Sasso mountain in the Abruzzi.

To replace the deposed Duce, the King appoints Badoglio, a monarchist general of the Regime and the conqueror of Addis Ababa. Badoglio simultaneously proclaims the end of Fascism and the continuation of the war at the side of the Nazis, ordering the Italian army and the police to repress fiercely any attempt at popular uprising. Meanwhile, the general and the King engage in secret negotiations with the Allies on one hand and with the Germans on the other.

Rejoicing throughout Italy at the end of the dictatorship, while large Nazi contingents gather at the border, ready to intervene in the peninsula.

SEPTEMBER–OCTOBER

Signing of the armistice with Italy, announced by the Allied radio. The King of Italy, the Government, and the High Command flee towards the South, already occupied by the Allies, abandoning the army, Rome, and the rest of Italy to their fate. By order of the Führer, the prisoner Mussolini is freed by a unit of Hitler's paratroops, who land on the Gran Sasso in helicopters. Headed by Mussolini, under Hitler's control, the Nazi-Fascist Republic of Salò is founded in the North of Italy.

The Italian army collapses, both in the peninsula and in the Axis-occupied territories, where Italian units are massacred by the Germans or else deported to Germany for forced labor in the war industry. Those who manage to escape seek refuge in the South of Italy, or join local partisan bands.

The Allies, after landing at Salerno, arrest their advance north of Naples. Above this line, all Italy is under German military occupation. Groups of armed resistance against the occupying forces begin to be formed, especially in the North.

Through the Spanish Embassy, the monarchist Badoglio government in the South communicates Italy's declaration of war against Germany, while the Salò republic publishes decrees calling up young men for the formation of a Nazi-Fascist army.

More workers' strikes in the industries in the North.

As in other occupied territories, also in Italy the Nazis proceed to the "final solution of the Jewish problem."

In Moscow, the "International," official anthem of the USSR, is replaced with a new anthem in praise of "Great Russia."

NOVEMBER–DECEMBER

In Italy, bloody reprisals by the Nazis, assisted by Fascist squads, which have returned to action, in the service of the occupiers.

In the cities and countryside of central and northern Italy, the partisans' armed resistance is becoming organized, coordinated by the clandestine political parties, and especially by the Communist Party.

The German counteroffensive in Russia breaks down. Violent air raids on Berlin. The Big Three (Churchill, Stalin, Roosevelt) meet in Teheran . . .

Where are we going? Where are they taking us?
To the land of Pitchipoi.

You leave when it's still dark, and you arrive in the dark

It is the land of smoke and screams

But why have our mothers left us?
Who will give us the water for death?

1 Nino, in that year, had grown much taller. And his physique adapted itself to this growth in an unruly way, changing without order or measure, creating a disproportion and an awkwardness, which, still, in their fleeting duration, gave him a different grace. As if the shape of his childhood were rebelling, in a dramatic struggle, before surrendering to his impatience to grow.

When he looked at himself in the mirror, he made furious grimaces, observed by his brother Useppe (who followed him always) with profound interest, as if at the circus. The chief cause of his fury was his wardrobe, all makeshift and ill-matched in the impossible race against his growth. And on some days, spitefully, he would go out in a bizarre camouflage: for example, with a dirty towel as a scarf, an old woolen blanket around his shoulders, and a half-crushed hat of his father's on his head making him resemble a goatherd or a bandit. And he was capable of turning up at school in this costume.

Always hungry, he would rummage in the kitchen cabinet and scour the pots, even eating dishes before they were cooked, he was so rabid. One evening he arrived, waving an enormous piece of dried cod like a banner, not even bothering to hide it. He had stolen it at Piazza Vittorio, he said, because he felt like eating steamed cod with potatoes. Ida, frightened, cowed by her respect for the law, refused to cook it, telling him to take it back; but he declared that, if she wouldn't cook it for him, he would eat the whole thing raw, there on the spot. Then, martyrlike, Ida did cook it; but she wouldn't eat a morsel. So he feasted blissfully with Useppe and Blitz.

This skillful theft marked, for him, the discovery of a new entertainment. Another evening he arrived with a string of sausages around his neck, and yet another evening with a live pullet on his shoulder, saying he would take care of killing it and plucking it, and then Ida would cook it. But since the chicken promptly revealed itself to be a comical, bold animal (instead of running off, it crowed and pecked at Nino's locks as if they were grass, and played tag with Useppe and Blitz), Nino became fond of him and didn't want to kill him then. So in the days that followed, the chicken lived in the house like a boarder, threatening the cockroaches with spread wings, jumping on the beds, and soiling everywhere. Until finally Ida made up her mind and traded it for some cans of sardines.

Now (along with the shame of being—she, a schoolteacher—practically an involuntary accomplice in these thefts), Ida turned pale every time Ninnuzzu was late, thinking they had caught him red-handed. But he said, with self-assurance, that if such a thing happened, he would display the black scarf with a skull printed on it, which he wore around his neck, declaring himself a musketeer of the Duce, authorized to requisition supplies.

For Nino, this was a season of frenzy. The lousy winter hindered his daily and nightly roving through the streets; and on some evenings, when he also lacked the money for the movies, the boy was forced to stay home and go to bed early. But since his little brother and his dog fell asleep before he did, he was left alone, deprived even of his faithful gnomes, and he didn't know where to fling himself until it was time to sleep, or how to release his energy. So he was even reduced to talking with his mother, loquaciously exalting the plots of the latest films, or the future era of the great Reich, or the secret weapon; while she, seated at the kitchen table, already under the influence of her sleeping pills, lowered her heavy eyelids and let her head slump until it banged against the marble tabletop. In his boyish oratory, meanwhile, he was never still a moment; an irresistible urgency seemed eager to express itself through every muscle of his body. He would kick a rag that had happened to be in his path, and slam it vehemently all around the kitchen, as if it were a football field; or he would strike a blow in the air with one fist, then with the other, as if in the ring . . . Until, when a futile whistle addressed to his mother proved she was asleep, he would give up talking by himself and sullenly go off to his room.

Not even reading his sports magazines, his cheap novels of adventure or scandal, could amuse him any more; instead, they increased his restlessness, stirring up his desire for action, or for making love. At this point, on some evenings, he would go out into the street, even in the rain, hoping for some chance encounter, maybe even with a cheap, lost little whore who, for the charm of his curls, would receive him free of charge in her cot, or (if she was without fixed address) would follow him silently up the stairs to the seventh floor, to his daybed. There, Blitz, already carefully trained for these eventualities, would welcome them soundlessly, barely greeting them with his tail.

But he rarely had such strokes of luck, which had actually befallen him during the fine season, and even a couple of times towards Christmas. As a rule, Ninnarieddu encountered only the freezing desert of rain and darkness. And he came home alone, all soaked, to go to bed, head down against the pillow, infuriated at having to sleep so early!, while life, with its cots of love, its bombs, its engines, its massacres, was still raging everywhere, merry and bloodthirsty!

School, by now, had become an impossible constraint. And not infrequently, in the morning, especially in bad weather, after grumbling a reply to Ida's usual call, he would roll over again under the blankets when she had gone out, and would continue sleeping voluptuously at least another two hours, indifferent to the missed class. When he did get up then (all charged with free and fresh energies, happy to have had a vacation), even the tenants on the floor below took fright and started complaining, hitting the ceiling with a broom. The house was transformed into a stadium, a circus, a jungle. The morning's greatest amusement was the search for *Roma* and *Lazio*, fatally given to vanishing in the heat of the usual contests. In an epic hunt furniture was shifted, upset, explored, turned inside out, and everything was flung in the air, until Blitz, all dusty, would reappear from some cranny, carrying the retrieved prey in his teeth, exultant, applauded like a champion.

Such childish games did not exhaust, but rather exacerbated, Nino's turbulence, driving it to excess, like a tribe aroused by its own yells. In the midst of those crazy competitions, in a furious and almost tragic gaiety, he would start running around the rooms, imitating the leaps and roars of lions, tigers, and other wild beasts. Then he would jump on a table, shouting; "Achtung! Everyone to the wall!! In three seconds it will be H hour! Three . . . two and a half . . . two . . . one and a half . . . one . . . H HOUR!!! Heil Hitler!" with such fierce verisimilitude that even Blitz was bewildered, and Useppe peered into the air, expecting the appearance of the famous H HOUR, which for him was identified with a kind of *airpane*.

In the afternoons, sometimes, persecuted by Ida's sulks, Ninnuzzu would sit at the little table to do his schoolwork. But he would immediately start yawning, like a malaria case. And he would leaf through the books with a bitter frown, as if he didn't know what to do with them, every now and then tearing off a bit of page and chewing it, promptly spitting it on the floor. Finally, nauseated by that absurd torment, he would get up, saying he needed a breath of air before settling down to study. Blitz would rush to him, enthusiastic at this decision; and the pair would not be seen again in the house until suppertime.

Often, however reluctantly, he did without Blitz's company, to be freer in his actions; and these actions, even if they were only trips to the movies or on the tram, loomed menacing and nefarious in Ida's puzzled mind. On top of everything else, he had developed a quarrelsome character. Once he arrived home with the knuckles of his right hand bleeding; and he said he had beaten up somebody who had insulted the Duce. And how had he insulted him? He had said the Duce was an old man now, maybe sixty.

Another time, coming home with a torn jersey, he said he had been in a fight caused by jealousy. Not his own, but somebody else's; some girl's boyfriend had become jealous of him.

Yet another time, he turned up at the house with a black eye. And he said he had taken on two characters by himself and they had had a fight, two against one. Who were they? How should he know who they were? They were two shits he'd never seen before, but as he went past, with his hat pulled down and his blanket around him, they had nudged each other and murmured: "Hey, look at the Negus!"

That blackened eye (as Ida had refused him the money for a pair of dark glasses) was an excuse for him to stay away from school for several days. But for that matter, his absence from school by now was more frequent than his presence; and on his own initiative, he signed his excuses with his mother's name. When the Principal finally summoned him to report with his father or his mother, that is with the responsible head of his family, Nino explained that his only family was a little brother, and a dog, and a widowed mother (occupied all day long as a teacher in the school); so he himself was the head of the family. After which, since the Principal (a blustering man with white mane, vaunting a youthful, com-radely manner) was a decorated Fascist, who moreover was named Arnaldo like Mussolini's brother, Nino became filled with self-confidence, and taking advantage of this conversation, asked for a recommendation so that he could be immediately accepted as a volunteer in the war. But the Principal answered that at his age his duty as a Fascist was to study, until the Fatherland called on him; you do not serve the Fatherland only on the battlefield, but also in the classroom and the factory, etc. And, to conclude, eager to be rid of him, quoting the Duce's motto *Book and Musket*, he dismissed Nino with a Roman salute.

The torment of classes drove him nearly crazy. The desk was too narrow for him, and, even without being aware of it, every now and then he gave it a shove, or sighed. For all the subjects discussed in class he cared absolutely nothing: it seemed comical to him that people should assemble for this purpose, wasting whole mornings. And he was gripped by the downright physical temptation to burst from the benches, upsetting every-thing, to launch into his imitation of the tiger or the lion, as he did at home. Then, not knowing how to save himself from such temptation, he would suddenly pretend to have a deep cough, deliberately, to have himself sent into the corridor.

To make his presence less disruptive, the teachers had isolated him, like a reprobate, at a desk in the back row. But under his occupancy, that lonely abode seemed no longer a pillory, but rather the cock's single cage in a common hen run. And from that special isolation, his presence stimu-lated even more the almost enamored vassal-obeisance his classmates in general felt for him.

When the mood seized him, he was capable of mobilizing the whole class in his enthusiasm. So one sirocco morning, to enliven the Greek lesson, at a certain point he planted his feet against the desk in front of his and began to shove, unobserved. And at his prearranged signal, his accomplices imitated him, all together; thus, in a shameless silence, the whole row of desks began to advance like Birnam wood towards the teacher's dais. The teacher, always culpable because of his suspect political ideas, unnerved by hardships and half-crazed with hunger, at this phenomenon displayed a blanched face, as if for a moment he really felt himself nailed, like Macbeth, to the spot marked by his destiny.

But these wretched schoolboy pranks no longer allayed Ninnuzzu's boredom, which, towards the spring equinox, became tragic. During school hours he yawned constantly; and when, with the best of intentions, he suppressed his yawns, the effort forced him to clench his teeth or make frightening faces. Involuntarily, he would sprawl on the bench of his desk as if on a triclinium; and when scolded by the teacher, in sitting up straight, he would assume the sinister air of a murderer in the patrol wagon.

Unable to resist the incessant yearning to smoke and to move his feet, he invented a form of dysentery for himself (as an excuse for leaving the room more often). And so in the end he spent a good part of his school mornings in the latrine. Where he lingered to turn slips of paper and random scraps of tobacco into his wartime cigarettes, sucking on them afterwards with fury and voluptuousness, to the last mangy shred, which burned his hand. Then, if he was in the mood, he would amuse himself by fouling up the place, decorating a door or a corner of a wall with some drawing of fabulous wickedness. And when, taking his time, he went back into the classroom (as already before leaving it) he didn't bother to act his sick man's role; but rather, he had a proud, anarchistic manner. So his schoolmates looked at him with laughing glances of admiration and silent solidarity.

One of those days, during a recess, the Principal sent for him, to warn him that if he didn't show up the next day with his mother, he would not be admitted to the school. He said all right, and went back to the classroom. But the moment he was back inside, he immediately regretted being there; and he produced the familiar excuse of his ailment, to leave the room. This time, however, he didn't go to the latrines, but went down the steps, and passing the porter's lodge, he said: *Special permission!* with such a hard look that the porter himself took fright, and didn't dare argue. Since the gate was locked, he climbed over it. And just outside, he peed against the wall, bidding the school his last farewell.

That same evening he announced to Ida that now he knew all that was to be known, and was quitting school. He would have to stop soon anyway, to go to war. When the war was over, they could discuss the matter further.

This news had the power to shake Iduzza, for a few moments, from her evening weariness, and even to stir some of her extreme ambitions. At heart, her first idea, when Ninnuzzu was little, had been to see him become a great professor, a scientist, a man of letters, in short an important professional man; and she still felt, in spite of everything, the inexorable obligation to have him take a degree. No other expense seemed so necessary to her; so, recently, to keep intact at least her famous treasure hidden in her corset, she had sold off her little gold objects, various furnishings of the house, and every other salable thing: even the wool mattresses, which she had exchanged for others of kapok, plus a few pounds of pasta.

At Nino's catastrophic announcement, she seemed to swell out, her hair actually on end, like certain small helpless animals when they want to assume a frightening mien. As usual, in a poor and comical resurrection of her mother Nora, she found on her own lips the tragic invectives of the children of Zion against Tyre or Moab . . . And amid these insults and lamentations, she flung herself here and there about the kitchen, as if she hoped that from the chimney or beneath the sink, some ally would appear before her, some help . . . But there was nothing to be done; she had to combat Nino alone. And her protests had more or less the effect on him of the voice of a cricket or a frog on a pistolero riding across the pampas.

His few interjections, into Ida's implacable monologue, were only to say to her, in a conciliatory voice: "Aw, mà, why don't you cut it out?" until, finally, with some signs of impatience, he went off into the living-room-study. And Ida followed him.

Then, exasperated, so as not to hear her, he began to sing the Fascist anthems, like an immense chorus, improvising some obscene variants on them, to make things worse. At this point, as could have been foreseen, fear annihilated Ida. Ten thousand imaginary policemen spurted from her brain within that explosive room, while Nino, proud of his success, actually began singing "Red Flag." Nor was Blitz's accompaniment wanting: disconcerted by the unequal dialogue, he came out with wild, scattered barks, as if he saw two moons in the sky.

". . . that's enough. Go off then . . . to the war . . . anywhere you like . . ." Ida began repeating, aside, her throat dry. Her voice was a bare murmur. And swaying, she sank down in a chair, like a bundle.

Meanwhile, Useppe, wakened by the racket from his first sleep, and unable, with his small stature, to reach the door knob, was calling out in alarm: "Màà! Ino! Aièèèè!" Promptly, pleased with this diversion, Nino moved to liberate him; and to refresh himself after the tormenting scene with his mother, he abandoned himself to the usual games with Useppe and the dog. A wondrous gaiety was released in the rooms. While Ida, mute on her chair, began to write the following message, leaving it then clearly visible on her son's table:

> *Nino!*
> *all is over between us!*
> *I swear it!*
> > *your mother.*

Because of her trembling wrist, the letters of this piece of writing were so crooked and confused they seemed the work of a first-grade pupil. On the following morning, the message was still where she had left it, and the daybed was untouched, empty. That night Nino had slept away from home.

.   .   .

After that evening, not infrequently Nino spent his nights outside the house, nor did anyone know where or with whom. Once, towards the beginning of the third week, he disappeared in the company of Blitz for two days. And Ida, frightened, in her helplessness, wondered if she should summon her resolve and search for him in the hospitals, or even (for her, the most horrible menace of all) at the Police Station; then he was seen reappearing, followed by Blitz, joyous and all newly dressed. He wore a black oilskin windbreaker with a pale blue lining, a powder blue shirt, neatly pressed pants of simulated flannel, and brand new shoes, positively de luxe, with crepe soles. He even had a wallet (and he showed it with great display) containing a fifty-lire note.

Ida observed these novelties, dazed and uneasy, perhaps suspecting further thefts; but Ninnuzzu, anticipating all questions, announced to her, radiant and smug: "They're presents!" "Presents . . . who gave them to you?" she murmured hesitantly. And he, with bold and sibylline promptness, replied: "A virgin!"

Then, seeing his mother somewhat perturbed by this word, he immediately reacted, correcting himself, with a shameless face: "Well then, a whore! Okay?" But at this clearer answer, his mother's already distraught face actually became covered with blushes, so he burst out heatedly:

"Hey! If I say a *virgin*, you nearly faint. If I say a *whore*, you throw up. So I'll give you another choice: a *fairy!*"

At this new reply, Iduzza, more innocent than a nun as far as certain terms were concerned, looked at him with inert simplicity, understanding nothing. Meanwhile Useppe had arrived; and even amid the impassioned assaults of Blitz he remained dazzled at the sight of his new, elegant brother. As if he were at the Puppet Theater, when from the top of the stage, Roland the Crusader descends in his silver armor.

And in his overflowing happiness and desire to play, Ninnarieddu took his little brother off to one side. First of all, he immediately taught him a new word: *whore*. And he laughed blissfully at the readiness with which Useppe learned to say it, naturally in his own way: *ho*. Now, seeing Ninnarieddu's unfailing amusement whenever it was repeated, Useppe remained convinced that the word was, in itself, comical; so afterwards, every time he said *ho*, he already laughed madly, on his own.

After this, as a secret between the two of them, his brother announced the marvelous news that he would soon take him out on a bicycle ride all over Rome: because in two, or at most three days, he was sure he would own a racing bike, which had been promised him as a present. And leaving this divine promise with Useppe as a pledge, he disappeared again in his wealth and splendor, like genies in tales.

But his promise of the bicycle was not kept. After staying away another two days and three nights, he returned on foot, at an incredible hour—about six in the morning!—when Useppe was sound asleep, and Iduzza, just up, still in gown and robe, was at the stove cooking some greens for the midday meal. As usual, he was followed by Blitz, who, however, seemed unusually depressed, and so hungry that he even took advantage of a cold cabbage stalk found under the kitchen table. Nino himself, even in his same new clothes, seemed poor, dirty, and disheveled, as if he had slept under a bridge. On his very pale face and on the back of his hand, he had some raw, violent scratches. And without even stepping into the rooms, the moment he arrived he sat on the chest in the entrance, where he remained, frowning and silent, as if under a malediction.

To Ida's excited questioning, he answered: "Leave me alone!" in such a grim and peremptory manner that his mother was dissuaded from insisting. More than an hour and a half later, when she went out, he was still there, in the same position as before, with Blitz sleeping in wretched repose at his feet.

The night had been interrupted by air-raid alarms, more threatening with the approach of spring; and Useppe, less of an early riser than on other days, woke up after eight. Something in the air alerted him to a surprise (in which there flashed, among other things, the vision of a bicycle ride); and promptly, with a daredevil feat, which he now, however, could perform expertly, he lowered himself, on his own, from his cot. A moment later, he appeared at the entrance, and at the sight of Nino sitting there on the chest, he immediately rushed towards him. But Ninnarieddu shouted

"Leave me alone!" with such raging brutality that it froze Useppe halfway in his dash.

This was the first time, in the twenty months and more of their community, that his brother had treated him badly. And though Blitz, moving at once to greet him, did his best to cheer him with rasping licks and fanning tail, Useppe remained numb in his amazement, breathless, glued to the spot. With a bitter gravity on his face, and all filled with a strange solemnity; as if confronted by an absolute and undecipherable decree of fate.

Nino, in driving him away, naturally took a glance at him; and the sight of his person, even in that tragic dawn, produced instantaneously a comical effect. The fact was that, in the already warm spring weather, Useppe wore at night only a little woolen undershirt, so short that it barely covered him to the waist, leaving him, from the belly down, completely nude in front and behind. This, on his rising, was the costume in which he found himself; and if no one bothered to dress him, he remained in it throughout the morning and perhaps even for the rest of the day. In his innocence, however, he went around the house like that, with the same naturalness and nonchalance as if he were clothed.

But on the present occasion, his simplicity of dress contrasted so curiously with the extreme gravity of his face that Nino, as soon as he glimpsed him, burst into irresistible laughter. And, at his laughter, as if at a liberating signal, Useppe immediately ran to him, all joyful, in a return of total faith. "Hey, leave me alone!" Nino warned him again, resuming his thug's look; but all the same, to please him, he gave Useppe a little kiss on the cheek. Useppe (so content, by now, that he had even forgotten the absent bicycle) promptly returned another little kiss. And this moment, in the history of their eternal love, remained one of the most cherished memories.

After the exchange of little kisses, Nino pushed Useppe away, and Blitz too; then he stretched out on the chest, falling into a downright sepulchral sleep. He woke towards noon, still with the same grim pallor, as if a revolting taste had remained in his throat, and he could neither spit it out nor swallow it. And when Useppe came again to greet him, Nino, his face dark and frowning, taught him a new word: *bitch*, which Useppe promptly learned with his usual bravura. But not even this new didactic success sufficed, today, to brighten Nino's gloomy expression; so afterwards, whenever Useppe said *bits*, he assumed a suitable gravity.

Until nearly the end of the week (also because he didn't enjoy being seen outside so disfigured by scratches), Ninnarieddu, for the first time in his life perhaps, spent most of his hours in the house, both day and night. But his mood, in becoming domestic, had become at the same time unusually sulky. Even towards food he showed a glum indifference, since his hunger was also spoiled by his black humor. And almost constantly he chose to be alone, locking himself into his room, which was also the family living room; so Useppe and Blitz were forced to release their energies in the few confined rooms of the rest of the house. Being unable to smoke unhinged Nino's reason, until the wretched Iduzza, rather than see him go mad, forswore her oath and gave him money for some cigarettes, even at black-market prices. But those few were not enough for him; and to make them last longer he mixed the tobacco with certain surrogates, stinking weeds. Moreover, by the bed in his room he kept some flasks of wine, which made him nasty drunk: he would suddenly come out of the door, lumbering, as if on a deck in a storm, shouting insults and obscenities; or else yelling: Death! Death!! Death!!!

Then he strode up and down the hall, saying he would like to squeeze the whole universe into a single face, so he could beat it to a pulp with his fists; but if by chance that face was a woman's, after having beaten it with his fists, he would then smear it with an ointment of shit. He even had it in for the Duce, for whom he threatened fantastic, but unrepeatable punishments. And he went on repeating that, anyway, despite the *cock-s* . . . (sic) Duce and the *assho* . . . etc. of a Führer, he, Nino, would go to the war anyway, to screw both of them up the a . . . He said Rome stank, Italy stank; and the living stank worse than a corpse.

During these abominable monologues, which she pitifully called his *gutter talk*, the terrified Iduzza would take refuge in her room, sealing her ears with her palms, not to hear. While, forgotten in the tumult, Useppe would stay in a corner to gaze at his brother with great respect, but with no fear: as if he were facing a volcano too high to strike him with its lava. Or as if he were in the midst of a stupendous storm at sea, through which he was recklessly passing his tiny boat. Every now and then, from his corner, erect and filled with courage, in his little nightshirt, he would remind his brother of his presence, calling him in a faint voice: "ino ino," clearly meaning: "Never fear, I'm keeping you company. I'm not running away."

As for the foolish Blitz, it was obvious that the matter, whatever it meant, gave him some pleasure. So long as his chief love didn't remain locked in his room, excluding him from his presence, for Blitz all was merriment.

After a while, weighted by the wine's indigestion, Ninnarieddu would sink down to sleep on the daybed, snoring, to Useppe's supreme admiration, with a voice that made it seem an airplane was flying around right inside the house.

Because of the scratches, he had to give up shaving for those days: his beard, new and wild, still a half-grown boy's, sprouted irregularly, like patches of dirt. And, to make himself even more disgusting, he didn't even wash or comb his hair. On Saturday morning, finally, he woke up with the scratches reduced to little more than a trace, and he could shave. It was a sunny Saturday, breezy, and you could hear a radio singing a popular song in the courtyard. He washed his hands, ears, armpits, and feet; he wet and combed his curls. He put on a clean white jersey, which was rather tight on him, but at the same time, fully displayed his chest muscles. In front of the mirror, he tested the muscles of his arms and chest; and with great leaps, he started playing lions and tigers, through the room. Then he went back to the mirror, to examine the marks of the scratches, which luckily had become almost invisible. There was, all the same, a brief flash in his eyes. But meanwhile, his face in the mirror pleased him; and in an immense outburst of all his nerves, muscles, breath, he shouted happily:

"Ah, life!! Life! . . . Now we're off into town . . . Rome! Come on, Blitz!"

On leaving, to console Useppe, who was remaining alone, Nino said to him:

"Useppe, come here! You see this sock?"

It was an ordinary dirty sock, which he had dropped there on the floor: "You see it? Be careful! Stay here and watch it! Not a peep out of you! Don't make a move: you have to stand still and guard it for a minute and a half AT LEAST. You got that? Don't you dare move! And you'll see it turn into a rattlesnake, that moves and rattles: ta-tum-ta-tum! Tum-tum!"

Filled with extraordinary faith, Useppe stood for some time by the sock, waiting for the apparition of the marvelous creature; but it failed to materialize. Life's disappointments. Similarly, there was no further talk of the bicycle. However, one of those days, Nino brought home instead a half-broken wind-up phonograph (the previous similar machine, his former property, had been traded for cigarettes) with a single worn record, which still continued to play, as best it could, its sentimental little tunes: "The Old Organ-Grinder" and "Illusion, My Sweet Dream" . . . repeating them by incessant request during the hours Nino was in the house, an average of twenty performances a day. For Useppe, it was a sublime portent, no less than the rattlesnake. But on the third day, its now sexless voice, its enunciation incomprehensible, sounded more pained than usual; and with a jerk it died, in the midst of a song. Nino ascertained there was no remedy for the phonograph; it was broken. He put it on the floor, near the wall, and, after giving it a kick, left it there.

Another time, one afternoon, Nino brought up on a visit a casual girl of his, met only a short time before; to Useppe she seemed another stupendous spectacle. She wore a colored dress with roses on it, which rode up behind as she walked, showing a second dress, black with lace; and she advanced, calm and shapely, with a distorted gait because of her orthopedic soles. On her hands she had as many dimples as she had fingers; her nails were a cherry red, her eyes starry, and her mouth perfectly round, small, of dark carmine. She had a slow, singsong voice and, speaking, at every cadence of that voice, she would sway. On entering, she said:

"Say, what a cute kid. Who does he belong to?"

"He's my brother. And this is my dog."

"Aaaah! What's your name, kid?"

"Useppe."

"Ah, Giuseppe, right? Giuseppe!"

"No," Nino spoke, with frowning absolutism, "his name really is USEPPE, just like he said!"

". . .? Us . . . I thought it was different . . . You mean he's really Useppe? What kind of name would that be?"

"We like it."

"It sounds funny to me . . . GIUseppe, sure, but Useppe . . . Useppe doesn't sound like a real name to me!"

"That's because you're a dimwit."

2 As the fine weather progressed, the air raids on the Italian cities that year multiplied, gradually more furious; and the military bulletins, though they feigned optimism, reported destruction and massacre every day. Rome still was spared; but the people, unnerved by now and frightened at the strange talk that circulated everywhere, began to feel less secure. The wealthy families had moved to the country; and those remaining (the great crowd), meeting one another in the street, on trams, in offices, peered into one another's faces, even strangers, all with the same absurd question in their eyes.

In some part of Ida's mind, not clear to her reason, there was in that period a little, brutal shift, which made her morbidly sensitive to the alarms (which had previously seemed usual, indifferent to her), suddenly rousing in her an almost impossible reserve of energy. For the rest, her life of scholastic and domestic toil dragged on the same as before, in a kind of negative ecstasy. But at the first cry of the siren, she was immediately seized by a confused panic, like a machine plunging down a slope, out of gear. And whether she was awake or asleep, at whatever moment, she would rush to fasten on her corset (where she still kept her savings); and taking Useppe in her arms, with an unnatural nervous strength, she would flee downstairs carrying that burden, to seek safety in the shelter. Which, for her and the other tenants of her wing, had been established beyond the building, in that very basement-tavern where, three winters before, the German boy Gunther had gone down to drink.

Sometimes, Useppe was not a docile weight in her arms; he would wriggle and cry, in response to the grief of Blitz, who accompanied them with his incessant whining from behind the closed door. For the dog, in fact, Ida felt no concern, leaving him in the house during the alarms, abandoned to his fate; but he, for his part, could not resign himself to the separation.

Ninnarieddu, when he was at home, laughed at those flights of Ida's; and he contemptuously refused to follow her to the shelter. But not even the presence of his chief love sufficed to console Blitz, who, for the duration of the alarm, would keep running back and forth between the front door and Nino, returning to lick his hands and stare into his eyes with his own brown eyes, impassioned and persuasive. Always insisting in his catastrophic lament, which repeated, on a sole note, never stopping, like an obsession: "Please, let's go with them! Then, if they're saved, we're all saved; if we have to die, we'll all die together."

Finally, rather than condemn Blitz to such maniacal torment, Ninnarieddu, though bored and reluctant, decided to satisfy him once and for all, going down with him—the whole family together—into the cellar-tavern. And from then on, whenever Nino was at home, the air-raid alarms became an occasion of amusement, awaited and desired, especially if they came at night, because then, at last, Useppe and Blitz could join in Nino's nightlife.

As soon as the notorious howl shattered the darkness, Blitz was immediately ready, as if at the transcendental announcement of a prime festivity. And, with one bound, leaving his place on the daybed (where he always slept, huddled against Ninnarieddu) he would bustle about, waking everybody, running from one to the other, barking with joyous urgency, and flapping his tail like a little flag. For that matter Useppe, already wakened on his own, would repeat, thrilled: "Larm! larm!"

The most maddening job was waking the grumpy and sleepy Nino, who played deaf; so Blitz had, somehow, to pull him down from the bed; and then he went on nagging, while Nino, all yawns, slipped on his jersey and pants, not without cursing and blaspheming, even against dogs. But as he grumbled, he woke up completely. Until the happy moment when, now lively, he picked up the leash: amid the applause of Blitz, who rushed up, to be leashed, with the haste of an eager viveur taking a carriage to go dancing.

Then they hurried into the next room, where Nino rapidly loaded

Useppe astride his shoulders. And with no other luggage (at most, Useppe might sometimes carry *Roma* with him or the walnut), Nino, Useppe, and Blitz—truly three bodies and one spirit—would fly down the steps, leaving Ida behind to follow alone and grumbling, her purse clutched to her bosom. Meanwhile, from the other doors and through the courtyard, all the families, in nightshirts, in underclothes, with babies in their arms, dragging suitcases down the steps, would be running towards the shelters. And over their voices, from the high distance, already the roars of the air fleet were approaching, with an accompaniment of shots, flashes, explosions, like a formidable fireworks display. All around, families could be heard calling one another. Some child would be lost. Some people, running in terror, would stumble and fall. Certain women screamed. And Nino laughed at this universal fear, as if at a great comic scene, echoed, in chorus, by the ingenuous hilarity of Useppe and Blitz.

Those nights in the cellar were not entirely unpleasant for Ninnarieddu: because, among other things, down there he had the opportunity of meeting some neighborhood beauties who usually, because of their family's protectiveness, were not easily allowed out. However, when he entered the cellar, he never failed to display his personal scorn; and remaining near the doorway, his back against the wall in a contemptuous pose, he let the audience know (in particular the young girls) that he was stuck down there only because of his dog; as for himself, he didn't give a damn about the bombs, in fact he enjoyed bombs even more than firecrackers! And if only these alarms were at least the real thing! But unfortunately these Rome alarms were all a farce, because everybody knew there was a secret agreement between Ciurcíl and the Pope, declaring Rome a holy, untouchable city, and bombs would never drop here. Having clarified these points, not condescending to add anything else, Nino would enjoy the air raids as best he could.

For that matter, Nino really cared little about the possible destruction of the house and the loss of the family property, which after all consisted of a couple of beds, or springs, with kapok mattresses, a clothing-bag (with winter sweaters and his camel's-hair coat, now too small for him, and a coat of Ida's, turned inside out), a few tattered books, etc. In fact, if the house was knocked down, the Government, after the victory, would compensate them for the damage, with a bonus. And Nino had already agreed with Useppe and Blitz that, with this compensation, he would buy a completely furnished trailer-truck, where they could live the life of roving gypsies.

As for the city of Rome, Nino personally objected to the idea of sparing it out of exaggerated special respect. On the contrary, in his opinion it wouldn't be such a bad thing if bombs fell on Rome, seeing that Rome's greatest assets were ruins: Colosseum, Trajan's Forum, etc.

Not infrequently, during alarms, the electricity failed; and to illuminate the cellar, an acetylene lamp was turned on, which recalled street fairs and stands selling sliced watermelon. An acquaintance of the proprietor had supplied the place with a portable phonograph for the occasion; and when the alarm was prolonged, Nino and his friends, to overcome their boredom, spent the time dancing with some girls in the confined space. The one who enjoyed these sounds and dances most was Useppe; crazed with happiness, he would scramble among the dancers' legs, until he reached his brother, who, laughing to find him underfoot, would abandon his partner and start hopping around with Useppe.

Sometimes, in the confusion of the flight, Ida neglected to dress him, merely wrapping him in an ironing cloth, or a shawl, or any rag. And then, when this fell away, Useppe would find himself in the shelter clothed only in his usual little nighttime undershirt; but it was all the same to him. And he had no thought of modesty, skipping and dancing as if he were in elegant evening dress.

Blitz, too, had the opportunity of meeting other dogs there in the shelter. Apart from the exceptional hunting dog, and an old fox terrier that belonged to an elderly lady, these were always dogs of the lowest sort, bastard mongrels like himself, usually scrawny and starving because of wartime privations; but all delighted, as he was, with the fun. And after the usual greeting ceremonies practiced among dogs, he would start frisking around with them.

Some women nursed babies, or knitted; some old crones said the rosary, making the sign of the cross every time there was a heavier thud over the city. Some, as soon as they came in, flung themselves down wherever they could, to resume their interrupted sleep. Certain men made up a table, playing cards or morra, with the tavern's wine as the stakes. And at times arguments sprang up, which could even end in quarrels or brawls, stilled by the proprietor or by the air-raid warden.

We already know that Ida, through unsociability and scant opportunity, had never had anything to do with her neighbors, who for her had remained transient figures, casually encountered on the stairs, in the courtyard, or in shops. And now, running into them in her flight and finding them all around her, half-familiar and half-alien, still not quite awake, she confused them sometimes with the bawling crowds of her just-interrupted dreams. She had only to sit down on a bench, and the action of her evening sleeping-pill would promptly take hold of her again; however, she didn't deem it proper for a schoolmistress to sleep in public; and huddled there in the midst of the racket, she would make an effort to keep her eyes open; but every now and then she would slump, then recover herself, wiping the saliva from her chin, and murmuring with a little smile: "I'm sorry, so sorry . . ." She had charged Useppe to wake her from time to time. And whenever he remembered, he would climb up on her knees to shout in her ears: "Mà? maà!!" and tickle her under the chin, to his own private and enormous amusement, because his mother, when tickled, would laugh like a little girl. "Wake, mà?" he would then inquire, eager and curious, when she reopened her drugged eyes, dazzled by the acetylene. For a moment she wouldn't recognize that cellar; and dazed, she would clutch the baby to her, in protection against those strangers, perhaps assassins or informers . . . She was always afraid of making a spectacle of herself while asleep; and maybe even saying compromising things: for example, "My mother's maiden name was ALMAGIÀ" or else, "My baby's a bastard, the son of a NAZI."

In the shelter, besides the usual families from those parts, some other people also happened in: casual passersby, or else some homeless characters: beggars, cheap prostitutes, and black marketeers (with whom Nino, always on the prowl for money, on those nights plotted certain minimal and mysterious deals). Some of them, coming from Naples, told how that city, after the hundred air raids it had undergone, was reduced to a cemetery and a charnel house. Everybody who could run off had gone; and the poor beggars who had remained, seeking refuge, went every evening to sleep in caves, where they had carried mattresses and blankets. By now the city's streets were a desert of rubble, infested with decomposition and smoke, under the fire of the Flying Fortresses which attacked every day.

On that single, memorable occasion when she had been in Naples, for a two-hour visit, Iduzza had still been a novice who had never seen anything outside her own province. And so in her memory Naples had remained a legendary Baghdad, far grander than Rome. Now that unique, unparalleled vision of hers was replaced by a ruinous expanse, vast as Asia, and caked with blood: where even the thrones of the kings and queens and the myths of the great cities studied in school, with other fantasies of hers, were swept away.

But Ninnarieddu, in the Neapolitans' tales, felt instead the seduction of that adventurous existence in caves and sea-grottoes, which promised to be full of surprises and amorous fortune, risk and anarchy. And as someone from the provinces wants to escape to the metropolis, he was already thinking of going off to Naples in the company of one of his new black-marketeer friends. In fact, for several weeks now, he had stopped all pretense of studying; and the schools meanwhile had closed on their own. The war, ended in Africa, was approaching Italian territory; all countries were aflame. He was fed up with the Holy City, where they only played at the war, arranged in Vaticans and Ministries; and a desire for places without holiness, where what had to burn burned, attacked him at times almost to the point of nausea, like an incendiary fever. If the Regimes wouldn't admit him as a combatant, because he was too little (!), he would manage to make war on his own!

But during those very days, instead, his constant desire was fulfilled. The Fascist war's disastrous turn favored the enrolling of volunteers, ready to give their lives for the Duce; and before the end of June, Ninnarieddu, though still half a child, found a way of being accepted into a battalion of Blackshirts, leaving for the North.

Dressed as a fighter, he really did look like a little boy; but his expression was haughty, indeed aggressive; and he already betrayed a certain intolerance of military discipline. A serious concern of his, on going off, was Blitz, whom he necessarily had to leave behind in Rome; and having absolutely no faith in his mother, he recommended him to his brother Useppe, solemnly shaking his little hand, in a real pact of honor and importance.

3 His farewell to Blitz had been heartbreaking, despite his assurances that he would be back in a week at the latest, at the head of a motorized column, laden with tripe and bones for all the dogs of Rome. Blitz was not credulous like Useppe; and taking those assurances as products of imposture and megalomania, he remained inconsolable. For a whole day, refusing even to eat his hard-won ration, he never stopped running from the door to the window, shouting to Nino to come back, though at heart he knew Nino was now too far away to hear him. And if, from upstairs, he saw the form of a boy more or less Nino's size, he would whine with bitter longing.

That first evening, Ida, dazed, shut him in the bathroom to sleep; but inside, he never stopped moaning and scratching at the door, and so Useppe also refused to go to bed, determined to sleep in the bathroom too, rather than leave Blitz in there alone. And finally Blitz was allowed refuge in Useppe's bed, where, in the exuberance of his gratitude-joy-distress, he licked the naked Useppe from head to foot, before falling asleep in his arms.

Blitz never strayed a step from the two of them, except at shopping time. Since it was the vacation period, Ida would go out shopping around ten in the morning; and during those days she had begun taking Useppe with her almost every time, leaving Blitz to guard the house, since while she was waiting in the various lines, Blitz with Useppe would be a double encumbrance. When they left, the dog already knew he was not part of the company on such occasions, and circling around them without wagging his tail, he would watch their preparations to go out with a mortified look, resigned to his lot.

On their return, from the street they could hear him greeting them with all his voice, on sentry duty by the open window on the top floor. And when they arrived, they found him waiting inside the door, ready to receive them with unrestrained effusions, chiefly addressed to Useppe, repeating to him a hundred times: "You're all I have left in the world now!"

.   .   .

One of those mornings, Ida was coming back from shopping, with two heavy bags over her arm, holding Useppe by the hand. The weather was calm and very hot. Following a habit she had got into that summer for her wanderings around the quarter, Ida had gone out, like a working-class woman, in her housedress of printed cretonne, without a hat, her legs bare to save her stockings, and canvas shoes with high cork soles on her feet. Useppe wore only a faded little checked shirt, some makeshift shorts of blue cotton, and a pair of sandals too large for him (because purchased with the idea of his growing into them), which slapped against the pavement as he walked. In his hand, he carried the famous ball *Roma* (the walnut *Lazio* during that spring had been irretrievably lost).

They were coming out of a tree-lined avenue not far from the Freight Station, turning into Via dei Volsci, when, unannounced by any alarm, they heard advancing through the sky an orchestrated clamor of metallic humming. Useppe raised his eyes, and said: "Airpanes." And at that moment the air whistled, while in an enormous thunder, all the walls were already crashing down behind their backs and the ground was leaping around them, crumbled in a hail of fragments.

"Useppe! Useppeee!" Ida screamed, flung into a black and dusty cyclone which blocked her vision: "Mà, I'm here," he answered, at the level of her arm, in his little voice, as if reassuring her. She picked him up, and in an instant there flashed through her brain the instructions of the NAPU (National Antiaircraft Protection Union) and of the building warden: when bombs fell, it was best to lie down on the ground. But instead her body started running, with no direction. She had dropped one of her shopping bags, while the other, forgotten, still hung from her arm, beneath Useppe's trusting little behind. Meanwhile, the sound of the sirens had begun. In her dash, she felt she was sliding downwards, as if she were on skates, along an uneven terrain that seemed plowed, and was smoking. Towards the bottom, she fell in a sitting position, Useppe clutched in her arms. In her fall, the shopping bag had emptied its load of vegetables, among which, scattered at her feet, there shone the colors of the peppers green, orange, and vivid red.

With one hand, she clutched at a crushed root, still covered with shattered earth, which protruded near her. And settling herself better, huddled over Useppe, she started feeling him, his whole body, to make sure he was unharmed. Then she placed the empty shopping bag over his head as a helmet of protection.

They were at the bottom of a kind of narrow trench, protected from above, as if by a roof, by the thick trunk of a fallen tree. Nearby, over them, they could hear its broad foliage stirring in a great wind. All around, there was a whistling, ruinous din, in which, among crashes, lively little bursts, and strange tinklings, there were weak, human voices at an absurd distance, and the whinnying of horses. Useppe, crouching against her, looked into Ida's face from beneath the shopping bag—not frightened, but rather curious and pensive. "It's nothing," she said to him, "don't be afraid. It's nothing." He had lost his sandals, but he still clutched his ball tightly in his fist. At the louder jolts, she could feel him tremble ever so slightly.

"Nuffing . . ." he said then, half-persuaded, half-interrogatory.

His bare feet were swaying calmly next to Ida, one on either side of her. For all the time the two of them waited in that refuge, he and Ida stared into each other's eyes, intently. She couldn't have said the duration of that time. Her wristwatch was broken; and there are circumstances in which, for the mind, calculating time is impossible.

At the all-clear, when she looked out, they were inside an immense dusty cloud which hid the sun and made them cough with its tarry taste; through this cloud, they could see flames and black smoke from the direction of the Freight Station. On the other part of the avenue, the side-streets were mountains of rubble; and Ida, advancing with difficulty, Useppe in her arms, sought an exit towards the square, among the massacred and blackened trees. The first recognizable object they came upon was a dead horse, at their feet, its head adorned with a black plume, amid wreaths of crushed flowers. And at that point, a soft, warm liquid wet Ida's arm. Only then, the dejected Useppe started crying: because for some time now he had stopped being a little baby that wet himself.

In the space around the horse, more wreaths could be glimpsed, more flowers, plaster wings, heads and limbs of mutilated statues. In front of the funeral establishments, broken and emptied, all around there, the terrain was covered with glass. From the nearby cemetery came a damp smell, sugary and stagnant; and beyond the breached walls, you could glimpse black, twisted cypresses. Meanwhile, some other people had reappeared, growing into a crowd that wandered around as if on another planet. Some were stained with blood. Screams could be heard, and names, or else: "there's a fire over here, too!" or "where's the ambulance?!" However, these sounds also reechoed hoarse and outlandish, as in a yard of deaf-mutes. Useppe's little voice repeated to Ida an incomprehensible question, in which she seemed to recognize the word *home:* "Mà, when do we go home?" The shopping bag fell down over his eyes, and he was dominated by a fierce impatience. He seemed filled with a mixed worry he wouldn't utter, not even to himself: "mà? . . . home? . . ." his little voice continued stubbornly. But it was difficult to recognize the familiar streets. Finally, beyond a half-destroyed apartment house, from which the up-rooted beams and shutters were dangling, amid the usual dust-cloud of ruin, Ida recognized, intact, the building with the tavern, where they went to take shelter on the air-raid nights. Here Useppe started wriggling with such freenzy that he managed to free himself from her arms and get down to the ground. And running on his little bare feet towards a thicker dust-cloud, he began to shout:

"Biii! Biiii! Biiiii!"

Their building was destroyed. Only a slice of it remained, open onto the void. Raising your eyes to the place of their apartment, you could glimpse, through the cloud of smoke, a piece of landing, beneath two water-tanks which had remained in place. Below, some howling or mute forms roamed among the cement slabs, the smashed furniture, the piles of wreckage and refuse. No moan rose; beneath, they must all be dead. But some of those forms, driven by an idiot mechanism, were rummaging or scratching with their fingernails at those piles, searching for someone or something to save. And in the midst of all this, Useppe's little voice continued calling:

"Biii! Biiii! Biiiii!"

Blitz was lost, along with the double bed and the cot and the daybed and the chest, and Ninnuzzu's tattered books, and his enlarged picture, and the kitchen pots, and the clothing bag with the altered overcoats and the winter underwear, and the ten packets of powdered milk and the twelve pounds of pasta, and all that was left from the last pay envelope, kept in a drawer of the kitchen-cabinet.

"Come away! Come away!" Ida said, trying to lift Useppe into her arms. But he resisted and struggled, developing an incredible violence, and he repeated his cry: "Biii!" with a more and more peremptory demand. Perhaps he believed that, urged in this way, Blitz would necessarily have to pop out, tail wagging, from behind some corner, any moment.

And dragged off bodily, Useppe wouldn't stop repeating that single comical syllable, his voice convulsed in sobs. "Come away, come away," Ida repeated. But the truth was she didn't know where to go now. The only asylum that presented itself to her was the tavern, where she found some people already gathered, so many that there was no place to sit. An elderly woman, however, seeing her come in with the child in her arms, and recognizing them, from their appearance, as *bombed out*, invited her neighbors to push together, and made room for Ida next to herself on a bench.

Ida was gasping, tattered, her legs scratched, and all soiled right up to her face with a greasy soot, in which you could make out the minuscule fingerprints left by Useppe, as he clung to her. As soon as the woman saw Ida more or less settled on the bench, she asked her solicitously: "Are you from around here?" And at Ida's silent nod, she informed her: "I'm not; I come from Mandela." She was just passing through Rome, as she did every Monday, to sell her produce: "I'm a countrywoman," she explained further. Here at the tavern she was to wait for her grandson, who, as usual on Mondays, had come along to help her, but at the moment of the air raid he was off in the city, God knows where. A rumor had it that in this raid ten thousand planes had been used, and the entire city of Rome was destroyed, even the Vatican, even the Royal Palace, even the markets of Piazza Vittorio and Campo dei Fiori. All gone up in flames.

"I wonder where my grandson is now? I wonder if the train for Mandela is still running?"

She was a woman of about seventy, but still healthy, tall, and big, with rosy complexion and two black rings in her ears. In her lap she held an empty basket with an unrolled headcloth inside; and she seemed prepared to wait for her grandson, seated there with her basket, perhaps for another three hundred years, like the Brahman in the Hindu legend.

Seeing the desperation of Useppe, who was still calling his *Bi* in a voice more and more faint and weak, she tried to amuse him, by swaying in front of him a tiny mother-of-pearl cross she wore around her neck, on a little string:

"Bi bi bi baby! What are you saying? Eh? What do you want?"

In a low voice Ida stammered the explanation that Blitz was the name of the dog, buried under the rubble of their building.

"Ah me, humans and animals, we all have to die," the other woman remarked, moving her head only slightly in placid resignation. Then, addressing Useppe, filled with matriarchal gravity and without coyness, she consoled him with the following speech:

"Don't cry, kid, your dog's sprouted wings. He's turned into a dove and he's flown up into the sky."

In saying this, she raised her palms and imitated the flutter of wings. Useppe, who believed everything, suspended his weeping, to follow with interest the little movement of those hands, which settled again on the basket and stayed there, in repose, their hundred wrinkles blackened by earth.

"Wings? Why?"

"Because he's turned into a white dove."

"Wite dove," Useppe agreed, carefully examining the woman with his tearful eyes, which were already beginning to smile. "And now what's he do?"

"He flies, with lots and lots of other doves."

"How many?"

"Lots and lots!"

"How many?"

"Three hundred thousand."

"Thee huned ousand are lots?"

"Eh! More than a ton!!"

"That's lots and lots! What they do?"

"They fly around and have fun. Yes."

"And wallows? Are wallows there too? And osses?"

"They're up there, too."

"Even osses?"

"Even horses."

"They fly too?"

"Oh my yes, indeed they fly!"

Useppe gave her a faint smile. He was covered with blackish dust and sweat, he looked like a chimneysweep. The black locks of his hair were so sticky they stood straight up on his head. The woman, seeing his little feet were bleeding from a few scratches, authoritatively called to a soldier who had come in looking for water, and ordered him to treat them. And Useppe submitted to the rapid medication without even paying any attention to it, he was so enthralled by Blitz's happy career.

When the soldier had finished, Useppe absently waved goodbye to him. His two little fists were empty: the ball Roma was also lost. A little later, in his filthy clothing and wet shorts, Useppe was sleeping. The old woman from Mandela, after that moment, remained silent.

In the cellar a throng of people were coming and going; the place stank with the crowd and with the gusts from outside. But, unlike the air-raid nights, there was no confusion, no shoving, no raised voices. Most of those present looked one another in the face, dazed, not saying a word. Many were wearing tattered or scorched clothes; some were bleeding. Somewhere outside, in an endless and incoherent murmuring, every now and then a death-rattle seemed perceptible, or else a fierce scream suddenly rose, as if from a blazing forest. Ambulances began to circulate, fire engines, soldiers armed with picks and shovels. Someone had also seen a truck arrive, loaded with coffins.

Among the people inside, Ida knew hardly anyone. Through her thoughts, which spun in an inconclusive raving, from time to time there passed the faces of some of her neighbors in her building who, on air-raid nights, had run to take shelter down here with her. On those nights, dazed with sleeping pills, she had hardly glimpsed them; but today her brain presented them to her, though they were absent, with the precision of a photograph. *Messaggero*, with his trembling limbs and his stunned face, carried by his daughters like a puppet. Giustina, the farsighted concierge, who used to hold her needle way out to thread it. The clerk on the second floor who always said *Greetings* and *Prosit*, and had planted a *victory garden* in the courtyard. The plumber, who resembled the actor Buster Keaton and suffered from arthritis, and his daughter, who recently had started wearing a tram-conductor's uniform. A mechanic's apprentice, friend of Ninnuzzu's, who wore an undershirt with *Pirelli Tires* printed on it. Proietti, the house-painter, who though unemployed, always kept on his head a working cap made of folded newspaper . . . In the present uncertainty of their fate, these faces appeared to her suspended over a no-man's-land, from which in a moment they might reappear in flesh and blood, scrounging around the San Lorenzo quarter, available as usual and cheap; or from whence they might, instead, have set forth towards an unattainable distance, like the stars that had burned out millennia ago, now irretrievable at any price, beyond even a treasure sunk in the Indian Ocean.

Until this morning, nobody had been more available than the dwarf bastard Blitz, prompt at any call, even if it was from the garbage collector or the rag man. She herself had never given him much consideration, believing him, in fact, an intruder and a sponge. And at this hour, on the contrary, he was so inaccessible that all the police of the Reich could never catch him again.

The first thing about him that came back to her memory, giving her a special little stab, was that white star on his belly. That sole elegance of his life became also the supreme pathos of his death.

What would Nino say when he didn't find Blitz again? In the earth's enormous laceration, Nino was the single point of tranquillity and heed-lessness in Ida's mind. Was it perhaps because people swear that rogues, as a rule, always survive? Even though, since the day of his departure, he had sent no news of himself, Ida felt splendidly assured, as if by an angel's vow, that Nino would come back from the war safe and sound, and, indeed, would show up again soon.

They looked inside to say that, in the street, the Red Cross was distributing clothes and food; and soon the old woman from Mandela with her youthful, slightly swinging gait, went out to seek provisions. She wasn't able to collect any clothes; but she got hold of two packages of powdered milk, a bar of ersatz chocolate and another of concentrated jam, almost black; and she put this stuff in Ida's empty shopping-bag, to her gratitude. Ida was thinking in fact that Useppe should eat something as soon as he woke up, since his only meal so far that day had been his morning breakfast, shared with Blitz. That breakfast had consisted, as usual, of a piece of rationed bread, elastic and soft, perhaps kneaded with chaff and potato peelings; and a cup of watery milk. But still, as she remembered it, up there in their sun-filled kitchen, it seemed now the picture of extraordinary wealth. As for herself, she had drunk only a little cup of fake coffee; but still she felt no hunger, only nausea, as if the destroying dust-cloud had coagulated in her stomach.

The old woman's grandson appeared, returning with an empty suitcase, tied with a length of cord. And he promptly carried his grandmother off, asserting haughtily that Rome wasn't destroyed at all, and anybody who said so was talking balls, but they had better run off in a hurry, since an observation plane had already been sighted, heralding several thousand Flying Fortresses on their way. "But the train to Mandela? Is it running?" his grandmother was asking him, climbing up the steps with him to the door. Before going away, she left her headcloth as a present with Ida, telling her it was a good piece of new cloth, woven in Anticoli on a handloom, and she could make an overall for the baby from it.

Ida would have liked never to move again from that bench: she couldn't bring herself to muster her strength and face the end of the day. A horrible stench lay in the cellar; but damp with sweat, the child clutched in her arms, she had sunk into a kind of unfeeling, almost ecstatic peace. Sounds reached her muffled; on her eyes a sort of gauze had spread. Suddenly she noticed, looking around, that the tavern had emptied and the sun was beginning to set. Then she became afraid she had taken too much advantage of the proprietor's hospitality; and with Useppe asleep in her arms, she went outside.

Useppe was still asleep, his head hanging from her shoulder, when, a little later, she was walking along the Via Tiburtina. On one side, the street followed the wall of the cemetery; and on the other, it was flanked by apartment buildings partially destroyed by the bombs. Perhaps because of her fasting, Ida was overcome with sleepiness, her sense of identity was escaping her. She was wondering vaguely if the house in Via dei Volsci in San Lorenzo, where she had lived for more than twenty years, were not instead the Cosenza house, destroyed by the same earthquake that had destroyed, together, Messina and Reggio Calabria. And if this broad street were San Lorenzo, or the Ghetto. There must be some infection in the quarter; that was why they were demolishing it with picks! And was that body, caked with blood and plaster, male or female? Was it a dummy? The policeman wanted to know, because of the Registry. That's why he was arguing with the soldier. Were those festering flames for burning the dead bodies? And if the tracks had been ripped up, and the tram reduced to this carcass, how would she go to school in the morning? The dead horses, that made her stumble: were they Aryans or Jews? The dog Blitz was a bastard, and therefore Jewish for the Registry. That's why she was being deported, because at the Registry she was listed as a Jew, there was an accent on her last name. Ah, that explained everything . . . Her surname was Almagià . . . but luckily Useppe was named Ramundo . . . Is Ramundo accented on the middle syllable or the last? . . . And there were the words: *Israelitic Coemetery:* spelled like that: *coemetery.* And *Israelitic* . . . Wasn't that a forbidden word?!

Reading that sign on the cemetery gate, she was convinced this was how things really stood: she was being deported as a non-Aryan. She tried to walk faster, but she felt she couldn't make it.

At the suggestion of the tavernkeeper, she had fallen in behind a group of bombed-out families and fugitives, heading in the direction of Pietralata, towards a certain building where, so it was said, a dormitory had been set up for the homeless. Almost all the people ahead of her or following her carried bundles or suitcases or household goods; but except for Useppe, she had absolutely nothing to carry. The only property left her was the shopping-bag hanging from her arm, with the Red Cross packets inside and the headcloth of the old woman from Mandela. But luckily, safe inside her corset (which she never failed to wear, even in summer) she still had the precious little bundle of her savings. After so many hours, to tell the truth, that corset was becoming a hairshirt for her. Now her only desire was to arrive, anywhere, even at a concentration camp or a ditch, to release herself at last from that ferocious corset.

"Silence! The enemy is listening! Victory . . . Victory! . . ."

A little man, at her side, alone and elderly, kept repeating in a loud voice similar war slogans, which could be read here and there along the way, on the scorched walls and the smoke-stained posters. And he seemed to be amusing himself privately very much, since he snickered as if he were telling himself jokes, commenting on them with various grumblings. His right arm was in a cast to the shoulder, so he had to hold it up, extended, as if he were giving the Fascist salute; and that also seemed to exhilarate him. He looked like an artisan or a clerk, skinny, not much taller than Ida, with lively eyes. Despite the heat, he wore a jacket and a brimmed hat set squarely on his head; and with his free hand he was pushing a barrow where he had loaded some household goods. Hearing him always muttering to himself, Ida decided he was a madman.

"Signora, you're Roman?" he suddenly addressed her, in a merry Roman accent.

"Yes, sir," she murmured. In fact, she privately thought you must always answer madmen affirmatively and respectfully.

"Roman born and bred?"

"Yes, sir."

"Like me. *Roma Doma*. I'm Roman myself, and as of today, a war invalid." And he explained to her how a slab had hit him on the shoulder-blade just as he was coming back to his workshop-home (he was a marble-cutter, near the cemetery). His little house had been spared, luckily, but he preferred to clear out all the same, taking with him the bare necessities. The rest, if thieves or bombs didn't screw him out of it, he would find when he went back.

He chattered with increasing gaiety, and Ida kept staring at him, frightened, not following his talk.

"Lucky kid! He's asleep," the madman remarked a little later, nodding towards Useppe. And, seeing how exhausted she was, he suggested she put the baby in his barrow.

She glanced at him with enormous distrust, imagining that, under the pretext of helping her, the little man meant to steal Useppe from her, carrying him off in the barrow. Still, since she was at the end of her strength, she accepted. The man helped her settle Useppe (who continued to sleep serenely) amid his possessions and then he introduced himself to her with these words:

"Cucchiarelli Giuseppe, hammer and sickle!" and as a sign of understanding and greeting, he clenched the fist of his good hand, winking at her with both eyes.

Ida's poor dazed head went on reasoning: if I tell him the baby's named Giuseppe the same as he is, it's more likely he'll steal him from me. Following this logic, she chose to say nothing. Then to protect herself against any dark intention on the part of the little man, she clung to one handle of the barrow with both fists. And though she was now almost asleep on her feet, she wouldn't let go of that handle, not even to stretch her numbed fingers. Thus, having passed the Jewish cemetery, they followed the sharp curve of the Via Tiburtina.

And so Useppe made the rest of his journey as if in a coach: still sleeping, settled on a quilt, between a cage inhabited by a pair of canaries, and a covered basket containing a cat. The latter was so terrified and bewildered by the whole obscure event that for the entire journey it didn't breathe. The two canaries, on the other hand, huddled side by side at the bottom of their cage, occasionally exchanged minimal chirps of solace.

4 About another two and a half months went by, with no news of Nino. Meanwhile, on July 25th, the Duce, left without any following in his bad luck, had been deposed and arrested by the King, and Fascism had fallen with him, replaced by the Badoglio provisional government, which lasted forty-five days. On the forty-fifth day, which was the 8th of September 1943, the Anglo-American Allies, masters by now of much of southern Italy, signed an armistice with the provisional governors. And they immediately fled southwards, leaving to the Fascists and the Germans the rest of Italy, where the war continued.

The Italian army, however, scattered through the country, without any leadership or order, had disintegrated, so only the Blackshirt militia remained fighting at the side of the Germans. Freed by Hitler's men, Mussolini had been set up in the North at the head of a Nazi-Fascist republic. And at present the city of Rome, left without a government, was in fact under Nazi occupation.

During all these events, Ida and Useppe had continued living at the edge of the Pietralata area, in the refugee shelter that had received them that first night after the air raid.

Pietralata was a sterile country area on the extreme outskirts of Rome, where a few years earlier the Fascist regime had set up a kind of village for pariahs, or rather of poor families driven by the authorities from their old homes in the center of the city. The same regime had hastily constructed for them, with ersatz materials, this new neighborhood, composed of rudimentary, identical dwellings, which now, though still recent, seemed already decrepit and rotting. They were, if I remember rightly, little rectangular houses all in a row, all the same yellowish color, in the midst of a barren terrain, unpaved, which produced an occasional bush, born withered, and for the rest, only dust or mire, according to the season. In addition to these hovels, you could see certain cement constructions, used as latrines or public washing-places, and some clotheslines, like gallows. And into each of those dormitory-hovels whole families and generations were crammed, mingled now with a stray population of war refugees.

In Rome, especially in the last few years, this territory had been considered virtually a no-man's-land, beyond the law; and in general the

Fascists and the Nazis didn't dare show their faces much in the area, though its view was dominated by a military fort, standing high on a hill.

But for Ida, the Pietralata settlement, with its inhabitants, remained an exotic region where she ventured only to make purchases at the market, or for similar reasons, crossing it always with her heart pounding, like a rabbit's. The shelter where she lived was, in fact, about half a mile from the built-up area, beyond a desert of uneven fields, all dips and embankments, which hid the building from view. It was isolated, quadrangular, at the end of a crumbling ditch; and it wasn't clear what its original function had been. Perhaps it had first served as a place for storing farm produce, but later it must have been used as a school, because there was a pile of desks inside. And probably some further work had been started, then suspended, because on the roof, flat like a terrace, a part of the railing had been demolished, and a trowel and a pile of bricks had been left there. Practically speaking, it consisted of a single ground-floor room, rather vast, with low grilled windows, and one exit which opened directly onto the ditch; but it boasted some conveniences truly rare those days in the outlying slums, namely a private latrine with cesspool, and a cistern feeding a water tank on the roof. The only faucet in the building was in the latrine, in a narrow basement, and from there the apparatus for the flow of water into the tank was also regulated. Now, however, at the end of summer, the cistern was dry, and Ida, like the other women, had to go to a public faucet in the slum-settlement for water. Later, with the rainy season, the situation improved.

No other dwelling existed nearby. The only building this side of the main settlement, about three or four hundred yards away, was a tavern, a kind of plaster shed, where they also sold salt, tobacco, and other rationed goods, scarcer and scarcer with the passing of time. If there were threats of raids in the area, or round-ups, or the mere presence of Germans or Fascists, the proprietor found a way of alerting the refugees, with certain signals of his.

From the entrance to the shelter at the end of the ditch, in the direction of the tavern, a rough path had been made, reinforced as far as possible by some stones. This, in the area, was the only trodden path.

Since Ida had been there, many of the little crowd that arrived with her had moved elsewhere, to live with relatives, or to go farther into the country. In their place, there had been some newcomers, left homeless after the second bombing of Rome (August 13th), or refugees from the South; but even these, gradually, had scattered to other places. Among those who had remained, like Ida and Useppe, since the first evening, there was still Cucchiarelli Giuseppe, the marble-cutter who had brought Useppe in his barrow. It seems that, falsifying some documents for the list of the dead, he had recently managed to have himself included among the bomb victims trapped under the rubble. He preferred to stay incognito with the refugees, counted as dead by the Rome Registry, rather than work as a marble-cutter at the cemetery under the Fascists and Germans.

With him there was also his cat (who proved to be a female, of a handsome striped red-and-orange, Rossella by name); and the pair of canaries, named Peppiniello and Peppiniella, in their cage, hung from a nail. And the cat, obeying her master's teachings, always gave these two a wide berth, as if she didn't even see them.

The only other inhabitants of the shelter at present were a single family, half-Roman and half-Neapolitan, and so numerous, in itself, that Cucchiarelli Giuseppe nicknamed them *The Thousand*. The Neapolitan components of this family, left homeless that spring after the bombing of Naples, had come to move in with their relatives in Rome; but here again they had remained without a roof, along with their hospitable relations, in the July air raid. "We," they boasted on the subject, joking, "are a military objective." It was difficult to make a precise count of them, because they were a fluctuating tribe; however, they were never less than twelve and, as some of them improvised various activities and jobs, they enjoyed a relative prosperity. There were some young men, who appeared only at intervals, generally staying off God knows where, also for fear of the German round-ups. There was a very fat old Roman woman, named Sora Mercedes, who was always seated on a bench with a blanket around her because of her arthritis, and under the blanket, she guarded a store of provisions. There was the husband of Mercedes, a Neapolitan, also a Giuseppe by name. There were two other old women (of whom the more talkative, named Ermelinda, was known to Useppe as Dinda), another old man, some young daughters-in-law, and the little ones, several kids, boys and girls. In their number (besides one Currado and one Impero) there was also another Giuseppe, so to distinguish the many Giuseppes, they used to call Mercedes's husband Giuseppe Primo; Giuseppe Secondo was Signor Cucchiarelli (whom Ida, to herself, continued to call the Madman); and Peppe the little Neapolitan. To them was added finally (not counting the canaries Peppiniello and Peppiniella) our own Useppe, who of all the Giuseppes was, without doubt, the most lively and popular.

Among The Thousand there was a noticeable gap in the middle-aged generation because two parents (already grandparents of Impero, Currado, etc.) had died, suffocated, in Naples. In addition to various sons, already adult, they had left an orphan daughter, here present among The Thousand, a last girl by the name of Carulina. She was over fifteen but looked thirteen; and with her little black braids twisted and pinned over her temples, she suggested a cat, or a fox with its ears pricked up. About a year

155

before, in Naples, when they spent the nights in the caves to escape the bombings, this Carulina, then aged fourteen minus one month, had been made pregnant, they didn't know by whom. She herself, in fact, would answer the insistent interrogations of her tribe by swearing that if somebody had done it, she hadn't noticed anything. However, there was no relying on her word, because her head was made in such a way that she believed blindly in all fantasies and inventions, not only other people's but also her own. For example, in the Easter season, her relatives at home had told her, teasing, that the Americans, as Easter presents, instead of the usual destructive and incendiary bombs, would drop on Naples some egg-bombs, recognizable even up in the sky because of their gaudy colors. Naturally, these would be harmless projectiles which, exploding on the ground, would release surprises: sausages, for example, chocolate, sweets, and so on. From that moment on, the convinced Carulina was alert, always running to the window at the hum of every plane, peering into the sky towards the hoped-for apparition. Finally, on Holy Saturday morning, when she went out to do the shopping, she returned looking as if she had been touched by a miracle; and she offered her grandmother a sweet pastry, saying that just when she was going by Porta Capuana, from a Flying Fortress an egg-bomb had fallen, the shape of a huge Easter egg, all covered with tinfoil, painted with the designs of the American flag. This bomb had exploded just in front of the Gate, without doing any damage. On the contrary! it had spurted lights and sparks like a beautiful Catherine-wheel; and out of it stepped the movie star Janet Gaynor, in a long evening dress, with a jewel on her bosom, and she had promptly started distributing pastries all around. The famous actress had beckoned with her little finger to Carulì in person, handing her the pastry in question, with the words: *Take this to your grandma, poor old woman, she doesn't have many Easters left to her in this world.*

"Ah? Is that what she said? What language did she speak to you in?"

"What do you mean? Italian. Neapolitan. Of course!"

"And afterwards, how did she get back to America? If she hangs around here too long, they'll take her hostage, she'll be a prisoner of war!!"

"Nooo! Nooo!" (hotly shaking her head) "What are you talking about? She went right off, five minutes later! She had a kind of balloon tied to her, a parachute, only the opposite, that flies up instead of down. So she got back into the Flying Fortress up there waiting for her, and off she went again."

"Ah, fine. Thanks a lot and goodbye!"

A few weeks after this extraordinary event, Carulina reached Rome with her family. And when she arrived, she looked like a kind of freak of nature: small as she was, and with that enormous belly, so big you couldn't understand how she could carry it along, on her tiny feet. In the month of June, back in Rome, in the San Lorenzo quarter, she had given birth to twin girls, healthy, normal, and plump, while she was thin, though in good health. The pair were named Rosa and Celeste; and since they were, and remained, identical in every respect, their mother, to tell them apart, tied ribbons around their wrists, one rose-colored, the other a celestial blue. Unfortunately, with the passing of time, the two ribbons had become almost unrecognizable in their filth. And their mother would examine the ribbons each time scrupulously, before certifying, content: "This one's Rusinella." "This here's Celestina."

Naturally, her scant milk wasn't enough for the two babies; but one of her Roman sisters-in-law helped her out. She was actually suffering from an excess of milk, having barely and forcibly weaned her last son (Attilio). Otherwise, he would have been too addicted to tittie, where he wanted to stay attached always; he might grow up to be a mamma's boy.

Carulina, even if she now had a family, was still childish for her age; so she wasn't interested, like her sisters-in-law, in *Film Parade* and other magazines of great success with the female audience; but spelling out the words aloud, she still read stories with illustrations and comic books for babies; and she loved to play tag and hide-and-seek with the kids of the place. However, at even the slightest whimper from Rosa, or from Celeste, she could be seen running, worried, her eyes wide, protruding, like a car's headlights, in the direction of her offspring. She conscientiously shared her scarce milk between the twins, baring her little breasts in public without shame, as something natural. And during this nursing operation she assumed an air of great importance.

To put them to sleep, she sang a very simple lullaby that went like this:

"Ninna ò ninna ò
Rusina and Celesta go to sleep, go
ò ò
ninna ò."

And this was all, repeated always the same, until that pair fell asleep.

The corner reserved for her tribe, in the vast shelter room, was always bedecked, especially on rainy days, with diapers and the infants' little shirts, hung up to dry. She worked constantly, excessively, changing and cleaning her daughters, brusquely turning them upside down. She was, in other words, a good mother: but with brisk, authoritarian ways, without coyness or simpering, indeed, yammering at the daughters when necessary, as if they understood. Perhaps, too unprepared for motherhood, instead of little babies, she saw in them a pair of her contemporaries, dwarfs, who had emerged from her as a surprise, like Janet Gaynor from the egg-bomb.

At the same time, however, in her unexpected promotion to the position of mother, she had somehow promoted herself to be mother of all. She was always to be seen working, fanning the fire here, or washing a rag there, or combing her sister-in-law's hair in the style of the actress Maria Denis, etc., etc. One eternal occupation of hers, also, was to wind up the gramophone, the family's property, which (since their last radio had inevitably crashed with the bombs) was kept going from morning till night. The records were few and always the same: two songs, already a couple of years old, which were entitled "My Country Queen" and "The Vamp of La Scala"; an old Neapolitan comic song, "The Photo"; another of the same ilk, called "Fan Me," in which a certain Carulì was also mentioned; and in addition three dance tunes (tango, waltz, and fox trot) and a piece of Italian jazz, with the band of Gorni, Ceragioli, etc.

Carulì knew all these titles and names by heart, just as she knew magnificently the names of movie actresses and the titles of pictures. In fact, she was crazy about movies; however, if you asked her the story of the films she had so enjoyed, you discovered that she hadn't understood a thing. In the place of stories of love, rivalry, adultery, and such, she saw only fantastic movements, like a magic lantern's. And for her, the stars must have been something on the order of Snow White or the fairies in children's magazines. As for the male stars, they interested her much less, because they were less readily identified, in her imagination, with fairy-tale characters.

As she had been born into a tribe, obviously, there had been nothing secret about sex to her eyes, from her earliest childhood. But this fact, oddly, had fostered her sexual indifference, so innocent it resembled absolute ignorance, to be compared, actually, with that of Rosa and Celeste!

Carulì was not beautiful: her graceless little body was already sagging after the double pregnancy, so that it made the movement of her legs unsteady, giving her a disjointed and comical gait like that of certain mongrel puppies. From her scrawny back, her shoulder blades were excessively prominent, like a pair of plucked, trimmed wings. And her face was irregular, the mouth too big. To Useppe, however, this Carulì must have seemed a world-shaking beauty, if not actually divine. And at present, the name he called most often and repeated (after *mà*) was *Ulì*.

For that matter, Useppe had soon learned the names of everybody: Eppetondo (Giuseppe Secondo, alias the Madman, namely Cucchiarelli, who was not *tondo*, or round, but quite skinny), Tole and Mémeco (Salvatore and Domenico, Caruli's two older brothers), etc., etc. And he didn't hesitate to call them by name joyously, whenever he felt like it, as if they were all little kids like himself. Often, intent on their own affairs and schemes, they wouldn't even notice him. But after a moment's bewilderment, he would already have forgotten the affront.

Without doubt, for him there existed no differences of age, or of beauty and ugliness, or sex, or social station. Tole and Mémeco were, really, two misshapen, stubby boys, of uncertain profession (black marketeers, or thieves, according to circumstances), but for him they were the same as two Hollywood strong men or two patricians of high degree. Sora Mercedes stank; but when he was playing hide-and-seek, his favorite hiding-place was the blanket she kept over her lap; and at the moment he vanished under it, he would murmur to her in great haste, with a look of complicity: "Don't tell, eh, don't tell!"

A couple of times, towards the end of the summer, a few German soldiers happened by there. And immediately, panic spread in the shelter, because by now among the common people the Germans seemed worse than enemies. But though the announcement *the Germans* acted in those surroundings as a kind of malediction, little Useppe seemed unaware of it, and he received the unusual visitors with an intent curiosity, with no suspicion. Now, in these cases, to tell the truth, the Germans were only simple soldiers passing by; they had no evil intentions, nor did they demand anything beyond a road direction or a glass of water. However, it is certain that if an SS troop had turned up in the room with all their paraphernalia of massacre, the comical Useppe would not have been afraid of them. That tiny, defenseless being knew no fear, but a universal, spontaneous trust. For him strangers apparently didn't exist, only members of his family, returning after an absence, whom he recognized at first sight.

On the evening of his arrival after the disaster, unloaded, sleeping, from the barrow, he hadn't waked till the following morning, and Ida, to force him to eat something, had had to feed him almost in his sleep. In the night, during that long, long sleep of his, she had heard him start and moan; and, touching him, she thought he was feverish . . . In the morning, however (a fine sunny morning), he woke fresh and lively as always. The first presences he had glimpsed, the minute his eyes were open, had been the two canaries and the twins (the cat was off on business of her own). And he had immediately rushed towards them, greeting this sight with much spellbound laughter. Then, like a cat, he had started exploring his new, unexplained dwelling, as if to say: "Yes, yes, I'm quite satisfied with it," mingling with all those unknown people, seeming to announce: "Here I am! At last we meet again!" He hadn't yet been washed since the previous morning, and in that intrepid face, dirty and black with smoke, the joy of his little blue eyes was so funny it made everyone laugh, even on that tragic first day.

Afterwards, the promiscuous life in the single, huge common room, which was a daily torment for Ida, for Useppe was all a festivity. His minuscule life had always been solitary and isolated (except on the happy nights of air-raid alarms); and now he had the sublime good luck to find himself, day and night, in numerous company! He seemed positively insane, in love with all.

For this reason, too, the other children's mothers forgave his remarkable precocities, commenting on them without envy. Comparing him with their own children, they could hardly believe he was barely two years old; and, among themselves, they suspected that Ida was bragging on this score, feeding them a story. On the other hand, to confirm the kid's scant age, however, there were his unlimited ingenuousness and his physical dimensions, still inferior to those of his contemporaries. Certain charity ladies had left there, as an offering for the homeless, a pile of used clothing, from which his autumn wardrobe had been pieced together: a pair of long pants with suspenders, which Carulì had taken in for him at the waist, but which elsewhere were far too loose, so that they looked like Charlie Chaplin's trousers; a cloak and hood of black oilskin, lined with red quilting, which fell all the way to his feet; and a little blue wool sweater which, on the contrary, was short on him (it may have belonged to a new-born baby) so that it always hiked up behind, exposing a bit of his back.

Moreover, Carulì had produced two little shirts for him and several pairs of underpants from the headcloth of the old woman from Mandela; and with the scraps of a goatskin, stolen by her brothers from a tanner, she had fixed him some footgear, the kind shepherds wear, tied up with string. It could truly be said that, among all the guests of the room, Useppe was the poorest. Or rather, he was during the first period: for, later, as we will see, another guest arrived who, at least for a time, was even poorer than he.

Like all lovers, Useppe had absolutely no sense of the inconveniences of that life. While summer lasted, the inhabitants of the dormitory were joined by mosquitoes, fleas, and bedbugs. And Useppe scratched himself above and below, performing true natural gymnastic feats, like cats and dogs, and grumbling only as a slight comment: *"lies, lies,"* that is to say *flies,* since he called all insects flies.

In the autumn, with its windows closed, when it was time to cook, the room filled with a stifling smoke; and not bothering too much about it, he was content to wave his two hands now and then, saying: "Go 'way, smoke." These discomforts, in any case, were made up for by the wonders of the room which, with the autumn rains, was always densely populated, offering programs of ever-various novelty and attraction.

First and foremost, there were the twins. The other kids of the troupe, more or less his own age, displayed, in their way, a certain sense of superiority towards those nursing infants. But for him they were such a fascinating sight that at times he would stand and gaze at them for whole minutes, in ecstatic amusement. Then, all at once, irresistibly, he would burst into certain joyous and incomprehensible speeches of his, convinced perhaps that to converse with those infants, an Ostrogoth language was required. And perhaps he was right, because they answered him with delighted gesticulations and special cries, so enthusiastic that, in producing them, they soaked themselves with saliva.

Seeing such harmony, the relatives one day suggested he should marry one of the pair. And he promptly accepted the proposal, grave and convinced; however, when it came to making a choice, he hesitated between the two (and in fact they looked identical), so there was general agreement on the solution of marrying him to both. The wedding was celebrated without further delay. Sora Mercedes was the priest and Giuseppe Secondo the best man.

"Useppe, do you take Rosa and Celeste as your lawfully wedded wives?"

"Ess,"

"Rosa and Celeste, do you take Useppe as your lawfully wedded husband?"

"We do, we do," the two brides declared, through the mouth of the best man.

"I hereby declare you man and wife."

And this said, as the hands of the bridal trio were solemnly joined, the officiating Mercedes pretended to slip three imaginary rings on their fingers. Useppe glowed with fervor, but also with responsibility at this double consecration, which Carulì approved with great contentment, in the presence of Impero, Currado, and the other kids, all witnessing open-mouthed. For the wedding feast, the best man offered two sips of a sweetish liqueur of his own making; but Useppe, after tasting it dutifully, didn't appreciate its flavor at all and unceremoniously spat it out.

The failure of this refreshment, however, did not spoil the festivities; in fact, it aroused general laughter, which promptly released the bridegroom from his gravity. And in an immense and radiant good humor, Useppe flung himself on the ground with his legs in the air, giving way to an unrestrained acrobatic celebration.

Another wondrous sight was the pair of canaries, before whom Useppe would actually emit little cries of rejoicing: ". . . naries?" he would repeat, "naries??" But he tried in vain to understand their speech, sung or chattered.

"Ulì, what're they saying?"

"How should I know? They don't talk our language, they're foreigners."

"They come from the Canary Islands, don't they, Sor Giuseppe?"

"No, Sora Mercedes. These are domestic. They come from Porta Portese . . . the flea market."

"What're they saying, Eppetondo? Eh, what is it?"

"What can they say? Hmph . . . They say: cheep cheep, I'm skipping here and you're hopping there. Does that suit you?"

"No."

"Ah, it doesn't suit you, eh? Well, then you tell me what they're talking about."

But Useppe, chagrined, could find no answer to this.

Unlike the canaries, the cat Rosella would converse with no one. Still, when necessary, she had a vocabulary of certain special sounds, which everyone, more or less, was able to understand. To ask for something, she said: *myew* or *mayeu;* to call, she said *mau,* to threaten *mbrooooh,* etc., etc. But very rarely, to tell the truth, was she to be found inside the building. Her owner Giuseppe Secondo had decreed, *When human beings are starving, cats have to live on mice,* and in consequence, she spent the greater part of her time hunting, expending dexterity and boldness, because the hunting grounds were treacherous. "You be careful," Giuseppe Secondo warned her from time to time, "there's that tavern not far away, and they roast cats there." And at present, so it seemed, even mice were in short supply. In fact, the huntress's body, beautiful in its feline elegance, during the last few months had grown thin and mangy.

According to general opinion, she was an underworld sort, evil and untrustworthy. In fact, if you tried to catch her, she would escape; and when nobody was looking for her, she would come up unexpectedly, brushing against one person or another, purring, but darting away as soon as you tried to touch her. Towards children, moreover, she harbored a special distrust; and if at times, distracted by her sensuality, she happened to rub up against one of them, he had only to make the slightest movement and she would promptly hiss at him with a fierce air. And so Useppe, every time she condescended to graze him, held himself motionless, without breathing, in the thrill of that difficult and fleeting sign of favor.

Another outstanding luxury of the big room, for Useppe, was the gramophone. He varied its songs to infinity, and he would start dancing, not the monotonous and prescribed steps of the tango or the fox trot, but dances of instinct and imagination, in which he finally lost all restraint, drawing the other kids along with him in authentic feats, like a champion. Among his premature abilities, his athletic talent was the most universally admired. You would have said his little bones contained air, like birds'. The supply of school desks that had remained in the room were all piled up, occupying a whole wall; and for him that pile must have represented a kind of adventurous cliff! He scrambled up as if on wings, to the top, springing and running, balanced on the highest edges like a dancer, to leap down, all of a sudden, weightless. If somebody shouted to him from below: "Come down! You'll hurt yourself!" he, usually so prompt to reply, became deaf now and out of reach. Applause and encouragement—"Bravo! Go!"—met with an equally carefree lack of response. He had no taste for showing off; in fact, on occasion, he even forgot about the presence of others. You had the sensation that his body was carrying him beyond himself.

In addition to the pile of desks, the room was cluttered on all sides with bundles, stoves, tubs, basins, etc. as well as sandbags for fire protection, and rolled-up mattresses. In the air, from one end to the other, ropes had been stretched, all aflutter with clothes and linen.

The entire surface, fairly vast, was an irregular quadrilateral, an obtuse angle occupied, with its adjacent areas, by The Thousand, who at night slept all in a mass on a row of mattresses pulled side by side. The acute angle was inhabited by Giuseppe Secondo, who, alone among all the people there, personally owned a wool mattress. He had, however, left the pillow at home, and used his jacket in its place, with, on top, his hat, which he put back on his head every morning, never taking it off, not even indoors. He explained this habit by saying he suffered from rheumatic arthritis. But the truth was that inside the lining of the hat he kept hidden, in smoothed thousand-lire notes, a portion of his private liquid capital, having distributed the rest, a part inside the lining of his jacket, and a part under the inner sole of his single pair of shoes, which at night he laid to rest beside him, under the blanket.

The next angle was Ida's corner. Unlike all the others, she had separated it from the rest of the dormitory with a kind of curtain, made of sacks crudely sewn together and hung from a string. And in the fourth corner, at present uninhabited, a succession of transient guests had passed, of whom the only remaining souvenirs were two empty flasks and a large sack of straw.

In this period, on waking in the morning, Ida rarely recalled having dreamed. But the few dreams she did remember were happy, so that it was all the more bitter to find herself, on rising, in her present state of wretchedness. One night, she seems to hear again the cry of the fishermen heard in her childhood when she visited her grandparents during the summer: FAA-LEIU!! And, in fact, she finds herself in the presence of a turquoise sea, inside a calm and luminous room, in the company of her whole family, the living and the dead. Alfio refreshes her, waving a colored fan, and Useppe on the shore laughs to see the little fish jumping up above the surface of the water . . .

Then she finds herself again in a very beautiful city, such as she has never seen. This time, too, a vast blue sea is present, beyond immense seaside terraces where a vacationing crowd is strolling, happy and calm. All the city's windows have varicolored curtains, which flap ever so slightly in the cool air. And this side of the terraces, among jasmines and palms, extend outdoor cafés, where the people, reposing restively under bright beach umbrellas, admire a fantastic violinist. Now this violinist is her father, tall and regal, on a bandstand with a decorated railing: he is also a famous singer, and he plays and sings "Celeste Aida, forma Divina . . ."

.   .   .

The reopening of the schools, which in her new refugee condition had worried Ida since the summer, was now indefinitely postponed in the city of Rome; and Ida's only activity outside the house, at present, was the difficult hunt for food, for which her salary proved more inadequate each month. Sometimes, from The Thousand, who, among other things, also carried on a contraband activity, she bought some pieces of meat, or some butter, or eggs, at high black-market prices. But she allowed herself these luxuries for the exclusive benefit of Useppe. She herself had grown so thin that her eyes seemed twice as big as before.

A strict division of property reigned in the room, so at mealtimes a true but invisible boundary was set up among the three inhabited corners of the quadrilateral. Even Useppe, at that hour, was confined in his own corner by Ida, who feared that the child, among the banqueting Thousand and Giuseppe Secondo intent on heating up his private cans, would involuntarily assume the guise of a mendicant. In that time of famine, even the generous became mean; and the only one who, every now and then, peered in at the sackcloth curtain bringing a taste of his dishes as an offering, was Giuseppe Secondo. But she, who continued to consider him mad, would blush in confusion at such offers, repeating: "No, thank you . . . excuse me . . . thank you . . . so kind . . ."

In the refugee group, she was the most educated, but also the poorest; and this made her more shy and frightened. Even with the children of The Thousand, she couldn't shake off her feeling of inferiority, and only with the twins did she achieve some familiarity, because they too, like Useppe, were born of an unknown father. The first days, if anyone asked her about her husband, she answered, blushing: "I'm a widow . . ." and the dread of further questions made her still more antisocial than she already was by nature.

She was always afraid of disturbing, of being in the way; and she left her corner only rarely, living huddled behind her curtain like a prisoner in solitary confinement. When she dressed or undressed, she trembled for fear some outsider might look in at the curtain, or catch a glimpse of her through the holes in the sackcloth. She was embarrassed every time she went to the latrine, outside which it was often necessary to wait in line; but still, that fetid little room was the only place that granted her, at least, a respite of isolation and peace.

In the common room, the rare moments of silence affected her like a breath of open air in the depths of a circle in hell. Those alien noises, which assailed her from all sides, were now reduced, in her ears, to a single, eternal roar, with no more distinction of sounds. However, on recognizing Useppe's bright voice in their midst, she felt the same little glory that stray cats feel when their enterprising kittens venture into the public square, out of their hole in the cellar.

Usually, when supper was over, Useppe was dropping with sleep and he was seldom to be found at the hour when The Thousand prepared their great pallet for the night. He considered such rare occasions a great stroke of personal luck, witnessing those preparations with profound interest, trying to mingle in their midst. Then, as Ida's hand drew him beyond his own private curtain, he would look back with longing.

Now one night, in the universal darkness, he happened to be waked by a call of nature; and in satisfying it heroically without any help, so as not to disturb his mother, he felt curious at the enormous choir of snorers from outside the curtain; and he lingered on his pot, pricking up his ears until, rising, he went out, barefoot, to explore the dormitory. How did they manage, the sleepers, to produce such varied sounds? One seemed a combustion engine, one a train-whistle; one brayed, and another sneezed repeatedly. In the shadows of the room, the only glow came from a small votive candle, kept always burning by The Thousand in front of certain photographs, on a kind of little corner altar at the end of their pallet. That dim light could barely reach the opposite corner, where Useppe stood, on coming from behind his curtain. But he gave up the idea of going farther, not for fear of moving in the dark, but because, instead, his curiosity in observing the mechanism of the snores prevailed at that point over any other attraction. And with a little laugh, seeing that the pallet of The Thousand, at the point nearest him, left a tiny empty space towards the edge, he promptly settled there, covering himself as best he could with an available blanket's hem. He could just make out the shape of the sleepers nearest him. The one at his side, to judge by the enormous swell beneath the blanket and also by the odor, had to be Sora Mercedes. At her feet, a much smaller shape was lying, the blanket pulled over its head, and this might be Carulina. Before stretching out entirely, Useppe tried calling her very softly: "Ulì . . ." but she showed no sign of hearing. Maybe it was somebody else.

None of The Thousand noticed Useppe's intrusion. Only the big form beside him, in sleep, instinctively moved a bit farther in, to leave him a little more space, then drew him closer, perhaps believing him a grandchild. Huddled next to that great warm body, Useppe fell asleep again at once.

That same night, he had the first dream of which any trace remained in his memory. He dreamed that on the grass there was a little *sip* (ship) tied to a tree. He jumped into the boat, and almost immediately it came loose from its rope, while the field had become very glittering water, where the boat, with him inside, swayed rhythmically as if it were dancing.

Actually, what his dream translated into the gay roll of the boat was a real movement going on meanwhile at his feet. The little infantile form covered almost to the head had become a couple. A male of the tribe of The Thousand, seized by a sudden stimulus, had slipped noiselessly down along the row of mattresses, and without a word to her, lying on her, was releasing in brief jolts his nocturnal urge. And she let him have his way, answering only with an occasional little somnolent grumble.

But Useppe, sleeping, noticed nothing. At dawn, Ida, upset at not finding him beside her, rushed out into the dormitory. In order to see, she opened a window slightly, and in the faint light she glimpsed him at the edge of the great couch, serenely sleeping. Then she picked him up and replaced him on his own mattress.

5 That early autumn brought various remarkable events to the refugees in the room.

At the end of September, the summer heat still continued, and to keep from suffocating, they slept with the windows open. It was the 29th or 30th of that month when, late one evening, around eleven, shortly before the curfew, the cat Rossella jumped into the room from one of the low windows over the ditch, announcing herself—she usually so taciturn—with a long, ardent mewing. Everyone was already in bed, but not all were yet asleep; and a moment after Rossella's announcement, Giuseppe Secondo, still awake, was the first to see a male shadow outlined in the frame of the window:

"Is this the shelter for the refugees?"

"Well? What do you want?"

"Let me in." The voice sounded hoarse and exhausted, but peremptory. In that period, anybody who turned up by surprise was suspect, especially at night. "Who is it? Who is it?!" various alarmed voices asked around the room, from the common couch of The Thousand, while two or three of their number hastily got up, summarily covering their hot, almost naked bodies. But Giuseppe Secondo, the only one who wore pajamas to bed, was already going towards the window, with his shoes on, his jacket around his shoulders, and his hat on his head. Meanwhile Rossella, with unheard-of concern, never stopped urging him on with her special call MYEEEEW! running back and forth from the window to the door, clearly insisting this man be welcomed without delay.

"I . . . I ran away . . . from the North! a soldier . . . !" The stranger was shouting, heightening his highwayman's manner. "O *màma mia* . . . I'm going to fall . . ." his voice suddenly changed, and he was talking to himself in a Northern dialect, in a desperate and helpless abandonment, leaning back against the outside wall.

It wasn't the first time passing soldiers had happened by, men who had thrown away their uniform and wanted to reach the South. As a rule they didn't stay long, they ate something, rested a bit, and then resumed their journey. But they generally turned up during the day, and were more polite.

"Wait . . ." Because of the wartime blackout, they closed the window before turning on the central lamp. He must have believed they were shutting him out, because he started hammering on the door with his hands and feet.

"Hey!!! Hang on a minute . . . Come in!"

Immediately, the moment he was inside, almost sinking to his knees, he sat down on the floor, resting against a sandbag. Obviously he was at the end of his strength, and he was unarmed. The entire tribe of The Thousand (except for some of the kids and the twins, who were sleeping) had crowded around him, the men bare-chested or in undershirt and shorts, the women in slips. Useppe had also popped out from behind his curtain, all naked as he was, and he followed events with extreme interest, while Ida looked out cautiously, always afraid any newcomer might conceal a Fascist spy. And the canaries, wakened by the light, remarked on what happened with a few cheeps.

But the most obsequious was Rossella, clearly smitten with that man. After rubbing flirtatiously against his legs, she sat before him in the pose of the Egyptian sphinx, never taking her copper eyes off him.

The man, however, paid no attention to the cat's special welcome. On

167

entering he had not given the room the slightest glance, nor had he addressed anyone in particular. Indeed, even in asking for hospitality, he openly declared, with his demeanor, a total rejection of places and their inhabitants, animal and human.

The ceiling lamp, though faint, bothered him, so that, once seated, he moved his face away from it, grimacing; and then, with jerky movements like a paralytic's, he shielded his eyes behind a pair of dark glasses, dug out of a filthy sack he was carrying with him.

That canvas bag, with a shoulder strap, about the size of a schoolboy's bookbag, was his only luggage. His haggard face, beneath a several days' growth of beard, was of a gray pallor; but, on his arms and chest, covered with wispy hair, his natural coloring could be seen: dark, almost a mulatto's. His hair was very black, stiff, cut short over his brow; and his rather tall physique, even in its present deterioration, seemed healthy and fairly sturdy. He was wearing a pair of summer pants and an unbuttoned knit shirt, with short sleeves, all in a condition of indescribable filthiness. And sweat poured off him in streams, as if after a Turkish bath. He looked about twenty.

"I want to sleep!" he said in a weak voice, but still with his truculent manner, full of menace and rancor. He continued making certain strange grimaces, distorting his facial muscles in such a way that Carulina was irresistibly moved to laugh, and had to hide her mouth with both hands to keep him from seeing. But he wouldn't have noticed anyway, since his eyes, concealed by the dark glasses, looked at nothing.

All of a sudden, he frowned in a meditative expression, as if better to pull himself together; and planting both his hands on the ground, he made an attempt to stand. Instead, he turned his face to one side and threw up a little whitish foam on to the floor. "Màma mia . . ." he murmured, his breath tainted with vomit. Then Carulì, perhaps repenting her earlier laughter, came forward, barefoot, in her rayon slip (which, like the other women, she kept on when she went to bed). And on her own initiative and responsibility, she went to the fourth corner, shaking out as best she could the straw-filled sack that was there, at anyone's disposal.

"If you want," she said to the man, "you can sleep here. It doesn't belong to anybody."

Nobody expressed opposition. And Giuseppe Secondo, seeing the young man had trouble getting to his feet, came to his aid considerately, as if helping a wounded dog. However, once he was standing, the stranger repulsed him brutally. And, alone, he went and flung himself on the sack, like a dead weight.

"Meeeew!" and the cat leaped to join him, settling herself near his feet, at a point where some straw spilled from a large hole in the sack. Before curling up there, she busily arranged the straw more neatly with her paws, amusing herself by playing with the wisps for a while; but when this momentary diversion was over, she crouched down with her belly over that hole, and stayed there, calmly contemplating the stranger with her huge open eyes. She was purring with pleasure, but at the same time in her eyes you could perceive a glow of sincere concern and responsibility.

The others present couldn't believe their eyes, seeing her so different: she who never made friends with anyone, and, rude by nature, spent all her nights away from home. But in reality, unknown to all, she was now pregnant and perhaps was developing some instinct which made her feel upset and strange, having so far experienced nothing of the sort in her life. This was, in fact, her first pregnancy, and at the age of less than ten months. And she had been pregnant already for several weeks; but the swelling of her belly had remained minimal, so nobody had noticed it.

.   .   .

The stranger, the moment he dropped on the sack, fell at once into a sleep that resembled total unconsciousness.

He had left his bag on the floor, where he had sat down on entering, and one of Carulì's sisters-in-law, before putting it at the head of his bed, explored its contents. It contained the following objects:

three books, one of Spanish poetry, another with a difficult philo- sophical title, and a third entitled: *Paleochristian symbols in the cata- combs*;
a grease-stained notebook with ruled pages, which bore on every page, lengthwise and sideways, in pencil, in larger or smaller writing, but always in the same hand, only these repeated words: CARLO CARLO CARLO CARLO VIVALDI VIVALDI VIVALDI;
a few stale crackers, soft, as if they had been in water;
some ten-lire notes, crumpled and scattered in disorder among the other objects;
and a personal identity card.

This was all.
On the identity card, facing the photograph of its owner, they could read:

Surname: VIVALDI
First name: CARLO

Profession: student
Birthplace: Bologna
Birth-date: 3 October 1922

etc., etc.

In the photograph, taken some seasons earlier, the young man sleeping on the sack was still recognizable, though now he suffered by the comparison. His cheeks, emaciated at present, in the portrait were full and fresh, in their intact oval form. There he looked neat, even elegant, with his half-open collar, white and pressed, and a handsome, loosely knotted necktie. But the most indecent change affected his expression which, in the portrait, even that ordinary passport-snapshot, had an amazing innocence. It was serious, to the point of melancholy; but that seriousness resembled a child's dreaming loneliness. Now instead his features were marked by something corrupt, which perverted them from within. And these marks, filled with a terrible stupor, seemed to have been produced not by a gradual development, but by a lightning violence, like a rape.

Even his sleep was degraded by it; and in those present, unconsciously, it created an uneasiness close to dislike. Other lost and exhausted characters had happened into this place before, but in him you could feel a difference, which almost excluded him from the communal sympathy.

Towards one in the morning, when in the vast room's shadows, all had long been asleep, he suddenly began to writhe on his sack, screaming obsessively: "Stop! Stop! I'm thirsty! I want to get out of here! Turn off that light!"

The profound snoring of the sleepers was interrupted. "What light?" one of them grumbled lazily. And, in fact, all lights were out. The first to move was Useppe, who jumped down from his mattress and ran towards the corner with the sack in an alarmed dash, as if the stranger were a close relative of his.

He was followed by Carulina, who first of all saw to closing the windows and turning on the central lamp. Little Useppe, all naked, was standing there, a step from the sack, his gaze fixed, interrogatory. The cat, still half stretched out on her straw, pricked up her ears, and sniffed the time with her little dark nose still warm from sleep, widening her dazed pupils on the man who was writhing so wildly. At a certain point, she jumped to the floor in alarm, moving around him. He was sitting up on the sack, still inveighing in an obscene manner. He was delirious. He kept repeating: "Take that light away!" but it was clear he wasn't accusing the lamp that had just been lit in the room. His black eyes, aflame and bloodshot, watched only a stony point outside himself, like the eyes of the demented. His face, livid before, was now fiery. His temperature must have risen to well over 100 degrees. Giuseppe Secondo tried to take it with a thermometer, but the stranger pushed him away. In his raving, he ripped his shirt, which here and there was striped with brownish stains, either mire or blood, it wasn't clear which. And he scratched his chest so fiercely that he tore the skin. He was surely teeming with lice.

Then he started bouncing here and there on the sack, as if he were being pounded from below: "*Màma mia*," he moaned desperately, "I want to go home, home . . ." and he clenched his eyes shut with such force that his eyelids seemed ready to crush his sockets. Then his lashes were noticed, soft, and so long and thick they must have bothered him.

After about a quarter of an hour, he calmed down a little, perhaps because they had forced him to swallow an aspirin tablet with some water. His delirium became milder. Absorbed in a strange cogitation, he began to work out certain calculations: additions, multiplications, divisions which came to his lips in a nonsense murmur that seemed a joke: "Seven eights," he was saying, "seven nines . . . three hundred sixty-five days, makes eleven per minute . . ." He frowned with terrible gravity: "And eighty an hour, that's the maximum . . . Forty-six plus fifty-three, eleven thousand . . . Don't think! Don't think!" he repeated at this point, dazed, as if someone had interrupted him. And he turned over on the sack, again trying to count on his fingers: "Minus five . . . minus four . . . minus one . . . how much is minus one . . . ? DON'T think! Minus one . . ." It seemed he couldn't make any sense of his countdown any more: "Forty dozen shirts," he grumbled sternly, "not enough for a complete service . . . For twenty-four table settings . . . twelve tablecloths . . . one thousand five negative exponent . . . how many dozen?! this is algebra, goddammit . . ."

After a while, Carulina as usual couldn't contain herself, and she had to stifle a laugh with her hands: "Why's he counting?" Useppe asked her, concerned, in a low voice. "How should I know?" she answered him, "he's got a delirious fever, that one . . . he's not thinking like a human being!" "A dowry . . . he's arguing about a dowry!" Granny Dinda spoke up, for her, with knowledgeable pedantry. And Carulina couldn't restrain another laugh, which made her two braids dance on the top of her head, where she had left them last night in her laziness, not undoing them.

To make up for her rudeness, she considerately collected the ill man's dark glasses, which he had dropped on the floor; and she put them in his bag. Then, seeing he hadn't even removed his sandals, she slipped them off his feet. His feet were black with filth and encrusted dust.

He had dozed off. And Rossella, also calming down, curled herself again in her hole, covering her head, to sleep.

That night Ida had a brief dream, which she was never to forget afterwards, in all its vividness. It seemed to her that screams and groans were coming from the sack again, as they had in reality a little earlier. But there was nobody any longer on the sack, all red with blood. The people around did their best to hide that blood under heaps of sheets and blankets; but it seeped through everything; and in an instant sheets and blankets were soaked in it.

.   .   .

The following morning, the new guest had already recovered. His temperature was normal, and as soon as he waked, around nine, he got up on his own. He avoided conversation, and he always wore his black glasses, even indoors; his attitude, however, seemed very changed since the previous evening: now he moved awkwardly, almost shyly. And the others, who had previously felt jarred by his presence as if by a scandal, gradually recovered from that first unnerving effect, regarding him with greater indulgence and liking.

Not knowing what to say to all those people, he tried to apologize for having forced himself on them: "They gave me an address, here in Rome, where I could stay, with some acquaintances, but the address turned out to be wrong. I didn't know where to turn . . ." he explained in his untamed way, half-embarrassed and half-curt. "This here," Giuseppe Secondo answered him, "isn't private property! This is a public shelter, at the disposal of the community." "I'll pay everyone back, at the end of the war!" the young man declared, high-handed and grouchy, "I'll reward everyone generously!" He didn't feel like eating, for the moment; but he asked ("I'll pay, of course," he added) for a cup of hot ersatz coffee. "I didn't want to stay any longer . . ." he kept saying to himself, barely holding the cup in his shaking hands. "I didn't want to stay on . . . but I can make it . . ." He didn't so much drink the coffee as suck it, his breath whistling.

He was no longer ghostly, as he had been on arrival; but even after he had shaved with a Gillette razor lent him by Giuseppe Secondo, his pallor was frightening, malarial. At noon, he flung himself on a dish of pasta, attacking it brutally, with the fury of a starving puppy.

After he had eaten, a more natural color returned to his cheeks. From Giuseppe Secondo he accepted the present of a shirt which was very big on its donor, but was small on its recipient, in spite of his thinness. He was apparently pleased, all the same, to be wearing something clean. Carulina washed his pants in the tub, making him pay only for the soap: black-market price, because it was a special pre-war laundry soap, not the kind you got with your ration card, which seemed made of sand and gravel. Then while the pants were drying, he clumsily covered himself with a rag around his waist (he had sturdy, hairy legs, of an almost naive, primitive roughness), and asked for the loan of a basin, to wash his body with the remainder of the purchased soap. And Rossella, who never failed to show up promptly wherever he was, accompanied him even into the latrine, where he withdrew to bathe.

After that first, angry introduction at the window, he gave very little further news about himself: and he revealed such information reluctantly, under pressure, only to explain his presence there. He was heading, he said, for the South, for the Naples area, where he had some relatives. And he planned to resume his journey as soon as possible, perhaps tomorrow. He wasn't ill, in fact, but only tired, since he had come this far on foot, and in disastrous conditions. This was the first night he had slept under a roof. The other nights, before, he had spent in the open, sleeping behind a bush, in a gulley, wherever he happened to be. "I'm not sick!" he repeated with some hostility, as if they had accused him of being contagious.

Carulina's two brothers, who moved back and forth for their affairs between Rome and Naples, told him that if he would wait two or three days, he could take advantage, along with them, of a truck belonging to a friend, who had the necessary passes and was going, in fact, to Naples. This friend knew how to handle any eventuality, being a lot smarter than the Germans and the Fascists. Maybe he would find a way to hide him in the midst of the truck's merchandise, as he wouldn't want to be seen, logically, since he was a deserter.

They added, however, that according to the latest news they had gathered, the Allies were nearing Naples, and the Germans were about to leave the city, driven out by a popular uprising. Once Naples was occupied, the Allies would have the road open to Rome. It was a matter of days, perhaps of hours. In a little while Rome too would be liberated, and it would be all over. Seeing that he had waited this long, he might just as well wait to the end, to find the way free, and without risk of being held up along the road.

Carlo, although uneasy, ended by accepting the suggestion. In reality, even if he insisted he felt great, you could see his bones and his nerves were battered. Sometimes he would make a grimace and stand still, staring into the void, under the lingering effect of the nightmare.

Almost with shame, he asked Giuseppe Secondo if he could also have for his own corner a curtain on the order of the Signora's (he was referring to Ida). Among them all, for his requests, he preferred to address Giuseppe Secondo, perhaps because, seeing the man kept very busy around the place, he had taken him for a kind of head of the family. And in asking for these poor favors (the loan of the basin, the ersatz coffee, which he paid for) he would frown, assuming an arrogant mien; but his voice came out upset and hesitant, as if he were asking for a huge sum, a million.

From the summer's many old rags, Carulina fixed him up a kind of composite curtain, which looked like Harlequin's cloak, and which protected him from the others' gaze up to a point. You could still see the lower part of his body, half stretched out; and every now and then, his hand was visible at the side of his pallet, rummaging in his bag, as if its contents didn't consist, entirely, of three tattered old books and an identity card and some stale crackers and some ten-lire notes; as if, instead, it might harbor possible pastimes for him, some help against his wretchedness and delirium, and maybe even a surprise.

Moreover, you could see, at intervals, from beyond his feet, the little form of Rossella appear, sinuous and a bit stunted, with her imperceptibly swollen belly, as she stretched after a nap and walked undisturbed over his legs. She had observed the hanging of the curtain with a look of expertise and approval, and then she had established her permanent residence behind there; so the kids, respecting her now as the property of that isolated character (who frightened them with his grim manner), no longer dared chase her, bother her, and tease her, as they had often done in the past.

The young man, to tell the truth, was too concerned with his own thoughts to pay attention to the cat; while she, beyond any doubt, was already convinced she meant a great deal in his life. He had only to shift his position, or move on his pallet, and she would promptly rise up on her forepaws, extending her face and going: "Muhí," which was her special answering call: like someone saying *present!* at a roll call; when, he, in reality, didn't see her or hear her at all, as if she didn't exist. Only rarely, by chance, his hand would stretch absently and give her a pat; and she would close her little eyes, blissful, answering him in the intimate feline language of purring: "Ah, yes! This is really the right moment. That pat was just what was needed, to complete our contentment in staying here, the two of us alone, together and independent."

Carulina's sisters-in-law began to remark: "Rossella has found her man." "The little witch" (this is what they called her at times) "got a crush at first sight" and meanwhile they would snicker at Giuseppe Secondo, trying to get a rise out of him, her legitimate owner. But he would wave his arm, with an air of generosity and indifference, which meant: "Let her do as she pleases. It's her business."

It happened, now and then, that the kids would venture to look in, beneath the curtain, to spy on that lonely couple. And Vivaldi Carlo neither rejected them nor made friends: he ignored them. The only one who never came to bother him, contradicting his usual sociable ways, was Useppe: perhaps because he had sensed the other wanted to be left alone. Once, however, playing hide-and-seek, he completely forgot this consideration. And he burst in under the curtain, crouching behind the sack and whispering to the young man, as he did to Sora Mercedes: "Don't tell, eh? Don't tell."

Every now and then, perhaps suffocating in that dark and stinking corner, the young man would emerge from the curtain and take a few steps in silence, as if to say: "Oh my God, what shall I do? Where shall I put this body of mine?" But, repelled by the room's pandemonium, he would withdraw at once to his lair.

The second day he went out and came back a little later with a new purchase, a candle which was to serve him for reading, since the light in his corner was insufficient, both during the day and at night. He also bought two packs of black-market cigarettes from Carulina's brothers. And he spent the rest of the day behind his curtain smoking and reading, or trying to read, the books he had with him.

The third day he went out again, without saying goodbye to anyone, with a conspirator's ambiguous, grim air, and he returned towards evening, with a relieved look. Inside Rome, he must have had some private postal address, since from his sortie he brought back two letters, without stamps on the envelopes (as the women noticed immediately). He had already torn open the envelopes, surely to take a rapid glance at the two letters, waiting to read them properly, in greater safety, behind his curtain. But, too eager and anxious to concern himself with anything else, the moment he was back, he began rereading them, sitting half outside, on the edge of his pallet, without drawing the curtain or lighting the candle, in the presence of all. "Good news?" they asked him. "Yes," he answered. And, with an unexpected need to communicate, he added, with an indifferent look: "From my family. From home."

Actually, he was too full of this liberating emotion, precarious though it was, to keep it all to himself. He delayed pulling the curtain, which he left folded back behind him, against the wall, as if the arrival of that correspondence had restored him, at least temporarily, to the human race. "And so they're all well back home?" one of the sisters-in-law went on, merely to encourage him to chat. "Yes, they're all well." "And what's their news, eh? What do they say?" Granny Dinda inquired. With a certain palpitation in his voice, though making a show of contemptuous nonchalance, as if the matter didn't concern him, he answered: "They send me their best wishes. Today's my birthday."

"Aaah! Many happy returns! Happy birthday!" they all shouted around the room, in chorus. And at this, he made a discontented face, and closed himself inside his curtain of rags.

That same evening, Carulina's brothers brought the news that Naples had been abandoned by the German troops. The Allies were at the gates of the city, but meanwhile the Neapolitans, tired of waiting, in the space of a few days had taken care of cleaning out the city on their own; starving as they were, homeless gypsies, dressed in tatters, armed with drums of gasoline and old sabres and anything they could find, they had merrily overpowered the German armored troops. "Naples's won the war!" Tole and Mémeco proclaimed to all present. "Does that mean it's all over now?" Carulina asked. Nobody had any doubt: Naples-to-Rome for the Anglo-Americans was merely a hop, skip, and a jump. For the moment, the road to Naples was cut off: America was on the other side, the Reich on this. But it was a matter of being patient a few more days, a week at most, and the way would be clear. "And then we'll all go home!" said granddad Giuseppe Primo (forgetting that their *home* no longer existed).

The only one who wasn't so sure was Giuseppe Secondo: the way he saw it, the Anglo-Americans, being capitalists, were spoiled boys, who took things easy: "They've got the victory in their pockets by now . . . A month more, or a month less . . . Why should they break their neck getting to Rome? Maybe they like the weather in Naples, the blue sea . . . A big holiday! They might decide to spend the winter on the cape of Posillipo . . ." But these remarks of Giuseppe Secondo's couldn't mar the enthusiasm of The Thousand.

In that period, The Thousand managed to acquire, God knows from where (apparently there were some Germans who first requisitioned it, then sold it), a great quantity of contraband meat: at times even whole quarters of beef, which they stored in the latrine, where it was cooler, hanging them on the wall from a butcher's hook. Since this was a perishable item, they sold it at such a fair price that even Ida could allow herself the expenditure, enjoying that unhoped-for luxury almost every day of the week.

But for some time, Useppe had shown an occasional reluctance to eat meat, and he had to be forced. The fault, as could clearly be seen, lay in his nerves rather than in his stomach; but this bitter caprice of his, which he himself couldn't explain, in some cases seized him to the point of horror, making him vomit and cry. Luckily, however, when cleverly distracted by some little game or improvised story, he soon forgot all his repugnance, with his natural carefree nature. And he trustingly followed the others' example, eating the dish he had detested yesterday, now without even a hint of revulsion. So those providential meals helped prepare him better for the approaching winter.

The one who profited most by the unusual abundance was Vivaldi Carlo, who, coming from the North, was naturally carnivorous. For his birthday, along with the letters, he had obviously also received some money, for that same evening he grandiosely extracted a thousand-lire note from his frayed pocket, purchasing a quantity of cigarettes and an enormous steak, which he devoured with his usual childlike voracity. He offered everybody something to drink; but, clumsy and bewildered, as soon as he had paid for the wine, he withdrew behind his curtain, not sharing in the general festivity.

And in the days that followed, having become a customer of The Thousand's new butchershop, he quickly bloomed again. His limbs, naturally sturdy, regained their elasticity and energy, and the unhealthy gray patina completely disappeared from his skin. Now more than ever, with his dark coloring and strong features, he resembled a nomad Arab-Ethiopian rather than a boy from Bologna. His rather protruding upper lip revealed, even too much, with its mobility, the feelings kept hidden by his silent mouth. And in his eyes, elongated like a stag's, there returned now and then that dreamy shadow, helpless and subterranean, which could be seen in his picture. But his face retained, like an indelible brand, that strange mark of brutal corruption.

Only once, during those days, was he seen to smile: and it was when, at the abrupt and unexpected appearance of three or four kids beneath the curtain, Rossella arched her back, swelling up in that attitude known in zoology as *terrificans*, with all the fur of her tail as stiff as quills. And baring her teeth, she emitted an authentic little roar, like a bloodthirsty feline of the tropical forests.

His healthiness exacerbated the torture of those immobile days, for the guest of the fourth corner. He could be heard yawning, with a kind of heartrending death-rattle, stretching to his full length, like a martyr on the wheel. In addition to his reading, now he spent a part of his time writing in a newly acquired notebook, which he carried with him always. And Carulina's sisters-in-law, among themselves, maliciously guessed that perhaps this notebook, too, like the one before, was being filled to all its length and breadth with CARLO CARLO CARLO VIVALDI VIVALDI.

In those days, for young men of military age, and worse still for deserters, it was more dangerous than ever to show yourself in the street. The same day their withdrawal from Naples was announced, the Germans had held a great parade in Rome, a show of strength, filing along the main streets with their armored vehicles. The streets were papered with posters calling up all ablebodied men to the defense of the North, or to forced labor in Germany. From time to time, without any warning, streets were blocked off, and buses, offices, and public places were invaded by German soldiers or by Fascist militia, who arrested all young men present, herding them into trucks. These trucks, filled with young prisoners, could be seen moving through the streets, followed by screaming women. The Italian corps of the Carabinieri, which the Germans considered untrustworthy, had been disarmed: those of its men who hadn't succeeded in escaping had been sent off to concentration camps, and the rebels were massacred, the wounded and the corpses abandoned in the middle of the street. Posters ordered all weapons to be turned in, warning that any Italian citizen found possessing arms would be executed immediately on the spot.

Now in the room, either Carulina, or one of the others, provided he wasn't too little to reach the window, was always keeping watch inside the bars. If any uniform of the Reich or the Fascists was sighted in the neighborhood, they immediately warned, in their secret code, "Light the lamp!" or else "I've got to shit!" and without delay all the men present would run to the corridor towards the inside staircase, which led from the basement to the roof, remaining ready, up there, to leap down and escape through the fields: The Thousand took care also to load themselves hastily with their quarters of beef. Even Giuseppe Secondo followed them, though he was old, asserting he was Wanted because of his subversive ideas. And Vivaldi Carlo got up from behind his curtain to join them, but without running, raising his mobile upper lip in a grimace that bared his incisors, as if he were laughing. It wasn't a grimace of fear, or of ordinary aversion. It was a phobic contraction, which in an instant perverted his features with its almost deformed brutality.

And Rossella would stretch at once and go to him, her tail erect as a banner, with merry little contented steps, which clearly said: "Thank goodness! It was time to move a bit!"

6 A few days after the arrival of Vivaldi Carlo (I can't establish now the exact date, but it was surely before October 10th), a new event distinguished those autumn evenings: and this time it was a sensational surprise.

It was pouring rain: the light was on, door and windows closed, the panes masked with gray-black paper, and the gramophone was playing: "My Country Queen." The mattresses were still rolled up against the walls; it was the hour when supper was being prepared in every corner. And all at once, Useppe, who insisted on operating the gramophone, abandoned this fascinating task and dashed towards the door, shouting, in a transport of wonder:

"Ino! Ino! Ino!"

He seemed out of his mind, as if through that door he had had a vision of a golden sailing-ship with silver masts, about to land inside the room all its sails unfurled, its decks alight with hundreds of little colored lamps. At that moment, in fact, two youthful voices were heard outside, more and more distinct in the downpour. In turn, Ida popped out of her corner, trembling from head to foot.

"Mà, Ino's here! Open, mà, open!" Useppe shouted at her, dragging her to the door by her skirt. Meanwhile somebody outside was knocking vigorously at the door. Ida didn't hesitate, though her convulsed fingers, wet with sauce, fumbled at the bolt.

Nino and another youth came in, both huddled under a single waterproof tarpaulin, the kind used to cover the goods in the back of open trucks. Nino was laughing heartily, as if it were all a detective adventure. As soon as he set foot inside the room, with one movement he flung the tarpaulin on the floor, all glistening with water; and having taken a red rag from inside his clothes, he tied it around his neck with an air of glorious defiance. Beneath the tarpaulin, he wore a little striped jersey, like a cyclist's, and a windbreaker of common rough corduroy.

"Ino! Ino!! Ino!!!"

"Hey, Usè! It's me! You know me? Going to give me a little kiss?"

They exchanged at least ten. Then Nino, introducing the other youth, announced: "This is *Quattropunte*. And I'm *Ace of hearts*. Hey, *Quattro*, this here's my brother, the one I've told you all about." "Oh, you've talked about him plenty, all right!!" the other boy confirmed, his face beaming. He was more or less Nino's own age, with the ordinary look of the Lazio peasants, his eyes small, good-humored, and sly. But you could see easily that his slyness, his good humor, every muscle of his sturdy little body, every breath of his lungs and beat of his heart, he had dedicated, without debate, to Nino.

The latter, meanwhile, was thinking of other things; and when his friend was already beginning his sentence, "Oh, you've talked about him!", without listening further, he was seeking everywhere with impatient and pensive eyes. "How did you find us?!" his mother kept repeating; she had been covered with blushes since his entrance, like a lover. But instead of answering, he asked her, urgently:

"Blitz? Where's Blitz?"

Useppe was so transported with joy that he hardly caught this question. Just faintly, at the passage of Blitz's poor shadow, his radiant gaze clouded for a moment, perhaps without his knowing. Then Ida, afraid of summoning back the memory, murmured aside to Nino:

"Blitz is gone."

"What? . . . Remo didn't tell me that . . ." (Remo was the name of the famous proprietor of the San Lorenzo tavern, near their house) "Remo didn't tell me anything about that . . ."

In an apologetic tone, Ida began to stammer: "The house was destroyed . . . nothing was left . . ."

But Nino burst out furiously: "I don't give a shit about the house!"

His tone proclaimed that, as far as he was concerned, all the houses of Rome could have collapsed: he spat on them. What he wanted was his dog, his beloved companion, the starred-belly. This was what mattered to him. A tragic, childish suffering had come over his face, and he seemed almost ready to cry. For a while he was silent. Under his tangled curls, which covered his head like a helmet, his eyes conversed from an abandoned and bottomless darkness with a tiny ghost, sprung up to receive him in this alien place, dancing, crazed with joy, on his four little crooked legs. Then Nino reacted with wrath, as if Blitz's loss were everyone's fault. He sat down angrily on a rolled-up mattress, his legs outstretched, and to the whole assembly that had gathered around him, he announced, with grim arrogance:

"We're partisans of the Roman Castelli zone. Good evening, comrades. Tomorrow morning we're going back to the base. We want a place to sleep, something to eat, and wine."

He saluted with clenched fist. Then, with a kind of carefree wink, he pulled his jacket aside to show a belt, worn high up, almost across his chest, where he concealed a pistol.

You would have said that his meaning, displaying it, was "Either you give us food, etc., or else you'll pay with your lives." But instead, he promptly brightened with an ingenuous, self-satisfied smile, and explained:

"It's a Walther," giving it an affectionate glance. "Spoils of war," he continued. "A German had it . . . An ex-German," he clarified, making a gangster face, "because he's not a German now, or Spanish, or Turk, or Jew . . . or . . . or . . . he's fertilizer."

Suddenly his eyes, always so lively, had a strange, frowning stare, drained of images, like the glass of a lens. Since his birth, Ida couldn't remember ever having seen those eyes on him. But it lasted only an instant. Then Ninnuzzu was again shining in a fresh, exhilarated mood, spilling out his boyish boasts:

"These boots, too," he declared, showing his huge foot, size twelve, "are the same brand. DEUTSCHLAND. And Quattro's watch. Hey, Quattro, show them that watch of yours. It winds itself up, you don't have to wind it, and you can even tell the time at night, without the moon!"

He stood up, and moving rhythmically, as if in a dance hall, he began singing a popular song about the moon, very famous at the time.

". . . Hey, what about opening the window a little? It's hot in here. If the blackout patrols go by, we're armed. And besides, in a storm like this, the Blackshirts don't come out. They're even afraid of rain water."

He seemed to enjoy provoking everyone: the submitting Italians, the occupying Germans, the Fascist renegades, the Flying Fortresses of the Allies, the posters with their requisitions and their death penalties. Currado, Peppe Terzo, Impero, and the complete raft of kids was already on top of him like so many suitors, while Ida followed him with her eyes, keeping to one side, her palpitating mouth almost laughing. The thorns of anxiety could barely scratch her thoughts, promptly blunted by her mysterious faith in Nino's hoodlum invulnerability. She was sure, beneath the level of her consciousness, that he would pass through the war, the Germans' hunting, the guerrilla fighting, and the air raids without being hurt at all, like a heedless little horse galloping through a swarm of flies.

Quattropunte, who seemed more cautious, stopped him in time, as he was trying to force the window open. Nino gave him a sweet and charming smile and hugged him: "This guy," he said, "is our best comrade and my best friend. They call him Quattropunte because his specialty is those nails with four points, that blow up the Germans' tires. His specialty is nails, and mine is aiming. Hey, comrade, tell them how many we've knocked off. For me, the Germans are like ninepins. If I see a bunch standing in a row, I knock them flat!"

"Eh, those Germans, they've got meat by the ton," was the enthusiastic, but ambiguous comment of Tore, Carulì's brother. Nobody bothered to find out if he was referring to human flesh or to those famous quarters of beef. At the same moment, Ida felt such a fierce, sharp ache that for a moment all she could see before her were some blackish spots. And at first she couldn't understand what was happening to her, when through her brain there passed a boy's voice, foreign and drunk, saying to her: "Carina, Carina." It was the voice that, in January of 1941, had said those same words to her, not perceived then, in her unconscious state. But, recorded on an instrument hidden in her brain, suddenly they came back to her, along with the kisses that had then accompanied them, and which now, resting on her face, gave her an impression of sweetness, no less piercing than the ache. Into her conscious mind a question rose: in that *row* that Nino had mentioned, could that blond boy also have been standing? . . . She didn't know that, almost three years ago, he had decomposed in the Mediterranean sea.

Useppe stayed close to his brother, moving wherever he moved, and slipping between people's legs to run after him. Though he was in love with the whole world, now he saw clearly that this was his greatest love. He was able even to forget all the others, Carulì included, and the twins, and the canaries, for this supreme love. Every now and then he raised his head and called him: "Ino! Ino!" with the obvious intention of telling him: "I'm here. Do you remember me or don't you? This is our big night!"

At that point, from the end of the room, where the inner door opened, an old man's voice shouted at the top of its lungs:

"Long Live the Proletarian Revolution!"

It was Giuseppe Secondo, who had not witnessed Nino's arrival at first, since he was momentarily in the latrine. He had come back just when Nino was proclaiming, "We're partisans. Good evening, comrades . . ." and immediately an extraordinary spark had flared up inside him. Still, he had remained watching, discreetly, an ordinary spectator, until he could contain himself no longer. And darting like a spurt of flame, he made his way forward, hat on his head, and introduced himself to the pair:

"Welcome, comrades! We're completely at your disposal. This evening you're doing us a great honor!!" And with a boy's joyous smile, he lowered his voice slightly, to reveal, convinced he was making an important announcement:

"I'm a Comrade, too! . . ."

"Hi," Nino said to him, with serene condescension, not stunned by the news. Then, with great eagerness, Giuseppe Secondo started rummaging in his mattress, and with a triumphant wink, he came and displayed to the visitors a clandestine copy of *L'Unità*.

Recognizing it at once, although illiterate, Quattro smiled with pleasure. "*L'Unità*," he stated gravely, "is the true Italian newspaper!" Nino looked at his friend with a kind of respect: "He," Nino explained to all, eager to do him honor, "is an old fighter in the Revolution. I'm new to it myself. I . . ." he declared with sincere honesty, but not giving a damn, "until last summer, was fighting on the other side."

"Because you were only a kid," Quattro rebutted in his defense. "All kids make mistakes. The right ideas come when you're older, and can use your head. When you're a kid, you're not ripe yet for the struggle."

"Yeah, well, I'm grown up now!" Nino remarked with happy arrogance. And, joking, he attacked Quattro with a playful jab. The other parried, and the two engaged in a mock fight, punching and fending off blows, like real boxers. Giuseppe Secondo stood beside them, to act as referee, with great expertise and with such enthusiasm that his hat slipped to the back of his head, while around them, Peppe Terzo and Impero and Carulina and all the horde jumped and cheered like genuine fans at the ringside.

The game brought Nino's excitement to a climax. And, abruptly, he quit the match and jumped to the top of the pile of desks with the impetus of a barricadiero:

"Long live the Revolution!"

All applauded. Useppe ran after him. The other kids, too, scrambled up the pile.

"Long live the Red Flag!" Giuseppe Secondo, beside himself, shouted in his turn. "We're almost there, comrade partisans! The victory is ours! The farce is over!!"

"Soon we'll revolutionize the whole damn world!" Ninnarieddu proclaimed. "We'll revolutionize the Colosseum and St. Peter's and Manhattan and the Verano cemetery and the Swiss guards and the Jews and the Lateran . . ."

"Everything, everything!" Carulina yelled, from below, jumping up and down.

"And we'll have a regular airline Hollywood–Paris–Moscow! And we'll get drunk on whisky and vodka and truffles and caviar and foreign cigarettes. And we'll ride around in an Alfa Romeo racer and a personal biplane . . ."

"Hurray! Hurray!" the kids applauded, at random, all breathless in the task of climbing up on the dais of the political rally. Only Useppe had already arrived there, and from above, sitting astride a bench, he also shouted: "Hurray!" and slapped his little hands on the wood, to contribute to the noise. Even the twins, forgotten on the ground on some rags, gave out some soprano trills.

". . . and turkey, and ice cream, and foreign cigarettes . . . and we'll have orgies with American girls and we'll screw the Danish blondes, and the enemy will have to jerk off . . .

"Hey! When do we eat around here?!"

Ninnuzzu had jumped to the ground. Useppe flew after him.

"It's ready, all ready," Giuseppe Secondo hastened to reassure him. And the women returned to their supper preparations, with a great commotion of dishes and pots. At that point, in the fourth corner, from behind the curtain of rags, a meowing was heard.

Vivaldi Carlo hadn't shown his face, remaining in his lair the whole time. "Who's in there?" Nino inquired. And unceremoniously he pulled the curtain aside. Rossella hissed and Carlo half sat up on his pallet.

"And who's this?" Nino said, displaying, for the first time since he had come in, a hint of suspicion. "Who're you?" he asked the man in the lair. "Who're you?" Quattropunte repeated, promptly intervening to support his Chief.

"I'm just somebody."

"Somebody who?"

Carlo made a grimace.

"Talk," Nino said to him, proudly assuming a guerrilla fighter's proper attitude during an interrogation. And Quattro, in turn, insisted: "Why won't you talk?" driving his little eyes into Carlo's face like two nails.

"What are you afraid of, anyway?! Don't you trust me?"

"We're not afraid of anybody, including God Almighty! And if you want us to trust you, then unbutton your lip!"

"What the fuck do you want to know?"

"What's your name?"

"His name's Carlo! Carlo!" the kids intervened, in chorus.

"Carlo what?"

"Vivaldi! Vivaldi! Vivaldi!" shouted the women, from the opposite corner.

"Are you one of us?" Nino asked, maintaining his austere and threatening demeanor.

"Are you one of us?" Quattropunte repeated, almost in unison.

Carlo looked at them with a gaze so transparent it seemed amused. "Yes," he answered, with a baby's blush.

"You're a Communist?"

"I'm an anarchist."

"Well, if we want to be fussy," Giuseppe Secondo spoke up, conciliatory, having immediately joined the conversation, "our great Master Carlo Marx was more against the anarchists than for. The red flag is red, and the black flag is black. That's for sure. Still, in certain historic hours, all those on the Left march united, in the struggle against the common enemy."

Nino remained silent for a moment, his brows furrowed, meditating on a philosophical suspicion of his own. After which he smiled, satisfied:

"If you ask me," he decided, "I like anarchy."

Carlo, apparently pleased, smiled briefly (the second smile since the day of his arrival). "And what are you doing in here all by yourself?" Nino confronted him. "Are you against other people?"

Carlo shrugged.

"Come on, comrade anarchist," Giuseppe Secondo urged him, "come eat with us! Tonight I'm host!" he announced with a grandiose, billionaire's tone, proceeding towards the center of the room.

Carlo advanced, hesitant and gawky, without looking at anyone, and Rossella promptly skipped after him. In view of the exceptional evening, the supper was set out communally in the center of the room, on a single table made of packing cases placed side by side. Around them, mattresses, pillows, and sandbags were pulled up on the floor as chairs. Giuseppe Secondo brought to the table some bottles of special wine, which he had been saving to celebrate the victory (that is, the defeat of the Axis). "We start celebrating the victory," he said, "tonight."

Carlo and Nino had taken their places on two mattresses almost opposite each other, seated in the pose of Buddhist monks. Next to Nino sat Quattro, and behind them the kids were fighting, all wanting to sit near them. Useppe had clung tight to his brother, and his eyes, always raised to that face, were like two little beams cast on him to see him in more light. His attention was distracted only every now and then, as he went *mew* . . . *mew* . . . to the cat, offering her some morsel.

The menu of the supper was: spaghetti all'amatriciana, with canned tomatoes and real country sheep cheese; steak alla pizzaiola; bread made with real flour, bought on the black market in Velletri; and various fruit jams. The rain that continued pouring down gave all a feeling of isolation and of safety, like being inside the Ark during the flood.

Nino remained fairly silent, he was so taken up with observing Carlo Vivaldi: no longer suspicious but intent, like kids, when an exotic or somehow problematical character comes to join their gang. At every moment, his eyes returned to the face of that other youth, who, on the contrary, looked at no one.

"You from Milan?" Nino asked him.

"No . . . Bologna . . ."

"Why're you here then?"

"And why are you here?"

"Me? Because the Fascists were beginning to stink, as far as I was concerned. That's why. I got fed up with the stink of black shirts."

"Me, too."

"Were you a Fascist?"

"No."

"You were an anti-Fascist even before?"

"I've always been an anarchist."

"Always! Even when you were a kid?"

"Yes."

"Ace of Hearts, will you show me your pistol?" a voice begged, at that moment, in Nino's ear. It was Peppe Terzo, Carulì's Roman nephew, besieging him from behind, along with his little brother and his cousin Currado; but Nino with a shove sent all three sprawling on the mattress, and warned them fiercely:

"That's enough of that, eh! Clear out!!!"

"Hey, you little bastards . . . leave the gent alone! What makes you so impolite!!" they were warned in turn by Peppe Terzo's mother from her place, with a hen's gentle lament. Meanwhile, the cat Rossella, reappearing from beneath people's feet, was rubbing against Useppe, to ask him for another tidbit; but when Nino sighted her and reached out to give her a passing pat, she ran off in her usual way. Carulina's three nephews, then, rising from their sprawl, began to chase Rossella to release their energies; but with one dart she promptly took refuge beneath Carlo's leg; and from there she hissed at the whole table.

Giuseppe Secondo, who was sitting beside Carlo, suddenly gave him a smug, sly look:

"Comrades," he said, addressing Nino, and Quattro, "this cat belongs to me. And you want to know what her real name is?"

"Rossella!" Carulina cried triumphantly.

"Eh, thanks a lot!" Giuseppe Secondo said, shrugging haughtily. "Rossella! that would be her . . . governmental name, you might say . . . less compromising . . . if you follow me. But her real name, the one I gave her when I took her, is different, and I'm the only one who knows it!"

"Doesn't she know it herself?!" Carulina asked, with curiosity.

"No. Not even her!"

"What might this name be?" the two sisters-in-law asked together.

"Tell us! Tell us!" Carulina urged.

"Well, tonight, among ourselves, maybe I can whisper it," Giuseppe Secondo resolved. And with a conspirator's air, he revealed:

"RUSSIA!"

"Russia! You mean Rossella's real name is Russia?" a sister-in-law asked, not convinced.

"Yes, ma'am. Russia. Yes, indeed."

"Well, Russia may be a nice name, I'm not saying it isn't," Sora Mercedes remarked, "but where does it come in? Russia's a place, a whaddayacallit, a locality? Russia!"

"If you ask me," Granny Dinda stated, "I like Rossella better."

"Well, everybody to his own taste," Giuseppe Secondo replied.

"Russia's Russia, all right," Granny Dinda sustained, "but for a female, Rossella seems nicer to me."

Giuseppe Secondo shrugged, with a sense of slight mortification, but also of definitive, misunderstood superiority.

"Rossella . . ." one of the sisters-in-law remarked at this point, "Scarlet . . . isn't that the name of the actress in that movie . . . what was it called?"

"Gone With the Wind," Carulina cried. "Vivia Leik, in Gone With the Wind!"

"She was the one that got married and then died?"

"No, her little girl died," the Neapolitan sister-in-law clarified, "and he had married that other one . . ."

The little group began discussing the film; but this subject bored Giuseppe Secondo. He gave the two comrades a look, meaning: "That's women for you! . . ." Then he rose from his seat and came to stick his face between Nino and Quattro. He was determined to take any risk, to demonstrate his own faith to the two of them; his comically infantile face glowed with liberating pleasure.

"And do you want to know why," he announced, in a proud voice, "why that little pair" (pointing to the canaries) "are named Peppiniello and Peppiniella?"

"? . . ."

"In honor of comrade Giuseppe Stalin!!"

Quattropunte answered him with nods full of approval and gravity; but Nino, on the contrary, gave him no satisfaction. To tell the truth, though he ate and drank a great deal, Ninnarieddu had become listless and paid little attention to the chatter. Giuseppe Secondo went back to his place. For her part, meanwhile, Sora Mercedes, with the idea of pleasing him (and not even counting the other Giuseppes present) said to him, "You have the same name, too, Sor Giusè . . ." but he, shocked, held out his arms, as if to say: "Good heavens! don't speak of me in the same breath!"

Here the mentioned Peppiniello and Peppiniella, perhaps believing it was daybreak, sang a few notes. Carulina, to heighten the festivities, went and put on the jazz record; and at this, the twins, who had fallen asleep on a corner of the mattress, woke up yelling. Carulina hastened to them and started singing:

"Ninna ò nanna ò
Rusinella and Celesta go to sleep, go . . ."
etc., etc.

But even before the twins, Useppe seemed to be affected by the lullaby, and he soon lowered his eyelids. Ida then took him on her lap, and so she was sitting next to Ninnarieddu.

"How did you manage to find us?! . . ." she repeated to him in a low voice once more.

"Aw, mà, I told you: I went by Remo's. First I went to find the house, and when I saw there was a hole in its place, I asked him!" Nino explained to her with some impatience. And he immediately shut his mouth again, with a grouchy expression, perhaps because his words had once more summoned up his recent grief for Blitz.

"Ninna ò nanna ò
Rusí and Celestina go to sleep, go . . .
ò ò ò ò ò . . ."

Useppe was sleeping. Ida went to put him to bed on her own mattress behind the curtain of sacks. And when she came back, her place beside Nino had been occupied by the usual huddle of Carulì's nephews and they were already closely examining the German boots, studying the laces, the sole, etc. as if admiring a monument.

". . . Were you in the army?" Nino asked.

Vivaldi Carlo raised his eyes, with the wild melancholy of an animal peering from its den, uncertain whether to venture forth and attack. That evening, he was devoting himself more to drinking than to eating, and already the uneasiness that had gripped him at first was dissolving some-what in the wine.

"Yes, he was a soldier! He came on foot all the way from North Italy!" two or three women answered for him, including Carulina, pleased to show she was informed. But at this further unasked interference, Nino emitted an impatient whistle; in his gaze, which met Carlo's, there was no longer the terrorism of the gang leader, but only a stubborn demand for dialogue, undisguised, to the point of innocence.

"You ran away from the army?"

Carlo's upper lip began to throb: "No," he declared honestly, and almost meekly, "I told *them*, here, that I was a soldier, just to tell them something . . . But it wasn't true. I don't belong to any army!" he stated with a bitter tone, whether claiming honor or dishonor, it wasn't clear.

Nino shrugged. "Well, talk, if you feel like talking," he said, indifferently. And with prompt arrogance, he added: "I don't give a shit about your business."

Carlo's face hardened, the eyebrows meeting on his forehead. "Then why do you ask?!" he said, with aggressive modesty.

"And you? What've you got to hide?" Nino rebutted.

"You want to know where I ran away from?"

"Yes! I want to know!"

"I ran away from a convoy of deportees, from a sealed train, heading for the Eastern frontier." It was the truth, but Carlo accompanied it with an odd laugh, as if he were telling a joke.

"Aaaah! thank the Lord! The Turk's told us the truth at last!" Granny Dinda spoke up now, with a little sigh of relief. "Aaaah! Granny! shut up!" Carulì scolded her softly. Carlo looked at the two women, without seeing them, his eyes inexpressive.

"They caught you in a round-up?" Ninnarieddu asked further.

Vivaldi Carlo shook his head. "I . . ." he mumbled, "I was in the underground . . . I was distributing political propaganda! Somebody informed . . . they reported me to German headquarters." Here he came out with another, almost obscene laugh, which corrupted his features like an infection. At his awkward movement, Rossella, from below his leg, made her special cry of whining protest, which went: "Mememiè! Mememiè!" And almost absurdly embarrassed at having disturbed the cat, he straightened up, looking around with his dreamy gaze, like an orphan's. But at that point, with sudden brutality, and addressing Nino exclusively, he said: "Do you know what they're like? The bunker security cells? They're known as the *antechamber of death?*"

"I've got an idea!" Nino had shifted position, stretching his feet on the table, putting his shoulders against the knees of his friend Quattro, who was glad to act as his backrest. "Say, comrade," he said to Carlo, after crumpling between his fingers his own empty pack of Popolari, throwing it away, "gimme a cigarette." He made a show of nonchalance, acting like an American gangster, hardened by every sort of experience. Carlo threw him a cigarette across the table. And at the same time, with a forced, almost evasive little smile, he informed him: "Me, I was in one." "I was there . . ." "I was there . . ." he repeated several times, isolating himself in an abstract stare, in a kind of absurd and disgusting vision. And for the moment, assuming a monotonous, scientific speech (only interjecting a few words of dialect, *lus* for *luce*, light, or *dona* for *donna*, woman, or such things, along with an occasional grimace), he entered into a description of that special kind of cell.

According to his description, these were single storerooms, like air-raid bunkers, made by pouring cement over a domed armature, employed at present by the Germans in Northern Italy because they could be built rapidly and were simple and practical. The interior, measuring approximately 6 feet by 3 feet 6 inches with a height of 4 feet 2 inches, was just big enough for a plank-bunk, and a man was unable to stand erect. In the ceiling there was set a light bulb of perhaps three hundred watts, which remained burning day and night and pierced even closed eyes like a blowtorch (here Vivaldi Carlo instinctly covered his eyes with his hand). And the only opening to the outside, about halfway up the barred door, was a little peep-hole or air vent, hardly wider than a rifle's barrel. He pressed his lips to it constantly, crouched on the plank on all fours, sucking that breath of air through the little hole. In that courtyard of the SS Headquarters (a kind of garage on the city's outskirts) they had built about fifteen of those bunkers, one next to another, with an adjacent crematorium.

As a rule, none of the bunkers remained empty for long. You were shut up in them, usually, after the interrogation, while waiting to be sent elsewhere. At night especially, voices emerged from them; often voices that were no longer reasoning, but rather senseless screams of matter. One man, still conscious, repeated that he had been in there for thirty-five days; he did nothing but ask for water, but nobody gave him any. Sometimes, when he asked for water, in reply he saw the barrel of a gun thrust through the vent. In the next bunker on the left, there was a *dona*, a woman, who during the day seemed dumb, but every night she fell into a screaming lunacy, and she even called to the SS guards, addressing them as *my sons*. But the moment the footsteps of the sentry on patrol approached, suddenly all voices were silent.

In fact, at every creak of a lock being opened, a sound of shots there in the courtyard followed a little later. The bunkers had got that name, *antechambers of death*, because, at night in particular, you left them only to be executed in that same courtyard, with a shot at the back of the neck. There was never any knowing who would be next, nor the reasons for the daily choices and exceptions. At every shot, the SS men's dogs howled.

Here, Vivaldi Carlo, as if waking from his long vision, started laughing again, like a drunk who, to act tough and damned, publicly confesses some shameful personal act:

"I was in there for seventy-two hours," he narrated, not directing his words at anyone. "I counted them, by the churchbells. Seventy-two. I counted them. Three nights. In three nights, ten shots. I counted them."

At the table, all remained respectfully silent; however, the only ones listening with real involvement were Nino and Quattro. The Thousand, and with them even Giuseppe Secondo, exchanged dejected glances, dismayed at the grim subject which was spoiling their feast; while the kids, and Ida no less than they, were already dropping with sleep.

". . . in there, all you do is count . . . you spend the days counting . . . any kind of nonsense . . . to keep from thinking . . . You count . . . the important thing is to concentrate on some stupid exercise . . . lists . . . weights and measures . . . the laundry list . . ."

(At this phrase, Sora Mercedes nudged Carulina; and Carulina, though considerably upset by the subject, barely managed to stifle a compulsive hilarity.)

". . . subtraction, addition, fractions . . . numbers! If you start thinking of your mother, your father, your sister, your girl . . . then start figuring out right away what their age is in years, months, days, hours . . . Like a machine, without thinking . . . Seventy-two hours . . . three nights, ten shots . . . One shot apiece, and that's that . . . One two three four . . . and ten . . . They said they were partisans . . . most of them . . . bandits . . . that was the charge . . ."

"What? You were a partisan, too?" Nino asked, putting his feet on the floor, with a sudden interest that made him actually glow.

"Not me! I told you! I was *not* a soldier!" the other boy protested, almost becoming angry. "I . . . I worked in the city . . . (but I won't tell you what city) . . . Posters . . . pamphlets . . . propaganda . . . Political prisoner . . . that's why they sent me to the train! But I didn't know, not the sentence . . . Early in the morning, when they came to take me out of the cell, my only thought was: *This is it! Number eleven!* I already felt the thud in my brain . . . *March . . . march . . .* shit. Keep marching . . . ah, *màma mia* . . . the world's disgusting."

"The world STINKS!! Are you just finding that out?" Ninnarieddu confirmed, triumphantly. "Eh, I caught on to that a long time ago! It's lousy, and it STINKS! But all the same," he added, having second thoughts, and beginning to move his feet, "for me . . . this stink . . . gets me excited! Some women, you know? they stink like . . . like what? . . . like women! And that stink of women gives you a hard-on . . . For me," he proclaimed, "all the stink of life gives me a hard-on!!"

At that, his feet, on their own, had started moving to the jazz rhythm of a moment earlier. "Then what? How did you get away?!" he asked, with curiosity, as he danced.

"How did I do it? I did it . . . I jumped down . . . at a stop . . . Villach . . . no, before. I don't know where . . . There were a couple of dead bodies to unload: an old guy . . . and an old woman . . . No! I don't want to talk about it any more! That's enough!!" And here Vivaldi Carlo frowned, with a nauseated but oddly helpless and naked expression, like a capricious child who has finally spilled his whole story and says, exhausted: now leave me alone.

"Bravo. We won't talk any more about it. Have a drink!" Sora Mercedes urged him. "Anyway, it'll all be over soon. In a little while, thank God, the liberators will be here!"

"When are they going to come, then, these Messiahs? . . ." Carulina's other grandmother sighed at this point, in a whining little voice. Unlike Granny Dinda, she was usually quiet. "They're coming, Granny, they're coming. It's a matter of hours!! Let's drink to it!" was the general chorus from The Thousand. And Carulina, who, in spite of her emotion, still continued to harbor her treacherous hilarity, seized the occasion to turn it loose, coming out with a laugh that sounded like a horn's honking. Carlo then raised his eyes towards her, and gave her a sweet, childlike smile.

His face seemed drained but relaxed, in convalescence after a raving illness. There was no longer any sign of that corrupt expression which had disfigured it until a moment before. And the very excitement of the wine, burning in his eyes, had now been transformed by the putrid fire of a moment earlier into a tremendous radiance, shy and ingenuous. He was crouching in an uncomfortable position, with one leg half-extended and the other raised, to leave room for Rossella, and he seemed a messenger from some defeated and scattered tribe, sent perhaps also to ask for aid.

Following the general example, he poured himself more wine, but with a clumsy movement, so that he spilled some over the edge of the glass. "That brings good luck! Good luck!" all shouted then, "spilled wine means good luck!" and they fought to dip their fingers in that wine, to wet the skin behind their ears with it. Even those who hadn't moved from their places were included in this little baptism, especially by the hand of Carulì, who didn't forget anyone: not even Useppe, immersed in sleep behind his curtain, or the other kids sleeping about the room, or the half-dozing Ida, who reacted to the tickle with a faint unconscious laugh. The only one excluded was Vivaldi Carlo himself; but in the end, overcoming her awe, Carulina took care of him, too. "Thank you . . . thank you!" he kept repeating. "Thank you!" And not knowing how to respond to this profusion of thanks, embarrassed by their excess, she remained there, swaying on her legs, in a kind of courtly ballet.

"A toast to the liberators! A toast to our comrade partisans!" Giuseppe Secondo shouted. And after having clinked glasses with this one and that, he came over to Carlo. "Cheer up, comrade!" he encouraged him, toasting, "it's only a few more months now. In a little while, we'll break through in the North too. And by spring at the latest you'll see your home again!"

Vivaldi Carlo responded with an uncertain smile, which expressed a kind of gratitude, without wanting to give way to exaggerated hope.

Examining him, Giuseppe Secondo felt an immediate and sociable need to drag him too, at once, into the general festivity. "By the way, comrade," he said to him then, expansively, "I meant to ask you a while ago: instead of staying here, with this anger that's rotting your insides, why don't you go and join in the armed struggle, along with our partisan comrades? You're a smart boy, and a brave one, too!"

Perhaps Vivaldi Carlo had been expecting just such a question! In fact, even before the old man could put it into words, his features had become taut in an urgent, aware determination which dispelled the wine's fog. He frowned sternly, and, with a glum bitterness, declared:

"I CAN'T."

"Why can't you?" exclaimed Nino, who had meanwhile come around to that side of the table.

Vivaldi Carlo blushed, as if he were about to confess something illicit:

"Because," he stated, "I can't kill anyone."

"You can't kill? What do you mean? Not even the Germans?! Why not? Is it some kind of vow you made in church?!"

The interrogated boy shrugged. "Me?" he declared with an almost contemptuous smile. "I'm an atheist!" Then he trained his eyes on Nino's face, and speaking slowly and forcefully, despite his lips being sticky from drink, he explained, in a tone of insurrection:

"My—ideals—REJECT—violence. All evil is derived from violence!"

"Then what kind of anarchist does that make you?"

"True anarchism cannot admit violence. The anarchist ideal is the negation of power. And power and violence are the same thing . . ."

"But without violence how can you manage to have an Anarchist Government?"

"Anarchism rejects Government . . . And if the means has to be violence, then it's no good. We don't pay the price. In this case, Anarchism isn't achieved."

"Then, if it isn't going to get done, I don't like it. I like things that get done."

"It depends on what you mean by ACTION," Vivaldi Carlo rebutted, crossly, in a low voice. Then, expanding again, with intent, persuasive ardor, he declared: "If the price is betraying the ideal, then the end has failed before it begins! The ideal . . . the idea isn't a past or a future . . . it's the present in action . . . And physical violence kills it at the roots . . . Violence is the worst thing of all."

This resolute defense of his ideals seemed to have heartened him, but made him shy, at the same time. As if ashamed of his eyes' natural fervor, he lowered them, so you could see only those lashes, too long and thick, recalling his still recent boyhood. "So then," Ninnuzzu persecuted him still, "tomorrow if you bump into that German who stuck you into the bunker or the other one who loaded you onto the freight train, what'll you do? Let them live?!"

"Yes . . . " Vivaldi Carlo said, while his upper lip curled in a grimace that again corrupted his features, like a passing shudder. And at the same time, in Nino's eyes there reappeared that new, blind flash, like a photographer's bulb, which had already amazed Ida at the beginning of the evening.

"*Non-violent anarchists*," Giuseppe Secondo decreed meanwhile, puzzled, "as an idea, is something to be taken into consideration . . . But, when you need violence, you need it! Without violence, the socialist revolution won't be achieved."

"I like the revolution!" Nino exclaimed. "I don't believe in anarchy without violence! And you know what I say? YOU KNOW? That the Communists, and not the anarchists, will bring on the real anarchy!"

"The real liberty is the red flag," Quattro approved, with contented eyes.

"In Communism, everybody'll be comrades!" Nino went on, at full tilt, carried away. "There won't be any more officers, or professors, or titles, or barons or kings or queens . . . and no Führers or Duces!"

"And Comrade Stalin, what about him?" . . . Giuseppe Secondo inquired, concerned.

"Him! He's different!" Nino decided firmly. "He's above discussion!" And in his voice, beyond his peremptory rhetoric, there was a certain familiar and intimate note, as if they were talking about an old relative who had held him, as a little boy, on his lap and had let him play with his moustache.

"Nobody touches him!" he further declared, and this time the earlier note was accompanied by another, fiercer: to assert if necessary to all present that this exclusive privilege was due Stalin, not only for his own well-known personal merits, but also, and in a special way, because of the particular protection of Ace of Hearts.

At that moment, emerging from beneath Vivaldi Carlo's leg, Rossella made a daring, sudden leap and landed on his stomach. And looking him square in the face, in a polite but also demanding fashion, she addressed him directly with the sentence: "Nian nian nian nian?!" which, in translation, would mean: "Don't you think it's time to go to bed?!"

This brief cattish action distracted Nino's interest from the matters under discussion, mentally transporting him to the field of cats in general, a particularly humorous breed in his opinion (though, obviously, less important than dogs). At this fleeting notion, some futile and laughing sparkles could be seen to play, briefly, in his eyes. Then, all of a sudden, remembering his imminent rising at dawn, he emitted an enormous yawn.

It was the signal for retiring. Vivaldi Carlo was the first to stand, swaying a bit at the knees. "*Màma mia*, it's all gone to my legs, that wine," he grumbled, following Rossella towards their corner. Giuseppe Secondo arranged to bed down on the floor, in a blanket, ceding his mattress to the guests. And Nino accepted the offer in all simplicity and without thanks, as his logical right. Following a habit acquired as guerrilla fighters, he and Quattropunte, as they stretched out side by side on the single mattress, rejected any idea of undressing, removing only their boots. On the floor, near their heads, they placed their belts with pistols, and the flashlight. And at the initiative of Giuseppe Secondo, who thoughtfully set his alarm clock for them, they asserted that when necessary they could also do without it, because Quattropunte had a precision alarm inside his brain.

But long before the sound of the alarm clock, perhaps about four o'clock, an urgent shuffle of bare feet, after a hazardous journey in the semidarkness, arrived at Nino's pillow. And a little voice, faint but intrepid and determined, began repeating into his ear, almost into the pavilion: "Oh, oh! Ino! Ino!! oh!"

A first, instantaneous effect on Nino was a certain shift in the plot of his dream. The scene is taking place in a movie theater where he, who is seated in the orchestra seats with the audience, is also directly engaged in the action on the screen, riding over a prairie out West, among other horses in a wild chase. At present his horse begs him to scratch his right ear, where there's an itching sensation. But, as he scratches the horse's ear, he realizes he isn't on an animal's withers, but is hoisted astride a Stuka in flight; and the itching sensation is inside his own ear, caused by an urgent telephone call from America . . .

"Pass it to the squadron leader." Nino rolls over on one side and continues zooming in the Stuka at an altitude of twenty thousand feet, to the engine's tranquil hum. But that American telephone, meanwhile, continues teasing him with its calls, also tugging occasionally at his hair, and putting a paw on his arm . . .

At this point (thanks to a new and special nervous mechanism which acted as a signal on his bandit nights) Nino stirred and raised his head, still not waking up entirely; and instinctively he grabbed his flashlight. In a brief glow, he perceived the clear blue of a pair of eyes blinking towards him, surprised by the light, but also full of a festive complicity as if it were Christmas Eve; and then, immediately reassured, he flung himself down again to sleep.

"Who is it?!" Quattro's sleepy voice grumbled beside him in alarm.

"Nobody."

"Ino . . . Ino . . . it's me!"

Before he started snoring again, Nino gave an answering grumble of understanding, which could have corresponded to an *aw right* or *okay*, as it could have meant the opposite, or nothing at all. His transitory half-wakefulness had barely been infiltrated by the comical and curious impression of an almost imperceptible presence, the size of a gnome, which he recognized as some kind of entertainment, even if its identity was confused. Perhaps a fantastic animal, more lively and pretty than the other animals which notoriously sought his vicinity, and somehow belonged to him. And it made him laugh, jumping around him to greet him from the four cardinal points of the universe. And it wouldn't go away, and at present was walking on top of him.

And, truly, his brother Useppe, after pondering for a moment beside the mattress, had resolutely climbed onto it and was advancing there, between Nino's knee and Quattro's leg. Given his dimensions, he could easily settle into that minimum available passage. He let out a glorious little laugh, and fell asleep.

And so, for the rest of that great night, Useppe slept naked between the two armed warriors.

When, on rising promptly at dawn, they discovered that uninvited guest in the bed, they were delighted and surprised, as if by a gag in a comic film. Immediately Quattropunte thought of returning him to his mother, and so while Ace of Hearts, first of all, absented himself in the little room on the landing, his friend fulfilled the assignment of carrying the visitor to his proper address, holding him in his arms with the utmost deference. Shyly then, at the moment he passed the curtain, he asked: "May I come in?" out of respect for the Signora, though she, stirred by the sound of the alarm, was already peering out, a blanket around her shoulders, against a just-lighted candle's glow, which filtered through the holes in the sacks.

"Excuse me, Signora, here's the kid," Quattro murmured, with no further explanation, settling his burden on the bed with a wet-nurse's delicacy. Despite this delicacy, however, Useppe's eyes were already half-open and dazed. And, seeing his brother appear, now ready to leave, he opened them wide.

Quattro went off, to take his turn in the little room. And Nino, who disliked candles, calling them dead people's lights, blew out the flame, putting his own glowing flashlight in its place on the ground. Then he asked Ida if she could give him a little money, at least for tobacco, since he didn't have a lira. And when Ida, from her familiar purse, had collected a few ten-lire notes for him, he lingered a bit to converse with her, as if to give her a just and deserved recompense.

The object of the conversation was Vivaldi Carlo, presently sleeping, whom Nino indicated without naming him, pointing an elbow towards his curtain. In a low voice, Nino revealed to his mother that, after some thought, he had decided that character wasn't really from Bologna. "I know the Bolognese accent. I had a Bolognese girl friend, who always said sh . . . sh . . . for s . . . s . . . and he doesn't say sh . . ." If anything, he might come from Friuli . . . or Milan . . . In short, Ninnuzzu's opinion was that he came from the North, all right. That was true. But Bologna was a lie. Similarly, it was true he was an anarchist. However, beyond the anarchism, Nino sensed some other matter he had kept hidden. Maybe even the name Carlo Vivaldi was a fake. "I've thought about it, and you know what I say, mà? . . . That guy, if you ask me, might even be a . . ." Here Nino seemed even on the point of making Ida his secret accomplice. But, thinking it over, he must have preferred the possibility of a future alliance with (the so-called) Vivaldi Carlo himself. And he left his remark unfinished.

On her side, Ida had been on the point of whispering to him: "He's an anarchist, like your grandfather . . ." but her shyness restrained her.

Ever since the previous evening, the news that Vivaldi Carlo was an anarchist, and hence of the same persuasion as her father, had immediately stirred her emotions. And at supper, afterwards (even though she was half dead with sleepiness), hearing him tell his adventures, she had said to herself, again recalling her father's sorrows, that the anarchists evidently encountered little sympathy in this world. Moreover, his Northern accent, here and there, reminded her of her mother Nora . . . And consequently she felt an instinctive liking for Vivaldi Carlo, more than for all the other occupants of the vast room, as if a tie of solidarity and kinship united her to that moody dark-haired boy. But in the face of Nino's reticence, she didn't insist on knowing any more.

Dawn was breaking outside, but the room, protected by its masked windows, lay stagnant in the night's darkness. And all the others inside continued sleeping, undisturbed by the alarm's early signal, which didn't concern them. Only in Giuseppe Secondo's direction, already at the clock's first sound, a certain busy movement could be noticed. And the ghostly little flame of some makeshift wick could be seen flickering (in fact, at that hour, there was no electricity; and along with candles, all ordinary sources of illumination or fuel were becoming scarcer every day).

Quattro had reappeared, and Nino collected his flashlight from the ground, while Ida lay back on the bed, deciding not to relight her candle stub. At this point, Useppe, seeing his brother heading for the exit, climbed urgently to the edge of the mattress and began dressing with furious haste.

In a few moments he had reached the outside doorway, from which the two visitors were already moving off. He was all ready, in his shorts, jersey, bound shoes, even his rainproof cloak over his arm: as if it were understood that he was leaving too. For a few more moments, he stood still and stared after the couple, now at a distance of perhaps ten yards from the threshold, on their way along the grubby little field beyond the ditch. Then, saying nothing, he started running after them.

From inside, meanwhile, Giuseppe Secondo arrived in great haste, completely dressed as usual, with his jacket buttoned up and a hat on his head. "Just a minute!" he cried in agitation, running towards the two, and stopping them halfway along the path: "Are you going to leave without having your coffee?!

"I was fixing you some coffee, REAL coffee!" he explained, as if promising a paradisiacal delight. And, in reality, the offer of true coffee, in those days, was no small matter. However, after exchanging a look of consultation, the two answered that there was no more time. A friend was waiting for them, at an agreed spot, to go back with them to the base. They had to hurry, Ninnuzzu explained with some regret.

"I won't insist then. But I have to talk to you, right here and now, about a secret matter. It'll only take half a minute, but it's urgent!" And Giuseppe Secondo feverishly drew Ninnuzzu aside, though still addressing his discourse to Quattro as well. "Listen, comrades," he said, gesticulating to them both, "I won't give you a lot of chat. I just want to say this: MY PLACE IS WITH YOU! I was telling myself as much yesterday evening, and then last night I made my decision! What am I staying here for? My decision is to go right to the heart of the struggle! I want to come with you, to join the ranks!!"

Though in a low and hasty voice, he had spoken with some solemnity; and in his eyes you could read the virtual certainty that the comrades would applaud the offer. But Nino, making no comment, gave him a look which said clearly: "You want to be a partisan? You, you little old crow?" glancing, at the same time, at Quattro with a kind of half-amused wink. Quattro (who, while listening, kept discreetly at a slight distance), on the contrary, didn't bat an eye; he was serious, gripped by the importance of the subject.

"Don't judge by appearances! I'm as tough as an ox. My arm is okay and in good working order now!" With this, Giuseppe Secondo, in a prompt athletic display, began to swing his right arm, injured in the July bombing. "And I know all about military science," he went on commending himself, in the face of Nino's skepticism, "I was in the First World War. I haven't been cutting statues all my life." Then he quickly informed them, with extreme urgency: "I also have a little liquid capital set aside, and I would be honored to place everything I have at the service of the Cause!"

This final piece of information must have seemed more persuasive and reliable to Nino. He considered Giuseppe Secondo with an air of greater compliance; and then (after interrogating Quattropunte with a glance, to be sure of his approval), he cut things short, saying briskly:

"Do you know Remo, by any chance, the one who has the tavern in Via degli Equi?"

"Of course! He's a comrade!" Giuseppe Secondo assured him, his heart pounding with joy.

"Well, talk to him; use our names. He'll give you all the instructions."

"Thanks, comrade! I'll be seeing you soon then! Very soon!!!" Giuseppe Secondo burst out, radiant with jubilation and impatience. Then, like someone waving a triumphant banner, as a way of saying au revoir, he concluded: "For our ideal, just existing isn't enough. The time's come to live!!"

He saluted them with clenched fist. Quattropunte responded with the same salute, an expression of profound responsibility on his face. But

Ninnuzzu, hurried and distracted, was now turning his back to go on. Then he noticed Useppe, who had already run and overtaken him, and dragging the red-lined raincloak on the ground, was now raising his eyes towards him, like birds when they drink.

"Ah, Usè," Nino said, "ciao! . . . Something you wanted to tell me?" he added, after a glance. "Give me a little kiss?" And the little kiss was given; but Useppe, seeing his brother move away, began chasing after him again.

The dawn was wet and dark: the first drops of rain were falling. Hearing Useppe's footsteps after him, Ninnarieddu turned.

"Go back," he said, "it's starting to rain . . ." And he stood still for a moment, two paces away, to wave goodbye to him. Hesitant, after stopping too, Useppe dropped his raincloak on the ground, to free his hand and return the farewell. But, hanging from his limp arm, his little fist opened and closed ever so weakly, cross and reluctant.

"Useppeeeee!" Ida's voice could be heard calling from inside.

"Well, Usé? Eh? What're you doing here? Can't you see it's raining?" Seeing his brother paralyzed and mute in the middle of the path, Nino made a carefree little dash backwards, for a final kiss.

"What're you doing? Eh? You want to come with us?" he asked, joking.

Useppe looked at him without answering. Again Ida's voice could be heard from inside. Suddenly Ninnuzzu's eyes laughed, raised to the leaden sky, as if they reflected clear weather.

"Usè," he began, bending over his brother, "listen to me now. Today I can't take you with us. You see how lousy the weather is?" . . .

. . . "Usepeeee!"

. . . "But I want to ask you something," Nino continued, looking around and whispering into his brother's ear, as if it were all a plot, "mamma still goes out, doesn't she? Early every morning?"

"Ess."

"Well, then, listen to me. Will you believe me if I give you my word of honor?"

"Ess."

"Okay, don't say a word to mamma or to anybody else. And I give you my word of honor that one of these mornings, as soon as the weather's nice, when mamma's gone out, I'll come and get you, with a car some friends of mine have, and I'll take you to see the partisans' camp. Then, in plenty of time, before mamma gets home, we'll bring you back here."

7 After that conversation, there wasn't a day that Useppe didn't run to peer at the sky the moment he was awake, sticking his head out of the door, from time to time, also during the course of the morning, occasionally lingering a fairly long time, seated on the outside step, waiting. But several days went by, days of good weather too, before Nino kept his promise. And in the meanwhile, the passage of that October was marked by other events of significance for the inhabitants of the big room.

First of all, there was the departure of Giuseppe Secondo for the guerrilla battlefields. One Sunday morning (only a very few days after the famous night of the banquet) he was seen returning, joyous and impatient, from one of his expeditions into the city. For the first time since they had known him, he no longer wore his hat on his head. He crossed the room in one gust, paying only hasty, distracted attention to those present and their talk. In two minutes he had collected a little emergency bundle, his essential baggage; then he said goodbye to all, adding that, in any case, he would be coming back to the room, to pick up some other objects belonging to him which he might need in the future. But if by chance, he added, he were to lose his life in the meantime, he declared here and now, before witnesses, that he left to Signora Ida Mancuso and her little boy, here present, all his personal property which, after the event, might be still found in the room, including the two canaries and the cat. While he was on the subject, he didn't forget to hand a small sum to Carulì, so that, in his absence, she could somehow take care of the two birds. As for Rossella, he said, she could perfectly well manage on her own, with garbage and mice.

At that hour, in fact, Rossella was off hunting. For various reasons, surely including her pregnancy (it was already in its last stages, though still unsuspected and invisible), with the coming of autumn she had developed a perpetual and ferocious hunger, and she had also become a thief: so all provisions had to be protected against her claws. Every time Carlo went out, she too, disdaining all other company, went off on her own, into the open, on her private hunting parties. And so she wasn't there to say good-bye to her owner, who, for that matter, didn't bother to look for her or ask after her. It was clear that all these family matters were trivia for Giuseppe Secondo, in the face of the happy, thrilling adventure towards which he was rushing today.

Before leaving, he took Ida aside and, in confidence, whispered two things to her. One: for any sort of message to her son Ace of Hearts, or for any news of the same, she could always rely completely on her old acquaintance, Remo, the tavernkeeper. And two: starting today, he himself, Giuseppe Secondo and Cucchiarelli, had as a partisan a new and single name:

Moscow, his own choice. Of these two pieces of information (the old man explained to Ida), she could, without hesitation, transmit the second to trusted mutual friends; whereas she was to be the only one to know the first, until the day of victory, when all the red flags would be unfurled in the free air. Having said this, the partisan Moscow gave Ida a wink of political complicity, then flew out of the room.

Flew is the word. In fact, Giuseppe Secondo was in such an aerial mood today that he had assumed an ecstatic tone, like a schoolboy on vacation, even as he hypothesized, for himself, the mortal possibility. And Ida, who since that first day had privately continued calling him *the Madman*, saw her personal opinion confirmed. When he had gone, however, she was left with a feeling of sadness, as if this goodbye today were the Madman's last farewell, and they would never see each other again. And during the rest of the day, the sight of the rolled mattress among Giuseppe Secondo's other piled-up possessions clutched at her heart, despite her personal interest as his heiress: so she avoided looking towards that abandoned corner.

Rossella, on the other hand, when she came home around dinnertime, seemed not even to notice her owner's absence, though he was usually there at that hour, busy over his stove and his cans of squid in tomato sauce or his boiled beans. Skittishly avoiding all other human contact, she ran at once, head low and tail high, towards Carlo Vivaldi's curtain, and there she settled herself as usual against him on the pallet, stretched full length for the comfort of her pregnant little belly. Nor did she give any sign, even in the days that followed, of remembering that other man, who, for better or worse, had taken her in from the street as a kitten, giving her a home and a name.

That week, the partisan Moscow, as he had already announced and contrary to Ida's sad foreboding, turned up a couple of times. He came to collect some objects that might be useful *up there*—a blanket for example, or provisions—and he seized the occasion to lock himself in the latrine and have a wash, since *up there*, he said, there was no water for washing, though, to make up for it, there was a great quantity of good Castelli wine. And he explained that he happened to be here, passing by on his rounds, because his special job with the comrades was that of messenger: "from the outpost to downtown, and back again."

Happiness was bursting from his every wrinkle and pore, and he was bearing secret, exciting news: Ninnuzzu and Quattro and other comrades were performing amazing feats and were aglow with epoch-making valor and health. And certain girls of the Castelli were already sewing elegant partisan uniforms for them to wear in the Liberation parade: an ultramarine blue, with a red star on their beret. And the English pilots, flying over the countryside, greeted them from their planes, and two English prisoners, who had been guests of Ninnuzzu and Co. for a night and a day, had predicted the liberation of Rome by the end of the month at the latest (there was a rumor they were waiting for the fateful date of 28 October, the Fascist anniversary). Having given this news, the little herald waved a general goodbye to all, and was off again like an elf.

Now that even Giuseppe Secondo (previously rather skeptical on the subject) had announced the liberation was near, The Thousand actually began to collect their luggage, to be ready to set off for Naples as soon as the Allies entered Rome. It was agreed that Carlo Vivaldi would take the same route; but after the interlude of the banquet, Carlo had withdrawn again into his isolation, if anything more sullen and suspicious than before, seeming ashamed of his brief lapse. After hearing his tales, the women among The Thousand, in their chatter, had, among other things, ventured the supposition that he might be a Jew. But this conjecture circulated in the big room with great caution, and in low voices, in everyone's instinctive solidarity with the hunted young man. It seemed as if such a thing, even whispered, might single him out, assisting the hated German police.

One Sunday, Carulì's brother Tore, returning from some of his dealings in the city, pointed out to Ida in the newspaper, *Il Messaggero*, the news that schools would reopen on November 8th. Among all The Thousand, Tore was the least illiterate, and he liked to display his culture by commenting on items in the papers, especially the sports page. That Sunday, among his other comments, he remarked that in the *Messaggero* there was no trace of a piece of news that was, however, circulating inside Rome, and that had even been broadcast, they said, by Radio Bari: yesterday, Saturday (October 16th) the Germans had rounded up all the Jews of Rome at dawn, house by house, and loaded them into trucks for an unknown destination. The Ghetto had been totally stripped of all its Jewish flesh, and only its skeleton was left; but also in the other sections and neighborhoods, all of Rome's Jews—individuals and families—had been rooted out by some SS who had come on purpose, a special company, supplied with an exact list. They had taken them all: not only the young and the healthy, but also the old, the seriously ill, even pregnant women, even babes in arms. It was said they were all being taken off to be burned alive in big ovens; but this, according to Tore, was maybe an exaggeration.

At that moment, the gramophone was playing a dance tune, and the kids were all jumping around: so the comments on this news were lost in the uproar. And in the course of that same Sunday, the Jews' story was actually forgotten among The Thousand, in the flow of news that arrived every day by direct or oblique routes, collected in the city or brought by acquaintances of listeners to Radio Bari or Radio London. After their journey, however brief, these items usually reached the big room distorted, or expanded, or confused. And Ida had learned to protect herself by ignoring them all, treating them like folk tales; but not this last piece of news, no, because she had been expecting it for some time, even without admitting it to herself. From the moment she heard it, fear never stopped thrashing her, like a spiked scourge, until every hair on her head ached at the root. She didn't dare ask Tore for further clarification, impossible at any rate; nor did she know to whom to turn, to find out if halfbreeds were also written down in the list of the *guilty* (this was the very term she used in her thoughts). And in bed, with the darkness, her terror increased. When curfew struck, she heard Carlo Vivaldi return—in that period he wandered around the city more than ever—and she was almost tempted to get up and ask him. But she heard him cough; and she thought she could sense, in that cough, something terrible and rejecting. It's true that some (also Nino?) murmured that he might be a Jew; but others (given, to tell the truth, scant credence) also insinuated that he was perhaps a Nazi-Fascist spy. She suspected that, merely hearing her utter the word *Jews*, he, like the others, would immediately see her secret written all over her face, and tomorrow might report her to the Gestapo.

She had gone to bed with her clothes on, and she had left Useppe dressed, too; and she hadn't even taken her sleeping pill, so that the Germans, if they came for her in the night, wouldn't catch her unprepared. She held tight to Useppe, having decided that, the moment she heard the soldiers' unmistakable tread outside and their knocking on the door, she would try to escape through the fields, dropping from the roof with her baby in her arms; and if pursued, she would run and run all the way to the marsh, to drown herself there, along with him. The terrors brooded over for years, erupting in the immediate fear of this night, grew in her to a raving fantasy, without release. She thought of going out into the streets at random, with the sleeping Useppe in her arms, heedless of the curfew, since night-wanderers, when terrestrial horror reaches a certain degree, become invisible . . . Or else of running towards the mountains of the Castelli, hunting for the Madman, to plead with him to hide Useppe and herself in the partisans' lair . . . But most of all she was soothed by the thought of going off with Useppe into the Ghetto, to sleep in one of the empty apartments. Again, as in the past, her contradictory fears finally followed a mysterious comet, that invited her in the direction of the Jews: promising her, there in the distance, a maternal stable, warm with animals' breath, and with their big eyes, not judging, but only pitying. Even these poor Jews from all of Rome, loaded into trucks by the Germans, tonight hailed her like Blessed Spirits who, unknown to themselves and even to the Germans, were going off, through a splendid deceit, towards an Oriental realm where all are children, without consciousness or memory . . .

> "Do not look at my black skin,
> for the sun darkened me,
> my beloved is white and ruddy,
> his curls are golden.
> There, my beloved's voice knocks:
> open to me, my dear, my dove.
> I rose to open but I could not find him,
> I sought him and could not find him.
> The watchmen searching the city found me:
> have you seen my soul's beloved?
> I have not tended my own vineyard
> and he took me into the house
> and his banners of love were over me!
> I sought him in the streets and squares and did not find him
> I called him and had no answer.
> Before the day ends and the night,
> return my stag, my beloved kid.
> Oh if you were my brother
> who sucked my mother's breasts!
> then on meeting you, I could kiss you
> and no one would scorn me.
> In his body I rested
> and he savored me with his lips and his teeth,
> come, my brother, let us see if the vine has blossomed.
> I beseech you, should you find my beloved
> tell him I am sick with love . . ."

Where had she learned these verses? In school perhaps, as a little girl? She had never recalled knowing them, and now, in her confused wakefulness, it seemed to her that her own voice, as a child, was reciting them in a languid tone, affected and tragic.

Around four she dozed off. The usual dream returned to her, the one that had visited her often, with some variants, since the previous summer: about her father, sheltering her under his cloak. This time, in the cloak's shelter, she wasn't alone. Useppe was there too, all naked (even smaller than in real life), and Alfio her husband, also naked and stout. And she herself was naked, but it didn't embarrass her, for all her being old as she was now, and decrepit. The streets of Cosenza became confused with those of Naples, and of Rome, and of who knows what other metropolises, as usual in dreams. It was pouring rain, but her father had a large, broad-brimmed hat on his head, and Useppe amused himself by kicking his feet in the puddles.

In the dream it was pouring, but instead, when she woke, the morning was sunny. Ida got up hastily, knowing that on this Monday morning she had planned to buy Useppe a pair of new shoes (with the points of her clothing-ration card), since the homemade bound sandals had become unserviceable, especially as winter was approaching. She and Useppe were quickly ready, having slept in their clothes. At first, there had flashed into Ida's brain the bizarre notion of going, for her purchase, to a certain little cobbler in the Ghetto . . . But she had second thoughts in time, remembering the Ghetto had been emptied; only its skeleton remained, as Salvatore had said. And then she decided on a shoeshop in the Tiburtino quarter (which she had already patronized when she lived in that area) where she counted on still finding remainders of the very smallest sizes and, among them, some pre-war shoes of real leather, which she had had her eye on since last spring. And she decided to take this opportunity also to drop by Remo's tavern (in her eyes he had become a Gray Eminence, thanks to the Madman's hints) with the thought of receiving, perhaps, some information from him about the guilt, or innocence, of half-breeds . . .

After a fairly long stretch on foot, they had to wait more than half an hour for the bus to the Tiburtino. To make up for this bad luck, they were fortunate in the purchase of the shoes, being able to discover, after much searching (the shoes noted by Ida had unfortunately been sold just a few days before), a real pair of little boots, covering the ankles, the like of which Useppe had never owned. They actually seemed of real leather, the soles were of crepe; and to his mother's satisfaction (since in making such exceptional expenses for his wardrobe, she was worried about his *growth*), they were almost two sizes too large for Useppe. But he was especially attracted by the laces, which were a handsome carmine color, in contrast with the pale brown of the footgear. In fact, the shopkeeper explained, these were *two-tone boots*.

Useppe wanted to wear them immediately: and this was an advantage, because, as soon as they were outside the shoeshop, near the station, the disastrous traces of the air raids appeared around them; but he was too intent on his new feet, and paid no attention.

Meaning to go to the tavern, Ida chose some little side-streets, avoiding, as a doubly frightening sight, the Via Tiburtina, with the long wall of the Verano cemetery. She was beginning to feel tired after her almost sleepless night; and as she turned towards the familiar places of San Lorenzo, she stupidly began walking faster, at the blind stimulus that drives mares and donkeys towards the manger. But a resistance from Useppe's little hand, imprisoned in hers, restrained her. And in a sudden reawakening she lost the courage to continue on that route which for her had once been the way home. Then, giving up the visit to Remo, she turned back.

In reality, she no longer knew where to go. Her night-suspicion that she was wanted by the Germans was growing to a paranoid certainty in her weakened mind, blocking off like a colossus the return roads to the big room in Pietralata. Nevertheless, she followed Useppe's little footsteps, which went again towards the bus stop, convinced and spellbound even if somewhat unsteady in the oversized and still stiff boots. At Piazzale delle Crociate a middle-aged woman passed them, running like a lunatic in their same direction. Ida recognized her: she was a Jew from the Ghetto, the wife of a certain Settimio Di Segni, who ran a little store, buying and selling second-hand goods, behind Sant'Angelo in Pescheria. On various occasions, in recent years, Ida had gone to his place to offer some household object for sale, or some piece of personal property; and sometimes she had happened to deal with his wife, running the shop in his place. On some days, in their minuscule storeroom, she had met a few of their numerous children and grandchildren, all of whom lived with them in a couple of rooms over the shop.

"Signora! Signora Di Segni!"

Ida called, walking faster after her, with a voice of almost exultant surprise. And when the other woman didn't seem to hear her, she immediately took Useppe in her arms and ran after her, clinging to that alien encounter like an earthling lost in the deserts of the moon who has run into a close relation. But the woman didn't turn or listen; and when Ida was beside her, the woman barely glanced at her, with the grim and hostile eye of a lunatic rejecting all relationship with normal people.

"Signora! . . . Don't you recognize me? I . . ." Ida insisted. But the woman was paying no attention to her; indeed, she seemed not to see or hear Ida, though, at the same time, she had started walking faster, to shake her off, suspiciously. She was sweating (she was rather fat), and her bobbed yellow-gray hair was sticking to her forehead. Her left hand, with the "patriotic" steel wedding ring, clutched a wretched little change-purse. She had nothing else with her.

Ida ran along beside her, jolting the baby, in a kind of gasping panic: "Signora," she said suddenly, getting as close to her as she could and speaking in a very low voice, as if to an intimate confidante: "I'm Jewish, too."

But Signora Di Segni didn't seem to understand her, nor did she listen to her. At that point, shaken by some sudden alarm, the woman moved away from there, bursting into an animal dash across the square, towards the railroad station opposite.

After the bombings, the station had been promptly reopened; but its low rectangular facade, of a yellowish color, was still scorched and blackened by the smoke from the explosions. Since it was a secondary station, there was never much of a crowd, especially on Monday; but today the movement seemed even less than usual. In these times of war, and especially since the German occupation, troops were often loaded or unloaded there. But there were no soldiers in sight today, and only a few civilians moved around, without haste. On that late morning of a Monday, the building had an abandoned and temporary look.

But Useppe gazed at it as if it were a monument, perhaps also in a vague reminiscence of the days he had gone there with Ninnuzzu to enjoy the spectacle of the trains. And he remained quiet, looking all around with curious eyes, momentarily forgetting his private, personal impatience: he was in a big hurry, in fact, to go back to Pietralata, instead of bouncing around here in his mother's arms; he couldn't wait to carry, finally, to Ulì and to all of them, today's big news: the boots!

And Ida, meanwhile, had almost forgotten he was in her arms, since she was bent solely on not losing sight of Signora Di Segni's isolated form, which drew her along like a will-o'-the-wisp. Ida saw her head towards the passengers' entrance, then come back again, in her great and furious untouchable's solitude, expecting no help from anyone. Not running any more, but stumbling in haste on her old summer shoes with enormous orthopedic soles, she was now moving along this side of the station's facade, then she turned left towards the freight yard, towards the service entrance. Ida crossed the square and took the same direction.

The gate was open: there was no one on guard outside; and no one shouted at her even from the police sentrybox, just inside the gate. Perhaps ten paces from the entrance, she began to hear, at some distance, a horrible humming sound, but for the moment she couldn't understand precisely where it was coming from. That station area, at present, seemed deserted and idle. There was no movement of trains, or traffic of freight; and the only people visible were beyond the boundary of the yard, distant, within the precincts of the main station: two or three ordinary employees, apparently calm.

Towards the oblique road leading to the tracks, the sound's volume increased. It was not, as Ida had already persuaded herself, the cry of animals packed into cattle-cars, which could sometimes be heard echoing in this area. It was a sound of voices, of a human mass, coming, it seemed, from the end of the ramps, and Ida followed that signal, though no assembled crowd was visible among the shunting tracks, which criss-crossed the gravel around her. In her progress, which seemed to go on for miles, and sweaty like a march through the desert (in reality it was perhaps thirty steps), she encountered only a solitary engine-driver, eating from a piece of wrapping paper, beside a spent locomotive, and he said nothing to her. Perhaps the few watchmen had also gone to eat. It must have been just past noon.

The invisible voices were approaching and growing louder, even though they sounded somehow inaccessible, as if they came from an isolated and contaminated place. The sound suggested certain dins of kindergartens, hospitals, prisons: however, all jumbled together, like shards thrown into the same machine. At the end of the ramp, on a straight, dead track, a train was standing which, to Ida, seemed of endless length. The voices came from inside it.

There were perhaps twenty cattle-cars, some wide-open and empty, others closed with long iron bars over the outside doors. Following the standard design of such rolling-stock, the cars had no windows, except a tiny grilled opening up high. At each of those grilles, two hands could be seen clinging, or a pair of staring eyes. At that moment, nobody was guarding the train.

Signora Di Segni was there, running back and forth on the open platform, her legs without stockings, short and thin, of an unhealthy whiteness, and her mid-season dust-coat flying behind her shapeless body. She was running clumsily the whole length of the row of cars, shouting in an almost obscene voice:

"Settimio! Settimio! . . . Graziella! . . . Manuele! . . . Settimio! . . . Settimio! Esterina! . . . Manuele! . . . Angelino! . . ."

From inside the train, some unknown voice reached her, shouting at her to go away: otherwise *they* would take her, too, when they came back in a little while. "No-o-o! I won't go!" she railed, in reply, threatening and enraged, hammering her fists against the cars, "my family's in there! Call them! Di Segni! The Di Segni family!" . . . "Settimiooo!!!'" she burst out suddenly, running, her arms out towards one of the cars and clinging to the bar on the door, in an impossible attempt to force it. Behind the grille, up above, a little head had appeared, an old man's. His eyeglasses could be seen glistening over his emaciated nose, against the darkness behind; and his tiny hands clutched the bars.

"Settimio!! The others?! Are they there with you?"

"Go away, Celeste," her husband said to her. "Go away, I tell you: right now. *They*'ll be back any minute . . ." Ida recognized his slow, sententious voice. It was the same that, on other occasions, in his cubbyhole full of old junk, had said to her, for example, with sage and pondered judgment, "This, Signora, isn't even worth the cost of mending . . ." or else, "I can give you six lire for the whole lot . . ." but today it sounded toneless, alien, as if from an atrocious paradise beyond all access.

The interior of the cars, scorched by the lingering summer sun, continued to reecho with that incessant sound. In its disorder, babies' cries overlapped with quarrels, ritual chanting, meaningless mumbles, senile voices calling for mother; others that conversed, aside, almost ceremonious, and others that were even giggling. And at times, over all this, sterile, bloodcurdling screams rose; or others, of a bestial physicality, exclaiming elementary words like "water!" "air!" From one of the last cars, dominating all the other voices, a young woman would burst out, at intervals, with convulsive, piercing shrieks, typical of labor pains.

And Ida recognized this confused chorus. No less than the Signora's almost indecent screams and old Di Segni's sententious tones, all this wretched human sound from the cars caught her in a heart-rending sweetness, because of a constant memory that didn't return to her from known time, but from some other channel: from the same place as her father's little Calabrian songs that had lulled her, or the anonymous poem of the previous night, or the little kisses that whispered *carina, carina* to her. It was a place of repose that drew her down, into the promiscuous den of a single, endless family.

"I've been running all over the place the whole morning . . ."

Leaning towards that bespectacled face at the grille, Signora Di Segni had started chatting hastily, in a kind of feverish gossip, but also in the familiar and almost ordinary manner of a wife who is accounting for her day to her husband. She told how that morning around ten, as planned, she had returned from an expedition to Fara Sabina with two flasks of olive oil she had managed to find. And arriving, she had discovered the neighborhood deserted, doors barred, nobody in the houses, nobody in the street. Nobody. She had inquired, she had asked here, there, the Aryan café keeper, the Aryan news-vendor. And questions everywhere. Even the Temple deserted. ". . . and I ran this way and that way, to this one and that one . . . They're at the Military Academy . . . at the Termini station . . . at Tiburtino . . ."

"Go away, Celeste."

"No, I won't go away. I'm just as Jewish as you! I want to get into this train too!!"

"*Reschut*, Celeste, in the name of God, get out, before *they* come back."

"Nooo! No! Settimio! Where are the others? Manuele? Graziella? The baby? . . . Why can't I see them? Why don't they show their faces?" Suddenly, like a madwoman, she burst out screaming again: "Angelinooo! Esterinaaa! Manuele!! Graziella!!"

A certain shifting could be heard inside the car. Having climbed somehow to the grille, a head with a mop of hair, two little black eyes, could be seen behind the old man . . .

"Esterinnaaa! Esterinaaa! Graziella!! Open up! Isn't anybody in charge around here? I'm a Jew! A Jew! I have to go with them! Open up! Fascists! FASCISTS!! Open the door!" She shouted *Fascists,* not as an accusation or as an insult, but as a natural form of address, as one might say *Ladies and Gentlemen of the Jury* or *Officers,* to appeal to Order and Authority in the situation. And she insisted doggedly in her impossible attempt to force the bars.

"Go away, Signora! Don't stay here! It's best for you! Go away quick!" From the central offices of the Station, beyond the yard, some men (porters or clerks) were gesticulating to her from a distance, with agitated urging. But they didn't approach the train. They seemed, indeed, to avoid it, like a funeral or infected chamber.

No one had yet shown any interest in the presence of Ida, who had remained a bit behind, at the end of the ramp; and she, too, had almost forgotten about herself. She felt invaded by an extreme weakness; and although the heat wasn't excessive there in the open, on the platform she was covered with sweat as if she had a fever of 104 degrees. However, she abandoned herself to this weakness of her body as if to the last sweetness possible, as she became confused in this throng, mingling with the sweat of the others.

She heard bells ring; and there flashed through her head the warning that she had to hurry to conclude her daily round of shopping; perhaps the stores were already closing. Then she heard some deep and cadenced blows, echoing somewhere near her; and she thought at first they were the puffs of the engine starting, and imagined that the train was preparing for its departure. She promptly realized, however, that those blows had been with her for the whole time she had been on the platform, even if she hadn't paid any attention to them before; and that they were resounding very close to her, right against her body. In fact, it was Useppe's heart beating that way.

The child was quiet, huddled into her arms, his left side against her breast; but he held his head turned to look at the train. In reality, he hadn't moved from that position since the first moment. And as she peered around to examine him, she saw him still staring at the train, his face motionless, his mouth half-open, his eyes wide in an indescribable gaze of horror.

"Useppe . . . " she called him, in a low voice.

Useppe turned, at her summons; the same stare, however, remained in his eyes, which, even as they encountered hers, asked her no question.

There was, in the endless horror of his gaze, also a fear, or rather a dazed stupor; but it was a stupor that demanded no explanation.

"We're going, Useppe! We're going away!"

At the moment she turned to hasten off from there, among the persistent shouts behind her a man's voice could be distinguished, calling: "Signora, wait! Listen! Signora!" She turned: those calls were addressed to her, all right. From one of the little grilles that allowed her to glimpse a poor bald head with intense eyes that seemed ill, a hand stretched out to throw her a piece of paper.

As she bent to pick it up, Ida realized that there, scattered on the ground along the cars (from which a foul smell was already emanating), there were other similar crumpled notes among the rubbish and garbage; but she didn't have the strength to stay and collect any. And as she ran away, she stuffed that little scrawled piece of paper into her pocket without looking at it, while the stranger behind the grille continued shouting thanks after her, and indistinct instructions.

In all, no more than ten minutes had passed since her entrance to the yards. This time, the Italian policemen on guard at the gate came briskly towards her. "What are you doing here? Get out! Hurry! Get out of here!" they ordered her, with an angry urgency, which seemed intended simultaneously to scold her and to safeguard her from a danger.

As she was going out of the gate with Useppe in her arms, a brownish truck arrived from the street, leaving a confused sound behind it as it passed, like a subdued echo of that other chorus from the train. Its load, however, locked inside, was invisible. Its only visible occupants were, in the cab, two young soldiers in SS uniform. Their appearance was normal, calm, like that of the usual Municipal truckdrivers who loaded up their meat supplies at this freight-yard stop. Their faces, clean, a healthy pink, were ordinary and stolid.

Ida completely forgot she had to finish her shopping, feeling only the haste to reach the bus stop. Driven by the exclusive desire to be back behind her sackcloth curtain, she had dismissed her weariness and preferred not to put the child on the ground again. Feeling him in her arms, near and tight, consoled her, as if she had a shelter and a protection; but for the whole distance she lacked the courage to look him in the eyes.

There were many people waiting at the bus stop; and inside the overcrowded vehicle it wasn't easy to maintain one's balance, standing. Unable to reach the straps because of her short stature, Ida, as usual in these instances, performed ballerina exercises to remain on her feet in the crush, to spare Useppe too many shoves and jolts. She noticed his little head was swaying, and she carefully settled it against her shoulder. Useppe had fallen asleep.

In the big room, everything was the same as usual. The gramophone was playing "The Vamp of La Scala" and at the same time Carulì's sisters-in-law were quarreling over a pot, amid atrocious insults; however, that familiar racket could not disturb Useppe's sleep. Ida stretched out immediately beside him, and closed her eyes tightly, as if they were being hit by fists. Then all at once her muscles jerked faintly, and the sounds and scenes of the whole earth suddenly abandoned her.

If anyone had been near her, he would perhaps have thought her dead, she was so still and pale; but perhaps he wouldn't even have had time to notice that little spell of hers, which really was of infinitesimal duration. A moment later, her eyelids relaxed, opening gently again over her cleared eyes like two slow little wings, while her mouth formed a calm and ingenuous smile, a dreaming child's.

Almost at once, she let herself sink into deep sleep, without dreams and full of silence, beyond the continued din of the room. She woke after several hours. It was almost evening. And immediately, as she sought Useppe in the cot beside her, she recognized, beyond the curtain, the unmistakable little music of his laughter. Useppe had waked before her and was already sitting there on the ground, blinking his carefree eyes, rapturously displaying his new boots to the familiar company: Peppe Terzo, Impero, Ulì, etc. The least convinced, among them, seemed Ulì, who had promptly noticed the excessive size of those *two-tone* shoes; however, she set to fixing them for him with a pair of inner soles made from a lady's felt hat (residue of the Charity Ladies of July) . . .

Ida lived through the rest of the day in an almost absent dreaminess. During the night, she woke with a start, hearing beside her in the cot a shrill little cry, of piercing anguish. She realized Useppe was twitching in his sleep, and after a silence he resumed moaning in a spasmodic stammer. Then she called him; and making a light with her usual, precious candle stub, now reduced to its last flickers, she saw him all in tears, pushing her away with his tiny hands, as if refusing any comfort. And still without waking entirely, he continued his incomprehensible stammer, in which she seemed to recognize the word *horse*, mingled in confusion with *kids* and *grownups*. Calling him by name several times, Ida tried to rescue him from the dream that was invading him; and finally she showed him the new boots with their red laces, saying: "Look, Useppe! Look what's here!" At last then the child's pupils brightened amidst their tears. "Mine," he stated with a smile. Then he added, "Shoos!" and with a brief sigh of satisfaction he went back to sleep.

The next morning, merry as usual, he had forgotten the events of the previous day and night; nor did Ida mention them to him again (to him or anyone else). In the pocket of her housedress she had the message thrown to her at the station by the Jew in the train; and she examined it, aside, in the daylight. It was a piece of lined copybook paper, sweat-stained and crumpled. On it, in pencil, there was written in a shaky hand, large and laborious:

If you see Efrati Pacificho tell him we're all in good health Irma Reggina Romolo and everyboddy going to Germany hole family all-right the bill pay Lazarino another hundred and twenty lire debt becau

That was all. There was no signature, no address (omitted through caution or lack of time? Or perhaps simple ignorance?). *Efrati* was one of the most common family names in the Ghetto: where, for that matter, according to what people said, nobody was left any more. Still, Ida placed the message in a compartment of her purse, though with no precise intention of seeking its addressee.

In the big room, they had already stopped talking about the Jews and their fate. Almost every day, if he turned up at home, Salvatore read, syllable by syllable, more news from the *Messaggero*. A Fascist had been killed in the city, and a bulletin from the police force of the Open City (so Rome had been declared since August) threatened severe measures. There was talk also of the famous hand-made nails with four points, which disabled the German vehicles, and of how the Germans were arresting smiths, mechanics, etc. The Fascist Action Squads were being formed again, etc., etc. However, the predominant news, which, though not written in the papers, circulated as a rumored certainty, was the event already predicted by the partisan Moscow: namely that on October 28th, the feast and anniversary of Fascism, the Allied troops would enter Rome.

Meanwhile the Nazi-Fascists in Rome began to be concerned with certain groups of *snipers* who were operating in the outlying slums, Pietralata among them. The tavernkeeper's long-distance signals had become more frequent; more often now, Carulì or some other member of The Thousand on sentry duty at the windows would warn: "*Light the lamp!*" or "*I have to take a shit!*"; and the young men in the room, these days, prudently avoided being found at home. Carlo, too, stayed out most of the time, God knows where, still returning regularly at the curfew hour, surely because he didn't know where else to go and sleep. And always on schedule, Rossella would punctually reappear in the big room a bit before him, to be ready to receive him behind the curtain with her special miau.

On October 22nd, there was a real battle between the Germans and the crowd at the Forte Tiburtino. More than once, since September, the starving people of the district had attacked the fort, carrying off not only food and medicines, but also weapons and ammunition; and the few Italian soldiers inside, besieged, had let them get away with it. But this time there were German sentries, who had given the alarm to their Headquarters. An SS unit in full battle array had promptly been sent to the scene of the disorders; and the news of this disturbing presence had flown, in advance, beyond the borders of the slum.

In the meanwhile, Granny Dinda had gone out to collect some wild salad greens in the area. And at her hasty return, she brought the thrilling news, heard God knows where, that the German army was marching against the American army, which was arriving from the big highways; and the decisive battle would take place within minutes, right on the fields around them, just outside their room!

At the echo of the shots, which followed a little later, the unenlightened inhabitants present wondered whether they should really believe Granny Dinda. With some hope, but also with great fear, the women took shelter in the corners, as if they were in the trenches, while Granddad Giuseppe Primo saw to arranging the sandbags at the windows, with a slow and haughty manner, like a gouty old general. Carulina, for her part, was quick to throw a rag over the cage of the canaries entrusted to her care; and the whole business intoxicated the gang of kids present, who rampaged heroically, amused at the women's fright. Merriest of all, as usual, was Useppe, who jumped up on the pile of desks and ran and crouched, then flung himself to the floor, shouting: bang! bang! bang! Though Ida had beseeched him to wear his old sandals around the house, saving his new footgear for when they went out, he wouldn't hear of this; and so at present, his footsteps, in his constant running around the room, could be distinguished by a new, characteristic sound: plop, plop, due to the still somewhat excessive size of the boots with their thick crepe soles.

The shooting didn't last long, and a little later the room was visited by the Germans. It seemed they were searching for the hiding place of some local *snipers* who had escaped capture after the conflict at the Fort. Awed by their grandiose equipment (they had huge helmets down to the nose, and held their automatic guns aimed), Useppe, who had understood nothing of the whole episode except the racket, asked in a loud voice if these were *Mericuns*. Luckily, these men couldn't know that this term, in Useppe's language, meant *The Americans*; and for that matter, Carulina immediately signaled Useppe to keep quiet.

They shoved all the inhabitants into the road, and began searching every corner of the interior, even the roof and the latrine. Luckily, there was no meat being kept in the latrine today, and they didn't bother to examine the other victuals store, under Sora Mercedes's blanket, confident because, a moment before, they had seen the heavy, arthritic lady emerge from beneath that same blanket. Again, thanks to luck, at that hour the ablebodied males of the room were all absent. And so, after having barked some incomprehensible warnings in German, the armed men went off again, and never came back.

Some days later, also at Pietralata, the following proclamation was seen posted, in German and in Italian:

On 22 October, 1943, Italian civilians, members of a Communist band, fired on German troops. They were taken prisoner after a brief skirmish.
The Military Tribunal has sentenced to death 10 members of this band for having taken part in an armed attack on units of the German forces.
The sentence has been carried out.

The sentence was carried out the day after the attack in a field near Pietralata, where the corpses were immediately buried in a ditch. But, later, when the ditch was discovered, there were actually eleven corpses, not ten. The eleventh was a harmless cyclist, who had happened by, and was shot along with the others, because he was there.

8   The weather was variable, and there were numerous sunny mornings, but Nino still hadn't kept his promise to Useppe. It's hard to say whether Useppe remembered it or not. True, he still went often to the doorway to look towards the sunny road, as if he were waiting; however, perhaps in his mind, distance (almost two weeks had gone by) was confusing Nino's promise with the mornings and with the sun in one vague mirage. Meanwhile, before the mirage could finally become incarnate, destiny began, through a precipitous series of events, to reduce the number of people in the room.

On about October 25th, early in the afternoon, a monk knocked at the door. At that moment, only Ulì, the kids, Sora Mercedes, and the grandmothers were present. The grandfathers had gone to sit at the tavern. Ida was behind her curtain, and the sisters-in-law had climbed to the building's little terrace, to collect in great haste some laundry they had hung out.

In fact, it was beginning to rain. The monk had covered his head with his hood, and he had that busy and circumspect manner that marks religious. He greeted them with the customary phrase *Pax et Bonum* and asked for Vivaldi Carlo. Being told the young man was out, he sat down on a packing-case to wait, in the circle of kids who looked at him, wide-eyed, as if watching a movie. But after a few minutes' waiting, he got up, having to run off to attend to some other matters. And, crooking his little finger, he called aside Carulina (who must have seemed, among those around him, the most trustworthy secretary) and said to her softly: to tell Sig. Vivaldi Carlo very promptly and in strict secrecy that he was to go as soon as possible to the *place he knew about*, to receive urgent news. Then he repeated *Pax et Bonum* and went off.

The sisters-in-law, arriving at this point, had time to glimpse him as he left; Carulina, however, valorously braving their interrogation, refused to repeat the message. This silence cost her an effort so great it actually made the veins in her neck swell; but the test, luckily for her, was not imposed long. No more than a quarter of an hour after the monk's departure, Carlo Vivaldi, perhaps alerted by some presage, reappeared, off schedule, in the big room. Carulì quickly rushed towards him, shouting in a loud voice, "There was a monk here asking for you . . ." and he started, visibly. His face and hair wet with rain, he resembled at that point a sparrow battered by the bad weather. Without a word, he turned his back and rushed out into the road again.

In his absence, several conjectures followed, among Carulina's grand-mothers and sisters-in-law. At that time, every adventure story became true to life. It really happened, for example, that high officers or well-known political figures disguised themselves in various ways to foil the search of the occupying enemies. And the women conjectured, among other things, that the monk was a false monk, perhaps a disguised anarchist, or even some generalissimo of the loftiest circles.

Instead, the man really was a poor simple monk, sent by a Roman convent where a distant cousin of Carlo's was hidden at present. Because of his proud ideals, Carlo was revolted at the thought of taking refuge in a convent. He preferred to remain without a fixed address, and so correspon-dence and news from the North were sent to him through the little cousin. Now, today's news, awaiting him, was of the most atrocious sort. But the truth about him was learned only later.

Meanwhile, the curfew hour passed without his showing up again. And the inhabitants of the room inferred that, after the mysterious monk's visit, he had vanished forever. In their eyes, Carlo Vivaldi was still an ambiguous and strange adventurer: perhaps in the service of some foreign power? or connected with the Vatican? The mother of Currado and Im-pero even advanced the hypothesis that he was a nobleman incognito, in attendance on His Majesty the King-Emperor, and that by now he had probably already flown to Brindisi or to Bari, on a special plane placed at his disposal by the Pope . . .

Instead, Carlo Vivaldi was not far away, perhaps in that same neighborhood, or perhaps in some other undefined neighborhood of the city, wandering alone through the rainy streets, immersed in the blackout's darkness, infested by patrols. From the moment that afternoon when his cousin had given him the *secret urgent news* until late at night, he did nothing but roam the streets, without choosing any direction, or knowing what time it was, or caring about the curfew. There's no telling how he escaped the dangers of that aimless walk: protected, perhaps, by the insuperable barricade of outrage and delirium that at times surrounds the desperate. We can believe the armed patrols out searching crossed his path several times that night, all of them, however, turning away and stifling their *who goes there?* for fear of offending his shade.

He himself could never have said where he was taken by that measureless walk of miles and time uncalculated (perhaps nine or ten hours). He may have gone from one end of the city to the other, or he may have continued roaming in a confined space, always the same, back and forth. At a certain hour of the night he went back to take refuge in his only available lodging, at Pietralata, behind the curtain of rags. All were asleep; the only one who heard him come in was Ida, who had a hard time falling asleep on those nights, even with her pills, and stirred at the slightest rustle. First she heard his footsteps on the path, then the prolonged meow of Rossella, who bade him welcome at the door. And afterwards, for the rest of the night, she thought she could hear him coughing constantly amidst a repetition of dull thuds, as if he were beating his fists against the wall.

In fact, the next morning, his knuckles were all skinned and bleeding, but nobody in the big room had time to observe them. It so happened that around eight, Giuseppe Secondo turned up, on one of his periodical hasty visits. He came in with his usual jovial manner, bringing excellent news again today: Ace of Hearts was fine, so was Quattropunte, and so were all the comrades of the glorious band . . . Thanks to them, another ton or so of evil German meat had been sent to fertilize the earth of the Castelli . . . A week ago, the Germans had attempted a round-up of partisans, with some losses; but they, of the *Liberty* (the band's code name) were too smart to let those cowards catch them . . . And as for predictions for the future, beyond doubt the war's end was imminent. Of course, they could no longer count on the Allies entering Rome on October 28th . . . "It would of been a clever trick, of course; that would of spoiled their celebration, all right! . . ." However, before Christmas, it was a sure thing, Giuseppe Secondo concluded.

After such brilliant confidences, the merry little man rummaged for a few more minutes in the heap of his belongings; and then with a broad wave of goodbye to left and right, he headed for the door. At that point the rag curtain was yanked violently; and Carlo, with vehemence, as if he were going to tear it apart, emerged from behind it with a great laugh. "I'm coming with you! . . . With your band!" he said abruptly. He already had his bag over his shoulder—all his luggage, in other words. In the light that fell obliquely through the half-open door, his gaze, from eyes hollowed and shadowed by insomnia, seemed deeper, more grim than usual. And following his laugh, which had left an almost obscene echo in the air, the obscure corruption, returning at intervals in his face, now actually transfigured it, like a twisted mask. However, from all this, into the muscles of his body there poured a kind of unleashed, athletic gaiety. Giuseppe Secondo, dumbfounded for an instant, brightened with a smile of rejoicing, which made wrinkles all over his face: "Ah! High time!" he cried, and added nothing else. Going out with him, Carlo Vivaldi waved a half-ironic farewell behind him, as if to say that this room, too, with all its occupants, was now dissolving for him into the foam of the dead past. Though Rossella followed him with her little eyes from the pallet, he forgot even to say goodbye to her.

The clouds had shredded; but in the cool wind that was beginning to rise, there were still brief, passing showers, springlike. Giuseppe Secondo no longer wore his famous hat on his head; however, he protected himself with an umbrella; and those remaining laughed at it behind his back (truly, a partisan with an umbrella was a rather odd thing). And so the two went off together, beyond the muddy field: the old man walking briskly, under the umbrella; and the young man preceding him with his lanky, somewhat uneven gait, like the walk of certain young blacks.

At their departure, Rossella had hastened to the door. And now, motionless on her four paws by the step of the threshold, she watched them go away, her nose extended towards them in an expression of surprise, already alarmed, as if she could sense that a signal of her destiny was striking at this moment. Nevertheless, in the hours that followed she couldn't help seeking Carlo; in some way, however, she must have known from the beginning she would never see him again. And she tried not to be caught in that ridiculous search of hers, wandering in the vicinity of the curtain with a sidelong, evasive walk, slipping away menacingly whenever anybody came near her. Then she went and hid under the pile of desks, and she stayed there for the rest of the day, flattened between two planks, in a corner where nobody could reach her, fixing her suspicious pupils on the bustle of the room.

As evening fell, when everyone had forgotten about her, suddenly she let out a strange, uneasy meow, and she came from beneath the pile, drifting about, with that unfamiliar lament, which was crying: help help. She was driven by a stimulus of terrible strength, which she had never experienced before. And then she went to settle in her straw hole behind the curtain, where, a little later, she gave birth to a kitten.

Nobody was expecting it, since they hadn't noticed she was pregnant. And it was, in fact, a single, scrawny male offspring, so tiny it seemed to belong to the race of mice rather than of cats. Though new at this, and still young herself, she promptly got busy, tearing the membrane from it with impatient, almost angry bites, already expert, like all mother cats. And then she began to lick it in furious haste, like all mother cats, until the kitten gave out his first meow, so faint he sounded like a mosquito. Then she huddled over him, perhaps confident that she could nurse him. But probably because of her too many fasts, as well as her immaturity, her teats were dry. Abruptly, suddenly, she moved away from him, looking at him with pensive curiosity. And she went off and curled up on her own, at a certain distance, where she remained a bit longer, idle, her eyes aware, filled with melancholy, no longer replying to that lonely little mewing. Then all at once she pricked up her ears, having caught the familiar voices of Caruli's brothers coming home; and as she heard the front door open, casting a last indifferent look towards the kitten, she was quick to spring from behind the curtain into the road.

She didn't show up again that evening or the next day, while the kitten lay dying in the straw, from which he could hardly be distinguished because of his fur's reddish color, inherited from his mother. Every time the racket in the room died down for a brief interval his faint mewing could be heard again, continuing almost uninterruptedly. It seemed strange that this wisp of a voice (the only sign of his presence—you might say—he gave in the world) could maintain such resistance: as if inside that imperceptible little animal, already doomed from the start, an enormous will to live was contained. Useppe couldn't make up his mind to leave the kitten abandoned to his orphan lament; crouched there on the floor, not daring to touch him, he observed every slight movement with anxious eyes. And looking out into the street a hundred times he called desperately: "Ossella! Ossellaaa!!" But Rossella made no reply, and wandering by now who knows where, she had perhaps already forgotten she had borne a son. As the hours passed, meanwhile, the mewing behind the curtain became more and more timid, until it was silent, and a little later, a sister-in-law of Carulina's came to take a look, picked up the kitten by the tail, and cursing its unnatural mother, went to throw it in the latrine.

Useppe, at that moment, was busy making a rumpus with his friends in The Thousand's corner. And when, coming back to see the kitten behind the curtain again, he no longer found it, he didn't ask for news of it. He stood there, silent, staring with big, grave eyes at that little straw lair, stained with Rossella's blood. And he never spoke of it again with Ida, or with anyone. A minute later, distracted by some trifle, he flung himself into playing once more.

Rossella didn't come home for three days; then on the afternoon of the third day, perhaps only because driven by hunger, she turned up again in the room. "Ah, you dirty, nasty, awful thing!" the women screamed at her, "aren't you ashamed to show your face in here, after you let your baby die all alone like that?!" She entered running, grim, not looking at anyone. Who knows what she had gone through in those days? Her fur was worn, yellowed, filthy, like an old cat's; and her body was so emaciated that, now she was no longer pregnant, in the place of her flanks she had two holes. Her tail was reduced to a string; and her muzzle had become an acute triangle, with enormous ears, dilated eyes, gaping mouth, and bared teeth. She had become even smaller than before; and in the expression of her face, she looked like certain dejected pickpockets who have grown old and do nothing but steer clear of all other living creatures, having known only hatred. At first she went and huddled under a desk, but since the kids made a great effort to dislodge her from there, she darted away, and with a bound of her skeletal body, she reached the top of the pile, where she remained perched like an owl. She was on her guard, her ears flat, her bloodshot eyes staring menacingly down. And every now and then she hissed, convinced that in this guise she was presenting herself as a terrifying creature, to keep the whole world at bay. At that moment, her instinct was attracted by something moving down below, in midair, towards the corner of The Thousand. She was the first to notice it, and immediately it was too late to forestall her. Her speed was such that, at first, she gave the impression of a red ray cutting the air obliquely; and already, in place of the two flying canaries, she had left two bloody little rags on the ground.

Almost with the same fantastic speed, at once, as she was frightened by the yells and insults that assailed her from all sides, she ran off again into the road from which she had arrived. Three or four of them chased her, indignant, to give her a beating; but they couldn't catch her, and were barely able to glimpse in the distance her wasted tail disappearing precipitously down a slope. And after that nobody ever saw her again. It's possible that, thin as she was, she still whetted the appetite of some neighborhood cat-hunter, in those days of hunger. Having lost her former agility, in her decline, perhaps she let herself be fatally caught and ended up eaten, as her owner Giuseppe Secondo had foretold, when putting her on her guard.

With reproaches, Carulì was also blamed for the massacre of the canaries. It had been she, in fact, who had carelessly left their cage door open; she had been distracted by Rossella's unexpected apparition just as she was busy cleaning it out. Peppiniello and Peppiniella, perhaps for the first time in their existence, and perhaps mindful of their ancestors free in the Canary Islands, had let themselves be tempted by adventure; but unskilled in flight, having been born in captivity, they had managed only to flutter awkwardly in the air, as if they were two fledglings.

"And what will Sor Giuseppe say now? After he even paid you to take care of them!" all present yelled at Ulì, who was sobbing disconsolately at the sight of the slaughtered pair. Meanwhile Useppe, in the face of those little clumps of spent, bloodstained feathers, had turned pale, and his chin was trembling: "Say, mà, won't they fly any more?" he repeated softly, as Ida thrust him away from there towards their corner, "not fly any more, mà? Can't they fly any more?"

The women, in their repugnance at touching blood, didn't have the heart to pick them up from the floor, and pushed them out into the street with the broom. The next morning, they had vanished from the spot, and it's not impossible that they too were eaten by some living creature: perhaps a dog, perhaps a cat, but perhaps also a human. In that period, the people in the neighborhood who hunted for their food among the garbage were becoming more and more numerous every day; and to somebody who is content at finding some potato peelings or rotten apples, a pair of roast canaries can look like an Archbishop's dinner.

In any case, Ida told Useppe they had flown away.

The sun, that morning, was shining so warmly that summer seemed to have come back; and a little after Ida's daily exit, Nino's promise, finally, was kept.

He was radiant, no less thrilled than Useppe. "I'm taking my brother out with me!" he declared to the others, "he'll be home before lunch"; then he wrote a note in pencil, and left it on Ida's pillow:

> *Back in 4 hours*
> *Useppe*
> *Guaranteed by Nino*

and beneath this guarantee, he drew his personal coat of arms: an ace of hearts over two crossed swords.

He hoisted Useppe astride his shoulders, and running and jumping down along some vacant fields, he came to a grassy space at the edge of a dirt road, where a little truck was waiting for him, with a man and a woman of middle age. Useppe recognized them at once: they were the tavernkeeper and his wife (Remo had a special permit to transport foodstuffs). Inside the truck there were demijohns, baskets, and sacks, some already full, others still to be filled.

The journey lasted about three-quarters of an hour, and it proceeded without hindrance. Nobody stopped them. It was the first time in his life Useppe had traveled in a car and seen the great open countryside. Until now, of the whole world he had known only San Lorenzo, the Tiburtino and environs (Portonaccio, etc.), and the slum of Pietralata. His emotion was so great that, during the first part of the trip, he remained silent; until, in his joyous rapture, he began to chatter to himself or with the others, trying to comment, in an unthought-of and incomprehensible vocabulary, on his discovery of the universe.

If it hadn't been for an occasional passing German vehicle and some burnt-out automobiles abandoned at the edge of the road, you wouldn't have known the war existed. The sumptuous autumn splendors seemed ripened in a legendary peace. Even where the terrain was in shadow, the sun breathed through the air in a gilded veil that calmly stretched over the whole sky.

At a little country crossroads, Remo and his wife unloaded the two passengers and continued on their own, agreeing they would meet at the same place later. Again Nino put Useppe on his shoulders, and leaping and skipping with him, crossed gulleys, slopes, and muddy paths, amid rows of vines and rivulets that glistened in the sun. At about two-thirds of the way, they stopped at a little house, where a girl was up in an olive tree shaking the branches, while a woman below collected the olives in a tub. This girl was Nino's mistress, but in the presence of the woman, who was her mother, she didn't want to let it be seen. The woman, however, knew (and they were aware she knew), and at Nino's arrival she gave him an ecstatic smile, as the girl climbed down from the tree, and, casting him only a fleeting glance, went into the house with an arrogant stride. She came out a little later, to give him something wrapped in newspaper. "Hello there!" Ninnuzzu then said to her pompously, and she grumbled hello, in a grouchy, cross tone. "This is my brother!" Nino announced to her, and she answered "Is that so?" with hauteur, as if to pay no further compliment, meaning: if he's our brother, he can only be a rascal the same as you. Nino, who knew her, laughed and then said to her: "Ciao!" "Ciao," the girl answered, through pouting lips, going back to the tree, with a high, reluctant step.

"What do you think of her?" Ninnuzzu asked Useppe, resuming his way, as if speaking to his confidant. "Her name's Maria," he went on. "Her mother's a widow, and she's an orphan. When the war's over," he concluded, joking cynically, "I'm going to marry her." And turning back towards the tree, he called: "Mariulina! Mariulina!"

The girl, perched in the tree like a fantastic eaglet, didn't even look around. However you could tell from her secret wriggling, from the way her chin was hidden against her throat, she was laughing a little laugh of jealous pleasure.

After another stretch of road, Useppe, impatient to run on his own legs, began to kick at Nino's chest; and Nino put him down. In this last stretch, too, the terrain was rather steep, and Nino admired Useppe's athletic prowess, amused at introducing his brother to the realm of adventure. At a certain point they stopped to have a pee, and this was a source of further amusement, because Nino, as he used to do when a kid with his ignorant friends, showed Useppe his virtuosity, sending the stream high into the air, and Useppe imitated him with his own little jet. The countryside was deserted: Nino had purposely avoided the mule-track, where Germans could be encountered; and there weren't even any houses, only a few straw huts. Not far from a hut hidden in a depression of the hill, a little mule was cropping grass. "Horse!" Useppe shouted at once. "Not horse," a familiar voice said from inside the hut, "that's a mule." "Eppetondo!" Useppe shouted then with enthusiasm. In the low, medium-sized hut, the partisan Moscow was busy peeling some potatoes in a basin; and at the pair's entrance, he smiled with his mouth, his eyes, his wrinkles, and even his ears. Besides him, there were two young men seated on the ground, cleaning some rusty, mudstained weapons with rags soaked in kerosene. And around them, in the hut, there was a disorder of army blankets, heaps of straw, shovels, picks, knapsacks, flasks of wine, and potatoes. From beneath one blanket some gun-barrels stuck out; next to the door a submachine gun was propped against the wall; and nearby, on the ground, there was a little pile of hand grenades.

"This is my brother!" The older of the two guerrillas, a short boy of about twenty, with a round face and some wisps of beard, wearing a few dirty tatters (even on his feet, he had rolled-up rags instead of shoes), barely raised his eyes from the job that was absorbing him. But the other gave Useppe a fine smile of friendship, ingenuous and festive. This youth, though his body was already grown, perhaps six feet tall, still betrayed his age in his pink and beardless face: he was sixteen. He had a low forehead, and his broad eyes, of a milky blue, avoided other people's gaze, in a kind of still-adolescent shyness, contrasting with a certain tough expression of his. He was wearing a whitish trench coat, now filthy, over his bare torso; pants and boots originally belonging to the Italian army (the pants were too short for him); and on his wrist, a German watch of which he seemed extremely proud, for every minute he happily held it to his ear to make sure it was working.

"This is Decimo, and this is Tarzan," Ace made the introductions.

"Here!" he added, throwing the younger man (Tarzan) the package received from Mariulina, which contained some tobacco leaves. And temporarily abandoning the cleaning of the weapons, Tarzan took a switchblade knife from his trench-coat pocket and began at once to chop up those thick brown leaves, to make some cigarettes with newspaper immediately.

"Everything okay?" Ace inquired, having been absent since the previous night, spent in Rome with another girl friend of his from the old days. And meanwhile, with an air of knowledge and mastery, he was examining those weapons, now being restored, which represented his latest exploit. It was he, in fact, who had discovered them, the day before, at the edge of a wood where some Germans were camping, and yesterday, as soon as it was dark, he and two other comrades had gone to take them by stealth, eluding the camp's sentries. He personally, however, had shared only in this first phase (the most dangerous, really) of the expedition; leaving to the other pair the more toilsome part (namely the transport of the load to their base), in his anxiety to catch the last tram and to keep his Roman date.

"You can see for yourself . . ." Decimo answered his question, still intent on his work, with an almost grim determination. Decimo was new; he had just joined the band, and for this reason he still hadn't conquered himself some shoes. He didn't even know how to use weapons, and Ace was teaching him how to take apart the Breda automatic guns, how to unscrew the breech of rifles, etc. The new weapons, just looted (ten pieces in all), were of Italian origin, having fallen into the Germans' hands after the dispersal of the Italian army. And Nino displayed a certain contempt for Italian arms (outmoded stuff, according to him, and rejects). But for him, in any case, handling arms was always a passionate delight.

"We're running out of kerosene," Decimo remarked gravely, "we have to get hold of some more." "I believe," Tarzan said, "Quattro and Pyotr will take care of that." (Pyotr was the guerrilla pseudonym of Carlo Vivaldi.)

"Where are they?" Ace inquired.

"They went up the hill, for provisions. But they're late already. They should be back by now." And Tarzan seized the opportunity to consult his watch.

"What time did they leave?"

"At 0730 hours."

"What did they take with them?"

"Quattro has the P.38, and Pyotr took Harry's Sten."

"Where's Harry?"

"He's outside, in the vineyard, naked, taking the sun." "Ah, getting some rest," Moscow intervened, reproaching Ace (but in fun), "after he had to take two turns of guard duty last night. And after all that work he did in the evening, left alone there in the middle of the road, with all that artillery in his arms . . ."

"I would of missed my tram! And I didn't leave him alone, anyway. Wild Orchid was there. There were two of them."

"Eh, Orchid. He's a big fighter, all right! Fine company, eh!"

"And where's he now?"

"Who? Orchid? He's probably lying outside too, somewhere in the garden."

"And the Chief?"

"He slept in the village. He'll be back in the afternoon. By the way, Ace, you haven't heard the news . . . Him and me, last night, we fixed that PAI character."

In communicating this information, Tarzan curled his lips in a hard and contemptuous grimace. But a childish blush rose to his cheeks at the same time.

"Ah," Ninnuzzu said, "high time. Where?"

"A few feet from his house. He was lighting himself a butt. The flame of the lighter helped us recognize him. He was alone. It was all dark. Nobody saw a thing. The two of us were around the corner. We fired at the same time. It all took a couple of seconds. We were already safe when we heard his wife yelling."

"The bereaved widow," Ace of Hearts commented.

"Yeah, but all the same," the partisan Moscow exclaimed emphatically, "I bet she wasn't crying, the Signora, when there was that German round-up thanks to her late husband's good offices!!"

"He was a lousy spy," Ace remarked again. "A fat-ass," he concluded, the definitive judgment. In the meanwhile, he never stopped gazing at the weapons scattered there on the ground before him, with the air of a capitalist inspecting his personal wealth. "At the present moment," Tarzan summed up for him, about to glue his newspaper-cigarette with saliva, "we have eight shotguns and six '91's . . ."

Even the partisan Moscow took part every now and then in the arms count with an expert's haughtiness: "These are German projectiles," he informed the beginner Decimo, indicating the grenades with his foot.

"They're good for the explosive in them," Ace spoke out. "Later I'll show you how they're used . . ."

"We take out the charge and make gunpowder from it, and when you mix that with TNT . . ."

"Eppetondo! What kind of horse's that?" Useppe spoke up at this point, still interested in the mule.

"I told you: that's not a horse. That's a mule."

"Ess! Mule! Mule! But what kind of horse is it?!"

225

"Aw, come on! A mule's not a horse. It's half horse and half donkey."

". . .? . . ."

"It had a mare for a mother, and a donkey for a father."

"Or vice versa," ventured Tarzan, who, having been born and bred in the city, wanted to show a proper knowledge of these rustic subjects, all the same.

"No, if it's vice versa, it's not a mule. It's a hinny."

Tarzan had a mortified smile. "Where's his mother now?" Useppe inquired meanwhile, insistently, at Moscow's side.

"Where do you think she is? At home, with her husband."

". . . is she happy?"

"I'll say! Happy as a lark."

Useppe laughed, reassured. "What's she doing? Playing?" he insisted, with fervor.

"Playing. Jumping and dancing!" Moscow assured him. Useppe laughed again, as if this reply corresponded fully to an uncertain hope of his. "Why doesn't he play?" he asked, nodding towards the mule, grazing alone on the grass.

"Eh . . . he's eating! Can't you see he's eating?"

With this, Useppe seemed satisfied. But still another question was suspended on his lips, as he considered the mule. Finally, he asked:

"Do mules fly, too?"

Tarzan laughed. Moscow shrugged. And Ninnuzzu said to his brother: "Hey, stupid!" Of course, he was unaware of the information given Useppe, on the day of the air raid, by that big lady from Mandela. But seeing Useppe smile an uncertain and somewhat sad little smile, he surprised him with this communication:

"By the way, you know what that mule's name is? He's called Uncle Peppe!!"

"So that makes three Giuseppes here: me, you, and the mule!" Eppetondo observed, boasting. "Four, really," he corrected himself, giving Decimo a sly look. The latter blushed, as if at the revelation of a state secret; and that blush, despite his bearded face, revealed his still-immature mind. In fact, his real name wasn't Decimo, but Giuseppe; and he, in particular, had a double reason for concealing himself behind an alias. First, as a partisan; and second, as someone wanted by the Roman police for theft and contraband dealing in cigarettes.

Useppe's eyes widened at the thought of all the Giuseppes there are in the world. At that moment, outside, in the vicinity of the hut, an explosion was heard. They all stared at one another. Ace went to the door to take a peek.

"Nothing, nothing," he announced towards the interior, "that dope Orchid as usual, hunting hens with hand grenades."

"If he only would catch some!" Moscow remarked. "He aims at the hens, and he never catches so much as an egg."

"When he comes back, we'll give him a kick in the ass."

Ninnarieddu armed himself with binoculars and went outside. Useppe ran after him.

Beyond the little wooded rise which hid the hut from view, a valley opened out, of olives and vineyards, all crisscrossed with glistening little streams. The air carried rural sounds of people and animals; and every now and then planes flew by with a hum like guitar-strings. "They're English," Nino said, observing them with the binoculars. At the very very end of the countryside, the Tyrrhenian could be glimpsed. Useppe had never seen the sea, and that blue-violet strip, for him, was only a different color of sky.

"Want to take a look through the binoculars?" Nino suggested to him. Useppe leaned towards him on tiptoe. It was the first time he had had such an experience. Nino, holding the instrument in his own hand, set it against Useppe's eyes.

At first, Useppe saw a fantastic red-brown desert, all interwoven with shadows that spread out, upwards, where there were two marvelous golden globes hanging (it was, in reality, a vine tendril, not very far away). And then, as the binoculars shifted, he saw a pale blue patch of water, which throbbed, changing into other colors, and kindling and extinguishing some bubbles of light: until suddenly, festively, it burst into a flight of clouds.

"What can you see?" Ninnuzzu asked him.

"The sea . . ." Useppe whispered, in an awed voice.

"Yes," Nino confirmed, kneeling beside him, to follow the same line of vision, "you guessed it! That's the sea."

"And . . . and where's the ships?"

"There aren't any now. But one day, Usè, you know what we'll do, the two of us? We'll get on an ocean liner and sail off to America."

"MERICA!"

"Right. Are you game? Give me a little kiss now?"

From below the hill Wild Orchid appeared. He was a boy with an angular, hollowed face, with black tufts over his eyes; he wore a Fascist Youth fez on his head. To it he had applied red stars, hammers and sickles, varicolored ribbons, and similar ornaments. Beneath a red jacket full of holes, he wore a mechanic's overall in very bad shape, bound at the waist by a belt with grenades hanging from it. On his feet he had Italian army shoes of light calf, almost new.

He was carrying no hens or booty of any other sort. He dashed towards the hut, and Nino, after shouting *shit* after him, paid him no further attention. Followed by Useppe at every step, he was inspecting the surrounding country with his binoculars, when he sighted something towards the mountain that immediately aroused his interest. At no more than six or seven hundred yards' distance as the crow flies, three German soldiers were just coming out of a clump of olive trees along a narrow trail that, after crossing some villages, joined the main road on the other side of the mountain. One of the three, stripped to the waist, was carrying on his shoulder a sack containing, as it later proved, a live piglet, surely requisitioned from some peasant family. The three climbed without haste, as if out for a stroll, and indeed, their gait suggested they were rather drunk.

Even before they had vanished behind the curve in the trail, Nino impatiently reentered the hut, to announce at once that he was going *to have a look*, hunting for their overdue comrades (Pyotr and Quattro), who, by now, should be on the descending path, also on that part of the mountain. To Useppe, left on the little patch of grass in the mule's company, he shouted to wait for him and play there, he would be right back. And he hastily gave the others various instructions in the event of his being delayed.

Tarzan decided to go with him. Taking some short cuts through the brush (the same path, more or less, probably being followed by Pyotr and Quattro in their descent) the two planned, with their goatlike agility, to move ahead of the Germans in their climb; so they would be ready and waiting at a lookout point, hidden towards the peak; and from there, they would take the Germans by surprise at the elbow of the trail.

While the two, with feverish gaiety, agreed on this plan (the space of a minute), from the side of the mountains, borne on the still air, firing reechoed: at the beginning some isolated shots, followed at once by a series, a volley, and then by a few more single reports. A prompt inspection of that zone with the binoculars revealed no one on the trail or anywhere around. The two hurried. On leaving the hut with Ace, Tarzan had hidden under his trench coat the sub-machine gun that was propped by the door.

Meanwhile, Useppe was obediently prepared to wait for Ninnuzzu, inspecting on his own the limited territory around the hut. First he chatted with the mule, who, however, though repeatedly called by the name of Uncle Peppe, gave no answer. Then he found a naked man, with many red tufts on his head, groin, and under his armpits, who was snoring, his arms wide, in a clearing among the rows of vines. And afterwards, exploring on all fours the little patch of woods on the lower slopes of the hill, among other curiosities and wonders, he saw a kind of mouse (with velvety fur, a tiny tail, and its forefeet much bigger than its hind ones) run suddenly towards him with dizzying speed, peering at him with a pair of sleepy little eyes, then, still with the same look, run with the same speed, but backwards, disappearing inside the earth!

These, however, were secondary events compared with the main event, of extraordinary importance, which happened to him at that point.

Among the olive trees, behind the hut, there was a different tree (perhaps a small walnut) with luminous, merry leaves that cast a dappled shade, darker than the olives'. Passing nearby, Useppe heard a pair of birds chattering together and kissing. And immediately, at first sight, he recognized the couple as Peppiniello and Peppiniella.

In reality, these two can't have been canaries, and were more likely goldfinches: birds more suited to woods than cages, who come to Italy for the winter. But in their shape and their yellow-green color, they were easy to mistake for the two Pietralata canaries (a bit hybrid themselves, to tell the truth); and Useppe had no doubts on this score. Obviously the big room's two songsters, this morning, as soon as they were cured of their sanguinary illness, had flown here, perhaps following the little truck, from above.

"Ninielli!" Useppe called them. And the two didn't fly off; on the contrary, they began a musical dialogue in reply. More than a dialogue, really, theirs was a little song, composed of a single phrase which the two repeated in turn, alternating it with skips between two branches, one lower and one higher, and marking every reprise with lively movements of the head. It consisted of a dozen syllables in all, sung on two or three notes— always the same except for imperceptible caprices or variations—to a tempo of *Allegretto con brio*. And the words (quite clear to Useppe's ears) went exactly as follows:

It's a joke a joke all a joke!

The two creatures, before flying off again into the air, repeated this little song of theirs at least twenty times, surely with the intention of teaching it to Useppe, who, in fact, after the third repetition had already learned it by heart, and later kept it always in his personal, private repertory, so he could sing it or whistle it at will. However, without explaining why, even to himself, he kept this famous song, which accompanied him all his life, as his own, and never communicated it to anyone, then or later. Only towards the end, as we shall see, he taught it to two of his friends: a little boy whose last name was Scimó, and a dog. But it's probable that Scimó, unlike the dog, forgot it immediately.

From inside the hut, Moscow called Useppe, wanting to give him a boiled potato. And in addition, Wild Orchid, climbing up then from a turn around the vineyard, made him a present of a little bunch of wine grapes: the skin was fairly hard—to be spat out, in other words—but they were very sweet inside. "Ninielli! Ninielli!" Useppe hastened to explain meanwhile to Eppetondo, tugging him by the sleeve in great excitement; but since Moscow, involved in other matters, paid no attention to him, he gave up trying to inform him of his canaries' salvation. And after that, he never spoke with anyone about his meeting with that fortunate little couple.

In the hut, the remaining three discussed the emergency situation, calculating that Ace wouldn't soon return from his excursion on the mountain. Perhaps it would be best to send someone to consult Eyeglasses (that was the Chief's name) because, if the battle with the three Germans took place in a nearby stretch of the terrain (and in the present uncertainty of its outcome), they could fear, they were saying, a subsequent search of the area . . . And it was also a question of getting rid of Useppe promptly, turning him over to some trusted person who would take him back in time to meet the truck on the main road.

Meanwhile, after those shots earlier, nothing more had been heard.

Among his heterogeneous equipment, Moscow also possessed some small binoculars. They weren't war loot, however, but a little instrument of his own property, which in the past he had used in the peanut gallery to enjoy theatrical performances, in particular *Tosca*, Petrolini, and Lydia Johnson, his special favorites. Now, in the course of the discussion, Moscow went out from time to time to examine the mountainside with his opera glasses. And it was a surprise for all when, ahead of every expectation, the band of the absent was seen, complete, appearing from behind some undergrowth not a hundred yards from the trail, and advancing up from the dip towards the hut. In front, side by side, came Ace and Quattro, with Tarzan only a short distance behind them, pulling a torn and blood-stained sack by a rope; and farther back came Pyotr, alone. Besides their bulging knapsacks, all carried supplementary loads; and at their arrival they emptied everything into the hut, except for the slaughtered booty, the piglet that Tarzan had taken upon himself to quarter outside in the woods. There was kerosene and provender (polenta, cheese, salt) and, in addition, waterproof German boots, two German revolvers with their cartridge-belts, a cigarette lighter, a Contax. Almost feverish, Decimo tried on a pair of boots. At this point, from outside, Harry also made himself heard; he had slipped on some corduroy peasant trousers and was repeating: "Mag-nificent! Mag-nificent! . . ." still half-asleep. *Maggnificho*, as he pronounced it, was one of the few Italian words he knew. He was, in fact, an Englishman who had escaped from prison camp in a movie-sequence adventure (in his escape he had even stolen back his own gun!)

and had recently joined up with the band. From the loot, he was offered a watch.

By this time, the bodies of the three Germans, covered with boughs and earth, were lying in a ditch by the side of the trail, about two-thirds of the way from the crest. Quattro and Pyotr had performed the job on their own. And when, coming obliquely down through the brush, they had run into Ace and Tarzan, it was all over. However, neither of the two victors seemed to want to talk about it. Pyotr, with his murky, dead-man's eyes, his face sagging and brutalized by an enormous weariness, as soon as he had taken off his knapsack, went and flung himself down in the grove behind the hut, where he fell sound asleep, breathing with his mouth open, like an addict in an opium stupor. And Quattro sat himself down in a corner of the hut, huddled there, complaining of exhaustion and dizziness. There was an unusual, nauseated pallor on his face, and a feverish look in his eyes. He said he didn't feel like eating, or talking either, and he wasn't even sleepy. All he wanted to do was rest like that a while, off to one side, and his sickness would pass.

Only later, he confided to Ace some details of the encounter, in which Carlo-Pyotr had played such a terrible role that Nino himself seemed shaken by his friend's description. "And to think," he remarked to Quattro, as they spoke together in low voices, "that night we ate at Pietralata, you remember? . . . he said he rejected all violence . . ." In Ace's view, anyway, Pyotr's action was justified. In fact, as Nino had sensed from the beginning, Pyotr-Carlo, in addition to being wanted by the police, was a Jew (neither Vivaldi nor Carlo was his real name) and he had decided to join the band after receiving word that his parents, his grandparents, and his little sister, hiding under false names in the North, had been discovered (certainly through some anonymous denunciation) and deported by the Germans. But still, in spite of all this, Quattro, merely at recalling the scene of the clash, felt his blood run cold, and you could see the skin wrinkle on his bare forearm.

The news that the three Germans were roaming around that part of the mountain had reached Quattro and Pyotr early that morning, when they had stopped for a fresh supply of provisions at a friendly peasant's. The neighborhood families, spreading the word from one to the other, had been warned to hide their livestock and food stores and to be on guard, because the three characters were "hunting provisions" among the little houses with the usual brutality of the Nazi troops, who made themselves hated wherever they passed. It hadn't been hard for Quattro and Pyotr to pick up their trail, thanks especially to the presence of Quattro, who was a native of that countryside and knew every place and every person in it; and they had decided to keep watch, hidden on the Germans' path, to take them by surprise at the right moment. The wait had lasted longer than they had foreseen, because the three men, exasperated by their meager haul, had taken successive diversions, becoming more and more drunk on wine. Finally, from the hiding place in the underbrush, Quattro and Pyotr had seen them appear on the trail, preceded by their drunken voices, which were singing in Italian, half-swallowing the words, a popular song of the time:

"Sea, why do you invite me
    To dream tonight . . ."

They were singing together, a jolly chorus, their cheeks flushed, their jackets unbuttoned; the youngest and fattest, the one with the sack on his shoulder, had actually taken off jacket and shirt, remaining naked to the waist. Quattro was the first to shoot, from a very short distance, hitting with deadly accuracy the one who seemed the oldest: a thin, balding man of about thirty, who clutched both hands to his chest with a hoarse, stupefied cry; and, after a strange spin in the air, he fell, face to the ground. Immediately, with a convulsive, instinctive movement, his companions grabbed for their revolvers; but they didn't have time even to draw them from their belts before the volleys of Pyotr's machine-pistol, from his position a little farther on. For an imperceptible space of time, the Germans' eyes held the eyes of Quattro. One man sank to his knees and advanced perhaps a yard, kneeling, murmuring incomprehensible syllables. And the third, the bare-chested one, who was still absurdly carrying the sack by its rope in his left hand, let his grip relax with a strange slowness; and in a sudden shout of panic he took a step to one side, his hand to his abdomen. But an instant later, at a final volley of shots, both fell, near the first man.

No further sound came from the three inert bodies lying on the trail; in that petrified pause, however, from a bush towards the opposite slope a kind of blood-curdling imploration echoed, of extreme terror, like the crying of a newborn infant. It was the imprisoned pig, who, hit by the last volley, had rolled or had dragged himself into the bush, and from there was emitting those spasmodic human-sounding screams, usual with animals of his species when they sense the end is near. Then silence fell immediately, and Quattro stepped out onto the trail. Two of the Germans seemed already dead; only the oldest, the one Quattro himself had shot, was still jerking weakly; and at that point he tried to move his face from the ground, spitting a bloody saliva and murmuring "Mutter Mutter." Quattro finished him off with a revolver-shot in the head; then he turned the second man over, and found him wide-eyed and lifeless; while the last, the one naked to the waist, lying supine, whom Quattro believed already dead, grimaced at his approach, and painfully raised one arm.

Quattro was about to shoot this one too; but then Pyotr burst from the brush onto the trail, saying with a twisted laugh: "No, wait. This one's mine." And Quattro offered him the revolver, thinking Pyotr wanted to be the one to give him the coup de grâce. But Pyotr rejected the revolver, and in determined, raging hatred, aimed a terrible kick, with his heavy boot, at the man's flung-back face. After an instant's pause, he repeated the action, exactly the same, and again, several times, always with the same mad violence, but with a strangely calculated rhythm. Quattro, who had stepped back a pace, and was turning his head not to see, could still hear those kicks, in their grim heaviness, following one another at regular intervals, as if marking an incredible time in an immense space. At the first blow, the German had reacted with a stifled, rattling scream, which still sounded rebellious; but his screams had gradually weakened until they were reduced to a little feminine moan, like a question steeped in a nameless shame. The thuds continued at more rapid intervals after the moan had stopped. Suddenly, Pyotr, with his long, lanky stride, came to face Quattro. "He's had it," he announced, panting slightly, like someone who had completed a physical task. His gaze was still glaring beneath his sweating brow, and his cleated boot was spattered with blood. Now they had only to strip the dead of their weapons and everything else that was of use—according to guerrilla regulations—then hide the bodies. Beforehand, when choosing the spot, the two had kept in mind the neighboring field, beyond the trail, with a broad ditch, its bed still muddy from the recent rains. And, first of all, dragging the bare-chested one by the feet, they threw him into it. He had no face any more, only a shapeless, bloody residue; and, in contrast, the extraordinary whiteness of his fleshy torso looked unreal. Blood, which had flowed copiously from the wounds in his abdomen, soaked the pants of his blue-gray uniform. His shoes, however, were not stained; but the two partisans didn't remove them. They also left his pistol and the rest, even his watch. With the other bodies, on the contrary, they followed the usual rules, and then they threw them on top of the first, covering the ditch with earth and boughs. Finally, Quattro saw to recovering their loot, the pig, now silent, on its back behind the bush. In all, from the moment of the first shot, the action had taken only a few minutes.

. . .

Immediately after the return to the hut, Ace and the others got busy loading the mule. A little later the girl appeared, Maria (known to Ace as

Mariulina), who among other things assumed the assignment of taking Useppe, on the mule, back to the rendezvous on the road. Ace couldn't go with him, being occupied with various urgent preparations, and waiting, moreover, for the arrival of the famous Eyeglasses. In saying goodbye to his brother, from the ground, he promised they would see each other again soon. Winking to him, secretly, as if to a guerrilla comrade, he confided that on one of the next nights he was to participate in a big action on the Via Tiburtina; and afterwards, perhaps, he would come and sleep with them at Pietralata.

The mule, Uncle Peppe, set off, overloaded. In addition to Mariulina and Useppe, he was carrying on his back a big burden of faggots and branches, under which, in reality, were hidden weapons, grenades, and ammunition, which Mariulina was to deliver, on her way back, to a villager, accomplice of other guerrillas. Useppe had been set in front, against Mariulina's breast; she sat astride the mule, her legs outstretched, like a horseman. She had a short little black dress, and some homemade black stockings rolled up above her knees. As she rode, her pretty round thighs were bared on either side, and they, like everything that could be seen of her flesh, were a pink-peach color, gilded by very fine, dark freckles. On her face, she had her usual grumpy expression; and during the journey (ascent and descent of the trail, and path towards the paved road) she spoke only to the mule, saying to him, as the situation required: "Geeeee!" or else "Aaaaaah!" To Useppe's various questions, she answered, at most *yes yes* or *no no*, at times incorrectly. Uncle Peppe advanced calmly, also because of the huge burden he was carrying, and for certain stretches she would get down and pull him by the halter, shouting at him angrily: "Aaaaaah!" her reddish hair falling over her eyes, as Useppe clung tight to the harness to keep from falling.

Useppe enjoyed the journey very much. He also had one leg on either side of the mule's back, like a knight of olden times. He huddled against Mariulina's breast, as if against a warm pillow, and under his little behind he had Uncle Peppe's hairy withers, also warm. Before his eyes was Uncle Peppe's dark brown mane and his two erect ears, neither a horse's nor a donkey's, which had between them, as ornament, a frayed green plume. For Useppe these, and other, even minimal, specialties of the mule were curiosities of the maximum interest. Around him he had the spectacle of the countryside with its lights, different now from those of the morning. And if he turned to look up, he saw Mariulina's eyes, an orange color, with black lashes and brows, and her face which, in the sunlight, was all covered with a down, as if she had a great veiled hat on her head. In Useppe's opinion, Mariulina was a universal beauty, to be gazed upon in awe.

When the descent ended, they saw some Germans go by, in the valley, also leading a heavily laden mule. "Mule! Mule?!" Useppe exclaimed, waving to them festively. "No, no . . ." Mariulina replied, fed up with answering him. "Inglish?" Useppe exclaimed further, echoing the remark he had heard his brother make at the passage of the airplanes. "Yes yes!" she answered impatiently.

The truck was already waiting at the crossroads of the highway. And after delivering Useppe to the tavernkeeper, who scolded her for the delay ("Are you stupid or crazy?"), she, having deigned him neither a greeting nor an answer, shouted promptly to the mule: "Geeee!" and left them, going back on foot, beside the mule.

9 This time, Ninnarieddu didn't keep his promise. Almost a year was to go by before he turned up again. After that splendid morning of Useppe's on the guerrilla war's fields, cold and rainy days followed. The slum of Pietralata was a swamp of mud.

In the big closed room, the stink was terrible, also because the twins, with the cold and the scant air and their unhealthy diet, had developed diarrhea. They were wasted, had lost their gaiety, and cried and kicked, skinny, in their filth.

The Thousand, suffering the cold, had completely given up undressing. They all slept in their clothes, and also during the day they spent most of the time wrapped in their blankets on their mattresses, one against the other. Males and females made love at every hour of the day, no longer caring who watched them; and among them intrigues developed, jealousies, scenes, in which the old people also took part. Promiscuity made them all quarrelsome: the gramophone's songs were constantly mingled with yells, insults, blows, and tears of the women and the kids. There were also broken panes, which were mended as well as possible with strips of glued paper. Night fell early; after some disorders in the city, the Germans had advanced the curfew to seven P.M. Bicycles were forbidden to circulate after five in the afternoon, and public transport (already greatly reduced, to tell the truth) stopped at six.

And so, in the evening, all were imprisoned in the room. One of the pastimes of those evenings was hunting cockroaches and mice. One evening, a mouse was kicked to death before the eyes of Useppe, who cried: "No! no!"

Mice, already frequent visitors to that half-basement room in former times, encouraged to new audacity after Rossella's flight, now hastened more numerously to The Thousand's provisions, perhaps prescient of an imminent abandoning of the ship. In fact, The Thousand, fed up with waiting there for the famous Liberation that never came, were beginning to emigrate towards other shelters. The first family to leave was Salvatore's, with his children Currado, Impero, etc., the result of an angry separation following a quarrel; but soon the same Salvatore invited those left behind to come share a finer abode, empty and cheap, obtained through some acquaintances of his in Albano. And so also Domenico and family, with Granny Dinda, Sora Mercedes, Carulina, and the others went to join the rest of the tribe.

The morning of the farewell remains marked in the memory by a chaotic disorder. Carulina was so nervous she cried, and she ran here and there, as the twins, as their diarrhea had worsened, were soiling themselves constantly. Their few diapers, which she stubbornly washed over and over again with every sort of ersatz soap and very poor soap powder, never dried; and hanging from the lines in the room, still with yellowish stains, they dripped their water onto the floor, the provisions, and the rolled-up mattresses. Carulina was assailed from all sides with reproaches and screams, and she also received a backhand slap from a sister-in-law. From somewhere in the distance came echoes of bombardments; and the grandmothers, frightened by that thunder, and sulky at the thought of leaving, invoked the Pope, the dead, and the biggest saints in heaven in very shrill voices, while Domenico cursed. I have heard all private cars were forbidden to circulate at that time; the young men of The Thousand, however, thanks to their aptitude in underhand dealings, still managed to procure a little Balilla pickup truck, supplied with all the necessary permits, in addition to another three-wheeled motor vehicle sent by Salvatore. But, unfortunately, when the moment came, these means of transport were insufficient to carry the departing company and their property (among other things, The Thousand had decided to take away also their mattresses, previously lent by the hospital for the use of the homeless: since, even in their move, they remained, by right, homeless) . . . And the preparations, the packing and loading, finally became a dramatic disease. The exasperated Domenico started kicking the mattresses, which, having been used to wrap up cooking utensils and bound with cord, had assumed gigantic dimensions; Peppe Terzo, Attilio, and their mother burst into a chorus of screams. And then the oldest grandfather (husband of the silent grandmother) started crying like a baby, begging them to leave him there to die, or rather, to bury him then and there at Pietralata, maybe drowning him in some marsh: "Bury me," he kept repeating, "bury me, that way I'll sleep peacefully tonight in heaven!" And the grandmother, his wife, hearing him, exclaimed in a shrill voice: "Gesù! Gesù!"

The least agitated was Sora Mercedes, who remained seated on her little stool till the last moment, her knees covered by the blanket (from beneath which the provisions had been removed), merely repeating, in a chanting tone: "Aw, shut up a while, damn you all!" while her husband, Giuseppe Primo, seated beside her with a kind of wool bonnet on his head, relieved his emotion by hawking and spitting on the floor.

It was decided that a part of the company, including Carulina and her daughters, would reach the new headquarters by tram. Before the farewell, Carulina left Useppe, as a souvenir, the record with the comic scenes, which, unfortunately, without the gramophone (already packed away with the load of luggage) could no longer play; but for that matter, from excessive wear, for some time it had been able to emit only rasping sounds and coughs. She also made him a present (winking at him secretly, that he was to tell no one) of a little sack forgotten by her kin, containing about two pounds of dried beans.

At the departure, an uncertain sun was peeping out in the sky. The last of all was Carulina, immediately preceded by her Roman sister-in-law, who carried Celestina in her arms and, on her head, a crammed suitcase that wouldn't close; while Carulina carried Rusinella in her arms and the bundle of damp diapers on her head. If it hadn't been for the piercing cries that came from them, it would have been hard to tell which of the two bundles carried by each of the departing women contained babies. In fact, Carulina, as a last resort, had wrapped the little girls in every sort of rag available—Carlo Vivaldi's former curtain, leftovers from the Charity Ladies, even wastepaper—because of her shamed fear that, on the Castelli tram, all the passengers would be able to tell, from the odor, that her daughters were soiled from diarrhea.

Urged by the others who went ahead of her and turned to call her sharply, she hastened, with effort, in the mire, still in her summer shoes, reduced to clogs. The hand-me-down stockings she wore, too big for her feet, bagged at her ankles, and because of the weight that made her tilt to one side, her walk was more crooked than usual. As an overcoat, she wore a kind of uneven three-quarter-length garment made from a jacket of her brother Domenico; and under the bundle of diapers you could see the precise parting of her hair, divided into two even bands to the nape, with the braids at either side pressed low by her burden.

Before passing the curve of the path, she turned to wave to Useppe, with a smile on her broad, turned-up mouth. Useppe was standing motionless, this side of the ditch, watching her leave, and he answered her with his special wave that he made on such occasions, opening and closing his fist very slowly and sadly. He was grave, with only a little, hesitant smile. On his head he wore a cyclist's cap she herself had found for him, with his usual Chaplinesque pants, his two-tone boots, and the rain cape down to his feet, which opened as he waved, displaying its red lining.

A few months later, a terrible air raid on the Castelli destroyed a great part of the city of Albano, and at the news Ida thought of The Thousand, wondering if by chance the tribe had all been wiped out. Instead, they were unharmed. In the following summer, Nino, in Naples for certain dealings of his, happened to run into Salvatore, who on that occasion took him home for a visit. They lived in the remains of a handsome building half-destroyed by the air raids, in a room on the second floor which—since the stairway had collapsed—was now reached through the window by a kind of drawbridge made of planks. And Carulina was also there, having become, through the natural logic of destiny, a prostitute with the Allies. Though a bit taller, she was even thinner than at Pietralata, so that in her reduced face, her eyes, smeared with mascara, seemed doubly broadened. And the gait of her scrawny legs, on high heels, was more clumsy than ever. Still, her way of looking and acting, her speech, hadn't changed at all.

There was no sign of the twins, and Ninnuzzu didn't bother to ask for news of them. In the brief course of his visit, an Afro-American soldier arrived, Carulina's lover; he was happily preparing to return to America the next day; and as a present, at Carulina's own choice, he brought her one of those all too well-known Sorrento music boxes, that are wound up and play, off pitch, a little song. On the box's inlaid top there was a little celluloid doll, dressed in a bodice and tutu of lilac rayon. Thanks to a stick inserted in her body, every time the music box was wound up, she made a turn around the lid. Carulina was spellbound by that ballet to the sound of music; and as soon as the device ran down, she would immediately rewind it, with an owner's eager self-importance. There, along with the other grandmother and the two grandfathers, their husbands, was also Granny Dinda, who, to justify Carulina's overexcitement to the visitors, explained that this was the first doll she had ever owned in her life. Meanwhile, the same Granny Dinda sang the words of the box's old song, accompanying them with café-chantant movements. As refreshment, the guests were offered whisky and potato chips.

But Ninnuzzu never remembered, afterwards, to report this meeting to Ida, who certainly, in view of the vastness of Naples and its countless throngs, never thought to ask him if he had encountered any of The Thousand in that immensity. And so Ida remained forever with the thought that The Thousand might have been buried beneath Albano's rubble.

．　．　．

When the last of The Thousand had gone around the curve, Useppe, coming back inside, discovered the room had become huge. His little steps reechoed there; and when he called "Mà" and Ida answered "Eh?" their two voices sounded different from before. Everything was motionless, amid the wastepaper and the garbage scattered on the ground; not even a cockroach or a mouse ventured forth at that hour. In the obtuse angle, the glass of the little votive candle holder, broken in the uproar, lay on the ground next to the greasy wick and a patch of spilled oil. In the center of the room, a packing case had remained, formerly used as the twins' crib, with a layer of old newspapers inside, all soiled with their feces. In Eppetondo's corner, there was still his rolled-up mattress; and in the corner beside the door, where the rag curtain had been torn away the better to wrap up Rosa and Celeste, there was the straw pallet, still stained with the blood from the birth of Rossella's kitten.

Ida had lain down on her own mattress, for a brief rest. But her organism must have become habituated to the racket, as if to a drug, since the incredible silence which had suddenly fallen in the room exacerbated her nervous tension rather than calming it. Rain had begun falling again. Neither from the city nor the slum came any sign of other existences. And the rustle of the rain, with the returning echo of distant bombing, enlarged the silence around that room, half-sunk in mud, where only she and Useppe remained. Ida wondered if Useppe realized The Thousand's departure was definitive. She could hear his little steps slowly cover the room, all around, as if on a tour of inspection; then suddenly that slowness of his walking was transformed into an excited haste, until, seized with a frenzy, he began to run. On the ground there was a rough ball of cloth that, on days of fine weather, had allowed other, older boys to imitate football players out in the open field. And he, in turn, imitating those boys, began kicking it furiously, but there were no teams, no referee, no goalie. He scrambled madly up the pile of desks, and jumped down with one of his usual flights.

The faint thud of his booted feet was followed by a total silence. A little later, peering from behind the curtain, Ida saw him seated like an emigrant on a sandbag, examining the record left him by Carulina, scratching his finger around the grooves. His eyes looked up, grave and bewildered, at Ida's movement. And he ran to her with the record:

"A' mà, play it!"

"It can't be played, like this. You need the gramophone to play it."

"Wy?"

"Because, without a gramophone, a record won't play."

"Without a gammapone, it won't play . . ."

The rain was falling harder. In the air, a hiss, like a siren, made Ida start. But probably it was only a truck, going by on the Via dei Monti. It stopped at once. Darkness was falling. The vast abandoned room, cold, filled with rubbish, seemed isolated in an unreal space, this side of a besieged frontier.

Waiting for the rain to let up a little, Ida looked for some pastime to entertain Useppe. And for the umpteenth time, she sang for him the story of the *ships:*

"And the ship turns and the ship veers . . .
. . . Three the lions and three the big boats . . ."

"Again," Useppe said to her, when she had finished.
She told it to him another time.
"Again," Useppe said. And meanwhile, with a hinting little smile, to announce a surprise that would surely find her incredulous, he revealed to her:

"A' mà, I saw it . . . the sea!"

It was the first time that, in some way, he referred to his adventure on the guerrilla fields. As a rule, when questioned, he kept his mouth shut, maintaining a proper secrecy on the subject. However, this time Ida interpreted his obscure phrase as a simple fantasy and asked him nothing.

"And the ship turns and the ship veers . . ."

For a certain period, in that month of November, the two of them remained the room's only occupants. The schools, though with some delay, had been reopened; Ida's school, however, had been requisitioned by the armed forces, and her classes had been transferred to another locality, even farther away than the previous one (with afternoon sessions, because they had to have shifts) so it was practically impossible for her to reach it, given the present scarcity of public transport and the curfew hour. Ida, therefore, thanks to her status as an air-raid victim, obtained a temporary dispensation from teaching. She was still obliged to leave the house every day, on her usual hunt for food; and especially on days of bad weather she had no other solution but to leave Useppe alone, his own guard, locking him in the room. It was then that Useppe learned to pass time *thinking*. He would press both fists to his brow and begin to *think*. What he thought about is not given to us to know; and probably his thoughts were imponderable futilities. But it's a fact that, while he was thinking in this way, the ordinary time of other people was reduced for him almost to zero. In Asia there exists a little creature known as the *lesser panda*, which looks like something between a squirrel and a teddy-bear and lives on the trees in inaccessible mountain forests; and every now and then it comes down to the ground, looking for buds to eat. Of one of these panda it was told that he spent millennia thinking on his own tree, from which he climbed down to the ground every three hundred years. But in reality, the calculation of such periods was relative: in fact, while three hundred years had gone by on earth, on that panda's tree barely ten minutes had passed.

Those solitary hours of Useppe's were, however rarely, interrupted by some unexpected visits. One day it was a striped cat, so thin it seemed a cat's ghost, which, still, with the strength of desperation, managed to break through the paper that replaced the windowpane and enter the room in search of food. Naturally, the mice, on his arrival, avoided looking out; and Useppe had nothing to offer him but some leftover boiled cabbage. But with that peculiar aristocratic haughtiness cats retain even in decline, he sniffed the offering and, without condescending to taste it, went off, his tail erect.

That same day, three German soldiers arrived: obviously, as on other occasions in the past, they were ordinary army privates (neither Polizei, nor SS), without evil intentions. With the common custom of German troops, however, instead of knocking, they hammered violently on the door with the butts of their guns. And since Useppe, locked in, couldn't open the door, they finished tearing away from the window the rest of the paper already broken by the cat shortly before, to search the interior's length and breadth with their eyes. Useppe had gone towards them, below the window, pleased at receiving a visit, from anyone at all; and, seeing only him in the room, they addressed him in their language. What the devil they were looking for, nobody knows; and Useppe, not understanding their Ostrogoth words, but presuming that, like the cat, they were looking for food, tried offering them that same leftover cabbage. But like the cat before them, they also refused the offer; and indeed, laughing, they offered Useppe a candy in return. Unfortunately, however, it was a mint candy—a flavor Useppe didn't like—and he promptly spat it out. Dutifully, after having spat it out, he started to return it to the donor, saying to him with a smile: "Here!", at which, laughing harder than ever, they went off again.

The third unexpected visitor was Eppetondo, who had his own key and thus could enter the room. In the place of his old hat, he had found himself a cap like an American gangster's to protect his head from the cold. And he was as merry as ever, though his arm, put in a cast and healed after the fracture of the previous summer, had developed rheumatism. He didn't want anyone to know his arm hurt, however, for fear of being dismissed from the partisans for being too old and decrepit. And he confided his fear to Useppe. Moreover, he brought him news from the camp, as if by now he were speaking with a guerrilla comrade. All the comrades were well; and they had performed new, splendid feats. One night, the *Liberty* and other squads had scattered four-pointed nails on the roads into Rome, working with the RAF, which, attacking the blocked German vehicles at the right moment, had massacred them with volleys of automatic fire, ordinary bombs, and incendiary bombs, so the great Roman consular roads were all a bloodstained orgy. And, on another night, Ace and some comrades, after various minor actions of road sabotage, had dynamited a whole train of German troops; it had exploded immediately, in an inferno of flames and twisted iron.

The *Liberty* group had abandoned the hut, moving its base elsewhere, into a little stone house. Ace and Quattro and Tarzan, etc., sent greetings and love to Useppe. In spite of the cold and the bad weather, which made underground life much harder, all were in good spirits and fine shape, with the single exception of Pyotr, who, after the first days of ardent participation, had fallen into a kind of listlessness, and didn't do anything, spending all his time getting drunk. Actually, Comrade Pyotr for some time had been unusable as a guerrilla: so much so that the others, in fact, were arguing about whether or not it would be a good idea to send him away, or even liquidate him, with a shot in the head. But instead they went on tolerating him: first, because they figured when this bad period was over he would be himself again, the way he had been at the start; secondly, because of his bitter situation as a Jew; and thirdly, because of the friendship of Ace, who still trusted and respected him, and considered him a hero, defending him fiercely against the stubborn hostility of the other comrades.

Though he understood little of it, Useppe listened to all this epic news with the same fervor as when he listened to the song of the *ships*; and, indeed, at the end of Moscow's report, he said to him, "again!" but with no results.

Unfortunately, the chief reason for Eppetondo's visit proved a severe frustration for him. He had come, in fact, with the idea of taking to the camp the last supplies of canned goods he had left in the room—sardines, mussels, and octopus in tomato sauce—but he discovered that everything had been carried off, and of his belongings only the mattress and the empty cage were left. All the rest, clearly, had departed along with The Thousand; and assailing them with various insults, of which the less unrepeatable were "bastards" and "sonsofbitches," Eppetondo took the initiative of unrolling his mattress on top of Ida's, so that at least someone would enjoy it, since as a partisan he slept very comfortably on straw. For that matter, this big room was even less comfortable than the *Liberty* squad's little base, where at least a wood fire could always be managed. Inside the room, on the contrary, there was no means of heat; your teeth chattered; the dampness made stains on the wall; and Useppe, rather pale and wasted, wandered around, wrapped in so many old woolen castoffs (ex-Charity Ladies') that he seemed a walking bundle. "Now at least you'll sleep on two mattresses," Eppetondo said to him when it was time for their goodbyes, "and mind you: don't let them steal this too, eh! It's all wool, and be careful the mice don't eat it, either!" The empty cage remained in the corner, as a souvenir.

Frequent visitors, on those lonely days of Useppe's, were the sparrows, who arrived to hop and chatter at the barred window. And since his talent for understanding the language of animals came to him only on certain days, Useppe understood nothing of their chatter except their ordinary cheep cheep cheep. Still it wasn't hard for him to understand that even these guests were looking for a snack. Unfortunately the bread ration was so scant that it was hard for him to find a few leftover crumbs to offer these other starving creatures.

10

TO ALL PROVINCIAL AUTHORITIES, TO BE CARRIED OUT IMMEDIATELY, THE FOLLOWING POLICE ORDER HAS BEEN SENT:

1 — ALL JEWS RESIDENT IN ITALIAN TERRITORY, EVEN IF GRANTED SPECIAL STATUS, TO WHATEVER NATION THEY MAY BELONG, MUST BE SENT TO CONCENTRATION CAMPS SET UP FOR THE PURPOSE. ALL THEIR PROPERTY, REAL ESTATE AND OTHER, MUST BE IMMEDIATELY SEIZED, UNTIL IT CAN BE CONFISCATED BY THE ITALIAN SOCIAL REPUBLIC, WHICH WILL DISTRIBUTE IT IN THE INTEREST OF INDIGENT VICTIMS OF ENEMY AIR RAIDS.

2 — ALL THOSE BORN OF MIXED MARRIAGES WHO, IN APPLICATION OF THE EXISTING RACIAL LAWS, WERE RECOGNIZED AS MEMBERS OF THE ARYAN RACE, MUST BE SUBJECTED TO SPECIAL SURVEILLANCE BY THE POLICE FORCES.

ROME, 30 NOVEMBER 1943

This double ordinance, by which the Italians sanctioned the *Final Solution* already initiated by the Germans, covered the case of the widow Ida Mancuso née Ramundo, both in the first article (because she was an air-raid victim) and in the second (because an Aryan of mixed blood). But it doesn't seem to have had any practical effect on Ida, all the same. In fact, she received no benefit from the Jews' confiscated property. And, as for the second article, it's true, apparently, that in the course of the following season, after her transferral to a new temporary domicile, some policemen came to question the concierge about her situation. But the concierge-informer kept his information to himself; or at least, if he reported it to anyone, it was under the seal of secrecy. She never knew about it. And probably her file ended up lost in the subsequent annihilation of all destinies.

However, the double ordinance, which she happened to see at the beginning of December, meant for her that she was officially under special police surveillance from that moment. Her guilt was thus contemplated by the law, without ambiguity or compromise, and denounced to the world on the city walls: *Wanted, a certain Ida, alias Iduzza, of mixed race, mother of two children, the older a deserter and a partisan, and the second, a bastard of unknown father.* For Ninnarieddu, she wasn't too afraid: the moment she thought of him, she could see him, with his dancer's gait, his long, straight legs and his feet flung out, kicking aside any obstacle or tumult, her invulnerable son. But she was persecuted by horrible fears for Useppe. It was known that during the round-up of the Jews, the Germans had grabbed children, even babes in their mother's arms, flinging them into their funereal trucks, like rags into a rubbish pile; and that in certain villages, in reprisal or merely out of drunkenness, they had killed children, crushing them with tanks, or burning them alive, or slamming them against the walls. Few people, at that time, believed these reports, considered too incredible (though, to tell the truth—it must be reported—they were later confirmed by History and, indeed, represent only a small part of the reality). But Ida couldn't dispel those visions: so the streets of Rome and of the world for her seemed crowded with possible executioners of her Useppetto, her little pariah without race, underdeveloped, under-nourished, poor valueless remnant. At times, not only the Germans and the Fascists, but all human adults seemed murderers to her; and she ran through the street, aghast, to arrive, exhausted, her eyes wide, in the big room, starting to call from the road "Useppe! Useppe!" and laughing like a sick little girl when the tiny voice answered her: "A' mà!"

The Nazi-Fascists, actually, still didn't dare show themselves too often in the slum. The October shootings hadn't sufficed to frighten the population of those huts drowned in mud and hunger. With winter, the attacks on bakeries and food trucks became more frequent. Bands of guerrillas were formed within the slum itself, and it was said that in the caves, in the hovels and little rooms where families of ten people slept, even under the beds, weapons were hidden, stolen back in September from army outposts and barracks. Even the young males, who in the rest of the city mostly remained hidden in the fear of raids, here displayed themselves defiantly, with hard, grim faces, in the courtyards and the holes and the garbage dumps of their outlying ghetto, among their worn and disheveled mothers, the wasted girls, the lice-ridden kids with their little bellies swollen from lack of nourishment. Ida avoided going too far away from the slum, so as not to leave Useppe alone; but to bring him something to eat, she forced herself to desperate exploits. Even the famous nest egg of savings sewn into the stocking had now been consumed in black-market shopping, and like the other kids', his little belly had also swollen slightly. Every time she went to the Bursary to draw her monthly pay, Ida felt her legs buckle beneath her, expecting the clerk to announce to her indignantly: "Wicked halfbreeds like you are no longer entitled to any salary!"

The big room had remained uninhabited only for a few days. At the beginning of December, once the news had spread that over there, at the end of that avalanche of mud and garbage, a roof was available, new lost creatures had begun to turn up, in whom Ida, with her confused prejudices, saw a threat rather than a protection. She was even more afraid to leave Useppe now in that company than she had been, before, to leave him alone.

Among the many newcomers, there happened to be the family of a little shopkeeper from Genzano, dazed with terror of air raids. Apparently some one of The Thousand had directed them here. The head of the family, a ruddy and corpulent man, who suffered from high blood pressure, had been seen only at their arrival, then he had rushed back to Genzano, where his shop had already been bombed out, but the house was still standing. The fact was that in a wall of the house he had secretly bricked up, for safe-keeping, all the money and valuables he had left, and for this reason he wanted to stand guard. Until one day, in a raid, which still left the house intact, he died of a heart attack, from fear. A relative came from Genzano to bring the news to the family, all women. And the room filled with screams and weeping. But after some argument, between sobs, the women, also overcome by terror of the bombings, left the relative the task of burying the dead man and watching the house; and they stayed where they were, in the room.

They were also obese, but pale; and the mother's legs were all swollen with varicose veins. They spent the day around a brazier, mourning, in total inertia and dejected silence. They were waiting for the arrival of the Allies, who, according to them, were at the gates, and then they would go back to Genzano, where, however, they no longer had a shop, or a man, nothing but that hypothetical, walled-up treasure. And they spoke of the imminent Liberation in spent voices, like enormous hens on a peg perch, saddened in the swelling of their feathers, reduced to waiting for the arrival of the master, to carry them off in a sack.

If Useppe approached the brazier, they pushed him away, saying in a whining voice, "Go back to your mamma, kid."

A woman from Pietralata also turned up, mother of one of the boys shot on October 22nd. When her son was alive, she had nagged him all the time because he came home late at night, until her son, exasperated by her constant yelling, had even beaten her, and she had also, in the past, reported him for this to the police. Now, every evening, she went wandering from one house to another because she was afraid to sleep at home, where she said her son's ghost came back every night to beat her. This boy of hers was named Armandino, and the Germans had arrested him before her eyes, after she too, that day as on previous occasions, had joined in the attack on the Fort, hoping to get some flour. Every now and then, during the night, she could be heard saying: "No, Armandino, no. Not your own mamma!" Often, in the daytime, she would boast of Armandino's beauty, famous in Pietralata for his resemblance to the actor Rossano Brazzi. And, in fact, she herself must also have been good-looking when young: she still had very beautiful long hair, but gray now, and lousy.

These new refugees in the big room had brought their own mattresses; and in addition, left by transient guests, there was some kapok scattered on the floor at the disposal of other temporary vagabonds. Carlo Vivaldi's pallet was occupied by a young man of whom Ida was especially afraid, as if of a werewolf. It's true he had made some improvements in the room, applying pieces of plywood to the broken windows, replacing the paper; but for the rest, he resembled not so much a man as some other starving mammal, of a nocturnal species. He was tall and muscular, but bent, and he had a cadaverous face, with protruding teeth. No one knew where he came from, or what his profession was, or how he had landed there; but from his speech, he seemed Roman. He also, if Useppe approached him, sent him away, saying: "Clear out, kid."

The days of The Thousand were past! The only one who occasionally paid any attention to Useppe was the mother of the executed boy; when it was dark, she would accompany him down to the latrine, if necessary, holding his hand as Carulina used to. And one evening, in helping him pull up his pants, touching his fleshless little ribs, she said to him: "Poor little bird, I have a feeling you won't make it, you won't grow up. You're not long for this world. The war slaughters kids."

She entertained him, too, with a game, or rather a fairy tale accompanied by mime, which she had already used with her own children when they were little. It was always the same, and it consisted of this: as a beginning, she tickled the palm of his hand, saying:

"Square, pretty square,
  Here passed a crazy hare,"

and then, pulling up his fingers, one by one, beginning with the thumb,
she continued:

"This caught him,
  this killed him,
  this cooked him,
  this ate him,"

and reaching the little finger, she concluded:

"and this one was left all alone,
  because for him there was none."

"Again," Useppe would say to her at the end of the story; and she
would start over at the beginning, while Useppe would look at her intently,
hoping that, one of these times, the crazy hare would manage to escape,
leaving the hunters empty-handed. But invariably the tale proceeded and
ended always in exactly the same way.

. . . . **1944**

JANUARY

In the cities of occupied Italy, and chiefly in Rome, the police set up special units, which employ professional sadists, German and Italian, with license to arrest, torture, and kill, at their whim, according to the Hitler system of "Night and Fog."

In Verona, the Fascist court of the Republic of Salò sentences to death the Fascist leaders guilty of having voted against the Duce in the July meeting of the Grand Council. Among those sentenced is Ciano, the Duce's son-in-law. The sentence is immediately carried out.

Allied landing near Anzio blocked by vast German forces. The advance in Italy is held up at Cassino.

FEBRUARY–APRIL

After new ordinances of the Italian police, the Fascists, assisted by local informers, proceed to seek out and arrest Jews who eluded the previous German round-ups.

In Rome, in reprisal for a partisan attack on an SS patrol (32 killed), the German Command orders the massacre of 335 Italian civilians, whose bodies are flung into a cave (the Fosse Ardeatine).

The potential of the Red Army steadily grows, through the increased efficiency of the USSR war industry and shipments of Allied material. Engaged all along the front in a series of attacks (Stalin's ten offensives), the Soviet troops advance victoriously westward, reaching the Czechoslovakian border to the south.

JUNE–JULY

With a landing in Normandy, opening a new western front against the Germans, the Allies begin the reconquest of France.

In Italy, there is a breakthrough on the Cassino front; and resuming their advance from the south, the Allies enter Rome.

The Italian resistance forces, in the part of the country still occupied by the Nazis, organize into a single army (Volunteers of Freedom Corps), while the regular Italian troops of the Italian Liberation Corps, set up by the King and by Badoglio, take part in the Allies' actions.

From the East, the Russian troops continue their advance towards the Reich.

In the Reich, an assassination attempt against Hitler, organized by some high German officers, fails. The conspirators are executed, along with other persons involved or suspect (about five thousand).

AUGUST–OCTOBER

On the western front, the Allied advance continues. The Allies enter

Paris. In Italy, they face the enemy along a new line north of Florence (the Gothic Line).

On the eastern front, a last-ditch German counteroffensive temporarily halts the Soviets on the Vistula; while beyond the river, the city of Warsaw, rising up against the Nazis, is destroyed in reprisal, its last remains burned, practically ceasing to exist (300,000 Poles massacred).

In the Pacific, there is a succession of kamikaze attacks (Japanese suicide pilots), in a vain attempt to destroy the American fleet. The naval battle of Leyte, near the Philippines, ends with a disastrous defeat of the Japanese navy.

In Germany, the Führer orders general mobilization of all ablebodied males between sixteen and sixty years of age.

NOVEMBER–DECEMBER

In German-occupied Italy, a proclamation of the British High Command, ordering the demobilization of the resistance, in view of the imminent Allied victory, goes unheeded. The coordination of the Italian resistance is now the task of the CLN (Comitato Liberazione Nazionale, National Liberation Committee), composed of the six clandestine opposition parties which have survived the Fascist regime. With the active participation of the populace, the partisan forces keep the Germans engaged in a wearing struggle, driving them from various areas, which declare themselves autonomous, forming little temporary republics.

In autumn and winter, Allied operations in Italian territory are blocked at the Gothic Line . . .

1 The thunder of the bombings around Rome was becoming more frequent, and more constant; and the women of the Genzano shopkeeper, each time they heard them, sprang to their feet with hysterical screams of terror. After the Allied landing at Anzio on January 22, from the slum came songs and shouts of joy, as if the war were over by now. The very few Fascists of the neighborhood went into hiding, while all the young men came into the streets, and some even showed themselves armed: they seemed to be openly preparing the revolution. They took bread, flour, and other foodstuffs, with violence, from the shops or wherever it was still to be found, and freely distributed copies of the clandestine *Unità*, special edition.

Ida left the room as little as possible, and always held Useppe close to her skirts, afraid that the Germans, responding to the provocation, would invade the slum and kill or deport all males, not sparing her little man Useppe. During those days, the Werewolf vanished; and she wondered if by any chance he was a spy, who had hastened to report the people of Pietralata to the German High Command. In any case, that extreme, popular festival ended in another bitter frustration. Within a few days the Germans had succeeded in containing the operation, nailing the Allies to the Anzio beach. The shopkeeper's women huddled together, no longer screaming, not even breathing, their lips yellow with fear: for the thunder of the shellings around Rome was now steady, day and night. To these thunderclaps, there was added the enormous racket of the German supply trucks, which drove along the highways, not to retreat, but to attack with new reinforcements. The Anzio landing was only a hamstrung episode. The real front was still blocked at Cassino. The imminent liberation was again the usual lie. The war wasn't ending.

In late January, Ida received an unexpected visit from Remo the tavernkeeper, who called her outside, apart, having urgent news to communicate from her son Nino. Ace was in excellent health, and sent her greetings and hoped to see her soon, and sent kisses to his little brother. However, the recent war events, with the approach of the front, the destruction of the villages, and the constant German round-ups, had forced him and his men to suspend fighting in the zone. The *Liberty* group had been disbanded; some of its members had fallen, others had given up the struggle. Ace and Pyotr (Carlo) had gone off together, determined to reach Naples, crossing the front line; and it was sure that, alert and brave as they were, they would succeed in their enterprise. Moscow and Quattro were dead, and, by the way, the tavernkeeper brought Ida a posthumous message from Giuseppe Cucchiarelli. In fact, some time earlier, in absolute and universal secrecy, he had charged Remo, in the event of his death, to inform Signora Ida that the mattress already left her contained a surprise for her. In the wool, in the corner marked on the outside by a knot of red thread, there was something that he, as a dead man, couldn't use any more, even for the latrine, while for her and the kid, on the contrary, it might now come in handy.

As for himself, Remo brought Ida some presents: a flask of wine, half a liter of olive oil, and two candles. He felt it unnecessary to tell her the details of Moscow's death, and she didn't ask him. It had taken place on January 21st in the city of Marino, and for more than two days his body had remained exposed in the middle of the street, where the Germans had forbidden its removal, kicking it whenever they passed by. In death, his body seemed even smaller and skinnier than in life, and his face, even though swollen from torture, had taken on the characteristic look of the neighborhood granddad, because of his sharp chin that almost touched his nose. The Germans, in fact, before shooting him, had ripped out the fifteen teeth he still had in his mouth, as well as the nails from his fingers and toes, so his bare feet and his little old man's hands were puffy and black with clotted blood. He had gone to the city of Marino on duty, to deliver a coded communication from Eyeglasses to the commander of another band. And he was walking along with comrade Tarzan, assigned to collect a radio, when, seeing a vague form in the shadows of the little street, he had promptly ordered: "Halt there!" in a military tone. In reply, from behind the houses, came some voices grumbling in German, and Tarzan then fired; but afterwards, quickly, in the shooting that followed from the other side, he managed to run off, while Moscow was surrounded and captured. On him they found the message whose meaning he himself was really unable to reveal, since he didn't know it (the text was: *the clean laundry is in the bucket*). Obviously, he did know, however, many other things, which his torturers wanted to make him tell. But as visible marks demonstrated, those German boys, despite their labor, extracted nothing from him but noisy sobs, like a child's; until they gave up, finishing him off with a shot in the back. His dream, at this point, would have been to die shouting: "Long live Stalin!" but he had barely enough breath to emit a moan no louder than a sparrow's.

Less than a month earlier, on Christmas day precisely, he had reached the age of sixty. He was born in the same year as Benito Mussolini: 1883.

Quattro's end followed soon after Moscow's; and it was on the night between the 25th and 26th of January. Three days after the Allied landing, the Germans had had time to collect reinforcements from north and south; and the traffic of their vehicles invaded the roads towards Anzio. Still, it was believed the Allies would prevail; and the *Liberty* comrades were eager to participate in this final battle of Rome. Adventure on those roads excited them with its risk, like a real decisive battle. And beneath his polite and laconic manner, Quattropunte (or *Quat* as he was now more often called), was inwardly leaping and dancing with enthusiasm: finally they were in the front line, now reduced to a thread. On this side, there was the infamous past; and over there, the great revolutionary future, almost present, now, you might say. It's true that the Anglo-Americans were capitalists; however, behind them, as allies, there were also the Russians; and once the Fascists and Germans had been driven out, the proletariat—all together—would take care to establish true liberty. On the night of the 25th, it was pouring rain, and Quattro had covered his head with a little topee, which he had painted black for camouflage, and beneath which his round boyish peasant face disappeared almost to the nose. He had his submachine gun with him, looted from the enemy; on his feet were his waterproof boots, looted from the enemy; and he was carrying, naturally, his usual nightly ammunition of four-pointed nails, which, to tell the truth, on this night, were rather few. In fact, getting supplies of nails had become difficult since certain blacksmith friends who produced them (Romans, mostly) had been arrested and taken to the slaughterhouse. And recently, Quattro had taken to making them himself, at a village forge with the complicity of the apprentice, unknown to the proprietor.

The *Liberty* group's first enterprise, on that night, involved the telephone wires, of which they cut and carried off about a mile's length. Then on the Anzio road, the squad broke up into two groups: the first, with Quattro, especially assigned to the preparatory scattering of the nails, took positions on the edge of a crossroads; and the second, led by Ace (the commander, Eyeglasses, was in bed, wounded), stationed itself on a rise a bit farther on, at some distance from the first, with sub-machine guns ready for the passage of the German convoy, already *fixed* by the nails.

The crossroads, that night, was a site of extreme danger. There the traffic from Cassino encountered the traffic from Rome and the north; and, to regulate it, there were two men of the Feldgendarmerie. Only a quick and clever character like Quattro could succeed in pulling it off: and on such nights, too, his body had developed the senses and muscles of a wildcat, the wings of a hawk. With his little eyes blazing, he observed every slight distraction of the two gendarmes, who were rather heavy and slow; and without missing an instant, he would slip from his hiding-place, almost beneath the hoods of the cars, hurling his nails into the road with precise aim and with the same fun as when you play marbles on the sidewalk. Then he would dart back, so quick he was invisible or, at most, mistaken for some little night animal in flight. Having used up his supply of nails, he drew back behind the edge of the road with the other two of his group (one was Decimo, and the other a boy from Ariccia known as Negus). And, in file, bent over and silent, they worked their way south, with the idea of joining the rest of the band if possible, to support them, without overlooking, however, any tempting proposal of destiny along their way.

They were walking blindly over traveled territory, through mud and water. Every now and then, from the road, in the rustle of the rain, they could make out the sound of German vehicles, laboring, with flat tires, and then, with a contented smile, Quattro would make the Sign of the Cross. This gesture, which had remained with him from his first childish lessons at the parish house, now held no ecclesiastical significance for him; but it was a familiar gesture of good luck or to ward off the evil eye (as others make horns with their fingers, or tug at the curls inside their pants).

Arriving at the foot of an embankment a little less than three yards high, they climbed to the top, to observe, from the protection of some dry brush there, the enemy traffic on the road. First they saw a row of heavy trucks go by, continuing their journey though some of their tires were pierced. After an interval, a powerful closed car, of a kind generally reserved for high-ranking officers, sped unharmed before their eyes. But not half a minute later, at some distance to the south, they heard a bold crackle of automatic fire, then a crash, then silence. It must have been Ace's men, on the job. A great excitement gripped the three comrades watching from the embankment, their guns ready. At that moment, below them, a little open truck was passing, packed with soldiers, their metal helmets glistening in the rain. Immediately, the three opened fire, in unison, aiming first at the driver. And then they continued firing, not lifting their finger from the trigger, while the riddled and broken truck, after skidding on the wet pavement, rolled towards the opposite side of the road, amid wild, tormented screams. Two bodies could be seen falling from it onto the road, just as confused shooting began from the vehicle. Suggesting a carnival dancefloor, the tracer-bullets' red lines crisscrossed the air, striped by the rain. Suddenly flames rose from the truck, illuminating the lifeless bodies of the Germans on the asphalt: though disfigured, they could be recognized as young boys, of the most recent draft. The truck's carcass danced for a while on its side then stopped. A few last shots came from it, immediately spent in a definitive volley from the top of the embankment; some raving voices were still heard from inside, murmurs of *Mutter Mutter* among other incomprehensible words. At the same time the fire raged; and finally that mass of metal, in its death agony, jerked and fell silent. This side of the steady shelling heard from the sea, now only the hiss of the flames was audible, and a crackle of burning supplies; and the anguished barking of a guard dog somewhere among the olive groves and the vineyards.

In the shadows, the three on the embankment called one another softly: "Quat? . . . Decimo? Negus? . . ." "Yes . . . yes . . . yes . . ."

At that point, from the north, a still-distant clank of tracks signaled the arrival of armored vehicles on the road, and the three boys hastily withdrew from the embankment, fleeing together towards the fields behind, through the rows of vines and the ditches and the water pouring from the heavens.

It was only after they had gone about three or four hundred yards that Negus and Decimo realized Quat was no longer with them. But they supposed he had turned off in some other direction in the confusion of the darkness, and it was now too late to track him down anyway. The arriving convoy had stopped at the little truck. The sound of cleated boots could already be heard on the road, while shouts and orders in German began to reecho in the vicinity, among the groping shoots of the withered, soaked vines, and the flashing of the masked lanterns. Holding their breath, and crawling on all fours through the mire, Negus and Decimo managed to slip into a canebrake, and from there, fording a pond, they found themselves in a wood where, already, the sounds of the hunt pursuing them were faint and scattered. Still, panting, in a low voice, they tried calling: "Quat . . . Quat . . . !" There was no reply. And they resumed their flight, until dripping with rain and sweat, livid and breathless, they came into a valley of a few dark little houses, definitely safe from the pack.

In the last phase of the duel with the little truck, and while it was already giving its final jerks, a bullet had pierced Quat's chest; but he had felt no pain, any more than if they had hit him with a fist; so he had imagined the blow came from a piece of stone or a clod of earth dislodged by the shooting; and this sensation hadn't even reached his consciousness, it had been so brief. He hadn't dropped his gun (in fact, he had settled it over his shoulder), and had hastened off in flight with the others, sliding down the embankment with them. But, having reached the bottom, suddenly he had felt faint, unable to take another step. There, in fact, at the foot of the embankment, his companions later found his little topee. And Negus remembered having heard, when he fled from there, a groan just behind him, but so slight he hadn't given it any thought.

Quat, left behind, alone, had bent double, his knees in the water. And while his consciousness ebbed, his muscles had nevertheless obeyed him, in the instinctive action of setting the gun on the grass, on (relatively) dry ground, before stretching out where he was, as if he were lying down in his bed. So he had let himself sink, in the darkness, his head on the muddy grass and the rest of his body in a puddle, while the other two boys, unaware, continued their flight.

He was already dying. And he didn't know if it was night, or morning, or where he was. After an interval of time no longer calculable for him, he suddenly saw a great light, and it was a German's portable lamp, which illuminated him, full in the face. Behind the first German, another promptly appeared; but who knows what Quat thought he saw in those two very tall figures, with metal helmets and spotted, camouflaged overalls. He gave a shy, contented smile, and said: "Hello." In reply, he received spit in his face; however, it's likely he didn't feel it. Perhaps he was already dead, or perhaps drawing his last breath. The two soldiers grabbed him, one by the arms and the other by the feet, and rapidly climbing back up the embankment, they flung him from up there into the middle of the road below. Then they hastened along a little path beside the column of vehicles, where their other comrades were already gathering, after their useless pursuit. The dead bodies of the two young Germans had been removed; from the black hulk of the truck, twisted towards the grade, an occasional flame still spurted, and a ghastly, revolting odor came from it. An order was shouted twice, and the motorized convoy moved, advancing over Quat's small body, which lay there, the arms a bit away from the body, the head thrown back because of the knapsack and that trusting, peaceful little smile still on the lips. The first of the vehicles gave a slight jolt, which already, with the next one, was less perceptible. The rain persisted, but more calmly. When the last vehicle had gone by, it must have been about midnight.

Quattro's real name was Oreste Aloisi, and he was not yet nineteen, born in a village near Lanuvio. His father owned a patch of vineyard there and a house of two rooms, one over the other, with a little cellar for the wine barrels; however, years before, after deciding to emigrate, he had rented his little property.

Another death in those days was that of Maria, the girl Ace called Mariulina generally known to the comrades as *the redhead*. She was taken with her mother in a round-up, and in her fear of dying, she betrayed; however, her betrayal proved of no help to her or to the Germans.

Towards evening, three or four German soldiers had shown up at her house. They came, in reality, because this place had been indicated to them; but at the beginning, perhaps to amuse themselves by making a show of an innocuous pretext, they entered nonchalantly and asked for some wine. And Mariulina, not even getting up from her chair, replied by jutting her chin out in a spiteful gesture, to say they didn't have any. Then they exclaimed: *search, search* and amid the mother's screams, they promptly started tearing up the house, which consisted of a single room with a stall for the mule attached to it. With a kick they knocked over the sideboard, reducing all the crockery inside to smithereens (a total of five or six items, counting dishes and bowls, two glasses, and a little porcelain doll). They shattered the mirror; and having found two flasks of wine behind the bed, they ripped up the sheets, broke the picture on the wall;

and then they forced the women to drink that wine, in their company, as they also drank. Maria had witnessed the whole scene standing still and silent, frowning; at the order to drink, she began gulping down the wine at once, with an air of shameless determination, as if she were at the tavern. But her mother, who was crawling among the wreckage on her hands and knees, waving her arms awkwardly, like a swimmer, had no stomach for drinking; and so she swallowed and spat and swallowed and spat, all soiled with saliva, wine, and dust mixed together. And meanwhile she was shouting, explaining to those men that she was a poor widow, etc., etc. While Maria, with a scornful and icy smile, reproached her: "Aw, shut up, mà! What's the use talking? They can't understand you anyhow."

Actually, one of them did understand some Italian, and spoke it haltingly, distorting the words in such a comical way that Mariulina, already half-drunk, laughed in his face. For drink, instead of *bere*, the man said *trínchere*, and Maria talked back to him, as if speaking to an idiot: "Sure, trinchete, trinchete. I'll trink, too."

Meanwhile it had grown dark. The acetylene lamp had been smashed with the rest, and the men turned their portable lamps, big as headlights, on the women's faces, ordering them to lead them to the stable and the other storage places. They found the mule Uncle Peppe, and oil, and more wine, and they decreed: *rekvisition, rekvisition!* Afterwards, in a half-buried little grotto, under a pile of faggots and potatoes, they uncovered some cases of ammunition and hand grenades. Then, squawking in German, they roughly pushed the two women into the house and, holding them against the wall, they began to shout: "Partizani! Banditti! Where partizani?! We find! You tell, or dead!" It seemed, to hear them, that they were proposing alternatives. And the mother, who had begun whining on a long, faint and unchanging note, turned to Mariulina, imploring her: "Talk, girl, talk!!!" Through a kind of shrewd opportunism, she had always kept herself ignorant of her daughter's guerrilla doings, although she suspected them. And now, she was reduced to helplessness, inert, within those few inches of wall.

"I don't know nothing! Nein! NEIN!" Mariulina proclaimed, shaking her red head with an extreme ferocity ("If they ask you, deny everything, everything!" Ace of Hearts had indoctrinated her). However, as soon as she saw a pistol aimed at her, her lips went white, and her big eyes of a pale wheat color, almost pink, opened wide in terror. She wasn't afraid of snakes, or of bats, and not even of Germans, or of other people. But she had an enormous fear of skeletons and of death. She didn't want to die.

At that point, she felt a little warm spasm in her kidneys, which seemed gently to dissolve her joints, relaxing the weight of her lower body. And she immediately blushed, clenching her legs tight and glancing at her feet, which in the sudden and violent flow were already being stained with menstrual blood. At this unforeseen incident, which took her by surprise, in the presence of those young men, shame mingled with her fear. And hurled between shame and fear, trying to hide her feet and at the same time to wipe the wet floor with the soles of her heavy shoes, all trembling like a reed, she told everything she knew.

She didn't know much, really. The guerrillas, realizing she was a young girl, not even sixteen, had confided in her only what was indispensable, and they had left her in ignorance of the rest, or perhaps had told her some tales. For example, her "fiancé" Ace of Hearts had revealed to her, in great secrecy, that his real nam was Luiz de Villarricca y Perez, with a brother, José de Villarricca y Perez (known as Useppe); both born in some Argentine pampa (among caballeros, caballos, etc.) and other stories along the same line. When it came right down to it, she knew her guerrilla neighbors, mostly, only by sight and by nickname. The only names and addresses she knew were: 1) the leader Eyeglasses, resident in Albano and at present wounded in the leg: who, however, in those days, because of Albano's forced evacuation after the air raids, had been taken away on a stretcher God knows where; 2) Quat, that is to say Aloisi Oreste, who had died a few days earlier (while his brothers were scattered at some front, and his parents, farm laborers, after emigrating in search of work, had returned and had taken shelter in some undefined locality); 3) and finally a certain Oberdan, from Palestrina, who, having now returned to Palestrina, slept like his fellow townspeople in caves, among the ruins of the city. But of all these rapid events, no news could yet have reached Mariulina.

As for the information that especially interested the Germans, namely the refuge where the comrades hid out, the last certain headquarters Mariulina knew about was the little stone house where the *Liberty* command had moved for the winter, leaving the hut of their early days. The *redhead*, however, was not aware that the boys had recently deserted that hiding-place also, shifting without fixed residence from one hill to another, to avoid the German round-ups; nor, for that matter, did she know that all links had now been broken not only between *her* band and her, Mariulina; but also among all the bands that had existed in the area (which, to tell the truth, for her had always been ghost-bands, without precise headquarters or distinguishing names . . .); or that, lately, Ace's comrades had separated and scattered; or finally that, while she was speaking about him unawares, her Ace had already gone off with Pyotr for their adventure beyond the front.

When Mariulina's confession was over, she and her mother were beaten and flung on the ground by their enraged guests, who then took turns raping them. Only one didn't share in this last violence, though he had enjoyed himself worse than the others in the beatings, seeming almost transported by a perverse ecstasy. He was a corporal of about thirty, though he had an old man's face with oblique wrinkles that gave his expression a tormented quality, and with the staring, colorless eyes of a suicide.

That hasty and rudimentary orgy was accompanied by more drinking of the wine requisitioned in the stable. And at this point, Mariulina, who until that evening had never had more than one glass at a meal, became drunk for the first time in her life. However, her drinking had actually not been excessive: so her intoxication was of the sort that does no harm, but on the contrary has a magic effect, at the age of sixteen, when the body's channels are healthy and fresh. As soon as they had been pulled to their feet, the two women were pushed outside again and ordered to lead the patrol towards the farmhouse the girl had mentioned. When the company moved, Mariulina had the real sensation that other armed men were rising from the night outside, forming a little crowd around the two of them; but this fact, in her present mood, aroused neither alarm nor wonder in her. It all seemed to her an innocuous scene, like the figures in a dance. That house was three or four miles away, beyond the valley where, about three months ago, Nino and Useppe had looked down with the binoculars. The night was not very cold, it wasn't raining, and the previous days' mud had partially hardened on the trails. The crests of the hills were covered by a mist, but, over the valley, the few moving clouds, light and unfurled like ribbons, left broad starry spaces exposed. Towards the sea, the artilleries rumbled almost uninterruptedly, amid flashing glows and signals that flared on and off in the haze. However, that noisy spectacle, which for more than a week had constantly accompanied existence in the valley, on this night, over here, made no more effect than a sea storm on the horizon. Of the two women, the older (her age, really, was not even thirty-five) was stupefied, staggering as if on the point of throwing up, so the soldiers of the escort had to push her forcibly by the shoulders; while the girl, all warmed with wine, was borne by a passive excitement, with no thought. As guide, she walked at the head of the expedition, a slight distance from her mother, who, put in the middle like a prisoner, followed with the rest of the unit. In her little black dress, with her short stature, the woman disappeared from view among those gigantic soldiers; Mariulina, however, didn't even look back for her, since everything seemed inoffensive and fantastic, estranging her and yet inspiring trust. Accustomed as she was to those hikes, she walked on, limber and heedless as a little animal; and indeed, at some points, in her natural readiness, she jumped ahead of the soldiers. The shame, the fear, and even the nuisance of her physical filth were dissolved in the sole carefree pleasure of her body in movement, as if she were dancing along. And she didn't notice her damp, disheveled hair falling in her face or her torn jersey that left her bosom half revealed; even the sensation of blood between her legs or the saliva in her mouth gave her an affectionate feeling of warmth. The familiar landscape ran towards her obediently; while the destination seemed far, far away, left in the infinite like the little clouds speeding through the sky. And meanwhile she was distracted by fleeting impressions, following with curiosity the little gusts of steamy breath in the air, or the whims of the shadows on the ground. One fine moment, from the zone between the Castelli and the sea, some luminous balloons, of every color, were seen rising towards the sky by the hundreds. At first they hung suspended, making a pattern like an ear of corn, then they came down in cascades, loosened in a long varicolored necklace through the air; and at the end they were fused in a grand finale, which dazzled the whole countryside with its single, white splendor. Her eyes raised, wide, towards the sight, Mariulina made a misstep and stumbled; and the soldier at her side, in putting her back on the trail, seemed to embrace her. Glancing at him, she recognized him. He had been the last to rape her, tearing her aggressively from the one ahead of him; and she was convinced, seeing him now, that he hadn't then behaved with the filthy coarseness of the others. He was a handsome boy with irregular features, a pert nose, a curled mouth that seemed always about to smile, and small pale-blue eyes beneath golden lashes, short and hard. "He must love me," Mariulina said to herself, "if he wasn't disgusted with me, back home, the way I was . . ." (during her menstrual period, Ace, her first and only lover, avoided her). And in a spontaneous gesture, she rested her head against the boy's chest. He looked at her with an unsure, elusive air, but almost kindly. A moment later, down among the folds of the hill, about two hundred yards away, they could glimpse the house they were looking for.

The little whitish building, without windows on that side, seemed to sit crooked, on uneven terrain, with its battered roof and its little closed door. Impulsively, Mariulina made a leap forward, as if to run to Ace of Hearts, waiting for her down there as usual, on his shaky cot, all ready, his mouth brimming with kisses. But alien arms blocked her, amid menacing voices that questioned her in German. "Ja, ja, yes, yes . . ." she stammered, bewildered; then suddenly she started wriggling, her eyes wide in a dazed, horrified gaze. "Mà! Màààà!" she called, turning around, seeking her mother, and bursting into childish tears. And it was only after a while that she heard her mother's voice, calling her, in turn: "Maria! Marietta!" from some place, near but indistinct, among the soldiers who were holding both of them, plunging down the slope towards the little house. Their masked lamps searched the darkness; but there was no sign of a sentry anywhere around, nor was any sound heard except their own footsteps. All in battle-dress with sub-machine guns aimed, some of them took up positions outside among the olive trees, while two or three went around the hut, and others stood at the door. In the rear, the house's one little window was wide open; and a soldier circumspectly explored the dark interior with his lamp, his free hand on the grenades hanging from his belt, as he muttered a remark in German and, at that same instant, his companions in front bashed in the door with their feet and the butts of their guns. In the dazzling beams of the lamps, the interior of the hovel proved uninhabited, completely abandoned. On the floor some straw was scattered, rotten from the rain that had come through the open window; nor were there other furnishings except for a metal cot, without mattress or blankets, where a missing leg had been replaced by a pile of bricks; and some iron springs, with a little straw pallet, shrunken and soaked with rain. On the pallet there was a mashed mess-tin; on the ground, the broken handle of a tin fork; and hanging from a nail a torn piece of a shirt, with a blackish stain, as if it had served to bind a wound. Nothing else: no trace of weapons or of food. The only sign of recent life was, in a corner, a pile of shit, not yet hardened, deposited there by Ace and Company as an insult to possible patrols, a gesture of certain nocturnal malefactors, at the door of a cracked safe.

Moreover, on the walls, damp and filthy, they could read some enormous slogans, still fresh, written with coal: LONG LIVE STALIN, HITLER KAPUTT, DOWN WITH THE GERMAN MURDERERS. Just as on the outer walls of the hovel, above a previous Fascist slogan, CONQUER, there had been freshly added WE WILL in much larger letters.

Inside there, a couple of days later, some country people found the bodies of Mariulina and her mother massacred by bullets, shattered even in the vagina, with knife-stabs or bayonet wounds in the face, on the breasts, everywhere. They had been flung at some distance from each other, on opposite sides of the deserted room. But they were buried together, in the same hole, there on the land near the hut, in the absence of any relations or friends to provide for their funeral. In the sequel of his very eventful days, Ninnuzzu never bothered to come back to those places; and as far as we can suppose, he never learned of Mariulina's death, or of her betrayal.

2 After the visit of the tavernkeeper Remo, that same night, as all were sleeping, Ida, behind her curtain, by candlelight, unstitched the mattress at the point indicated, taking care not to wake Useppe, who was lying asleep on it. Rummaging in the wool, she drew out a clump of ten one-thousand-lire notes, which for her, especially at that moment, represented an enormous fortune. And she immediately placed them in the familiar old stocking, which she put in a safe place, as before. That night, to set her mind at rest, she spread her precious corset between one mattress and the other; but this was surely not sufficient guarantee against the movements of her cohabitant refugees, who all seemed to her thieves and murderers, of whom she was in constant fear. Now, she felt a certain homesickness for The Thousand, who had tormented her with noise, but had made up for it by their fondness for Useppe. Not knowing their fate, however, after the recent destruction of the Castelli, she saw them in an ambiguous aspect, halfway between living forms and ghosts. And a surge of panic, stronger than homesickness, choked her as she crossed the room, all bustling with their vague forms—and invaded now by shifting, suspect masks—and where, final point of squalor, the late Madman's corner was usurped by outsiders, with no trace of him left except the canaries' empty cage. Although, when he was alive, she had never addressed more than two or three words to him ("excuse me" . . . "don't trouble yourself" . . . "thank you" . . .) now she was in anguish at the injustice of that sprightly little body's being prevented from running about and keeping busy, with that hat on its head. And she would truly have been happy to see him come back in the big room, to tell her the story of his death as a fairy tale, even if she would be obliged, in consequence, to return the ten thousand lire.

This sum, among other advantages, then helped her escape from the room. These were days, obviously, when luck was with her. At the Bursary, where she went to draw her salary as usual, she met this time an elderly colleague, another schoolmistress. Who, seeing Ida so lost, suggested a prompt and advantageous move to her. The woman knew that the needy family of a former night-school student of hers was prepared to sublet his little bedroom, since he had gone off in '42 to the Russian front. The price was low, because the mother didn't want to empty the boy's room, but to leave it as it was, with all his things in their place, until his return: so in fact she would be renting out the bed. It was a sunny room, however, and clean, and kitchen privileges were included. Thus, three days later, Ida and Useppe bade farewell to Pietralata. Theirs was, this time, a proper housemove, with a cart, because, in addition to the little supply of oil, cloths, and candles, they also carried with them the inheritance from Eppetondo: the real wool mattress and the Peppinielli's empty cage.

Another advantage of the new home was that it was in Via Mastro Giorgio, in Testaccio, only a short walk from the school where Ida and that elderly fellow-teacher of hers had taught. At present, the school building had been requisitioned for military purposes, and the classes were held in other rooms, on the Gianicolense; however, the distance to the Gianicolense, from Testaccio, was not insuperable, like the distance from Pietralata. And so Ida managed to obtain permission to resume her teaching position. And for her it was a special blessing in those days, for the exile from school was becoming entwined, in her fears, with her racial guilt.

And yet it seemed almost impossible to her that the guilt of her mixed blood, now that it was also denounced in ordinances, and under police surveillance, couldn't be read in her face. If one of her pupils raised his little hand to ask a question, she would start and flush, suspecting the question would be: "Is it true, Teacher, you're a half-Jew?" If somebody outside knocked at the classroom door, she already felt faint, expecting a visit from the police, or at least a summons from the principal, who had to inform her that as of today she was suspended from teaching, etc., etc.

Testaccio wasn't an outlying quarter, like San Lorenzo. Though it, too, was prevalently inhabited by poor or working-class people, only a few streets separated it from the middle-class neighborhoods. And the Germans, who rarely visited Pietralata and the Tiburtino, were encountered here in greater numbers. Their presence, for Ida, transformed her daily journey into a revolving track where she personally, ridiculous target, was marked out by spotlights, followed by iron footsteps, encircled by swastika signs. Again, as once before in the past, all Germans looked alike to her. She had finally given up the chimerical anxiety of recognizing, perhaps one day or another, beneath one of those helmets or visored caps, the desperate blue eyes that had visited her at San Lorenzo in January of 1941. By now all these soldiers seemed to her unvarying copies of a supreme mechanism, judging and persecutory. Their eyes were flashes of light, and their mouths, megaphones prepared to shout in loud voices, through the squares and streets: *Catch the halfbreed!*

From her new neighborhood, only a few hundred yards separated her from the Ghetto. But on her daily return journeys, she always avoided crossing the Garibaldi bridge, beyond which she could glimpse the squat form of the Synagogue, which made her look away, with a heaviness in her legs. In her purse, there was still that note she had picked up from the deportees' train at the Tiburtina station; she had never tried to look for its addressee. It was known that the Ghetto's surviving Jews, who had happened to escape the round-up of 16 October, had almost all come back to their homes on this side of the Tiber, having nowhere else to go. One survivor, talking about it later, compared them to condemned animals, who docilely enter the slaughterhouse pen, warming one another with their breath. And this trust of theirs makes people consider them foolish; but isn't the opinion of outsiders (he remarked) often foolish?

Ida was afraid of that little besieged quarter: and all the more so because of a suspicion that among the survivors who had returned to the neighborhood there might also be Signora Celeste Di Segni. She didn't know, in fact, whether on that Monday, October 18th, the Signora had then been allowed to leave with the train or whether, excluded, she had stayed in Rome. And remembering how on that morning, in the street towards the station, she had insanely whispered into her ear, *I'm Jewish too*, Ida since had been more afraid of coming upon the Signora than of encountering a bogey-man. That little whisper now returned to her, with a grim echo, like a mad self-accusation.

In reality, the witness she feared had managed, on that Monday morning, to leave with the other Jews. And it was only after the war's end that the sequel and conclusion of that departure were learned.

The progress of the sealed train was very slow: the prisoners had been inside it for five days when, at dawn on Saturday, they reached the concentration camp of Auschwitz-Birkenau, to which they were assigned. Not all, however, reached there alive: and this was a first selection. Among the weakest, who hadn't resisted the trial of the journey, there was a pregnant daughter-in-law of the Di Segnis.

Of the living, only a minority of about two hundred individuals was judged able to work in the camp. All the others, numbering about eight hundred and fifty, promptly on arrival were sent to death, unaware, in the gas chambers. In addition to the ill, the handicapped, and the less strong, this number included almost all the old people, the children, and babies. Among them were Settimio and Celeste Di Segni, along with their grandchildren Manuele, Esterina, and Angelino. And, of our acquaintance, there were also with the notions-vendor Signora Sonnino and the author of the message to "Efrati Pacificho" as well as Iduzza's namesake: Ida Di Capua, that is to say the midwife Ezekiel.

For the remaining two hundred, destined to the life of the camp on that Saturday of their arrival, the journey begun on October 16th, 1943, was of varying duration according to their strength. In the end, of the one thousand fifty-six who had left, in a body, from the Tiburtina station, a total of fifteen came back alive.

And of all those dead, the luckiest were surely the first eight hundred and fifty. The gas chamber is the only seat of charity, in a concentration camp.

.   .   .

Ida's landlords, Marrocco by name, were natives of the Ciociaria region (they came from the little village of Sant'Agata), and had left their mountaineers' hut and their fields of flax only a few years before to move to Rome. The wife, Filomena, worked at home as a dressmaker, shirtmaker, and seamstress, while her husband Tommaso was an orderly at the city hospital. Their son Giovannino, whose room Ida was at present occupying, was born in 1922. In the summer of 1942, from Northern Italy, where he and his unit were waiting to leave for the Russian front, the boy had married by proxy Annita, a Ciociaria girl who had grown up near him in the mountains. It was impossible for him to obtain a leave at that time; and so the young couple, practically speaking, had remained only engaged. The girl-bride, now twenty, had recently come to live with her in-laws, along with Filomena's aged father, left a widower a short time before. Neither the girl nor the old man had ever been out of Ciociaria until now.

All these people shared the apartment in Via Mastro Giorgio, which consisted of a total of two rooms plus a rather spacious entrance hall that Filomena used as her workshop, while her double bedroom, with the mirrored wardrobe, served as a fitting room for her customers. At night, Annita slept in the workroom on a little folding bed, and the old grandfather on a cot in the kitchen.

The little bedroom of Ida and Useppe opened off the entrance and, through another door, led directly into the kitchen. Thanks to its window's southern exposure, on fine days it was filled with sunlight. And despite its minuscule proportions, compared to the corner behind the curtain at Pietralata, it seemed to Ida an almost luxurious lodging.

The furniture consisted entirely of a little bed, a wardrobe about a yard wide, a straight chair, and a little table that served both as dressing-table and desk. In fact, the room's absent owner, as a boy, had barely reached the second grade; but before being called to the war, he had started attending night school (during the day he worked for a mattress-maker). And neatly arranged on the little table, there were still his few school texts and the notebooks with his homework, written in a diligent, but hesitant and labored hand, like a child's.

And in the wardrobe, his civilian clothes were also still hanging. Kept in a clothing-bag, along with his sweater, there was his good suit of mixed wool and cotton, dark blue, almost black, the shoulders cut rather square, neatly cleaned and pressed; and on a special hanger next to the bag, his best shirt of special white muslin. His other two shirts, more ordinary, for everyday wear, were in a lower drawer of the wardrobe, with a pair of cheap pants, four pairs of shorts, two undershirts, some handkerchiefs, and some darned colored socks. In addition, on the wardrobe's lower shelf, there was a pair of shoes, almost new, stuffed with newspaper and, folded over them, his Sunday socks, also practically new. And on a string stretched across the inside of the door, there was a rayon tie, a pale blue and white check pattern.

In the corner, then, two little printed pamphlets were kept: one was entitled *New and Practical Method for learning to play the GUITAR without a teacher and without knowing music*; and the other *Easy Method for the MANDOLIN*. No mandolins or guitars, however, were to be seen. The only musical instrument that existed in the place was inside the drawer of the desk-dressing table, next to a pen and a pencil: one of those little reed pipes cut with a knife, which mountain boys play when following their goats. In fact, Giovannino (as his mother Filomena always boasted) had had a passion for playing music ever since he was little; but except for that reed pipe, till now, he had never owned any other instruments.

To complete the list: under the bed there were his everyday shoes, resoled many times, but with the uppers all worn. And hanging from a hook behind the door there was a mangy leatherette windbreaker. These were virtually the entire contents of the little room.

There were no comic books or picture magazines or pictures of film beauties or football players, as in Ninnarieddu's room. The walls, covered with cheap wallpaper, were bare except for a free calendar, the kind with twelve pages, still for the year 1942, with propaganda photographs of works of the Fascist regime.

No individual photograph of the room's absent owner existed, here or elsewhere. His mother possessed and displayed two pictures of him, in groups; but you could tell little from either of them. The first, taken perhaps by some village amateur, portrayed him, still a little boy, along with another dozen mountain kids his age, at Confirmation; and in the confused and blurred whole, of him in particular you could discern only that he was thin, rather blond, and that he had a cap on his head and was laughing. The second picture, brought back by a soldier who had met him in Russia, was a little snapshot, showing a landscape of undergrowth, with a watery stripe in the background. In the foreground, you could see a thick, crooked stake that crossed the whole landscape from bottom to top; and to the left of the stake, fairly close up, a mule's behind, near a bundled-up little man with puttees on his legs, who wasn't, however, Giovannino. To the right of the stake, on the contrary, but farther to the rear, you could see some dark forms, all in a huddled mass, so you couldn't even say whether they were soldiers or civilians, or if there were helmets on their heads or, rather, some kind of limp little hat. Among them was Giovannino; but really it was impossible to distinguish him, or even to indicate him at a precise point within the pile.

After she had taken over the room from Filomena—who on that occasion had made a careful inventory of it—Ida never again allowed herself the liberty of opening the wardrobe, which still was without a key and with a door that wouldn't close tight. And on this score, she never stopped warning Useppe, who obediently avoided even grazing with his finger the absent proprietor's belongings, content merely to observe them with profound respect.

For their personal possessions, Filomena supplied them with a cardboard box and also cleared space for them in the kitchen cupboard. Thanks to the Madman's bequest, Ida, feeling rich, had purchased some reserve provisions and also a remnant of red ersatz wool, from which the same Filomena made a little overall for Useppe. With that overall on, Useppe no longer resembled an Indian or Charlie Chaplin, but a gnome from an animated cartoon.

The little room was certainly not as noisy as the vast place at Pietralata; but here too, noises were incessant. During the daytime, from the entrance-workroom, there was the almost constant racket of the sewing machine, the voices of visitors and customers, etc. And at night, from the kitchen, there was the Ciociaria grandfather, who slept little, in his sleep often had nightmares, and in his waking intervals did nothing but hawk and spit. His long body, thin and bent, was a cavernous well of catarrh that could never be drained. The old man kept always beside him a big, chipped basin, and hawking, he emitted sounds of extreme anguish, like donkeys' braying which seems to charge the silence with the total sorrow of the cosmos. For the rest, he conversed little, was simple-minded, and never left the house, frightened by the city streets as if by a siege. If he happened to glance out of the window, he drew back at once, complaining that here in Rome you couldn't see any empty air outside. From his house in the mountains, when he looked out (for "look," instead of *guardare* he said *tr'mintare*) he could see lots of empty space and here, instead, the air was all full of walls. At night, too, you could hear him exclaim, in his nightmares, that stubborn complaint of the full and the void ("Tr'mint! tr'mint!! Look, look! It's nothing but a wall!"). And if, as often happened, some shots resounded from the streets or some planes passed through the sky or perhaps the windows shook because of bombs in the neighborhood, every time he would be jolted awake with a kind of hoarse, desperate howling, which meant "Here I am, awake again!" From time to time in his vigil he would repeat: "Oi mà, oi mà" and he would answer himself, in his mother's place: "Son! Son, what is it?" Or else he would be overcome by self-pity, calling himself "little gypsy" and claiming he was "a little gypsy in the strawstack" (the strawstack was his hut of straw where, in the mountains, he had finally been reduced to living alone). Then he would start hawking, with such torment that he seemed to be vomiting blood.

During the day, he remained seated always on a little chair in the kitchen, his basin beside him. His emaciated body, all bones, ended in a great clump of dirty, wispy white hair, over which, also indoors, he would wear his hat, following the mountaineer custom. On his feet, even here in Rome, he wore the bound *cioce*; but for that matter his walking was limited to the distance from the kitchen to the WC and back. His supreme, insatiable desire was for wine, but his daughter allowed him very little.

The kitchen window was long and extended in a tiny covered balcony, where, those first days, a rabbit lived. Immediately, on his entrance into the new lodging, Useppe had glimpsed it there, hopping on its long rear paws. And after that, his greatest pleasure in the house was to stand behind the panes of the balcony to contemplate the rabbit. Its color was pure white, with a touch of pink in the ears, and its pink eyes seemed unaware of the world. Its only attitude towards the world was a certain fright that seized it, quickly and unpredictably (even without any apparent motive), and made it flatten its ears and run for shelter inside its little house made from a plywood box. But as a rule it would remain crouched to one side, in an intent calm, as if it were brooding on some baby rabbits; or it would fervidly gnaw the cabbage stalks Annita furnished it. A hospital patient had given it to Tommaso; and the family, particularly the daughter-in-law Annita (though accustomed, of course, as herdsmen, to the slaughter of animal flesh), had taken it—who knows why?—to their bosoms, as if it were a kind of relative, so they couldn't make up their minds to sacrifice it in a pot. One day, however, Useppe, who ran to the balcony every morning when he woke up, found Annita alone there, sweeping up the remains of the stalks with a sad face. The rabbit was gone: the family, resigned, had traded it out of necessity, for two cans of meat.

"... where's the abbit?"

"He's gone away . . ."

"Who'd he go with?! . . ."

"With an onion, some oil, and tomatoes" . . . (the mother-in-law answered, sighing, from the entrance-hall).

In the workroom, along with Filomena and Annita, there was always a *piccinina,* a little one, that is to say a girl apprentice, whose duties also included errands and shopping. She was from the Abruzzi, about fourteen, already developed, but so thin that in the place of a bosom she had a cavity. Sewing, mending, or at the machine, she always sang a popular song that went:

". . . my joy, my *tormend*
    you are . . ."

The three women were rarely alone. When no customers were about, there was never any lack of visitors. Every day a neighbor woman dropped by; she was about thirty-five, named Consolata, and she had a brother who had gone off to the Russian front at the same time as Giovannino, in his same unit, and his fate had also been unknown for a long time. A man, who late at night listened to Radio Moscow, had said, months ago, that this brother's name had been mentioned in a broadcast list of prisoners; however, another man, who listened to the same program at night, said the first name mentioned by the radio was his, all right, Clemente; but the last name was different.

This, their relatives in Russia, was the sole, eternal subject of the women's talk; it even eclipsed the other subject, famine. Ninnuzzu, also had sent no news, as he was off wandering somewhere or fighting as a guerrilla; and Ida preferred not to speak or even to think of him: a kind of unconscious exorcism. But she kept the tavernkeeper Remo always informed of her movements, in case Nino should pass through Rome again.

Another visitor to the Marrocco women was a certain Santina, who lived alone near Porta Portese. She was about forty-eight, rather tall, and with excessively large bones, which, despite her extreme thinness, made her body seem heavy and bulky. She had large dark eyes, with a deep gaze, without light; and as she was losing her teeth from lack of nutrition, and an incisor was missing in front, her smile had something helpless and guilty about it, as if she were ashamed of her own ugliness, and of herself, every time she smiled.

Her hair was turning gray, and she wore it loose over her shoulders, like a young girl; however, she used no powder or cosmetics, and didn't try to hide her age. Her ruined, pale face, with broad, jutting bones, expressed a crude and resigned simplicity.

Her chief profession, even now, was whoring. However, she also contrived to make some money washing clothes, or giving injections, among the neighborhood families. Every now and then she would fall ill and go to the hospital, or else she would be caught by the police; but as a rule, she

271

wasn't accustomed to baring her wounds, and on her return after an absence she would say she had been *back to the village*. She also said she had a mother, back in the village, whom she had to support. But everyone knew she was lying. She had no relatives in the world and that *mother* was, in reality, a pimp, many years her junior, who lived in Rome, but rarely let himself be seen with her. Apparently he lived in another quarter, and there were some who had glimpsed him, but like an apparition or a shadow, without precise outlines.

Santina's frequent visits to the Marrocco home were due, especially, to her ability to read the unknown in cards. For this, she had a personal system not to be found in texts of cartomancy, learned nobody knows where. The Marrocco women never tired of consulting her about Giovannino; and as soon as she arrived, they would hastily clear the worktable of snippets, scissors, pins, and other clutter, to make room for the deck of cards. Their questions were always the same:

"Tell us if he's well."

"Tell us if he's thinking about us."

"Tell us if he'll come home soon."

"Tell us if his health is good."

"Tell us if he thinks about his family."

Filomena asked these questions of hers in a tone of insistent urgency, as if she were begging an answer from a very busy and brisk Authority; while Annita ventured them slowly, in her usual reserved and melancholy way, her head bent slightly towards one shoulder, her habitual pose. Her dark-skinned, oval face seemed paler because of the black weight of her chignon, which she left loose, to one side. And in commenting, with her mother-in-law, on Santina's replies, her voice was hesitant and discreet, as if she was afraid of being a nuisance.

Santina never raised her dense, opaque eyes from the cards, and she gave her answers in the tone of a slightly backward girl reciting an obscure prayer. Her replies, like the questions, did not vary much from one time to the next:

"Swords . . . swords upside down. Cold. It's cold out there," Santina says.

"You see!" Filomena reproaches Annita, "I kept saying we should have sent his heavy sweater, too, in the package!"

"He wrote us he didn't need it, and to send him more socks instead, and chestnuts . . ." Annita justifies herself.

"But is his health good? Tell us that: if he's in good health."

"Yes, here I see good news. There's a powerful person near . . . a good recommendation. Somebody important . . . King of Coins . . . a man with rank . . ."

"Maybe it's that lieutenant . . . what did he say the lieutenant's name was, in the letter . . . ?" Annita suggests meekly.

"Mosillo! Lieutenant Mosillo!"

"No . . . no . . ." Santina shakes her head. "King of Coins . . . not a lieutenant . . . more! Somebody higher up . . . A Captain . . . or . . . General!"

"General! ! ! ?"

"And now here we see the Queen and the Two of Cups . . . and the Trump! A dark woman . . ."

At this, Annita looked away, to hide the sadness of her black eyes, which were almost in tears. Among the dangers of Russia, from what people were saying, there were the women out there, who fell in love with the Italians and held onto them, not letting them go off again. This was perhaps the sharpest of the various aches that tore the anxious bride's heart.

A last letter from Giovannino, in the family's possession, was over a year old, dated 8 January 1943. It was written in watery ink of a reddish black color. On the envelope, and also at the beginning of the letter, there was written CONQUER, because it was said that letters got by with a simple rubber stamp, without censorship, if they bore that Fascist slogan written on them.

CONQUER
Rusia 8 January 1943, XXI
Dearest memmbers of my Fammily
I write this letter to let you know I am well and hoping you are the same the epifany was not bad here I can tell you that here for cold they say olodna (. . . three words censored) the pakkage didnt arrive but dont worry for christmas the government gave us some pasta in hot water and an old Rusian lady made cakes for us lucky civilians here its so cold it splits your toenails and all these nights laying barbwire and digging for the gun we live underground like rats and eat lice Dear Parents keep your morale up were going to win I enclose money-order for three hundred and twenty lire dear Mother and Wife dont believe the bad news its all the defeattists (. . . five words censored) Ill be home soon the importunt thing is your haelth here Im learning some Rusian words like for potato they say kartoshy dear Mother I cant wait to come home and kiss you all this is all I think about day and night theres never any letters dear Parents let me know if the last money order came now Ive got to run and theres no more space all my love your Son and Husband

Giovannino

Besides this letter, another had arrived, a little earlier, addressed to Annita, and since then there had been no further mail or news from Giovannino. In the spring of that same year 1943, that soldier passing through, who brought the photograph, had told of meeting him a few months before, in November, and they had shared a loaf of bread and a can of meat. As for the other missing soldier, Clemente, Consolata's brother, the man had never met him or known him and had no news of him.

Filomena and Annita were both almost illiterate; but whereas Filomena often took Giovannino's letters from the cupboard in her bedroom to have them reread to her and to comment on then, Annita was very jealous of hers and showed them to nobody. One evening, however, when the other women had gone out, she knocked at Ida's door and, blushing, asked her the favor of reading his last letters from the front. At the time when she had received them, she was still in the mountains, and since then, here in Rome, she hadn't had anybody to *explain them* to her, so she almost risked forgetting them . . . From beneath her pullover she drew the little packet of paper. They weren't all letters, there were also some franked postcards with propaganda phrases printed on them, such as: IN EVERY HOUR OF HER GLORIOUS HISTORY ROME HAS CARRIED OUT HER MISSION OF CIVILIZATION . . . As usual, on the envelopes and on the letters, the boy, as a clever stratagem against the censor, had written CONQUER. Because of the ersatz ink, made of dust and water, the writing was all faded, as if it were a century old.

"Beloved Annita please if you can get a foto taken for me so I can look at it at least for example ask that hospittal worker santospirito who has a codak and please dont worry about me Ill get home and I cant wait to give you a milion kisses and well have a nice honneymoon I want to take you all the way to Vennice . . . (a line censored) *dearest Wife dont be afraid Im well and here we have lice races and the one who had the fastest wins a cigarete I won two Africas and a Trestelle and please dear Wife next time you write send me a one lira stamp there arent any around here" "please remember to put lice powdder in the package" . . . ". . . the women here are called Katusha but dont think about that!! for me theres only one woman in the world the queen of my Heart! Youre the whole world for me and a milion kisses . . ." "Last night I dreamed I was with you but you werent grown up like now you were a little girl like the old days and I said to you how can I marry you now? Your too little! And you said when you get back from Rusia Ill be grown up and I said here I am back and I held you in my arms and you grew up right in my arms and I gave you a milion kisses! Ah my beloved Wife this is hell nobodys*

unhappier than me but well be together again soon because I cant wait (. . . one word censored) *but this is the army I send you a milion kisses"* . . .

Refusing, in her shyness, to take a seat on the single chair or on the edge of the bed, Annita remained standing throughout the reading, barely resting her stubby, chapped hand on the little table. But as her eyes followed, one by one, the words Ida read aloud, she had an overseer's expression, as if those little sheets of paper were a most precious codex and deciphering them were another kind of cartomancy that somehow compelled destiny. She made no comment, except for a very brief sigh in taking the bundle back at the end. And she left, with the rather clumsy gait of her sturdy legs, which had been made for the long and ample skirts of the Ciociaria women and now—exposed beneath the short, shrunken little dress, with knee-length black stockings, leaving bare a strip of flesh—seemed of a rustic and animal heaviness in contrast with her tiny body. From the winter of 1943 until today, she and her in-laws had continued to make the rounds from one office to another, seeking news of Giovannino: Ministries, Army Headquarters, Red Cross, Vatican . . . And the reply was always the same: *There is no news of him. Missing in action.* This reply, from certain functionaries or soldiers on duty in the offices, by now, was sometimes given in a brutal tone, or bored, or actually mocking. But what does *missing* mean? It can mean taken prisoner, shipped to Siberia, or still in Russia, guest of some family, or married to some woman there . . . And in the first place it can mean *killed.* But this hypothesis, among all the possible ones, was ignored by Annita and Filomena as impossible. They continued to expect Giovannino any day, airing his good suit every now and then, and they finally denied all credence to official news sources. They had more faith in Santina's cards.

Their friend Consolata criticized them for their ignorance:

"Only peasants like them," she murmured aside to Ida, "can believe in these frauds with the cards." In fact, she was more educated than the Marrocco women, a clerk in a notions shop, and a Northerner originally; however, no less than they, she also optimistically expected her brother's return from Russia. "Missing means he can be found. And with so many of them there, a few thousand are sure to come back. They can't all have disappeared. My brother isn't the kind who gets lost. Before he went to the Russian front, he'd been at the front in the Alps, in Greece, and Albania. He carried a compass to find his way, and he always wore a miraculous medal of the Madonna." She had great faith in the Madonna's protection, especially in a country of Godless heathens like Russia; and she would make a grimace at the talk of some people, who said: "Russia is the grave of Italian youth." "It's all propaganda," Consolata would say. There were some who would remark cruelly, "They say *missing* rather than say *desperate cases*," and they would make fun of Annita because of her condition, "Married but still a virgin . . ." they would taunt her; and maybe they would wink and suggest she get herself a new husband. Then Annita would cry, and her mother-in-law would become infuriated with those wicked people, who insulted a young bride's purity and cast doubt on Giovannino's fidelity.

Both mother-in-law and daughter-in-law were, by nature, faithful and chaste; but their language, common to the peasants of their parts, in some instances sounded obscene to the bourgeoise Ida. It seemed that, for them, every named object was supplied with a sex, an ass, etc., and made for the purpose of copulation. If the door wouldn't open, they would say, "It's that cunt of a lock that isn't working," and if they couldn't find some pins, "Where the fuck are those buggers?" and so on. Ida was aghast, hearing little Annita casually utter certain words which, for her, inspired fear and shame.

The master of the house was seldom seen, because if he worked the day shift, he came home late; and if he worked at night, he slept during the day. In one of his brief intervals at home, he taught Useppe a song of his village, which went like this:

The bad shepherd who eats the cheese
In church never goes down on his knees
He keeps his hat right on his head
That's why the shepherd is so bad.

As a rule, in the Marrocco home, as during the latter period at Pietra-lata, nobody paid much attention to Useppe. There were no other kids; the *piccinina*, half-stupefied by her hunger pangs, barely had enough breath left to sing, more and more listlessly, *my joy and my tormend are you;* and the women of the family, like their visitors or customers, were too busy or concerned to bother with him. Mostly, they treated him like a kitten, to be tolerated as long as he plays on his own, but to be driven off when he gets in the way. The days of The Thousand were receding farther and farther into the past, like an ancient legend.

In Ida's long hours of absence, and after the rabbit's obscure departure, Useppe, when he didn't *think*, stayed in the company of the grandfather, who, to tell the truth, didn't seem to notice his presence. Though the old man spent all his days sitting on a chair, he never had a moment's rest, badgered by the life which still persisted in his organism, as if by a swarm of horseflies who refused to leave him alone. His eyes could still see and his ears could hear, yet every object of his senses was reduced, for him, to a tormenting irritation. Now and then he dozed off, but only for a little while, coming to again with a start. Or else, with the effort of someone setting forth on a toilsome journey, he would shift his body's weight from the chair to the window, where he was immediately repelled by the *full* of the buildings and walls which attacked him from outside: "There's no emptiness! Empty air!" he would say in despair, gazing out with his spent, bloodshot eyes. And if he saw somebody looking at him from a window opposite, he would say, "He's looking at me, and I'm looking at him!" as if establishing a law of unbearable anguish. So he would go back again to his chair and resume his spitting into his usual basin. Useppe would watch him with intent, eager eyes, as if gazing at an enormous landscape, tormented by the cold:

"Why you spit so much?"

"aaaagh . . . aaaaaaak . . . rrrrhhaaaa . . ."

"What's wrong? Want a drink? Eh? . . . Want a drink? Want some wine?" (in a lowered voice, so as not to be heard by Filomena).

"Uuuuuh . . . muuuuuuuuuuurrrhau . . ."

"Here! WINE! Here . . . WINE!!! But don't tell, eh? Don't let anybody hear . . . hey . . . here . . . drink!!"

3 During the last months of the German occupation, Rome took on the appearance of certain Indian metropolises where only the vultures get enough to eat and there is no census of the living and the dead. A multitude of beggars and refugees, driven from their destroyed villages, camped on the steps of the churches or below the Pope's palaces; and in the great public parks starving sheep and cows grazed, having escaped the bombs and the confiscations in the countryside. Despite the declaration of *open city*, the Germans were encamped around the inhabited area, speeding along the consular roads in the clatter of their vehicles; and the disastrous cloud of the air raids, which constantly crossed the territory of the province, spread over the city a great tarpaulin of pestilence and earthquake. The windowpanes in the house shook day and night, the sirens wailed, squadrons clashed in the sky amid yellowish rockets, and every now and then in some outlying street, with a thunderclap, a dust-cloud of ruin burst up. Certain frightened families had settled in the air-raid shelters or in the labyrinthine basements of the great monuments, where there was a stagnant odor of urine and feces. In the de luxe hotels requisitioned by the Reich Commands and guarded by armed sentries, fantastic suppers were held, where the waste was obsessive, to the

277

point of indigestion and vomiting; and in there, at the supper tables, the massacres for the next day were orchestrated. The Commander, who had himself called King of Rome, was a big compulsive eater and drinker, and alcohol was the customary stimulant and narcotic for the occupiers, both at the High Command and in the lower ranks. In secondary, remote streets of the city, you could remark some little building or villa, in middle-class style, with rows of windows recently walled up on the various floors. They were former offices, or family-style boarding houses, now converted by the occupying police forces into torture chambers. Inside, all the wretches infected with the vice of death found employment, like their Führer, masters at last of living, helpless bodies for their perverse practices. From inside those buildings, day and night, there often came a deafening din of cheap dance music and songs from gramophones turned up to full volume.

Every day, in every street, you could see a police wagon stop in front of a building, with orders to search every room and the rooftops and terraces, in the hunt for someone whose name was written on a piece of paper. No regulation limited this perpetual hunt, without any forewarning, in which the masters' power was total. Often an entire building or quarter would suddenly be barred off by cordons of troops, with the order to round up, within that enclosure, all males between sixteen and sixty, to deport them to the Reich for forced labor. Instantly, public transport would be stopped and emptied, a helpless and mad throng would run in confusion towards escapes with no exit, followed by volleys of automatic fire.

For months now, to tell the truth, the streets had been papered with proclamations printed on pink paper, which ordered all ablebodied men to present themselves for obligatory labor under pain of death; but nobody obeyed, nobody heeded those edicts, by now they didn't even read them any more. It was known that, in the city's cellars, there were stubborn little squads of guerrillas in action; but the sole effect of their enterprises on the crowd's apathy was the nightmare of the reprisals that followed from the occupiers, carried away by the convulsions of their own fear. The populace had fallen silent. The daily news of round-ups, torture, and slaughter circulated through the neighborhoods like death-rattle echoes without any possible response. It was known that, just outside the city's girdle of walls, ineptly buried in mined ditches and caves, numberless bodies were thrown to decompose, sometimes heaped up by the tens and the hundreds, as they had been collectively massacred, one on top of the other. Communiqués of a few lines, with no explanation, announced the date of their decease, but not their place of burial. And the crowd avoided speaking of their ubiquitous, shapeless presence, except in some evasive murmurs. Every contact and every substance gave off a funereal, prison stench: dry in the dust, damp in the rain. And even the famous mirage of the *Liberation* was being reduced to a fatuous dot, subject of sarcasm and mockery. For that matter, it was said that the Germans, before abandoning the city, would blow it up completely, from the foundations, and that already, underground, miles and miles of sewers served as a deposit for mines. The architectures of the metropolis "of which not a stone will be left upon a stone" seemed a panorama of phantoms. And on the walls, meanwhile, day after day, the pink posters of the city's masters multiplied, with new orders, taboos, and persecutory vetoes, niggling to the point of ingenuousness in their bureaucratic delirium. But finally, inside the isolated city, sacked and besieged, the true master was hunger. Now the only food distributed by the Food Office was, in a ration of one hundred grams per person, a bread made from rye, chickpeas, and sawdust. For other provisions, practically speaking, there was only the black market, where the prices rose so recklessly that, towards the month of May, Ida's salary was no longer enough to buy even a flask of olive oil. Moreover, in these last months, salaries were paid irregularly by the city offices.

The Madman's bequest, which had seemed to her a huge patrimony, had been dissipated much sooner than she had foreseen. The supplies bought with that money were also about to run out: she barely had a few potatoes left and some dark pasta. And little Useppe, who thanks to the Madman had begun to put some flesh on his bones again, was now losing weight every day. His eyes took up nearly all the room in his face, small as a fist. Around his well-known central cowlick, always erect in an exclamatory air, the black clumps of his hair had become lank and dull, as if covered with dust; and his ears stuck out from his head like a nestling's featherless wings. Every time the Marroccos put their pot of beans on the stove to heat up, he could be seen roaming around their legs, like a poor begging gypsy.

"Join us, join us," Filomena would say, according to the dictates of proper manners, as she sat down at the table. And at this ritual phrase from the good old times, now those present, in general, retired, prudently, discreetly. But at least a couple of times it so happened that Useppe—to whom, since he was only a tiny kid, nobody ever said: join us!—would step forward naively to prompt: *Join?* on his own initiative. And his mother, blushing, had to call him away.

Ida's wretched war against hunger, which had engaged her for more than two years, was now a hand-to-hand combat. This single daily imperative—find food for Useppe—made her insensitive to any other stimulus, her own hunger's to start with. During that month of May she lived, practically speaking, on a little grass and water, but it was enough for her; indeed her every mouthful seemed a waste, because it was robbed from Useppe. At times, to take still less from him, she decided to boil some peelings for herself, or ordinary leaves, or even flies and ants; they were still a sustenance . . . or perhaps gnaw on some stalk from the garbage, or tear the grass from the walls of the ruins.

In appearance, she now had white hair and the bent shoulders of a little humpback, having become so tiny that she was only slightly taller than some of her pupils. And yet, at present her physical resistance was greater than that of the giant Goliath who was six cubits and a palm tall and wore a cuirass of five thousand shekels of copper. It was an enigma, where that drained little body drew certain colossal reserves. Despite her malnutrition, which was visibly consuming her, Ida felt neither weakness nor appetite. And truly, from her unconscious, an organic certitude promised her a kind of temporary immortality which made her immune to needs and diseases and spared her all effort for her personal survival. This unnamed instinct for preservation, which regulated her body's chemistry, was also obeyed by her sleep, which for that period, as if to serve her as nightly nourishment, was unusually normal, empty of dreams, uninterrupted, despite the external noises of the war. However, at the hour of rising, an internal din of grand peals would shake her. "Useppe! Useppe!" was the cry of those tumults. And immediately, even before waking, with urgent hands, she would seek the child.

At times, she found him huddled against her bosom, grasping her breasts in his sleep, in a blind, anxious movement. Since the time when she had nursed him during his first months of life, Ida had become unused to the sensation of those little hands clutching her; but her breasts, scant even then, had now dried up forever. With an animal and useless tenderness, Ida detached her little son from herself. And at that moment she began her daily quest through the streets of Rome, driven on by her nerves, whipping her like an army of men in parallel rows.

She had become unable to think of the future. Her mind had narrowed to the day, between the hour of her morning rising and the curfew. And with all the many fears she had borne innate within her, now she feared nothing. The racial decrees, the intimidatory ordinances, and the public news had on her the effect of buzzing parasites, swirling around her in a great strange wind, without attacking her. That Rome was all mined and would collapse tomorrow left her indifferent, like an already remote memory of Ancient History or an eclipse of the moon in space. The only threat to the universe, for her, was summed up in the recent sight of her little son she had left sleeping, reduced to such a trifling weight that he made almost no hump under the sheet. If she happened to see herself in a mirror, in the street, she saw an alien thing in the glass, without identity, with which she barely exchanged a dazed glance, then immediately moved away. A similar glance was exchanged among the early-morning passersby, who avoided one another, all run-down and ashen, hollow-eyed, their clothes sagging on their bodies.

For these adults, she had no pity. On the other hand, she felt compassion for her little pupils, because they were children, like Useppe. But the most wretched and wasted of them still seemed to her better nourished than he. Even their little brothers, however small they were, seemed more grown than he. Lacerating fantasies took her thoughts back to certain pink, plump babies in ads; or certain blessed children of wealthy families, whom she remembered having glimpsed in their embroidered baby-carriages or in their wet-nurses' arms. Or else her thoughts returned to when Ninnuzzu was in his cradle, so pretty and big that Alfio, his father, in picking him up would cry: "Allez-oop! Weightlifting!!!" raising him high in the air, with a boastful, triumphant laugh. Useppe, instead, had had to fend for himself since infancy, to put a few little rings of fat on his wrists and thighs; but compared to today, that period of the little rings was to be recalled as a time of abundance. And it seemed incredible to her that in all of enormous Rome she couldn't collect enough to fill such a tiny belly.

Several times, during that May, she retraced her steps to San Lorenzo (walking obliquely and keeping her eyes off the ruin of her house) to beg something from the tavernkeeper Remo. She also went to plead for some leftovers or scraps from the father of a student of hers, who ran a delicatessen, and from another who worked at the Municipal Slaughterhouse. Armed with a little pot lent by the Marroccos, she would stand in line for the economic soups distributed by the Vatican; but although called economic, those soups, at the price of two hundred lire, were a luxury for her finances; and she allowed herself this expense only rarely.

Gradually, she lost all sense of honor or of shame, as well as fear. Once, coming home around noon, she encountered a lot of people with packages in their hands, coming from Piazza Santa Maria Liberatrice, where the Germans were distributing free food. This exceptional donation in the working-class districts, prompted in those days by fear, was meant as propaganda, a show. In fact, the general in charge of the Germans (the well-fed *King of Rome*) presided over the distributions, and in the square, around the trucks, photographers and movie-cameras were at work. This increased the repugnance of the district's inhabitants, and a number of them, suspecting some German machination, abandoned the square. But at the sight of those packages, Ida felt only an impetuous greed, which sucked at her from inside. Her brain emptied. The blood raced through all her body, until it spread in some enflamed patches on her skin. And pushing her way through the crowd in the square, she held out her hands towards the truck, to collect her kilogram of flour.

Until a few weeks before, whenever decorum required, she still wore a second-hand felt cloche, formerly derived (along with a pair of slippers, two old brassieres, unmatched stockings, and other odds and ends) from the famous gifts of the Charity Ladies at Pietralata. But now she no longer wore stockings or hat; and recently, for practical reasons, she had cut her hair, which, short like this, crowned her head with a crinkly mop. For some time, indeed, whenever she combed her hair, many strands were left in the comb; but it was still thick. So her head, though white, with this little crown of curls involuntarily took on the aspect of her childhood years in Cosenza. Her face, of a waxen pallor, though grown smaller and hollow, remained oddly free of wrinkles, its natural round form resembling the muzzle of an animal, pointing aimlessly.

Already that past winter, more than a few shops had closed down. Many shutters were lowered, and all the display windows were bare. The few provisions still available were requisitioned, or confiscated, or looted by the occupiers, or taken over by black marketeers. Wherever there was a legal store open, you could see long lines waiting outside; but those lines still stretched along the sidewalks after the supplies being sold had run out. When she found herself among the last, left empty-handed, Iduzza would go off dazed, with the tread of a guilty person who has received a deserved punishment.

At the sight of any edible substance, alas inaccessible to her means, she remained spellbound, with a heart-rending envy. Nothing made her mouth water, even her secretion of saliva had dried up; all her vital stimuli had been transferred to Useppe. There is a story about a tigress who, in a chill solitude, kept herself and her cubs alive by licking the snow and distributing to her little ones some scraps of meat that she ripped from her own body with her teeth.

At the Gianicolense, near the school, there was a modest little villa with a few square feet of garden, enclosed by a little wall that, as a protective measure, had some sharp fragments of glass set in the top. The gate must originally have been of iron; but perhaps as a result of the scrap collections for the war industry, at present there was a wooden one, rein-forced on the outside by a network of barbed wire. Not far from the gate, against the inner wall, you could still see a little shed with a sheet-iron roof, which had formerly served as a chicken coop; but now the few surviving hens were prudently raised inside the house.

The first weeks she taught at the Gianicolense, Ida often rang at the little villa's gate, to purchase eggs; but lately their price had risen to twenty lire apiece . . . It was the latter half of May. One afternoon, coming out of her class, Ida glimpsed through the gate, lying on a rag on the ground, in the shade of a bush, a beautiful, intact egg. Clearly a hen, during a brief escape from the house into the garden, had just laid it there, and nobody was yet aware of it. The windows at the front of the house were closed, the owners were perhaps even absent. The little street, almost rural, was peaceful and deserted.

The egg lay on the path to the old hen coop, sheltered between the bush and the base of the wall, no more than two feet from the gate. A flush rose to Ida's brain. She calculated that, if she raised the barbed wire with her left hand, and thrust her other arm through the low slats of the gate, she could easily reach the egg. This calculation, which lasted an instant, was not really made by her; but by a second, spectral Ida, who was released from her material body, bending it in great haste, down on all fours, using her hand to clutch. In fact, calculation and action were simultaneous. And Ida, having placed the little egg in her purse, was already slipping away from the scene of that unpunished and unprecedented crime. In her haste, the barbed wire of the gate had scratched her fairly deeply on her hand and wrist.

There had been no witnesses. She had got away with it. Now she was well beyond the Gianicolense, and an unusual cool feeling, with the physical pleasure of speed, rejuvenated her from the age of mother to that of older sister. Her booty, like an enormous oval diamond, shone in the open sky before her, in the collapse of the Tables of the Law. This first theft was the most thrilling, but it wasn't the only one. The second was even bolder, downright foolhardy.

It was around the twentieth of May, early in the morning. She had just gone out of the house, leaving Useppe, for breakfast, a little piece of rationed bread, saved from the day before, and a bit of ersatz cocoa, to be dissolved in water. At that hour, only a few workmen were out in the streets. Coming from a side alley out onto the street along the Tiber, she glimpsed a little truck, parked in front of a food storeroom.

Two armed Fascists, in uniform, with parachute-troopers' berets, were guarding the operation of a young man in faded overalls, who was going to and from the storeroom, unloading some cases of goods on the sidewalk. Just as she was coming around the corner, Ida saw the two militiamen enter the storeroom together. Their voices, chatting gaily, reached her.

In fact, bored by this peaceful operation, the two boys had sat down on some cases inside, continuing an argument they had already begun. The subject was a woman, Pisanella by name, and the argument was about love. Ida, however, caught nothing but the murmur of their voices, which resounded vaguely in her ears. Her powers of perception, in that instant, were all concentrated in her eyes, cast on two simultaneous images: the man in the overalls, who was in his turn going into the storehouse; and on the sidewalk, a step away from her, a large cardboard case, its top open, and only three-quarters full. On one side, it contained little cans of preserved meat; and on the other, packets of powdered sugar (the contents could be recognized by the shape, and the blue color of the wrapping paper).

Ida's heart started throbbing so violently it was like the flapping of a pair of huge wings. She reached out one hand and appropriated a can, which she slipped into her purse, promptly taking refuge around the corner of the street. At that very moment the man in overalls came out of the storeroom with another load: without having noticed anything, however, Ida believed. Actually, with a sidelong glance, he had caught her in the act, though he pretended to see nothing, out of sympathy for the little woman. Two ravenous beggar types, appearing on the broad street at that same moment, as their gaze met hers, gave her a wink of understanding and congratulation. They, she was sure, had seen her: but they too, out of sympathy, walked right on casually, as if nothing had occurred.

Everything had happened in the space of three seconds. And already Ida was slinking away, through the back streets. Her heart continued pounding, but she felt no special apprehension, and no sense of shame. The only voice that rose from her conscience was a shrewish cry that insistently reproached her: "While you were about it, you could have grabbed a pack of sugar with the other hand!! Damn you, damn you, why didn't you take the sugar, too?!!"

The ersatz cocoa, which Useppe drank in the morning, was already sweetened at the factory, with some artificial powder, suspected of being harmful to the health. Sugar cost more than a thousand lire the kilogram . . . With these thoughts, her face frowning, Ida scratched her wooly mop, which looked like a clown's wig.

In those last ten days of May, she carried out, on an average, one theft per day. She was always alert, like a cutpurse, ready to snatch at the first opportunity. Even at the Tor di Nona black market, where the vendors were more vigilant than mastiffs, with her incredible dexterity, she managed to loot a pack of salt, which at home she then shared with Filomena, who gave her some white cornmeal.

Suddenly, she had fallen into an unscrupulous depravity. If she had been less old and ugly, she might have taken to the sidewalks like Santina. Or if she had been more practical, she might have followed the example of an old retired woman named Reginella, a customer of Filomena's, who went to beg every day in Rome's rich neighborhoods, where she was unknown. But those luxurious districts were not only, by now, the fief of the German High Command, but had always been situated, for Ida, in a foreign and unattainable distance, no less than Persepolis or Chicago.

And yet, in this unexpected Ida, as in a double phenomenon, a natural shyness of nature continued, indeed grew morbidly. After she had rushed about the streets stealing, at home she hardly dared use the stove in the common kitchen. From the (fairly scarce) food of the family, she stayed not just her hand, but even her eye, like savages before taboos. And in the classroom, she seemed not so much a schoolteacher as a frightened little pupil: so her children, though speechless from hunger, already threatened to degenerate into a disrespectful gang. (Luckily, the early closing of the schools came in time to spare her this affront, never undergone before in her career.)

But most of all she was shy of asking help from her acquaintances, whose number lately had shrunk to one: the tavernkeeper Remo. On days of extremity, when she had no other resource, she made herself take the familiar, long way to San Lorenzo, where at the usual hour the proprietor was punctually in his lair behind his counter, beneath which he defiantly kept ready a rolled-up banner, the red flag. With his dark face, lean as a woodman's, his black eyes sunk above harsh, bony cheekbones, he seemed always locked up in dominant concerns of his own, and at Ida's entrance he remained seated in his place; in fact, he didn't even greet her. Ida came forward, embarrassed, full of blushes, half-stammering. Nor could she bring herself to confess the primary and urgent reason for her visit; but he would forestall her. And without even opening his mouth, with a silent signal of his chin, he ordered his wife to find, again today, a free portion of something for the mother of comrade Ace. Now that little basement kitchen was becoming, truly, emptier and emptier, as the tavernkeeper Remo became more and more laconic; and Ida emerged, confused, carrying her little packet of food, ashamed even to say thanks . . .

. . . .
"Weg! Weg da! Weg! Weg!"

Some German exclamations, interrupted and drowned by women's voices, reached her one of those mornings, when, after a futile trip to the closed Bursary, she was heading for Remo's tavern. She had just turned into a cross-street of the Via Tiburtina, when she heard the voices from the direction of Via Porta Labicana, a short distance away. As she stopped, hesitant, she almost bumped into two women, who came running from another side street to her right. One of them was old, the other younger. They were laughing excitedly, the young woman holding the other's clogs in her hand, while the old woman ran barefoot. By its hem, the old woman was holding her skirt up in front of her, swollen with a white powder: flour, spilling a bit behind her on the cobblestones as she went by. The other was carrying a black oilcloth shopping bag, also bulging with flour. As they passed Ida, they shouted at her: "Hurry, Signora, run! Tonight we eat!" "We're taking back what's ours!" "They have to give our stuff back, those lousy thieves!" Word was already spreading, other women were coming rapidly out of the doorways. "You, go back upstairs," a woman passing by fiercely ordered, letting go of a little boy's hand; and on the spoor of the spilled flour, they all ran in a pack, Ida among them. They had only a few yards to go. Halfway between Via di Porta Labicana and the freight station there was a blocked German truck, from the top of which a soldier of the Reich was yelling, confronting a crowd of poor women. Obviously, he didn't dare put his hand to the pistol in his belt, for fear of being lynched on the spot. Some of the women, with the supreme audacity of hunger, had actually clambered up on the truck, which was loaded with sacks of flour. And having slashed the sacks, they were filling their skirts, their shopping bags, and any other receptacle they happened to be carrying. Some even filled coal scuttles or pitchers. A couple of sacks lay on the ground, already half-empty, amidst the assault; a quantity of flour had poured out on the ground and was being trampled. Ida desperately forced her way forward. "Me, too! Me, too!" she screamed, like a child. She couldn't break through the siege that encircled the sacks flung on the ground. She made an effort to climb onto the truck, but she couldn't manage it: "Me, too! Me, too!!" From the top of the truck, a beautiful girl laughed above her. She was disheveled, with very thick black eyebrows and strong teeth like an animal's. She was holding her brimming little dress out in front of her by the hem, and her thighs, bared to her black rayon underpants, shone with extraordinary whiteness, like a fresh camellia's: "Here, Signora, but hurry up!" And crouching towards Ida, with a laugh, she hastily filled her shopping-bag with flour, pouring it directly from her own lap. Ida in turn had started laughing, like a halfwitted little girl, trying to get away now with her burden, through the screaming crowd. The women all seemed drunk, excited by the flour as if by a liquor. Intoxicated, they yelled the most obscene insults against the Germans, things even a whore in a brothel wouldn't have uttered. The least brutal words were: bastards! cowards! murderers!! thieves! Emerging from the crowd, Ida found herself in a chorus of young girls, the last to arrive, who were doing their share, screaming in loud voices, skipping as if in a ring-around-the-rosy:

"Dirty pigs! Dirty pigs! Dirty piiiiigs!!!"

At that point she heard her own voice, shrill, unrecognizable in her infantile excitement, shout with the chorus:

"Dirty pigs!"

For her, this was already a brothel obscenity; she had never said anything like it before.

The German guard had taken flight in the direction of the freight station. "The PAI! the PAI!" Ida heard someone shout behind her. In fact, as she was fleeing towards the Tiburtina, from the opposite side the German soldier had appeared with reinforcements, some Italian militia of the PAI. They held up their arms, pistols in hand; and to intimidate, they fired some shots in the air, but Ida, hearing the shots and the women's confused screams, thought it was a massacre. She was gripped by a terrible fear of falling, mortally wounded, leaving Useppe alone in the world, an orphan. She ran blindly, screaming, mingling with escaping women who almost ran her down. Finally she found herself alone, not knowing where she was, and she sat on a step beside a ditch. She couldn't see anything, except for some imaginary dark bubbles of blood, which burst in the sunny air. That same hammering racket, which always woke her in the morning, now had come back to throb inside her temples, with the usual rumble of an uprising: "Useppe! Useppe!" she felt a spasm in her head, so sharp she touched her scalp with her fingers, suspecting she might find them wet with blood. But the shots hadn't wounded her; she was unharmed. Suddenly, she jumped up, no longer seeing the shopping-bag over her arm! But she found it nearby, on the uneven lot, with the flour intact to the brim: she had lost very little, fortunately, in her flight. Breathlessly then, she started searching for her little change-purse, finally remembering that it must have remained at the bottom of the shopping-bag. And she dug it out feverishly, staining her whole arm with flour mixed with sweat.

The shopping-bag, too full, wouldn't close. From a pile of refuse there on the ground, she picked up a piece of newspaper to hide the stolen flour before heading for her tram.

．　　．　　．

At home, that morning, there was not only no gas, but also no electricity or water. Filomena, however, grateful for a little gift of flour, managed to make Ida some *pèttola* (pasta) and to cook it along with her own, adding a little fistful of beans, already boiled.

Ida took another portion of flour with her when she went out that afternoon. That day (like every Thursday since the schools had closed) she had to go give a private lesson in the neighborhood of the Trastevere station. And she planned, on her return, to go as far as Via Garibaldi, where she knew a man who, in exchange for the flour, would give her some meat for Useppe's supper.

This plan for the day was tangled in her head like wire. It was the first of June, and, oddly, it was like a due date, for all the accumulated fatigue of the month of May to fall on her at once. After the fear of death that had gripped her as she fled from the truck, she found herself again, worse than before, bewildered and cowardly like a pariah dog persecuted by the dogcatchers. As she headed for Via Garibaldi, she felt her legs buckling, and she sat down to rest on a little bench in the garden this side of the bridge. Her mind was distracted, so she could barely perceive, in confusion, some voices conversing nearby, in the little garden or at the tram stop not far off. The subject was not new: they were talking about an air raid that same day, in the outskirts: some said twenty deaths, some two hundred. She remained aware of being seated there in the garden, and at the same time she found herself running around the San Lorenzo quarter. She was carrying in her arms something of supreme value which must have been Useppe; but though it had the weight of a body, this thing had neither form nor color. And also the quarter, which was now enfolded in an opaque dust cloud, was no longer San Lorenzo, but a foreign space, without houses or form. She wasn't dreaming, since she heard meanwhile the tram clanking on the tracks and the passengers' voices at the stop. However, at the same time, she knew she was mistaken: that wasn't the tram's clanking, but another sound. Recovering herself with a jolt, she was embarrassed to find her lips drooping and saliva running down her chin. She stood up, unresolved, and having walked only halfway across the Garibaldi bridge, she realized she was heading for the Ghetto. She recognized the call that was tempting her there and that came to her this time like a low and somnolent dirge, still loud enough to engulf all exterior sounds. Its irresistible rhythms resembled those with which mothers lull their babies, or tribes summon their members together for the night. Nobody has taught them, they are written already in the seed of all the living, subject to death.

Ida knew that the little quarter, for months now, had been once more cleared of all its population: the last evaders from the previous October, having stealthily returned to their narrow rooms, had been rooted out again in February, one after the other, by the Fascist police in the service of the Gestapo; and even refugees and vagabonds avoided the area . . . However, in her head, today, this news was lost amid reminiscences and older habits. In some confused way, she still expected to encounter there the usual gang of little families with curly hair and black eyes, in the streets, at the doorways and windows. And at the first intersection, she stopped, puzzled, no longer recognizing the streets or the doors. In reality, she was at the head of a street she had often visited in the past: narrow at the start, among low houses, it opens into a small square, then continues among other little ramifications to the central square. Its name, unless I'm mistaken, is Via Sant'Ambrogio. And from here, more or less, Ida used always to set off, in her past wanderings. Around here were the little shops and courtyards and the familiar alleys where she had busied herself with her buying and selling and where she had heard from Vilma, "a bit upset in the head," the radio-information of the Signora and the Nun, and where once she had learned from a little old woman in a tiny hat about the official halfbreed race, and another time she had met the midwife Ezekiel . . . It was an enclosure more minuscule than the most minuscule village, even if within it thousands of Jews were crowded, in families of ten to a room. But today Ida dragged herself through it as if in an enormous maze without beginning or end; and no matter how much she roamed about, she always found herself at the same point.

She vaguely realized she had come here to deliver something to somebody; indeed, she knew this somebody's last name: EFRATI, which she kept repeating to herself in a low voice so she wouldn't forget it. And she looked for someone she could ask for directions. But there was nobody, not even a passerby. No voice was heard.

To Ida's ears, the perpetual roll of the cannon in the distance was confused with the echo of her own solitary footsteps. Here, separated from the traffic along the Tiber, the silence of these sunny little alleys isolated the senses like a narcotic injection, excluding all surrounding, populated territory. Through the walls of the houses, you could strangely feel the resonance of the inner voids. And she kept on murmuring EFRATI, EFRATI, entrusting herself to this uncertain thread to keep from being completely lost.

There she was again in the broader space with the fountain. The fountain was dry. Dead plants trailed from the narrow street's little loggias and decrepit balconies. At the hovels' windows there was no longer the usual array of underpants, diapers, and other rags strung out to dry; at either side, from the outside hooks, the little broken lines were still hanging. And some windows had shattered panes. Through the grille of a street-level room, formerly a shop, you could glimpse the damp, dark interior, stripped of the counter and the merchandise, and invaded by cobwebs. Some of the doors seemed barred, but others, bashed in during the looting, were ajar or half-open. Ida pushed at an unhinged door, with only one leaf, then closed it behind her back.

The entrance hall, the size of a closet, was almost in darkness, and it was cold there. But the little stone stairway, all worn and slippery, received light from a window at about the level of the third floor. On the second landing there were two closed doors; but one of the two had no name. The other had, written in pen, on a little glued card: Astrologo Family, and on the wall, above the bell, two more names, in pencil: Sara Di Cave, Sonnino Family.

Along the wall of the stairs, peeling and covered with stains, you could read various writings, most of them obviously by childish hands: *Arnaldo loves Sara—Ferruccio is hansome* (and below, added by another young hand: *he's a shit*)—*Colomba loves L—Roma's the winner.*

Frowning, Ida examined all the writings, in an effort to decipher her own confused reasoning in them. The house had two upper stories in all, but the stairway seemed very long to her. Finally, at the next landing, she discovered what she was looking for. Actually, the number of people named EFRATI in the Rome Ghetto was beyond counting. There was no stairway, you might say, where one wasn't to be found.

Here there were three doors. One, without a name and off its hinges, opened into a windowless cubbyhole, with the springs of a bed on the floor and a basin, both battered. The other two doors were closed. On one, there was a little plate with the name: Di Cave, and above it, written on the wood, also the names: Pavoncello, Calò. And on the second, a broad piece of paper was glued, which said: Sonnino, EFRATI, Della Seta.

In her weariness, Ida couldn't resist the temptation to sit down on those iron springs. From the broken window over the stairs came a swallow's shriek and she was amazed by it. Heedless of air raids and explosions, that little creature had flown across the sky—its fragile body unerringly oriented—as on a domestic path. While she, a woman, and over forty years old, found herself lost.

She had to make an enormous effort not to give way to her desire to stretch out on those springs and spend the whole night there. And certainly it was this effort which, in her state of extreme weakness, then provoked an auditory illusion. First she was surprised by an unreal silence in the place. And within this, her ears, buzzing from her fasts, began to perceive some voices. It was not, actually, a true hallucination, because Ida realized that the manufactory of those voices was in her brain, indeed she herself did not sense them elsewhere. However, the impression she received from them was that they were spreading through her auditory canals from some unspecified dimension, which no longer belonged to exterior space, or to her memories. They were alien voices, of various tone, but predominantly female, unconnected with one another, without dialogue or communication among themselves. And they distinctly pronounced phrases, some exclamatory, some relaxed, but all of ordinary banality, like assembled fragments of the common life of every day:
. . . "I'm on the roof collecting the laundry!!" . . . "If you don't finish your homework, you're not leaving this house!" . . . "I'm going to tell your father when he gets home!" . . . "They're distributing cigarettes today . . ." "All right, I'll wait for you, but hurry . . ." "Where've you been all this time? . . ." ". . . I'll be right there, mà . . .!" "How much are you asking?" "He told me to start dinner . . ." "Put that light out; electricity costs money . . ."

This phenomenon of hearing voices is fairly common, and at times even the healthy experience it, more frequently when they are about to fall asleep, and after a hard day's work. For Ida, it wasn't new; but in her present emotional fragility it seized her like an invasion. The voices in her ears, before dying away, started reechoing one after the other, overlapping at a turbulent rhythm. And in this haste of theirs she seemed to sense a horrible meaning, as if their poor gossip were exhumed from one confused eternity into another confused eternity. Without knowing what she was saying, or why, Ida found herself murmuring, to herself, her chin trembling like that of a child about to cry:

"They're all dead."

She said it with her lips, but almost without voice. And at this murmur, within the silence, she felt a weight like the plunging of an acoustic probe in her memory. She was then able to establish that she had come here today to deliver the message picked up from beneath the train on October 18th at the Tiburtina Station; and she immediately began to rummage, with restless fingers, in her bag, where she had kept it since that day. On the little paper, worn and filthy, the penciled writing had been almost entirely rubbed away. She could just read: . . . *see Efrati Pacificho . . . family . . . lire debt* . . . The rest was illegible.

She was gripped by an anxiety to leave this place. In hunting for her purse, she had seen again at the bottom of her shopping-bag the packet of flour she had put there on leaving home: it recalled her to some vague but very urgent matter to which she had to attend before evening . . . Half-drunk, she came out again on the landing. The electric bells, at the two closed doors, made no sound; then she began to knock on one, then the other, at random, on either side of the narrow landing. She knew she was knocking without effect or intention; and soon she gave up. However, as she descended towards the front door, those absurd raps in the void, instead of stopping, came at her, striking her between the throat and the breastbone. The useless message from the Tiburtina Station remained upstairs in the cubbyhole, where she had dropped it.

Meanwhile, the thought had returned to her mind that she had to go immediately to Via Garibaldi and try to barter the flour for a piece of meat for Useppe's supper. But here fortune came to her aid. In the vicinity of the Portico d'Ottavia, still on the margins of the Ghetto, in a doorway at the top of three or four steps, she glimpsed an almost-closed door from which a trickle of blood was flowing. Looking in, she found a sordid little room, badly illuminated by an interior window, and converted for the moment into a semi-clandestine butcher shop. A young man in an undershirt, muscular, with a bony face, his hands covered with blood, was standing behind a bench beside an enormous suitcase lined with bloodstained newspaper. With a cleaver in his hands, he was chopping into pieces the already-skinned and halved body of a kid. Both he and the few customers were in a hurry, also because the curfew hour was near. On one side of the bench, all stained and bloody, there were two bleeding kids' heads, and a pile of bills of small denomination in a basket.

A sweetish, warm smell hung over the room, nauseating. Ida approached unsteadily, shy, as if she had come to steal. And without saying a word, her mouth drawn down and her features trembling, she set her packet of flour on the bench. The young man barely glanced at it, with an almost grim eye; wasting no time in argument, he flung into her hands, wrapped in a piece of newspaper, the last bit that remained of the kid: a leg and part of the shoulder.

The passersby were emptying the streets in haste, but Ida had no idea of the time. In reality, since she had half dozed off in the garden, more time had passed than she thought. Now curfew was already striking; and at the corner of the Tiber, at Piazza dell'Emporio, she found herself, unawares, the only transient in a depopulated world. Buildings were already closing their front doors, but at that moment no patrol was policing the area. The sun, just beginning to set, seemed a strange, desert star, like the midnight suns. And as she walked along the Tiber, the river, struck by the sidelong light, looked whitish to her. On her way home, she saw nothing but this white, dazzling liquid in all the air; and she hastened, uneasily suspecting she had dropped onto a kind of exotic planet, though familiar to her footsteps. In her crooked and fluttering gait, she was careful to clutch jealously the shopping-bag with that piece of kid inside, like a battered sparrow returning to his tree with a rich worm. And when, beyond the opposite sidewalk, she recognized her own front door, she looked up with eyes filled with gratitude to seek along the lines of windows for those of home. To her gaze, all the windows looked like black crevasses on the face of an iceberg. The downstairs door was being closed. As she hastened, her body, in its weakness, had no weight.

That night, after such a long time without dreaming, she had a dream. Her dreams, as a rule, were colored and vivid, but this one, on the contrary, was in black-and-white, and blurred like an old photograph. She seemed to be outside an enclosure, something like an abandoned refuse dump. There was nothing but piles of shoes, worn and dusty, which seemed to have been thrown away years ago. And she, alone there, was desperately searching in that pile for one little shoe of very small size, like a doll's, with the feeling that, for her, this search had the value of a definitive verdict. The dream had no plot, only this one scene; but though it had no sequel or explanation, it seemed to tell a long, irremediable story.

.   .   .

The next morning, for the first time after many months, Ida couldn't manage to get up early. Nor could she force herself to any enterprise, except, around eleven, another futile pilgrimage to the Bursary to see if the payment-window had reopened today.

On her return, Filomena persuaded her to eat a portion of *pèttola*. Having lost the stimulus of hunger, she swallowed the first mouthfuls reluctantly; but then she consumed the rest with such voracity that, a little later, her unaccustomed stomach had some fits of vomiting. She then lay supine on the bed, her eyes wide in the effort to restrain herself, and to avoid such a squandering of that most precious pasta.

The weather was splendid, already summer, but she felt a great cold and a constant somnolence that every now and then flung her, bullyingly, on the bed. In those dozes, she saw again, in a very remote Beyond, that other Ida who till yesterday trotted and galloped through the streets like a racer, and lurked, and stole . . . "A teacher!! A schoolmistress!!!" she said to herself, shuddering at this last vision. And she actually saw herself under accusation, taken into Court: among the judges there was her Headmistress, the Schools Inspector, the General in command of the German Forces, and some men in PAI uniforms. Now she was very hot, her throat dry. She was running a temperature. From time to time, however, a little air came to refresh her, as if a breeze of leaves or little wings fluttering near her face:

"Hey, mà, why you're sleeping so much?!"

"I'll get up now . . . Have you eaten?"

"Ess. Filomena gave me some pèttola."

"You must say *Signora* Filomena . . . Did you say thank you, eh?"

"Ess."

"How did you say it?"

"I said: *join?* and she said to me: *here!*"

"*Join!!* Is that what you said to her? You mustn't . . . I've taught you not to ask . . . But afterwards, at least, you thanked her for her trouble? . . ."

"Ess-ess. First I said *join* and after I said *ciao.*"

Filomena and Annita were happy those days, because Santina had read in the cards that peace would come soon and they would have news of Giovannino. Tommaso, the head of the household, was pessimistic, on the other hand. He told them how he had heard, in the hospital, that the Germans meant to make a last-ditch stand, and anyway they would first explode all those famous mines; and that even the Pope was planning to escape with the "Vatican fleet" in an armored plane, towards the unknown.

All the roads around Rome were loud with vehicles and with squadrons of planes. Towards the Castelli, only an enormous cloud of smoke could be seen. On the evening of June 3rd, Tommaso, who was a football fan and favored the Lazio team, came home more dejected than ever: as if all the rest weren't enough, something unheard of had taken place: Tirrenia had eliminated Lazio. And so, the latter was excluded from the finals, favoring the hated local rival, Roma.

Starting today, Tommaso was on vacation, since he was unable to reach the hospital. Effective immediately, crossing the bridges over the Tiber was forbidden. Thus the city was divided in two territories, unable to communicate with each other. At this news, in Ida's poor feverish mind, the real topography of Rome became confused and upset. All her regular urban itineraries—not only the school on the Gianicolense and Trastevere, but also Tordinona and San Lorenzo and the Bursary—appeared to her, today, unreachable, situated on the other side of the river. And the little village of the Ghetto moved away from her to a nebulous distance, beyond some bridge miles and miles long.

Tommaso also said that, from Piazza Venezia along the Corso, he had seen an endless procession of trucks file by, filled with German soldiers, all black with soot and stained with blood. The people looked at them and said nothing. The soldiers didn't look at anybody.

The evening of June 4th, because of the electricity shortage, everyone went to bed early. Testaccio was calm beneath the glowing moon. And during the night, the Allies entered Rome. Suddenly, a great clamor was raised in the streets, as if it were New Year's Eve. Windows and doors were flung open, flags were unfurled. There were no more Germans in the city. From above and below, shouts were heard: Hurray for peace!! Long live America!!

The grandfather, wakened with a start, began to groan "oi mà oi mà" hawking into the basin.

"oi mà oi mà . . ."

"son, son . . . what is it?"

"I want . . . rruhuhur . . . oi mà . . . son son . . . oi mà . . . save me save me . . . these Germins here . . . oi mà the Germins . . . the Germins are jumping on me . . . uuuhrrh . . . rrrrrruhuhu . . . they're killing me . . . poor naked gypsy . . . rrhu . . ."

There was a bustle in the house. "The Americans! The Americans have come!!"

Useppe, thrilled, ran around in the dark on his bare feet. "Hey, mà! màààààà!!!! The Mericuns! The Mericuns are here . . . !"

In her dream, Ida was back in Cosenza, a little girl, and her mother was calling her insistently to get up, it was time to go to school. But outside it was cold, and she was afraid of putting on her shoes, because she had chilblains on her feet.

Too tired to get up, she barely mumbled something, and sank back into sleep.

After the attack on the flour truck, Ida didn't believe she could go back again to the San Lorenzo quarter, which had become for her the very center of fear. But when two weeks had gone by after the reopening of the roads and there was still no news of Ninnarieddu, she ventured as far as Remo's tavern.

Here, she learned the surprising news that Nino had already been in Rome around the beginning of June, shortly after the Allies' entrance, dropping by the tavern for a rapid visit with Remo, who had naturally given him his mother's address in Testaccio. He was in excellent health, and high spirits, and had brought good news also of Carlo-Pyotr, who was alive and well, now living with some relatives (it was his wet-nurse, in reality) in a little village halfway between Naples and Salerno. The pair, having crossed the front lines together unharmed, had maintained, indeed strengthened their guerrilla friendship; and they often had chances to meet in Naples, where Nino was conducting some important business.

This was, in its entirety, the news, scant and brisk, which the tavern-keeper had received from Nino, who had been on an army jeep in the company of two American sergeants, and in a great hurry. Since that day Remo hadn't seen him again.

After this reassuring information, Ida heard no more from Nino until August. In that month, a card came from him, postmarked *Capri*, with the color photograph of a luxurious palace entitled *Quisisana Grand Hôtel*. Mistakenly, the recipients conceived the fabulous notion that Nino was actually lodged in that palace. On the correspondence side of the card, among other signatures of strangers, he, over his own signature: *Nino*, had written only, in English, *See you soon*. These words were undecipherable to those present: some thought they must be American, and some, instead, Japanese or Chinese. But Santina, who now plied her trade with Allied soldiers, consulted a Sicilian-American on the subject. And she reported, from him, that the words meant, more or less, *Arrivederci presto*.

Still autumn came, in continued, total silence from Ninnuzzu. Who, to tell the truth, during those six months, had been in Rome more than once, coming and going. But always in transit, involved in certain urgent deals of his, he had so far neglected to get in touch either with his friend the tavernkeeper or with his mother.

Meanwhile, the Allied armies, after landing in Normandy, had opened their attack on the Germans in Europe, reconquering France; and in August they had entered Paris with General de Gaulle. In all the countries formerly subjugated by the Germans, the revolt progressed, while the Red armies advanced from the East. And in Italy, after Rome, the Allies had taken Florence, stopping at the *Gothic Line*, where the advance was now held up.

Other events of that summer: not long after the liberation of Rome, Annita, exploiting the opportunity of a lift, had seized the occasion to pay a visit up in the mountains, where the family hovel, and the others near it, were undamaged. However, of all the cities and villages in the plain below or up towards the hills, which you used to pass along the way, nothing was left, she reported on her return: in their place you could see nothing but a big cloud of dust. Her in-laws would name this or that locality, village, orange-grove; and shaking her head slowly, her eyes disconsolate, she would repeat that it was the same everywhere: nothing left but dust. It seemed that the strange sight of this dust cloud had invaded all the other impressions of her journey, so she could remember nothing else.

The second event was, in August, the grandfather's death. On one of those torrid nights, the old man, on his own initiative, lowering himself from the cot in the kitchen, had lain down on the floor, perhaps to feel cooler. And in the morning he was still stretched out there, grumbling to himself, paying no attention to the line of ants marching across his half-naked body. The first to enter the kitchen, waking at dawn, had been Useppe. Amazed, staring at the old man, he had tried offering him the basin to spit in, the chair, the flask of wine. But the old man answered only with insistent muttering, in a tone of refusal, nor would he get up again. From the kitchen that same morning he was transferred to the hospital, whence, a little later, he was carried, dead, directly to the graveyard and emptied into the common paupers' grave. Useppe, who asked where he had gone, was told by Annita that he had returned to the mountains; and at this reply, Useppe stood there puzzled, imagining that emaciated old man, naked, covered with ants, and without even his *cioce* on his feet, climbing up amid the notorious dust cloud. After that, however, Useppe asked no more about him.

Ida, meanwhile, after the inevitable confusion in all public services, had resumed collecting her salary from the Bursary in bank notes of a new kind, known as am-lire. But also with these am-lire it was hard for her to manage meals every day; stealing, however, was out of the question for her from now on. Her old school building, there in Testaccio, requisitioned by the armed forces, had been occupied by a unit of South Africans, who every now and then gave Tommaso Marrocco the leftovers from their mess, in exchange for some errand. And then it happened that Ida, through Tommaso, found a job there: giving Italian lessons to a member of that unit. Never having taught an adult before, Ida was quite scared at the trial; but at first, she believed a South African would be a black-skinned man, and this fact, for some unknown reason, she found more reassuring. Instead, she found herself facing a white man, blond, with freckles; he spoke very little, in an incomprehensible language, and had rather rough manners, somewhat like a recruiting sergeant. He was heavy and square, and slow to understand; but here, I believe, the fault lay more with the teacher, who in that lesson hour, gasped and stammered, filled with embarrassment, looking like an idiot. The lessons were held in the school building, in an airy room on the ground floor, formerly the gymnasium; and in payment Ida received some little bags of powdered soup, cans of corned beef, etc. The job ended in late summer, when the South African was transferred towards Florence; and this remained, from then on, Ida's only connection with the victors.

Of Giovannino, there had still been no news. And so Ida, at the end of summer, was still occupying, with Useppe, the little room in Via Mastro Giorgio. Here one afternoon, late in September, there was an unexpected visitor: Carlo.

He turned up looking for Nino, declaring that the latter had been in Rome for some days now, though without a specific address. And Carlo had hoped to find here, at least, some idea of how to trace him; but on realizing that nobody in the house knew anything, he didn't conceal his own impatience to leave promptly, announcing in a grumble that he had to catch the train back to Naples before evening.

Still, in the face of Ida's anxiety and the others' consideration, to leave so abruptly must have seemed too rude to him. And when invited, he sat down awkwardly at the work table, where they promptly served him some white Frascati wine. Running from the little room, Useppe, on recognizing him, had shouted at him joyfully: Carlo! Carlo! and Ida, stammering in her surprise, had introduced him to the others: "Signor Carlo Vivaldi." But as he sat down, he announced with a stern, brusque manner, as if all should have known it already:

"My name is DAVIDE SEGRE."

In the room, besides Ida and Useppe and the women of the house and the *piccinina*, there were Consolata and two other lady acquaintances plus an elderly little man, a family friend, who was a news-vendor by profession. Ida would have liked to ask the guest a hundred questions, but his usual mien, sullen and shy, checked her. Further, she was ashamed that Nino had left her in the dark, so uninformed that she, his own mother, had to ask news of an outsider.

He who once had been called Carlo, then Pyotr, and now Davide, sat uneasily amid the little domestic throng. Those present, having already heard Ida speak of him, had immediately identified him as that famous partisan, companion of the heroic Ninnuzzu, who had crossed the lines with him. And consequently, they treated him as a guest of supreme worth, all excited at his presence. But these honors seemed to embarrass him still more, indeed to irk him and make him gloomy.

At that time, he was much the same as in the past; however, he somehow seemed more of a boy than in the Pietralata days. He wore a freshly laundered white polo shirt, over pants which were, on the contrary, incredibly filthy, of blue denim, like a sailor's. And though shaven, and with his hair cut nice and short in his old style, he had a neglected look in his face, in all his body, as if he had let himself go. His nails were black with dirt, and his feet were filthy in his worn sandals. Though Ida introduced him with the title of "Signor," he looked more like a gypsy or a proletarian. And the intense sadness of his dark eyes seemed to drown in an inner stubbornness, almost desperate, like an incurable, brooding obsession.

He looked at no one; and between sips of wine, instead of setting down the glass, he clutched it in his nervous hands and stared into it, seeming more interested in the bottom of a glass than in his own peers. When someone urged him to tell something of his adventures, he answered only with a shrug of one shoulder, and a crooked smile. He was, clearly, very timid; but there was also something arrogant about his silence, as if he refused all conversation to avenge the civil obligation that had led him, against his will, to stay here in company. The center of general curiosity and consideration, he behaved exactly like a deaf-mute. Only when Consolata and the Marrocco women inevitably began expounding to him the crucial problem of their missing men, he raised his eyes for a moment, and with a snap of his jaws, he said, gravely and brutally absolute:

"They'll never come back."

All were silent. And then the news-vendor, to distract the women a bit from the terrible shock, promptly changed the subject to Santina, who had promised to come to read the cards right after dinner, and instead was keeping them waiting. On this subject, the little man, assuming a light tone, began making easy guesses about the business that might be keeping Santina, explaining her delay. And he didn't use vague terms, but quite precise ones, enriched with obscene allusions, aiming at a comical effect.

The young man named Davide didn't seem any more interested in this subject than in the previous ones. When Santina appeared at the door a few minutes later, however, he, who till then had paid no attention to anyone, accompanied her with his eyes as she came towards the table with heavy steps. And he went on watching her, beneath his slightly lowered lashes, even after she had taken her seat, finding herself almost opposite him. Thanks to the horde of soldiers old and young, who weren't choosy, and who poured into Rome in those months from every continent, Santina was now enjoying some good fortune, compared to her usual lot, and she had had her long, partly gray hair waved by a hairdresser; but otherwise she hadn't changed. Nobody bothered to introduce her to Davide; nor did she seem to notice those black eyes observing her with an obstinate wildness. But when her ruined, washerwoman's hands, heavy and gnarled, were about to shuffle the cards lent her by Annita, Davide stood up, announcing firmly:

"I have to go."

Then, addressing her at once, he suggested, or rather he almost ordered her, bullying, though he blushed like a little boy:

"Please, will you come down with me? There's still an hour and a half before my train. *Afterwards*, you can come back here for the cards."

He had spoken without ambiguity, but there was no lack of respect in his tone; indeed, in his final words, he almost seemed to be asking charity. Santina's backward, docile eyes barely moved in his direction; she gave a little, hesitant smile, showing the incisor's gap in her upper gum.

"Go on, go with the gentleman; we'll wait for you," the news-vendor encouraged her, with a cordial, slightly malicious festiveness. "We'll wait for you here. Take your time."

She followed the young man simply. When the sound of their paired footsteps disappeared down the steps, in the workroom there were various comments, but all, more or less, harping on the main theme "such a handsome boy, going off with that old tramp!!"

Meanwhile the old tramp was leading this unexpected customer to her ground-level room on the edge of the Via Portuense, not far from Porta Portese. It was at the bottom of a solid, isolated building, with two stories over the ground floor (these upper stories seemed to have been added more recently, though they were already in bad shape and decaying) at the end of a vacant lot, without cobbles, beyond some huts with gardens. You entered the place directly from the street, through a narrow door without nameplate or bell, and the interior, a single damp little room, looked out onto a kind of garbage dump, visible through a barred window, which, however, was always hidden by a curtain. On the same side as the window, there was a wooden bed, not very broad, guarded by two holy pictures: one was the usual, repeated image of the Sacred Heart, and the other the figure of a village saint, with bishop's crook and vestments, and a halo around his miter. The bed was covered by a piece of reddish cotton damask, and at its side there was a cheap little Oriental-style rug, worn almost to the nap.

The rest of the furniture consisted of an armchair with half the springs showing and a little table bearing a celluloid doll dressed in tulle, a small frying pan, and an electric hot plate. Under the table, there was a big fiber suitcase, which served also as wardrobe, and above, hanging on the wall, there was a little cupboard.

In one corner of the room there was a curtain of the same flowered and striped material as the one at the window, and equally worn. Behind it there was a small tin-plate washstand with jug, basin, and bucket, a very clean towel hanging from a nail, and on the floor even a bidet, also of tin plate.

The latrine, shared with the other tenants of the upper floors (on the ground floor, Santina was the sole inhabitant), was in the little courtyard inside the main entrance. To reach it, you had to come out of the room on the street and go around the building to the front door. In any event, in the little room, under the bed there was a urinal, which could also be emptied directly into the street.

Santina didn't undress, taking off only her shoes before lying down under the cover beside Davide, who had already stripped naked. They stayed together about an hour, and in that hour he released himself in an animal aggressiveness, greedy, almost frantic. At the moment of goodbyes, however, he looked at Santina shyly again, with a kind of tender gratitude, whereas for that whole hour he had avoided looking at her, turning his grim and lonely eyes elsewhere in the fury of his body. He gave her all the (little) money he had, digging it from the pocket of his trousers (where he also had his Naples-Rome round-trip ticket); and piling it up in her hand, the bills all crumpled like waste paper, he apologized to her, ashamed that he couldn't pay her better. But then, realizing it was late, he had to ask her to give him back some change for the tram to the station. And this request made him blush, mortified, as if at a guilt difficult to pardon; while Santina, at this little exchange, seemed to apologize in turn, her eyes obedient and dazed, because really the money received from him (however little) was more than twice her usual rate.

In any case, he hastened to inform her that, after the liberation of the North, he would have a lot more money than now, so he would be able to pay her much better. Meanwhile, with what money he could scrape up at present, every time he came to Rome he would visit her.

She accompanied him to the tram stop, afraid that, unfamiliar with the neighborhood, he might get lost. Then, with the weight of her mauled and patient body, she went back up to the Marroccos; while he, jolted in the crowded tram, pushed his way forward, nervous as a wrestler without style.

. . .

The reappearance of Carlo-Davide, like a dispatch-rider, preceded Nino's only by a little. Barely two days later, just after dinner, Ninnarieddu presented himself at the Marrocco home; and his visit was the opposite of Davide's, though equally brief.

Since on the door of the house there was the nameplate MAR-

ROCCO, even before knocking, he called excitedly: "Useppe! Useppe!!" As chance would have it, however, Useppe, since it was a beautiful sunny day, had gone out with Annita. On learning this, Nino was disappointed, especially since he couldn't stay long. He had brought his little brother some bars of American chocolate, and he put them there on the shelf, with an irked expression. Then Filomena promptly dispatched the *piccinina* to recover the pair, who for that matter couldn't have gone far: they had probably stopped at the little garden in Piazza Santa Maria Liberatrice. But, after a speedy disappearance below, the *piccinina* reappeared running, in such a hurry she seemed to be gulping the air: she had looked for the two of them in the garden and in the square, but hadn't found them. To tell the truth, she had carried out the errand reluctantly, eager not to lose a spark of this new and dazzling guest. Never, except perhaps among movie heroes, had she seen such a sensational figure.

He was curly-haired, tall, well-built, sunburned, bold, elegant, all dressed in American style. He had an American leather jacket, short at the waist, with civilian shirt and trousers, but of American army cloth. The pants were neatly pressed, held up by a magnificent leather belt, the legs tight, ending in some little rawhide boots, the arrogant kind seen in Westerns. And at the open neck of his shirt you could see a gold chain dancing on his chest, a little gold heart hanging from it.

The epic of his feats, now legendary in the family, passed back and forth before her eyes, in little moving, shameless illustrations. And even his hands suggested destruction and turmoil: so that at his casual approach, the *piccinina* promptly threw herself back slightly, laughing, and trembling, as if to say: Help! help! He's going to beat me!

And yet, she went towards him, in an impertinent, even defiant way, to have him show her more closely a big fake-silver ring he wore on his finger. On the bezel there were engraved the letters A.M. (Antonino Mancuso): "Those," he explained to her, "are my initials." She sank into contemplation of the ring, with the importance of a connoisseur examining the treasure of the Great Khan. But suddenly she ran off to the other side of the table, laughing wildly at her own nameless audacity, which actually broke her heart.

He had no time to talk about his great war exploits and his adventures of the past few months. But it was clear, in any case, that for him those were already ancient events, which he recalled only fleetingly and absently; he was too involved with today and too impatient to rush to the immediate tomorrow. Whatever the important occupations that presently engaged him might be, they remained a riddle; indeed, he enjoyed playing the mystery man on the subject.

He was sorry to hear Carlo-Davide had come looking for him in vain;

but he immediately resigned himself, with a shake of his curls, saying: "I'll see him in Naples." And he amused himself by telling jokes, whistling the tunes of songs, and at every moment he burst out laughing like a chaffinch. All were thrilled by his festive presence.

Truly, now that he was eating and drinking his fill and was free to do as he pleased, Ninnuzzu was blooming; and in this present season of his flowering, his greatest joy was in making everyone love him. Whether it was the street-cleaner, the begging nun, the women selling watermelons, the policeman, the mailman, the cat: even them. A fly, even, if it came to light on him, perhaps meant to say to him: "I love you." And since he so loved being loved, he was always glowing, devilish and wild as if he were playing with a rainbow ball. He would throw it, and the others would catch it and toss it back to him; and he would make a leap and catch it. Now, excess, in this exhibitionistic game of his, was inevitable; however, a kind of ingenuous question, timid and propitiatory, appeared every now and then, the following (more or less): "Well, do you love me? Yes or no? Ah, say yes: I enjoy so much being loved . . ." And here in his eyes, in his aggressive and capricious mouth, there appeared the hint of a threat: "If you say no, you'll torment me. I want to be loved. It would be a shitty thing, to torment a boy like that . . ."

This note made his every vanity forgiven, and nobody could resist him. Even the news-vendor (who always turned up at the Marroccos about this time, to drink a glass of wine in company) abruptly banged his fist on the table and said to Ida, in an almost thunderous voice: "This son of yours, Signora, he's really something!!" And a little old woman of seventy, a customer who had come to try on a new jacket, sat down deliberately to enjoy him, and she murmured into his mother's ear: "Signora, I could just eat him up with kisses!"

Ida herself, who always had some grudge against him for varying reasons, every now and then broke into bright laughter, meant to make others take notice: "I made him, this boy! I'm the one who made him!"

Saying he had spent the summer dancing, he promptly wanted to teach some new dances to the women present; and the *piccinina*, in her great fear he would embrace her, almost dived under the table. But luckily, forgetting about dancing, he lighted a cigarette with an American (or English) lighter which he called *the cannon*. And for the occasion he offered all a smoke, holding out, to one after the other, including the old lady, his pack of American cigarettes, Lucky Strike. But the only one of the company who smoked was the news-vendor, so Nino gave him the whole pack, except for one cigarette which he kept in reserve, brashly sticking it over his ear. And then, to play the clown, he started imitating the poses of a Mafioso.

Meanwhile, every two minutes he fell to grumbling at Useppe's absence, until, frowning, he declared he couldn't wait for him any longer. It was clear that the most important reason for his visit had been to surprise his little brother and deliver the American chocolate; and he was really angry and impatient, at this plan of his gone awry. "Want me to take another look in the square?" the *piccinina* volunteered quickly, in the hope of keeping him there. "No, it's late now. I can't stay any longer," he answered, his eye on his watch.

And after saying goodbye to all, he started to leave; then an idea came into his head. He sighed, half-cross, and ran a couple of steps towards his mother, grandly placing before her, as a present, a handful of am-lire. She was so stunned by this unprecedented act that she didn't even thank him. Instead, she called him, when he was already at the door, having forgotten before to make him repeat (to avoid future misunderstandings) the new first and last names of Carlo Vivaldi, which she had not properly learned the other day.

"DAVIDE SEGRE! They're Jew names," he explained. And he added, in a proud, smug tone:

"I knew all along he was a Jew."

Here, in a flash, something comical and odd came back to his mind, stopping him at the door and prodding him, with the urgency of a communication that couldn't be postponed: so even in his haste to be gone, he ran back, almost leaping: "Hey, mà, I got to tell you something," he stated, glancing at Ida in amusement, "but it's private. I got to tell you by yourself."

Whatever could it be?! Ida didn't know what in the world to expect from him. She took him into the little room, closing the door. He drew her aside in the corner, bubbling with sensational impatience:

"You know what they told me, mà?!"

"? . . ."

"That YOU'RE A JEW."

". . . Who told you that!"

"Eh, I've known a long time, mà! Somebody here in Rome told me. But I won't say who it was."

"But it's not true! It's not true!!"

". . . Aw, mà!! You think we're still in the days of Pontius Pilate or something? If you're Jewish, what difference does it make?"

He reflected for a moment, and then added:

"Carlo Marx was a Jew, too."

". . ." Ida, breathless, was shaking like a string in the wind.

. . . "And papà? What was he?"

"No. Not him."

Ninnarieddu thought this over for a moment, though without too much earnestness: "Women," he observed, "you can't tell when they're Jews. But men you can tell, because when they're kids they peel off the end of their prick."

Then he concluded, as if making an indifferent statement:

"Me, I'm not a Jew. And Useppe isn't either."

And without further ado, he ran off. A little later, the old woman also took her leave, while the news-vendor was happily smoking his own Lucky Strikes. The sewing machine, operated by the *piccinina*, resumed hammering with worse racket than usual; and Filomena went back to making chalk marks on a piece of brown wool spread out on the table.

A quarter of an hour later, Annita and Useppe came home. They had been to look at the merry-go-round in Piazza dell'Emporio, and on the way back Annita had bought Useppe an ice-cream cone, which he was still licking when they came in. Ida, after the dialogue with Ninnarieddu, had remained in her room; and the *piccinina*, who didn't feel like singing *joy and tormend* any more today, raised her long, saddened eyes from the machine at their entrance and promptly announced to Useppe:

"Your brother was here."

Puzzled, Useppe continued mechanically licking his cone, though no longer tasting its flavor. "Your brother! Nino! He was here!" the *piccinina* repeated. Useppe stopped licking the cone.

". . . Now where's he gone?! . . ."

"He was in a hurry. He left . . ."

Useppe ran to the window over the street. A little truck could be seen going by, overloaded with people, then the ice-cream man's cart, a little group of Allied soldiers with their *segnorine*, an old hunchback, three or four kids with a balloon, and nobody else. Useppe turned quickly towards the room:

"I'm going down . . . to call him . . . now . . . I'm going . . ." he declared with desperate insistence.

"Where'll you call him, kid? By now he's already in Naples!" the news-vendor, smoking, advised him.

Useppe cast an irreparable look around, of loss. Suddenly his little face seemed all crushed, and his chin began to tremble.

"Look what he brought you! American chocolate!" the news-vendor said, to console him. And Filomena, taking the bars down from the shelf, put them all in his arms. He clutched them to himself with an expression of almost menacing jealousy, but he didn't even look at them. His eyes, in their sadness, had become huge. He had a stain of vanilla on his chin, and in his dirty fingers, he was still clutching the ice-cream cone, melted meanwhile in his hand.

"He said he'd be back soon, didn't he, mà? That's what he said? He's coming back soon?" Annita said to Filomena, secretly winking one eye.

"Oh, yes, yes indeed. He said that this Saturday, Sunday at the latest, he'd be back here."

. . .

And instead, the thoughtless Ninnarieddu showed up again only in the month of March, no less, the following year. In all this interval, they didn't receive so much as a postcard from him. Comrade Remo, again consulted by Ida, said that after their famous meeting in June he hadn't seen Nino again. In his opinion, they could presume he had gone back to fight with the partisans in the North, maybe with the Garibaldi assault brigade . . . Later, however, through Davide, who every now and then came back to visit her, Santina learned that Ninnuzzu, on the contrary, had become involved with some Neapolitans, driving all around liberated Italy with them in a truck, dealing in contraband goods. On various occasions, he had also been in Rome, always in a rush however and, so to speak, incognito. More than this, Santina couldn't report from Davide, who, to tell the truth, had now become less taciturn with her; indeed, at times, he let himself go and talked, in their ground-floor room, especially if he had been drinking. And among his various subjects, one of the most fervid was Nino. But Santina understood almost nothing of Davide's talk, though with her usual meek patience she was able to listen to him in silence even for a full hour. For her, Davide remained an obscure figure, irregular and inexplicable: virtually an exotic species like the Moroccans or the Indians. And as for Nino, she had never seen this famous hero in person, not having been at the Marrocco home on the day of his visit. All the reports she had heard from the others might leave her awed, but without curiosity. And in her poor, backward imagination, she managed to retain, at most, the few bits of substantial, practical information.

As soon as Davide started talking about Nino, his face would brighten, like the face of a little boy, forced into long confinement by heaven knows what abstruse tasks, when suddenly the door is opened and he is allowed to run outside again. And as if he were telling of a Vesuvius or a flood, which are not judged for what they do, he never criticized Nino's actions, indeed he boasted of them with the greatest respect, displaying, at times, an obvious partiality towards his friend. But from this partiality of his, free and spontaneous (as if owed to Ace's superior merits), he seemed to derive an innocent pleasure, and a kind of consolation.

According to Davide, Comrade Remo didn't understand Ninnarieddu at all, if he could imagine him a partisan in the North. The partisans in the North were organized like an army, and from the beginning (since the summer of '43) this aspect had infuriated Nino, who couldn't stand officers and chevrons, respecting no hierarchies or institutions or laws; and if he had turned to contraband dealings now, it wasn't because of the earnings, but because of the illegality! In fact, the older Nino grew, the less he could adapt to Power; and even if, on occasion (through some inner, fatal need of his), he worked up a certain excitement for Power, he soon reversed it, into the most extreme defamation: with double enjoyment, in fact. Nino was too intelligent to allow himself to be blinded by certain false stars . . .

And at this point, Davide, carried away by the subject, began to argue in a loud voice, with impassioned rhetoric . . . Power, he explained to Santina, is degrading for those who submit to it, for those who administer it, and for those who control it! Power is the leprosy of the world! And the human face, which looks up and should mirror the splendor of the heavens, all human faces, instead, first to last, are deformed by such leprous aspect! A stone, a pound of shit will be worthier of respect than a man, as long as the human race is infected by Power . . . Davide unburdened himself in this vein in Santina's little room, gesticulating with his arms and legs, shaking and flapping the bed-cover. And Santina listened to him, her big eyes wide, lusterless, as if, in a dream, she were listening to a Kalmuck or Bedouin shepherd reciting verses to her in his own language. Since Davide, with his unruly movements, took up almost all the bed, her broad behind was half hanging out of it; and her feet, covered with chilblains, were cold beneath her stockings: but she avoided drawing the cover too much to her side, out of consideration for her lover. Really, in the little room, pleasantly cool in summer, the damp in winter oozed from the walls, like the floor of a wine cellar.

But the cold and the icy water that give her chilblains, the heat that enervates and makes her sweat, the hospital and the prison, the war and the curfews, the Allies who pay well and the young pimp who beats her and takes all her earnings, and this handsome youth who likes to get drunk and talk and wave his arms and kick and slaughter her in bed, but is *nice*, since he then always gives her the last cent he has in his pockets: all good and all evil, the hunger that makes her teeth fall out, the ugliness, the exploitation, wealth and poverty, ignorance and stupidity . . . for Santina are neither justice nor injustice. They are simple, unfailing necessities, for which no explanation is given. She accepts them because they happen, and she undergoes them without any suspicion, as a natural consequence of being born.

. . . . 1945

JANUARY

In Italy, as in the other occupied countries, the Nazi-Fascists multiply their acts of repression and genocide, with murders and incalculable destruction, slaughtering entire populations, and deporting people to the concentration camps or the industries of the Reich (where the number of forced laborers, from all over Europe, now exceeds nine million).

On the Eastern front, the Soviets resume the offensive along the Vistula, forcing the Germans to abandon Warsaw and the rest of Poland. The Soviets reach the Prussian border. In Berlin the Führer moves into his private air-raid shelter (Bunker) at a depth of about sixty feet beneath the Chancellery buildings.

FEBRUARY

In Germany, tribunals are set up which mete out capital punishment to anyone unwilling to join in the death-struggle.

Near Yalta (the summer residence of the Czars) a new Conference of the Big Three, the Allied Powers (Russia, Great Britain, United States), who foresee imminent victory. The future disposition of the world is outlined, agreed on by the three, according to the familiar pattern of blocs or spheres of influence of the Great Powers, which already draw their respective portions on the map.

MARCH

From his underground Bunker, beneath the rubble of the bombed Chancellery, the Führer orders the destruction of all military and civilian installations, all systems of transportation and communication, all industrial plants and provision supplies of the Reich.

Before the advance of the Soviets, who have now broken through all along the front as far as the Baltic, the German populace flees on the wrecked roads, in the severe winter, towards the west, from which the victorious Allies on the Rhine are already advancing.

APRIL

The Führer orders the last-ditch defense of the German cities, insisting on the death penalty for any transgressors.

President Roosevelt of the United States dies. He is succeeded by Vice-President Truman.

In Italy, after having broken through the Gothic Line and occupied Bologna, the Allies advance rapidly northwards towards Milan, where the retreating German forces abandon the city to the partisans. German capitulation along the entire front. Attempting to escape into Switzerland, disguised as a German, Benito Mussolini is discovered and captured by the partisans. He is hastily taken to a place of execution near Como, with his mistress Claretta Petacci. The corpses of the executed couple, with those of other Fascist chiefs, are exposed to the crowd, hung by their feet, in a Milan square.

In Germany, the great Soviet offensive develops, leading to the encirclement of Berlin, while the American forces advance from the Brenner. From his Bunker, Hitler (still commander-in-chief of the army) continues issuing feverish orders which, if they could still be carried out, would be translated into the total self-destruction and self-genocide of the German Reich. While the advancing Soviet units are already entering destroyed Berlin, Hitler kills himself in his Bunker along with his mistress Eva Braun and his closest followers. His corpse, burned in haste by the survivors, is identified by the Russians.

In Yugoslavia, Tito's partisans definitively liberate the country from the Nazis, who have already evacuated Greece.

MAY

With Germany's unconditional surrender, war activity ceases on the European front. Among the new products of the war industry, the most recent, tested in this sector, are some refined products of rocket propulsion, such as the German Nebelwerfer, with its multiple charges, and its Soviet counterpart, the Stalin Organ, and, finally, Hitler's famous secret weapons, the V-2 missiles.

JUNE–JULY

In Italy, the Parri government is formed, made up of the six Resistance parties, along the line of the CLN (Comitato Liberazione Nazionale), which had already assumed control of the country. Unresolved—awaiting a referendum—is the question of the monarchy, which the Papacy and the relentless supporters of Fascism, still very much alive and active behind the scenes, would like to see retained, with a view to further restorations.

In Rome, the torturer Koch is executed, shot in the back.

In the United States, the first atomic bomb is made. On the project—developing since 1943—thousands of scientists and technical experts have been working in secret.

In the Far East, Japan, despite defeats, persists in the continuation of the war. The United States issues an ultimatum: surrender, or total destruction.

AUGUST

Japan makes no reply to the ultimatum of the United States. On the sixth day of the month, the United States drops on Japan (city of Hiroshima) a first atomic bomb (the energy released equals twenty thousand tons of TNT). On the eighth of the month, the Soviet Union declares war on Japan, and invades Manchuria and Korea. On the ninth, the United States drops on Japan a second atomic bomb (city of Nagasaki).

With the unconditional surrender of Japan, the Second World War comes to an end. Fifty million dead (plus thirty-five million wounded, and three million missing).

The Big Three, the victorious Powers, meet at a Conference in Potsdam, where they calculate the shares, or spheres of influence, due to each of them in the new division of the world, proportionate to their respective power. Italy, in the new revision of the map of Europe, finds herself in the Anglo-American sphere of influence. Elsewhere, a source of disagreement is Germany, which is broken up by the litigants into two zones (East and West), with the capital, Berlin (Eastern zone), divided into sectors by the Powers involved. Already, in the course of this dispute, between the two opposing European spheres the Iron Curtain begins to descend, meant to safeguard the East from Western contagion, and vice versa, like an off-limits sign between two adjacent hospital wards.

Asia still remains to be divided, along with the colonial territories, which have become spoils of war. Of the latter, Korea (formerly property of the Japanese Empire) is cut, at the 38th parallel, into two occupation zones, Russian and American. And Indochina (formerly under French domination) is entrusted, in the South, to British occupation; while North of the 16th parallel, it is claimed by the Liberation Movement and its Communist leader, Ho Chi Minh, who announces the free Republic of Vietnam.

In Italy, in the process of national pacification, the disarming of the partisans is decreed, with the approval of the Communists.

SEPTEMBER

The American banks inform Italy that the economic aid of the United States (only resource at present for the exhausted peninsula, destroyed by the war) is compromised by the action of the Parri government, in which the left wing's policies are prevalent.

In Indochina the French colonialists begin to demand restoration, sending an expeditionary corps which, from the South, protected by the English, aims at the armed reconquest of Vietnam.

OCTOBER–DECEMBER

In China, the definitive evacuation of the Japanese troops has ended the truce between the Communists of Mao Tse-tung and the National Government of Chiang Kai-shek, who is favored by all the Powers, including the

Soviet Union. Talks between the two groups aiming at a coalition government are broken off at the eruption of a violent battle between the two opposing armies, which ends with the victory of the Red Army and signifies the inevitable resumption of the civil war.

In Italy, the end of the Parri government. The newly chosen Prime Minister is De Gasperi (a moderate Christian Democrat), who includes also the Communists in his cabinet, with Togliatti as Minister of Justice. One of this Ministry's first actions is the definitive end of trials purging the Fascists, in accordance with the policy of national pacification, already initiated . . .

1 "What bad luck! You always miss him!" Filomena deplored, when Santina, on Ninnarieddu's second visit, arrived about an hour after he had left. Nor, in fact, did they ever meet; but for that matter, it's improbable that an encounter between the two would have had much effect on either of them.

Obviously, for Nino, time was a relative phenomenon. After so many months of absence, he turned up again as if a couple of days had gone by. On this occasion, the *piccinina* remained in her corner, glancing at him timidly, like an animal that had been chased off. Useppe was trembling, and he clung to Nino's jacket, to keep him from running away again.

Since the famous day at the partisans' camp, in October of '43, the pair hadn't seen each other. Useppe, just over two at that time, was now more than three and a half; and Nino's appearance also had changed somewhat in the meanwhile. From their immediate and spontaneous recognition, however, it seemed that, to each other's eyes, both had remained at the same age. Only, after a little while, Nino said to Useppe:

"You're different from the way you used to be. Your eyes are sadder."

And he tickled him to make him laugh. Useppe poured out a little cascade of laughter.

This time, too, Nino was in a hurry. And as he was taking his leave of Useppe, he slipped into his overall pocket a pocketful of paper money that, at a glance, in Useppe's opinion, amounted surely to a million. "It's all yours," Nino said to him, one foot already on the stairs. "Now you can buy yourself a bike." But Useppe remained actually deaf to the idea of the bicycle; his only thought or feeling at that moment was that Nino was going away. And a short time later, he himself, with his little fingers, helped Ida dig the "million" out of the pocket of his overall, so she could take possession of it. To Useppe's mind, millions—or even billions—were mothers' responsibility. In his hands, they had no more value than ordinary paper.

.   .   .

During the last days of that April, from the various points of Europe where the Germans were still fighting, the fortunes of war, all together, took a precipitous turn towards conclusion. The Reich's famous *secret weapons* had failed; on this side, the Gothic Line had given way, like all other lines, fortifications, and fronts in other places. In Italy, the German army, after retreating from Milan, capitulated; and in Berlin, encircled from all the cardinal points, the first Russian soldiers were already entering the ruins. At the distance of a few hours from each other, Mussolini, attempting to escape disguised as a German, was caught and shot near the Italian border; and Hitler killed himself with a pistol (fired by his own hand or someone else's) in the final dwelling where he lived underground, his private air-raid shelter under the Berlin Chancellery . . .

About a week later, the total surrender of Germany, after six years of slaughter, ended the Blitzkrieg in Europe.

The dreamer Mussolini's vision (of himself crowned, supreme victor, on a white horse) had gone up in smoke; but that of the dreamer Hitler, on the contrary, had come true over a very great area. Territories, cities, and countries of the New Order were reduced to fields of skeletons, rubble, and slaughter. And more than fifty million unnatural deaths: including his own, the Führer's, and the death of the Italian Duce paired off with him as, in circuses, the clown is paired with the straight man. Their little bodies were eaten by the earth, like those of the *Jews*, the *Communists*, the *outlaws*; and those of Moscow and Quattro and Esterina and Angelino and the midwife Ezekiel.

Beyond Europe, in the Orient, the Second World War still raged; while here it was a time of settling accounts and holding trials, as happens after a fraud or a murder in the family. Even the final, scandalous secrets are stripped naked, which till now have tried to disguise themselves at least partially.

The jails were opened, and graves and ditches were dug up. Scenes of crimes were revisited; justice was done. Hidden documents were recovered. Lists were made and names ticked off.

Since the previous summer, on posters and in newspapers, strange photographs had already begun appearing in Rome; and naturally they already circulated with the first news bulletins, also in our Testaccio quarter and in Via Mastro Giorgio. At that time, however, little Useppe was still "protected by 'Saint Baby'" as they say in Rome of innocent children: and in this perhaps you could see the first sign of certain backward traits of his, which contradicted his other precocities. Almost like infants, or indeed like dogs and cats, he had a hard time recognizing, in the single dimension of print, any concrete forms. And for that matter, in his casual walks around Testaccio, always held by some adult's hand, he was really too busy, too attracted by the world's great variety, to pay attention to those flat images. At home, the books in the little bedroom were forbidden, untouchable, being the personal property of Giovannino; and the few newspapers that turned up in the family failed to arouse his interest, since he was totally illiterate.

The only painted or printed forms he consorted with, besides playing cards (which were kept under lock and key) were those in certain comic books about the house, and a syllabary which Ida had placed at his disposal. But although he amused himself occasionally by communicating to the others, with the air of a great mind-reader, the signs he had deciphered ("house!" "flowers!" "people!"), such papery entertainments soon bored him.

But during that spring of '45, one day his mother, having left him waiting a few moments outside a shop, found him studying some illustrated magazines, attached to the side of a kiosk, some distance above him. On the lowest, opened to a double spread, the page was completely taken up with two news photographs, both of hanged people. In the first, a shady city street could be seen, along the railing of a half-destroyed bridge. From every tree of the avenue bodies were hanging, all in a row, in the same, identical position, with the head bent to one ear, the feet a bit apart, and the hands tied behind the back. They were all young, all shabbily dressed, poor-looking. On each of them a sign was fixed, with the word: PARTI-SAN. And all were males, except for a single girl at the beginning of the line, who had no sign and, unlike the others, was not hanged by a rope, but with a butcher's hook through her throat. In the photograph, she was seen from behind; but her figure, still in bloom, suggested she was very young, under twenty. She was shapely, in dark slacks, and over her bloody torso, whitish in the picture, so that it seemed naked, fell her long black hair: it wasn't clear whether loose or in braids. Near the wall of the bridge, a man could be seen, a sentry perhaps, in military trousers, tight at the ankle. And on the other side of the avenue, a group of people had gathered to watch, with the casual appearance of passersby, including two little boys more or less Useppe's age.

In the second photograph on the same page, an old man was seen, with a fat, bald head, hanging by his feet, his arms wide, over a large, blurred crowd.

Higher up, on its cover, the magazine displayed another recent photograph, without hangings or dead people, but still mysteriously horrible. A young woman, her head shaved like a dummy's, holding a baby wrapped in a blanket, was advancing through a throng of people of all ages, snickering and pointing to her and laughing at her obscenely. The woman, who had regular features, seemed frightened, and was hurrying, struggling along in some run-over men's boots, preceded and pursued by the crowd. All those around her were shabby and poor as she was. The baby, a few months old, with a little head of pale curls, had its finger in its mouth and was peacefully sleeping.

Useppe, his head upraised, was there studying these scenes in a hesitant awe, still bewildered. He seemed to be confronting an enigma, deformed and ambiguous by nature, and yet obscurely familiar. "Useppe!" Ida called him; and obediently giving her his hand, he followed her, puzzled, but without asking her anything. A little later, attracted by some new curiosity, he had already forgotten the kiosk.

And in the days that followed, it seemed this new discovery of photography, belated and only vaguely perceived, had had no effect on him except as a fleeting impression, leaving no trace at all in his memory. In the street, Useppe had become the same ignoramus as before, who passed amidst signs and print without seeing them, too taken by the other dimensions of the universe that surrounded him, minuscule though it was. And at home, he never mentioned to anyone the abstruse spectacle of that kiosk; only if he happened to glimpse some photographs in an unfolded page of the newspaper, his eyes would widen in a vague reminiscence towards those others that, at a distance, appeared to him as patches of shadow: and so his reminiscence dissolved, at the same moment, beyond recall.

Once, later, the news-vendor (who actually called himself a *journalist*), finding a paper on the table, to amuse Useppe made a hat from it, like a carabiniere's headgear, and put it on his head. Seeing the "journalist" with his round face and his jutting chin like a dwarf's, clowning beneath that hat, Useppe laughed loudly. Then, jumping on the chair, he promptly took the hat from the news-vendor's head to try it on the *piccinina*; then he wanted to try it on Ida, and finally on himself. Now, his head was so small that it vanished entirely inside the hat; and he, in all this, laughed and laughed, as if a crazy refrain had got stuck in his throat.

Unfortunately, Filomena intervened a little later, to recover the newspaper, which she duly folded and put to one side. However, after that same afternoon, seeing the master of the house intently leafing through some old publications of his (including some of a lovely pink color) Useppe immediately asked him to make him a hat with one of them. Perhaps, after the *journalist's* example, he had decided this was the logical and, to him, most interesting use for printed pages. He accepted with docile resignation, nevertheless, the refusal of Tommaso, who then, seeing Useppe's new interest in journalism, seized the occasion to boast that this was a collection of sports papers, with historical games from the times when the war hadn't yet interrupted the great championships. And in this illustration you could see a pass in the famous Italy-Spain game; and this player was Ferraris Secondo, and this was Piola . . .

I remember that day was a Sunday; and the month, I believe, was June. The next morning something happened, similar to the previous episode at the kiosk, and it seemed at the time equally insignificant and fleeting.

Coming home quickly from the market, between one errand and another, Ida had left a half-opened package of fruit in the kitchen. And a little later, Useppe, tempted by the fruit, found in his hand the sheet of paper it had been wrapped in; was he already thinking, perhaps, of making himself a carabiniere's hat from it?

It was a page of an illustrated weekly, badly printed, in a purplish hue: the cheap kind that, as a rule, are full of sentimental little stories and gossip about actresses and crowned heads; however, at present, as was inevitable, most of the space, even here, was taken up with accounts of war experiences. The page reproduced some scenes of the Nazi prison camps, of which, until the Allied invasion, there had been only subdued and confused reports. Only now were these secrets of the Reich beginning to be revealed and photographs of them published, in part taken by the Allies on entering the camps, in part recovered from files which the defeated hadn't had time to destroy, and in part found on the prisoners or the dead SS, who had kept them as a documentation or a souvenir of their personal action.

Because of the magazine's popularizing, unscholarly nature, the photographs printed on that page weren't even among the most terrible of those to be seen at that time. They depicted: 1) a heap of murdered prisoners, naked and sprawling, and already partly decomposed; 2) a huge quantity of piled-up shoes, which had belonged to those or other prisoners; 3) a group of prisoners, still alive, seen behind a metal fence; 4) the "death stairway" of 186 very high and irregular steps, which the forced laborers were made to climb under enormous loads right to the top, from which they were then often flung down into the pit below as a spectacle for the camp authorities; 5) a sentenced man on his knees before the ditch he himself has been made to dig, guarded by numerous German soldiers, one of whom is about to shoot him at the nape of the neck; 6) and a little series of frames (four in all) which show successive stages of a decompression-chamber experiment, performed on a human guinea pig. This kind of test (one of the many and various experiments doctors carried out in the Lagers) consisted of subjecting the prisoner to sudden changes in atmospheric pressure; and it normally ended in madness and death through pulmonary hemorrhage.

All this was explained, as far as I can recall today, by brief captions underneath each picture. For an ignoramus who couldn't even read, however, that page's unusual spectacle must have seemed an insoluble riddle, especially since the cheap magazine's poor printing made some images ambiguous and unclear. You see there a chaotic heap of whitish, stick-like objects, whose forms cannot be distinguished, and, elsewhere, an enormous waste of piled shoes which, at first sight, could be mistaken for a pile of dead bodies. A long, long stairway, which reaches beyond the frame, with some tiny, crumpled forms at the bottom, among brownish spots. A bony young man with big eyes, crouching at the edge of a hole, a kind of bucket beside him and around him many soldiers, who seem to be amusing themselves (one of them is making a blurred movement with his arm). And on the other side of the page, some little skeletal human shapes, staring behind a fence, wearing striped tunics, loose and sagging, which make them look like puppets. Some of them have bare, shaven heads; others wear caps; and their faces show an agonizing smile, a wretched, definitive depravity.

Finally, at the foot of the page, you can see, in four successive photographs, the same man with a dazed face, all tied up with heavy straps, under a low ceiling. In the center of the ceiling there seems to be some kind of apparatus, looking like a funnel; and the man raises his eyes up towards that undefined object, as if he were praying to God. You might think the different expressions in the four photographs are caused by the incomprehensible actions of that sort of God. From a stupefied cowardice, the dull face passes to a horrid suffering, then to an ecstatic gratitude, and then again to stupefied cowardice.

It will be forever impossible to know what poor illiterate Useppe may have understood of those meaningless photographs. Coming home a few seconds later, Ida found him staring at them all together, as if they were a single image; and she thought she recognized in his pupils the same horror she had seen there that noon at the Tiburtina station, about twenty months earlier. At his mother's approach, he raised his eyes to her, drained and discolored, like a little blind child's. And Ida felt a shudder run through her whole body, as if a huge hand were shaking her. But with a soft, gentle voice, so as not to upset him, she said, as you would have spoken to kids much younger than he:

"Throw away that nasty paper. It's ugly!"

"It's *uggy*," he repeated (he still hadn't learned to pronounce certain combinations of consonants). And he immediately obeyed Ida's words; indeed, almost impatient, he helped her tear up that bit of newspaper as if it were rubbish.

A minute later, a peddler's cry could be heard below the windows, as he passed along the street with his barrow. And this was enough to distract Useppe. He ran towards the front window, curious to see the peddler. "Onions! Garlic! Greens!" the man shouted, in his sing-song chant. And Annita, to spare herself the steps, lowered to him from the window a little basket tied to a string. Standing on a footstool at the window, Useppe followed the basket's journey with the same interest as if it were an Earth-Moon airship, or, at the very least, Galileo's first experiment on the Leaning Tower of Pisa. Today's incident, as usual, seemed to have gone by without leaving a trace in his little head.

Still, in the first days that followed, at the sight of certain newspapers or picture magazines, he would keep his distance, like a puppy after a whipping. And in the street he seemed a bit uneasy, dragging Ida off by her dress from the proximity of any wall poster or the famous kiosk. There was a visit from Nino, who this time invited him out for an ice cream. And on the way back, Nino seized the opportunity to dash to the kiosk on the other side of the street, saying to the boy: "You wait for me here." But Useppe, on seeing him approach the kiosk, began to shout from the sidewalk:

"Back! Come back! Baaaack!" with a tone of desperate alarm, as if to defend his brother against some unknown threat of the street. "You," Ninnuzzu teased him then, coming back to him, "the more you grow, the more you make me laugh! What're you yelling about? I'm not going to run away!" Then with his laughing mouth, he concluded: "Hey, how about giving me a little kiss?"

. . . During that summer, there were another two visits from Ninnuzzu. At the first, he glanced at his mother, remarking: "Your hair's turned all white, mà, you look like my grandmother!!" as if he hadn't already seen her white hair on his previous visits and were noticing the novelty only now.

And on the second visit, he announced he would soon become the owner of a motorcycle, a foreign make, good as new, a terrific bargain! And next time he would come to Rome on that!

So it happened that the *piccinina* (who now, in Ace's presence, always remained demurely to one side) that same night dreamed she was being chased furiously by a motorcycle, speeding on its own, with nobody on the seat. And she fled left and right, so frightened that all of a sudden, in her fear, she learned how to fly.

.   .   .

Meanwhile, during the month of August, after the dropping of the atomic bomb on the cities of Hiroshima and Nagasaki, Japan had also signed an unconditional surrender.

The news of the atomic explosion was such that people talked of it reluctantly, as they speak of repulsive abstractions. They couldn't talk about time, because the phenomenon's duration (if that was the word) was so minimal it couldn't be calculated (they tried to figure it in twenty-thousandths of a second). Within this *duration*, the two doomed cities, with their inhabitants, had ceased to exist down to the molecules of their matter. There could be no talk of destruction or of death. They talked about such a *mushroom* of light that people blind from birth had perceived its unreal glow, at a distance. And of everything previously existent within its range, the mushroom had left only, here and there, some shadows on the ground, like ghost-images printed on a plate. Beyond the mushroom's range, the *first tornado* is unleashed, and then the *second tornado*, and then a putrid rain of strange poisons or embers. Impossible to count the victims: because the physical consequences of the *mushroom*, and of the *tornadoes*, and of the *atomic fallout* cannot be evaluated only by the number of the *annihilated* and the dead (at Hiroshima, at a first calculation, these came to eighty thousand). The *demolition and incendiary* bombs and their impacts, fires and *clouds* seemed still earthly phenomena; while Hiroshima and Nagasaki no longer seemed places of this world. It wasn't possible even to feel compassion for the Japanese.

And so the Second World War was over. In the same month of August, the Big Three (Messrs. Churchill and Truman, and Comrade Stalin) met again in Potsdam to define the peace, that is, to mark the reciprocal boundaries of their Empires. The Rome-Berlin Axis and the Triple Entente had vanished. The Iron Curtain was appearing.

2 With autumn, peace brought a series of new events.

The first to return were the Jews. Of the one thousand fifty-six passengers on the Rome-Auschwitz train from the Tiburtina Station, the survivors were fifteen: of the poorest class, like almost all the people deported from Rome. One of them, on his arrival, was taken to the Santo Spirito Hospital, where Tommaso Marrocco was working as an orderly, and from there he brought the first news home. The man, a peddler by trade, a young man not yet thirty, at present weighed no more than a child. He had a number branded on his skin, and his body, once normal and sturdy and now decrepit-looking, was covered with deep scars. He was feverish, delirious all night long, and he vomited some blackish stuff, though he was unable to swallow any kind of food. On their arrival in Italy, the fifteen, only one woman among them, had been received by a welfare committee, which had given each of them a second-class railway ticket, a small cake of soap, and (the men) a packet of razor blades. The oldest (aged forty-six), as soon as he arrived in his empty house, had locked himself inside and was still lying there, weeping, after several days. When others happened to see one of these survivors go by, they easily recognized him at first sight, pointing him out and saying: "That's a Jew." Because of their ridiculously scant weight and their strange appearance, people looked at them as if they were jests of nature. Even those who were tall seemed little and walked hunched over, with a long and mechanical tread, like puppets. In the place of their cheeks were two holes; many of them had hardly any teeth left and, on their shaved, emaciated heads, a feathery down had just begun to grow, like a baby's. Their ears stuck out, and their hollow eyes, black or brown, didn't seem to reflect the images of their present surroundings, but some host of haunting figures, like a magic lantern of constantly changing, absurd forms. It's odd how some eyes visibly retain the shadow of who-knows-what images, impressed on them before, no telling when and where, in the retina, like an indelible writing that others cannot read—and often don't want to. This was the case with the Jews. Soon they learned that nobody wanted to listen to their stories: some people's minds wandered at the start, others interrupted them promptly with an excuse, and others actually stepped away from them, snickering, as if to say: "Brother, I feel sorry for you, but I have things to do right now." In fact, the Jews' stories didn't resemble the tales of ship-captains, or of Ulysses, the hero returning to his palace. They were spectral figures like negative numbers, beneath all natural sight, inconceivable even for common friendliness. People wanted to censor them from their days as normal families remove the mad or the dead. And so, along with the illegible visions swarming in their black eye-sockets, many voices accompanied the lonely walks of the Jews, echoing vastly in their brains, in a fugue, below the ordinary threshold of the audible.

. . . .

USEPPE: ". . . say, mà, why is that man hitting the wall with his hand?"

IDA: ". . . nothing . . . it's a game . . ."

". . . he sick?"

"No, he 's not sick."

"No? No, eh? Can he see?"

"Of course, he can. He's not blind. He can see."

". . . he's not blind . . ."

This man was someone Ida saw often, passing by Piazza Gioacchino Belli, on this side of the river. He was the regular customer of a bar in the neighborhood, where she herself had been allowed to display a little personal advertisement, written in ink, seeking private tutoring. The man's age was beyond guessing. He could have been an adolescent, or else an old man of sixty (actually, he was thirty-five). The only thing you recognized about him, on sight, was that, in addition to being a Jew, he must always have been poor; and his trade, in fact, as Ida learned from the bar's proprietor, had been handed down from father to son, junk-collector. He always wore a little cap on his head, even though it was hot, and in his big brown eyes, very close to his long sharp nose, there was that kind of very sweet trust you can see in the eyes of certain dogs when they are sick. One day (all blushing like a country girl making her first approach as a prostitute) Ida summoned her courage and, in a stammer, asked him confidentially, if, among the survivors of the Lagers, he knew of a Signora Celeste Di Segni and an old midwife . . . "No, no," he answered, smiling with a clumsy, simple-minded innocence, "no kids, no old people. They've *gone up to heaven* long ago . . ."

And, immediately, rummaging in his pocket, he asked Ida in reply if she would like to buy a lady's wristwatch, a bargain . . . Then, when Ida evaded it, he suggested the same purchase to the barman, perhaps in exchange for a bottle of cognac, or grappa, or something else.

. . . Ida hadn't been into the Ghetto, not since that afternoon of June first, the year before. Nor, as far as I know, did she ever set foot there afterwards, as long as she lived.

. . . . . .

Towards the end of November, there was another homecoming, which filled the Marrocco family with hope: Clemente, Consolata's brother, came back from Russia.

His return, after such a long silence and so many futile inquiries, was hailed as a miracle. Less than a week later, however, Consolata could already be heard murmuring, with a sidelong glance: "Maybe it would of been better for him if he hadn't come back . . ." He had, in fact, left Rome healthy and whole, and he had come back missing the toes of one foot and three fingers of his right hand, because his limbs had frozen during the retreat in '43. As a civilian, he had been a carpenter by trade. And how could he, now, resume his work, half-maimed, an invalid? Consolata would have to work twice as hard, for herself and for him.

On his arrival, he had kept his mutilated hand hidden in a dirty little scarf, as if he were ashamed of it. Then Filomena made him a black wool glove which covered his hand, leaving only the two sound fingers exposed; and after that, in the quarter, he was given the nickname of the Black Hand.

He could say nothing specific about Giovannino. The last time he had seen him had been during the retreat, this side of the river Don, in January of 1943, maybe the twentieth, according to his calculations—or else the twenty-fourth or the twenty-fifth (who could keep track, there, of nights and days?). They were escaping together, he and Giovannino, on a road or a frozen swamp, in an enormous confusion of little trucks, sleds, oxen, horses, and men on foot. He and Giovannino were on foot, stragglers from their unit, which had been broken up and dispersed. At a certain point, Giovannino, exhausted, had sunk to his knees under his knapsack. And Clemente, after slipping the pack off him, had helped him to stand up again and continue; but after another mile or so, Giovannino had fallen again, and then again, two or three times. Until, unable to resist his own weariness, he had lain down to rest at the side of the track, waiting for some sled or wagon to stop and pick him up. He wasn't wounded, only he complained of thirst; and Clemente, before resuming his march alone, had collected a handful of snow from the ground, holding it out in his palm for Giovannino to drink. After that, they lost sight of each other definitively. Later, then, Clemente had surrendered, a prisoner, to the Russians, but among his prison mates of those years in Siberia and Asia, he had never met any mutual acquaintance who could give him news of Giovannino.

The day of his arrival, Clemente had turned up at home, leaning on a crutch, wearing a German army greatcoat, with a few lire in his pocket. At the Italian border, against the pay he hadn't received, they had given him fifteen hundred lire, which he, unaware of the new Italian prices, had considered wealth. Instead, he had spent nearly all of it on the trip from the Brenner to Rome, to buy himself a few liters of wine and some sandwiches. "Two slices of salami, two hundred lire!" he remarked, sarcastically. And in all his infinite adventure, this was the one point he kept coming back to, insistently. Of all the rest, he spoke as little as possible, and with reluctance.

He was born in 1916, so at present he was getting on for thirty; but since everyone remembered him from civilian days as fat, he now seemed almost more of a boy than when he was young. His weight when he left for the front had been over two hundred pounds; now it was under one-forty. And his complexion, formerly ruddy, had turned yellowish, because of the malaria he had caught in Asia, in the prison camp. Now he felt well and in good health, according to what he said. He also declared that his mutilation didn't in the least prevent him from working, and in the prison camp he had always done his share: picked cotton, gathered dry grass to burn, chopped wood, and, when necessary, also performed carpentering jobs. For example, by himself, back there he had made for his broken and sore-covered foot a sort of wooden support fitted out and attached with some laces to his leg, so that he could walk also without a stick, normally.

In saying all this, he would take on a grim expression; and though he addressed no one in particular, it was clear his words were aimed chiefly at his sister, to let her know he wasn't a poor sickly cripple, as she seemed to believe, and he had no need of her or of anyone else. To tell the truth (though he wouldn't admit it), in the Asian prison camps, the Russian medical officers had already observed his intermittent fevers and for a time had exempted him from work, putting him in the hospital there, known as *lazaret*. However, in the end, they had discharged him, like the healthy prisoners; and according to him, the constant weariness that weighed on him now was only the result of his very long return journey, which had lasted two months.

Before, as a youth, *Black Hand* had had a rather slow and lazy personality; for example, he was always irked that (except on Sundays) he couldn't have a siesta after his midday meal; and when it was time to go to the shop, early in the morning, he had to be called a dozen times before he could bring himself to get out of bed. But now it was all different; his willpower no longer sufficed. The slightest exertion tired him; on some days, even if he stood still on his feet for a few minutes, his eyesight would suddenly fail through weakness, and he would be able to see again only when he was lying down.

Another source of humiliation for him was not being able to drink as in the past. Wine had never been a vice with him, but a pleasure. Besides liking its taste and the excuse to be in company, he had found real self-satisfaction in wine, which made him lively, talkative, even eloquent; and, more, allowed him to boast how he could hold it, because he could drink quantities without getting drunk. Now, instead, as everyone celebrated his return from Russia and, especially during the early days, fought to offer him drinks, any wine, whether white Frascati or Orvieto, or Chianti red, like the Nebbiolo of prime quality bought on his arrival in the North, had the same bitter taste in his mouth. And from the first sips he felt depressed by it, worse than ever, his stomach burning as if he had swallowed coals. And yet a nostalgia for his old habit still drove him to the tavern, where, with a little jug of wine, he was capable of spending whole days at the same table. But nobody recognized now the jovial boy of the past in this grouchy mute with yellow skin.

Like his sister, his acquaintances had long since given up any hope of seeing him come back alive; and they had welcomed him with incredulous exclamations as if he had risen from the dead, spreading the word and running to greet him. However, in the center of such general wonder, he, though celebrated, felt himself, God knows why, set aside, as if he were an encumbrance; and in company, he withdrew into himself, like a Lazarus in his shroud. The presence of others, all the same, was necessary to him: to be alone, even for a few minutes, filled him with anguish and fright.

In the tavern, not only the friends at his table, but also the other customers at first besieged him with demands that he tell his adventures. But he evaded the subject, saying with a grimace and a reluctant tone: "What's the use of talking about it!" ". . . people who weren't there can't understand it . . ." ". . . anyway, what I saw, nobody would believe . . ." At times, rabid from his bitter wine, instead of a reply he would hurl insults: "You slackers," he would cry, "what do you want to know, now?! You should of been there, on the spot!" Or else, at their insistence, he would toss out some fragment of information, snickering: "You want to know what I saw? I saw dead bodies by the hundreds, from here to the ceiling, like piles of beams, hard, without any eyes! . . ." "Where?" "Where! In Siberia! There were crows there . . . and wolves . . ." "I saw the wolves come running, at the smell of the convoys . . ." "I've seen WHITE CANNIBALS!"

". . . and that's nothing!" he would add each time with a spiteful pleasure and a sad gaze, hinting at all the rest he wasn't telling.

Once, without anyone's asking him anything, he suddenly stretched his black hand out beneath his neighbor's eyes. "You see this masterpiece of surgery?" he said with a strange hilarity in his eyes, like somebody about to proffer an obscene secret, "performed by a friend, an Alpino, in a half-burnt-out barn, with a pair of pruning-shears!" "And this!" he continued (displaying his mutilated foot, bound in some rags, still with an unhealed sore), "there was no need of an operation! Running away, God knows where, from the trap, on the ice, I sat down to take off my shoe, because it was as hard as an iron vise. And as I pulled and pulled, my foot—gangrene—came away with the shoe: I was left with the heel and some pieces of bone."

Then, another of those present, insulted because he had been called *slacker*, said to him: "Well, and did you remember, at least, to send a postcard of greetings and thanks to your Duce?" And Clemente gave him a grim look, but found no answer. In fact, he couldn't deny that as a young man, he had been in favor of Fascism. He trusted the Duce, and the generals, too, even after his own experience in the Albania-Greece campaign for which he absolved the Italian leaders, explaining it, for some reason, as a "betrayal by the Greeks." And in the summer of '42, ready for his new departure to the Russian front, he had proclaimed, proposing a toast in that same tavern: "Them, our Leaders, they know their job! If they're shipping us there, poorly equipped, unprotected against the cold, it's because they already know that, for the Soviets, by now, the game's all over! In one or two months, before winter comes, Russia'll be kaputt! And we Italians have to be there, for the victory!"

To the Marroccos' incessant questions, especially about the circumstances of the retreat, he made an effort to give some kind of answer, prised out of him with such difficulty that his face seemed to become almost swollen with repugnance: "But were there any houses around there?" "Villages, yes, villages . . ." "With homes, with families, that is . . . ?" ". . . yes . . . peasants . . . country people . . ." "What are they like? Kindhearted? . . ." "Yes, the Russians in general are good people." ". . . . but why give him snow to drink?! Wasn't there any water?! . . ." Black Hand looks away, with a twisted smile. "Eh," he answers in a contracted, grimmer voice, "we were lucky even to have snow to drink. In the prisoners' train to Siberia, we drank piss . . . THIRST! HUNGER!" he turns back, brusquely, listing on the fingers of his good hand, with one finger of the maimed one, "cold! epidemics! hunger!

HUNGER!" and at this point he stops, realizing how cruelly he is assailing the hopes of these poor idiots. However, in his hollow eyes, marked by his illness, more than pity a certain contempt glows: is it possible they can't finally realize that the ones who couldn't make it, and who dropped by the wayside during the retreat, were all lost? Nobody could carry them. They had to be left there, and they were all dead in advance.

·　　·　　·

Now we'll try to report, at this distance, from memory, the last hours in the life of Giovannino.

While his companion Clemente (better known, there at the front, by his last name, Domizi) continues his escape without him, Giovannino remains on his knees at the edge of the track, waiting for some vehicle to pick him up. His confused mind is tormented by a recollection of the fallen bodies, already half covered by snow, which were sown on the terrain of his march with Clemente; at times, he stumbled over them. And so he resists his desire to lie down and stretch out; but he is no longer able to pull himself to his feet. To attract the attention of the crowd of stragglers, he begins waving his arms, shouting at random: "*Paesano! Paesano!*" His voice is lost in the din: there are cries, battalions being called together, numbers of companies or Christian names, yelling at mules; but all are alien voices. The name of his battalion and the surname Marrocco are not heard anywhere.

There, a sled goes by, drawn by oxen, with a bundle inside, groaning, and an infantryman walking behind it. Giovannino moves towards it, on his knees, gesticulating and pleading. But the soldier gives him only a hesitant glance, then turns away and goes off with the sled. A little later, at some distance a cart is glimpsed, laden with supplies, with three bundled-up forms: maybe they can find room for him? "*Paesani! paesani!*", but the cart also goes off in the confusion, paying no attention to him. Shifting on his knees, Giovannino moves back, so as not to be run over; and he waves his arms, to explain himself, towards a corporal who has just dismounted from a little horse so thin its vertebrae protrude like teeth. The horse's legs have become entangled in some object; while his master frees them, the animal turns towards Giovannino his big eyes, which apologize like a human's. And the man, also glancing at Giovannino, makes a disconsolate gesture of refusal; then looking ashamed, he sets off again on his horse. The snowstorm begins, the sky is dark gray, at two in the afternoon night is already falling. An Alpine soldier, with staring eyes, passes before him, marching barefoot, his feet swollen and black as lead. "*Alpino! alpino!* help me! carry me!" Giovannino thinks to shout at him. But the soldier is already far off, toiling through the snow on his huge black feet.

Giovannino draws back. His fever is worse. Now, amid the explosions and the broken shouts, bells can be heard ringing, and he can't understand where he is any more. Finally, seeing a very high wagon go by, with gilded candles big as columns, he begins to realize he is watching the procession at Ceprano, and the figure up there, carried in procession on the wagon, is the General, giving orders, his arms folded. But why are they throwing petals of snow at him from all the windows? Giovannino recognizes him, and he even remembers how this same General said to the troops: "Burn the vehicles, throw away the supplies, everything. Every man for himself. Italy is to the west. Keep going on and on, to the west; Italy is there."

"West," Giovannino reasons, "means where the sun sets." Over there, in the distance, through the storm, he sees a fire blazing somewhere, and he understands it is the sun. So, leaving behind him the crowd that begins to fade in his ears, still proceeding on his knees, and also using his hands to push himself forward, he undertakes his journey to the west.

His swollen feet, without shoes, awkwardly wrapped in pieces of blanket, don't ache in the least, though they encumber him. Instead of his feet and his legs, from the knee down, he seems to be carrying two sand-bags. The cloth of his uniform has stiffened on him like metal plate, creaking at his every movement, and his body, pierced by thousands of needles, is all an ache and a numbness. The gusts jolt him and slap him, whistling, and he grumbles against them: "go fuck yourself," "goddamn cunt," and other such homely protests, familiar to him since childhood . . . In reality, from his lips, a gurgle of confused syllables barely emerges, as if his tongue had been cut off.

He continues for a few more yards, stopping every now and then to pick up a crust of frozen snow, which he sucks greedily; but then the fear of falling persuades him to tolerate his parched throat. Reaching the crumbling edge of a crevasse, he comes upon someone, all wrapped up, sitting and resting on the ground, against a big stone. It's a little soldier, no taller than a child, dead; but Giovannino doesn't notice he's dead, and insistently asks him for directions. The soldier looks at him with a faint mocking smile and gives him no answer.

But, in any case, there can't be such a long way still to go: these are already the *macère*, the narrow terraces of Sant'Agata in Ciociaria, with the young flax growing, and there in the background, by the little lighted fire, the family hut is visible.

And now his grandfather has come from the hut, threatening him with his belt because Giovannino has left behind the new kid, called Musilla, a new name. "Musilla! Musilla!" and many bleats answer, but they are from the east, and he doesn't feel like going back there. To elude his grandfather's thrashing, as the old man stares at him with two eyeless holes, Giovannino decides to hide here behind the field. And, in fact, he has slipped gently down the slope, almost to the bottom of the crevasse, where at least he is a bit sheltered from that incomprehensible tumult above.

Damn you, Granddad! I'm going to leave home soon anyway, and go to Rome, to be a Carabiniere. Now Giovannino no longer knows whether this torment that burns him is ice or fire. He feels his brain boiling, and chills squeeze his heart like a lemon. Constantly, between his legs, a slimy warmth trickles, promptly frozen and encrusted against his flesh. With his incessant thirst, he would like to lick the frozen sleeve of his coat, but his arm and his head drop down, exhausted. "Meh! Meeh! Meeh!" This is the bleating of the lost Musilla; and this tortured, piercing scream is explained because today, on the meadow above, in front of the house, they are slaughtering the hog. The hog, when they catch him to kill him, makes a sound like a human. And in a little while, up in the hut, they'll eat the blood puddings, the heart, the liver . . . But hunger, which during the past days was the worst suffering of this army service of Giovannino's, is no longer making itself felt; in fact, the very image of food produces in him a surge of nausea.

He raises his eyes, and he becomes aware that a big tree is spread over him, a transparent, luminous green, from which his dog Toma is swaying, hanged from a bough. It is known that Toma a little while ago allowed himself to be tempted by the bladder of the freshly slaughtered pig, and he swallowed it and died; after which Uncle Nazzareno, who didn't go to the war because he's blind in one eye, hung the carcass from the tree as bait for the foxes. "Toma! Toma!" Giovannino moans, a little boy in short pants; but Toma, though dead, snarls and bares his teeth. Then, filled with fear, Giovannino calls his mother: and the syllable "ma ma ma" said by the voice of the boy Giovannino reechoes through all the fields.

Here is his mother coming out of the house above, with her distaff under her arm and her spindle in her hand, and even as she walks, she tends to her spinning, plucking the flax from the distaff and working it through her fingers. She is angry, and with her mouth wide, she rails at Giovannino, for the stink of shit he has about him: "Shame on you! Doing it in your pants at your age! Go away! You'll stink up the whole house!" There, outside the crevasse, where he sees his mother, a beautiful summer sun is shining; and on the hay illuminated by the moonlight his fiancée Annita goes by. His mother, here at the Sant'Agata house, still wears the long, full skirt of the Ciociaria women, with the little black corselet and blouse; but Annita, on the contrary, has on a short dress, without a belt, hardly more than a shift, her feet bare and clean. On her head she has a big white kerchief, tied in two knots at her nape, so her hair is invisible.

And she is coming back from the well, carrying the filled bucket, the dipper in it, all ready for drinking; at her little running steps, the cool water spills from the brimming bucket onto the hot hay.

"Annita! Annita!" Giovannino calls, with a yearning to drink from the bucket; but Annita also makes a disgusted face and drives him away: "You're all full of lice!" she screams. And at this point, from inside the hovel where Granddad is, a resounding bass voice asserts clearly: "A good sign. Lice run away from dead bodies."

Giovannino doesn't know what's coming over him. Now he doesn't feel like doing anything but sleep. The open sunny light lasts another instant and immediately afterwards, also here at Sant'Agata, it has become dark. There is a cool, restful, little evening breeze, which comes and goes, with a fan's slight movement. And, before sleeping, Giovannino would like to curl up, as he always has enjoyed doing; except that his body, because of all the cold, has become so stiff he can't bend any more. But at the same time Giovannino realizes, as if it were a natural thing, that he also has a second body which, unlike the first, is supple, clean, and naked. And, content, he crouches into his favorite position for lying in bed: with his knees almost touching his brow, huddled until a comfortable hole is hollowed out in his mattress beneath him; and as he nestles there, the dry leaves inside the mattress make a rustle, as if the wind were blowing them, summer and winter. This is the position he has always assumed to sleep, as a baby, as a little boy, and as a grown man; however, every night, at the moment he curls up in this way, he feels he has become tiny again. And, indeed, little, big, grown up, young, elderly, old, in the dark we are all the same.

Good night, Giovannino.

. . . . **1946**

JANUARY–MARCH

Revolutionary movements begin among the peoples of the colonies. Clashes with the British police in Calcutta and in Cairo, with a high number of victims among the demonstrators.

In Europe, to the consequences of the bombings and the mass flights (millions of homeless and refugees) are added the expulsions and forced transferrals of whole populations (thirty million Europeans, mostly Germans) as a result of the post-war boundaries agreed on at Potsdam.

In Italy, the radical steps demanded by the disastrous situation (war ruins, inflation, unemployment, etc.) are opposed by the dominant reactionary powers, who for their own repressive ends still foment disorder in the country, and especially in the South. The revolt of the peasants and farm laborers against the desperate living conditions is followed by bloody clashes with the police. Numerous victims among the protesters in Sicily.

In the USSR, a new regime of terror under Stalin (named, after the victory, Generalissimo and Hero of the Soviet Union), who, in the country drained and ravaged by war, has personally assumed all political and military power, through changes in the Constitution. The Leader, at his own caprice, can decide the life and death of all citizens. The list of the executed reaches incalculable figures. The slightest oversight by workers (forced to killing labor and virtually locked to their machines) is punished by deportation. The concentration camps in Siberia are now crowded with, among others, civilians and ex-soldiers released from Lagers and forced labor in Germany, consequently accused of treason for having surrendered, alive, to the Nazis. The Iron Curtain hides this reality of the Russian scene from the world, and even the little that leaks out is rejected, as reactionary propaganda, by the countless people "condemned to hope" who populate Europe, the colonies, and the rest of the world, and who continue to look to the Soviet Union as the ideal fatherland of socialism.

In China, battles between the Red Army and the Kuomintang continue.

JUNE–SEPTEMBER

In Italy, the first universal-suffrage elections for the Constituent Assembly and the choice between republic or monarchy. The republic wins. The Savoy family goes into exile. The Constituent Assembly convenes.

In Sicily, more victims in a clash between police and peasants.

In Palestine, impossible coexistence of Arabs and immigrant Jews. Terrorism and counter-terrorism.

Civil war in Greece—British sphere of influence—where the partisans have taken up arms against the monarchist reaction supported by the British. Prompt and violent repression from the established powers. The Soviet

Union—conforming to the Potsdam agreements—maintains diplomatic silence on the matter.

At Berkeley, California (USA), the 340 Mev synchrocyclotron is installed.

OCTOBER–DECEMBER

In Rome, during a clash between police and workers, two workers are killed and many wounded.

In Nuremberg, with twelve death sentences, the trial of the Nazi leaders ends. Through the various stages of the trial, a kind of public autopsy has taken place of the body politic of the Reich, that is to say, of an industrial-bureaucratic machine of perversion and degradation promoted to essential function of the State ("a page of glory in our History").

In North Vietnam, the French fleet shells Haiphong (six thousand dead) and occupies the Ministry of Finance at Hanoi. Ho Chi Minh calls the Vietnamese people to a war of liberation against the French . . .

1 Early in January of '46, the Marroccos received news that a relative of theirs from Vallecorsa (a village not far from Sant'Agata) had also come back from Russia, just in that period; and their hope of seeing Giovannino again, already stirred by Clemente's return, became higher than ever. Every morning, with the day's light, hope rose in the Marrocco home ("maybe today . . .") and then, towards evening, it wilted, to spring up again the next day.

The Vallecorsa relative, whose health had also been ruined in the Russian campaign, was suffering from TB and was hospitalized now in Rome at the Forlanini Sanatorium, where the Marrocco women visited him frequently. But though he answered their tireless questions with good will, he actually knew less than Clemente about Giovannino. And in fact, he and Giovannino had lost sight of each other even before the final rout, when the withdrawal had barely begun. Giovannino at that time was well, etc., etc. But from then on, all orders had become confused, there were no means of defense or survival, it wasn't a war any longer, or a retreat, but a massacre. Of the Italians surrounded in the *pocket*, it was a lucky thing if ten in a hundred came out alive. He, for his part, at the beginning had sought refuge with a family of Russian peasants (poor, starving people, just like us up at Vallecorsa) who had taken him in and fed him as best they could in their *izba*, in a village which was later burned down.

Filomena and Annita made him repeat these stories God knows how many times, plumbing every detail. Any story brought back by the veterans, even if negative or pessimistic, offered them new excuses to hope and to expect Giovannino. The father, on the contrary, didn't share their expectations; in fact, he seemed to consider the women deluded.

At every footstep coming up the stairs, they both raised their eyes at once from their work, in a moment's interruption, each time with a slight start. Then they would lower their eyes again, saying nothing to each other.

One day Santina's cards answered that Giovannino was *on the way*, with no further or more precise information. Another day, the *piccinina* arrived, breathless, and said she had seen Giovannino standing in a corner of the landing, on the second floor. They all rushed down; there was nobody on the landing. But the *piccinina* insisted hysterically she hadn't made a mistake: it was a man dressed as a soldier, with hob-nailed mountain boots, and a cloak. He was huddled in the corner between two doors, and, according to her, he had looked at her, frowning and staring, signaling her to say nothing. But how had she recognized him, since she had never seen him before? "He was blond, not very tall!" the *piccinina* answered, "just like him! It was him all right!!"

"Why didn't you talk to him then?"

"I was afraid . . ."

The father, who was present, shrugged his shoulders; but for the whole day Filomena and Annita kept going down the stairs and coming up again, and looking out of the front door into the street, to see if they could see that soldier. They suspected that Giovannino, for some reason, was angry with the family: perhaps because of his room, which wasn't ready for him . . . occupied by outsiders . . .? Already in November, Ida had begun to realize it was time for her to find a new lodging, and chance came to her aid. A little old woman, a customer of Filomena's (the same one who, at Nino's first visit, had said: "I could eat him up with kisses" . . .) was planning, in February or March to leave her own little private lodging in that same Testaccio quarter to go and stay with a daughter who lived in Rieti. For a payment of a few thousand lire, she was prepared to cede Ida her lease. And Ida, who was still saving some of the am-lire she had received from Nino, managed to make the old woman accept them as a down payment, promising the rest in a short time (she was counting on collecting some damages as a *bombed-out refugee,* or at worst obtaining a loan from the Ministry against her future wages . . .). And so, in a little while, Ida and Useppe would finally have a home again. Ida was eager and pleased with it, also because she hoped, among other things, that a more comfortable situation would immediately improve Useppe's health and spirits.

Useppe was pale. He was having a hard time recovering his strength, and he was no longer able to remain calmly on his own, as he had done the previous winters, "thinking" or watching the rabbit or the grandfather. Towards evening especially, he would be seized by a turbulent restlessness, and would start running around the rooms of the house, his head lowered, grumbling, as if he wanted to butt down the walls. The Marrocco women, bewildered, protested with their usual bad words, but luckily, in view of his imminent move, they had recently become more tolerant towards their unruly tenant.

In the evening, though he was sleepy, Useppe never wanted to go to bed; and Ida thought she could recognize in this whim of his a frightened apprehension, because for some time he had rarely enjoyed sound, uninterrupted sleep. The series of these abnormal nights had begun the previous summer, and one of them especially was marked in Ida's memory like a bitter speck. It had been after the episode in the kitchen, when he had diligently torn up the illustrated magazine with the strange pictures, repeating his mother's words: "It's *uggy*" (ugly). This episode, like so many others that had preceded it, soon seemed expunged from his capricious mind. But instead, perhaps a week afterwards, Ida was wakened in the night by a curious prolonged sob. And when she had turned on the light, she saw Useppe sitting beside her, half out of the sheet, waving his little hands frantically, in the gesture of certain ill people the doctors call *clastomanes*, when they rave and tear their hospital gown. Useppe, however, in the summer heat, was naked; and in that movement of his, he gave the impression of wanting to rip away his skin. "It's *uggy* . . . It's *uggy!* . . ." he moaned, with the menacing tones of a little animal who presumes to drive away, with his own defenses, an armed hunter. And he didn't even see his mother; he was alienated by unknown images that belonged, really, to his sleep, while with his wide eyes he stared at the wall of the room, as if he saw them there. When called, he was deaf. And even the usual, futile charms with which Ida distracted him on such occasions went unheard. For a few seconds, he remained staring, on guard; then, overcome by that thing of undefined fear which he had to confront all alone, he suddenly flung himself down again and huddled up, hiding his head. And almost immediately he plunged once more into sleep.

This incident came at the beginning of a long series of nights, in which her own dreams and Useppe's uneasiness overlapped, foggily, in Ida's mind at every waking. She herself, in fact, had resumed dreaming extravagantly; but her complicated oneiric adventures, passing through her memory, left only a painful streak, with no other recollection. She had simply the sensation that their preordained plot always ran towards a violent rupture, translated, externally, into some disturbance, perhaps only slight, of the child. What, in her dream, she had believed the crash of a storm or an earthquake, had been, in reality, only a jerk, or a moan of Useppe's; and this was enough to wake her with a start. At times, they were ordinary little upsets, the kind that can affect anyone, child or adult: she would find him muttering something in his sleep, his lips trembling, his face contracted, his teeth chattering. Or else she would hear him shout, or call: "Mà! màà!" asking help. She might also find him already awake, sobbing as if over some enormous disaster, because he had wet the bed. But more often he woke up, crying for no apparent reason, or he would cling to her in his sleep, as if pursued by some extraordinary threat. And all sweating, he would open his little blue eyes, still filled by that unspeakable fear. When questioned, he could give only disjointed or confused information: always repeating he had too many *deams*. "I don't want those *deams*," he would say in a frightened little voice. "But *what* dreams? What do you dream?" "Too many *deams*. Too many," he would repeat. The very task of explaining those too many dreams seemed to alarm him. From what could be reconstructed, he apparently dreamed of very tall buildings, as a rule, or else of chasms beneath houses, or abysses. But the dream he complained of most frequently was fire. "Fire! . . . fire!" he would weep on some of his sudden wakings. Once he also mentioned an *"uggy* woman, big, big" and "lots of people running" and "lots of fire, lots and lots" and "the kids and animals running from the fire."

Only once did he report a complete and precise dream, frowning in the effort to tell it properly. He had dreamed of his mother, "not all, just your face." This face of Ida's had closed eyes: ". . . but you were awake, and you weren't sick or anything!" And on her mouth first Ninnuzzu's hand was placed, and afterwards, over it, Useppe's hand. Suddenly, the two hands were torn away, and somewhere a big scream could be heard "big big big big big!" But Ida's face, with the eyes still closed, and the mouth closed, had meanwhile started smiling.

.   .   .

Useppe's nighttime spells of anguish, as was only natural, cast their long shadows also over his days. As the day's hours advanced, the child seemed to grow tense and retreat, like a person trying to escape somebody always waiting in ambush for him and threatening him, without his knowing why. One day Ida decided to take him to a doctor, a woman she had heard mentioned at school, a pediatrician. In the waiting room, a woman came in, just after them, carrying a ruddy character perhaps three months old; he smiled at Useppe. And when Useppe's turn came, and the character was left waiting there, Useppe turned to say to him: "Aren't you coming, too? . . ." The doctor was still a young woman, carelessly dressed, almost gruff in her manner, but basically conscientious and kindly. Useppe gravely allowed himself to be examined, as if he were witnessing some exotic ceremony; and, his curiosity aroused by the stethoscope, he inquired: ". . . Does it make noise?", thinking it was a toy trumpet. Then, a little later, again concerned for the other client left in the waiting room, he asked the doctor:

"Why doesn't he come in? . . ."

"He? Who?"

"That other one!"

"His turn comes after yours!" the doctor answered. And Useppe seemed disappointed, but didn't insist.

The doctor declared she could find no organic ailment in Useppe: "He's tiny, to be sure," she said to Ida. "You tell me he was four last August, and from his height he might be two and a half . . . he's thin . . . obviously, he's a war product . . . but he's very lively!" Then, leading him by the hand, she observed him in the full light from the window, "His eyes are strange," she remarked, half to herself, ". . . too beautiful," she went on, as if spellbound, but suspicious at the same time. And she asked Ida, in the tone of one who already foresees the answer, if the child had, by chance, proved more precocious than the norm.

"Yes, yes," Ida answered. And she added hesitantly: "as I told you, he was also born prematurely . . ."

"We already know that! And as far as his later development is concerned, that wouldn't be important!" the doctor replied almost angrily.

And, frowning and puzzled, in her rough way she went on asking Ida if she heard him talking to himself at times, perhaps in long and rather confused chatter . . ."Yes, sometimes," Ida answered, more and more shy. And going off to one side with the doctor, she murmured to her hesitantly, like someone divulging another's secret: ". . . I believe . . . he tells himself stories . . . or poems perhaps . . . or fairy tales . . . but he doesn't want anyone else to know them."

The doctor prescribed a tonic for him, and a mild sedative for the night. And finally Useppe sighed with relief, because the recondite ceremony was over. On leaving, he waved to the infant in the waiting room and gave him a knowing, confidential smile, as between old acquaintances.

The good doctor's prescriptions proved useful. Thanks to the sedative, Useppe's nights passed more serenely. And the tonic, which tasted of egg and syrup, was so sweet that Useppe, every day, even licked the spoon. Ida promptly hastened to lock away the bottle, for fear he would drain it all at once.

2 Though belatedly, Ninnuzzu kept his word and came with the motorcycle. To avoid leaving it alone in the street, where they could steal it from him, he didn't come upstairs but whistled at the Marroccos' windows from below, then called: "Useppe! Useppeeee!" blowing the horn full blast. When, from above Useppe saw him looking up, beside the dazzling machine, he began to tremble from head to foot with impatience; and without saying a word, he immediately rushed towards the stairs (as if afraid the motorcyclist would vanish meanwhile), so Ida had to run after him to put on his little overcoat and cap. She also wrapped around his neck a scarf of many colors, which Filomena had made specially for him at a modest fee.

At the first signals of the event, the *piccinina* had frozen over her machine, dazed as if she had received a blow; now she hastily resumed stitching, pretending not to have heard or seen anything.

It was winter, but the January day seemed like April. The tepid air, especially in the sun, smelled of bread. Once outside the front door, not even waiting for Nino's invitation, Useppe, all excited, grabbed the machine to climb into the seat, as if mounting a pony. Nino was wearing a leather jacket, big gloves, and a helmet. A bunch of kids had already gathered around the motorcycle like so many lovers; and Nino was explaining with smug superiority: "It's a Triumph!" even condescending to grant those poor lovers some detailed information about the horsepower, the gearbox, the brake-drum, the carter, etc.

The start was sensational, and the trip was a genuine science-fiction expedition for Useppe! They covered all of monumental Rome, from Piazza Venezia to Piazza del Popolo, and then to Via Veneto, Villa Borghese, and back again to Piazza Navona, and the Janiculum, and St. Peter's! They hurtled through all the streets with a gigantic noise, because Ninnarieddu, to show who he was, had abolished the muffler. And when they went by, people scattered in all directions on the sidewalks, and protested, and policemen blew their whistles. Useppe had never known those neighborhoods, which in a shining cyclone now rushed at Nino's motorcycle, as if at a space-probe launched across the planets. Raising his eyes, he could see statues flying with spread wings from domes and terraces, dragging the bridges in their race with their white tunics in the wind. And trees and flags spun. And characters never seen before, always of white marble, in the shape of men and women and animals, were carrying the palaces, playing with the water, sounding water trumpets, running and galloping in the fountains and around the columns. Drunk with the joy of adventure, Useppe accompanied the motor's thunder with a constant little explosion of laughs. And when Nino started to set him down, he frowned and clung to the machine, pleading with him: "Agin!" "Agin! Agin!" Ninnuzzu imitated him, teasing, as he sped off again, to satisfy him, "Hey, kid, it's time you learned to talk right!" then after the third trip, he declared: "Okay, that's enough! . . . How about giving me a little kiss?" he added, to say goodbye, leaving him at the door of the building. "Agin," Useppe murmured once more, though without hope, raising his eyes to him. But Nino, this time, definitive, didn't even answer him, bending right over to give him a little farewell kiss.

And giving it to him, he suddenly had the same notion he had had once before: that in Useppe's eyes there was something new and different. Even in his familiar little laugh, to tell the truth, there was now something different (a feverish tremolo, almost imperceptible, not due to the speed: rather an inner cracking, like the constant tug of a nerve). But Nino hadn't noticed this; half-astride his bike, he watched his brother from behind, as he reluctantly climbed the stairs, always putting the same foot first at each step, the way beginners do (in him a sign of bad humor), and perhaps with some grumbling . . . Between the cap and the scarf, you could see his smooth, wispy hair. And from his little overcoat, made with "room to grow in," his pants appeared, also too long, American style. "Ciao!" Nino shouted to him, laughing at that comical sight, "see you soon!" and Useppe turned again to wave at him, opening and closing his fist. "Make way, you kids! Clear out!!" Nino said, setting off again in a huge roar amid the crowd of worshipers.

.   .   .

After his reappearance in liberated Rome, Ninnuzzu hadn't been heard to make any further reference to the Communist revolution, or to Comrade Stalin. The subject came up again one day when Ninnuzzu, taking out Remo the tavernkeeper on his powerful bike, stopped off with him at the Marrocco home. In Filomena's workroom, the *piccinina*'s place was empty today, because she had been kept home with 'flu; however, the thoughtless Ninnarieddu didn't even notice this gap: he hardly saw the *piccinina*, to tell the truth, even when she was there, before his very eyes!

This time the bike had been left in the care of the concierge, who, devoted to motors and racing heroes, guarded it as if it were a harem princess. The tavernkeeper brought Ida a present, a jug of olive oil, and Nino brought her a packet of American coffee; and it was clear from some remarks that the two men's current relationship involved business more than politics. However, already on the stairs they had started a political discussion; their arguing voices had announced them from the landing below. And when they came into the house, they resumed their argument almost immediately.

Remo seemed embittered by Nino's present indifference towards the Communist Party; recently, in that month of January, the Party Congress had been held in Rome, followed with enthusiastic faith by Remo and by all the comrades; but Ninnarieddu hadn't taken the slightest interest in it; indeed he had barely heard news of it. When they suggested he take out a party card, he snickered, as if they had suggested he become a monk . . . And now, among these and similar complaints from Remo, he began softly to sing "Red Flag" in the tone of someone singing a song from an operetta, like *The Merry Widow!*

"In the old days," Remo said bitterly to the others, "he used to talk like a real comrade . . . But now, when we should all stick together for the struggle . . ."

"In the old days I was a kid!" Nino exploded.

". . . What struggle?" Consolata, also present, supported him, with a sad gaze, "we struggle and struggle, and we're left at the gate. Without a pot to pee in!"

"I'll struggle for ME and for anybody I like!" Nino proclaimed, on his side angrily, "but for the Cell Leaders, NO! Do you know what REVO-LUTION means? It means, first of all: no Leaders! When I was a kid, I fought for that other one. And you saw what happened? Our Magnificent Leader, who never retreats?! He was so scared, he was running away, dressed up like a German!! He might of dressed up like a nun!! When I was a kid, none of the Leaders bothered to tell me that black shirt meant dirty shirt! But when I left the Blackshirts, those other Leaders up North, acting like genuine officers, didn't want me with their partisans, because they didn't trust me! And now, I'm the one who doesn't trust them!!" And Ninnarieddu slapped his left arm, knifelike, with his right hand, in a well-known obscene gesture.

"But Comrade Stalin is a true Leader! You believed in him too!"

"I used to believe in him! . . . but not all that much!" Ninnuzzu reflected. ". . . well, I believed in him . . . and now, if you want to know, I don't believe even in him any more. He's another Leader like the rest, and wherever there are Leaders, there's always the same stink! Ask anybody who's been there, in the kingdom of Siberia! The people work their ass off, and he licks his lips!"

"You didn't talk like this before . . ." Remo repeated bitterly.

"Before! Before! BEFORE!" Nino shouted at him, so loud he was deafening, "you know what I say, Remo? We don't have much time!" and in a loud tenor voice he started singing,

"play your balalaika, Ivana, and wait some more . . ."

"Remo . . . this is my life, not theirs! The Leaders aren't going to screw me again . . . Remo, I want to live!" Nino burst out with such violence that he sounded like a fire alarm.

He expounded this concept of his, a second time, in Ida's new home in Via Bodoni, where he turned up with his Triumph after another argu-ment with Comrade Remo. As if continuing the quarrel with him, he raged, striding grandly about the kitchen; but really he was talking to himself, his only audience being Ida and Useppe, who kept quiet. Furi-ously, he repeated that Stalin was a Big Cheese like the others, and for that matter History said so, too. Hadn't Comrade Stalin flirted with the Nazis, to screw Poland?! And, lately, hadn't he taken advantage of Japan's being KO'd, in order to jump on them? Stalin and the other Big Cheeses, it's all one system: they play footsies with each other to screw everybody else and to screw each other, too. And Nino doesn't give a shit about them. Nino wants to live, he wants to enjoy all life and all the world, all the universe! with the suns, moons, and planets!!! Now, 1946, it's America's big mo-

ment: and as for the Revolution, it's a sure thing it won't come for now
. . . "Maybe it'll come in a hundred years. But my time—and I'm twenty
—is today. In a hundred years, when I'll be a hundred and twenty, we can
talk about it again!" . . . Nino in the meanwhile wants to get rich, a
superbillionaire, and go off to America in a special extra de luxe plane.
He'll take Useppe along, too: "Hey, Usè, you want to come, on the plane,
to America?" "Yes, yes, yes." "Then we're off!" . . . The Revolution won't
come for now because the guys in charge here now are the Americans and
"they don't want it." And not even Stalin wants it, because he's an imperialist, too, like those others. Russia's imperialist like America, but the
Russian empire's on the other side, on this side there's America's empire.
Their fight's all a fake. Meanwhile, the two of them flirt and divide up the
loot: you there and me here; and then if you make a wrong move, we'll see
who has the best atomic bomb, and so the rest of us can go out on the
balcony with our binoculars and enjoy the atoms. The Big Cheeses have it
all figured out among themselves, they're all buddies.

"Me! They make me laugh! I'm the king of anarchy! I'm the outlaw
bandit! I'll empty their banks, I will! And to hell with the big guys! I'll
smash their empire in their faces . . .

. . . "Hey, Usè, how about taking a ride now, on the bike?"

"Es! Es! Essss!"

"Es es es! Now you've lost your 'y' again! Come on, Useppe, come on,
come on, come on!"

And they run off together, the two lunatics. The enormous explosion
of their departing engine makes everybody look out into the courtyard. All
the tenants of Via Bodoni are at their windows, to watch the Triumph's
departure.

.   .   .

The new home in Via Bodoni, where Ida and Useppe had moved that
spring, was made up of two rooms, one of which was very small, hardly
more than a closet. In addition, there was the entrance, a dark space
without windows; on the left the WC opened, very tiny and without a
sink. The kitchen, instead, was to the right, at the end of a short corridor,
and its window looked onto the courtyard, as did the little room, while
from the larger room you could see the square of Santa Maria Liberatrice.
In this square stood a church decorated with some mosaics that Ida, according to her taste, considered beautiful, because in the light they glowed
with gold.

At a very short distance from the house was Ida's famous school,
which, after its wartime occupation, had already announced its reopening
with the next school year; and this meant a great advantage and solace for

Ida. The little apartment was at the corner of the building, on the top floor, next to the water tank and the common terrace where laundry could be hung; and this position, like the topography of the interior, reminded Ida of her old home at San Lorenzo.

Here, too, the building was vast, more vast even than at San Lorenzo, with two courtyards and numerous entries. Ida's was Stairway Number Six; and in her courtyard a palm tree grew: Ida liked this, as well. Partly on time and partly from a junk man, she purchased the necessary furniture, which, for the moment, was limited to a table and cupboard for the kitchen, a couple of straight chairs, a second-hand wardrobe, and two sets of bedsprings, with feet, which the dealers pompously called *sommiers*. She placed the broader *sommier* in the large room, for herself and Useppe; and the other, a single bed, was put in the little room, in the hope that sooner or later Nino would come to stay there. But to tell the truth, he showed no intention of returning to the family; and indeed, during his stays in Rome, he left his addresses shrouded in mystery. It was clear, at any rate, that he had no permanent home; and that, on occasion, a woman put him up. Not always the same one, however, because Nino's relationships, as in the past, were always intermittent and irregular.

In this department, on two successive motorcycle jaunts with Useppe, he was accompanied by a girl, seated on the crossbar. Her name was Patrizia, but she was no patrician; she worked at the tobacco factory. She was beautiful, even more than the guerrillas' *redhead*; and she displayed a terrible fear of the bike, begging Nino, every time they set out, please not to go so fast. He would promise, but only to enjoy himself the more when, instead, he let himself go in excesses of speed. And then the girl would cling to his waist, furious in her terror, her clothes and hair streaming in the wind, as she shouted: "Murderer! Murderer!" Once, on a country road, her screams alarmed some motorized police, who ordered the Triumph to halt, suspecting a kidnaping; however, the same Patrizia, tidying herself amid many little laughs, excused Nino and explained the misunderstanding. And they all laughed; in fact the policemen apologized and saluted, adding a few polite compliments.

We may believe, actually, that Patrizia said "Don't go fast" on purpose, for the subsequent pleasure of being frightened and shouting: "Murderer!" In fact, also on the meadow, behind the trees, where, both times, she and Nino lay down on the ground, holding each other tight, she would struggle first and shout at him: *let go of me, help, help!* and she would try to drive him off, slapping him and hitting his throat and biting. But then she would suddenly close her eyes, with a saintly little smile, and would start saying: "Yes yes yes . . . Ninuzzo . . . it's so good . . . you're so handsome . . ." On the first excursion, whispering with Nino, she was concerned by the presence of the kid running around on the field there and making her uneasy; but Useppe paid little attention to the lovers, having already seen people copulate who knows how many times in the big room at Pietralata, particularly during the last nervous days of The Thousand. Sora Mercedes, at his *why*'s, had explained to him that it was a sports competition, those were the finals. And Useppe, satisfied, hadn't concerned himself with them any more, accepting them in his heedlessness. He was concerned, however, on the first excursion with Patrizia, seeing her hit his brother like that, and he immediately rushed to defend him. But Nino, laughing, said to him: "Can't you see we're only playing? Can't you see how little she is, beside me? Eh, if I wanted to, I could smash her with one punch." And with this, he reassured him. Nino then, knowing his little brother's ingenuousness, was not the least troubled at seeing him appear from behind the trees at any moment of the game with Patrizia. In fact, on the second excursion, catching him having a pee nearby, he said to him: "Come here, Useppe, show Patrizia what a nice little cock you have, too!" And spontaneously, as if it were nothing, Useppe came forward and showed it. "When you're bigger," Nino said to him merrily, "you'll screw with this, too, and you'll make some *Useppolini.*" And Useppe was amused, delighted at the thought of the useppolini, but without pondering it at all: no more than if Nino had told him, joking, that those future useppolini would be born from his eyes. Truly Useppe was a living refutation of the science of Professor Freud (or perhaps the exception to it?). He was a male, no doubt about it, he lacked nothing; but for the present (and you can believe my sworn testimony) he took absolutely no interest in his own virile organ, any more than in his ears or his nose. The embraces of The Thousand, and, now, Ninnuzzu's, passed before him without troubling him, like poor Blitz's affairs with other people's bitches, or like the exchanged compliments of the Peppinielli. He felt no offense in them; however, a mysterious feeling alerted him, meanwhile, that they were taking place beyond his limited present space, in a distance still denied him, like the games of the clouds. And in accepting them, carefree, without any curiosity, he left them where they were. Especially in the country, on those fields in spring, he now had other, personal things to do.

Still, he liked girls; indeed, each of them seemed to him, when he looked at her, a supreme beauty: the ugly Carulina of The Thousand, and the beautiful redhead Maria, and this other beautiful Patrizia. He liked their colors, and their softness, and their fresh voice, and their tinkle if they wore some little bracelet or necklace of metal and of glass. Patrizia also wore, among other things, two long earrings, like little bunches, whose tiny glass grapes struck one another, sounding all the time; and she took them off carefully, putting them in her purse, before making love.

On the second outing, as he ran around the fields, Useppe turned up in the clearing among the trees where, at that moment, Nino and Patrizia, having just made love, were stretched out on the ground, resting. Still flung heavily on top of Patrizia, Nino had his face buried in the grass, his cheek next to hers. And Patrizia, supine, her arms out in a cross, like a blissful martyr, had her head thrown back amid her disheveled hair, so black it had a bluish cast. Beneath her lashes touched with mascara, her eyes resembled two dark stars with hard little rays. In the corner of one eye, a tear had remained. Her half-open mouth, in the halo of the darkish, smeared lipstick, suggested a little bitten plum, its juice trickling from it. And beneath the foliage that dappled the ground in contrasts of light, she seemed to be lying on damask. Useppe considered her so beautiful that, crouching for a moment beside her, he gave her a little kiss on the elbow. Then, content, he went off again.

The lovers paid no attention to him then. But Patrizia must have remembered Useppe's little tribute, because afterwards, when they were all three preparing for the homeward journey, she said to Nino: "I like your brother" (instead, as was later learned, she was jealous of him). And she added, teasing: "Will you give him to me? What do you want with him anyway? You don't even look like brothers. You don't look a thing alike."

"You're right," Nino answered, "we have different fathers. Mine was a sheik, and his was a Chinese mandarin."

This time, too, Useppe laughed loudly at his brother's new joke. He knew very well, in fact, that mandarins are a kind of fruit, and logically the only children they can have are little fruits . . . This was the only thing in Nino's remark that struck him as curious. And for the rest, he was all agog now to get back on the motorcycle. Any other interest, for him, was secondary.

That chance witticism to Patrizia remains Nino's only reference to Useppe's alien birth: at least in Useppe's presence, or Ida's. After the famous day of his first meeting with the baby at San Lorenzo, Nino never bothered to inquire about his mother's unknown adventure. Perhaps, among his other clandestine attractions, he enjoyed keeping this brother mysterious: an unexpected arrival from no one knows where, as if they really had picked him up from the ground, wrapped in a bundle.

3 In that period, Davide Segre had been for some months in Mantua, at his family's house, where he wrote Nino from time to time. Now, it was known beyond any doubt that of his whole family, deported in 1943, no one had survived. His maternal grandmother, very old and already ill, had died during the journey. His grandfather and his parents had been exterminated in the gas chamber on the very night of their arrival at the Lager of Auschwitz-Birkenau. And his sister, seventeen at the time, had died in the same Lager a few months later (apparently in March of 1944).

The house, however, must have been occupied in the meanwhile by some stranger, because Davide, among other things, had found some cartoons hung on the walls that had never been there before. At present the rooms were abandoned, dusty and half-empty, but not too untidy. Much of the furniture and many family belongings had been carried away, no one knew where or by whom; but certain things, strangely, were still intact in the same place where Davide had always seen them. A simpering doll, which his sister had never taken from a high shelf, was still there, in the same pose as always, its hair filled with dust, its glass eyes open.

Some of those objects had been familiar to Davide since his earliest childhood; and as a boy, he had taken a dislike to them because of their mediocre, constant presence, which resembled a kind of wretched eternity. Now, he almost felt repulsion at finding them again before him, inviolate survivors of the dead. But he had no wish to move them, or to touch them. And he left them there, where they were.

At present he was alone in the house (of five rooms). In the city, an uncle had recently returned (father of that little cousin formerly hidden in Rome by the monks); he had managed to save himself, in time, with his own family. But Davide had never been close to his relations; and he considered this uncle a stranger, to whom he had nothing to say, and so he avoided his company.

Already during their shared days of guerrilla warfare, Nino had understood, from certain remarks of Carlo-Pyotr, that he had been alienated since childhood not only from his relations, but to some extent also from his parents and his sister, because they were bourgeois. In all their habits, which he had liked as a child, he had learned, on growing up, to recognize more and more the common social vice, distorting and deceptive. Even the smallest things: the fact that his father had the words *Engineer* and *Commendatore* printed on his visiting cards; that his mother, full of pride, would accompany his little sister to a certain party of important children and both would dress up for the occasion; and their chatter at table; and their acquaintances; and his sister's smug tone when she mentioned certain rich families' names; and his father's manner when he boasted of Daviduccio's success at school; and his mother's way, when she caressed him, even as a grown boy, of saying: *my little baby, my angel, my little gentleman*— these for him were all sources of a physical disturbance, like a paralysis. And with age, this daily annoyance gradually developed, more clearly, in his fundamental great rejection, which, on the other hand, proved incomprehensible to his hopeless family, like the code of another world. In fact, they lived sustained in their every action by the conviction of being honest and healthy; whereas in their every action or word he always found another degrading symptom of the maximum perversion infecting the world; and its name was *bourgeoisie*. This new attention of his, always in revolt, was a kind of negative exercise, which necessarily sentenced his family to his contempt. And even of racism—that is to say Fascism—he held them responsible for their share, since they were bourgeois.

And so, while still in High School, Davide began to evade the family's contagion, waiting until he could run away from it. When he was home, he locked himself in his room; and anyway, he spent barely the necessary amount of time at home. He took his holidays alone, wandering around Italy like a penniless gypsy; but from the places he happened upon, he would send his family long, fervent letters, which were read and reread as if they were novels by a celebrated author. In fact, he, the only son, and the firstborn, was the family favorite, and they adapted themselves to his demands (everyone, for that matter, considered him very earnest, not spoiled or eccentric). When the racial laws excluded Jews from state schools, he decided he didn't need school anyway, and he would finish his studies on his own. And when his parents, at whatever sacrifice, both wanted to send him to safety across the ocean like other Jewish youngsters of his class, he passionately refused, saying he had been born in Italy, and his place, now, was here! There was no dissuading him; indeed, from its tone, his refusal would seem to constitute for him an ultimate, even if somewhat puerile, rescue: as if he, Daviduccio Segre, had some unknown mission to carry out in his hapless native land; and exile, at the present time, for him would be a desertion and a betrayal.

It was in that period, in the course of his summer pilgrimages, that Davide met some militant anarchists in Tuscany and began some underground propaganda work with them; and there, in September of 1943, he was caught by the Germans, under a false name, after some stool pigeon had denounced him.

Now, he seemed to have broken off all political activity, and he saw no one. The only former acquaintance he had tried to seek out in Mantua was a girl, his adolescent lover, whom he designated in his letters to Nino only with the initial G. Baptized, not Jewish, she was a couple of years older than he and had been his only true love so far; and at the time she loved

Davide she had been a beautiful young girl, a factory worker. But, after 1942, she had been unfaithful to Davide with a Fascist; then, during the occupation, she had started making love with the Germans and had quit the factory, leaving Mantua. It was said that in Milan, after the Germans withdrew, she had had her head shaved as a collaborator; but nothing specific was really known. Of her parents, who had emigrated to Germany years ago to work, there was no news; and despite all Davide's inquiries, nobody could say what her end had been.

He had no other company; and his only correspondent was Ninnuzzu, to whom he wrote without any regularity; he might write him two letters in a day, or none for several weeks. For his part, Nino answered at most with an occasional picture postcard (to sit down and write, for him, was like a jail sentence: the mere sight of a blank page and a pen reminded him of school, and his fingers promptly developed writer's cramp and numbness). He chose brightly colored cards, gaudy and comical; however, he wrote only greetings and his signature, and if Useppe was there, he guided his little hand to add: *Useppe*.

He couldn't understand why Davide was extending his stay up there (he had left with the idea of remaining only a few weeks); and he wondered how he spent his time, alone, in that house in the provinces. "Maybe," he surmised, knowing him, "he spends it getting drunk." Sometimes he would blurt out: "I'm going up there to get him," but his excursions and his mysterious dashes north and south of Rome, for the moment, didn't take him to Mantua. And anyway, in every letter Davide insisted that he planned to come back as soon as possible, as soon as certain money became available: and when it was finished (he added once, on this subject) he would get a job as a farm laborer or a worker: any physical employment that prevented thinking. He wanted to devote himself to the most physical and exhausting toil; in that way at least, coming home at evening, in his weariness he would want only to fling himself on his bed, without any possibility of thought . . . But on this point, Ninnuzzu shook his head, incredulous: Davide, in fact, the very evening of their hazardous arrival in Naples, on his first drunk, had confided in Nino some plans for the future, dreams of his since childhood. And among these the first, perhaps the most urgent, was to write a book: with the writing of a book, he had declared, you can change the life of all mankind. (Then a moment later, he was almost ashamed of having revealed such a confidence; and frowning, he had stated that it was a lie and that he, if he set out to write, meant to produce only pornography.)

Moreover, Ninnuzzu was informed (having learned it, at one time, from Comrade Pyotr) that in the past, Davide had already attempted once to be a worker; but, in the event, he had failed the test. It had been about six years earlier, when Davide was just emerging from adolescence. His official status was unemployed student—banned, for racial reasons, from the public schools of the Realm—but, in reality, for him, this was the precise beginning of his period of greatest excitement, as outside school a new and fresh, though risky, freedom opened before him. For some time, in fact, Davide had been secretly pledged to his revolutionary choice, meditated, and now definitive (rather than betray it, he would have chopped off his hands!). And finally, the time to keep that pledge was announced to him.

By now, he considered himself grown up. And for his real initiation, he felt his first duty was to undergo directly and physically—he, born of the bourgeois class—the experience of the wage-earning factory worker. In fact, his IDEAL, as is well known, excluded, as an absolute principle—for the true anarchist revolution—any form of power and violence. And only at the price of personal experience, could he—in his opinion—feel himself the *neighbor* of that part of mankind which, in today's industrial society, is born already subjected by fate to power and to organized violence: namely, the working class!

So, that same year, he had managed, through some acquaintances of his, to get himself hired as an unskilled worker in an industry in the North (it is no longer known whether in Genoa or Brescia or Turin or elsewhere). It was the period of the Nazis' total victories; and we can imagine that, even in factories, this wasn't the happiest moment for Anarchism. Davide Segre, however, laughed at the Axis victories, convinced, indeed, they were traps prepared by destiny to send the Nazi-Fascists (that is to say, the bourgeoisie) to definitive and inevitable ruin: from which the song of revolutions could rise freely across the earth!

Actually, Davide Segre, the adolescent (and such, in reality, he was), saw all mankind as a single living body; and just as he felt every cell of his own body tending towards happiness, so he believed all mankind tended towards it, as its destiny. And thus, sooner or later, that happy destiny had to be fulfilled!

How that little runaway Jewish student then managed, when hired, to produce suitable documents, I couldn't say. However, I have been assured that (thanks to some clandestine intrigue) in the factory his real identity was unknown; nor did anyone, for that matter (not even his family), even find out about this worker's experience of his, which he kept secret from all, except a very few of his accomplices and confidants. For myself, the scant and fragmentary information I have been able to gather came, to a large extent, from Ninnuzzu; and he, for that matter, gave it a comic interpretation (even if, for Davide, it had been a real tragedy). And so my present memoir of the event remains rather patchy and approximate.

The place where he was sent the very first day was a hangar with a roof of sheet-metal, vast as a city square and crammed, for three-quarters of its volume, with monstrous machinery in operation. Davide crossed its threshold with the respect due a holy enclosure, because what had been for him a free choice was an imposed sentence for the other humans enclosed there. And in fact, inside him, with his sense of rebellion, there was also an exalted emotion, since he was finally penetrating—not as a simple visitor but as a true participant—into the *eye of the cyclone*, that is, into the lacerated heart of existence.

Since they put him immediately at the machine, he had at first only a confused and swirling view of the place. Above all, the huge room resounded incessantly with such a din that after a little while it made the eardrums ache, and a human voice, even shouting, was lost there. Moreover, the place couldn't remain still, but shook as if in an uninterrupted chronic quake, causing a faint seasickness, worsened by the effect of the dust and of certain caustic, piercing odors, he couldn't say from where, but which Davide, in his corner, felt constantly in his saliva, in his nostrils, mingled with every breath. In that vast space with few apertures, daylight entered murkily, scantily; and the electric illumination, in some points, was so blinding it pierced the eyes, as in third-degree interrogations. Of the few, narrow windows—all set high up, just under the roof—the closed ones had panes covered with a blackish crust; and through the open ones came damp, icy drafts (it was winter), clashing with the searing vapors which burned the air inside and created a weakness in the bones like a fever of a hundred and four. From somewhere in the back, through the dusty smoke, you could glimpse tongues of flame and incandescent streams; and around these, the human presences seemed not real, but the effects of nocturnal delirium. Inside there, the outside world, from which every now and then half-buried echoes arrived (voices, the clanging of a tram), became an improbable region, an Ultima Thule at the end of a trans-polar passage.

Davide, however, felt prepared for all this; indeed, he faced it fearlessly, like a raw recruit eager to prove himself in his *baptism of fire*. One fact, on the other hand, was new to him (although, really, it was a necessary consequence of all the rest), and this was the lack of any possible communication among the human subjects of the shed.

In here, the men (there were hundreds) couldn't even be counted as *souls*, as they used to be in the days of serfdom. In the service of the machines, whose monstrous bodies confiscated and almost swallowed the little human bodies, they were reduced to fragments of a cheap material, distinguished from the machinery's metal only by its poor fragility and its capacity for suffering. The frantic, iron organism that enslaved them remained for them a meaningless enigma, as was the direct aim of their own function. To them, in fact, no explanations were given, and they themselves asked none, for that matter, knowing questions were useless. In fact, for the maximum material output (which was all that was required of them, imposed like a life-and-death pact), their only defense was obtuseness, to the point of stupor. Their daily law was the extreme necessity of survival. And in the world, they bore their body like a brand of this unconditional law, which denies room even to the animal instincts of pleasure, still more to human demands. The existence of such States within the State was, of course, already well known to Davide Segre; and yet, till now, he had perceived it through a sooty mist, as if confounded in a cloud . . .

His precise job in the factory is not recorded in my information: however, from the same I can infer that, as a novice worker and without skills, he was at first put at a press, with the later possible alternative of a milling-machine or something else. But from one machine to the other, his fortune changed little; indeed, certain insignificant variations, within the same order of eternal monotony, confused him uselessly instead of giving him relief.

In any case, for him, it was always a question of repeating at dizzying speed some elementary operation of the usual sort (e.g. pushing a bar into a slot, stepping on a pedal at the same time . . .), exact and identical, with a minimum average of five or six thousand pieces in a day—at a pace measured in seconds—and never stopping (except to go to the latrine, but this parenthesis was also clocked). Nor was any relationship allowed him, in all that time, except with his press, or his milling-machine.

And so, fixed there to his automaton-demiurge, from the first day Davide found himself plunged into a total solitude, which isolated him not only from all the living people outside, but also from his companions in the hangar, all of them abstracted as he was, like somnambulists, in their frenzied work and in their incessant obligatory gesticulation, all of them subjected to his same undifferentiated fate. It was like being in a penitentiary where solitary confinement is the rule, and where, moreover, each convict is given the bare minimum for survival at the price of spinning without respite, and with the extreme number of turns, around a point of incomprehensible torture. Under the torment of this leech, which drains from within, every other interest is thrust aside like an enemy snare, or like a sinful and disastrous luxury which must later be paid for with hunger.

This unexpected solitude was a new experience for Davide, too different from that other solitude—known to him—of contemplation and meditation, which, on the contrary, gives the sense of communicating in unison with all the creatures of the universe. Here, imprisoned within a mechanism that locked him to passive obedience—and always intent on the same, uninterrupted pursuit, foolish and sterile—Davide felt overwhelmed by the double horror of a crushing bulk and an absurd abstraction. And the annihilation didn't leave him even at the exit, where his temporary *freedom* resembled that of a prisoner, taking his hour of fresh air, with irons on his feet. For a long while, beyond the factory gates, he still had the impression that everything around him and the earth beneath him, was vibrating disgustingly, the way you feel after a rough crossing, nauseated. And until he flung himself on his bed, the machines' daily siege continued to clench him, concentrated in a kind of invisible pliers that held his head in their jaws, with piercing pains and a horrible sizzling. He felt his cerebral matter being deformed, and every concept or thought that came to him, in those hours, irked him, and he wanted to drive it away immediately, like a parasite. From the first evening on, at the moment of retiring, the effect of Davide Segre's working day had been to make him vomit—there, as soon as he had set foot in his little room—all the scant food he had eaten and the great amount of water he had drunk (in that period he still drank only water, or, on occasion, orangeade and nonalcoholic beverages, when his finances permitted).

And every evening after that, punctually, when he came in, the same vomiting phenomenon recurred, which he found himself unable to resist, against all his will (besides, it made him angry thus to waste his dinner, which he had earned with such suffering . . .). Nor was he spared, every morning, a certain struggle, at the sound of the alarm calling him for his shift at the factory. Suddenly, in fact, with this announcement of his new day, the thousands and thousands of "operations" of his quota lay before him like an immense advance of black ants over his body; and he felt an itching everywhere, so his first gymnastics, to wake himself, were to scratch desperately. He had the strange, twofold feeling of heading for a sacred duty which nevertheless involved him in a kind of crime against nature, demented and perverse. And such an abnormal law irked his conscience, at the same moment that it summoned him with total fervor, like a voice from on high! In reality, Davide told himself, the true meaning of his present act lay precisely in his subjecting himself voluntarily to such an aberrant misdeed. This, in fact, was his pledge: to write the infamy of the worker's experience not on paper, but on his own body, like a bloodstained text: in which his IDEAL would become living, to cry the Revolution and to liberate the world!! Now, such faith sufficed to make the boy Davide gallop towards the factory shed, like a front-line fighter enamored of his flag!

The first days, during the usual labor, he consoled himself occasionally by directing his imagination—or rather, the last thread of it left to him intact—towards some refreshing visions: young girls of his acquaintance, mountain trails, the sea's waves . . . But these momentary vacations, alas, regularly ended in minor disasters or accidents, earning him reproaches (and threats of discharge) from the foreman, who wasn't the type for niceties (his most usual compliments were *pirla*, prick, and *vincenso*, a dialect term that means idiot there). On these occasions, Davide was immediately seized with a desire to use his fists, or at least to drop everything, give the box with the finished pieces a kick, and clear out. And naturally, with his willpower, he managed to suppress his temptation; however, it made his viscera roil with nausea, and always brought a return of his usual morning itch, as if he had nests of ants beneath his clothes, or an invasion of lice.

In any case, even those threadlike reserves of imagination were soon consumed. In the brief course of a week, for him the earth already existed no longer, with its woods and shores and meadows, nor the sky with its stars: because these things no longer gave him any desire or pleasure; indeed he didn't see them any more. Even girls, when he left the factory in the evening, didn't attract him. The universe, for him, had shrunk to that shed; and he was even afraid of escaping its prison coils, suspecting it would perhaps be impossible for him, afterwards, to go back in, if he were to look directly at the joy of living. Even his pleasure in art (he particularly loved painting and music, especially Bach)—and poetry—and his studies, his reading (not excluding the texts of his political masters) now teetered in the distance, like alien figures, expelled to an Eden beyond time. On occasion he had to snicker, thinking of Socrates of Athens, accustomed to arguing with his aristocratic friends in some luminous room, or seated at a banquet . . . and of Aristotle, who taught logic while strolling on the banks of the Ilissus . . . Here, among his companions in the shed, communicating the IDEAL (apart from the objective impossibility) would have been like talking about mothers in a desperate foundling asylum. A grim feeling of fraternal modesty, and also of bitter ethics, denied him such a right, like a forbidden luxury. And so, also certain propaganda aims of his (no secondary motive in his present enterprise) became another, constant frustration for him, as he continually postponed them. Only on one of the last evenings, as far as I know, was he inspired to distribute stealthily a little clandestine pamphlet to three of his companions, just outside the gates, though he had no further word from them later. Perhaps, in that atmosphere (with the Nazi-Fascist terror triumphant), this silence on their part represented the only possible sign of complicity towards him; but for him (who in his heedlessness didn't even consider the risks) it meant that his intentions of an anarchist apostolate in the factory had failed, without response.

Otherwise, his relations with his companions in the shed were limited, as far as I know, to a few casual and ephemeral exchanges. I have heard about a Saturday evening when he found himself eating with some of them. They were in a crowded place near the factory (portraits of the Duce, bellicose slogans, and the presence—all around—of plainclothes police, informers, and Blackshirts), and at table they talked exclusively of sports, movies, and women. Their language, or rather their allusive slang, was limited to a minimum vocabulary; and, in particular on the subject of women, it was reduced to a comical-obscene entertainment. Davide realized that to the machines' convicts such wretched evasions are the only allowed repose; and with a feeling which to him seemed *charity* (but was, really, far more his own need of being liked) he eagerly set out to tell a dirty story, which didn't then enjoy much success. It was a complicated anecdote, about a guy who for a costume party had decided to go dressed as a prick; but in the end, unable to find a suitable headcovering, he resigned himself to going as an ass, etc., etc. Now, the others present (without his suspecting, in his ingenuousness) looked around alarmed, imagining, in the climate of fear of those times, that the character in the anecdote referred to the Duce, or the Führer, or to Marshal Goering . . . That evening, Davide had a bandaged finger (in the shed he had squashed the pad of a fingertip) which was infected and was hurting him. Moreover, contrary to his habits at that period, out of friendliness towards his companions he had drunk some wine. And during the night—perhaps as he was running a slight fever—he had a nightmare. He dreamed that, in the place of his fingers, he had heavy bolts screwed too tightly into the nut, and around him, in the shed, there were no longer men or machines, but only some amphibians, half-man and half-machine, with trolleys from the waist down instead of legs, and drills or pulleys for arms, and so forth. They, and he with them, had to run and run without stopping in a clammy, boiling mist. And running, they had to emit screams and deafening laughter, because this, too, was part of the job. They all wore huge, thick green eyeglasses, since they were all nearly blind from certain acids in the foundry, and they spat out a dark, dense saliva, like black blood . . . For that matter, Davide had been having for some time, if not nightmares, kindred dreams. There were always drills in them, pulleys, vises, cauldrons, and screws . . . Or else there were complex calculations of speeds and pieces, which he had to make and remake constantly, quarreling with someone who insisted that his pay, in all, came to two lire and forty centesimi . . . and so on. Even in his dreams, obviously, he now wanted to avoid any temptation to happiness.

That famous Saturday evening supper was, according to my information, the only occasion when Davide met his companions outside the factory. And here it must be stated that Davide—already misanthropic by nature—with the workers became more shy and glum than ever. And as he grew worse, the more, in his heart, he really longed to be the opposite. He would have liked to address them in the locker room, pursue them outside the gates, embrace them, tell them all sorts of things meant specifically for them; but more than *good morning* and *good night* would never come from his mouth.

Though nobody in the factory knew his real class and identity, he still felt himself treated as an outsider among the workers. And, for him, worse than an outsider, he felt repugnant to them, knowing that for him this factory work was only a temporary experience, an intellectual adventure after all, while for them, it was their whole life. Tomorrow, and the day after, and in ten years' time: always the shed and the racket and the pace and the pieces and the foremen's reproaches and the terror of being fired . . . with never an end, until the moment of the definitive disease, or old age, when you're cast away as useless junk. To this end their mothers had borne them: men sound in mind and body, no less than he! men, or rather "the elect seat of conscience," in every way equal to him! To escape the burden of such an injustice, the only remedy seemed to him then to become a worker like them for the rest of his life. That way, at least, he would be able to call them brothers without remorse. And thinking about it, at times, he made up his mind, in earnest. But a moment later, he could glimpse the happiness that beckoned to him from a hundred thousand little open windows, saying to him: What!? you want to betray me?! In fact, Davide, as we have always mentioned, was a devotee of happiness, in which, he felt, man's true destiny resided. And even if his personal destiny announced itself to him, in those days, as hostile and threatening, we have seen that certain threats didn't weigh on him. Davide Segre's happiness, really, despite everything, could be sung in three words: HE WAS EIGHTEEN.

Meanwhile, he dedicated himself to his position as a worker beyond the confines of the possible. According to him, in fact, what he chiefly lacked was experience and training, so to train himself, he not only hastened to all his shifts, but also sought to work overtime, including Sundays: he was so suspicious of parentheses. And though that damned vomiting was repeated every evening, and every day his body lost weight and he was more and more enervated, he was convinced he could make it physically (his morale depended on his will). Was he perhaps less strong than the other workers in the shed?! There, in the factory, you could find men of fifty, and women, and little boys who looked consumptive . . . His body was healthy and strong; in the past he had even won athletic competitions, and very few could beat him at Indian wrestling. For him, to survive the test *physically* at least to the time he himself had fixed (that is, till summer—it was then February) was not only a pledge, but a question of honor. And instead, it was his body that betrayed him. It happened on the Monday of the third week. Saturday had gone badly for him: he had produced I don't know how many hundreds of defective pieces (he had been distracted by an unforeseen resurgence of jealousy concerning a little girl friend of his in Mantua), and the foreman, a new one, had called him, among other things: *balosso, maroc,* and *romanso gialo* (all truly incomprehensible terms to me, but they were apparently serious insults). In the evening, he skipped supper; and yet, on coming in, he vomited twice as much as the other evenings: a gray vomit, all dirty water, soot, and dust, and with even some sawdust and shavings in it! Then, in bed, he couldn't get to sleep. Always that itching everywhere, and those hateful pliers at his head, and in his brain, instead of thoughts, nothing but nuts and bolts, screws, pieces, and bolts and screws . . . Suddenly, like a searing whiplash, there flared up in his head this sole, frightening thought:

As long as men, or even a single man on the earth, is forced to live such an existence, all talk of freedom and beauty and revolution is a fraud.

Now, such a thought made him draw back, worse than a ghostly or demoniacal temptation; for to heed it would mean, for him, the end of his IDEAL, and therefore of every vital hope.

The next day, Sunday, he stayed in bed, feverish, and he slept almost the whole day. He also had some dreams, of which he remembered nothing precise; but certainly they had been dreams of happiness, because they left him with a sense of healing and also of extreme weakness (as in convalescences). Also the thought of the previous evening, which had seemed so terrifying to him, now came to him, instead, with the air of a promise and a stimulus: "In the face of the obvious *impossibility* of certain human damnations," he told himself, in fact, "you have to dedicate yourself more than ever to the IDEAL which, alone, acting mysteriously, like miracles, can free the earth from the monsters of the absurd . . ." That evening, as usual, he set the alarm; and in the morning he rose with frenzied urgency to return to the job. But then, as he was going off, at the thought of himself marching towards the shed, standing at the machine, etc., etc., he felt those fatal pliers fall on his head with an echoing thud, squeezing so fiercely he had to stop, at the stairs, his legs paralyzed! He was overcome with seasickness, he saw flashes, heard whistling—and, worst of all, he was filled, through all the channels of his will, with intentions which were resolute but, on the other hand, decidedly to be rejected: not only because they were contrary to his present commitment, and—beyond a certain point—also to the very IDEAL; but because they were foolish in practice, negative in tactic; and such that, in reality, in the present political and social situation, even a Bakunin (who was anything but nonviolent) would have repudiated them contemptuously! And yet, they were the only imaginings capable, at least *physically*, of giving him a certain impulse in the legs, and a little shiver, if not of joy, surely of gaiety . . . They were, actually, variations on the same theme, such as, for example, hitting the foreman who had called him *balosso* and the other things, jumping onto the machinery waving any old black-and-red rag and singing the "Internationale"; shouting to all present: STOP! in a voice of invincible volume, such as to silence all the notorious clangor of the shed; still shouting, and in increasing volume: "Let's run away from here! Let's tear down the whole place!! Set fire to the factories! Murder the machines! Dance in a universal ring around the owners!!" etc., etc. At heart, he was undoubtedly determined to resist such aleatory stimuli, with a *moral* force of his will; however, a physical CERTAINTY, like a cry from his bowels, warned him that perhaps no will of his would avail against another stimulus: the urge to VOMIT! He felt, in short, that as soon as he was back at his place, intent on counting the pieces produced and on suppressing the other stimuli, that famous vomit, which usually came to him in the evening, would pour out there, in broad daylight, and while he was at work! shaming him, like a kid, in front of everybody!

But, in any case, this didn't make him give up; he was determined to march on, all the same, as usual, towards the shed. But unfortunately, of all the long stairway from his lodging (five floors) he was unable to descend even the first steps! At the simple, imminent prospect of the shed, the effect of his paralysis followed immediately. His *moral will*, in short, was to go there; but his legs did NOT want to go there any more.

(It was—as he himself later explained to Ninnuzzu—*the paralysis of unhappiness.* For any real action, no matter whether toilsome or dangerous, movement is a phenomenon of nature; but at the unnatural unreality of a total unhappiness, monotonous, wearing, stupefied, without any response, even the constellations—he thought—would stop . . .)

And so, Davide Segre's experience as a worker, which according to his plan was to last, in the minimum hypothesis, five or six months (and in the maximum hypothesis, his whole lifetime!), was miserably concluded in the space of nineteen days nineteen! Luckily, his IDEAL had not emerged from it destroyed; but rather, on the contrary, enlightened and strengthened (he had already counted on this). Still, it can't be denied that, at least *physically*, his attempt had ended in defeat, so afterwards, when he encountered any workers, Davide felt a sense of shame and guilt that made him so misanthropic that he kept silent.

Obviously—Ninnuzzu admitted—today Davide was no longer the same boy; maybe at that time he was still a bit spoiled . . . Nevertheless, his present insistence on repeating that enterprise, destined to fail, made his friend laugh, as if at a child's whim. But while he laughed, Ninnuzzu always spoke with supreme respect of his Comrade Davide; for, since the first days of their life together in the Castelli, he had considered him not only a hero by nature, but a thinker, surely meant for some glorious achievement: a great man, in other words, from every point of view.

Some of the present letters from Mantua were long, well-written (with a real Author's style!) and they discussed learned subjects—art, philosophy, history—so Ninnuzzu showed them off with a certain honor, though inevitably, when reading them, he skipped at least half. Others, instead, were convulsed and confusing, scrawled in big letters, crooked, almost illegible. Davide said he couldn't stand it up there, and he felt he had fallen into a trap.

Towards the end of August, he announced that in a couple of weeks at most, he would be back, with the intention of staying in Rome.

4 On the Ferragosto holiday, the fifteenth of the month, while Davide was still in the North, down here, in our parts, there was a crime, at the Portuense. Santina, the elderly streetwalker, was murdered by her pimp. A few hours later, he turned himself in to the police.

Davide knew nothing about it, since nobody bothered to inform him (his intermittent affair with her had been almost clandestine) and in that period he didn't even glance at the newspapers. It's probable, for that matter, the newspapers up North carried no mention of the event. It appeared in the Rome papers, and there were also photographs of Santina and of the murderer. Her picture was not recent; but, though more fresh and full, and less ugly, her face already showed that opaque resignation of an animal marked for slaughter, which today, when you looked at it, seemed the sign of a predestination. The murderer's photograph, on the other hand, had been taken at the police station at the moment of his arrest; however, he also seemed younger than his age. He was, in fact, thirty-two, but he looked ten years less in the picture. Dark, a smudge of beard despite the holiday, with a low forehead and the eyes of a mad dog, his was exactly what they call a "jailbird's face." He betrayed no special emotion; he merely seemed to declare perhaps, in an inexpressive and sluggish language of his own: "Here I am. I came on my own. You didn't catch me. Look at me. Go ahead and look. I don't even see you, anyway."

On this occasion, his name, never told anyone by Santina, was learned from the newspapers. It was Nello D'Angeli.

The crime, apparently unpremeditated, had taken place in the woman's ground-floor room. And the weapons had been more than one, things to be found there in the house: a big pair of scissors, the iron, and even the bucket of dirty water. Death, however, proved to have been caused by an initial stab with the scissors, which had cut the woman's carotid artery; but the murderer had continued striking the unconscious body with every object he could get his hands on. The newspapers, referring to the crime, spoke of "temporary insanity."

On Ferragosto, at that hour (between three and four in the afternoon) the surrounding area was deserted; and anyway, certain neighbors, at home taking their siesta, had heard neither screams nor quarreling. It hadn't taken long, in any case, to discover the crime, since the murderer hadn't gone to any pains to wipe out the traces. He even left the door ajar, so that a stripe of blood trickled through it from inside, soaking into the dusty ground. In the room, the blood formed a big puddle by the bed, the rug and the mattress were steeped in it, and it had also spattered on the walls; moreover, the criminal left his own bloody footprints and fingerprints everywhere. Santina's body was on the bed, naked (perhaps, with her one boyfriend, she agreed to undress, as she didn't with her transient lovers). And though it was known in the vicinity that, thanks to the presence of the occupying soldiers, the woman still enjoyed an unusual good fortune, no money was found in her clothing or elsewhere in her room. After the removal of her body, her purse was dug out from under the mattress, where she herself usually kept it; but, besides her identity card, the housekey, and some old tram tickets, it contained only small change.

At the time of Nello's arrest, however, they found on him a number of banknotes of medium and small denomination. He kept them normally in the back pocket of his pants, in an imitation-crocodile wallet; and though worn and dirty, they showed no signs of blood. When asked, nevertheless, if he had stolen the money from the woman, he answered, in his sly and arrogant way, "You've got it," whereas, actually, he had received it from her own hands, a few moments before killing her. But he couldn't be bothered to clarify certain minor details.

Except for the wallet buttoned up in his pocket, all his clothing, and also his hands, even under the fingernails, were stained with blood, partly blackened and mixed with dust and sweat. In fact, he hadn't taken the trouble to wash, and he presented himself to the police in the same clothes he had been wearing since that morning: a rather fine open shirt, of pink linen, with a four-leaf clover of green enamel hanging from a chain around his neck, some loose duck trousers, without a belt, and summer shoes on his bare feet. He said he hadn't returned to his house after the crime, but had gone off alone behind Via Portuense, across some fields towards Fiumicino, where he had even slept, maybe an hour. In fact, there were some wisps of dry grass in his hair. It was seven-thirty in the evening.

At the station, they already knew his present occupation as pimp. And it wasn't hard for those officials to explain his crime, which they defined *classic* in its typicality: the old whore he exploited had perhaps refused him, and perhaps hidden (or at least so he must have suspected) a part of her earnings, which, instead, belonged totally to him, according to his own law. And he, who was defined in the report as *amoral, unfit, of subnormal intelligence and lacking all restraining inhibitions,* had thus punished her . . . He himself, for his part, lightened the job of the investigators assigned to him. At their questions, now futile and obvious, he answered, as he had in the beginning about the bills, nothing but: "That's it," "yeah, right," "that's how it was," "it was like you say" . . . or even with a silent raising of his eyebrows, a Southern movement which means simply a confirmation. Indeed, as he gave those answers of his, he displayed an indifferent, grumpy laziness, like someone who, subjected to a superfluous exertion, finds it convenient to be relieved of it, at least partially, by the investigators' inductive logic . . . And it was with a kind of relaxation, half-cynical, half-idiotic, that, not arguing, he signed at the bottom of the report: *D'Angeli Nello.* His signature, decorated with curlicues, was so excessive it occupied all the width of the page, like the signatures of Benito Mussolini and Gabriele d'Annunzio.

"Homicide, aggravated by abject motive." *Abject motive* in his case, according to the authorities, meant *exploitation and monetary interest;* but Nello D'Angeli would have been far more ashamed of his real motive, if he had been aware of it.

For a young man to exploit an old whore was normal to him; but to love her was not. And instead, the unconfessable reality was this: in his way, he loved Santina.

In all his previous life, he had never possessed anything of his own. He had grown up in public institutions for abandoned children and minors. In his infancy, the nuns of the institution, once a year, at Christmas, gave him a teddy bear, which was taken from him after Christmas and kept in a closet until the following year. Once, in the course of the year, seized by a longing for the bear, he had secretly taken it, after breaking the lock of the closet. Discovered a few minutes later, he was punished by being beaten with a brush and, the following Christmas, was deprived of the bear, which remained locked up.

From that time on, he had got into the habit of petty theft. The punishments were various and also odd: besides beating him, they made him stay on his knees for many hours, at meals they gave him all the food jumbled together in a single bowl, they chased him waving burning newspapers behind him, threatening to set fire to his ass, and even, on one occasion, they made him lick his own shit. Since his thieving habit was notorious, he was sometimes punished for thefts that hadn't been his doing. He wasn't a likable child, or a quick one; nobody came to his defense, and nobody ever felt any desire to cuddle him. When he was a young boy, it sometimes happened that a companion at the institution, an abandoned child like himself, would slip into bed with him, hugging him and even kissing him, or would try to go off somewhere with him. But he had learned this wasn't normal; and since he wanted to be a normal male, he furiously fought off those caresses with his fists. His fists were hard as iron, and the others were afraid of them. Later, he always mistrusted any aspiring friends, suspecting they were abnormal.

Released from the institutions at about twenty, he had gone, on his own initiative, to seek out his mother. Originally the daughter of shepherds (she came from the interior of Sicily, and was of Albanian descent), she had turned, as a girl, to the same trade as Santina; but now she was living with a man, and with three small children she had had by him. "I'll let you sleep here and I'll feed you," she said to him, "provided you work to help out the family." He worked digging ditches, but his mother wouldn't give him money even for cigarettes, and besides she reproached him all day long for earning too little, considering how much he ate. One day, though she was his mother, he hit her with his fists, then never showed his face again. A few months later, he turned up in Rome.

It was in those years that he came into possession of a little dog, who might perhaps have been white in color, with spots, but its raw patches and its filth made it seem blackish and greenish. He found it in a hole, all bruised from sticks and rocks; God knows how, through his personal care, he brought it back to life. He named it Fido; and he took it with him everywhere. However, he didn't pay the dog tax for it. And, in consequence, one day a city employee came and, with a kind of harpoon, pulled Fido straight into a little truck where a number of other dogs had already been loaded: all of whom, Fido included, went directly to the slaughterhouse.

Later, every time he was alone and ran into a stray dog or cat, Nello D'Angeli took pleasure in torturing it, until he saw it kick the bucket.

He didn't feel like working. He lived from day to day, through casual thefts, never joining up with other thieves. He vegetated, like that, at the edge of society; and not being clever by nature, he was quite often clapped into the Regina Coeli prison, where, in and out, he spent several months of the year. Then, after he had met Santina, in the intervals he lived partly off her.

He wasn't really ugly, but not handsome, either. He was a peasant type, short in stature, grim, sullen, and in general he didn't appeal to girls. Still, if he had wanted, he could have found one more suited to his age, and less ugly than Santina; but he himself, instinctively, avoided youth and beauty, like a hydrophobe afraid of being bitten. His only woman was Santina.

Their bond was money. But since, in reality, he loved her, the financial interest, unbeknownst to him, served him rather as an excuse to be with her. He had nobody but her in the world, just as Santina, except for him, had nothing. But she, even with her scant intelligence, was able to recognize her own love; whereas he didn't recognize his.

Every time he appeared at her place, first of all he said to her, grim and threatening: "Where's the money?" And she promptly gave him all she had, only regretting she didn't have more to give him. If she had refused it to him, or perhaps had insulted him, the thing would have seemed more normal to him. But how could she, in her simplicity, deny him anything? If she went on plying her trade as a whore, it was for him; and it was also for him that, in hard times, she rushed here and there, working as laundress, nurse, laborer. If she had been alone, she would have let herself die, like certain animals without a master, when they become old.

And with the pretext of money, he had become truly attached to her person: to her old and awkward body, which gave itself to him in her rough, meek, and—oddly—inexpert way, as if in all those years of her trade she still hadn't learned how to do it; and he was attached to her melancholy smile, to her smell of poverty. When she was in the hospital, he brought her oranges; and when they arrested her and locked her up in the Mantellate, he shut himself in his own rented shack, in the dark, feeling nausea even at the colors of the day. When he saw her free again, his first feeling was of anger; he received her with curses.

At times, leaving her abruptly after having taken her money, he would continue hanging around the vicinity of her place, like a poor strange dog not knowing where to go. His home was that ground-floor room. He always kept his own rented lodging, in a hovel on Via Trionfale; towards the end, however, when Santina was earning a bit better, more and more often he would go and sleep at her house in the evening. If she had customers, he would stay outside, sprawled on that refuse dump, waiting till they had finished. He felt no jealousy, well knowing that other men, for her, didn't count. She belonged to him, her sole master. The only purchases she made were for him. For herself, she spent nothing, beyond the necessities of her business, such as a public bath every now and then or a hair set. And in these times of good fortune, the only luxury she allowed herself was giving him presents: for example, the fake crocodile wallet, or some fine linen shirts, or other nice things. The enamel four-leaf clover on the little chain was also something she had given him.

And she washed and ironed his clothes, his pants, she cooked his pasta and meat on her little stove, she bought American cigarettes as a surprise for him.

. . . There, a shadow of a strange man comes out of the door of the room. Inside, the sound of running water is heard . . . He stretches, stands up, and goes towards the door:

"Where's the money?!"

And, after taking the money, if he likes, he can also go away; she doesn't ask anything of him in return. But instead, like babies after their mother has given them their milk, he starts to yawn and flings himself on the little bed, as if waiting for a lullaby.

She meanwhile moves about, busy with her preparations, takes macaroni from the little cupboard, onions, potatoes . . . Reclining, he leans on one elbow and examines her with a sidelong glance:

"Jesus Christ, you're ugly! Those arms and legs of yours look like four poles, and your ass looks like two sides of rotten beef!"

She utters not a word of reply, but moves a bit aside, with her passive, uncertain, culprit's smile . . .

"What're you doing? What're you cooking up? You've already made me sick, Christ, with that stink of onions. Stretch out here on the blanket. At least I don't see you that way . . ."

And so it begins again almost every evening. He can't comprehend the heart-rending homesickness that calls him back to her. And meanwhile, wherever he is, he feels the need of her body. On certain evenings, out of hatred, he doesn't show up; but the next day, she doesn't reproach him for anything. In the summer sunsets, at times she waits for him, sitting on the doorstep; and when she sees him arriving, a spontaneous, almost ecstatic gratitude glows in her dim, ingenuous eyes. She smiles her shy little smile, and says to him:

"Nello!"

She gives him no other greeting. She gets up, and with her heavy feet precedes him into the dark, cool little room.

"Where's the money?!"

If, one of these times, she were to drive him away, he would hate her less. Santina's presence, in his life, is like a disease's reddish spot, spreading.

Man, by his very nature, tends to give himself an explanation of the world into which he is born. And this is what distinguishes him from the other species. Every individual, even the least intelligent, the lowest of outcasts, from childhood on gives himself some explanation of the world. And with it he manages to live. And without it, he would sink into madness. Before meeting Santina, Nello D'Angeli had furnished himself with his own explanation: the world is a place where everybody is the enemy of Nello D'Angeli. His only recourse against the enemy, his normality, in order to cope, is hatred. Now Santina's existence is a fragment of alien matter, which upsets his world and makes his dull brain spin, out of gear.

At times, in sleep, he was invaded by nightmares, in which Santina was always being taken away from him. He dreamed a squad of Germans, having surrounded the room, was dragging her towards a truck, aiming *Maschinenpistols* at her, or else some orderlies in white coats, preceded by an Inspector, came with a coffin, raised Santina's dress, and said, "She's got syph," and they took her away in the coffin. Then he would yell and rage in his sleep, and would wake up charged with hatred against Santina, as if the fault were hers. One night, at one of these wakings, finding her asleep beside him in the bed, he fell on her, his eyes bloodshot, shouting: "Get up, damn you!" And as he hit her, he thought he was in an enormous brawl, where he himself, beaten, was being lynched.

Not once did he sleep, even for a little while, without dreaming; and his dreams, whether Santina appeared in them or not, were inevitably murky and uneasy. On Ferragosto, when he dozed off in the field after the crime, he dreamed he was in that same field, walking towards a ditch. It was neither day nor night, there was a dull glow he had never seen before; and at the bottom of that ditch there was Santina, who had fallen and was no longer moving, her eyes open, staring. He climbed down to her and took her in his arms, carrying her up from the ditch, and to bring her round, he stripped her naked. And she lay there stretched out on the field beneath him, with her body all bones, white and flaccid, and her old woman's little breasts, thin and sagging. Slowly her eyes closed and her face was regaining color, and meanwhile she raised one hand, moving her finger as if joking. And she repeated to him with her usual little smile, trying to hide the gap of the missing tooth in her gums:

"It's nothing . . . it's nothing . . ."

And for the first time in his life, he felt content and trusting. Waking, as the sun set, he saw again the bloodstains on his pink shirt and immediately remembered everything. There was no home, now, where he could go.

One of the many things he had taken to hating, for some time, was freedom. He had never been free. First the institutions, then the brief stay at his mother's with daily forced labor, and finally the coming and going at Regina Coeli. As at the nuns' orphanage when he was little, also later, not all the crimes he was charged with were crimes of his. Known as a habitual thief, he was often arrested without his having done anything, because he was suspect. And in this way, even when he was back in circulation, he felt like a sewer rat, who as soon as he shows himself in the street expects to be driven away by the first person who sees him. And without giving it any more thought, he went straight to turn himself in. With his crime of murder, since he was now thirty-two, he was sure to grow to old age in prison. That was his only home.

.   .   .

Ahead of the dates he had written Nino, Davide came back down to Rome at the beginning of September. He arrived as usual without forewarning, and wandered in vain from one of Nino's possible addresses to another, not finding him. In the end he ventured to Via Bodoni; but even before he had looked in at the concierge's lodge for information, he heard a little voice call: "Carlo! Carloo!" He had already become unused to this name; however, he was not long in recognizing Useppe, coming towards him from the first courtyard in the company of a big white dog. Useppe was waiting for his mother, who would be coming down in a little while. And though with some regret at having to disappoint the visitor, he announced brightly: "Carlo! Nino left yesterday! He went with the *airpane* and said he'd be back soon, with another *airpane!*" Though he had passed the age of five, even now, and especially when an excess of vivacity or emotion overcame him, Useppe mixed up words and consonants, like a baby.

Davide yawned, or sighed, on learning of Nino's departure, without, however, commenting on the news. Instead, in a low voice he pointed out: "My name isn't Carlo. My name's Davide . . ." "Vàvide . . . yes!" repeated Useppe, recovering himself, a bit mortified at his earlier mistake. And he began again, dutifully: "Vàvide! Nino left yesterday. He went with the airpane . . ." etc., etc.

Meanwhile, the dog was jumping about to welcome the unknown passing visitor with friendliness and trust. And she still leaned forward, barking to greet him, while he, having no further reason for lingering, was going back towards the entrance. "Ciao, Vàvidee!" Useppe shouted to him at the same time, waving his hands and kicking happily. And Davide, turning to wave goodbye, saw the child pulling the huge animal to him by the collar, as if he were holding a horse by the reins; and the dog, in its constant ructions, turned to lick his cheeks and his nose, and the child, leaping, hugged the big white head. It was clear there was perfect and wondrous agreement between the two. Davide turned the corner of Via Bodoni.

He had traveled all night in an old third-class coach with wooden seats; and moreover, because of the crowd, he hadn't been able to stretch out, so he had simply dozed as best he could, his face half-hidden against a rented pillow; however, though he had eaten nothing since the day before, he had no appetite. And having crossed the Ponte Sublicio, he continued, almost running, beyond Porta Portese, to go to Santina. With Nino away, he knew nobody else in Rome.

The door of the room was pulled almost shut; and outside, next to the step, there was a pair of slippers. A sweating, barefoot woman, with deformed feet, was busy with some buckets inside; and turning slightly, in a reticent and unsociable manner, she said Santina didn't live there any more. It was sirocco weather, sultry and cloudy. Davide was seized by a terrible thirst and a desperate desire to take refuge somewhere in the shade; however, the only tavern of his acquaintance, around there, was a low dive from which a radio's din emerged. It was playing a samba record with voices and the loud rhythm of drums. At one of the two tables a couple of customers was seated; the other was free; and the young man who waited on the tables must have been new to the place. Davide didn't recall ever having seen him before, the few times he had happened in there. Still, he tried asking him news of *Signora Santina.* The young man remained puzzled, especially since, around there, Santina was known not so much by her real name as by a slightly derogatory nickname, inspired by the size of her feet. "Yeah, yeah, *Bigfeet,*" a customer spoke up, in fact, from the other table, "the Ferragosto one . . ." "It was in the paper," the other customer remarked, glancing at Davide. "Ah, that one!" the waiter said. And lazily, with few but expressive words, he informed Davide of Santina's nasty end. Finally, he held the side of his hand to his neck, the better to indicate how her throat had been cut.

At this news, Davide felt no particular emotion. It seemed to him, indeed, that he had just heard a natural, familiar announcement, as of an experience already undergone in some previous existence of his; or else it was like a book where, before reading the other chapters, he had already glanced at the last pages. He had by now drunk more than half of his liter; and mechanically he bit into the sandwich he had ordered along with the wine. He had sunk into total impassivity; but his senses were confounded by his fatigue, so even though there were no trees around, he heard an enormous buzzing of cicadas or insects. The radio's racket stunned him, and he was longing to get out of this place. He asked those present if they knew of a room to be rented in the neighborhood, as soon as possible . . .

They shrugged, then the young waiter, after some reflection, said: "It's for rent again . . . there . . . From the *gimp* . . . where she lived . . ." he clarified, after a pause, with some scruples about naming Santina's room. His manner in making the suggestion was skeptical, however, oblique and hesitant. And in fact, though there was a scarcity of lodging in Rome, especially of cheap rooms, it wasn't easy to find someone willing to adapt himself to a room branded like that, and barely yesterday.

Davide left the tavern. Outside, he found again the same cloudy sky, the same sirocco wind, and the same sultriness as before, along with that absurd buzz . . . And he started to run towards the room, as if in panic fear that meanwhile even that last possible refuge might have disappeared. The door this time was closed, but some boys, playing nearby, following his movements with a slightly curious indifference, came to his help, calling the proprietress from below. It was the same *gimp*, the woman with deformed feet, whom he had seen a little earlier inside there with the bucket. And in furious haste Davide paid her, took the key, and holed up in his own lodging, flinging himself bodily on the bed. The familiar little room, which still retained Santina's poor smell, received him on that day as a familiar, almost affectionate nest. It was cool, shady. And Davide wasn't afraid of ghosts. He had learned, in fact, on his own, that the dead don't answer, even if you call them. All means are futile, even praying them to show themselves if only in feigned and hollow guise, even as a hallucination's effect.

Santina's personal belongings, unclaimed by anyone, had remained the inheritance of the landlady; so the room's furnishing was more or less the same as before. The bed, repainted a darker color, was the same, except for the replacement of the mattress and the cover, which now was the kind made of hard, twisted threads, with arabesques of a Turkish nature, to be bought from street peddlers. Instead of the old rug, there was another, even more worn and threadbare. The table, the little cupboard, the chair, and the holy pictures had remained the same, and so had the curtains, which, freshly washed, had faded still further. On the walls, the bloodstains were hidden beneath patches of whitewash; while on the armchair, scrubbed away as far as possible, they mingled with the dirt.

In the evening, when the air had turned a little cooler, Davide went out to collect his suitcase, checked at the railroad station. And he sent a letter to Nino (addressing it, as usual: Poste Restante, Rome) to inform him of his Roman address and to say he was here, waiting to see him the minute he came back.

During all the past summer of 1946, despite his many excursions and departures and his mysterious deals, Ninnuzzu had been an unusually frequent visitor in Via Bodoni.

Now he no longer had to call or whistle tunes to announce his arrival to Useppe: his horn's blast was enough, or the roar of his engine, to announce him! Useppe would have recognized the special sound of the engine and of that horn even amid a great horde of speeding motorcyclists!

But one day, around the middle of July, instead of these habitual sounds, Nino's voice was heard calling from the courtyard below: "Useppee! Useppeee!" accompanied by a great, expansive barking. Filled with the presentiment of an unparalleled surprise, Useppe looked out of the kitchen window; and his pupils widening, he started feverishly down the steps, not even fastening his sandals. After the first few steps, he lost one; and instead of wasting time picking it up, he slipped off the other as well, and left both there. To save time, he made part of the descent sliding down the banister; but at the third landing he crashed into a white giant who, as if already a centuries-old acquaintance, caught him up in an enormous welcome. At this point, Nino hurried up from below, laughing, and meanwhile Useppe felt his bare feet being licked. "Hey, you forget your shoes?" Nino remarked, arriving. And at Useppe's uneasy explanations, he promptly said to the dog: "Go up and get them! Go on!"

Immediately, the dog flew up the steps and brought one sandal back down, and in another dash produced the other, with the satisfied air of total comprehension. This was Useppe's first meeting with Bella.

The dog, in fact, was a female; and she already had the name of Bella before encountering Nino. Who gave it to her originally, no one knows. Ninnuzzu had seen her the first time, barely a puppy, in Naples, in '44, in the arms of a business partner with whom he had an engagement in the port. The partner, who dealt in contraband American cigarettes, had acquired her only a short time before, by chance, from a kid passing by, in exchange for some odd packs of *Camels* and *Chesterfields* (known to him, in his language, as *Camelle* and *Just to feel*); and he insisted he had made a good deal, because this little dog was a thoroughbred, and worth at least four or five thousand lire! But though Nino, envying him this purchase, immediately offered him more on his own, the partner wouldn't sell at any price, declaring that, in those ten minutes he'd held her in his arms, he had already become fond of her, as a member of the family. Now, at the time of her purchase, she was already named Bella: with this name, in fact, the vendor had introduced her to the purchaser, and she already answered promptly to the name.

Ninnarieddu, from that day on, had never got her out of his heart; and every time he happened to run into that character (whose name was

Antonio), he renewed his request to buy her from him; but every time, no matter how Nino increased his offers, Antonio refused her to him. And Nino had even thought of stealing her, but had rejected the idea out of a sense of honor, since Antonio had been his partner, and they still worked together on occasion.

Then, in July of 1946, Antonio was caught in an armed robbery and locked up. And immediately, tormented by the thought of Bella, he found a way of letting Ninnuzzu know Bella was now his, provided he hurried to collect her wherever she was, to save her from a probable, ghastly end at the Pound.

Nino hurried; but not finding Bella at Antonio's house, he guessed the next place to look for her should be in the vicinity of the prison buildings. And, in fact, arriving at Poggioreale, when he was still at a distance of twenty yards, he saw a kind of white bear in the gathering darkness, roaming around those outer walls, lying down from time to time, and waiting God knows for what, and whimpering uninterruptedly. And though Nino called her, and insisted, and tugged at her, she refused to move from there. She didn't even utter a reply, continuing her disconsolate, always identical whimpering, in which an ear more sensitive than the human ear could understand the word: "Antonio . . . Antonio . . . Antonio . . ."

Finally Nino was able to persuade her by reasoning along this line:

"My name's Antonio, too (alias Antonino and Antonuzzo and also alias Nino, Ninnuzzu, and Ninnarieddu) and now, the only Antonio in your life is me, because that other Antonio isn't likely to come out of those walls until you're old. And in the meantime, if you keep hanging around here, the men from the Pound will come and kill you with those lousy gases of theirs. You know I loved you at first sight. After the only dog of my own I ever had, I didn't want any other; but the moment I saw you, I thought: this dog, or none. So if you don't come away with me now you'll be leaving two Antonios without a dog. And I might add that my grandfather in Messina was named Antonio, too. Come on, let's go. Fate has brought us together."

This explains the unknown dog seen by Davide in Useppe's company. Immediately, at the first encounter with her on the landing, Useppe recognized in her an extraordinary kinship with Blitz, although, to look at them, you would have thought them direct opposites. And yet, like Blitz, she also danced on greeting you; and, to kiss, she licked you with her rasping tongue; and she laughed with her face and her tail, just like Blitz. There was a difference, however, immediately noticeable, in their gaze. In fact, Bella at times had a special sweetness and melancholy in her hazel eyes, perhaps because she was female.

Her breed, known as Maremma or Abruzzi shepherds, came from Asia, where Bella's ancestors, from the dawn of history, had followed the flocks of the earth's first shepherds. So Bella was, as a shepherdess, almost a sister of sheep, whom she also had to defend skillfully against the wolves. And in fact, her nature, always patient and meek, on certain occasions could develop a wild beast's ferocity.

She had a rural mien, full of majesty; her coat was all white, thick, a bit ruffled at times; and she had a kind, jolly face, with a black nose.

At present, being two years of age, she corresponded to a little girl of about fifteen in the human species. At times, however, she seemed a two-month-old puppy, when a little ball, the size of an apple, sufficed to drive her crazy in fantastic amusement; and at other moments, she seemed an old woman, thousands of years old, of ancient memories and superior wisdom.

With the previous Antonio, though she had a master, she had led the life of the streets and had twice copulated with unknown dogs. The first time, it had obviously been a black or half-black dog, because of her seven subsequent puppies some were black with white spots, some white with black spots, and one all black except for a little white ear. The last one, also all black, had a white tuft at the end of his tail and a little white collar. She had tended and nursed them with passion in a closet under the stairs; but after a few days Antonio, not knowing what to do with those seven poor bastards, had taken them from her, however remorsefully, and had sent them in secret to die.

Still, when a few months had passed, she was pregnant again, by who knows what dog. This time the birth went badly; she herself came close to death, and had then to undergo an operation which meant that from now on she could never again be a mother.

Perhaps these memories of hers were the source of that sadness seen at times in her gaze.

Since he had become Bella's owner, rather than leave her, Nino gave up movies, shows, dancehalls, night clubs, and all places where dogs are not admitted. If, in some borderline case, he found himself rejected, because of Bella, with the words: "Sorry, really sorry, no dogs allowed . . ." he would wheel around promptly, with a dire and contemptuous grimace, and at times he would answer with infernal curses, or quarrel. One day, when they had gone into a bar, Bella not only licked some pastries kept on display there; but in a single mouthful she swallowed one, and having found pistachio inside or some other ingredient she didn't like, she disgustedly vomited on the floor everything she had in her stomach. Then the barman protested about fouling the place, etc., and his protest jarred on Nino's nerves. "My dog's vomit," he declared angrily, "is a lot better than your

371

pastries and your coffee!" "Ugh, it's lousy!" he added ostentatiously, having barely moistened his lips in the cup (he was having an espresso). And he rejected the drink with a nauseated face, as if he wanted to vomit too. Then, grandly throwing five hundred lire on the counter for the damages, he said: "Come on, Bella!" and went out of there forever, a man shaking the dust of a place from his soles. Nor did Bella, for her part, show any sign of shame or regret: on the contrary, she followed Nino at a gay and festive little trot, carrying, like a standard, her hairy tail (worthy, indeed, of a charger in its magnificence).

But Ninnuzzu's great sacrifice in Bella's honor was giving up the motorcycle. In fact, after a little while, he decided to sell the Triumph, planning to purchase in its stead, at the first opportunity, a car in which he and she could travel together. But since the motorcycle's price was paid him in three instalments, and instead of saving every instalment, he spent it, for that summer the new car remained a Utopia. Meanwhile, Nino could often be seen standing, fascinated and intent, in front of some motor vehicle, in Bella's company and at times also in Useppe's, all three in consultation, in view of the purchase, discussing pick-up, mileage, horse-power . . .

Nino was so taken with Bella's company, that in some cases he pre-ferred her even to girls! And Bella, for her part, requited him to the maximum, though never forgetting that other Antonio, in Poggioreale. If she should happen to hear, even in some strangers' talk, the ordinary word "Antonio," she immediately raised her floppy white ears, with an alert and anxious look. By herself, she had understood that the other Antonio, al-though alive in Naples, was now, alas, beyond reach. And Nino, who behaved very considerately towards her, avoided mentioning Antonio in her presence, so as not to reopen the wound in her heart.

On Bella, as on primordial creatures in general, names had a prompt and concrete effect. For example, if you said the word *cat* to her, she would move her tail slightly, her ears half up and half down, and her eyes glowing with a provocatory intent, though almost entertained (in fact, like Nino himself, she didn't seem to take the race of cats very seriously. When one of them, on meeting her, happened to threaten her grimly, she would at first accept the challenge, perhaps so as not to offend him. But after one or two well-meant feints towards him, she would go off, laughing, with the implicit idea: *who do you think you are? A wolf maybe?!*)

And now, since she had made Useppe's acquaintance, the very sound of his name made her go immediately wild in festive, eager leaps: so Nino, amused by this game, when they happened to be in Rome together, couldn't resist the fun of tempting her, suggesting: "Want to go see Useppe?" And afterwards, rather than disappoint her, he often ended up taking her there. In this way, Bella became one of the possible motives, mostly unconscious, which explain Nino's returns to the family, in those two months of July and August.

And yet summer's temptations lured him more than ever. And he did nothing but run, at every opportunity, from one beach to another, coming back always blacker, his eyes radiant, slightly reddened by the sun and the water, and his hair stiff with salt. Bella also had a briny smell, and she scratched herself often, because of the sand that stuck in her coat. Nino thoughtfully took her, every now and then, to have a bath at a public bath for dogs, from which she emerged somewhat dazed, though snowy, combed and new, like a lady leaving the beauty parlor.

From time to time, Nino promised Useppe to take him along too, one of these days, on an excursion to the sea, and to teach him how to swim. But his Roman days followed one another so feverishly that no room was left for the famous excursion. And even their outings in trio (Nino, Useppe, and Bella), though fairly frequent, were inevitably reduced to brief dashes. They never went farther than the Pyramid, or the Aventine.

Ninnuzzu, that summer, wore shirts with flower patterns and many colors, which came from America and were bought at Leghorn. And he also brought three similar little shirts as a present to Useppe. He didn't forget Ida either, making her a gift of some towels with RAF printed on them and some African straw slippers. Moreover, he brought her an ashtray, of metal that looked like gold, stolen from a hotel.

It was towards the end of August that Nino, having returned to Rome for a few days, had a serious quarrel with the nameless people who housed him, because of Bella. And promptly, in his fury, without stopping to think, he arrived with suitcase and dog in Via Bodoni, where Ida hastened to settle him as best she could in the room with the little daybed.

Bella wasn't a city dog like Blitz; and when she entered the minuscule apartment, it seemed to shrink still further, as if at an excessive invasion. But Ida at present would have gladly received even a real polar bear, she was so pleased to have Ninnuzzu home again, if only in transit. Bella slept with him in the little room, at the foot of the bed, waiting calmly and patiently in the morning for him to wake up. However, she was quick to catch the first sign, even the slightest, of his waking; as soon as he began to stretch a little, or yawn, or simply open his eyes a crack, she immediately sprang up in enthusiastic racket, like certain tribes at the rising of the sun. And so the house was informed of Nino's waking.

In general this happened towards the noon hour. Until then, Ida, in her usual bustling about the kitchen, took care to be quiet, not to disturb her firstborn, whose fresh snoring could be heard beyond the door. This sound gave her a sense of pride. And if Useppe, waking first, made a little noise, she admonished him to be quiet, as if beyond that door the Head of the household, a great worker, were asleep. In fact, it was certain Nino worked, because he earned money (not a great deal, to tell the truth); but what his job was exactly remained a confused point (that it involved contraband or the black market was more or less known; but such work constituted only another alarming enigma for Ida).

Two minutes after Bella had cast aside all restraint, Nino himself would burst from the little room, wearing only his briefs, and he would wash himself in the kitchen with a sponge, flooding the whole floor. A bit after noon, somebody would call him loudly from the courtyard below (and usually it was a young man in mechanic's coveralls) and he would rush downstairs with Bella, reappearing only casually, at intervals, during the course of the day. The greatest sacrifice, on Ida's part, had been to give him the house keys, of which she was, as usual, enormously jealous, as if they were the keys of St. Peter. At night, he came home very late and waked not only Ida on his return, but also Useppe, who would immediately murmur, half dreaming: "Nino . . . Nino . . ." A couple of times, Bella, having come back with him in the afternoon, remained in the house to await him at evening; and those two times she could be heard welcoming him on his entrance, as he grumbled at her: "Ssh . . . ssh . . ."

All this lasted barely five days; but it was enough to fire Ida's imagination. Especially in the morning, when she was in the kitchen cleaning the vegetables, and Ninnarieddu was sleeping to one side, and Useppe to the other, it seemed to her she had formed a real family again: as if there had never been a war, and the world were once again a normal place to live. The third day, as Nino, awake earlier than usual, lingered in his little room, she went to visit him there. And finally she ventured, though shyly, to suggest he actually resume his studies, to "guarantee a future" for himself. She could make an extra effort and support all three of them for the time still necessary, perhaps she could find some more private lessons . . . In fact, Nino's present occupation seemed quite temporary to her, not the kind, certainly, that offered him a sure, trustworthy career!

For some time, in her simplicity, she had been hatching today's proposal, and Nino, instead of rebelling, as he would have done in the past, heard her out with a kind of facetious forebearance, as if moved to pity for her. Since, at her entrance, he was naked, rather than shock her he had quickly covered his abdomen with his shirt, all colorful flowers. At that hour, pre-dawn for him (it wasn't yet ten) he lay there, lazily stretching and yawning; but now and then he responded to Bella's festive roughhousing with equal roughhousing, so despite his respectful intentions, he happened to display again the nakedness he had covered, before or behind. And in all this racket, he still lent an ear to his mother, with the air of a person hearing for the thousandth time a funny, but also silly, story, now being told him yet again by some hick. "Aw, mà, don't you see?!" he blurted finally ". . . Bella, cut it out . . . Aw, mà! mà!! What are you talking about? College again!!! Me . . ." (he yawned) "Mà, I've got lots of degrees already!!"

"I'm not talking about the University, but at least a diploma . . . A diploma always counts for something, in later life . . . I meant . . . high school . . . a high school diploma . . . that, at least . . . as a basis . . ."

"I've got a basis, mà . . . don't worry!!"

". . . It would be so easy for you . . . You had almost made it . . . in school, when you quit . . . It would take only a little effort on your part . . . You're bright enough . . . and after so many sacrifices . . . now that the war is over!"

Suddenly Nino frowned: "Bella, out! Get out!" he yelled, angry even with Bella. And sitting up on the mattress, heedless that he was now openly displaying all his nudity, he exclaimed:

"The war was a joke, mà!" And he stood up. Naked like this, dark, in the poor, hot little room, he seemed a hero: "But the joke isn't over yet!" he added threateningly.

His child's face seemed to have come back to him, aggressive and almost tragic in its own whims. And meanwhile, he was pulling on his briefs, hopping on one foot like a dancer.

". . . These characters think they can start over again, like before: don't you see that? Well, mà, they're wrong! They put real guns in our hands, when we were kids! And now we're having fun, making peace! Mà, we're going to SMASH EVERYTHING!"

Suddenly he became exhilarated. This idea of smashing things filled him with an extraordinary gaiety: "And you even think you can make us go back to school!" he went on, speaking polite Italian deliberately to mock his mother, "written Latin, oral Latin, history, mathematics . . . geography . . . Geography! I study that on the spot. History: that's their dumb joke, and it's got to end! WE'LL make it end! and mathematics . . . You know the number I like best, mà? It's ZERO! . . .

"Bella, keep quiet out there. I'm coming . . .

"We're the generation of violence! When you've learned how to play the game with guns, you keep on playing! *They* think they can screw us again . . . The same old tricks, job, treaties . . . orders . . . hundred-year plans . . . schools . . . jails . . . the royal army . . . and it all starts over again like before! Oh, yeah . . .?! Bang! bang! bang!" At this point, Ida saw in his eyes again that look like a photographer's flash which she had seen for the first time the famous night of his visit with Quattro to the big room. And as he said bang bang bang, his whole body pretended to aim at a target which was, in essence, the planet Earth, round and complete with its kingdoms, empires, and national republics. "We're the first generation of the beginning!" he resumed, at the height of his rhetoric, "we're the atomic revolution! We're not going to lay down our arms, mà! THEY . . . they . . . they . . .

"THEY don't know, mà, how beautiful life is!"

He had raised his flowered shirt with one arm, to dry the sweat trickling among the little black curls of his armpits. All of a sudden, he laughed happily and ran into the kitchen. And a moment later, to the merry sound of running water, the kitchen was already flooded.

"Beuh! beuh! beeeeeehuh!" From the bedroom Bella can be heard, acting crazy, running around the double *sommier*.

"Nino! Hey, Nino!! Ninooo!" Wakened early by the impatient Bella, who follows him in supreme rejoicing from the bedroom, Useppe has now arrived.

.   .   .

Of all Nino's great invective, one point had frightened Ida: the part where he had talked about weapons. Truly, in Ninnuzzu's presence, for some time now Ida considered herself a subaltern or an inferior, like a poor provincial woman before a superstar. And she submitted to his reasoning almost with trust, resigned to a total abdication, as if confronting some science-fiction machine. Among all the possible hypotheses, it could be that Ninnarieddu's present profession was bandit! But no hypothesis can turn the course of the constellations! And Iduzza didn't allow herself even to venture certain hypotheses. He, whom she had before her eyes in Via Bodoni, was a son filled with health, who needed no one, herself least of all.

But in Ninnuzzu's speech today, she had been given a very precise reason to worry. In fact, after the liberation of Rome, an order had been issued for all arms to be consigned to the authorities; and Ida had been aware of this order from the time of her lessons to the South African. The suspicion of a flagrant illegality assailed and invaded her, so deeply that while Nino was out, later in the day, trembling at her own unheard-of act, she locked the door of the smaller room and began rummaging in the absent occupant's baggage, to see if arms were hidden there . . . But luckily there were only the familiar shirts, some dirty and others clean, a few briefs, some dirty and others clean, a pair of sandals, an extra pair of pants, and sand here and there. There were also two or three picture postcards, and a letter on violet paper, of which Ida glimpsed only the signature (Lydia) and the salutation (O my unforgettable dream of love), hastily replacing the paper to avoid the indiscretion of reading it. More-over, there was a book: *How to Raise Your Dog*.

The only weapon (if such it could be called) was, at the bottom of the suitcase, a little switchblade knife, somewhat rusty (Nino used it to pry sea urchins from rocks). Ida could breathe again.

The fifth day, Nino announced he had to leave the next morning; and since he would be traveling by plane, where dogs were not allowed, he was leaving Bella to board in Via Bodoni in his absence. For her food, he gave Ida a bundle of money, also giving her totalitarian instructions, with an important tone and scientific precision: it was obligatory that Bella should have so much milk every day, so much rice, a grated apple, and no less than a pound of choice meat! Ida was aghast at the luxury of her carnivorous boarder, who spent, alone, at the butcher's, far more than she herself and Useppe together. She recalled the revolting gruels with which the wretched Blitz had been content, and she had a feeling of resentful injustice towards this giantess of the prairies. However, to make up for it, imitating her example, Useppe could now also be persuaded to eat some meat dishes, without his usual morbid repugnance; and this was enough to make Ida forgive Bella her millionairess banquets.

After almost two weeks, Nino came back to collect her. He announced that he had at his disposal, though only temporarily, a lodging on the city's outskirts, almost in the country, where Bella could live with him; as usual, however, he kept the address a secret. Informed that Davide had come looking for him the day after his departure, he said he knew it already. Davide had written him and they had met. Then he told Useppe he was discussing the purchase of a second-hand jeep, of which he displayed the photo, illustrating its advantages and its disadvantages. As to speed, unfor-tunately, the jeep wasn't so hot; but on the other hand, since it was an army vehicle, it was good at crossing valleys, difficult terrain, streams, and the sands of beaches and deserts. If necessary, bunks could also be installed in it, for sleeping.

This visit of Ninnuzzu's was one of his shortest; indeed, it couldn't really be called a visit. Somebody in fact (Remo perhaps) was waiting for him in the street with a little truck, to accompany him and Bella to his new home, and in his haste, he wouldn't even sit down. At his first running steps on the stairway, however, he had to turn around. In the little flowered shirt Nino himself had given him, his hands clutching the railing, Useppe was up above, with a fearless air, but all his muscles trembling like a rabbit's:

"Nino! Ninoo! Ninooo!"

Bella immediately rushed back up to Useppe, but without even stopping, she leaped down again towards Nino, as if she didn't know which way to go.

Ninnuzzu raised his head, slowing down. On Useppe's mouth there was already the tension of a question, and meanwhile he could be seen turning extremely pale, as if in that question were concentrated all his body's energy:

"Wy" (but he gravely corrected himself) "WHy are you going away?"

"I'll see you soon," his brother guaranteed, stopping for a moment on the step and holding the eager dog by the collar. "And this next time," he promised, "I'll come for you with the jeep." Then he waved goodbye, but Useppe remained with his fingers clutching the railing, obviously refusing to return the goodbye. Then Ninnuzzu ran back up two or three steps, to say goodbye more properly, near him:

"How about giving me a little kiss?"

It was the twenty-second or twenty-third of September.

6 In the month of October, when the scholastic year began, Ida's old school was reopened, a short walk from Via Bodoni. This year Ida had the first grade, and not knowing with whom to leave Useppe, she decided to take him with her every day. Useppe was still under the age to be officially enrolled in the school (he had a year to go); however, considering him, with proud certainty, more mature than normal, Ida was counting on the example and the company of the other children to stimulate him at least to learn the alphabet meanwhile.

Instead, from the very first days, she had to change her mind. Faced with the problems of letters and numbers, Useppe, now five years old, proved even more immature than he had been as a tiny boy. Obviously readers and notebooks remained, for him, alien objects; and to force him seemed unnatural, like demanding a little bird study the notes of the pentagram. At most, if he was supplied with colored pencils, he could start drawing on the page some curious forms, like flames, flowers, and arabesques all combined; but he soon tired even of this game. And then he would leave the paper there and scatter the pencils on the floor with a capricious impatience, tinged with anguish. Or else he would break off, as if exhausted by the effort, falling into a dreamy absentmindedness that estranged him from the class.

Such calm moments were rare, however. More often, to his mother's profound embarrassment, Useppe behaved terribly; and even his usual sociability vanished here at the school. All the regulations, the confinement, the bench, the discipline were impossible trials; and the sight of the pupils seated in rows must have seemed an incredible phenomenon to him, since he did nothing but disturb his classmates, chatting with them in a loud voice, hugging them, or giving them little blows with his fist as if to waken them from a lethargy. He was capable of jumping on the benches, perhaps confusing them with those other famous benches at Pietralata; and he ran around the classroom with savage cries, as if he were still among The Thousand, playing football or Indians. But then he would constantly clutch his mother, repeating to her: "Hey, mà, can we go? Is it time yet? *When* is it time?" Finally, at the closing bell, he would rush out furiously, and on the brief journey home, he did nothing but press his mother, as if there were somebody waiting at the house.

Ida thought she could guess in him an unavowed apprehension that, during their absence, Nino might have come by the house and found nobody there. She realized, in fact, that every time, before passing the entrance, he examined both sides of the street with eager eyes, perhaps seeking that famous jeep already admired in the photograph; and then he would anxiously hurry beyond the first courtyard, perhaps hoping to find the festive pair, Nino and Bella, waiting beneath the windows. After the last goodbye in September, the two had given no further news. And Useppe certainly felt their absence more than ever, after those happy days of living together; however, he didn't say anything.

Seeing that school age, for him, had not yet arrived, Ida gave up taking him with her and decided to entrust him, instead, to a kindergarten in the same building as her classes. Every day, at the sound of the closing bell, she would run to collect him, taking him, you might say, from the very arms of the teacher-supervisor. But this second attempt proved even more disastrous than the first; indeed, hearing the daily reports on him that the teacher gave her, his mother no longer recognized in this new Useppe the same child as before. It was a rapid and progressive mutation, which, after the first signs, was accelerating its pace from day to day.

Unpredictably, Useppe now avoided other children's company. When they sang in chorus, he remained silent, and invited to sing with the others, he would soon lose the thread of the song, constantly distracted by every trifle, even imperceptible ones. During their playing together, he kept to one side with an expression of uneasy and bewildered loneliness, as if he were being punished. You would have said that, for this punishment, someone had set between him and the others a half-opaque partition, behind which he insisted, as if in final defense, on hiding. And if the others then asked him to play, he would withdraw, immediately violent. But a little later he could be found huddled on the ground in some corner, whimpering, like an abandoned street kitten.

There was no following his moods, contradictory and unexpected. He seemed stubbornly to deny himself society and companionship: at snack time, however, if another child eyed his cookie, he would impulsively give it to him, with a friendly and contented smile. At times, when he was silent, he could be found with a tear-streaked face, for no reason. And then all of a sudden he would let himself go in riotous, desperate merriment, like a little African carried off from his forest in the hold of a slave ship.

Not infrequently he would doze in boredom; and when the teacher tried to rouse him (even very gently, in her sweetest tone of voice) he would reawaken with an excessive and brutal jolt, as if he had fallen abruptly from a high bed. One day, on one of these wakings, getting up, he dreamily unbuttoned his little pants and peed in the middle of the classroom: he, a boy over five, among the oldest in the class.

If he was given games requiring concentration, such as building things or the like, at the beginning he would set out with some interest; but long before reaching the conclusion, he would suddenly sweep everything aside. One day, in the midst of such a game, he burst into sobs, silent and aching, which tried to find release in sound and seemed to suffocate him; until, bursting, they broke into screaming weeping, of painful, intolerable revolt.

While the teacher spoke of this with Ida, Useppe stood nearby, his eyes wide and amazed, as if he himself didn't recognize that strange child; and yet he seemed to say: "I don't know why this happens to me, it's not my fault, and nobody can help me . . ." Meanwhile he would start pulling on Ida's dress, urging her to go home. And as soon as the conversation was over, he would dart off as usual, in an impatient race towards Via Bodoni, barely restrained by his mother's hand: as if in their absence, in Via Bodoni, the menace of a mysterious and inconceivable event might have come true.

At first, the teacher assured Ida her little boy would become more acclimated to the school in time; but instead his state of anxiety worsened. In the morning, actually, he went out with Ida, carefree, perhaps not recalling his daily trial, convinced he was going out for a stroll! But at the appearance of the school, Ida could feel his little hand tighten in a still-confused resistance, while his eyes sought in her some defense against the uncertain oppression that repelled him there. It was a torment, for her, to leave him alone like that. And he remained there, frowning, without rebelling, indeed waving her his usual goodbye, clenching and unclenching his little fist. However, less than a week after his first entrance in the kindergarten, the series of his escapes began.

At recreation period, in the yard, the slightest distraction of the teacher was enough for him to try to run off. The teacher was a girl of about thirty, who wore eyeglasses and long hair in a braid. She was very

serious and thorough about her job; she never took her eyes off her eighteen pupils, and during the time in the yard she counted them again and
again, careful to keep them around her like a hen. Then there was also the
presence of the concierge, always on guard in the entrance hall, which led
from the yard to the gate on the street. The teacher couldn't understand
how, with all this, Useppe managed to steal away, promptly seizing each
opportunity as if he had been waiting for nothing else. You turned around
for an instant, and he had vanished.

Most times, at least in the beginning, he didn't get far: he would be
found just outside the entrance, hidden under the stairs or behind a column. And when questioned, he never lied or attempted excuses, but said
right out with a bitter expression of panic: "I want to go 'way!" One
morning, however, he wasn't to be found; and after a long hunt, he was
brought back to the teacher by a charwoman who had discovered him
wandering around the corridors of another floor, seeking an unguarded
avenue towards the exit. For him, the school building, with all those closed
doors and those stairways and those floors, must have been an endless
labyrinth; but the day came when he found its thread. And Ida saw him
arrive in her classroom; in his little blue smock and his bow, he ran to her,
and clung to her, all trembling and crying. And he wanted to stay there
with her for the rest of the morning (distraught, she promptly sent word to
the teacher), continuing to tremble like a migrant swallow overtaken by
winter.

But his worst exploit came the following day. This time, despite the
vigilance of the doorman at the entrance, he somehow managed to get to
the street (it was perhaps the first time in his life that he ran the city's
streets alone), and he was brought back by the concierge of Via Bodoni.
She was a sixty-year-old widow, grandmother of many now-grown grandchildren, who at present lived alone in her lodge-apartment (consisting in
all of the porter's booth and an adjacent windowless hole with a bed for
sleeping). She had seen Useppe pass the lodge, alone and coatless, wearing
his school smock; her suspicions aroused, she had gone into the entrance to
call him. As a rule, Useppe always stopped with curiosity at the glass
window of the lodge, because in the cubbyhole inside, the old woman kept
a radio, a little stove "like Eppetondo" and a glass egg with the Madonna
of Lourdes on a snowy field (if you shook the egg, the snow rose in so
many white flakes). But today, he had gone past without stopping. He was
breathless, bewildered, and at the woman's insistence, he muttered he was
"going home" (though he didn't have the keys), adding a disjointed and
bewildering speech about "something" that was "catching him" and "not
the other children" . . . Meanwhile, he restlessly put his hands to his
head, as if that unnamed "thing" were inside it . . . "Have you got a

headache maybe?" "No, no ache . . ." "If it isn't an ache, what is it then? Troubles?" "No, no troubles . . ." Useppe continued shaking his head furiously, without explaining himself; gradually, however, after his great exertion, he was regaining his natural color: "You know what you have there, in your head?" The concierge then concluded: "I'll tell you! A bee in your bonnet! That's what!" And he, suddenly, forgetting his great haste, began to laugh at the old woman's funny idea: a bee in his bonnet. Then he meekly allowed her to take him back to school.

His escape had lasted less than a quarter of an hour; but in the meanwhile, already two men had been set off to seek him, while the teacher minded her other charges, still enjoying their recess in the yard. Every moment, she would look nervously towards the interior of the building, or beyond the entrance passage, at the gate on the street. And it was from this direction she saw the fugitive reappear, an old woman holding him by the hand and trying to distract him meanwhile with tales of bees and singing crickets.

Exasperated though she was, the teacher hadn't the heart to maltreat him (nor had anyone, really, since he was born, ever maltreated him). She received him fairly calmly, and with only a slightly hurt manner, she said to him, frowning:

"At it again! Now what have you done? You should be ashamed of yourself, setting such a bad example. That's enough now, however. From today on, the school is closed for you."

Useppe's reaction to her words was unexpected, almost tragic. Not answering, he turned pale in the face, as he looked at her with questioning eyes, all agitated by a strange fear: not of her, but rather (it seemed) of himself. "No! away! away!" he shouted then with a strange, altered little voice, as if he were chasing away shadows. And suddenly he burst into a scene no different, apparently, from a normal fit of temper: flinging himself on the ground, flushed with rage, inveighing and rolling around like a wrestler, kicking the air and hitting it with his fists. Usually, however, childish fits are meant to create a spectacle; while here you could sense a total isolation. You had the impression that this child, in his tininess, was really waging an immense fight against enemies present to him alone, and to no one else.

"Useppe! Useppe! Why are you acting like this? You're so nice and good! And all of us here love you . . ." Slowly Useppe calmed down at the teacher's blandishments, until he gave her a little consoled smile; and from that moment till the time class was dismissed he never let go of her skirt. At the gate, however, the teacher took Ida aside and informed her the child was *too nervous* and, at least for now, unsuited to school: so she couldn't assume responsibility for him any longer. Her advice was to leave him at home, in the care of some responsible person, until he reached school age, a year from now.

And Useppe the next morning didn't go to school. Contradicting himself, to the last moment, he followed Ida around the house and questioned her with eloquent eyes, in the uncertain hope he would go out with her, as on other mornings. But he asked no questions; he said nothing.

In the concierge's opinion, Useppe's case was simply that of an over-lively little boy, always eager to *get into trouble* without the school's realizing. But Ida didn't agree: she knew Useppe kept certain secrets to himself (as he had, for example, after that famous morning of his with the bandits), but they were, she thought, secrets of another order, who knows what. In any case, it seemed futile for her to question him (or, still more, to accuse him).

Lacking any resource, as she did, she could find no solution except to leave him alone in the house, closing the door and double-locking it. And entrusting an extra set of keys to the concierge, she begged her to go up and have a look at him at least once late every morning. In exchange for this service, Ida would give private lessons to a granddaughter of hers, who came and visited her almost every day.

So once more Useppe had to spend his mornings in prison, as at San Lorenzo in his infancy. Afraid that, looking out, he might fall, his mother took care even to lock the windows with some hooks at the top (where he couldn't reach, not even standing on a table). Luckily, winter was now coming, when there are fewer temptations to go outdoors or look out of windows.

With this new necessity, Ida also incurred various extra expenses. First of all, she applied for a telephone, which, however, because of "technical difficulties" could not be promised her before the period of February–March 1947. Also, recalling how much Useppe had enjoyed the music at Pietralata, to distract him in his loneliness, she bought him an almost new wind-up gramophone at the market. At first she had thought of a radio, but then she did without it, seized by the suspicion that, turning on the adult programs, he might learn nasty things from it.

She complemented the gramophone with a record, personally chosen from a series for children. It was one of those then in use, at 78 rpm. And it contained two children's ballads set to music, suitable for the family: "The Little Washer-Woman" and "My Dolly's the Prettiest of All." The latter, a kind of madrigal in honor of a doll, concluded her praises with the verses:

She looks exactly like our queen,
Out riding with the king.

The old concierge, lively though she was, found the climb to the top floor too toilsome, so she preferred to send up her granddaughter, who was often in Via Bodoni helping her. The girl's name was Maddalena, but she was called Lena-Lena by Useppe. Not infrequently, early in the morning, she could be encountered on the stairs, intent on giving the steps a hasty washing with a wet rag; or else she was seen sitting in the lodge, momentarily substituting for her grandmother. Keeping still in there was a sacrifice for her, however, since she preferred movement; and she didn't the least mind running up to Useppe's in the morning. She was a little girl of about fourteen, who was as a rule quite cloistered in the family; and she lived not far away, at San Saba, having arrived from the interior of Sardinia. She had a plump little figure, with short legs, also plump; and black hair, kinky and excessively long, which grew upwards, compensating for her very short stature, and making her look like a country hedgehog (or porcupine). She spoke an incomprehensible language, all full of *u*'s, which sounded foreign; still, with Useppe, she managed somehow to make herself understood. He would let her listen to his record, and in return she would sing to him, in a harsh, high voice, some Sardinian dirges, all with *u*, of which he understood not a word; but the moment she finished, he would say to her "again!", as he did after Ida's Calabrian songs.

On certain days, Lena-Lena, required to perform other duties, couldn't come; and the old concierge came in her place. After struggling up all those stairs, she had to go back down at once, so as not to leave her lodge abandoned. She preferred to turn up rather early in the morning, when Useppe was still asleep, and after having taken a look at him, she would leave again without waking him. It happened then that Useppe, on getting up, would wait in vain for some visit; and in these cases, during the morning, from the courtyard below, you could discern his form up there behind the panes, intently watching to see if Lena-Lena would finally appear from the courtyard. If he then continued hoping also for the arrival of *someone else*, we don't know. As a rule, when noon had struck, he could again be seen at his sentry-post, waiting for Ida.

Generally, on the days when she was free, Lena-Lena would go up to see him between ten and eleven, when he had just got up. For some time he had been waking later, because Ida, after an interval of many months, had resumed giving him in the evening the pills that the doctor had recommended to help him sleep. In fact, after the parenthesis of the good season, his nights were again uneasy; indeed, at present, among his nocturnal disturbances there was one in particular which defied even the medicine's effects. It was a short-lived but fairly violent convulsion which caught him, usually, when he had just dozed off: as if the undefined object of his anxiety were waiting for him just on the other side of the barrier of sleep. Even his features displayed the amazement, and the repulsion, of someone at a sudden, frightening encounter, during which he nevertheless went on sleeping, retaining no memory of it. And every evening, alert beside him, Ida kept watch over that sort of rendezvous, which awaited him, unknown to himself, with a fixed, mechanical punctuality.

The doctor, consulted again, prescribed a calcium cure for him: eggs, milk, and walks in the open air: "This boy," she observed, "isn't growing enough." And in fact, during the summer, Useppe had grown an inch or so in height, but his weight hadn't increased. To examine him, the doctor had made him undress, and in its nakedness his dark little body showed the bones of the sternum and the frail little shoulders, from which his tiny head nevertheless rose with that young male's special boldness which was naturally his. Among other things, the doctor asked him to show his teeth, thinking that his present nervous disorders might be the prelude, perhaps, to the loss of his baby teeth, which in certain cases, she said, provokes an actual crisis of growth. And he promptly opened his mouth wide, clean and pink like that of a month-old kitten, with the two tiny rows in which you could see the bluish gleam characteristic of baby teeth. Looking at them, Ida thought again of how good he had been, growing them all regularly, right in the midst of the war, without bothering anybody.

"When the first tooth falls out," the doctor said to him gravely, "remember to hide it somewhere in the house, for when Sora Pasquetta comes by. She's a relation of Santa Claus, and in the place of the tooth she'll leave you a present." For him, since he was born, there had never been Santa Clauses or Father Christmases or wizards or fairies or the like; but he had heard some rumor of their existence. "How will she get in?" he asked carefully. "In where?" "Where! In our house!" "Don't worry. She's like Santa Claus, she comes down the chimney!" "Eh . . . but our chimney's narrow . . . she'll get through, will she? She turns little?" "Of course!" the doctor confirmed, "she can shrink or grow, and get through any place she likes!" "Even a pipe like this?" (Useppe, with his fingers widened in a circle, demonstrated more or less the width of the flue in Via Bodoni). "Absolutely. You can count on it!" And Useppe smiled, reassured and triumphant at such an authoritative guarantee.

· · ·

The day that she drew her November salary, Ida went to buy him another record for his gramophone. Remembering his taste for dance tunes at Pietralata, she shyly consulted the salesman, who furnished her with a swing number, all the rage. And this novelty at first had a great success at home, where "The Little Washer-Woman" and "My Dolly" were immediately relegated to the rubbish. The gramophone from today on was used only for the new music; and as was to be expected, at the first notes Useppe promptly started dancing.

This new dance, however, was also to be considered a symptom of the course of those days. There were no longer the leaps, the somersaults, and the various improvisations with which our dancer performed at Pietralata among his friends. Now his body executed a single rotating movement, which he started with his arms wide, until a wild and almost spasmodic rhythm seemed to overcome him. In certain cases, he didn't stop this whirl until he had reached the point of blindness and dizziness; and then he sank back to rest against his mother, repeating, exhausted but blissful: "Everything's spinning, spinning, mà . . ." Or else, in other cases, without interrupting the wheel of his dance, he would slow its pace, at a certain point, and then his body, turning, would tilt to one side, with its two arms flung loosely to that same side, and his face would assume a funny expression between amusement and dream.

These sounds and dances took place in the kitchen—which was the only *living room* of the house—and more readily at the hour when Ida was cooking ("to keep her company"). But the new pastime's success was truly ephemeral. The third day (it was Sunday morning) Useppe, having energetically wound up the gramophone, about to put on the record, gave up the idea. He remained there, frozen, in an absorbed or puzzled air, and he made certain little movements with his jaw, like someone chewing a bitter morsel. As if looking for an escape route, he withdrew to the corner by the sink, and there, to one side, he emitted a confused stammering in which Ida, not without amazement, managed to distinguish clearly the name CARULINA. From the days of their farewell, when he still called her *Ulì*, Useppe had never mentioned her in his talk, and perhaps this was the first time, ever, that he pronounced her name fully and correctly (even rolling the R strongly, in his concern to say it right). This reminiscence, however, the moment it flared up, seemed to drop away from him. And in a different, shouting voice, he addressed Ida:

"Mà? Màaà? . . ."

It was a dazed question, but also a demand for help against some obscure aggression. Then a brusque impulse agitated him; and unexpectedly he went and tore his precious swing record from the gramophone and flung it on the ground. His face was flushed, and he was shaking; and when the record had broken on the floor, he even began to stamp on it with his feet. But rapidly, in this action, he released his amorphous wrath; and he looked on the ground again, with the dismay of someone discovering a crime committed by others. He crouched down by the shards of his record, and with tender, moaning tears, like a baby's crying, he tried to piece them together!

Ida was quick to promise him a new record for the very next day (had she been a millionairess, she was ready to buy an entire orchestra for him); but he thrust her aside, almost hitting her: "No! no! I don't want!" he shouted. Then, standing, in the same bitter act of refusal, he pushed away the wreckage with his feet; and as she was picking up the pieces and throwing them in the garbage, he put his fists to his eyes to see them no more.

His mother was gripped by the painful feeling that behind this eccentric disorder that slammed him aimlessly here and there, inside him some crucial knot was twisting, which no one could loosen, or find the ends of, and he least of all. Without peace, he had now gone to the window to peer down from his habitual sentry-post into the courtyard; and even from behind, looking at the dimple of his thin neck between his rumpled curls, you seemed to glimpse the worried expression on his face. That he was secretly cherishing his eternal expectation of his brother was, for Ida, beyond doubt (nor was it anything new, of course). But since, in his new morbid condition, he was silent about this disappointment, Ida avoided reminding him of it, as if it were taboo.

". . . Isn't Lena-Lena coming today?"

"No, no. Today's Sunday. I'm here at home. Aren't you glad?"

"Yes."

In one of his unpredictable changes of mood, he ran to her and kissed her dress. In his upraised, festive eyes, however, the next uneasy question was already appearing:

"You . . . you're not leaving, eh, mà?"

"Me! Leave? NEVER, NEVER, NEVER would I leave my Useppe!" The little man heaved a sigh, of satisfaction and of unresolved doubt. And his pupils were diverted, meanwhile, by the steam of the pot, which rose towards the flue:

"When's *she* coming?" he inquired, frowning.

"She? Who?" (Ida imagined he still meant Lena-Lena, or Carulina).

"That lady that comes down the chimney, mà! The one that's kin to Santa Claus! Didn't you hear the doctor lady?"

". . . ah, of course . . . But don't you remember what she said? You have to wait till your first new tooth comes in. When you feel one of these beginning to come loose, that's a sign it's about to fall out, and then that lady comes to take it."

Useppe touched his incisors with his finger, curious to see if by any chance they were loose. "Ah, it's early yet," his mother quickly explained to him, "you're not old enough. Maybe in a year."

". . . . ."

A ringing of bells was heard above them, announcing noon. The

Sunday morning was cloudy, but warm. Through the closed window, from the courtyard came the shouting of the kids of the building, roughhousing, waiting for their mothers to call them to dinner. Ida would have been pleased to recognize among the other voices also her Useppe's, as she used to in the days when they lived behind the curtain in the big room. And more than once she had tried sending him down into the courtyard, to play with the others. But always, peeping out of the window, a little later, she had seen him down there, in some corner of the wall, all alone to one side; and observed from above, he looked like a poor foundling, cast out from society. "Useppe!" she then called to him impulsively, flinging open the window. And raising his eyes towards her, he would come flying from the courtyard, to run up to her at home. As before with his schoolmates, so now, it was he really who segregated himself from the others (and with some of his gestures, putting his hands forward as if to thrust them away, or drawing back, looking at them with wide, bitter eyes, he actually suggested the image of an elementary being who, sensing some virulent germ in his blood, wants to protect the others from contagion).

After the doctor's advice to keep him in the open air, on fine days now Ida always took him for a walk, either towards Monte Testaccio or towards the Aventine or else, not wanting to overtire him, to some little park near the house. And again, wherever he was, Useppe kept far away from the other kids and their games. If one of them said to him: "You want to play too?" he would run off with no explanation, taking refuge by his mother, like a savage inside his hut.

And yet, from certain glances of his, you wouldn't say he was a misanthrope. And while he avoided companionship, from time to time he flashed in the others' direction an instinctive little smile, which involuntarily offered and sought friendship. Below his short pants, his knees stuck out, thicker than they should have been, compared to the thinness of his legs; but with those little legs he made great athletic leaps, by himself, which showed how good he was. There was something humorous in his person which caused people to smile, making him quite popular with that little audience of the parks. The women and girls complimented him on the contrast between his blue eyes and his dark skin and black hair, which in Rome is considered a beauty of the first rank; attributing to him, however, a maximum age of three or four; when hearing he was over five, they commented in chorus on his small size, until Ida, tormented and scared, came to shelter him from their indiscreet remarks.

But to these, actually, as to their praise, Useppe remained completely alien and indifferent, like a caged puppy at a fair. Perhaps, for that matter, he didn't even hear them; and, in fact, even if he was quiet, his two protruding ears, sticking from beneath the sides of his cap, were always alert to the world's various sounds, which at some moments overwhelmed him in a sole, feverish anthem. Every slightest event distracted his gaze; or else he remained calm, with pensive eyes, as if his mind were straying. But not infrequently a special rejoicing made all his muscles quiver, kindling in his eyes a precipitous merriment, mingled with nostalgia . . . It was when he saw a dog: of whatever class, purebred or stray, and even if it was ugly, deformed, or mangy.

Though, to tell the truth, she was ill-disposed to the idea of increasing the family, Ida couldn't resist this sight; and one fine day, returning from a walk, she finally asked him if he didn't want a little dog all his own. But Useppe turned to her, his face torn with bitterness, shaking his head no, no, with furious insistence. His refusal seemed irrevocable, but painful; as if it involved that mysterious, crucial knot which for weeks now had tormented him inexplicably. In the end, in a kind of breathless cry, resembling a sob, the words came out:

"Bella too . . . like *Biz!*"

And this allowed Ida to understand how her little boy was denying himself even a promised treasure, for terror of losing it! She was deeply shocked at this, with the strange sensation, felt today for the first time, of a physical presence: as if an Ogre had installed himself in their room, to threaten Useppe with many mouths and many hands. But it was still odder for her to hear again from Useppe, after years of silence, the name of that Blitz whom she believed erased from his memory, as happens with the various heroes of infantile prehistory, who remain outside of time. It truly seemed that in this autumn of '46 all the memories of his tiny life were pursuing the forgetful Useppe, scenting the concealed point of his illness. "What do you mean, Bella like Blitz?!" Ida teased him. And without hesitating this time to break the taboo, she assured him Bella was safe and sound, in the company of Ninnuzzu, and they would soon show up again at home, as they always did! At this news, guaranteed by Iduzza, Useppe laughed, reassured. And the two, laughing together like lovers, for the moment drove the Ogre from the room.

But it wasn't enough. To compensate Useppe for the rejected dog, the next morning (Sunday) Ida took him to the new Porta Portese market, where she bought him a duffle coat, known in Rome as a *mongòmeri*: that is to say a special coat (for those who don't know) then made fashionable by General Montgomery, who wore it in battle. Useppe's was an Italian imitation, Roman in fact; and though of the smallest size, it was a bit big for him in the shoulders and the sleeves were long. However, he was immediately eager to put it on, and he promptly assumed a bold stride, as if inside that mongòmeri he felt like a tough guy, not to say a General.

7 His nights, meanwhile, were troubled and restless. After the last visit to the doctor, he obediently took all the prescribed medicines; indeed, when he received them from his mother, he thrust his mouth up like a little bird, as if greedy to be cured. But their effectiveness, for him, remained slight. Almost every evening, despite the sedatives, that usual ambush was punctually awaiting him, to threaten his first sleep with who knows what gigantic shapes. In the second week of November, for two nights in a row, he jumped straight up in bed, sound asleep, breathing fast, his eyes wide but unawake, not even reacting when the central bulb was turned on. Settling him back and covering him again, Ida could feel his limbs stiffened (as if still tensed for an unequal combat) and all sweating; and taking his hand, she perceived the furious beating of his pulse, which then slowly subsided to its natural rhythm, as his eyelids closed once more. The episode had lasted less than a minute, and as always, escaped his consciousness. But, on the contrary, the night between November fifteenth and sixteenth was marked by a lucid episode. Half-awake, in the heart of the night, Ida had turned on the lamp at the head of the bed, hearing in the room a soft shuffling movement, no louder than the little paws of a wandering animal. And, in fact, Useppe was there, standing, awake, leaning against the wall at this moment. Over his cotton flannel pajamas he had put on his mongòmeri, because it was cold in the room; he had left his feet bare, however, perhaps out of concern not to make any noise while his mother was asleep. The same restlessness which had always disturbed his sleep lately must tonight have dragged him from the bed, shadowing him in his little wakeful excursion inside the room walled by darkness. He looked fiercely at Ida and said to her: "Sleep, mà!" It was an order; however, this peremptory tone of his actually served him as a weapon aimed against the vague suspicion that peopled his body with anxieties, never formulated into a thought. Suddenly, he came out with a faint, tortured weeping:

"Mà, where's Nino gone?!"

And then, as if abruptly yielding to a horrible siren, who had been luring him who knows how long with her fears, he went on:

"He hasn't gone to America, has he? Without me?! . . ."

It wasn't hard for Ida to connect this question with the promise that, in her presence too, Ninnuzzu had actually repeated more than once to Useppe: to take him to America. (Indeed, the last time, he had added: "And we'll take Davide along, too. Maybe, over there, he'll find himself a beautiful Jew girl . . .") Nor was it hard for her to find, on this score, indisputable arguments to reassure Useppe. Consoled, a little later, he fell asleep again beside her.

After his brief greeting in September, Ninnuzzu, in his usual fashion, had sent no news home. Instead, two postcards had arrived, addressed to him, from which it was clear that, as his own address, he gave his acquaintances that of Via Bodoni. One, on glossy cardboard, of a bunch of pansies and red roses, was from Antonio, Bella's former owner, and it bore the rubber stamp of the Poggioreale censor. On it was written: *Sincere best wishes and warmest greetings.* And the other, sent from Rome, with the Victor Emmanuel monument in black and white, said, in a big, second-grade hand, but without errors: *Where are you off to? Can't you at least let me know that?* —*P.* Both had lain in the house since October.

Towards the end of that same month of October, one morning in the street Ida had encountered Annita Marrocco, who at present, to help the family, was in service with some well-to-do people on the Via Ostiense. In fact, Filomena's dressmaking brought in less and less (her customers, mostly old women, were either going into the hospital or dying on her), and Giovannino's little room was left unrented, always in the hope of its owner's return. Still there was no news of him, good or bad: even a chaplain had taken an interest in the case, and a medical officer, and now the family was awaiting a reply from another veteran in Northern Italy, an Alpine soldier from the Julia Division, whom they had written to ask if by any chance he, or some acquaintance of his, on the fields of Russia, had encountered or had heard mentioned a Marrocco.

Among the other bits of news, Annita reported that her mother-in-law one of those days had met Davide Segre, who, questioned by the old woman, had answered that he had seen our Nino here in Rome even recently, and more than once, but always in transit. Nino's health was fine, and that was all Annita knew. Of the suburban house he had rented (or been lent) near Rome, which he himself had mentioned to Ida, neither Annita nor her mother-in-law could say anything. Perhaps, Ida thought, this house was a fib of Nino's, or perhaps by now he had already changed address. For that matter, Annita said, Davide as usual had answered Filomena's questions roughly, in a few words, anxious to get away. Whether he himself was now living in Rome, and where, naturally he hadn't said. Old Filomena, whom Ida then ran into at the Piazza Testaccio market, confirmed her daughter-in-law's news, but had nothing to add. Every time they met her, the Morroccos invited Ida to visit them with the kid at Via Mastro Giorgio. But Ida, after a couple of visits at the beginning, whether out of neglect or timidity, never went there again.

In reality, except for her pupils and Useppe, Ida saw no one in the world. At times, she thought of going to Remo, to ask for further news of Ninnuzzo, but the idea of returning to the San Lorenzo quarter aroused such a strong repugnance that she gave it up.

For that matter, not even two months had gone by since Nino's last appearance. He had accustomed her to far longer absences and total silences, in all these years. The fact that Useppe, this time, suffered more than usual in the waiting for his brother was, in Ida's eyes, another manifest sign of his abnormal state of health, like his *naughtiness*, loneliness, and unreasonable rages, in which our real Useppe was hardly recognizable any more.

And yet, Ida never even thought of hunting for Ninnarieddu to ask him to make more frequent visits for his little brother's sake. To expect such an exertion from Ninnuzzu Mancuso would be like insisting the wind blow a bit more in this direction, or a bit more in that, to please a flag. Slow as she was, even Ida, with her slight experience, was able to understand this.

On the morning of November sixteenth, Useppe had the first serious attack of the disease that was undermining him. After his brief reassuring dialogue with his mother (it was about one-thirty), the child fell back to sleep and slept calmly the rest of the night. And he was still sleeping early in the morning when Ida got up and went into the kitchen to make coffee. It was there, as she was lighting the stove, that she unexpectedly saw him appear before her, in his little flannel pajamas, barefoot, with a dazed expression; he gave her a brief interrogative glance (or so it seemed to her) then he immediately ran off again. And she was about to call him back when, from the bedroom, she heard a scream of horror and unheard-of devastation, which resembled no human voice: it paralyzed her for a few instants, as she wondered where that voice came from.

In medical manuals, these typical attacks, known by the name of *grand mal*, are described, more or less, like this:

Violent convulsive fit with total loss of consciousness. At the beginning of the first phase (tonic-clonic) the arrest of respiration causes a loud cry, while the body falls to the ground without any attempt at protecting itself, and the skin takes on a cyanotic color. There is a strong increase in arterial pressure and an acceleration of the cardiac rhythm to the point of paroxysm. The tongue may be bitten in consequence of the stiffening of the muscles of the jaw.

In the clonic, or tumultuous phase, there are violent jerking spasms, followed by coma, which can last from one to three minutes, with interruption of cortical activity and total motor inertia. During this phase control of the rectum and bladder may be lost, resulting in faecal and urinary incontinence. During the attack, the resumption of respiratory activity is labored and stertorous, accompanied by intense salivation.

A syndrome known from the most ancient times. The causes, and the physiopathology, are still unknown.

When Ida came running into the room, Useppe was lying supine on the floor, his eyes closed and his arms wide, like a swallow struck down by lightning in flight. The initial phase of his attack, which had lasted only a few seconds, was already past, however, and when Ida knelt beside him, the ugly color of death was already fading from his face, as he resumed breathing. Grateful that the screaming, passing stranger, heard a moment before, hadn't stolen him from the house and made him vanish, she called him in a low voice. And Useppe, as if calmed by the murmuring of his own name, heaved a great sigh and his whole body relaxed. His features, too, reposed in his unharmed little face; and they formed, while his eyes were still shut, an enchanted smile of healing; then, serenely, like a miracle, the eyes opened, more beautiful than yesterday, as if dipped in a sky-blue bath. "Useppe!" ". . . mà . . ."

Having stretched him out on the bed again, Ida wiped a little blood-flecked foam from the corner of his lips; and letting her do it, he dreamily touched his damp hair: "What happened to me, mà?" But already this question came from him confused in a yawn, and his eyelids lowered again almost abruptly. His first, great desire was to sleep.

He slept almost the whole day, but towards noon, he woke for a brief interval. He neither remembered nor knew anything of his own attack (these attacks—the doctors were to explain to Ida—*are not experienced by the subject*), however, he must have sensed somehow that he had undergone an offense, of which he was ashamed. He huddled up across the *sommier*. And first of all, hiding his face in the pillow, he urged her: "When he comes back, mà, don't tell Nino . . ."

Ida reassured him, shaking her head, promising to keep the secret: still all unaware that Useppe's insistence was already futile. Now there would be no more time to talk to his brother. A few hours later, in fact (barely another day and a scant night), an incredible thing was to happen: so incredible that even today, from this distance which makes the living and the dead equal, I continue to suspect it of being a fraud. But, instead, it happened. Like so many of his companions of the "violent generation," Ninnuzzu Mancuso–Ace of Hearts was also suddenly, roughly flung aside by life. In May of the following year he would have been twenty-one.

· · ·

Although she had been inclined since birth to believe in premonitions, Ida this time had had none. And so when a policeman turned up at the house early in the morning, and asked her: "Are you related to Mancuso Antonino?" her first question was: "Why? Has he done anything wrong?" She immediately realized the policeman's embarrassment. "I'm his mother . . ." she declared, stammering. But already the man's considerate information was coming to her from beyond an abnormal, hollow clamor. It was a road crash (actually, the man said *accident*) on the Via Appia. A truck had run off the road. "Your son was wounded . . . badly." They had taken him to the emergency station at San Giovanni.

From Via Bodoni to reach the San Giovanni hospital you have to cross half the city. Iduzza must have had to go to the tram stop, board the tram, buy a ticket, get off at the other stop, make inquiries; and someone must have had to direct her to the place. But of all this journey, her consciousness recorded nothing, marking only the point of arrival, like a torn picture. It is a whitewashed room: Ida knows this, because curiously, on first entering she seemed to taste that dusty lime, as if it were in her mouth. Whether it is an isolated room or a passage, with windows or without, this she can't tell: just as the presence of people accompanying her to the hospital is confused. In front of her are two stretchers, with the shapes of two bodies, entirely covered by sheets. A hand has raised the first sheet. It's not he: a bloodstained head of a young man with blondish hair, left with half a face, the other half disfigured. They have raised the second sheet, and this one is Nino, visible to the neck. No wound can be seen on him, only a line of blood beneath his nose. And perhaps because of an effect of the light, he doesn't even seem very pale. His unmarked cheeks and his curls are spattered here and there with mud. His upper lip protrudes, parted, his eyelids with their long curving lashes do not seem naturally lowered, but as if crushed over his eyes in a kind of bitter subjugation. The last expression which has remained on his face is an animal, hesitant ingenuousness, which seems to be asking, filled with amazement: "What's happening to me?! I feel something I've never felt before. Something strange, I don't understand."

On recognizing him, Ida immediately had a fierce lacerating sensation in the vagina, as if they were tearing him again from there. Unlike Useppe's, Nino's birth had been terrible for her, after a long and difficult labor, which had almost drained her of blood. At birth, the baby weighed almost seven pounds, too big for a tiny little mother bearing her first child, and they had had to rip him by force from her body. But then the little mother had let out such savage cries that she seemed a great, massive beast, according to what her husband Alfio told her afterwards, teasing her; whereas today, on the contrary, no sound could emerge from Ida's throat, as if they had poured concrete over her.

Here, after the scene in the morgue, is the second half-conscious sensation that was to remain with her from that morning: she couldn't scream, she had become mute, and she was walking along certain unrecognizable streets, where the light was a blinding zenith, giving all objects an obscene prominence. The photographs displayed at the kiosks laughed obscenely, the crowd was writhing, and the numerous statues on top of the basilica swooped down in monstrous attitudes. Those statues were the same she had seen in the days after Useppe's birth, from the midwife Ezekiel's windows; today, however, the basilica was distorted, and so were all the other houses and buildings around, as if in convex mirrors. The streets were twisted and stretched out in every direction, to an excessive degree, against nature. And so her own house, too, was shifted away: however, she had to run there urgently, because she had left Useppe alone, not yet awake.

Where was she now? *Porta Metronia* must have been the name of this place. Ida, Ida, where are you going? You've taken the wrong direction. The fact is that these villages are made of plaster, all plaster, which can crack and collapse any moment. She herself is a piece of plaster, and risks crumbling into fragments and being swept away before she reaches home. In any case, no telling how, she has made it. She has reached Via Bodoni, climbed to the door. She is inside the house. Here, at last, for a while anyway, she can fling herself down, let herself fall into dust.

Useppe had got up and had also dressed, by himself. Ida heard perhaps his voice asking her: "What you doing, mà? sleeping?" and her own voice answering: "Yes, I'm a bit sleepy. I'll get up soon," as her body was breaking into dust and rubble, like a wall. From her childhood, perhaps heard from her mother's lips, the words *wailing wall* returned to her. She didn't know, in reality, what this *wailing wall* was exactly, but the name echoed to her in the room, even if she could neither wail nor weep. Not only her own body, but the walls themselves rustled and hissed, turning to dust. But she still hadn't lost consciousness, because, in that enormous downpour of dust, she heard a constant tick tick tick. It was Useppe's little shoes. The whole time he did nothing but walk, never stopping, back and forth through the rooms of the house. Tick tick tick tick. He walked up and down, for miles, in his little boots.

Later, when the papers had come out, the doorbell started ringing. Besides the concierge and her granddaughter, Filomena and Annita Marrocco came, the teacher from the nursery school, the old colleague, Giovannino's former teacher, Clemente's sister Consolata. Ida answered the door to all of them, her face stiff and white as a plaster cast, to whisper: "You mustn't talk about it in front of the baby. He mustn't know anything." So the silenced visitors stood in the kitchen around Ida, huddled on a chair by the stove. Every now and then Useppe would peer in, wearing his mongòmeri, because the house was cold; he looked like a domestic dwarf. He would peep in and then withdraw. The Marrocco women suggested taking him out, to distract him a little, but Ida wouldn't have it. In reality, after the attack two days before, she was secretly afraid he might have another, in the presence of outsiders; and that people, in consequence, might begin treating him like an invalid or a backward child.

Towards evening, a telegram of condolence arrived from the headmistress of the school. There were no relatives to inform. After the death of her grandparents in Calabria, Ida had had no further communication with her uncles and cousins left down there. Practically speaking, she had no relations or friends in the world.

Annita and Consolata helped her through the necessary formalities, assisted by Remo the tavernkeeper, who lent the money for the funeral and also provided a wreath of red carnations with a ribbon saying: *from his comrades*. Ida lacked the strength to do anything. She was called to Police Headquarters to be asked some questions, but the Inspector, seeing her, felt pity and let her go without insisting. For that matter, it was clear she knew even less than the Inspector himself did about her own son.

She didn't want to know any details of the accident. If someone mentioned it, she would stammer: "No, not yet. Don't tell me anything, not now." It seemed there were three of them, on the truck. One, the driver, was already dead when help arrived. Nino had died at the door of the hospital. The third, wounded in the abdomen, his legs shattered, was lying in a ward at San Giovanni, under police guard.

There was, in fact, something shady about the episode, from what Ida herself could make out from her dazed conversation at Headquarters. It seems the truck was suspect, because of a stolen license plate, and under a load of wood, it was actually transporting illegal merchandise, with, moreover, some unauthorized concealed weapons, of the kind formerly issued to the German army. There were still some cases (as the Inspector had to explain to Ida) of ex-partisans, plotting vague future acts of subversion or pseudo-revolution, which, for the present, really came down to penal illicit activities in the world of smuggling or acts of minor banditry . . . All this was at present under investigation. The only survivor of the three, before losing consciousness, had had time to scrawl the names and addresses of the other two on a piece of paper. Already half delirious, he had also insistently asked for news of a dog which, it seems, was with them on the truck; but they knew nothing of this famous dog's fate.

The accident had taken place shortly before dawn. Apparently the highway police had first signaled the truck to stop, but instead of stopping, the driver had pressed on the accelerator, swerving into a side road, no one could say with what precise intention. Then the chase had immediately begun, and the occupants of the truck (so the policemen testified) had reacted by firing some shots from the cab. For their part, the police had returned the fire, but only to intimidate, aiming at the tires (on the scene they later found some cartridge-cases whose exact origin was still being debated). And in the course of the brief shooting, perhaps because of a miscalculation of the driver's, or perhaps because the road was slippery (it had rained during the night), at the first curve, the truck had run off the road, plunging down an embankment beside it. It was still dark.

Three days later the survivor of the trio, a mechanic by profession, also died, after a long, uninterrupted delirium. In his condition, they had been able to extract no information from him about his own activity or that of his companions and their possible accomplices, and even the further investigation (which confirmed the police version of the event) achieved nothing on this score. Among those questioned were also Proietti Remo, owner of a tavern in the Tiburtino quarter, member of the Communist Party since underground days; and Segre Davide, student, Jew: both former members of the same partisan group to which Mancuso had belonged. But both proved unconnected with the events. In the end, the case was filed away.

8 The mother hadn't gone to the funeral; and even afterwards, she could never find the strength to go to Verano, where Ninnarieddu had been laid, a short distance from the old house of San Lorenzo, where he had grown up. Her legs buckled at the very idea of seeking him out inside that ugly wall which, in childhood, he had run past so often, playing, as if it were an odd frontier that didn't concern him. Now, the red carnation wreath of the *Comrades* had dried up over that little hole, unvisited by his mother. And the little bunches of cheap fresh flowers, which every now and then appeared to decorate it, were not brought there by her.

She hadn't even wept. In front of Useppe, in fact, she had to make an effort of concealment; and with outsiders, a suspicion restrained her. She had the sensation that if she merely uttered a moan, after it, like the breaking of a dike, irrepressible screams would burst out, and screaming, she would go mad. Then people would lock her up, and the poor little bastard Useppe would be left with no one.

She yelled only in dreams. When she managed to doze off, she heard terrible cries, which were her own. But these cries resounded only in her brain. Inside the house, all was silence.

Her sleep was more of a drowsiness, fragile, often interrupted. And it happened that, stirring in the night, she would find Useppe awake, with a look as if he were questioning her, his eyes open. Still, he never asked her anything: nor did he seek news of Nino any more.

During the last years, Ida had become spellbound in the magic faith that her son Ninnuzzu was invulnerable. And now, it was hard for her suddenly to convince herself that the earth was living without Ninnuzzu. His death, for him so rapid, on the contrary was long for Ida, who began to feel it grow after the hour of his burial, at which she had not been present. From that moment, it was as if he had been divided into so many doubles of himself, each of which tortured her in a different way.

The first was still that merry and impudent Ninnarieddu seen the last time at Via Bodoni as he was dashing out of the courtyard with Bella. He, for Ida, was still running about the earth. Indeed, she told herself that, walking and walking along the whole terrestrial curve, and across all frontiers, perhaps she would end up by encountering him. For this reason, at certain hours, like a pilgrim abandoning himself to the great unknown, she would set forth looking for him. Every time she went out, she always found again that terrible staring, fixed noon light, those unreal dimensions, and those distorted and indecent shapes that, to her, constituted the city since the morning of the "identification" at San Giovanni. For some months now, because of her failing sight, she had had to wear glasses, and on going out, she slipped over their lenses a second pair of dark glasses, to blind herself, at least partially, against that dazzling sight. And so, in another false, eclipselike light, she hopelessly pursued her fugitive. At times she thought she recognized him in some mischievous little child who laughed and waved from the doorway, or in another, astride a motorbike, one foot on the ground, or in another who rapidly turned a corner, curly-haired, in a windbreaker . . . And she hurried breathlessly after them, knowing in advance she was chasing a mirage.

In this way she went on until she was rapt in weariness, and lost all notion of facts, names, even her own identity. She no longer remembered being Ida, or her own address; and for a while she would shift uncertainly from one wall to another, through the passage of the crowd and the vehicles, with no information, as if she had happened into a world of masquers. The first signal of awareness came to her from two little blue eyes, which glowed at her from the depth of her morbid haze like a pair of little lamps, promptly summoning her home, where she had left Useppe by himself.

Though the autumn season was mild, Useppe lived like a recluse those days, because Ida hadn't yet found the courage to take him to the park or towards the country. Even more than by the city, she was repelled by nature, because in trees and plants she saw an abnormal growth of tropical monsters, nourished on Nino's body. Here it was no longer that same Ninnuzzu who was still running about the world, making her pursue him with no trail; but the just-buried Nino, imprisoned under the earth, confined, in darkness. This other Nino appeared to her as if he had become a little baby again, crying and clinging to her, asking her for nourishment and company; and among Ninnuzzu's various doubles, this was the only one that belonged to her as part of her flesh, however, at the same time, untouchable, lost in a dizzying impossibility. His wretched den in San Lorenzo had become a point farther than the Poles and the Indies, unattainable by ordinary routes. At times, Ida fantasticated of joining him through trenches and subterranean canals; at times she flung herself all fours on the earth, listening infinitely, to hear his heart beat.

But there was still one Nino worse than all the others: since Ida, of this one, was afraid. He presented himself to her just as he had been the day she saw him on the stretcher, for the identification at San Giovanni: his curls and face stained with mud, and a line of blood from his nose, as if he had come home from a fistfight after a normal wicked evening spent out of the house. His lids seemed lowered as if he weren't even aware of her; but, instead, beneath the long lashes, his pupils peered at her with hatred. And with his mouth half-closed in a grimace of hatred, he said to her:

"Go away from me. It's your fault. Why did you make me be born?!"

Ida knew that this Nino, like the others, now existed only in her deranged mind. And yet, she feared his persecution so much that, especially at night, she trembled thinking she would see him assume a shape, she would find him waiting behind a door, or in some corner of the house, to reproach her: "Why did you give birth to me? You're the guilty one." Then, she took fright like a murderess at crossing the dark corridor, or even lying in bed with the light off. She had covered the lamp at the head of the bed with a rag, so as not to disturb Useppe's sleep, and she turned it till its light was full on her face, often lying this way till morning. It was a kind of third degree, really, that she unconsciously imposed on herself, to make Nino forgive her; and in which, like an informer against herself, she did nothing but denounce herself, instead of attempting a defense. It was she who had killed Ninnuzzu; and now, one by one, she dug up the countless proofs of her own crime: from his first breath and the milk she had given him to the final wickedness: not having prevented him, with whatever means (perhaps with the intervention of the law) from going off to die . . . Suddenly, the defendant Ida turned prosecutor; and she blamed Ninnarieddu, calling him gangster and criminal, as she had in the days when they lived together. This comforted her for a moment, as if he were really there to hear her; but immediately, with a shudder, the knowledge returned that he no longer lived in any place.

During the day, because of the weariness after her sleepless vigils, every now and then she would doze off. And in her drowsing she would still hear Useppe's incessant little steps, in his winter boots:

tick tick tick tick

"It's your fault, mà. It's your fault. It's your fault."

Ida's daily conflicts with Ninnuzzu's various doubles stopped, however, after the first weeks; until, gradually, those different doubles were fused into a single, poor creature. This final Ninnuzzu was no longer alive, but he wasn't yet dead; and he ran raving on the earth, with no place where he could stay any more. He wanted to suck the air, the oxygen of the plants, but he had no lungs to breathe with. He wanted to chase girls, call his friends, dogs, cats, but he couldn't make anyone see or hear him. He wanted to put on that beautiful, American-style shirt displayed in the shop-window, take that car and go for a spin, bite into that sandwich, but he had no body, and neither hands nor feet. He was no longer alive, but he continued, reduced to the most atrocious prison misery: the desire to live. In this impossible form, Ida felt him constantly moving around in the air, trying desperately to cling to any object at all, even the garbage can, if only to link himself once more with the earth of the living. Then Ida longed to see him even for an instant, barely the time to say to him: "Ninnuzzu!" and to hear him answer: "Aw, mà," even if only through an hallucination. She began to shift back and forth in the kitchen, calling (in a low voice so that Useppe wouldn't hear her in the bedroom): "Where are you, Ninnarieddu?" and she would bump into the walls. She felt with an irreparable physical certitude that he existed, not only here but anywhere around, always writhing, nailed to his own desire to live, worse than a cross, and envying even the least insect, or the existence of a thread that can enter the eye of a needle. Now without any further desire to accuse her saying "it's your fault!", this Nino was reduced to the single cry: "help me, mà."

Iduzza had never believed in the supernatural existence of any god; indeed, it never occurred to her to think of God, still less to pray to him. And this was the first and I believe the only prayer that escaped her lips during her whole lifetime, one of those afternoons, late, in the kitchen in Via Bondoni:

"God! give him rest if nothing else. At least let him finish dying."

.   .   .

The weather continued undecided, and always variable, more like March than November. And Ida, every morning, feared the reappearance of the sun, which poured out in the air the horrible shamelessness of the objects and the living, caring nothing for Ninnarieddu's impossible absence. She felt a bit alleviated, as if by a medicine, when rising from the night, she saw above the city a leaden sky, overcast to the horizon, without even a strip of light.

It was on one of these rainy mornings of true autumn (perhaps four or five days had passed since the funeral, and Ida still hadn't resumed her work at the school) when, towards eleven, someone was heard scratching at the front door of the house. Useppe started, alert to that little, still-uncertain sound, as if he had been unconsciously awaiting it, and he ran towards the entrance without a word, his mouth trembling and pale. His little steps were answered, from beyond the door, by a whimper. The door had barely begun to move on its hinges, when a thrust, from outside, pushed it wide. And immediately Useppe found himself struck by the full force of an embrace of canine paws, which swung around him in a crazed dance, while a rasping tongue washed his whole face.

If Bella had been transformed, let's say, into a black bear, or even into a prehistoric or mythical animal, he would have recognized her all the same. However, besides him, perhaps no one else would have been able today to recognize in this filthy stray the luxuriant shepherd dog of before. From a well-fed and carefully washed lady, in a few days she had become reduced in appearance to the lowest social level of the mongrel. Thin, her bones sticking out, her beautiful coat all a scab of mud and filth (so that her regal tail seemed a length of black string), she was almost frightening, worse than a witch. And only in her eyes, though veiled with mourning, fatigue, and hunger, could you still recognize immediately her clean and snow-white soul. It was clear that, despite exhaustion, she had recovered at this moment all her girlish energy again to hail the rediscovery of Useppe; nor will we ever learn what and how many trials she underwent before returning to her one, last family. Had she perhaps witnessed the disaster of the truck? Escaping, thanks to her instinct, the treacherous hands of the guards and the stretcher-bearers, had she followed the ambulance, galloping invisibly to San Giovanni, to wander then outside those walls, untouchable as a pariah, to accompany the hearse of her Ninnuzzu? Had she perhaps, afterwards, remained lying on his grave, keeping watch, like a statue? Or perhaps, like Ida, had she set out to hunt for him in the streets of Rome or even perhaps of Naples or who knows where, following the scent he had left in his movements, still vivid and fresh on the earth? No one will ever be able to say. The story of this evasion of hers remained always her own secret, about which Useppe himself never questioned her, not even later. Meanwhile, there in the entrance, in a little voice tinged with panic, he only repeated to her: "Bella . . . Bella . . ." and nothing else, while she was making a love-speech which to uncouth ears would sound merely like: "Grui grruii hump hump hump" but whose translation (superfluous for Useppe) would be: "Now you're all I have left in the world. And no one will ever be able to part us."

So, starting today, there were three of them in the house in Via

Bodoni; and starting that same day, Useppe had two mothers. Bella, in fact—unlike Blitz—from the first meeting, had felt for Useppe a love different from her love of Nino. With the big Nino, she behaved like a slave companion; and with the little Useppe, on the contrary, like a protectress and a guard. Now the arrival of his new mother Bella was a stroke of luck for Useppe; since at present his mother Iduzza not only was old (some strangers, seeing her with him, assumed she was his grandmother) but also strange in her behavior, and childish.

After a brief period of absence, she had resumed her daily lessons. And her little pupils, informed that the poor lady, in the meanwhile, had lost a son, at first displayed, in their way, a certain respectful sympathy. Some of them came and put on her desk, as a present, some bunches of flowers (which she avoided even touching, and looked at them with wide frightened eyes, as if she saw leeches). And, if not all, at least the majority tried to maintain a polite, calm deportment in class. But you can't demand the impossible of about forty wretched first-grade convicts, who, among other things, had known their teacher less than two months. The winter of '46 marked an irreparable decline in Ida's professional quality.

Till now, even through the various vicissitudes of the times, she had always remained a good teacher. Obviously her teaching had never been a model of progressive methods! On the contrary, she knew how to do nothing except transmit to her elementary pupils those ordinary notions that to her, as an elementary pupil, had been passed on by her teachers, who in turn had received them from their teachers, etc. On occasion, obeying the dictates of the Authorities, she introduced into their themes and dictation the Kings, Duces, Fatherland, glory, battles that History imposed; however, she did it in all mental innocence, unsuspecting, because History, no more than God, had never been an object of her thoughts. I say she was a good teacher, only to say that children were her sole predestined vocation (in fact, she herself, as has already been reported and repeated, had never managed to grow up completely). Even her respect for Authority was the kind found in children, and not that privately conceived by those Authorities themselves. From this she even developed, in the minimal territory of her classroom, and only there, a certain natural authority of her own: perhaps also because the children felt they were protecting her against the enormous outside Fears they themselves shared with her. And they respected her the way children respect anyone who entrusts himself to their protection, even if only a donkey. This spontaneous relationship, not desired or reasoned out, had been maintained virtually intact for almost a quarter-century of Iduzza's existence, surviving the loss of Alfio her husband, and of her father and her mother, and racism, war's destruction, famines, and slaughters. It was a kind of miraculous little calyx that reopened each morning at the top of her bodily stem, even if the stem swayed, roughly treated by arctic winds. But in that winter of 1946, her flowering, which seemed perpetual, was exhausted.

The deterioration had begun, really, at the beginning of autumn, with Useppe's exile from the school. Although Useppe himself had wanted the exile (through that instinct that drives wounded animals to hide), Ida, at that blow, perhaps without being aware of it, had felt carnally offended by the entire world of other people: as if they had flung Useppe into the lowest zone of outcasts. And in this zone, she herself chose to remain with him definitively: her real place was there. Perhaps she didn't even realize this choice of hers, but by now the final childhood on earth for her meant Useppe. And then the only others in whom she had found comprehension (children), they too, like the whole adult world, began to frighten her. The Iduzza Mancuso who returned to her little illiterate pupils after the period of mourning no longer seemed a teacher. She resembled a poor novice slave-laborer who arrives at the factory of the older laborers, dazed by the long march across Siberia.

After the first sleepless nights, now, in the evening, she was overcome by a somnolence that made her doze on her feet. And such was her furious longing to trace Ninnuzzu that she hoped, at least, to meet him in a dream. But in her dreams, Ninnuzzu never showed up; indeed, most of the time, all living forms were excluded from them. Before her, for example, there opens an endless sandy plain, perhaps an ancient buried kingdom of Egypt or of the Indies, with no sign of a horizon, all planted to infinity with perpendicular stone slabs, bearing indecipherable exotic inscriptions. It seems those inscriptions explain something important (or fundamental) for anyone who can read. But the only person present is she herself, who cannot read.

Then another infinity presents itself to her, a dirty, barely ruffled ocean where innumerable shapeless things are floating; things that may have been clothes, sacks, crockery, or other normal objects, but all now are limp, colorless, unrecognizable. Of organic forms, even dead, she sees no trace; but strangely, these materials, though inanimate, express death more clearly than if there were bodily remains in their place. Here, too, there is no sign of a horizon. And over the water, instead of the sky, there stretches a kind of concave, dull mirror, which reflects the view of the same ocean, chaotic and indistinct, like a memory about to fade.

Elsewhere, the solitary sleeper goes wandering inside an enclosure, amid a wreckage of rusting scrap-iron, the pieces gigantic as dinosaurs around her, so tiny. She listens alert, anxiously in the hope of some human voice, were it even the groan of a dying man. But the only sound in this space is a siren's whistle, which for that matter is also an echo, repeated from who knows what millennial infinity . . .

Springing up from these dreams at the summons of the alarm, Iduzza found herself always so bewildered and awkward she wasn't even able to dress herself. One morning, at school, having taken off her coat, she was writing something on the blackboard when she heard subdued laughter running along the desks behind her back. In fact, the hem of her skirt had been caught in her corset, exposing a little naked strip of her thigh, over the garter, all twisted and worn. Aware of it, she blushed purple with shame, worse than a soul displaying its sins before the Last Judgment.

Often, in that season, she had an accidentally comic effect on her pupils. One morning, shortly after she had installed herself at her desk, she happened to doze off (perhaps because of the sleeping pills she took in the evening) and waking at their racket, she thought, for some reason, she was in a tram and thus said to one of the desks: "Hurry, hurry, we get off at the next stop!" Every now and then she stumbled over the dais; or else, thinking she was going to the board, she headed for the door; or she got words mixed up (for example, instead of saying to a pupil, "take your copybook," she said to him, "take your coffee"). Her voice, as she imparted the usual notions to her little audience, sounded like an out-of-tune hurdy-gurdy; and at times she would suddenly break off, while her face would assume a dull, dazed expression, no longer remembering the subject she had been expounding a moment before. Still, she forced herself, as usual, to guide the more backward children's fingers over the paper; but her own hands trembled so that the letters came out crooked, ridiculous. On certain days her lessons, for the children, were better than a Punch-and-Judy show.

The relative discipline she had maintained in the past, familiarly and without effort, was diminishing from day to day and breaking down. Even a stranger could have identified at once, among all the others, the door to her classroom, by the incessant sound of voices, the disorder and shuffling heard from it. At times, there were such deafening outcries inside there that the janitor looked in from the threshold, concerned. And a couple of times the Headmistress herself appeared, though she withdrew discreetly, saying nothing. Unfortunately, in their faces Iduzza thought she could read pitiless threats: reports of unsatisfactory performance to the Ministry, and perhaps loss of her post . . . But, in reality, she was shown a special indulgence, however temporary, in consideration of her past merits and of her recent trials: bombed out in the war, the loss of her son, a former heroic partisan, and now her solitude with the other little boy without a name . . . (In the school, who knows why, there was a rumor that, after her widowhood, she had casually fornicated with a close relative, and in this way the child's neuropathic nature was explained.)

The pupils' parents, somehow informed of their bad conduct, took pity on Ida and urged her to beat them if necessary. But in all her life she had never hit anyone, not even in the days of her devilish little firstborn, and not even at the time of Blitz, who, having grown up in the streets, boorish and without any manners, at the beginning often went peeing around the house! The very idea of punishing, or even frightening, frightened her first of all. And so in the childish tumult of her classroom, she writhed, stupefied and helpless, as if at a lynching. All she could do was to beseech them saying: "Sssh . . . sssh . . . silence, silence . . ." with her hands clasped as if in prayer, trotting and staggering among the unruly desks. Those forty poor kids no longer seemed children to her, but a race of malign dwarfs, and she could no longer distinguish their individual faces, confusing them in a single hostile mass with adult, persecuting features. "Sssh . . . sssh . . ." Her only consolation, during those hours of purgatory, was that sooner or later the bell would ring and release her. And then, eager as the worst blockheads of the school, she would rush out towards Via Bodoni and Useppe.

All the same, she was obliged, before going home, to make the usual detours here and there for her daily shopping and other errands. And not infrequently, in those days, she would take the wrong street, so several times she had to retrace her steps, driven through that familiar neighborhood itinerary like a foreigner in a hostile country. It was on such an occasion that, one morning, beyond a street cluttered with tracks being repaired, she saw an elderly creature, shapeless and laughing, come towards her, advancing with great, rickety steps, waving her arms and greeting her with guttural cries of exultation and of agitation at the same time. Ida stepped back as at the sight of a ghost, having immediately recognized her (though changed) as Vilma, the "prophetess" of the Ghetto, whom she had never seen since and had long believed deported and dead in a Lager, with the other Jews of the quarter. Vilma instead had escaped capture (finding refuge in the convent of her famous Nun) and indeed a story is told of her, which I have actually heard in various versions, and which goes back to the date of the big German "round-up," Saturday, October 16th, 1943. They say that on the eve of that day, Friday, October 15th, towards evening, Vilma ran weeping and breathless into the little Jewish district, calling from below in a loud voice to the families, gathered in their homes at that hour for the Sabbath prayers. Like a tattered herald, running in tears through the narrow streets, she begged them all to flee, taking with them the old people also and the babies and saving whatever they had that they valued, because the hour of the massacre (already announced by her so many times) had come, and at dawn the Germans would arrive with trucks; and her *Signora* had even seen the lists of names . . . A number of people looked out of the windows at her shouts, and some came down to their front doors; but nobody believed her. Not many days before, the Germans (whom the Jews considered fierce perhaps but "men of honor") had signed an agreement guaranteeing the safety of the Jewish population of Rome, after receiving the desired ransom: fifty kilograms of gold! collected miraculously, with the help of the whole city. Vilma was treated, as usual, as a poor crack-brained visionary, and the Ghetto's inhabitants went back up into their homes to finish their prayers, leaving her alone. That evening it was pouring rain, and Vilma, returning to the convent, all sweating and soaked, had been seized by a raging fever, the kind that usually attacks animals rather than humans: from which she had then risen, on being cured, in her present state of chaos, perhaps without memory, and happy. Her language was no longer intelligible; but she did no harm to anyone, and she still worked like a mule, so she continued to earn her double protection: from the Signora and the Nun. The latter, indeed, had had her baptized one Sunday in the church of Santa Cecilia; except that later they discovered that in her infancy, through the intervention of a godmother, she had already been baptized. And so Vilma, in her existence, received baptism twice.

At present, she looked like a creature without sex, and also without age, though from many signs you could tell she was old. Her hair was white, and clumps had fallen out, leaving some pink bald patches here and there on her head. She tied her hair with a bluish ribbon, knotted over her brow. And though it was winter, she wore only a little cotton summer dress (clean and neat), her legs bare, with no stockings; and yet she seemed overheated. She laughed loudly, with enthusiasm, as if she had been waiting a long time for this meeting with Ida; and she made great feverish and disjointed gestures to her, assuming the poses, from time to time, of hieratic or bacchic dances. She seemed eager to tell some news or some joyous announcement; but from her mouth came only certain thick and inarticulate sounds, which she explained by laughing and touching her throat, as if to acknowledge some disease there. Her mouth was toothless, but the splendor of her eyes, abnormal before, had now become almost unbearable.

Still under the first impression, of seeing a ghost, Ida tried to move away from her; but in a moment, Vilma, as she had come, with the same urgent haste, crossed the tracks again, as if she were rushing to some appointment that couldn't be postponed, in the opposite direction.

Ida never saw her again; but I have reason to believe she survived a long time. In fact, I think I recognized her, not long ago, in the midst of that little bunch of old women who go every day to feed the stray cats at the Theater of Marcellus or other Roman ruins. She was still wearing her ribbon around her head, though her hair had been reduced to a few woolly clumps; and this time too she was wearing a light little dress, poor but decent, over bare legs, which now seemed dotted—perhaps because of some blood disease—by little brown spots. She was sitting on the ground among the cats, always talking to them in that broken and inarticulate language of hers, whose timbre, however, now resembled the voice of a little girl. From the way they came to her and answered her, the cats, at any rate, obviously understood her language very well; and among them, she was oblivious and blissful, like someone immersed in a celestial conversation.

·   ·   ·

Meanwhile, in the course of that post-war year, the "Big" men of the earth, with various "summit meetings," trials of the most notorious criminals, interventions, and non-interventions, were busy reestablishing some kind of appropriate order. The great social metamorphosis, however, formerly awaited with impatience by certain of our friends (such as Eppetondo and Quattropunte), on all sides, east and west, fell apart the moment it was touched, or else it fled in every direction, like a mirage. In Italy, with the republic established, the working-class parties also had a role in the government. And after so many wretched years, this was surely a luxury and a novelty, which nevertheless clothed an old indestructible skeleton. The Duce and his supporting cast had been buried, and the Royal Family had packed its bags; but those who pulled the strings remained backstage, even after the scenery changed. The landowners still held the land, the industrialists the machinery and the factories, the officers their ranks, the bishops their dioceses. And the rich were fed at the expense of the poor, who then aimed, in their turn, at taking the place of the rich, according to the general rule. But neither among those rich, nor among those poor was the place of Iduzza Ramundo, who belonged, truly, to a third species. It is a species that lives (perhaps endangered?) and dies, and gives no news of itself, except at times, perhaps, in the crime reports. And in this autumn-winter, moreover, our Iduzza lived surrounded by a haze which blocked even her usual—and nearsighted—view of the terrestrial planet.

Of that year's events—political battles, changes of government—she knew little or nothing. And her only social problem (added to the insufficiency of her salary, with the current inflation) was now the terror of being driven from her post for unsatisfactory performance. We already know that, by habit, she never read the newspapers. And since the war had ended, and the Germans had gone away, the adult world had again withdrawn from her, casting her back on the sands of her destiny like an infinitesimal bit of flotsam after an ocean storm.

In the month of June, for the first time in her life, she had been called to cast her personal vote in the elections. And since rumors were circulating that absenteeism would be recorded as culpable by the Authorities, she had turned up at the polls, among the earliest and most eager: voting *republic* and *Communism*, for so she had been advised by Remo the tavernkeeper. If the choice had been her own, she would have liked to vote *anarchy* in memory of her father; but Remo, irritated, had gravely disapproved, informing her at the same time that there was no such party on the ballot anyway.

Before the year's end, Remo appeared at Via Bodoni another couple of times, considering it an obligation not to leave the mother of Comrade Ace of Hearts always alone. During those visits, she would sit there filled with embarrassment, not knowing how to perform her duties, recompense the guest, or what to say to him, always telling Useppe and Bella breathlessly to behave themselves and not make so much noise. Remo, for his part, realized it was perhaps best not to mention Ninnuzzu at all to the poor lady; so he then diverted her with political matters, which were always his chief passion. On this score, unlike Ninnuzzu, he revealed himself optimistic and confident in the future, citing this or that contemporary occurrence on the earth (revolts in the Colonies, civil war in China and in Greece, Ho Chi Minh's struggle in Indochina, and in Italy strikes and clashes between police and peasants, workers, etc.) as a propitious sign the world was on the move. And this time nobody could stop the people's progress. This wasn't 1918 any longer. This time Communism had won the war! Hadn't it been the Red Army that destroyed Hitler's forces? And here in Italy, hadn't it been the Garibaldi brigades (Hammer and Sickle) that had organized the Resistance? And once the march was in progress, who could stop it?! The apparent retreats, betrayals, and delays (which had disgusted Ninnarieddu), according to Remo, were only a tactic, which you always had to calculate in politics; and the secret of this tactic, like every other secret of victory and final redemption, was kept in only one place, absolutely sure: namely, the mind of Comrade Togliatti. There were no evils, problems of society—Remo's talk seemed to indicate—for which Comrade Togliatti, guided by his inner genius, didn't already know the remedy and the solution, imminent or future. In his mind, all was settled; and Comrade Stalin himself—in Remo's view—made no important decision without first consulting Comrade Togliatti. Both then, between the two of them, knew best what the right line was: always the one pointed out by Comrade Lenin, and inspired by the wisdom of Carlo Marx. These were scientific truths, tested and ripened; and in fact the different peoples were now on the move, following the indications of the great Comrades of the present and of the past. Judging by all the signs, we were today on the eve of the New World: "The two of us, Signora, sitting here today and talking, tomorrow we'll see the New World!"

So Comrade Remo assured her, faith burning in his grave, hollow eyes, and in his thin, dark face, like a woodman's or a stone-cutter's. And Ida, seated opposite him in the cold little kitchen of Via Bodoni, wondered if, in that grand New World there would be a place, at least, for little ones like Useppe.

On the night of 31 December 1946, in Rome, the year's end was hailed with a general din of firecrackers and paper-bombs.

. . . . **1947**

JANUARY–JUNE

In Sicily, the landowners react to the peasants' and farm-laborers' struggle for the right to survive by organizing a series of assassinations of trade-union leaders.

In Rome, the Constituent Assembly (with the Communists voting in favor) confirms the Concordat between the State and the Church, a pact stipulated by the Fascist regime with the Vatican.

As the civil war in Greece continues, Britain asks the United States to intervene, supporting the monarchist reaction against the partisan resistance. For the occasion, President Truman, in a speech to Congress, reads a message in which he commits the United States not only to intervention in Greece, but in any country threatened by Communism, and he urges all nations to defend themselves against the Red menace (Truman Doctrine). This new line of United States diplomacy upsets the World War Two alliances and begins the cold war between the two blocs, on either side of the Iron Curtain.

To meet the immediate and future demands of the cold war, which requires, first of all, control of the smaller nations, the two Great Powers (United States and USSR) promptly recur to the means of power most typical of each: financial for the Americans, and directly coercive for Stalin's Russia. Through the Marshall Plan, the United States, with massive economic aid, intervenes in the internal crises of the countries of its own bloc, ruined by the war (Italy and West Germany included); while on the part of the USSR, Sovietization imposed from above begins in the satellite countries, with the exploitation of their material resources—already virtually exhausted—which are transferred to the Soviet Union.

Urgent revival of the armaments race, and especially, the competition for the atomic secret, till now a monopoly of the United States.

In the countries of the Western bloc, internal conflict is exacerbated between the right-wing and center parties and the parties of the Left.

In Greece, the civil war persists.

In China, victorious counteroffensive of the Red Army. In Vietnam, Ho Chi Minh rejects the armistice terms offered by the French.

In Sicily, a peaceful demonstration of peasants ends in a massacre treacherously carried out by a local bandit in the pay of the landowners.

A new government is formed in Italy, headed by De Gasperi (center party), with the exclusion of the Communists.

JULY–SEPTEMBER

After thirty years of struggle, led by Mahatma Gandhi, using the non-violent methods of passive resistance, against the British Empire, India obtains independence. The territory is divided into two Nations: India

413

(with a religious majority of Hindus) and Pakistan (with a majority of Moslems). Thousands of refugees of the opposing religious minorities seek safety, crossing the respective borders. A bloody conflict ensues between Hindus and Moslems, with a million dead.

The process of self-liberation of the colonized peoples (already in progress since the first decades of the century and accelerated by the political changes in the present world) now reaches a decisive phase. The breakdown of the colonial Empires has already been sensed by the Powers concerned, some (not all) of which are persuaded to give way. Colonialism is then replaced by neo-colonialism, namely the economic subjugation of the former colonies, supported by the Powers through the purchase of their raw materials, the ownership of their industries, and the transformation of their territories (necessarily underdeveloped) into immense markets for their own industrial products (arms included).

OCTOBER–DECEMBER

In the Eastern bloc, the Cominform is founded (Information Center of European Communist Parties).

Peace negotiations concerning the unsolved problem of Germany are broken off by the Powers of the two blocs.

Feverish race to capture the American atomic secret, with intense espionage between the two blocs, spy hunts, death sentences, etc.

In the United States, the first missiles are produced, along the line of those made in Germany during the Second World War . . . . .

. . . weightless in a world of weights . . .

. . . .

. . . measureless in a world of measures . . .

MARINA CVETAEVA

1 "Hello! Who's that? This is Useppe. Who is it?"

"Yes, it's me! This is mamma, yes. What did you want to tell me, Useppe?"

"I'm sorry, *Segnora*" (the voice of Lena-Lena has intervened) "he made me call the number and now he can't think of anything to say!!"

Lena-Lena's laughter, unsuccessfully repressed, is heard, accompanied by Bella's joyous barking. Then, after a very brief grumble of argument at the end of the line, the receiver is hastily hung up.

Towards the end of winter, a telephone had been installed in Ida's house, and this was the first call she had received from it (she had confided her school's number to the concierge and to Lena-Lena, warning them, however, to call only for urgent communications . . .). Useppe, especially at the beginning, couldn't resist the temptation of that speaking object attached to the wall, even if, in handling it, he was then as clumsy as a savage. At its daily ring (Ida telephoned every day at ten-thirty, during recess) he rushed to it, followed by Bella at a run; but when Ida greeted him, he could only answer, as a rule: "Hello! Who's that? This is Useppe. Who is it? . . ." etc., etc. The only person who called that number was Ida, and Useppe, for his part, had nobody else to call in Rome. Once he dialed a number at random, only two digits, and Correct Time answered. It was a lady's voice, and he continued insisting: "Hello! Who is it?" while she, irritated, went on doggedly repeating: "It is exactly eleven forty-one!" Another time, there was an unscheduled call, early in the morning, but it was somebody who had dialed the wrong number; and from the other end of the line, after having made a mistake, for some reason or other he took it out on Useppe! Then as the days went by Useppe lost interest in that awkward, irresolute object. At her usual daily call, Ida heard a shy, impatient and almost listless voice answer, saying "yyyes . . ." ("Have you eaten?" "*ess* . . . yyyes!" "Are you all right?" "Yyes . . .") which then rapidly concluded: "goodbye, goodbye!"

During the winter, Useppe had been completely spared his attacks. The day after that first fall in November, his mother had rushed to confide in the doctor, alone this time; and on this occasion Ida had revealed also the secret of her own childhood spells, which she had never ever revealed to anyone before, not even to her husband: seeing and hearing again in every detail, as she spoke of it, the excursion she had made as a child on the little donkey to Montalto with her father, and the visit to the doctor friend, who had tickled her and made her laugh . . . But the lady doctor, with her usual brusqueness, cut short these complicated confessions, declaring with authority: "No, Signora. No, no. It has been proved certain diseases are not hereditary! At most you can inherit a tendency, PER-

HAPS, but that hasn't been proved. And it seems quite clear to me, as far as I can tell, that your personal case was different. There it was a matter of ordinary hysteria; whereas here we're dealing with a different set of phenomena" ("I immediately saw something strange," she murmured, half to herself, at this point, "in that boy's eyes"). In conclusion, the doctor tore a page from her prescription pad and wrote out for Ida the address of a specialist, a Professor, who could give the little patient an *electroencephalogram*. And the abstruse word promptly frightened Iduzza. As we already know, everything pertaining to the invisible realms of electricity filled her with a barbarian distrust. As a child, when there were bursts of lightning and thunder, she would hide in fear (if possible, she would run beneath her father's cloak); and even now, as an old woman, she was afraid to touch wires or even to screw a light bulb into a socket. At the long threatening word, which she had never heard before, her eyes grew large, raised shyly to the doctor, as if the lady had mentioned the electric chair. But intimidated by the Signorina's peremptory manners, Ida didn't dare reveal her own ignorance.

A little later, the events surrounding Ninnuzzu estranged her from every other concern; and in consequence, the projected visit to the specialist abandoned her conscious mind. In reality, she feared this unknown Professor's diagnosis as a capital sentence admitting no appeal.

The deceptive course of Useppe's illness encouraged her defensive inertia. In fact, the unnamed tyranny which had usurped the strength of the little tyke since autumn seemed to move away, as if exhausted, after having felled him once: faintly and steathily accompanying him, and at times allowing itself to be forgotten, as if it had decided this was enough. In the evening, when bedtime came, Ida would give him the usual sedative to drink, and he would greedily stick out his lips, like an infant towards the breast; and he would soon fall into a heavy and untroubled sleep, to which he abandoned himself, supine, his fists clenched, his arms out on the pillow, motionless for ten hours or more. When the little wound of his bitten tongue had healed, he retained no visible trace of the *access* of November 16th. Only, anyone who had known him before could perhaps notice in his eyes (already *too beautiful*, according to the Doctor) a new, fabulous difference, such as perhaps remained in the eyes of the first seamen after the crossing of immeasurable oceans still nameless on the maps. Unlike them, Useppe knew nothing, before or afterwards, of his voyage. But perhaps, unknown to himself, there remained in his retina an upside-down image, as they say of certain migratory birds who, in their ignorance, during the day along with the sunlight can still see also the hidden stars.

For Ida, this testimony of Useppe's eyes was noticeable only in the color. Their mixture of dark blue and pale aquamarine had become, if that were possible, even more innocent and almost unexplorable in its double depth. One day, coming suddenly into the kitchen, she found him silent on the step of the stove, and their gazes met. Then at the encounter, she saw in Useppe's eyes a kind of impossible, childish awareness, unspeakably tormented, which said to her, "You know!" and nothing else, beyond any exchange of logical questions and answers.

.   .   .

In the month of February, Lena-Lena was sent to work for a stocking-mender, so she had to give up her little visits in Via Bodoni. But to look after Useppe now there was Bella, who was enough.

The times of daily steaks, for Bella, were over, and of baths at the beauty parlor, and of all the other distinguished comforts she had enjoyed in the days of Ninnarieddu, who used to brush her and comb her and even massage her with his own hands, and swab her eyes and ears delicately with wet absorbent cotton, et cetera. Now, for food, she had to be satisfied, in general, with pasta and vegetables, with the sole addition of some extra morsel that Useppe would take for her from his plate (not letting Ida see). And as for her toilet, it consisted exclusively of a kind of dry bath she would give herself during their walks, using her personal method: namely, rolling in the dust and then shaking herself fearsomely, imitating a cyclone cloud. However, she really preferred this private system to those other de luxe baths, with soaps from Marseilles and hot water, which she had always disliked.

She was upset, and not a little, on the other hand, at having to adapt herself to the minimum space of one or two little rooms: she, who had been used to journeys, excursions, and the life of the street, and even earlier (in her ancestral experience) to the immense grazing-lands of Asia! During that prison winter in Via Bodoni, on certain days she even had to perform her corporal functions on wastepaper and newspapers. Still, she was resigned to any sacrifice, if it meant being with Useppe night and day.

Even on her new diet of mush, good-naturedly making the best of it, she had regained her sturdy shape and her healthy muscles. Her snowy coat now seemed a bit blackish, disheveled, and full of snarls. And though she still wore her silver-plated collar with Bella written on it, some neighborhood kids had named her Crummy. She was often to be seen busily scratching her fleas, and she stank heavily of dog. Indoors, this stink of hers had been communicated also to Useppe; so at times various dogs circled around him, sniffing him, perhaps wondering if he too wasn't some kind of puppy.

They (the dogs) were, you might say, Useppe's only companions. He had no friends or playmates of his own species any more. With the first return of the fine season, Bella and Useppe were out much of the day; and in the beginning, during her free hours, Ida had forced herself to accompany them. She had soon realized, however, the impossibility, with her thin and weakened little legs, of keeping up with that pair. After the first minute in the street, she had already lost sight of them, finding herself at least a quarter of a mile behind. As soon as they came from the building into the open air, they could promptly be seen rushing off, veering, skipping, tumbling towards the unknown; and at her loud calls, Bella would reply from the distance with considerate barking: "All's well. Don't wear yourself out. Go on home. I'll take care of Useppe! I can manage flocks of a hundred, two hundred, three hundred quadrupeds! Don't you think I'm able to deal with one little man?"

Perforce, Ida finally entrusted Useppe entirely to Bella. She felt sure her trust was not misplaced; and for that matter, what else could she have done? The excursions with Bella were the little boy's only recreation. Even the gramophone, after the famous destruction of the swing record, had been put aside forever, to decay in the dust. Now, in the confinement of the little rooms, Useppe, like Bella, became as uneasy and restless as a tormented soul, so Ida no longer dared incarcerate him even in the morning, as she had during the winter. Usually, after the mother's daily phone call, the two immediately went out; Bella had therefore soon learned to recognize the phone's ring as an advance signal of freedom; and on hearing it, she would start making immense leaps, accompanied by loud hurrahs and little sneezes of contentment.

But (as if she had a precision watch inside her big bearlike head) she would bring Useppe home punctually again at mealtimes.

At first, the two didn't stray very far from Via Bodoni. Their pillars of Hercules were the Tiber on one side, the slopes of the Aventine on another, and farther on, Porta San Paolo (it must be stated here that, in any case, Bella directed Useppe's steps away from the sinister building of the Municipal Slaughterhouse, located in our vicinity . . .). Perhaps, even today some inhabitant of Testaccio remembers having seen that couple go by: a big dog and a tiny boy, always alone and inseparable. At certain points of special importance, for example at Piazza dell'Emporio where a merry-go-round was encamped, the two would stop, in a double and irresistible palpitation which made the boy sway on his little legs and the dog furiously wag her tail. But, on the other hand, it sufficed for someone to show he had noticed them, and the child would retreat in haste, meekly followed by the dog. Spring was already pouring out a throng of noises, movements. From the streets and the windows names were called: "Ettoreee! Marisa! Umbe'! . . ." and sometimes also: "Nino! . . ." At this name, Useppe would rush forward, transfigured, his eyes trembling, moving a few paces ahead of Bella in an unspecified direction. And Bella, in turn, would prick up her ears slightly, as if to share at least for a moment that fabulous summons, though she knew, really, its absurdity. In fact, she renounced following the child, waiting in her place and accompanying him with a gaze of forgiveness and of superior experience. Then, when Useppe almost immediately came back, ashamed, she would welcome him with that same gaze. There was no shortage of Ninos and Ninettos living in that neighborhood; and even Useppe, to tell the truth, was not unaware of this fact.

.   .   .

The fine spring weather, very early that year, was spoiled for three days by the sirocco, which brought clumps of clouds and dusty showers, in a hot and dirty air that smacked of the desert. On one of those days, Useppe had a second fall. The family had just finished their meal, and he, who had eaten little and reluctantly, had remained in the kitchen with Bella, while Ida went to stretch out on the bed. A little later Bella began to show signs of agitation and incoherence, as happens with certain animals who feel a forewarning of an earthquake or some other terrestrial upheaval. She ran constantly between the kitchen and the bedroom until Ida crossly drove her away, yelling. It was three o'clock in the afternoon. From the courtyard a few noises rose (a radio and some voices from the bicycle park), then a thunderclap was heard without rain from the swollen, dirty sky, and from the street the whistle of a passing siren. But as soon as these sounds had died, Ida heard a subdued little dialogue in the kitchen, where Useppe seemed to chant some broken phrases, in a frightened and stammering little voice, and Bella uttered tender whimpers of solicitude and panic. It often happened that the two chatted together; but hearing them today, Ida was shaken by an undefined alarm which made her rush into the kitchen. Useppe, still on his feet, was walking with unsteady steps, as if he were wandering half-blind around in a penumbra, and Bella was at his side, like a poor ignorant wet-nurse seeking some remedy. On Ida's entrance, the dog came to her, as if pleading with her. And this time Ida witnessed with her own eyes the whole course of the attack, from the moment when the *grand mal* released its cry, falling like a murdering predator on little Useppe.

The succession of the various phases, still, came so rapidly that Ida hardly had time to be aware of her own movements, finding herself, as at the first attack, kneeling beside Useppe, who already seemed to be coming round, as she called him. And though, at that precise moment, from an extreme depth of her own viscera, a definitive signal told her that her son was doomed, she didn't perceive it. For her, only one thing was certain, enough for her at the moment: the ugly invader of her house, back for the second time to steal her child, obeying his own dark laws, would not be long in releasing him again.

This time, when, after a great sigh, Useppe reopened his eyes in his enchanted smile, there were two of them to receive him: his mother on this side, and Bella Crummy on the other. The latter gave him a little lick on the hand and another on the nose, but very delicately, not wanting to disturb him. And for all the duration of his subsequent deep sleep, she remained stretched out at the foot of his bed.

Also at his first reawakening, late that evening, Useppe found the two of them with him: Bella and his mother, one on either side. "Useppe!" Ida greeted him, and Bella greeted him with a bark so discreet and tremulous it could have been mistaken for a bleat. He raised his head slightly and said: "The moon!" In fact, the sirocco had gone away, leaving in its place a spring wind that had already cleansed almost the whole sky, where the moon could be seen passing up above, cool and naked, as if after a bath. It was the same moon seen from the San Lorenzo house in the days when Useppe still called it *ttar* or *wallow*, as he called *ttars* or *wallows* (according to the circumstances) the lighted bulbs, the colored balloons, or tin cans or gobs of spit on the ground, if the light made them shine even a little. (At that time he was still crawling and he could confuse the earth with the sky.)

Ida couldn't allow herself any further absences from school; the next morning, however, on going out, she took care to double-lock the door, as she had done the past winter. Performing such an act weighed on her hand, since it seemed a mark of disablement for Useppe. She had left him still asleep, huddled around his pillow, with Bella dozing at the foot of the *sommier*. Hearing her go out, the dog had raised her head slightly, with a reassuring little flicker of her tail ("Go on, go ahead; I'll take care of Useppe"). Before eleven, as usual, she telephoned him.

Two or three rings, then the familiar little voice of every day:

"Hello. Who's that? This is Useppe. Who is it?"

"It's mamma. Are you all right?"

"Yes." (In the background, Bella's habitual barking.)

"Did you drink your milk?"

"Yes . . ."

The dialogue is the same as ever, but today Ida thinks she hears a trembling in his voice. She must immediately apologize, reassuringly:

"I locked the door," she hastens to explain, "because you had a little temperature yesterday. But as soon as you're well, you can go out with Bella again!"

"Yes . . . yes . . ."

"Then you're all right? Be a good boy, eh? . . . I'll be home before one! . . ."

"Yes . . . Goodbye. Goodbye."

Everything seemed normal, as if that thing hadn't happened, yesterday or ever. Only Ida was left with the suspicion of having heard that certain tremulousness in his voice . . . On her way home, for their dinner she even bought a dessert: two cream pastries, one for him and one for Bella. And she saw him brighten with a pleased expression because Bella had not been forgotten.

No apparent sign remained of his *temperature* of the day before, except for his still pale and weakened look, with a residue of listlessness and sleep, which was enough, luckily, to distract him also from Ida's betrayal in locking the door. In the course of the morning, apparently he had amused himself by drawing: all his colored pencils were scattered on the kitchen table, and a sheet of paper completely filled to the margins with drawings . . . An accident had happened in Ida's absence, however, and he bravely announced it to her, with a comical hesitant little smile:

". . . hey, mà, Bella shat on the dishcloth."

That morning, as a matter of fact, Ida had dropped the dishcloth on the floor, and Bella, reasonably, had made use of it, perhaps assuming it had been placed there for her convenience . . . A considerable smell still rose from the sink, where Useppe had taken care to soak the rag, after having dutifully emptied the contents into the toilet. And Bella, during this scene, remained a bit to one side, with a sinner's saddened look, though she didn't understand what her sin was . . . But Ida didn't even dare utter her usual reproach to Useppe, namely that you say *go to the bathroom*, because *shit* is a bad word! (He had inherited it, with others, from his brother Nino.) Rather, she thought she recognized, in his words, an accusation for having locked him up, a prisoner along with Bella. "It doesn't matter!" she hastened to say, "the cloth was already dirty." And Useppe, afraid Bella would be scolded, was immediately consoled.

The drawing left on the table was all an arabesque of rings, splashes, and red, green, blue, and yellow spirals; and he himself proudly explained to Ida: "It's swallows!", pointing beyond the window to his models, racing through the air. Ida praised the drawing, which in fact seemed very beautiful to her, though she personally found it incomprehensible. But after telling her the subject, he crumpled the paper in his fist and threw it in the garbage. This was the end to which he condemned all his drawings. And if Ida protested, he would shrug and grow cross, with a contemptuous sad look (if possible, she sometimes secretly rescued those pages from the garbage and put them away in a private drawer of hers).

Everything proceeded normally. But, at a certain hour just after lunch, while Bella was having a siesta, Ida found Useppe huddled on the floor nearby, against the wall of the corridor. At first, glancing at him, she thought he was only brooding; but when she approached him, she realized he was crying, his little face clenched like a fist, contracted, all wrinkles. Looking up towards her, he immediately burst into dry sobs. And with a little animal's bewilderment, he said in a desperate voice:

"Mà . . . *wy?*"

In reality, this question of his didn't seem addressed to Ida, present there, but rather to some absent, monstrous, and inexplicable Will. Ida, instead, again imagined he was accusing her for having shut him up in the house treacherously; but soon, in the following days, she became convinced this explanation was insufficient. That question: *wy?* had become, with Useppe, a kind of refrain, which returned to his lips from beyond time and place, perhaps involuntarily (otherwise, he would have taken care to pronounce it properly, with the *h*). He could be heard at times repeating it to himself in a monotonous sequence: "Wy? wy wy wy wy??" But though it seemed automatic, this little question had a stubborn and heart-rending sound, more bestial than human. It recalled, in fact, the voices of abandoned kittens, of donkeys blindfolded at the mill, of lambs loaded on a wagon for the Easter festivities. It was never known if all these anonymous and unanswered wys reached some destination, perhaps an invulnerable ear beyond all earthly places.

2 After Useppe's second attack, Ida had gone anxiously back to the doctor, who arranged for a special examination two days later by the Professor-neurologist she had already suggested. On this occasion, not without impatience, she assured Ida that the feared EEG (electroencephalogram) was nothing but a registration, harmless and painless, of cerebral electric tensions, traced by a machine on a roll of paper. Ida, for her part, led Useppe to believe that a law had decreed some obligatory examinations for all little boys, to protect them from fevers. He made no remark, beyond an impatient huff, so faint it resembled a sigh.

For the occasion, Ida gave him a thorough bath in the laundry tub, and dressed him in his most elegant clothes, namely American-style long pants and a new jersey with red and white stripes. They took the tram to the railroad station, but from there to their destination, Ida allowed herself the luxury of a taxi. Not only to avoid tiring Useppe, but also because the Professor had given an address in the Nomentano quarter, not far from the Tiburtino. And Ida no longer had the strength to enter that neighborhood on her own.

In the past, Ida had ridden in a taxi at least twice (in Alfio's day), but Useppe was getting into one today for the first time in his life, and the sudden novelty excited him. Without hesitation he promptly sat himself beside the driver; and from the rear seat, Ida heard him ask the man: "What's the horsepower of this car?" "It's a Fiat 1100!" the driver answered smugly; and again Ida saw the man, having shifted into gear, reply to other unspecified questions from his customer, his finger pointing to the speedometer: obviously, Useppe had asked him about the car's speed . . . With this, the brief dialogue came to an end. Useppe fell silent, and Ida realized he was swaying his head in the way he usually did to accompany that strange chant of his: wy wy wy wy? A little later, wanting to evade the sight of those streets, she closed her eyes until their arrival.

They were shown into the side wing of a hospital building, where there was also an outpatients' clinic; thanks to the doctor's recommendation, however, the Professor had set their appointment a bit earlier than regular hours. He received them at the very end of the corridor, in a little room that had on the door his name: Prof. Dr. G. A. Marchionni. He was a middle-aged man, tall and plump, with eyeglasses over his thick cheeks, and a drooping gray moustache. Every now and then he took off his glasses to wipe them, and without those spectacles, his near-sighted face lost its professional gravity and decorum, taking on a swollen, dull heaviness. He spoke always in the same tone, drawling and academic; however, he expressed himself with propriety and respect, and always with good manners, unlike the lady doctor. He was, in short, just an ordinary, distinguished gentleman; but Iduzza, on seeing him, was immediately afraid of him.

He glanced at some notes on a paper, and said he was to some extent informed of the anamnesis (the doctor must surely have informed him); before proceeding, however, he wanted some further information from the mother: "Meanwhile, Giuseppe can take a look at the garden . . . your name's Giuseppe, isn't it?"

"No. Useppe."

"Fine, fine. Now then, Giuseppe, you go down and have a look at the garden on your own. There's a little animal out there that might interest you." And he thrust Useppe towards a French window leading outside.

The garden was actually a yard, enclosed among the hospital walls, with a few scrawny plants. But in one corner, inside a cage, there was, in fact, a very pretty little animal, who so attracted Useppe's attention that he was even holding his breath. It resembled a squirrel, in miniature, but without a tail. Its fur was brown, with yellow and orange spots; it had very short legs and tiny ears with a pink lining. And it did nothing but run dizzyingly around a wheel suspended in the cage, paying attention to nothing else. The cage was only a bit more spacious than a shoebox, and the wheel was perhaps six inches in diameter; but making that circle at such a breathless pace, never stopping, perhaps by now, on his dwarf legs, he had covered a distance in miles equal to the circle of the Equator! He was so caught up in his extreme urgency he didn't even notice Useppe's timid calls. And his handsome little olive-colored eyes gleamed, immobile, like the eyes of the mad.

In the beginning Useppe remained standing there in front of the cage, ruminating on ideas of his own. But a little later, the Professor peered out of the French window to call him and caught him with one hand inside the cage, doing something that was clearly the crime of housebreaking. He had decided, in fact, to carry the animal away, hiding him under his jersey, and then, with Bella's complicity, to take him to scamper in a marvelous place of their acquaintance, from where with his swift legs he could run off wherever he liked, maybe even to the Castelli, and America, and everywhere.

The Professor arrived just in time to foil the theft. "No . . . no . . . come now!" he admonished, with his slow voice. But since the little boy wouldn't desist, and indeed looked at him defiantly, the Professor was obliged to pull his arm from the cage, which immediately closed again with a click. Then, still holding Useppe's wrist, he drew him along, reluctant, towards the entrance to the little room where Ida was waiting for them.

At this point, the little animal, which seemed dumb, let his voice be heard, a kind of imperceptible grunt. And Useppe, turning to look back, gave the Professor a shove and planted his feet on the step. But the Professor, with a minimal effort, soon pushed him inside again, shutting the French window behind them.

Useppe's face had begun to quiver, even inside his eyes. "I don't want! I don't want!" he exclaimed suddenly with great noise, like someone tearing himself from an unacceptable contingency. And in a flash of wrath, which burned him with a dark flush, he promptly gave the Professor a punch with his fist, at stomach-level. Ida came forward cautiously . . . "Nothing, nothing, the risks of the job," the Professor said, snickering in his sad way, "now we'll handle it . . . we'll handle it . . ." and calmly he telephoned for a nurse, who appeared in a few moments, handing Useppe in a spoon *something nice and sweet*. As she held it out, her manner was somehow insinuating and smooth, and one would have said irresistible; however, the *something nice and sweet* was violently flung back at her— soiling her white coat—by two feverish little hands, which thrust everyone aside.

In fact, Useppe at the moment was rolling on the floor, kicking at the Professor and at the nurse and at his mother, in total rebellion. When he calmed down a little, he took some fleeting glances at the French window, as if there beyond, in the little garden, a point of darkness was hidden; and at the same time, Iduzza saw him make as if to rip up the new jersey he was wearing, the way certain sick people in their fever tear the bandages from their wounds. She remembered having caught him in the same act one summer night two years earlier, in the little room in Via Mastro Giorgio, when his illness had showed its first signs. And the whole development of this illness till today reappeared to our Iduzza in a kind of blood-thirsty cavalcade, which galloped across the days and months to ravage her little bastard.

At first, she feared that a new *great* attack was threatening him at that moment. And against all logic, she felt an extreme repugnance at the idea that a doctor, especially, should witness it! Her heart turned over like an empty cup with the rapid sensation that the knowledge of doctors not only was of no avail in Useppe's malady, but even offended it.

She breathed, seeing that luckily Useppe was calming down; in fact, he had taken on a shy air, like a defendant in contumacy, and he underwent with resignation all the further tests to which he was subjected. To the end of the examination, however, he opposed a stubborn silence to the Professor's questions; and we can believe he didn't even hear them. I suppose his thoughts were still tending exclusively towards that little tail-less animal (but Useppe never again mentioned their very brief meeting to anyone, as far as I know).

When they finally came out of the room, the two passed among a little group of people waiting, almost all on their feet: there was a blondish boy, with very long arms and sagging lips, who jerked constantly; and a little old man with ruddy cheeks, very clean, who never stopped feverishly scratching his shoulders, with a distraught expression, as if he were assailed by revolting insects, never sated. From one room an orderly looked out, and through the half-open door an interior could be glimpsed, bars at the windows and a clutter of beds without blankets, where some people, all dressed, had been flung in disorder. In the space between the cots, a man in shirtsleeves, with a long growth of beard, was pacing furiously, laughing like a drunk, and suddenly he began to stagger. After a brief wait, Ida and Useppe were summoned beyond a glass door which opened onto a stairway.

The EEG laboratory was in some basement rooms, equipped with mysterious machines under artificial lights; Useppe, however, displayed neither curiosity nor amazement on entering, and even when they attached the electrodes to his little head, he let them have their way, with a kind of disenchanted nonchalance. It seemed now, when you looked at him, that, who knows when and how, he had already traveled through that basement and undergone those same tests; and he already knew that, for him, any-way, they were absolutely useless.

Still, on coming home, he announced to the concierge with a certain importance, though in a confidential tone: "I had a *fafogram*." She, however, was becoming deafer and deafer, among other things, and didn't bother to understand this disclosure.

A few days later, Ida went back alone to the Professor, for his opinion.

The analyses and the clinical examinations had revealed nothing alarming. Even though slight, and underdeveloped, the child showed no lesions, no aftereffects of infections, or organic diseases of any kind. As for the findings of the EEG, they equaled, in Iduzza's eyes, an oracle of inscrutable geomancy. It was a multiple graph of oscillating waves, on broad strips of oblong paper. And the Professor explained as best he could to her that the waves indicated the rhythmic activity of the living cells: when the activity ceased, the waves turned flat.

The file was accompanied by a report of a few lines, which concluded: The graph does not indicate anything significant. And in fact, the Professor explained, there was no specific alteration of the brain recorded. To judge from this report, as also from the preceding clinical examinations, the patient's health would seem normal. However, he added, considering the anamnesis, the practical value of such a result remains uncertain, or rather, relative and transitory. Such cases do not allow the formulation of a precise diagnosis or a valid prognosis. It is a syndrome generally unexplained as far as the cause is concerned and unpredictable in its course . . . Medicine today can still offer only symptomatic remedies (the Professor prescribed Gardenal). Obviously, the therapy must be followed systematically and regularly. The patient must be kept under constant observation . . .

The Professor had taken off his glasses to wipe them, and at this moment, Iduzza thought she heard, from some ward not far away in the hospital buildings, a child's cry. In great haste, with a hollow voice, she asked if, among the causes, there could be an inherited tendency, premature birth . . . "It's not impossible, not impossible," the Professor answered, in a neutral tone, toying with his eyeglasses on the desk. Then looking up directly at Ida, he exclaimed to her: "But is this child receiving sufficient nourishment?!"

"Yes! Yes! I . . . the best!" Ida answered, distressed, as if defending herself against an accusation: "Of course," she explained, "during the war, it was hard for everybody . . ." She feared, with this *everybody*, she might have offended the Professor, including him in the mass of paupers. And she even thought she saw a certain irony in his eyes . . . It was, actually, only the special obliquity some myopic eyes have. Iduzza, however, was frightened by it. Now, a woman's cry made itself heard, from some other (perhaps imaginary) ward of the hospital. And the Professor's face, without the glasses, seemed naked to her, to the point of indecency, sordid and threatening. She had the suspicion that in this complicated place of basements, passages, stairways, and machines, under his command, a plot was being hatched against Useppe!

In reality, the man facing her was a Professor of no great qualities, who was giving her his own scientific information with proper impartiality (and almost free, moreover, because of the lady doctor's recommendation). But Ida, at that point, saw him in the form of terrible Authority, as if all the fear instilled in her, always, by adults, today were condensed in this mask. The lady doctor, even with her bad manners (she treated Ida, truly, like a halfwit), had never seemed a real adult to her; and neither had the doctor friend who had tickled her. From today on, however, she became afraid of all Doctors. The word *patient*, used by the Professor to define Useppe, had suddenly pierced her like a slander, which she rejected and which drove her brusquely away from the walls of the Hospital. She didn't want Useppe to be a patient: Useppe had to be a little boy *like other little boys*.

She didn't neglect, in any case, to go to the pharmacy that very day to have Prof. Marchionni's prescription filled. But then it later occurred to her she had forgotten to ask him if the child was allowed to go out freely, in the daylight hours, under the guardianship of a sheepdog . . . But the fact is that on this question, Ida had already made up her mind. Only on that first morning after the attack had her hand dared double-lock the front door; then immediately, starting the next day, Useppe found himself free again with Bella.

It was April. And then May June July August, a whole great solar summer opened out for babies young kids boys girls dogs and cats. Useppe had to run and roughhouse in the sunshine, *like other little boys:* she couldn't imprison him within walls. (Had that voice, perhaps, which still pounded in her, unperceived, from some point beyond the threshold of sound, already warned her that her little sprite would not have many more summers?)

3 There remains to narrate, finally, that spring and summer of '47, with the wanderings of Useppe and his companion Bella, free, in the Testaccio district and environs. Without Bella as guard, to be sure, such liberty would have been denied Useppe. Not infrequently he had been gripped again by reckless impulses to flight, that is, to walk on and on not knowing where; and there is no doubt he would have been lost if Bella hadn't been there to restrain him and bring him home

again at the appointed hour. Moreover, from time to time, incredibly, fears stirred in him: the movement of a shadow was enough, or a leaf, to put him on his guard and make him shudder. But fortunately, as soon as he turned his restless eyes, the first thing he saw was Bella's face, with her brown eyes happy in the fine day, and her mouth open, panting to applaud the air.

In the course of the season, the couple, solitary as they were, didn't lack for encounters and adventures. The first adventure was the discovery of a wondrous place. This was the place "of his acquaintance" where Useppe had planned to bring the little tailless animal. And the discovery, in fact, only slightly antedated Professor Marchionni's examination. It was a Sunday morning; after the brief interval of their confinement, Useppe and Bella again had the way free. And they were so eager that at nine, having bidden Ida goodbye, they were already out of the house.

The west wind, in its swift passage after the rains, had left the infinite so limpid that even the old walls were rejuvenated, breathing it in. The sun was dry and glowing, and the shade was cool. In the little breath of air, you walked without weight, as if borne by a sailboat. And today, for the first time, Useppe and Bella went beyond their usual boundaries. Without even being aware of it, as they walked on, they passed Via Marmorata, following the whole length of Viale Ostiense; and when they reached the Basilica of San Paolo, they turned right, at which point Bella, lured by an intoxicating smell, began to run, followed by Useppe.

Bella ran with the cry: "Uhrrr! Uhrrr!" which means: "The sea! The sea!", whereas what really lay ahead, of course, was none other than the river Tiber. But no longer the same Tiber of Rome: here it flowed among fields, without walls or embankments, and it reflected the countryside's natural colors.

(Bella possessed a kind of lunatic memory, vagabond and millennial, which suddenly made her scent the Indian Ocean in a river, and the Maremma in a mud puddle. She was capable of sniffing a Tartar wagon in a bicycle and a Phoenecian ship in a tram. And this explains why she bounded off in certain misplaced monumental leaps, or stopped constantly to rummage with such interest among refuse or to hail with a thousand ceremonies certain odors of minimum importance.)

Here the city had ended. Beyond, on the other bank, you could still glimpse amid the green a few sheds and hovels, which gradually became sparser; but on this side, there were only fields and canebrakes, with no human construction. And despite its being Sunday, the place was deserted. With spring barely begun, nobody yet visited these banks, especially in the morning. There were only Useppe and Bella, who ran forward a bit, then flung themselves down to roll on the grass, then jumped up and ran forward another bit.

At the end of the fields, the terrain sloped down and a little wooded area began. It was there that Useppe and Bella at a certain point slowed their pace and stopped chatting.

They had entered a round clearing, closed off by a circle of trees whose highest boughs became tangled so as to form a kind of room with a roof of leaves. The floor was new grass, just born after the rains, perhaps not yet trampled by anyone, and with only a kind of minuscule daisy flowering in it. The flowers looked as if they had all blossomed together at that moment. Beyond the trunks, towards the river, a natural palisade of canes allowed a glimpse of the water; and the flow of the current, along with the air that stirred the leaves and the ribbons of the canes, varied the colored shadows inside, in a constant tremolo. Entering, Bella sniffed the air, perhaps believing she was inside some Persian tent; then she pricked up her ears only slightly, at the sound of a bleat from the countryside, but she immediately lowered them. She too, like Useppe, had grown alert to the great silence which followed the isolated sound of that bleat. She crouched beside Useppe, and in her brown eyes a melancholy appeared. Perhaps she remembered her puppies, and her first Antonio at Poggioreale, and her second Antonio underground. It really was like being in an exotic tent, far from Rome and from every other city, who knows where, having arrived after a great journey; and outside an enormous space seemed to stretch, with no other sound but the calm movement of the water and the air.

A whirring ran above the foliage; and then from a half-hidden branch came a chirped little song which Useppe recognized without hesitation, having learned it by heart one morning, in the days when he was little. Indeed, he saw again the scene where he had happened to hear it: behind the guerrillas' hut, on the hill of the Castelli, while Eppetondo was cooking the potatoes and they were waiting for Ninnuzzu–Ace of Hearts . . . The memory came to him a bit vague, a luminous quavering, like the shade of this tent of trees; and it brought him no sadness, but on the contrary, it seemed a friendly little greeting. Bella also seemed to enjoy the song, because, still crouched, she raised her head, listening, instead of bounding up as she would have done on another occasion. "You know it?" Useppe whispered to her very softly. And in reply she flicked her tongue and raised an ear halfway, to signify: "I'll say I do! Of course!" This time, there were not two singers, but only one; and to judge by what you could see from below, he was neither a canary nor a goldfinch, but perhaps a starling, or rather an ordinary sparrow. He was an insignificant little bird,

431

of a gray-brown color. Peering up, taking care to make no movement or sound, you could better discern his lively little head and even his tiny pink throat which throbbed at his trills. Apparently, the song was popular among birds and had become the fashion, seeing that even sparrows knew it. And perhaps this one knew no other, since he continued repeating it, always with the same notes and the same words, except for a few imperceptible variations:

"It's a joke
a joke
all a joke!"

Or else:

"A joke a joke
it's all a joke!"

or else:

"It's a joke
it's a joke
it's all a joke a joke
a joke ohoooo!"

After having repeated it about twenty times, he whirred again and flew off. Then Bella, content, stretched out more comfortably on the grass, her head resting on her forepaws, and she began dozing. The silence, after the interval of song was over, expanded to a fantastic dimension, such that not only the ears but the whole body listened to it. And Useppe, in listening, had a surprise that would perhaps have frightened an adult man, subject to a rational scheme of nature. But his little organism, on the contrary, received it as a natural phenomenon, even if never discovered until today.

The silence, in reality, was speaking! or rather, it was made up of voices, which at first arrived somewhat confused, mingling with the trembling of the colors and the shadows, until the double sensation became one alone: and then it was clear that those quavering lights, also, in reality, were all voices of the silence. It was the very silence, and nothing else, that made the space tremble, its roots twisting deeper into the fiery center of the earth, and rising in an enormous tempest beyond the clear sky. Its clarity remained clear, indeed more dazzling, and the storm was a multitude singing a sole note (or perhaps a sole chord of three notes), like a cry!

However, within it, you could somehow distinguish, one by one, all voices and phrases and speeches, by the thousands and thousands of thousands: and songs, and bleatings, and the sea, and the alarm sirens, and shots, and coughs, and the engines, and the trains for Auschwitz, and crickets, and the exploding bombs, and the tiniest grunt of the tailless animal . . . and "hey, how about giving me a little kiss, Usè? . . ."

This multiple sensation of Useppe's, not easy or brief to describe, was in itself, on the contrary, simple and rapid as a figure in a tarantella. And the effect it had on him was to make him laugh. In reality, according to the doctors, this, again today, was one of the various signs of his disease: certain hallucinatory sensations are "always possible in epileptic subjects." But anyone happening past, at that moment, in the tent of trees, would have seen only a carefree, dark-haired little boy with blue eyes, looking into the air and laughing at nothing, as if an invisible feather were tickling his nape.

4 "Carloo! . . . ? . . . Vàvide . . . Ddàvide!"
The young man who preceded them at the distance of a few paces along Via Marmorata barely turned sideways. After the rapid visit to Via Bodoni the previous summer, Useppe had not seen Davide Segre (formerly Carlo Vivaldi and Pyotr); but Bella, on the other hand, had had further occasions to meet him, in the late summer and the following autumn, the times that Ninnuzzu had happened into Rome without finding a moment to show up at the house. Recognizing Davide immediately, she flung herself towards him with such impetuous joy that Useppe let her leash slip from his hands. (There had been a rumor circulating for some time, that the City dogcatchers were after stray dogs, and Ida, frightened, had bought a leash and even a muzzle, urging both Bella and Useppe to use them. And afterwards, convinced, whenever they were in inhabited areas, the two always remained thus linked to each other: with the natural effect that Useppe, the smaller, was led on the leash by Bella.)

The little voice which, shouting his names, had made the young man turn, had left him indifferent, however, just as if someone else had been called; nor was he quick to recognize Ninnuzzu's Bella in the stinking, festive dog that overtook him in the street. "Clear off!" was his first reply to that unknown dog. Meanwhile, someone else came running up: "I'm Useppe!" this other one announced with a bold mien; and bending over, he perceived two blue eyes smiling at him, in a quiver of greeting.

Recognizing them, Davide was almost frightened. His only wish, at that moment, was to be alone. "Ciao, ciao, I've got to go home," he said curtly. And turning his back, he continued with his clumsy gait towards the Ponte Sublicio. But as he was crossing the bridge, he was seized with remorse and turned around. He saw the pair, who after having followed him a couple of paces had stopped, dumbfounded, at the beginning of the bridge, the dog wagging her tail and the boy swaying with an uncertain expression, clinging to the leash with both hands. Then, to apologize as best he could, Davide made a hasty gesture of goodbye with his hand, and sketched an embarrassed, vaguely promising smile. This was enough for the two to rush to him, like a couple of baby chicks. "Where are you going?" Useppe confronted him, blushing. "Home, ciao ciao," Davide answered. And to be rid of them, he added, almost fleeing towards Porta Portese: "I'll be seeing you, eh? Later!"

Useppe, resigned, at this point gave him his usual goodbye, opening and closing his fist. But Bella, instead, fixed in her mind those words "see you later" as if they constituted a valid appointment. Meanwhile (it was almost one o'clock) she dragged Useppe by the leash towards Via Bodoni for lunch; while Davide, turning the corner, vanished beyond Porta Portese.

In reality, he was hastening to another appointment of his own, awaiting him at home, filling him with a furious desire, like the call of a woman. It was, instead, only a medicine to which he had been resorting for some time, in certain difficult hours, as he had turned to alcohol in the past. But whereas alcohol warmed him, perhaps exciting him even to rage, this other remedy had for him the opposite effect, promising him a state of calm.

After Ninnuzzu's death, he had fallen at first into a feverish restlessness, which every now and then drove him from his little Roman domicile, towards those places which still, from his brief past, could represent a kind of family. First he had turned up at the village of his wet-nurse, from whence he had departed immediately for Rome. Then a day later, he had gone back to Mantua, but from there he had soon taken the train south again. Some of his own anarchist comrades had seen him reappear in a café in Pisa or in Leghorn, where they used to meet in the days of his adolescence. To their questions, he had replied reluctantly, in monosyllables, or with forced smiles; and then he had sat there, frowning, taciturn, his legs never still, as if the chair made him itch or numbed his limbs. After about thirty minutes, in the midst of their talk, he had jumped up, with the impatience of somebody answering a call of nature; but instead, he had abruptly said goodbye to all, announcing in a grumble that he had to hurry to the station not to miss the Rome train. And without warning, as he had appeared, so he vanished once more.

One day, in Rome, he had boarded the little train for the Castelli, but he had got off at the first stop, to rush back. And more than once he had chanced to be seen in Naples . . . However, in all the places where he went, he found always the sole, definitive conviction that, as in Rome, so in any other city or town, he had no friend. And then there was nothing left for him to do but hole up in his rented room at Portuense, where at least he found a familiar bed on which he could fling his body.

In the final analysis, however, those journeys of his and those muddled sorties had not all been in vain. He had derived, at least, one profit from them, which could serve him from now on in his loneliness. And in calculating it, without any irony, he considered it a friendship, even if not a human friendship, but artificial and, in his opinion, revolting.

It had begun by chance a few months before, during one of his brief trips to Naples. Late in the evening, a young doctor, who had just taken his degree (whom Davide had known as a student in the days he had crossed the front lines with Ninnuzzu) had seen him suddenly arrive in his house. "Pyotr!" he had cried, recognizing him (he had introduced himself, in other days, with that name), and even before hearing him, he had realized the boy had come looking for help. Later, he was to remember that his immediate impression, merely looking at that face, was that he was receiving the visit of a suicide. In the almond eyes, hollowed, there was a nameless darkness, tormented and yet shy; and the muscles twitched, not only in his face, but in his whole body, under a charge of savage energy which could be consumed only in the form of pain. As soon as he entered, without even greeting his host (whom he hadn't seen, however, for perhaps two years), with the brutal vehemence of a housebreaker with a threatening weapon, he said he needed some medicine, any medicine, provided it was strong, a remedy that would act promptly, immediately, otherwise he would go crazy. He couldn't stand it any longer, he hadn't slept for days, he saw flames everywhere, he wanted a *cold, cold* medicine that would keep him from thinking . . . He wanted his thoughts to be detached from him . . . life to be detached from him! Exclaiming these words, he threw himself on a little sofa, not seated, but tangled, half on his knees against the back, and he hit the wall with terrible blows of his fists, threatening to fracture his knuckles. And he sobbed, or rather sobs formed in his chest, racking his body from within, though they found no release through his mouth, emerging barely in some painful and disjointed rattles. The young doctor's apartment, where they were, wasn't an office, but still his student dwelling, hardly more than a bachelor's rooms. Fixed to the wall with thumbtacks, there were some cartoons, cut out of weekly magazines . . . And Davide started ripping away those cartoons, shouting insults and curses. The host, who had always respected and admired him for his partisan exploits, did his best to calm him, to be of help. Here in the house, he didn't have a very well supplied dispensary; in his bag, however, brought home from the hospital where he was an intern, he had an ampoule of Pantopon. He gave him that injection, and a little later he saw Davide grow more quiet, indeed serene, like a starving infant who sucks his mother's milk. Relaxing, he remarked softly in his northern dialect: *"L'è bona . . . it's good . . . it's refreshing . . ."* and at the same time he gave the young doctor smiles of gratitude, while his eyes, steeped in a radiant mist, were already closing. "Sorry to bother you, so sorry," he kept repeating, as his host, seeing him falling asleep, helped him lie down on the bed in the adjoining little room. There he slept profoundly the whole night, about ten hours; and in the morning he woke soothed, sober; he washed, combed his hair, and even shaved. He wanted information about the treatment he had had, and his host straightforwardly explained it had been an injection of Pantopon, a medicine with a morphine base. "Morphine . . . that's a drug!" Pyotr commented, pensively. And he added, frowning: "Then it's shit." "That's right," the doctor replied with severity and with professional scrupulousness, "it's not usually advisable. However, in certain exceptional cases, it can be advisable." Still Pyotr had a saddened look, like a boy who has done something cowardly, and he continued striking the bruised knuckles of his fists against each other softly. "Don't tell anybody, eh?, that I shot that stuff into my body," was the last thing he murmured, shamefaced, to his host, before going off again.

From boyhood Davide had conceived a disgust and contempt for narcotics and drugs in general. Among the Segre family memories, there was handed down the story of a great-aunt, a story told by the younger generations, about a relative identified simply as *Aunt Tildina*, who had died in the hospital, they said, through a habitual abuse of chloral. She had died a spinster, about fifty, and in the family album, at home, there was a photograph of her at the time. You could see a pathetic little person, a bit hunched, almost bald—however, with her scant hair arranged in a coiffure with a black ribbon and little beads—in a tight striped jacket, a fur stole around her shoulders. For him, as a boy, that senile creature, with her tight lips, thin nose and protruding eyes, sad and with an old maid's faint eccentricity, had represented the archetype of bourgeois ugliness and squalor. And drugs, which traditionally he had always identified with Aunt Tildina, seemed to him a characteristic vice of the degraded and repressed bourgeoisie, which seeks escape from its guilt and its ennui. Wine is a natural release, virile and plebeian; whereas drugs are an unreal and perverse surrogate, something for old maids. Shame, which had depressed him already after his initial and almost involuntary Naples experience, came back to humiliate him more disastrously later on, at his every, voluntary relapse. And this shame gave him the strength to resist his own desire, up to a certain point, keeping him from falling into a total dependence on the enchanted medicine. There were some days, however, when the strange excess of energy that lacerated him, all directed towards an insoluble grief, drove him to an unbearable degree of anguish and horror. It was the breaking-point of his resistance. From this extreme point, the promise of his medicine opened to him like a great airy cleft at the end of a crumbling tunnel, from which he can take flight!

During those months (while accusing himself, in his own opinion, of illicit wealth), Davide lived off private means. On his last trip to Mantua, he had given that surviving uncle, whom he didn't like very much, a complete power of attorney, to dispose of his personal inheritance, which amounted, in all, to that apartment of five rooms where he had lived since childhood with his family. And as an advance against the sale of the apartment, his uncle sent him a postal money-order at the end of each month.

It was almost a miserable amount, but for him it was enough to survive meanwhile, given the gypsy existence he led. In his present life, there was no mistress, except for some poor mercenary affair, picked up on his occasional nocturnal desperado prowls and consumed there on the spot (under a ruin, or beneath the steps of a bridge) without even looking the woman in the face. It seemed to him, in fact, that he could recognize, in each of these lost girls, his Mantuan G., whom others (the ruling class of the time) had used in the same way he at present was using this one! And such exploitation was the equivalent of pimping; he felt as disgusting as those men; he was unworthy to raise his eyes! Then he released his need with the angry haste of someone performing an act of disfigurement; and he vastly overpaid his pickup, as if he were a rich American, afterwards finding himself perhaps without a lira, not even cigarette money.

Sometimes he drank, but less often than before. For food, when he remembered it, he ate standing, without plates or cutlery, at a pizzeria counter. And besides the rent of the room, these were his maximum usual expenses, to which was added, now, the single luxury of the new medicines. The use of certain drugs, however, was not very widespread in Italy at that time, so there was no difficulty about buying them, even cheaply.

After the first weeks, the fear of a fatal physical habit (which for him represented the ultimate dishonor) counseled him to replace opiates, on occasion, with substances of different composition, and different effect. For the most part these were sleeping pills, freely sold in pharmacies, and Davide swallowed them not only against nights of insomnia, but also in the morning and afternoon and at any moment when his own presence became intolerable to him. With their help, he plunged rapidly into a lethargy, in which he could lie immersed for whole days. But when he came out again, for him it was as if a moment had gone by since his falling asleep. The interval was zero. And the burden of indestructible time awaited him at the door of his room, like a boulder he had to drag after him. Then he would duly load it onto himself, trying to react. He would go out, come back, linger on the bridges, look into movie theaters and taverns, leaf through books . . . What was he to do, with his body?

His only consolation, on such days, was the knowledge that, as a last resort, he still had his first medicine, the Naples one, of which he always kept a supply on hand. None of the various other medicines he had tried could give him such a consolation, especially at the beginning, like a caressing hand—"it's nothing, it's nothing"—relieving things of their weight and also clearing his memory. Even his solitude, in those moments, proved a light episode, casual and temporary: extraordinary beings did exist on earth, his future friends, already moving towards him . . . "There's no hurry, no hurry. When I go out, maybe tomorrow, I'll meet them."

And every so often, between one remedy and another, used as alibi or alternative, he would go back to that unique one, fascinated, like a rake returning to his first love. He called these his *gala* days. They were his nourishment, but, unfortunately, ephemeral. Chemical solaces behave like the light bulbs in certain small hotels: they are regulated to remain burning just long enough for you to climb the steps to the floor above. But sometimes they go out when you are halfway up the stairs, and you find yourself left there like a fool, groping in the darkness.

·   ·   ·

That day of their encounter with him, Bella and Useppe, after eating in great haste, immediately ran out of the house again, according to their custom when the weather was fine. And, in fact, it was a summery day in May, the kind when, in Rome, all neighborhoods seem made of air and the whole city, terraces, windows, and balconies, seem everywhere bedecked with banners. The pair's natural direction, in such weather, as the day's light lasted longer, would have been towards Viale Ostiense, and from there on and on and on to the famous place of their recent discovery (the tree tent beside the water). But today Bella turned in the opposite direction, towards Ponte Sublicio; and Useppe promptly guessed that, having taken Davide at his word, she was running on his trail, to the appointment with him. To tell the truth, Useppe hadn't allowed himself to be deceived by Davide's words, obviously spoken at random, just to say goodbye, indeed with the obvious aim of getting rid of them quickly. And now this anxious suspicion made him somewhat uneasy. But as Bella was pulling him on the leash, happy and determined, he followed her to the hypothetical appointment without arguing, indeed with ardent breath.

He had never known Davide's address; but Bella knew it on her own, having already been there in Ninnuzzu's company. And the prospect of this imminent visit made her gallop with enthusiasm. Here we must recall that Davide, despite his misanthropic ways which made everyone else, more or less, take a dislike to him, often enjoyed success with animals and with small children. Did he give off some mysterious odor, particularly endearing to kids, cats, dogs, and such types? It's a fact that some girls, after having slept with him, said his rather hairy chest at night smelled of grass.

When they had come into the Porta Portese square, Bella raised her head and barked at the windows of the Gabelli Reformatory, which immediately reminded her of Poggioreale, where her first Antonio was locked up. Then, beyond the Gate itself, she lowered her tail and ears, turning stealthily towards the right: because there, on the other side, rose the walls of the City Pound, from which some lost cry could be heard; but she preferred not to let Useppe know about this.

There was the tavern, from which the usual radio noises were coming; and the hovels, and the shapeless vacant lot sown with garbage and rubbish. At that hour, not many people were to be found in the area. You could see, on the other hand, various dogs, rummaging amid the garbage or sprawled napping in the dust; and Bella, in spite of her eagerness to keep the appointment, still lingered with them, to exchange the usual ceremonies. One of those dogs was a tiny little cripple, like a dwarf monkey; another, big and rather swollen, resembled a calf. But Bella, who seemed a bear herself, recognized them nevertheless as her relations, and she celebrated their canine identity, greeting them peacefully and contentedly. With only one, a sturdy but slender type, of dappled color and with erect ears, the meeting was not cordial; both he and Bella snarled and bared their teeth, ready to jump on each other. "Bella! Bella!" cried Useppe, worried. And at this cry, luckily, a youth from a hovel called in a masterful voice, "Wolf! Wolf!", his authority succeeding in averting the conflict. That dog obediently reentered the hovel, and Bella, forgetting herself and him and all those other dogs in a moment, headed gaily for the little door of the ground-floor room which she immediately recognized, and she scratched on the wood, like one of the family.

"Come in!" Davide's voice exclaimed from inside. It was certainly his voice, but welcoming, with a light and content tone, never heard before. "The door's locked!" Useppe informed him in reply, with great trepidation. And then Davide, not bothering even to ask who it was, rising for a moment from the bed, where he was stretched out, came to the door; but before opening it, with a kick he thrust under the bed, from the rug on which they had been lying, a broken ampoule and a wad of cotton, stained with a few drops of blood.

"Who is it? Ah, it's you!" he said, with that incredible voice of his, clear and relaxed, as if Useppe's visit were a completely natural phenomenon: "Funny: I was thinking about you!" he added, brightening with an intuitive tenderness, faintly tinged with wonder: "I didn't know I was thinking about you, but now I understand: it was you I was thinking about."

And he lay down again on the bed, which hadn't been made for God knows how long. On the striped mattress there was only, at the head, a pillow gray with dirt, and, at the foot, a twisted sheet, also grayish. The blanket was piled on the floor near the chair, his pants flung on it and some newspapers. His jersey was on the floor farther away, in another part of the room.

"Bella's here too!" Useppe announced, as if the sight of her weren't enough, for Bella had actually preceded him inside, still attached to him by the leash. She celebrated the meeting by wagging her tail, but she restrained herself from some of her excessive and crazy demonstrations, no doubt conscious of a guest's duties. Promptly eyeing the heap of the blanket and assuming it was a bed prepared here on purpose for her, she settled on it like a bayadère, still wagging her tail.

Davide's body, almost supine on the bed, wearing only some briefs, revealed his terrible thinness; all his ribs protruded, but his face had a childish vivacity, filled with surprise but also with trust, as at a meeting between children of the same age who have run into each other.

"I recognized your footsteps," he declared, still with that simplicity of a moment ago, accepting the unlikely as a normal event, "tiny little footsteps . . . tiny tiny . . . And I thought: *here he is, he's coming; but who is he?* I didn't recognize the name, and yet I know it very well: Useppe! Who doesn't know it? Today wasn't the first time I thought of you, after all; lots of other times I've thought about you again . . ."

Useppe brightened, in a hopeful stammering. Every now and then, on looking at him, Davide would laugh briefly.

"You and your brother," he remarked in one breath, changing position, "are so different, you don't even seem like brothers. But you're alike in one thing: happiness. Your happiness is the joy of . . . of everything. You're the happiest creature in the world. Always, every time I've seen you, I've thought that, since the first days I met you, there in that big room . . . I always avoided looking at you, I felt such pity! And since then—would you believe it?—I've always remembered you . . ."

"Me too!!"

". . . eh, you were just a baby then, and you're still a little kid, all the same. Don't pay any attention to what I say: this is my gala day, I'm giving a ball! But when you meet me, you should run away: especially when I'm dancing! You're too pretty for this world; you don't belong here. What do they say? *Happiness is not of this world.*"

He untwisted that dirty sheet from between his legs and now drew it up over his chest, gripped by a comical feeling of modesty, but also of cold (among other things, he hadn't eaten). Unlike the hair on his head, which was wiry and almost erect, on his chest and under his armpits he had wooly curls, like astrakhan. And their exuberant black was in contrast with the present extreme pallor of his dark body which, in its thinness, seemed to have returned to a first adolescence. He had flung himself down with his head thrown back, and his eyes roamed towards the ceiling in an ingenuous meditation, grave and spellbound. In his face, though wasted and smudged with beard, today you could recognize that little student of the identity-card photograph the women of The Thousand had examined curiously, in a circle, the first evening of his arrival.

"I've always loved happiness!" he confessed. "On some days, when I was a boy, I was so filled with it I would start running, my arms wide, longing to yell: it's too much, too much! I can't keep it all for myself. I have to give it to somebody else."

But Useppe, meanwhile, was there, still yearning to clear up a fundamental point of their earlier dialogue: ". . . Me too," he resumed, from that point, in a kind of whirr, "you shouldn't think I forgot, about you, when you lived there with us, and you slept there! You had sunglasses, and a bag . . ."

Looking at him again, Davide's eyes laughed.

"From now on," he proposed, "will we be friends? Will we ALWAYS be friends?"

"Ess-ss . . . Yyess!"

"You still have that cowlick standing up in the middle of your head!" Davide remarked, looking at him, and laughing softly.

In the room, with the door closed, the afternoon light barely filtered through the curtain of the little window; and there was a stagnant, almost cold semidarkness. Clearly nobody ever swept or tidied up in there: cigarette butts were strewn on the floor, and some empty, crumpled packs of Nazionali, and here and there cherry pits. On a straight chair which served as bedside table there had remained an empty syringe, next to a bologna sandwich, barely bitten into at one end. For the furnishing, everything had remained, more or less, as in Santina's time. Only there were a few books on the table, while the doll had been eliminated or put away somewhere; and the two holy pictures on the wall were covered with sheets of newspaper.

The place somehow reminded Useppe of the big room of The Thousand, and he liked it without reservations. His happy little eyes wandered about, and he also took a few exploratory steps.

"And where are you going, all alone, in Rome?" Davide asked, raising himself up on one arm.

"We're going to the *sea!*" Bella interjected. Useppe, however, aware that Davide perhaps didn't understand the shepherdess's language, translated for him, correcting:

"We're going to the *river!* Not this river here," he promptly confided, "but farther on, past San Paolo! and then farther, lots farther on!!" He was about to tell Davide of their encounter with that winged songster who knew the refrain: "it's a joke . . . etc." but he changed his mind, and after a pause, asked him instead,

"Have you ever seen a little animal" (with his two hands he indicated its size) "without any tail, brown with yellow patches . . . and short legs? . . ."

"What other animal does it look like, for example? . . ."

"Like a rat . . . only without a tail . . . and its ears aren't as big!" Useppe eagerly explained.

"It could be . . . a dwarf pika? . . . a guinea pig . . . a hamster . . ." Useppe would have liked to give and ask further information; but Davide, following his own train of thought, remarked with a futile smile:

"Me, when I was a kid like you, I wanted to be an explorer, I wanted to see everything, do everything . . . But now," he added with a gesture of weakness and almost nauseated lack of appetite, "I don't even feel like raising my hand, or going any place . . . But one of these days I'll have to go to work! I want to do manual labor, something hard, so when I come home at night I'll be tired and I won't be able to think any more! . . . Do you think much?"

"Me? . . . yes, I think."

"What do you think about?"

Here Bella made a sound, to encourage Useppe. He wriggled on his little legs, looked at her, then looked at Davide again.

"I make poems!" he told him, blushing with secrecy and trust.

"Ah! Yes, I had heard you're a poet!"

"Who from?!" Useppe glanced at Bella, the only one who knew . . . (But actually, it had been Nino who, boasting to his friend of his famous if spurious little brother, had said to him, among other things: "If you ask me, he'll be a poet or a champion! You ought to see him jump! And hear him talk!")

"You mean you already write poems?" Davide resumed, ignoring Useppe's question.

"Nnooo . . . I don't want to *wite* . . . I . . . no . . ." (as usual, in moments of emotion or confusion, Useppe lapsed into his erroneous, abbreviated baby's utterance) ". . . I think the poems . . . and I say them . . ."

"Who do you say them to?"

"To her!" Useppe nodded towards Bella, who wagged her tail.

"Say them to me, too, if you remember them."

"No, I don't remember . . . I think them, then I forget them right away. There's lots of them . . . but little! LOTS, though! I think them when I'm by myself, and even when I'm not by myself, I think some sometimes!"

"Think one now!"

"*Ess.*"

Immediately, Useppe frowned, beginning to think. ". . . But just one isn't big enough . . ." he remarked, shaking his head, ". . . now I'll think a lot of different ones, and I'll say them to you!" The better to concentrate, he shut his eyes so hard his eyelids wrinkled. Then a moment later, when he reopened them, his gaze, like songbirds', seemed to follow a shifting, luminous point out of eyeshot. At the same time, accompanied by a swaying of his legs, his airy, shy little voice began to chant:

"Stars like trees and rustle like trees.
"The sun on the ground like a handful of little chains and rings.
"The sun all like lots of feathers a hundred a thousand feathers.
"The sun up in the air like lots of steps of buildings.
"The moon like a stairway and at the top Bella looks out and hides.
"Sleep canaries folded up like two roses.
"The ttars like swallows saying hello to each other. And in the trees.
"The river like pretty hair. And the pretty hair.
"The fish like canaries. And they fly away.
"And the leaves like wings. And they fly away.
"And the horse like a flag.
"And he flies away."

Since each of these lines for him was an entire poem, between one and another he had marked the pauses with a breath; until, having said the last, he gave a louder breath, stopped swaying, and ran towards his audience. Bella welcomed him with a little festive leap; and Davide, who had listened with great gravity and respect, declared to him firmly: "Your poems all talk about GOD!"

Then throwing his head back on the pillow, he seriously began explaining his personal opinion: "All your poems," he said thoughtfully, rationally, "center about a LIKE . . . And these LIKES, taken all together, in chorus, mean to say: GOD! The only true God is recognized through the resemblances of all things. Wherever you look, you discover a single, common imprint. And so, from one resemblance to another, step by step, you climb up to one alone. For a religious mind, the universe represents a process where, from one testimony to another, all in agreement, you arrive at the point of truth . . . And the most reliable witnesses, obviously, are not clergy, but atheists. And it's not with institutions, or with metaphysics that you testify. *God, that is nature* . . . For a religious mind," he concluded gravely, "there is no object, not even a worm or a wisp of straw, that doesn't testify equally to the existence of GOD!"

Useppe had seated himself familiarly on the easy chair, from which his thin little legs swung in mid-air, his naked feet in sandals; while Bella, comfortably curled up between bed and chair, gazed blissfully first at Useppe then at Davide. And Davide, meanwhile, pursued his own meditations aloud, as if he were disputing in a dream with some great Doctor, no longer realizing he was speaking to two poor illiterates. As if, indeed, he no longer remembered who, among the three there in the room, was the cultivated student, and who the kid and who the dog . . . Still, all of a sudden, his eyes stared with attention at a place on his own naked arm, where a slightly swollen vein showed a dot of blood on the surface, like an insect's bite. Every time he had recourse to his medicine, Davide always injected it at that precise point of that vein, always the same one, because of a mysterious fixation which perhaps concealed his intention of deliberately creating a visible sign of his own recidivous cowardice. However, the intoxication, which now cradled him like a mother, promptly distracted him from that defaming brand. He was taken with the musical pleasure of his own voice, while his eyes had become limpid in their blackness, like pure and cool water reflecting the night.

"Me, too, before," he said, smiling, his forehead half-hidden by his arm. "Years ago, I used to write poems: all poems about politics, or else about love. I didn't have a girl, I didn't even have a beard, but every day I met an average of at least five or six new girls, most of them strangers, to whom I would have liked to be engaged, since I thought each was more beautiful than the last. But the poems I addressed only to one, known as *Beloved*, who didn't exist; she was an invention of mine, and she was by far the most beautiful of all. I couldn't even picture her: I knew only that she had to be a virgin, and, preferably, blonde . . .

"The political poems, on the other hand, I addressed to every sort of person, past and present. I wrote to Brutus the Elder and Brutus the Younger, to the Tsar, and to Karl Marx: always in verse. Some of those poems, the first ones especially, come back to me, pounding in my head, mostly on gala days . . . They're schoolboy stuff, beginner's verses . . . I remember one called:

To the comrades

The Revolution, comrades, is not read in the texts
of philosophers served at their banquet by slaves
or by professors who negotiate at the table
the sweated struggles of the others.
The great Revolution is taught by the air
which gives itself to all breaths and receives them all.
It is sung by the sea, our infinite blood,
whose every drop reflects the whole sun!
So every human pupil reflects the entire light.
Comrades, men of all the earth!
We read the word of the revolution
in my-your-our eyes, all born to the light
of thought and of the stars!
It is written:
Man: thinking and free!" . . .

. . . "More!" Useppe said, when the recitation of this poem was over.
Davide smiled, agreeably: "Now," he said, "I'll tell you a love poem. I believe I wrote it about ten years ago! The title is:

Spring

You are like the primroses, still closed, that open
in the first March sun . . .
. . . Open, my beloved!
It is time! I am March!
I am April!! I am May!!!
O shell of the meadow, primrose of the sea,
spring is here, and you
are mine . . ."

". . . More!" Useppe demanded, this time too.
"More what?" Davide replied, laughing. "That's the end of the poem.

I must have written five hundred, maybe a thousand, poems, but my memory's empty . . ." With this, he thought again: "Maybe," he said, wrinkling his eyelids, "there's one I can remember, the last one! I didn't even write it down, it's been a long time since I've written any. I only thought it. It's very new. It came into my mind on its own, not many days ago, another *gala* day, and I think it was a Sunday, like today. I say *I thought it*, but that isn't exactly right. I seemed to be reading it already written down, I don't know where, like in ideograms, colored figures . . . And I don't even know what it means; in fact, I'd say it doesn't mean anything. It's title is LUMINOUS SHADOWS."

Useppe's feet wriggled in his impatience to hear the poem. Bella raised one ear slightly. And Davide abandoned himself to his recitation with a passive and almost absent voice, as if those irregular verses, short and long, were returning to his memory from a moving, reflected scene, the same where he had invented them the first time:

"Luminous shadows
'And how to recognize him?' I asked.
And they answered me: 'His sign
is the LUMINOUS SHADOW.
You can still meet him who bears this sign
which radiates from his body but also confines it
hence we say LUMINOUS
but also SHADOW.
Ordinary sense is not enough to perceive him.
But how explain a sense? No code exists.
It could be compared to the desire
that summons lovers around a girl,
irritable, plain, slovenly, but clothed
in her own unconscious erotic visions.
Perhaps an example could be found
in the tribal favor that consecrates
those born differently from the others, visited by dreams.
But examples are of no use.
Perhaps it can be seen perhaps it can be heard perhaps
it can be guessed
that sign.
There are those who await it who precede it who reject it
some believe they glimpse it at the moment of dying.
And surely it was for that sign that on the river Jordan
amid all the confused anonymous crowd

to *one* the Baptist said: "You are the one
who must baptize me, and ask of me baptism!" '
Shadows shadows shadows luminous
luminous lu-mi-nous . . ."

. . . "More!" Useppe said.
"And he wants *more!*" Davide protested, as he was beginning to drowse. "But you," he asked Useppe then, vaguely curious, "do you understand these poems?"
"No," Useppe answered sincerely.
"And you like listening to them all the same?"
"Yes," Useppe cried, simply, from the bottom of his heart.
Davide gave a little eccentric laugh: "Just one more, and that's that," he decided, "but by some other Author. Let me think. Maybe a poem like yours, with LIKE in it . . ." "Like! . . . like! . . . LIKE . . ." he began to declaim, as if becoming inspired, and with a joking voice, now almost without breath, lazy.
". . . *Like* . . . Ah, I've got it! This is called COMEDY, and it's about Paradise!!"
Useppe prepared to listen, his mouth open. He could hardly believe it was allowed to deal with such a subject!

". . . LIKE a river, light
Streaming a splendor between banks whereon
The miracle of the spring was pictured bright.
Out of this river living sparkles thrown
Shot everywhere a fire amid the bloom
And there like rubies gold-encrusted shone . . ."

". . . more!" Useppe ventured.

"As, with my eyes in shadow, I have seen
A meadow of flowers flashed over by the sun,
When cloud breaks and a pure ray glides between,
Many a clustered splendor, blazed upon
By ardent beams, was to my eyes revealed,
Although I saw not whence the blazing shone!
. . . . . ."

". . . more . . ."
Davide gave a great yawn of weariness. "No," he protested, "that's enough for now! . . . And you?" he inquired, turning his head towards Useppe, "do you believe in Paradise?"

". . . In . . . who?"

"In PARADISE!"

". . . I . . . I don't know . . ."

"As far as I'm concerned," Davide suddenly declared, "paradise or hell's the same to me. I want God NOT to exist. I want there to be nothing *beyond*, nothing at all. Whatever there might be, it would cause me pain. All things that exist, here, or *beyond*, cause me pain: everything I am, everything other people are . . . I want not to be any more."

"Are you sick or something?" Useppe, worried, asked him at this point. In fact, Davide's pallor had become ashen, and his gaze murky, like someone on the brink of sickness, or just emerging from it.

"No, no, I just feel sleepy . . . it's normal!"

Useppe had got down from the chair, and Davide glimpsed the little blue eyes examining him anxiously, and on either side of them, the little head's disheveled locks, so shiny and black they seemed damp.

"Don't you want us to stay here, to keep you company . . . ?"

"No, no . . . I have to be alone," Davide answered, in a restless voice, "we'll see each other again soon . . . another time!" Imitating Useppe, Bella had also risen on her four legs, all ready to follow him, or rather to take him off with her. After a hesitant silence, Davide heard the creak of the lock, which Useppe was struggling to pull with his little hands, then the door being closed with the minimum noise, out of respect for his sleep, and some little murmurs of comment, with a scrape of sandals, moving off. Davide was already dozing.

Meanwhile, on the floor above, they had turned on a radio, which was echoed, from other directions, by other radios, with the identical notes. Also shouted names were heard, dogs barking, the muffled clang of some tram, in the distance . . . More than a sleep, Davide's was an exhaustion, involved in a hybrid compound with wakefulness. He dreamed he was where he actually was, on his little bed in the room, and at the same time he was in the street. But his daydream's street displayed a vast and un-recognizable area, struck by a dazzling noon sun which, in the excess of its splendor, seemed more blind and mournful than a midnight. Perhaps the place was a station, it was invaded by a din of arrivals and departures, but no one could been seen. Davide had rushed there like the others who were awaiting someone's return or at least had someone to greet . . . But he knew already that for him this was a futile delusion. Suddenly it seems to him that a hand is waving a handkerchief from a window . . . and this is enough to move him infinitely. He waves in reply, but he realizes that handkerchief over there is an ugly, bloodstained rag, and he senses that behind it, half-hidden, there is a horrible smile, of incrimination and irony. "It's a dream," he remembers, to console himself; but still he doesn't bother to hasten his waking, because he knows that, anyway, it will be nothing but a long long continuation of this dream.

.   .   .

The next day, at the same time after lunch, as if the *appointment* with Davide were tacitly understood for every day in the week, the familiar couple Useppe-Bella impatiently retraced the same route to the ground-floor room; but today Davide wasn't at home. When there was no answer to Bella's scratching or to his own knocking, Useppe, suspecting Davide might be inside sick, climbed up some outcroppings of the wall to the low barred window. And vainly calling from there, "Vàvide . . . Vàvide! . . .", as the window was open, he pushed the curtain from outside and glanced into the room. Everything was the same as the day before: the bare mattress, the tangled sheet, the butts strewn on the floor, etc.; but the master of the house was absent. At that same point, from the little door of the courtyard, the room's landlady came out, the lame woman, who perhaps at first took Useppe for a thief!? However, seeing how little he was, she surely changed her mind:

"What are you doing here, kid?" she asked him.

". . . Vv . . . Dàvide!" Useppe explained, all red in the face, as he climbed down.

"Davide? I saw him go out a couple of hours ago. He mustn't of come back yet."

"When's he coming back? . . ."

"How should I know? He comes and goes. He doesn't say anything to me, about when he'll be back."

Bella and Useppe walked around the house, and stayed there for a while, in case Davide, sooner or later, happened to show up. From various parts, the usual dogs of varying breed appeared, all eager to greet Bella; but luckily, Wolf was not among them today. In the end, the two, resigned, went home.

The next day, at the same hour, Bella with prescient wisdom tugged the leash towards Viale Ostiense; but Useppe pulled in the opposite direction, suggesting: "Vàvide!" and, meekly, she again turned with him towards the room. This time Davide was at home, but evidently he wasn't by himself, since some low talk could be heard through the door. Useppe, all the same, mustered his courage and knocked.

". . . Who is it?" Davide's voice, almost frightened, said from inside, after a silence.

"It's me . . . Useppe!"

Another silence.

"It's us . . . Useppe! . . . and Bella!"

"Ciao . . ." Davide's voice then said, "but I can't let you in today . . . I'm busy. Come back some other time."

"When? Tomorrow?"

"No . . . not tomorrow . . . Another time . . ."

"When then?"

"I'll tell you when . . . I'll come and call you when . . . I'll come to your house and call you . . . Understand? Don't come back here again, until I come to your house and call you."

"You'll come and call us?"

"Yes . . . yes! . . . yes! . . ."

Davide's voice sounded hoarse, broken, and labored, but friendly and tender.

"You remember the *address?*" Useppe inquired, to make sure.

"Yes, I remember it . . . I remember."

Every time she heard Davide's voice again, Bella gave some leaps and then whimpered, her forepaws against the wood of the door, protesting against the forbidden entry. And Useppe, also, erect there, swaying on his feet, couldn't bring himself to conclude that dialogue. Something, still, was lacking . . . One fine moment, a new and seductive idea brightened him, and after a final tap, he brought himself to say:

". . . Vàvide, why don't you come and eat, when you come to our house to call us?! We've got tomatoes . . . and a stove . . . and pasta . . . and tomatoes . . . and . . . and . . . wine!"

". . . yes, thanks. I'll come. All right. Thanks."

"When will you come? . . . Tomorrow? . . ."

"Yes, tomorrow . . . or later . . . another day . . . Thanks!"

"You won't forget? . . . eh?!"

"No, no . . . But run along now . . . go on home."

"Yes. Let's go, Bella." And Useppe was already running towards Via Bodoni, eager to inform his mother there would be this guest for lunch tomorrow! And they should in all haste buy some wine (an exceptional purchase in their house, where the only drinker had been Ninnuzzu). But neither the next day nor the days that followed, though a whole flask of wine was kept ready in the center of the table for the special guest, and Useppe himself busily arranged a place for him with plate, cutlery, etc., did that guest show up. Even after the meal was over, Bella and Useppe delayed their daily outing, in case he came late. And they lingered a long time at the door of the building, before going off, peering down Via Bodoni in both directions, and also in its vicinity . . . But Davide hadn't made up his mind to come that way.

More than once, in those circumstances, Useppe was tempted to venture towards the prohibited ground-floor room . . . But Bella, with a look and a tug of the leash, chided him, "He didn't make an appointment with us!" until both decided on renunciation. And they took instead the long road already learned, which led to the beautiful tent of trees. This had become, for them, a habitual route. And in those very days, they had there the second extraordinary encounter of the season, after the one with Davide Segre.

5 Their recent excursions in the Portuense area had kept them away from here for three days. And as soon as they returned, after this absence, they found a mysterious innovation. At this time (the end of May) the place was still visited only by the two of them. On the fields nearer the city, some young Roman bathers were to be seen along the shore, especially on holidays. But that wooded area beyond the hillocks and the canebrakes remained distant and unexplored, like a virgin forest. Once, coming from the sea, a gull flew over, which Useppe believed a huge white swallow. And after that sparrow or starling of the first day, even under the tent, other similar starlings or sparrows often appeared, but actually let nothing more than their commonplace *tweet tweet* be heard, and normally they were scared off by Bella's festive welcomes. Their ignorance of the song *All a joke* was certain, but apparently already foreseen by Useppe. There existed, in any case, a sure proof that in their circles the beautiful song was known by now; and so, in his opinion, it could be confidently assumed that one of them, sooner or later, would sing it again.

As for his ephemeral and joyous hallucination of the first day there, Useppe had accepted it naturally, as we have seen; so once it was past, he forgot it almost entirely. From it, there remained in him, suspended in a minuscule territory, only an enchanted recollection, a rainbow where colors and voices were a unity, presumably enormous, beyond the branches through which it shed a luminous dust or murmuring. Even inside the city sometimes, for the space of an instant, all sounds and forms around Useppe might become composed, rising in a flash, an incredible flight, towards the final scream of silence. When you saw him cover his face with both hands, in the smile of a little blind child intent on a beautiful sound, it meant his whole tiny organism was listening to that rising choir which in the language of music (wholly unknown to him) would be called a *fugue*. It was again that same reminiscence returning to him in a different form. Perhaps, in some other imperceptible form, it accompanied him everywhere, bringing him always back to the tree tent as to a happy home.

Still, that home remained too solitary for him. His native, irrepressible instinct was to share his own pleasure with others, and so far only Bella shared the tree tent with him. He had tried to lure his mother there, at least for one single excursion, waving his arms to describe the site with enthusiasm, as well as with geographical precision; but Ida suffered too much in moving on her half-broken little legs, where instead of bones she now seemed to have slack ropes . . . To compensate for this refusal, Useppe had lately conceived a supreme ambition: to receive there, under the tent, Davide Segre! But so far, unfortunately, he hadn't found the nerve or the opportunity to invite him . . . And as for others—all the other people of the earth—he had for some time felt himself outlawed. Indeed, the deserted abandonment of that little hollow by the river allowed him to inhabit it with Bella.

Behind the circle of trees, sunk deeper in the slope, there was a second hollow, where the wood dwindled to a few bushes, so the ground there was drier and sunnier and even a few poppies bloomed. Useppe and Bella know it by heart (like all the other hollows and slopes around), and it was precisely there that Bella was used to drying herself in the sun after her daily bath.

In fact, Bella now bathed in the river every day, observed with regret by Useppe, who didn't know how to swim. Once, actually, seized by the desire, thinking of nothing else, he had hastily taken off his sandals and pants, and had started to fling himself in the water after her, to play. But alerted by her shepherdess's prophetic instinct, she had immediately turned back, arriving at the shore just in time to restrain Useppe, catching his jersey in her teeth. And then she had turned around to bark furiously at the river, as if it were a wolf. "If you do that," she had promptly said to Useppe, with a heart-rending moan, "you'll force me to give up my swim forever, and it's hygienic for me, among other things, to counteract my latest name, Crummy." And after that, Useppe had overcome his own temptation to swim, waiting in the sun, on the bank, for Bella to return from her bath, which for that matter lasted barely the time to cool off.

Now on this afternoon we mentioned, peering inside, at their arrival in the sunny hollow, the two found a hut of branches, very well built, which hadn't been there before. At present, like every other place in the vicinity, it was deserted; however, it must surely have been inhabited, from what they could immediately observe in their prompt and curious exploration. They found there, in fact: a little mattress (or rather a mattress-cover, ripped open along one side and stuffed, it seemed, with rags) with an army blanket over it; nearby, glued to a stone with its own wax, a partly consumed candle; and on the ground, several picture magazines, with comic-strip adventure stories. Moreover, in a hole that had been dug, they also found two cans of sardines and one of corned beef, along with a medal gilded to look like gold, the size perhaps of a small slice of roll, adorned with two legends, one around the circumference and one in the center, and carefully wrapped in cellophane, all hidden under a pile of still-fresh leaves. On the ground, outside the hole, there was an unwrapped paper, with leftover salt lupins. And outside the dwelling, spread out to dry on a rock, and held fast by a couple of stones, there was a pair of briefs, of a very small size. After having considered all these items, Useppe put everything back in its place as it had been before.

Here, however, to tell the truth, when the exploration was ended, Useppe preceded Bella outside the hut, and at that point something happened behind his back which cannot be ignored. Bella, in short, having second thoughts, retreated a couple of steps and in an instant ate all the lupins in the paper. Then in her boorish ignorance, without even suspecting she was culpable, she trotted gaily and contentedly after Useppe, who had noticed nothing.

For that whole day, the hut's unknown inhabitant didn't show up; and likewise the next day, at their arrival, there was nobody. Somebody must have been there in the interval, however, because to the objects listed above others had been added: a tin alarm clock, wound up; a half-consumed flask of water; and an empty Coca-Cola bottle.

While Bella, having had her swim, was drying out in the sun, Useppe withdrew to their tent, where she joined him a little later, stretching out to nap under the tree. And Useppe, who wasn't sleepy, climbed up the same tree, to a certain limb where he used to perch, when he was tired of playing, to sing poems there which he always invented on the spur of the moment and promptly forgot. On the higher branches, over him, the sun beat down; and except for some little birds' hasty visits, there was a population of infinitesimal creatures of odd aspect and, if you examined them carefully, of marvelous colors, who lived in the trunks and frequented the leaves. These, too, in the sun, displayed to Useppe all the colors of the rainbow, and also others, unknown: with patterns of fabled geometry, which Useppe's eyes entered like travelers in an Arab quarter. Moreover, from that sentry-post, his eyes could cover a stretch of the river, and the sunny shore.

Useppe had been there perhaps half an hour when he glimpsed, in the rippled water of the river below, a pygmy head advancing, then two arms emerging, and an entire little boy sneezing as he came out of the water. Surely believing himself unobserved by anyone, as soon as he reached land, he slipped off his little bathing briefs. And all naked, he ran towards the downward slope, where he vanished.

Unquestionably, he was the inhabitant of the mysterious hut! At this discovery, Useppe called Bella from above; but sleepily, she answered him with a slight flick of her left ear, not even opening her eyes. And Useppe decided to wait, shifting towards higher branches to peep and see if there he could observe some other sign of life from the stranger. But even from up there, the hut was invisible to him; everything was deserted around them; and only the rustle of the current could be heard, amid the buzzing of the afternoon light.

Suddenly, Bella pricked up her ears and leaped up, warned, perhaps by her nose, of something new in the offing. And frantically wagging her tail, still alert, she let out a bark, grandiose but cordial.

This bark's effect was not immediate, but almost. Half a minute later, footsteps approached. And with the caution of an explorer advancing through a fierce jungle, the little boy of a moment earlier, no longer naked, presented himself beneath the tent of trees. At the sight of him, Useppe, as if at a sensational apparition, seized with great high spirits, slipped down his treetrunk in furious haste. Seeing this boy close to, Useppe thought he immediately recognized an undeniable resemblance to the unforgotten tailless animal.

The boy had, in fact, thin little arms and legs, exceptionally short in their proportions (though he himself was far from tall). His face, especially seen in profile, protruded like an animal's muzzle. His eyes were round and set apart, of a lively olive color; his nose, small and restless, was almost flat. And his mouth, so straight it seemed without lips, still stretched to his ears when he condescended to smile.

On his head, recently shaved, a thick wool was growing back, like a little brown coat; and some tiny tufts of hair also blossomed from his ears, which were minuscule, and stuck out somewhat. Finally, over his white polo shirt and his dark gray shorts, this character wore, at present, a comical makeshift garment, not even sewn, and with two holes for sleeves: it derived, apparently, from a piece of khaki tarpaulin, once hastily painted here and there with patches of greenish-brown paint!

From his height, you would have thought he was eight, or at most nine; whereas, in reality, he was twelve (nor did he fail, when necessary, to boast of this seniority, affirming a long past, a life full of experience).

Having arrived in the pair's presence, he eyed them, still cautious and on guard, but with a certain obvious superiority. And, irrepressible, his proud gaze betrayed a joyous satisfaction in resting on Bella. In fact, his hand (or little paw) reached out to touch her:

"Anybody else here, with you two?" he asked then, grimly.

"Nooo . . . Nobody else!"

"You're by yourselves?"

"Ess."

"And who are you?"

"I'm Useppe. And this is Bella."

"And what did you come here for?"

". . . To play . . ."

"Is today the first time you've come here?"

"Nooo . . . We've been here a thousand times . . . MORE than a thousand!" Useppe declared.

It seemed a real third degree. The mysterious being looked Useppe straight in the face, with an air of complicity, but also of authority:

"I warn you: you mustn't tell anybody in the whole world you saw me. You understand? NOBODY in the world!"

Useppe shook his head in reply, as if to say no, no, no, with such ardor that not even a blood-oath could better have guaranteed the secrecy due this stranger.

The newcomer then sat down on a stone; and as, with a worldly air, he lighted a cigarette he had fished from his shorts, he explained:

"The cops are after me."

From his tone, you might have surmised that all the police forces of Italy, and perhaps of Europe, were hot on his heels. A silence followed. Useppe's heart was pounding. Inevitably, in his imagination, all the stranger's pursuers appeared in the guise of so many Professor Marchionnis, heavy, bespectacled, elderly, and with drooping moustaches.

But the other boy's heart, meanwhile, was so irresistibly transported towards Bella, with such emotion, that on his little face, or muzzle as may be, a smile shone, his lips clenched, but extending from ear to ear, and multiplied in so many little wrinkles, while his eyes brightened smartly, intent, like a lover's.

"You want a smoke, too?" he asked her (while she, returning his feelings, made a fuss over him, close, almost nose to nose). And, joking, he blew a little smoke into her nose. At which, also joking, she reacted with a kind of merry sneeze.

"Is BELLA her real name?"

"Yes, her name's Bella."

"Is she old?"

"Nooo . . ." Useppe answered. And then he declared, with a certain personal emphasis:

"She's littler than me!"

"How old are you?"

Calculating, Useppe showed first one hand with all the fingers extended, then the other hand, with only one finger raised, which, on reflection, he crooked a little at the knuckle.

"Five, going on six!" the other deduced immediately. And in return, he declared, with great pride:

"I'm going on THIRTEEN!" Then, assuming a slow and condescending attitude, he went on to say:

"Down home, back in my village, we have a dog, too, but not this big, medium-size, with a black face and pointy ears. He only has one and a half ears, because his father ate the other half.

"He belongs to my uncle, my mother's brother, and he takes him hunting."

He paused, then concluded:

"His name's Tòto."

After this, they remained silent. Finishing his cigarette, the stranger took the last puffs from the butt with hasty and ostentatious voluptuousness. Then he buried the miserable remaining stub, in a very proper way, as if he were giving it a decent burial, and he stretched out on the grass, propping his head against the stone. Bella had sat down next to him, and Useppe, in turn, had huddled on the ground, facing him. They remained in silence, gazing at one another, finding nothing further to say. Suddenly Bella raised her head abruptly, but she didn't bark or move from her place.

A little bird had lighted on a high branch, directly above them. It was quiet for a moment, then it skipped two or three times on the same branch, then made several movements of its head (as if to tune its own song), and then it sang. A wondrous merriment flooded Useppe's veins. Bella also had immediately recognized the song, for she looked up, pleased, her mouth open, her tongue quivering slightly. For his part, the third listener remained quiet, peeping upwards with a single eye, distracted or absorbed in his own thought.

At the bird's parting whirr, Useppe started laughing, running towards the newcomer. "Hey!" he called him impetuously, with an exultant little cry. And without hesitation, he asked him:

"You know that song?"

"What song?"

"That one he was singing just now!"

"Him who? The *acedduzzo?*" the fugitive from justice asked suspiciously, one of his little paws pointing towards the branch.

"Yes!" And thrilled with secrecy, but impatient to tell him the news, Useppe revealed in one breath: "It goes like this:

It's a joke a joke all a joke!"

"Who told you that's how it goes?!"

Useppe didn't know how to answer this question; still, transported by the little song, he irresistibly repeated it, and this time without omitting the notes.

The stranger had an idle and luminous little smile, shrugging one shoulder at the same time: "The *aceddi*," he affirmed, "have a language all their own. How can anybody know it? . . ." He made a skeptical grimace, but a little later, in a self-important tone, he said:

"In my village, there's a wine-seller who's also the barber, and he has a real talking *aceddu*, it talks just like a human! But you don't find that kind of *aceddu* in the trees. It's not Italian. It's a Turk. And he says hello and says Happy Easter and Merry Christmas, and dirty words, and laughs. He's a parrot. All different colors. And he learned a song they sing in my village, and he sang it!"

"How does the song go?" Useppe asked.

"It goes like this:

I'm the king and cardinal,
I can talk and laugh.
But when I'm in company
I can also shut my mouth!"

At the sound of all these songs, Bella had started jumping, as if at a festival. Useppe, on the contrary, had sat down in the grass again, to contemplate the mysterious being.

"What's the name of your village?" he asked him.

"Tiriolo."

In uttering this name, the interlocutor assumed a smug look, like one mentioning, to a group of illiterates, a place of exceptional renown: "Last year, during the Giro d'Italia, Bartali went through, the champion cyclist!" he declared. ". . . I even have a medal I snitched from a Shell station! A medal made in honor of Gino Bartali in some big industrial factories in the Kingdom of the Mountain, near Milan . . ."

Here Useppe blushed, remembering, in fact, the cellophane-wrapped medal he and Bella had already observed inside the hut of boughs. Surely this stranger would have been displeased to know his house had been discovered . . . But he didn't notice Useppe's flush, having at that moment lowered his eyes, concealed by two thick fringes of lashes. Suddenly, a coughing fit, brutal considering his smallness, attacked him like a series of slaps. As soon as he had caught his breath again, he remarked proudly:

"Smoker's cough!"

And digging into the pocket of his shorts, he took out an almost intact pack of Lucky Strikes. "American!" he boasted, showing them to Useppe. "They were a present!"

"Who gave them to you?"

"A faggot."

Useppe was unaware of this epithet's meaning, but rather than seem too ignorant, he refrained from asking it.

Along with the cigarettes, he had taken from his pocket a piece of newspaper, which he examined with formal ostentation, as if it were a top-secret document. There was a little news item of a few lines, headed: *Three boys escape from Gabelli Reformatory. Two captured. One still at large.* And below, among other things, there was mentioned a certain *Scimó Pietro*, from Tiriolo (province of Catanzaro). After having examined the document at length, as if he hadn't known it by heart for some time, the fugitive made up his mind and, submitting it to Useppe, with his little black fingernail, he underlined the words *Scimó Pietro*. But for Useppe, who didn't know how to read, those two words, no less than the entire document, were an undecipherable enigma. Then the other boy revealed to him with braggadoccio: "That's my name. That's me. Scimó!"

(His full name, actually, as revealed also in the document, was Scimó Pietro. Scimó was his surname. But he was used to being called only by that surname.)

"Now you know my name. But I'm telling you: nobody else must know it. Don't tell anybody my name, or that you saw me here!"

Useppe guaranteed his secrecy with new and repeated shakes of his head, even more impassioned, if possible, than the earlier ones.

Then, with total trust and brotherhood, in a low voice, the above-named Scimó informed Useppe that he had escaped from the Reformatory, where his relatives, and in particular his brother, wanted to keep him locked up. But he didn't feel like staying shut up in there. During an outing to the Janiculum with his whole troop, he and a couple of others had slipped away. The undertaking had been planned by him, with them, in every detail. First of all, they had taken advantage of the fact that the instructor on duty that day, Signor Patazzi, had an intestinal ailment that forced him to retire now and then, leaving surveillance momentarily to the group leader. With clever stratagems they had managed to distract this boy's attention, and vanish. And while his other two companions in the escape had stuck together (and this surely had been the first thing to screw them, because, paired like that, they had been easy to find), he, with the true science of jailbreaks, had bidden them goodbye at the start, to go off on his own. A little later he had hastily removed the uniform jacket and cap; and for various hours he had hid in a garbage can full of leaves, dried grass, horse dung, and so on, emerging only under cover of darkness. In advance, he had cleverly supplied himself with some cards from the gift-package chocolate bars (these cards now had considerable trading value on the market), taking them with him, concealed in his shoes, along with his precious medal of the Giro d'Italia. And that same evening, in exchange for the cards, a character in Trastevere had given him these civilian pants he was now wearing. He had then tailored for himself this camouflage (it was the already-described khaki garment with colored spots) the better to hide, living underground. And now, maybe those other two had let themselves be caught, but he was never going to be captured, that was sure, living or dead.

Scimó's narrative had been followed by Useppe (and also by Bella) with the intensity of thrilling news, especially in the climaxes. Not only their ears, but their whole bodies were swept away by it. And as for Scimó himself, he had accompanied his speech with such a gesticulation of legs, head, arms, and fingers, that at the end he had to be quiet and rest. But a little later, as if to seal an exclusive triple pact with those present, by revealing, after his past, also his future, he said, in dazzling boldness:

"I'm going to be a bicycle racer."

A great silence followed. With the sun already towards the west, that invisible rainbow, always open and curved over the tree tent, scattered all its lights like little weightless wings, shifting and humming, where among the hundred thousand colors a golden orange predominated, with violet and Nile green. And their buzz resembled a mixed resonance, as of countless voices and strains of music, which came from far away; but here, too, certain special voices predominated, and these were soft, as of crickets, water, and tiny girls.

Useppe, delighted, started laughing. He wanted to return Scimó's great confidences, revealing to him some personal secret, unique and extraordinary; but he didn't know what to say to him, though he saw him already bent forward, impatiently. So, by whim, and without having thought about it, Useppe whispered into his ear, indicating with his hand the surrounding tent of trees:

"Here there's God."

Scimó grimaced, as an experienced and skeptical man, though the grimace still did not herald (as one might have thought) a profession of atheism. He declared, instead, with some self-importance:

"God's in church."

At this point, considering it had grown late, he said he would have to leave soon: "By now, the four-o'clock show must of begun a while ago!" he considered, with the tone of a businessman who has great responsibilities that can't be postponed. And he explained he had to be at the Ostiense Station to meet a friend of his from Garbatella (who had free tickets), to go to the movies with him afterwards:

"I don't care much," he added, "about the picture, because I've seen it twice already. But I want to get there at least in time for the end of the first show, because that's where you find the faggots, and they take me to eat a pizza afterwards."

Here were those Faggots again! Obviously, famous and munificent personages, of whom Useppe had no idea! Still, not even this time would he confess to Scimó his own ignorance. He heaved only a faint sigh (which nobody noticed); also because, on top of everything else, he had never been to the movies in his life.

In rising from the ground, Scimó displayed, with a certain careless ostentation, the white polo shirt he wore beneath his camouflaged jerkin. It was very elegant (unlike his shorts, which seemed to have come from a ragman's cart): new, clean, and decorated on one side with the drawing of an anchor, in blue. It was, Scimó said, Australian: and it turned out that this too had been given him by a FAGGOT! In fact, one—whether the same, or another, it wasn't clear—of these Faggots had also promised him a pair of summer shoes, tennis style, and maybe, in the future, also a wrist-watch and a pillow! Useppe was definitively convinced that these mysterious personages mentioned by Scimó must certainly be spectacular creatures, of a supreme magnificence! And in his mind he pictured them as a cross between Santa Claus, the Seven Dwarfs, and the Kings on playing cards.

Scimó said that now, before going into the city, he had to "go by his house" to take off his "camouflage jacket" (so he called it) which, in the city, he said, would be counterproductive. Here, having pronounced in full this very difficult word, he had to stop for a minute to catch his breath; but a moment later, looking around again with extreme secrecy, he went on to say that today it was too late, but tomorrow, if they happened by here, he would show them "his house": a hut he had built himself, complete, where he retired and lived clandestinely, which was in a hidden spot in the vicinity.

At this speech, as when the medal had been mentioned before, Useppe's face flushed with prompt redness, which this time didn't escape Scimó. He eyed it, puzzled and suspicious, until, in encountering those eloquent pupils, amid the general silence, he had a kind of illumination; and without further hesitation, he burst forth in a terrible tone of denunciation:

"Who ate my fusaie?!"

At this, Useppe was more upset than ever, since he knew nothing of the lupins incident. Nor was Bella herself, for that matter, able to understand the question. Among other things, in the human vocabulary known to her, the word *fusaie* was lacking: they were called lupins. And her misdeed in the hut had left not the slightest recollection in her big sheepdog's head. The only thing she understood was that Scimó, at present, for some obscure reason, was growing angry with Useppe; and then, in the urgent necessity of soothing him, filled with innocence, she flung herself on his neck, giving his whole face an amorous lick, plus a few painless nips at either ear.

And it happened that this gesture of peace was interpreted by Scimó as a self-denunciation on Bella's part! So on his own, if through a misunderstanding, he realized how things had actually gone. In the face of the shepherdess's confession he could only pardon her at once. Indeed, he promptly smiled at her, this time also revealing his teeth, which were very small, spaced, and already dark and in bad shape. And Useppe, in return, smiled with consolation (displaying, in turn, his own little baby teeth). Then Scimó decided to be bighearted:

"Hell, what's a few *fusaie?*" he said, with a lordly grimace, "and I had already figured, on my own, some animal going by had eaten them . . . The important thing," he added, lowering his voice, "is that the Pirates didn't come in!!!" And he went on to explain that, on the opposite bank of the river, there existed a notorious band of pirates, headed by a certain Agusto, who was over sixteen, and once had been a rival even of the superfamous Hunchback of Quarticciòlo! These Pirates had a boat at their disposal, and went roaming up and down the whole shore, taking things! and setting fire to huts! and killing animals! and attacking people! So far this year they hadn't been seen around those parts; but last year, in July and August, they had definitely been there. And they had thrown a car into the river with the people still inside! destroyed huts! beaten up a deaf-mute! and made love with a calf!

After this, Scimó took his leave. But on going off, he said to Useppe and Bella that if they happened to come back tomorrow afternoon, they could look for him directly at his house, since they already knew the place. But nobody else was to know! He then urged them to be on time, because tomorrow he had to leave earlier; there was a new movie at the theater, and he wanted to see this picture from the beginning.

"Tomorrow," he announced, "when you come, I'll show you a place, near my house, where the cicadas make their nests."

.   .   .

The next day all three met, extremely punctual, at the rendezvous. And in addition, Bella and Useppe had another unexpected encounter along the way. Obviously, this was a season of encounters for them. They were going along the last stretch of Viale Ostiense, the Basilica already in sight, when a woman's fresh voice called after them: "Useppe! Useppe!" There, waiting at the bus stop, was a girl with a little baby in her arms and a straw bag

461

over her shoulder. "Useppe! Don't you recognize me?" she went on, smiling sweetly. Bella was already sniffing her with some familiarity, but Useppe, for the moment, couldn't say who she was: rather, the small infant, though a stranger, had a face that seemed to recall somebody else . . . It was a little girl, still unweaned, clearly female because she wore earrings. Her cheeks were round and vermilion, her eyes very black, already bright and laughing. And her dark hair, moist and fine, an inch or so in length, was all neatly smoothed down, except for a single lock, curled with great care, which lay across the top of her head.

"Don't you recognize me? Patrizia! You remember me?"

" . . . . "

"Don't you remember any more? . . . eh? . . . when we went riding together on the motorcycle! . . . You remember!"

" . . . *ess* . . ."

"And this is Bella? . . . Isn't it? You're Bella, right? Hey, Bella, you knew me!? . . ."

Patrizia seemed much fatter, and at the same time with a worn and suffering look in her face. Now, she wore her black hair tied by a ribbon on top of her head, and hanging behind in a long swinging tail. Instead of all the various jewelry that used to tinkle on her, now she wore only a little bracelet of copper and other metals, which tinkled too, frequently, because it was made up of several strands that jangled together with her movements. And every time, at that tinkle, the baby would wiggle her hands and feet in amusement. She was wearing a white shirt with a little lace border, and the rest of her person was wrapped in a printed cloth, with colored drawings from animated cartoons, allowing her arms and part of her legs to remain free. On her feet she wore white booties, knitted by hand, tied with a lively pink ribbon. Her tiny earrings, like buttons, were of gold.

Patrizia shook her head, observing Useppe, who peered up with a little smile. "I knew you right away, Useppe!" she said to him. "And this," she added, "is your niece!"

Useppe seemed puzzled. "Yes, she's your niece! You're her uncle!" Patrizia confirmed, laughing with a tremulous face. And taking her little daughter's wrist and moving it, as if to wave, she began saying to her: "Ninuccia, say hello to Useppe! Wave to Useppe . . ." Suddenly, her laughter broke in a convulsive sobbing. She tried to dry her tears as best she could with the baby's little fist, still suspended in its wave, putting it to her eyes.

"Ah, I still can't believe it . . . All these months have gone by, and it still doesn't seem real to me! I expected anything but that. That I didn't expect! That he would leave me all alone with my big belly, and go off. I was expecting that. But not this other, not this!"

Then, again she smiled at Useppe, her face swollen from crying, and nodding her head, she said to him, in a voice a little maternal and a little infantile:

"Ah, Useppe, he really loved you, he did! I was even jealous, because he loved you more than me! He even hit me once, when I said something about you!"

". . . Our bus is coming," she observed hastily, drying her tears with a handkerchief fished from her bag with difficulty, ". . . eh, we'll be going . . . so long, Useppe."

You could see, from behind, her thickened hips swaying because of her high heels, then her naked legs were visible as she climbed into the bus, with the assistance of the conductor, who had leaned down to lend her support out of respect for her burden of the baby. At that time of day, there were few passengers on the bus. She immediately found a seat by the open window, and from there she waved again a vague goodbye, which seemed bitter, and already distant. Useppe went on waving, opening and closing his fist slowly, while the bus resumed its route, and Bella, sitting on the sidewalk, followed its movement with a troubled panting of her nostrils and tongue. The last glimpse they had of those relatives of theirs was Patrizia's immense, shiny-black mane; and, below her bent face, the coy curl of Ninuccia, in the center of her smooth, dark little head.

.   .   .

When they reached the place of the rendezvous, they found Scimó outside the doorway of his hut, as if he were waiting for them. Even before greeting him, Useppe almost breathlessly announced he had met, just a little while ago, a kid who was his niece, and he himself was her uncle! But Scimó received this amazing news without being too awed by it. He himself, he said, was the uncle of several nieces and nephews (children of his older brothers), including a niece fourteen years old! "And my mamma," he announced further, "back at the village has a niece that's her aunt, too!"

And after this, frowning with the mental exertion, assisting himself in the calculation with all ten fingers, he set to explaining that his grandfather Serafino, father of his mother, had about ten younger brothers, some dead and some living, and among these the youngest was an American (or rather an emigrant to America). Time went by, and he was left a widower.

Now, this same grandfather Serafino had, on his own, nine children: six girls and three males, and that meant his mother had five sisters and three brothers. And they were all married with children (except three: a nun, and another little sister who had died young, and another brother who was shot up). And some had four, some seven, or three or six boys and girls, big and little, and all were nieces and nephews of his mother: and amongst them there was one named Crucifera, already grown up, a young woman.

Time goes by, and that American widower (Ignazio by name), already nearly old, came back to the village to open a store. And one fine day he said: "How'm I going to manage here, without a woman?" and he took that young Crucifera, who, since she was already the niece of Scimó's mother, suddenly, having married the uncle, became also her aunt! The same Crucifera, moreover, Scimó's cousin, also became a kind of half-grandmother to him, because she was the sister-in-law of his grandfather Serafino, who was also her grandfather and everybody else's!

"Where is he now?" Useppe inquired.

"My granddad's at Tiriolo."

"And what does he do?"

"He treads the grapes."

Useppe asked no further information: especially since Scimó was dying now to show his guests the main thing: namely the famous medal of the Giro. He no longer kept it in the hole, where it was threatened by the damp, but at the bottom of the mattress cover that served him, as was seen, also as storage place for clothing and other things; and he had wrapped it also in a second protection of tinfoil, besides the cellophane.

It was, as far as I know, a little medal made to advertise a brand of tires, of very light metal, a gold-yellow color, and circular, bearing in the center the declaration: BARTALI the KING OF THE MOUNTAIN uses such and such tires, etc., etc., and around the edge the decorative legend *Giro d'Italia 1946*—with other appropriate data (all hieroglyphics, obviously, for Useppe). As soon as the double wrapping was undone and the medal appeared, Bella sang, celebrating it: "I've seen this before!" while Useppe inevitably blushed; but luckily, Scimó neither understood Bella's speech nor was he, at the moment, observing Useppe, since he was occupied with examining the medal fore and aft, to make sure the dampness hadn't damaged it too much. In fact, he didn't take his eyes off it even as he held it out to Useppe (barely time for a quick look); and he hastened to rewrap it and put it back where it had been before. He continued, however, rummaging among the old newspapers and the rags that stuffed his mattress, surely having some other interesting thing still to display. And in fact he first took out a varicolored little comb, the kind seen on stands selling American goods; then a shoe buckle with glass diamonds, found in the street; and then half a windshield wiper. He showed them the alarm clock that really worked; to tell the truth, it worked even too well (it was fast, but he could tell time by the sun); and moreover, the latest novelty, a battery flashlight, like the ones Useppe had seen with the partisans. He said this one lasted 200 hours! Actually it was at present without a battery, but the guy who had given it to him had promised to supply one very soon.

"Who gave it to you?" Useppe asked.

"A FAGGOT."

The cicadas' nest proved an attraction, but mysterious. About sixty yards from the hut, behind the little hill, a tree grew, its trunk rather short compared to the grand height of its crown of leaves. One of its boughs was marked by a long cut, and Scimó said that was a deposit of cicada eggs. Then, pointing out a little hole in the shifted earth at the tree's root, he explained that down there was a nest where the eggs went to be hatched. He further declared that he had discovered, the day before, a little cicada just hatched from the nest, at the very moment when, attached to the tree's bark, it was toiling its way out of its shell. Since he had to go into the city, he had left it there, still dazed and half stupid, waiting for the moment to learn to fly. At present, however, along with the cicada, the shell had vanished: maybe some preying animal had stolen it, or maybe the wind had blown it away. And the cicada, having learned to fly by now, maybe lived up above in the same tree or in some tree nearby; and soon they would hear it sing, provided it was a male. Because only the males can sing; the females can't.

Useppe had heard the song of cicadas in the past, but he had never seen one. Both he and Scimó, however, agreed on not disturbing the earth of the nest, so as not to interrupt the hatching of other little new cicadas. In fact, according to Scimó, the one he had seen was a cicada scout, who had come up ahead, and would surely be followed by a numerous family of mute females and singing males.

And they went off to the banks of the river, where Scimó wanted to have a swim, before going to the movies. Here Useppe had to confess, with regret, that he didn't yet know how to swim. And he remained on the shore, grief-stricken, while Bella and Scimó splashed in the water.

Coming out completely naked, Scimó showed Useppe his genitals, boasting that he was already a man: completely virile, so much so that, if he thought of certain things, for example of kisses in the movies or of his cousin-grandmother Crucifera, he could even swell up. And Useppe, curious, decided to show him, in turn, his own little cock, to find out how far he had progressed. Scimó told him that he, too, beyond doubt was also a complete male, but he still had to grow. And Useppe then thought that, when he had grown, he would also perhaps be able to sing in a full voice, like the male cicadas.

Scimó's body, scrawny and gawky, was marked by various scars, whose explanation he immediately furnished Useppe. One, the most recent, on the leg, had been given by an instructor in the Reformatory with a stick. Another older scar on his arm, almost at his shoulder, had been given him by one of his older brothers, aged twenty-one, hitting him with a mule-harness. This mean brother, according to Scimó, was, of the whole family, the most determined to keep him locked up with the reform-school boys.

The third scar, which marked his upper forehead, near the hairline, he had given himself, banging his head against the door and against the walls, when they had locked him up in solitary confinement at the Reformatory. Remembering this cell, Scimó gave a kind of groan; his little face seemed to shrink still further, his eyes wide and staring. And suddenly filled with unexpected desperation, he flung himself down on all fours, slamming his head furiously against the ground, three times in a row.

Now he had to leave. And Useppe, with regret in his soul, could already see him arriving at the pinnacled movie Palace, there to meet those creatures of mysterious splendor, givers of gifts, whose person, title, and everything, really, were incomprehensible to him. And finally, though without admitting this ignorance of his, he moved in front of Scimó and, swaying, ventured with a shy voice:

"Why don't you take me with you, to the Movies, to meet *the faggots?*"

And he showed him that, buttoned up in a pocket of his overalls, he even possessed some change (which Ida had given him before he went out, to buy himself an ice-cream cone).

But Scimó shook his head protectively, and looking at him with a paternal eye, said:

"No, you're still too little." Then, perhaps to make his refusal more plausible, he added:

"And besides, they don't let dogs into the theater."

After which, seeing Useppe's disappointed expression, he lingered a few more moments with him. But he said at last, "I've got to hurry!" and to console him he solemnly promised:

"I don't have time today, but the next time you come here, I'll teach you how to swim."

"We'll be back tomorrow!" Useppe hastened to answer.

"Tomorrow's Sunday; the first show starts at three. But if you come early enough, I can start teaching you how to float and do the dog-paddle."

As he ran towards the hut, leaving the other two on the bank, his "smoker's cough" could be heard in the distance, making him stagger on his short legs. His departure cast a sad gloom over Useppe, which grew as the minutes passed. Even the company of Bella, who blinked at him affably with her understanding eyes, wasn't enough to console him. He thought again of Davide, whom he hadn't in the least forgotten, despite the new friendship with Scimó; and not feeling like staying on the river till evening today, he tugged at Bella's collar slightly, tempting her with the proposal: "Vvàvide . . ." But Bella shook her head, reminding him that Davide had made no appointment with them; and if they went to him unannounced, they would be sent away, like the last time.

After Scimó's departure, Davide's unkept promise also came back to sadden Useppe's loneliness. A passing cloud covered the sun, and to him it seemed an enormous storm-cloud. Suddenly, from the opposite shore a boat was seen setting forth, the forms of several boys visible in it. With a start, Useppe said to himself: "THE PIRATES!" and rose to his feet, in battle position. He was determined to defend the tree tent and Scimó's hut against them at any price. But the boat went off to the south instead, flanking the shore it had left; and a little later it was out of sight.

Useppe sat down again on the grass, his heart pounding. His sorrows of a moment before were becoming confused in a kind of formless presentiment not new to him, though unrecognizable every time it came back. Each return of his *grand mal* was a violence he underwent without witnessing it. Only, he sensed ahead of time an ambiguous signal, like the arrival, at his back, of a featureless mask behind which he felt was an empty hole. And then he was overtaken by a nebulous horror, as already half-blind, he attempted to set off without a direction, only to be struck down after two or three steps. This obscure execution, however, found him already unconscious. And even that first signal left only a vague trace afterwards, like a fragmentary theme heard somewhere, somehow, no longer remembered. Its notes emerge again from *something* that resembles a laceration . . . but they do not say what the *thing* is.

Sitting on the grass by the river, his heart still pounding, Useppe had the sensation of having already lived, in the past, another identical moment. There was no knowing when, perhaps in another existence, he had once found himself on a radiant shore, among fields dotted with merry tents, awaiting an imminent horror that wanted to swallow him up. His face contracted in a boundless rejection: "I don't want! I don't want!" he cried. And he stood up, as he had a little earlier, when he was prepared for combat with the Pirates. Against this other *thing*, truly, he had no way out, except an absurd flight. And the one extreme avenue of escape offered him, there at the moment, was the water of the river, which flowed beneath his feet. His vision already blurred, Useppe flung himself down. At that point, the current was rather calm, but the water was well over his head.

A desperate barking echoed along the shore; and in a moment Bella was upon him, as he floundered in incoherent disorder, battered by the water like a poor little creature, of air or earth, wounded in the back. "Hang on, climb onto me," Bella pleaded with him, slipping promptly under his belly and thus keeping him afloat, as she swam towards land. In the space of two breaths, the rescue was carried out: in his soaked clothes, Useppe was again safe, on the edge of the field.

It may be that the sudden cold shock of the water blocked his attack at its first onslaught. This time there was no scream, or loss of consciousness, or that horrible cyanosis that disfigured him. The only sign of this attack (partial or incomplete) was a trembling of all his muscles which racked him convulsively, as soon as he was on land, along with a tormented crying: "No, no! I don't want! I don't want!" he went on repeating, while Bella hastily licked him, like a litter of puppies. Useppe finally transformed the weeping into a frightened little laugh; and he hugged Bella tight, as if he were in his bed at home, next to Ida. They fell asleep together, and the sun dried them.

After an attack, this exhausted sleep did not always bring dreams; or rather they were dreams Useppe forgot completely on waking. But this time, he had a dream of which, in his memory afterwards, there lasted not exactly a recollection, but a shade, palpitating and colored. He dreamed he was in the same place where he actually was: only the river had taken the shape of a great circular lake, and the little hills around were much higher than in reality, all buried under a snowfall. I neglected to say, at the time, that in the winter of 1945 snow fell in Rome: and it had represented an unusual spectacle for Rome, and an extraordinary one for Useppe.

Then Useppe had been just over three; and after that time, the spectacle of the snow had receded in his memory, until it was hidden in a mist; but now, today it emerged again in this dream. That Roman snow, however, had been a peaceful sight, of incredible calm and whiteness; and instead, this snow in the dream was a blizzard such as Useppe had never seen in his life. The sky was blackish, a whistling wind bent the trees of the little hollow and of all the shores around, and the snow whirled, a machine-gun fire of pointed, murderous bits of ice. From the surrounding peaks, the trees stretched, naked and black, like flayed bodies, perhaps already dead. And all along the range of hills the only sound was the whistle of the gusts: there were no voices, nobody in sight.

Useppe, in the dream, wasn't on the shore, but in the water of the river-lake. And this water, though enclosed in a circle by the hills, seemed of an infinite size. It was all an iridescent color, calm and luminous, and of a gentle, wondrous warmth, as if it were constantly crossed by unseen springs, which the sun heated. Useppe swam in this water naturally, like a little fish; and around him, all across the tepid lake, there emerged countless little heads of other swimmers, his playmates. They were all strangers to him; but he recognized them all the same. And in fact, it wasn't hard to understand that there present were all Scimó's numerous nephews and nieces, immediately identifiable by their protruding little muzzles, imitating the famous tailless animal; and also there was a great crowd of little round heads with bright cheeks, lively black eyes: all twins, or close relatives, of his niece Ninuccia.

But the most extraordinary thing about this festive lake was that the circle of hills, tormented by the grim storm, was reflected there, by contrast, untouched and blissful, in the full serenity of a summer just beginning. The tortured trees were doubled there, unharmed, in the vivid health of their leaves; their reflection, ramified all over the lake, traced a kind of green arbor there, beneath the blue water, resembling a garden hung in the sky. And the water's movement accompanied them like a summer breeze, with a sound of a faint song and a murmuring.

Nor was there any doubt the lake was real and authentic, while the panorama above was a trick, something like Chinese shadows on a screen. This was obvious in the dream, which was, all in all, comic. And the sleeper derived a delicious pleasure from it and emitted little joyous exclamations in his sleep. Beside him, Bella on the contrary meanwhile uttered some grumblings, perhaps reliving in her dream the emotions of that heroic afternoon of hers.

Left to himself, Useppe would probably have slept like that for at least twelve hours, uninterrupted. But after about three hours, when the sun was declining, Bella woke up, gave her coat a great shake, and wakened him with the warning:

"It's time to go home. Mamma's waiting for us, for supper."

Useppe's homeward journey was strange, because, though he moved his feet after Bella's leash, he hadn't completely come out of his dream. They passed beneath the tent of trees, and the cries that birds make, gathering towards sunset, still seemed to him the swaying of that water, where sounds and reflections played together. He raised his eyes, and in the roof of boughs he thought he saw again the wondrous green arbor mirrored in the lake, with his swimming companions playing, sticking up their little heads. Even the Saturday-evening city noises reached him muffled, like a vast whisper at the bottom of the water, and this subaqueous sound for him was mingled with the throb of the first stars.

He was so sleepy that his head drooped at supper. And the next day he went on sleeping past lunchtime, ignoring Ida's calls. When he finally did get up, it took him a while to regain his sense of time. Suddenly he remembered he and Bella were to meet Scimó at the hut.

They arrived at about four: late for the appointment with Scimó. And, in fact, Scimó wasn't there. Since today was Sunday, and the season was now summery, bathers must have rested on the little beach that morning. There were some Peroni beer-bottle caps and banana peels; but luckily no trace of pirates there, or anywhere around. The hut was as they had left it the day before. Flung on the mattress were Scimó's briefs, still damp; and the flashlight was on the ground, next to the stone with the candle, like yesterday. Useppe didn't notice the fact that the candle had grown no shorter since the day before. The only novelty: the alarm had stopped. Useppe supposed that Scimó, in his haste, had forgotten to wind it. And since he had learned to tell time on clocks, he saw it said two.

That *two* for him meant unquestionably two in the afternoon; whereas, really, the alarm, at the moment it had stopped, unwound, was marking two at night. Useppe didn't know, and was never to know, that after saying goodbye to them, Scimó hadn't come back to sleep in the hut, and had spent the night in the Reformatory. Some city acquaintance of his, perhaps out of legalistic scruples, had reported him and allowed him to fall into a trap. Yesterday, in Rome, Scimó had been recaptured; and today, perhaps, he was spending his Sunday locked in a cell, being punished for his escape.

Useppe had no suspicion of such an event. He said to himself, embittered, that Scimó, after having waited in vain for him and Bella to keep the appointment, had certainly gone off, tired of waiting, to be on time for the first Sunday show. And surely by now he was already at the movies, nor would he return to the hut before night. So, for today, they wouldn't see each other.

This idea was enough to grieve him. Out of due respect for Scimó's dwelling, he left the hut and sat on the ground, a step from the entrance. Seeing him sad, Bella sat beside him, without disturbing him, calm, only amusing herself now and then by poking her head in the air to frighten a passing gnat. Despite her age, and even in the gravest situations, she was always susceptible to temptations from her puppy past.

As for her daily swim, after what had happened yesterday, she was led to give it up, no longer daring to leave Useppe alone on the shore, even for brief moments. Indeed, she made an effort to keep a certain distance between him and the little beach, as if the water represented the wolf for her.

Today the sun was baking, like full summer; but they were sitting in the cool, in the square patch of the hut's shadow. Beyond the little hollow, some trees rose, and from one of them the solitary, precocious song of a male cicada was heard. He must surely have been a still-little cicada, intent on his beginner's exercises, because, despite his stubborn determination, he produced the sound of an infinitesimal violin, barely scraped with a thread. And so, at the sound, Useppe recognized him immediately as that very cicada barely emerged from the nest that Scimó had seen born a couple of days ago.

A certain weariness from yesterday still lingered in Useppe's body, and he had no desire to roll and run and climb as on other days. But at the same time he was overcome with a restlessness which tempted him to shift and change places, though it didn't tell him where to go. This impatience continued even inside the tree tent. The roof of boughs brought him a vague reminiscence of yesterday's dream, which already today, however, was mostly erased from his memory. He no longer remembered the details of its landscape, or the blizzard, or the little heads, or the reflections. What he saw of it again was an expanse of water in a gentle movement of colors, with a singing whisper that accompanied its rocking. And he felt again a desire for his little bed and rest, opposed by a fear of falling asleep while everybody was awake.

Seeing he needed solace and distraction, Bella, seated beside him, decided to tell him a story. And blinking slightly, in a fabulous tone, filled with melancholy, she began by saying:

"Once I had some puppies . . ."

She had never spoken of them to him before. "I don't know how many there were," she went on, "because I can't count. But when it was feeding time, all my tits were occupied, that's sure, every one!!! So there were lots of them, and each more beautiful than the other. One was black and white. One was all black with one white ear and one black; and one was also all black with a little goatee . . . When I looked at one, he was the most beautiful; but I would look at another, and this one was the most beautiful; then I would lick another, and meanwhile another would stick his nose up, and he was beyond doubt the most beautiful. Their beauty was infinite, that's the truth of it. Infinite beauties can't be compared."

"What were they called?"

"They didn't have names."

"They didn't have names."

"No."

"And where've they gone?"

"Where? . . . I don't know what to think about that. From one moment to the next, I looked for them, and they weren't there any more. Usually, when they go off, they come back later, at least that's what happened with other friends of mine, who also had puppies . . ." (Bella, like her friends, was convinced that each successive litter was another return of

471

the same puppies) ". . . but mine never came back again. I hunted for them, I waited for them a long time, but they never came home."

Useppe was silent. "Each more beautiful than the other!" Bella repeated, convinced, her eyes dreaming. Then, thinking it over, she added: "It's natural. The same thing happens with others . . . with all our people. Eh, take for example my Antonio, the Naples one . . . He is surely the most beautiful of all! But my Ninnuzzu, he too, you only have to see him: nobody exists who's more beautiful than he!!"

It was the first time Ninnuzzu's name had been mentioned between them. On hearing it, Useppe's face trembled, but then settled in an alert little smile. Bella's speech, really, barked out in canine accents, cradled him like a melodious soprano aria.

"And you," she resumed with conviction, looking at him, "you are always the most beautiful in the whole world. That's certain."

"And my mamma?" Useppe inquired.

"Her! Did you ever see a more beautiful girl? Ah, everybody in Rome knows that! She's an infinite beauty. Infinite!"

Useppe laughed. He was absolutely in agreement on this point. Then he asked anxiously:

"And Scimó?"

"What a question! Everybody can see: he's the most beautiful!"

"The most beautiful of all?"

"Of all."

"And Davide?"

"Aaaah! Davide's beauty is the greatest. Positively. The maximum."

"Infinite?"

"Infinite."

Useppe laughed with contentment, because to tell the truth on the subject of beauty there was complete agreement between him and the shepherdess. Giants or dwarfs, beggars or dandies, decrepitude or youth, nothing made any difference to him. And neither the twisted nor the hunchback, the paunchy nor the scrawny: to him none was less lovely than the world's Paragon, provided all were friends equally and smiling (asked to invent a heaven, he would have built a place along the lines of the "big room of The Thousand"). For some time, however, he had been rejected, and that was understandable: it was because he had this bad sickness.

"Let's go away," he said to Bella.

The streets were lively with the Sunday afternoon crowd. Beyond some houses under construction, on an open lot, a large carnival had pitched its tents. There weren't only merry-go-rounds, stands, shooting galleries, miniature cars, etc., but even a roller-coaster, and flying swings where you were spun in a circle at a dizzying speed. Useppe, who had irresistibly advanced with Bella to the edge of the carnival, had an involuntary little laugh of joy, in the presence of those fantastic machines. But he drew back at once, with a mixed feeling of yearning and nightmare, as if before a denied intoxication. It is a fact that, from the beginning of his illness, at night he had certain frightening dreams (even if he then forgot them) in which he plunged down into blind abysses, or was whirled in measureless orbits in a rutilant void with neither beginning nor end.

The possession, in his buttoned pocket, of his usual spending money, lured him forward, towards the stands where they sold cakes, brittle, and especially spun sugar, pink and yellow in color. But here too, the festive throng pressed him back, solitary. Then, on Via Marmorata, towards Testaccio, they came upon the isolated cart of an ice-cream vendor. And Useppe made up his mind to extend his little hand with the money, to purchase two cones: one for himself and one for Bella. Indeed, encouraged by the face of the vendor, a squint-eyed little man with a friendly smile, seeing his watch, he asked him: "What time do you have?" "Five thirty," the vendor replied.

It was still early to go home. And suddenly Useppe made the impulsive decision to pay a visit to Davide Segre. "Vvàvide!" he announced to Bella, right in her face, in such an irrevocable, though pleading, tone, that this time, making no objections, Bella trotted towards Ponte Sublicio. Here, however, Useppe had second thoughts and decided to take his friend as a present that flask of wine Ida had purchased days before especially for him. There was the hope that Davide, seeing him turn up with this gift, wouldn't send him away.

To retrace their steps towards Via Bodoni, this time, instead of Via Marmorata, they took the inner streets of the district. From the windows, from the cafés and the taverns, they were accompanied by the uniform voices of the radio, broadcasting the football scores; but on crossing Via Mastro Giorgio, they heard, inside a tavern, someone shouting: "war . . . history . . ." and other words, drowned out by the radio. It was Davide's voice. Useppe knew the tavern, having sometimes accompanied Annita Marrocco there, when she went to buy wine. Excited by this surprise, he immediately went to the doorway of the tavern; and having seen Davide, he said to him in a loud voice, "Hey!", making his familiar gesture of greeting with his hand.

6 There was only one table of customers, all poor people of the neighborhood, and all fairly elderly men, of whom a little group of four was playing cards; and the others, more numerous, were sitting beside the group, or a bit behind, observing the game without taking part in it. Davide was one of these, though he showed no interest in the play. Until a moment before, really, his place had been at a little table nearby, where he had sat drinking alone, and where there still stood a couple of quarter-liter pitchers he had left, one drained, the other nearly empty. On his own, he had suddenly turned his chair, taking a place at the next table, without anyone's having invited him. Here he ordered another double liter, which he offered to the others, pouring some from time to time into his own glass. All the same, he didn't seem drunk, but overeager and expansive. At the sight of Useppe and Bella, a sudden radiance, sweet and boyish, caressed his face for a moment. "Useppe!" he cried, like someone running into a friend. And Useppe, with Bella, was at his side in one bound. "Sit here," Davide invited him, pulling a free chair to his side. However, once Useppe, glowing with happiness, had sat down, Davide paid no further attention to him. After his fleeting gesture of welcome, his face resumed its same tense and burning expression of a moment before.

To tell the truth, nobody in there paid any attention to Useppe and Bella. But the two were so pleased with their present situation that they asked for nothing more. Indeed, rather than compromise their luck, they avoided even the slightest disturbing action. Bella had stretched out on the floor, between Useppe's chair and Davide's; and (except for a tiny, irrepressible flick of her tail) she forced herself into a perfect immobility, until she seemed the monument of a dog. Every now and then, she addressed a futile and blissful glance upwards, to say:"Well, what do you think of this? Here we are, all three of us." And Useppe, from the chair where he was settled, would look silently around, with wide and trusting eyes, even taking care not to kick his dangling legs. Davide's nearness, though it instilled respect in him, freed him from all uneasiness. And further, among those present (besides a couple of other neighborhood figures he knew by sight) he had promptly glimpsed an old acquaintance: Clemente, Consolata's brother.

Useppe gave him a shy, knowing nod, but the man didn't recognize him. Clemente wasn't playing; he was seated among the players, almost behind their backs, on the side opposite Davide. Shrunken by his extreme thinness, with a greenish pallor and hollow, clouded eyes like a dead man's, he was huddled up in a little autumn topcoat, despite the hot season, and even his head was covered by a cap. On his mutilated hand, instead of Filomena's black knitted glove, he now wore another, of very worn leather dyed a reddish-brown. However, he was still known by his nickname Black Hand. His status was that of a hopelessly unemployed invalid; and his definitive dependence on his sister had brought him to hate her, and to make her hate him. Especially on holidays, when she didn't go off to work, this hatred drove him from the house early in the morning; and he spent his whole Sundays seated in this place. From time to time, he could be seen to extend his arm and pick up his glass of wine, untouched; but after having looked into it, with a fixed and nauseated stare, as if he saw worms, he would put it back on the table, having drunk not a sip of it.

Though he sat among the others, he remained confined in a gloomy torpor of his own, almost without reaction now to external stimuli. He was interested neither in the cards nor in the news broadcast by the radio. He listened, though in an oblique and intermittent fashion, to Davide's talk; and only then did his wasted features have a certain vibration, which expressed animosity, bitterness, almost contempt.

He alone, at that table, belonged to the still-young generation (though in appearance, he was ageless). He was in fact only a little more than ten years older than Davide. The others (all, to look at them, over sixty, or thereabouts) treated Davide with detachment and patience, like an odd little boy, displaying tolerance even if his aggressiveness was clearly troubling their peaceful game. Not a few men, among those in the tavern, seemed to know him already, at least by sight; but no one hailed him as a hero any longer, like the time he had shown up at the Marrocco home. Rather, because of his different social class, they seemed to consider him descended from a kind of decayed nobility, if not actually from an obscure planet.

The game was played by partners. The player nearest Davide was an old man about seventy, but with an athletic build, bursting with health. A tan undershirt left his muscular sunburned arms bare and the whiter skin under his armpits. He had thick, graying hair, and over the undershirt a baptismal medal hung from a silver-plated chain. His partner in the game, seated at the opposite side of the table, was a bald man with a flat face, in a messenger's uniform. And of the two members of the second couple, one, obviously from outside Rome (as you could tell from his accent) was a rustic character, squat and very red in the face, perhaps a cattle-trader; and the other was somebody Useppe had seen before, because he went around the district with a box hung from his neck, selling chestnut fritters, cakes, and peanuts (he had, in fact, left nearby, on a windowsill, the box with his merchandise, towards which Bella occasionally cast yearning glances). He had a round face covered with wrinkles, very small eyes and nose, and his fellow-players teased him, because he was slow-witted.

Near the big old man with the medal, but a bit behind him, as a spectator, a seedy little man of about sixty was sitting, his thin, sinewy neck emerging from a patched Sunday jacket which betrayed his extreme poverty. His sickly eyes, the irises pale blue, were all bloodshot, but their gaze was resigned, simple, and it followed with lively pleasure the destiny of the game. These Sunday afternoons were the only social occasions in his entire lonely week; he was a pensioner who managed still to eke out a living with little odd jobs. From time to time, he would applaud, a bit ostentatiously, the moves of the player with the medal.

Of the others witnessing the game, some followed its progress with interest, others seemed simply to be resting, dozing, as if they were continuing their holiday siesta in the tavern. There were some who, from time to time, got up to collect news from the radio, then came back to report it to their friends. Or else some transient would linger a while to watch, while others would withdraw, leaving their seats for the newcomers . . . But in the midst of the discreet coming and going, Davide never moved from his place, held there by the heaviness of his legs, in contrast with his inner ferment.

As if he also celebrated Sundays, today he had carefully bathed and shaved. He had somehow combed his hair, which his neglect allowed to grow in a mop, smoothing it with water, and parting it on one side. And so, in his unusually kempt appearance and his pensive and (sometimes) almost ecstatic gaze, he resembled more than ever that beardless student of the old identification snapshot, despite his gaunt cheeks and his pallor. He had put on a pair of pants not actually pressed, but fairly new, and a white knit shirt, fresh and clean, with short sleeves. Right away, Useppe, who kept his eyes on him most of the time, noticed a swollen, festering little sore on his bare arm, in the crook of his elbow; and sympathetically, he would have liked to ask its cause, but he didn't dare interrupt the relentless speech he was making.

Why, or of what, he talked so much, Davide himself didn't know. In fact, what he expounded were not topics, but rather pretexts, to involve the others, but himself first of all, in some general—or perhaps personal?—problem. To such questions there is no answer, for in his unusual and morbid loquacity, he seemed to be seeking not so much a solution as the actual problem! And when I try to recapitulate his talk that afternoon in the tavern, I see it in the image of many horses chasing one another around a circular track, always passing the same spots. At present, his voice (with its special timbre, of a young bass) could be heard drilling on a point his listeners couldn't be persuaded to take up, no matter how stubbornly he reiterated it: he was accusing everyone—not only his audience, but all living people, in general—of willful reticence on the subject of the last war and its millions of dead. Nobody wanted to talk about it any more, as if the matter were settled: this was the point he kept hammering home. And he went on repeating, in a tone of dogged protest, but also of almost pathetic appeal: "*Nisún* . . . nobody . . . nobody . . ." Until the old man with the medal said to him, though without much conviction, and taking care not to be distracted from his cards:

"Then you talk about it. We can hear you . . ." Then, flinging a card on the table with decision, he exclaimed: "Face-card!" while Clemente, sniggering, also looked at Davide, as if to confirm: "That's right. What are you waiting for, before telling us your philosophy?"

The room, rather spacious, had two entrances. In the corner near the back door, beyond the refrigerator and the counter and the table with the card-players, a little crowd was standing around the radio to listen to the football results. Unlike the seated customers, these men, for the most part, were young; and they didn't drink or occupy any table, just stopping off here on their way by, for the news. As they left, others from the street took their place; and through this entrance, with some coming in, and some leaving, there was a constant movement and a mumble of football arguments, in which the proprietor, from his counter, also gladly joined. On this side, meanwhile, other elderly customers had formed a second table, with their pack of cards. And on either side, you could hear exclamations of "Low card!" "Play!" and similar expressions appropriate to cards, mingling with the voices and sounds from the street in an absurd, deafening confusion. But Davide didn't feel disturbed by the noises; on the contrary, a sudden silence would perhaps have thrown him into panic. He enjoyed a clarity of awareness so acute that he was excited by it, as if by a physical stimulus inside his brain; and yet he felt he was groping his way, like a lost kid who doesn't dare ask directions of the passersby. Over everything else, however, a kind of enthusiasm prevailed in him: so that gradually the sounds outside became involved in his own interior clamor and fervor, in a single, ultimate adventure!

He was—as we can easily understand—on one of his *gala days*; but unlike such days usually, this Sunday gala had made the solitude of his room intolerable and had driven him out into the streets, with the slightly apprehensive thrill of a debut. He wanted to meet the footsteps of other people, the voices of other people.

And he wasn't guided by a choice, but only by accident. However, passing by here, he had slipped into this tavern, which he occasionally visited, and which promised him, to some extent, a family atmosphere.

He didn't want wine; in fact, alcohol, chemically, did not mix well with certain *gala* states of his. He had been led to drink a little, but only for decorum's sake, to justify, in this way, his presence as a customer and not an intruder. Now, with the wine, he had developed the restlessness of someone who, having entered a dancehall, is dying to dance; but the dance didn't go with his legs' ponderous weariness, which had come over him at the same time. And this, moreover, was not a dancehall . . . It was an ordinary . . . place . . . in the world . . . Exactly! Exactly! An ordinary place in the world!

He didn't even know what had driven him, all of a sudden, to turn his chair towards the next table (still the only one occupied, at that moment, in the tavern), putting into this simple and normal act an impetus so excessive it seemed an aggression. Perhaps, in any place and in any company (in a tribunal, or an old people's home, or even at the Court of England) his movement would have been the same. He had obeyed one of those incongruous impulses, the kind that drive a person, while he is walking through a square, suddenly to strip naked

No doubt it had seemed to him, in turning his chair this way, that he was arriving at some important resolve, even if unpredictable to himself, and very confused. And it was only at the moment when he opened his mouth that he realized his real desire, today, was to *speak*. He himself—so it seemed to him—was a terrible knot, and all the others were tangled and stumbling in the same way. Only a dialogue with the others could perhaps undo the knot. It was a battle, to be faced today, without hesitation; and then, after the victory, he would rest. If he had to make a speech, or rather a lecture, he didn't care about knowing it ahead of time. He was certain of only one thing: that these were *urgent communications!*

The possible themes were too many, really: so many that they bewildered him. And though completely conscious, he still recognized that his mind was glowing not with health, but with a kind of lucid fever which he wanted to make an effort to restrain, even if, somehow, he meant to take advantage of it. *To speak*, yes; but beginning where? From when? He had started out with his words about the war, as if this were a Pole Star, or a wandering comet, which would indicate his direction to him; but meanwhile (even after the invitation of the old man with the medal) he only rambled on in his idle protests, with a pretense of toughness that already brought him some sneers from Black Hand.

"The war's over," the card-player who looked like a cattle-trader spoke up, glancing at him for an instant. "We have to think about peace now . . ." Then, immediately dropping the subject, he turned his eyes towards his partner, the dull-witted peddler of various merchandise, and urged him:

"Come on! Follow suit!"

"Yes, the war's over!" Davide repeated, in a polemical tone, "it's peacetime, that's right . . ." And having said this, he laughed raucously.

This laugh had a certain surprise effect on Bella, who pricked up both ears; but meanwhile Davide, giving way—despite himself—to an access of ill-humor, writhed in his chair, with a grim look: "These peaces . . ." he inveighed towards the trader, who was really paying no further attention to him, "have been made a hundred thousand times! And there'll be another hundred thousand still, and the war is never over! To use the word PEACE for certain intrigues is . . . is pornography! It's spitting on the dead! But, of course, as far as the dead are concerned, you make an approximate count, and then they're filed away: dead files! On anniversaries, gentlemen in mourning clothes carry a wreath to the unknown soldier . . ."

"Let the dead bury the dead," the little pensioner proverbialized, his bloodshot eyes winking in a way that was meant not to be ironic but to encourage Davide. "Cases filed and forgotten!" Davide insisted, writhing, in revolt. But here he was restrained by the thought that if he began like this, by growing angry, he would lose his way from the start. And with a great effort of will, he made a kind of mental leap, which brought him to a state of lucid split-personality. There was a Davide Superego who set the pace, and another Davide who obeyed, even if puzzled at times as to the means and the ends. This Davide Superego was then to reappear to him, as his speech continued today, in varying guises: sometimes as a flaming sword, sometimes as a parody . . . This time, in giving him the go-sign, he assumed the form of a Professor of History. And Davide forced himself, with brows knit, to collect in his mind his own basic information on the subject, from the primary notions already instilled in his schooldays: forcing himself to be calm, clear, and especially orderly and methodical, if he wanted to deploy the field in view of the imminent battle. He decided then to proceed through successive theses, establishing, in the first place, some fundamental points of obvious certainty, indeed already given, as in theorems. And setting out on this assignment, with the same seriousness as when, a schoolboy, he was called to the board, he began, with a speech so diligent and orderly he seemed to be reading from a breviary:

1) The word *Fascism* is of recent coinage, but it corresponds to a social system of prehistoric decrepitude, absolutely rudimentary, and indeed less evolved than that used among anthropoids (as anyone who knows something about zoology can confirm); 2) such a system is in fact based on the exploitation of the helpless (peoples or classes or individuals) by those who have the means to use violence; 3) in reality, from its primitive origins, and all through the course of human History, there has existed no other system but this. Recently, the name of *Fascism* or *Nazism* has been given to certain extreme eruptions of ignominy, madness, and stupidity, characteristic of bourgeois degeneration; however, the system as

such is still functioning everywhere (under different, even contradictory names and aspects . . .), always, everywhere, since the beginning of human History . . .

In this preparatory phase of his problematical undertaking, Davide moved his head, alternately, this way and that, as if calling all those present in the place to witness his postulates. And though, in reality, from his speech (uttered, for that matter, in a very restrained voice) only some fragments emerged, immediately drowned again in the general confusion, still, with a kind of blind faith, he continued for a fairly long stretch, speaking according to the preestablished order: ". . . that, in other words, all History is a history of fascisms, more or less disguised . . . in the Greece of Pericles . . . and in the Rome of the Caesars and the Popes . . . and in the steppes of the Huns . . . and in the Aztec Empire . . . and in the America of the pioneers . . . and in the Italy of the Risorgimento . . . and in the Russia of the Tsars and the Soviets . . . always and everywhere, *sèmpar e departút*, free men and slaves . . . rich and poor . . . the buyers and the bought . . . superiors and inferiors . . . leaders and herds . . . The system never changes . . . it was called religion, divine right, glory, honor, spirit, future . . . all pseudonyms . . . all masks . . . But with the industrial age, certain masks won't hold up . . . the system bares its teeth, and every day on the flesh of the masses it prints its real name and title . . . and it's no accident that, in its language, mankind is called MASSES, which means *inert matter* . . . And so, here we are . . . this poor matter, material for work and labor, becomes fodder for extermination and destruction . . . *Extermination camps* . . . they've already found the earth's new name . . . *Extermination industry*, this is the system's real name today! And it ought to be written on signs at factory gates . . . and over the doorways of schools, and churches, and ministries, and offices, and in neon on skyscrapers . . . and on the mastheads of newspapers . . . and the title pages of books . . . even the SO-CALLED revolutionary texts . . . *Quieren carne de hombres!!*"

He no longer knew where he had read this last sentence; but at the very moment when he was quoting it, he reproached himself for it, as a mistake, since surely nobody there knew Spanish! He could have spoken, really, in ancient Greek, or in Sanskrit, because his words were received, at most, as an acoustical phenomenon. At present, he was only partially aware of this circumstance; but already the calm his Superego desired had been lost; and he began to move his feet and hands impatiently, bursting into coarse laughter: "There are those who believed," he exclaimed, raising his voice aggressively, "this last war was a war . . . of world revolution!"

The news broadcast was coming to an end; some of the listeners lingered to argue, while others were drifting off. "Make the revolution yourself, if you're so smart!" said a shirtsleeved young man, who, at Davide's words, had come over to the table. Davide turned to him with a quarrelsome grimace: "I'm not one of those who believed in it!" he explained with rancor. "I don't believe in those revolutions! . . . there's never been a true revolution! I've given up hope in the true revolution! . . ."

But the shirtsleeved young man, shrugging a shoulder, had already gone back towards the group of sports fans. "What might this good revolution be, then?" the proprietor asked from his counter, giving Davide a lazy glance. Without awaiting a reply, however, he resumed the argument already begun with the fans, exclaiming in their direction, somewhat heatedly:

"If you ask me, it was the referee who screwed things up."

The radio was now broadcasting light music, and the proprietor turned down the volume the better to follow the discussion of the games. From the various scores of the day, the talk had gone back to the All-Italy team's more recent victories over foreign teams. The young man in his shirtsleeves, shouting, sustained the supremacy of Mazzola. And at this point, unable to contain himself, the little man with the sick eyes rose from his chair to dispute him: "The win in Turin, to begin with," he shouted, proud of his expertise, "was all due to Gabetto! Mazzola had nothing to do with it! Gabetto made two goals! TWO!" he insisted, triumphantly waving two fingers beneath the young man's nose.

Since the radio was now playing a recent hit song (I don't remember which), one of the young men, on his own initiative, turned up the volume again; and to the song's rhythm, he began making studied movements with his hips and feet. Another, boasting of being more up-to-date in the field of dance, intervened to teach him the proper steps; and this new subject distracted a part of the surrounding group from sports. An animated, youthful shuffling was thus added to the music and the various voices. But, as usual, the general confusion did not touch Davide, or at least it grazed him only superficially. The center of his powers was held fast, aimed at the presumed mission that today, suddenly, with tragic urgency, he had imposed on himself: and that indefinite goad shattered, dispersed, everything else around him. Convinced that the proprietor's question demanded a suitable answer, with frowning patience he went back to his previous, schematic lesson. And concentrating again on the point where he had interrupted it, returning to his earlier tone of goodwill, almost catechistic, he made a total effort to declare: that the famous established eternal universal system of exploitation, etc., by definition is always attached to property, whether private or governmental . . . And by definition it's racist . . . And by definition it has to produce itself and

481

consume itself and reproduce itself through oppression and aggression and invasions and various wars . . . it can't escape from this circle . . . And its vaunted "revolutions" can be understood only in the astronomical meaning of the word, which means: motion of bodies around a center of gravity. Which center of gravity, always the same, is: Power. Always one: POWER . . .

But at this point the speaker must have realized his fine words were not being received by anyone, unless by mistake; they were like scraps of wastepaper whirled by the wind . . . And in fact, he fell silent for a moment, with the upset and puzzled face of a child in the midst of a noisy dream . . . But he promptly frowned, clenching his jaws; and suddenly rising to his feet, he shouted in a defiant tone:

"I'm a Jew!"

Dazed by his outburst, the customers at the tables around looked up for a moment from their cards, while Clemente glanced at him, his lips curling. "What's wrong with being a Jew?" asked the little man with bloodshot eyes, who meantime had sat down again in his place. "The Jews," the man in the messenger's uniform stated with almost official gravity, "are Christians the same as anybody else. The Jews are Italian citizens the same as anybody else."

"That isn't what I meant," Davide protested, blushing. He really felt guilty, as if accused of having introduced some personal questions; at heart, however, he was pleased simply that someone at least had answered him. "Who did you take me for?!" he protested still with some embarrassment, hunting for the thread that had escaped him, "races, classes, citizenships, are all balls, tricks performed by Power. It's Power that needs the gallows: 'That man's a Jew, he's a Negro, he's a worker, he's a slave . . . he's different . . . that man's the Enemy!' all tricks, to conceal the real enemy, himself, Power! He's the one, he's the pestilence that overwhelms the world with his raving . . . A man's born a Jew by chance, and black, and white, by chance . . ." (here he thought he had found the thread again) *"but you're not born a human being by chance!"* he announced, with an inspired little smile, as if of gratitude.

This last sentence, in fact, was the opening of a poem, written by him several years earlier under the title "Total Consciousness," which now served him in good stead. But as his Superego advised him against setting out to declaim those verses here, he thought it better, for the occasion, to turn that poem into prose; but all the same he produced a chanting voice, rhetorical and shy at once, just like a poet reciting his works:

"From the alga to the amoeba, through all the successive forms of life, along the incalculable epochs, the multiple and continuous movement of nature has tended towards this manifestation of single, universal will: the human being! Human being means: consciousness. This is Genesis. Consciousness is the miracle of God. It is God! That day God says: *Behold man!* And then he says: *I am the son of man!* And so he finally rests, and takes a holiday . . .

"But consciousness, in its own holiday, is one, total: separate individuals don't exist, in consciousness. And no differences exist, in reality, between one human being and another. White black red or yellow, females or males, being born human means having grown to the highest degree of terrestrial evolution! And this is the sign of God, man's only real coat-of-arms: all other coats-of-arms, honors, and epaulettes are nasty jokes, a delirium, pestilence: talk and tin . . ."

"But what God do you believe in?" Clemente interrupted him, his mouth half-twisted, his question already denoting a derogatory opinion of the man questioned. "Eh, believers are lucky!" the man with the bloodshot eyes sighed, on this score . . . "What kind of question is that? I thought I had made myself clear," Davide grumbled, ". . . do I BELIEVE IN GOD? . . . The question's wrong from the start, one of the usual tricks with words. A trick, like so many others."

"Ah. A trick."

"A trick, a trick. Priests' talk, and Fascists'. They talk about belief in God, in the Fatherland, in freedom, in the people, in the revolution; and all these beliefs are just frauds, tricks for their convenience, like medals and money. Anyway, I'm an ATHEIST, if that's what you wanted to know."

"Then what are you talking about God for? If you don't even believe in him!" the cattle-trader spoke up, on his own, swelling his cheeks slightly with an annoyed air. Meanwhile, since his partner in the game, the peddler, scratching one ear in accord with their signals, was consulting him across the table about his next move, he authorized him with the words: "Play!" and the peddler promptly flung his card on the table.

"Believing in God . . . What kind of God would a God be, if you can believe or not believe in him?! Me, too, when I was a kid, I understood it in that sense, more or less . . . But this isn't God! . . . Wait! I remember once, not long ago, a friend of mine asked me: 'Do you believe God exists?' I thought it over and I answered: 'I believe only God exists.' But without thinking, he said: 'On the contrary, I believe all things exist except God!!' 'In that case,' we concluded, 'we're obviously not in agreement . . .' But afterwards I discovered he and I were saying the same thing . . ."

Such an explanation must have sounded to the listeners (if anyone had really been listening) like an insoluble puzzle. Perhaps they assumed it was some Hebrew theology . . . In any event, the only comment that followed was some coughing from Black Hand, tantamount to notes of sarcasm uttered for him by his ruined lungs; as well as a "Hey, Davide!" discreet, but fairly daring, from Useppe. It was already the third or fourth time in the course of the meeting that Useppe had made his presence known with that appeal to his friend: but it was only to boast, "We're here, too!" with no expectation of a reply. And in fact, Davide, this time as before, gave no sign he had even heard.

He had sunk down in his seat again, almost without realizing it, and he was stubbornly pursuing the course of his own argumentation with the expression of one who, awake, is trying to reconstruct a dream's adventure: "In fact, they say *God is immortal*, precisely because existence is one, the same, in all living things. And the day that consciousness knows this, what is then left to death? In the all-one, death is nothing. Does the light suffer, if you or I close our eyelids?! Unity of consciousness: this is the victory of the revolution over death, the end of History, and the birth of God! That God created man is another of the many fairy tales; on the contrary, it's from man that God must be born. And we're still waiting for his birth; but maybe God will never be born. There's no more hope in the true revolution . . ."

"You think you're a revolutionary?" Clemente spoke up again, always with that sly and reluctant manner of his, scorning the other's reply even before he had heard it. "This," Davide said, with a little bitter laugh, "is another trick question. People like Bonaparte, or Hitler, or Stalin, would answer *yes* . . . In any case, I'm an ANARCHIST, if that's what you want to know!"

Now he was speaking in a combative tone, but not against Black Hand: rather, against some invisible interlocutor. At times, he would confuse the hoarse, rasping voice of Black Hand with that of his own Super-ego!

"And the only genuine revolution is ANARCHY! AN-ARCHY, which means: NO power, of NO sort, for NO one, over NO one! Anybody who talks about revolution and, at the same time, about Power, is a liar! He's a cheat! And anyone who wants Power, for himself or for anybody else, is a reactionary; and even if he was born a proletarian, he's a bourgeois! That's right, a bourgeois, because by now *Power* and *Bourgeoisie* are inseparable! The symbiosis is established! Wherever you find Powers, that's where the bourgeoisie flourishes, like parasites in sewers . . ."

"Ah, they're the ones with the money," the proprietor said, in a yawn, rubbing his right thumb against his forefinger. "With money," came a carefree voice from the direction of the radio-listeners, "you can buy even the Madonna . . ." ". . . and God Almighty," a second voice, more sarcastic, insisted from the same group.

"Money . . ." Davide laughed. And with a confused notion of creating a spectacle, like a terrorist hurling a bomb, he took from his pocket the two little banknotes he had, flinging them away with contempt. But despite his impetuosity, those weightless little pieces of paper fell only a pace from him, just behind Bella's tail; and Useppe duly bent and picked them up, considerately returning them to his friend, not without exploiting the opportunity to say: "Hey, Davide!" Then he went back, properly, to his still-warm chair, received by Bella with a dramatic jolt of welcome, as if he were coming home from a great expedition.

Davide had meekly allowed his possessions to be returned to him, shoving them back into his pocket, paying no attention: perhaps having already forgotten his impulsive act, with which, nevertheless, he had not released all his aggressiveness: "Money," he cried, "was History's first screwing!" But meanwhile, the young man with the carefree voice was no longer listening to him. He was a lively boy with gleaming teeth, who, putting one ear to the radio, had covered the other with his palm, to hear the new songs on the musical program without too much interference.

"It was one of *their* first tricks!" Davide went on, all the same, "and *they*, with this trick of money, have bought our whole life! All money is fake! Can money be eaten!? They sell their garbageman's frauds at a high price. Selling it by weight, a million is worth less than a pound of shit . . ."

"All the same, a little million would come in handy for me." At this point the unexpected voice of the peddler was heard, with a sigh. And in his eyes, worn and small as two pennies, there was the expanse of a legendary vision: perhaps a stupendous supermarket of his own property, brimming with tons of fritters and peanuts . . . His vision made him forget for a moment the game in progress; and he was soon reproached by his partner, who shouted at him: "Wake up!", giving Davide a cross look.

At the peddler's interjection, Davide's mood changed; and he smiled a pacified, boyish smile. Then, with this new face, brightened and promising (as if a fabulous herald had, all of a sudden, touched his brow) he announced:

"In the Anarchist Community, money doesn't exist."

And here, without further ado, he embarked on a description of the Anarchist Community: where the land belongs to all, and all work it together, dividing its produce equally according to the law of nature. In fact, profit, property, hierarchies, are all depraved and against nature, where they are excluded. And labor is a celebration of friendship, like repose. And love is a guiltless giving of the self, without any possessive egoism. Children—all born from love—are, there, the children of all. No families exist, since they are really the first knot in the deceit, that is, in established society, which is always a conspiracy . . . There, the use of surnames is unknown, everybody's called by his first name; and as for ranks and titles, there they would seem as ridiculous as a fake nose or a paper tail. There, feelings are spontaneous, because the natural, reciprocal emotion is understanding. And the senses, healed from the pestilential raving of Power, return to communion with nature, in an intoxicating health! There taste, sight, hearing, intellect, are all stages towards the true unified happiness . . .

From the way he spoke, content and convinced, with a limpid smile in his Bedouin's eyes, it seemed that the Anarchist Community was really a station to be found on maps (such and such a latitude, such and such a longitude) and you had only to take the train and go there. This illusory hypothesis aroused only a few little laughs (more of futility than of skepticism) in the group of idle old men, sitting and looking on; while, beyond the table, the radio was broadcasting, at the end of a little dance-band piece, a recorded din of applause that, to Davide, seemed mocking. But the worst mockery came to him, actually, from within himself, from the usual Superego: "Here it seems to me we're marching in the wrong direction," the latter insinuated, giving him a pinch in the stomach. "You're launching yourself as a prophet of the Future, and meanwhile you're exalting the remote past: namely the garden of Eden, from which we emigrated, don't you remember? to be *fruitful and multiply*, towards the City of Consciousness!" "That's right," Davide spoke again, gulping and laughing, uneasily, "they tell us that man, at the beginning, rejected the innocence of Eden in favor of knowledge, of consciousness. And this choice required the test of History, that is the conflict between the Revolution and the puppet of Power . . . until, finally, the puppet won! thrusting man down lower than the lower animals!! And this, now, is what we're witnessing! In fact, all the other living species, at least, haven't regressed: they've remained where they were the first day: in Eden, in the state of nature! while mankind alone has regressed! And has declined not only from his historical degree of consciousness, but also from the degree of his animal nature. You only have to summarize biology, and History . . . Never, before, had any living species produced a monster below nature like that spawned by human society in our modern age . . ."

". . . what's that?" the man with the bloodshot eyes inquired, in spontaneous curiosity.

Davide had to force his lips and jaws, in order to give the answer, since it seemed so obvious: "It's the bourgeoisie!" he declared, with the reluctance of someone chewing a tasteless morsel. And the little man drew back from any sort of argument, with a meek and bewildered smile, tinged with a certain disappointment: surely he was expecting a more sensational reply.

Davide, meanwhile, in his compulsive loquacity, felt as if he were running a gratuitous race, toilsome and ineluctable, through prearranged obstacles. His quarrel with the class enemy, in fact, had grown up with him since puberty ("like the flower of manhood and reason" he had once written in a poem), and now he felt an uneasiness at having to face again that trite, squalid enemy! But yet, at the mere mention, a ferment of rebellion rose inside him; and the Superego ordered him not to retreat!

"At least the pre-bourgeois Powers!" he began, rushing headlong, with a grimace, "in their togas and wigs, on their thrones and altars and horses, though pestilential, perhaps retained still a residue of nostalgia, let's say, for *total consciousness*. And to compensate (at least partially) for their shame, they left some vital, useful work as a repayment or a hope of salvation . . . In other words, some luminous trace, before putrefying, they did leave . . . But the bourgeois Power, in its passage, leaves only a slimy, repulsive streak, an infected pus. Wherever it puts down roots, it reduces all living substance—indeed, all inanimate substance—to corruption and rot, like leprosy . . . and it feels no shame! In fact, shame is a sign of consciousness—and the bourgeois have amputated consciousness, which is man's honor. They think they are whole beings, whereas they're maimed. And their greatest misfortune is this stubborn, impenetrable ignorance . . ."

He had risen to a tone of wrathful exhibition, like a District Attorney! Nor was this certainly the first time he played the role of prosecutor in such a trial; indeed, his propositions today were all echoes and refrains of a hymn he had sung over and over again, God knows how many times, either by himself, or with his companions in the struggle, when, on occasion, he had felt keyed up . . . Only his well-known class-protest was redoubled today by a visceral, disorderly passion that threatened to engulf him; and when he tried to release its excess with one of his usual wild laughs, this same laughter seemed to strike him like a volley of blows, hardening his muscles for his vengeance.

The terms of the prosecution's summing-up which he was uttering seemed to him insufficient to nail down the defendant definitively; they sounded abused, overworked . . . And he was searching his invention to find new, resolutive ones for this extreme clash, when the strange aggression of his passion overwhelmed him; and finding nothing better, his tongue was unleashed in a series of atrocious obscenities (those usually known as *barracks language*), rather unusual in his speech. He himself, in uttering them, felt amazement, and also the devouring pleasure of self-rape. And he had the bizarre sensation of celebrating a kind of black mass.

"All right, all right, we get it!" the usual carefree voice arrived from the radio-listeners, "the bourgeois give you a pain in the ass." And Davide, in reply, charged with greater emphasis his uninterrupted series of *bad words*, which, for that matter, exploded as harmlessly as firecrackers amid his present audience. Even Useppe, in fact, from infancy, had frequented true masters of such language (and not least, among them, the Marrocco ladies).

Davide, in his paroxysm, felt himself the precise center of a universal scandal, exactly as if he were being struck with stones. His legs wobbled, and a feverish sweat trickled from his brow. Then he clenched his fists, pursuing the thread of his harangue: "Nature belongs to all the living," he hastened to explain once more, with a hoarsened voice, "it was born free, open, and THEY have compressed and paralyzed it to make it fit into their pockets. They've transformed other people's labor into stocks and bonds, and the fields of the earth into income, and all real values of human life, art, love, friendship, into merchandise to be bought and pocketed. Their States are banks, usurers, who invest the price of others' labor and consciousness in their own dirty dealings: factories of weapons and garbage, intrigues, robberies, wars, murders! Their factories of *goods* are cursed slave Lagers, in the service of their profits . . . All their values are false, they live on ersatz . . . And the Others . . . But can anyone still believe in *others*, to oppose to THEM? Maybe THEIR falsifications will remain the only subject of future History. This is perhaps the crucial point in the irreparable process of inversion, where the scholarly calculators of History, even the best unfortunately, have added things up wrong (the grim prognosis of Power, obviously, is suppressed by anyone who, in the clenched fist of the revolution, hides the same infected sore of Power, denying its malignancy)! They diagnosed the bourgeois disease as symptomatic of a class (and so, when the class was abolished, the disease would be cured!), whereas the bourgeois disease is the crucial, eruptive degeneration of the eternal malignant sore that infects History . . . It's an epidemic of pestilence . . . And the bourgeoisie follows the scorched-earth tactic. Before ceding power, they'll have infected the whole earth, corrupted the total consciousness to the marrow. And so there is no hope of happiness anymore. Every revolution is lost in advance!"

At the beginning of his invective, he had risen again to his feet (in fact, he had thrust the chair back with a kick). And he remained stubbornly, boldly, in his erect position, though the leaden weariness of this *gala* day, contradicted by his teeming brain, accumulated more and more in his muscles, defying him with its weight. In vain, then, his hoarse voice tried to clear a path in the din. And moreover, listening to his own voice, at every stage, he recognized in his supposedly *urgent communications*, as in a recorded radio play, only self-plagiarism.

Indeed, he had various selves: Davide Segre middle-school student, in short pants, and high-school student in sports jacket and red tie, and unemployed vagabond in cyclist's jersey, and apprentice factory-worker in coveralls, and Vivaldi Carlo with his knapsack, and the bearded, armed outlaw Pyotr (in his underground winter of '43–'44, he had let his handsome black beard grow) . . . All offered the present orator their famous ideal products, rushing to him from every side, and running off at the same time, like ghosts . . . With the air of starting here, at this very instant, the last revolution still possible, Davide resumed his invective, forcing his breathless voice to the maximum:

"The enemy must be unmasked! Shamed! His damned tin medals have to be recognized and devaluated, without delay! Salvation depends on the OTHERS! The day false values drop on the market, to shit . . . eh, you follow me . . ." In the tavern, meanwhile, the racket had increased. On the radio a very popular little dance-band was playing, and the group of music-lovers, all of one mind, had turned up the volume very loud. A syncopated tune was being performed, of which I remember nothing except that the musicians accompanied it, at intervals, with the words of the song, stammered to the same rhythm (Loo-loo-look at me, ki-ki-kiss me, etc.), thus redoubling its witty effect, and inspiring an imitative din in the younger listeners. Suddenly, Davide took umbrage, and breaking off his speech, he pulled the chair up behind him, silenced. But before flinging himself down on it again, with sudden resolve, he thrust out his chest towards the company seated around him. And in a self-accusatory tone (though with a provocatory brutality, which was the equivalent of a fist brought down hard on the table), he cried:

"I was born a bourgeois!"

"And I," replied the old man with the medal, not looking at him, but with a frank and kindly laugh, "was born a porter at the Wholesale Market."

"Not all bourgeois are mean," the little man with the sick eyes observed in his turn, conciliatory and judicious. "There are good ones and bad ones, and in between . . . It all depends." Meanwhile, he kept his eyes on the cards, visibly anxious to follow the play: "Take it!" he whispered eagerly, connoisseurlike, to his neighbor (the old man with the medal); while the latter, almost contemporaneously, had spread his thick hand over the cards in the midst of the table, announcing with victorious indifference:

"This one's mine."

The little man with the bloodshot eyes, all agog, wriggled in his tight jacket. They counted the points, but the victory of the old man with the medal and his partner was taken for granted. The victor then assembled the deck, to deal again.

Sinking heavily into his seat, Davide now sketched a hesitant, apologetic smile. In that action of his "fist brought down on the table," the last of his virulence had dropped away. Indeed, his aggressive gaze of a moment before was followed, in his darting eyes, by another special look of his, the exact opposite: enough to make you believe that inside him there lived a wolf, a fawn, and who knows what other dissimilar creatures, of desert, forest, and hearth. At moments he looked like a kid, happy to be allowed in the grownups' company, instead of being sent to bed as on week nights.

He had bent over the table, bone-tired, but still wanting to talk, as if today, having broken the long spell of silence, he had to seize the occasion at all costs. He recalled a sentence he had read as a child in a fairy tale, about a princess set free by a prince: *for seven hours they had conversed, and they had not yet said even the seventh part of the things they had to say to each other.*

The card games, at this table and at the other, continued hand after hand. Across the tables the usual words of the game flew back and forth: "give me a good one," "that's worth three points," "low card," "trump him," "I bid clubs," etc. The proprietor, on his side, had become spellbound, and half-dazed, listening to the generous radio program, which now offered another hit song, I don't remember which. And the few young people left sang that same song under their breath, echoed by other radios outside, through the windows opened to the light westerly breeze. But Davide seemed grateful because, perhaps without paying much attention to him, they let him talk on. Asking for comprehension, he cast around an affectionate look, in which from inside him (the Superego had got off his back, hiding God knows where) something terribly vulnerable could be glimpsed, a kind of risky concealment, in his stubbornness: "I," he mumbled in a low voice again, "was born into a bourgeois family . . . My father was an engineer, he worked for a building firm . . . a high salary . . . In *normal* times, besides the house where we lived, we also had a villa in the country, belonging to us, with a farm run by a tenant farmer—a couple of apartments rented out (which brought in income)—an automobile, of course (a Lancia)—plus I don't know what *stocks* in the bank . . ." Having ended, with this, his financial report, he stopped, as if after physical toil. And then, resuming, he informed them that in his family, from childhood, he had begun to understand the symptoms of the bourgeois disease: which revolted him more and more, to the point that sometimes, as a boy, at the very sight of his relatives, he was overcome by attacks of hatred. "And I wasn't wrong!" he clarified, assuming again, for a fleeting instant, his tough-man's look.

Then, bending forward, his voice reduced to hardly more than a murmur, until it seemed a futile and disjointed grumble, addressed to the wooden tabletop, he turned to various recollections of his family. His father, for example, had a whole range of different attitudes, even different voices, depending on whether he was talking with bosses, or colleagues, or workers . . . His father and his mother, with no suspicion of being offensive, called their employees *inferior;* and even their habitual cordiality towards them always seemed bestowed, like a gift from above . . . Their occasional beneficences or alms, always fundamentally insulting, they called *charity* . . . And they spoke of *duties* in referring to all sorts of social nonsense: such as returning a dinner invitation, or a boring visit, or wearing such-and-such a jacket on a certain occasion, or *putting in an appearance* at a certain exhibition or stupid ceremony . . . The subjects of their conversations and discussions were, more or less, always the same: gossip about the city or about relatives, hopes of typical successes for their children, wise or indispensable purchases, expenses, income, rises and drops in prices . . . However, if they by chance touched on ELEVATED subjects like Beethoven's Ninth or Tristan and Isolde or the Sistine Chapel, they assumed a pose of special sublimity, as if such ELEVATED THINGS were class privileges . . . They didn't regard the automobile, their clothes, the furniture in the house, as objects to be used, but as banners of a social order . . .

One of his first jolts—the first perhaps?—was something he had never forgotten . . . "I must have been about ten, or eleven . . . My father is driving me in the car, probably to school (it's early in the morning), when in the street he is suddenly forced to put on the brakes. Some man has stopped us, not aggressively, but almost apologetically. From what I can understand, he is a worker, discharged the day before from a building job because of the direct intervention—it seems—of my father. I never learned the reason . . . He's still a young man (maybe forty), but with some gray in his eyebrows; medium height, not heavy, but strong, so he seems taller . . . His face is broad, with solid features, though still a bit adolescent, the way men often look in our parts . . . He's wearing an oilskin jacket and a beret, with some plaster spattered on it; you can see he's a mason. At every word, jets of steam come from his mouth (so this must have happened in mid-winter) . . . And he stands there, waving his arms, wanting to explain himself, trying even to smile, to win my father over. But instead, my father doesn't even let him speak, shouting at him, swollen with anger: 'How dare you? Not another word! Step aside! Get out of the way!' At first, I think I see a twitch in the man's face; when already, inside, all my blood has started pounding in one desire, or rather one infinite determination: that man must react, with his fists, maybe even a knife, against my father! But instead, he steps back to the edge of the street, in fact, he even puts his hand to his beret, like a salute, while my father, furious, almost running him down, has stepped on the accelerator . . . 'You should hide yourself! Rabble! Scum!' my father goes on shouting; and I notice that, in his anger, the skin between his chin and his collar has made some reddish, vulgar furrows . . . In that other man, on the contrary, who has remained in the street, I saw no sign of vulgarity. Then I was overcome with a disgust, at being inside the Lancia with my father, worse than if I had been driving a tumbril to the guillotine; and I realized that we, and all our fellow bourgeois, were the world's scum, and that man left in the street, and his fellows, were the aristocracy. And in fact, could anyone but a noble being, of true dignity, immune to all meanness and deceit, be found at that man's age, humbly begging another man his own age, offering his labor in exchange for . . .? I remember that along the last stretch of the street, I was ardently wishing I had already become heavyweight champion, so I could wreak that sublime mason's vengeance on my father . . . And for the whole day I didn't speak to him or to my mother or my sister, I hated them so much . . . That, I think, is where it began . . . I no longer saw them with the same eyes: it was as if I were looking at them always through a magnifying glass . . . fixed . . . precise . . ."

"And where's your family now?" the man with the bloodshot eyes asked, with interest. But Davide didn't answer his question, nor did he show any reaction to the interruption except a vacant glance, returning at once, as if pressed, to tell his rosary of charges: there was nothing, in his family's existence, nothing that wasn't counterfeit and polluted: their actions, their vocabulary, their thoughts. And all their daily choices, even the most trivial, were foreordained, according to certain philistine Credos they honored as maxims of a higher ethics: such and such a person is invited because he's a Count; you don't enter that café because it's common . . . But when it came to the real laws of ethics, their confusion was such you would really believe they were the unknowing butts of a joke. In his father's opinion, a building worker who took a roll of copper wire was unquestionably a thief; but if someone had said to his father that his famous *stocks* were stolen from the wages of the workers, he would have taken this as an absurdity. If an armed robber had broken into their house, destroying and murdering, his father and mother would naturally have considered him an infamous criminal, deserving life imprisonment; however, when the Fascist robbers acted the same way against the Ethiopian territory, his parents offered their own gold to help them. A system in which they themselves lived comfortably gave them no cause for suspicion. Out of sloth, they ignored politics, and the government relieved them of concerning themselves with it, and of all responsibility. They were blind, led by the blind, and leading other blind, and they didn't realize it . . .

They considered themselves just—in complete good faith!—and nobody contradicted them in this error. His father was considered by all a respectable man, his mother a lady above reproach, his sister a well-raised little girl, a *putèla bene allevata* . . . Yes, and in fact she has been raised in conformity with the code of the two *veci* (the old couple, her parents) and she copies it with such naturalness that at times you would say it was a congenital scripture, transmitted to her, by the *veci*, in their genes . . . You can see reproduced in her—though in embryo—their same ordinances of justice! It's easy for her, for example, to let herself be waited on (and even have her shoes laced!)—her, a *putèla*—by a maid who has been in the household for half a century and who is old enough to be her great-grandmother . . . And it seems logical to her to insist the two *veci* buy her a little plaid cape seen in a shop-window (she who has a couple of new overcoats in her closet), for the reason that plaid is absolutely the latest thing, and the other girls her age have one! If by any chance, there are some, perhaps, without any coat or winter shoes, she doesn't count them: as if they were on another planet . . .

"Is she a pretty girl, your sister?" the old man with the medal asked him, directly, at this point.

". . . Yes . . ." Davide answered, dumbfounded, after a moment, "she's pretty . . ." And in this answer, despite his grouchy voice, there involuntarily emerged a brotherly satisfaction in which all his previous harshness was dissolved; while a colored mist flowed into his irises, only to flow out again at once, irreparably. He found himself suddenly suspended in a state of delirious youthfulness, which diverted him with its impossible consolation, as if he were chasing a cloud: ". . . but she's stupid . . ." he added, in the tone of certain fifteen-year-old brothers who, embarrassed, pretend to taunt. And he declared, comical and discontent: "You can hand her any silly story, and she'll believe it. If you yell at her, one morning: 'Good heavens! what's happened to you?! Your nose has grown a foot long overnight!!' she'll rush to the mirror, scared to death. Any nonsense is enough to make her laugh: you just have to whisper into her ear, pretending it's some big secret, a word you've invented at random, which doesn't mean anything, like *perepè* or *bomborombò*, and she'll explode right away in terrific laughter! . . . And in the same way she's ready to start crying over a trifle. 'When Davide was little,' somebody at home recalls, 'the French circus came to town, and he wanted to go every evening, to every show!' 'And me?' she asks right away, 'me no?' 'You weren't here,' they explain to her, 'You weren't born yet.' And she bursts into huge tears at this news! . . . She thinks that if you plant a pearl, a necklace will grow, or maybe that a donkey was born of the cart; and if her girl friends disagree with these opinions of hers, she says they're ignorant . . . She strokes her dolls as if they were cats purring, and she ties ribbons on the puppy, convinced she's doing him a favor . . . But she's afraid of big dogs . . . She's even afraid of thunder . . ."

This information about the nameless sister was received, on Useppe's part, with a series of laughs, in which you could sense, beyond his amusement, a hint of boasting. In fact, among the subjects dealt with today by Davide, all more or less abstruse and inaccessible to him, it was a matter of personal satisfaction to encounter one that belonged to him at last, within his experience.

Unfortunately, a fire siren, or some other public service passing through the street at that moment, partially drowned out, for the child's alert ear, his friend's last remarks: ". . . when she receives a present she likes, she takes it to bed with her at night . . . if she has good marks at school, she sleeps with her report card by her pillow . . . at bedtime, she never wants to put out the light in her room . . . A real pain . . . on the pretext of saying goodnight to this one or that . . . a pain . . ."

"And where is your sister now?" the man with the bloodshot eyes inquired again.

This time, Davide didn't leave his question unanswered. At first, he contracted his whole body, staring, as if at an insult or an intimidation. Then he smiled a miserable smile and answered curtly: "She's in the pile."

The little man, not understanding, remained expressionless. "And my father too, and my mother," Davide resumed, with a strange accent, neutral and mechanical, as if he were reciting a litany, "and . . . and the others. All in the pile. In the pile! In the pile!" Again, from his dilated pupils, the fawn's soul peered out; but this time it was a little animal, frightened in the extreme, hunted and blocked on all sides, in some wasteland, and he doesn't know where to run and tries to persuade himself: *there must be some mistake here . . . all this chase . . . these barrels aimed . . . they must be hunting some dangerous beast in the vicinity . . . but that isn't me . . . I'm another animal . . . not carnivorous* . . . Suddenly, this visible tumult was followed by the void; his eyes froze. And turning to his neighbors, he asked, with a cold little laugh: "Have you, any of you, ever heard tell of ZYKLON B?"

None of his neighbors had ever heard such an object mentioned; but they deduced it must be something grotesque, from the way it excited him.

"Hey, Vvàvide!" Useppe's voice made itself heard at this point. But this time it had a broken sound, useless and distant, like the waving of an invisible little hand behind a thick fence. For that matter, Davide seemed less than ever in a mood to reply to it: perhaps he didn't even perceive it.

His face had become walled-up in a directionless stare, a kind of white and void ecstasy, like that of a man accused but not confessing, when the torture machinery is shown to him. He seemed to have aged in a moment; and even his always latent sexual ardor (which gave him the tragic grace of a constant, burning stigma) seemed to have dried up and withered beneath the press of old age that was crushing him: "These last years," he reasoned in a dull voice, snickering, "have been the worst obscenity in all History. History, of course, is all an obscenity from the beginning; however, years as obscene as these have never existed before. The *scandal*—so the proclamation goes—*is necessary, but unhappy the man who is its cause!* Yes, in fact: it is only on the evidence of guilt that the guilty party is accused . . . And so the proclamation means: that in the face of this decisive obscenity of History, witnesses had two choices open to them: either the definitive disease, namely becoming definitive accomplices of the scandal, or else definitive health—because precisely from the spectacle of the extreme obscenity it was still possible to learn pure love . . . The choice was made: complicity!"

In drawing this conclusion, he assumed the almost triumphant air of one who denounces a misdeed, just discovered and irreparable: "And then," he said more harshly still, "how can you think of setting fire to the lazaret, when you, you yourself, are a carrier of the contagion and spread its stink around?!" This nameless *you*, whom he branded with infamy, seemed to be addressed to none of those present, but rather to some invisible spy, crouched behind his back.

Thanks to a fairly frequent phenomenon of certain *gala* states, in his inner ear now, his every word, as he uttered it, increased its duration, so in the last two minutes, he felt he had expounded a long theorem, which he considered somehow dazzling. Moreover, while his voice sank progressively lower (to the point of becoming, in the racket, an indistinct sound) it seemed to him, instead, grotesquely, that he was talking in a very loud voice, and the little crowd in the tavern for him had the effect of a multitude. This multitude, however, was fairly distracted (he was aware of that) or even alienated from him: some played cards, some listened to the songs; and though an old man or two, in the second rows, nodded at some of his phrases, he could see (with a curious lucidity) that those were almost mechanical movements, rather of vacuous amazement than of participation. "What the hell am I saying?" he asked himself curtly.

When he reached a climax, in the face of this total lack of success, he was disturbed by painful doubts about his own oratory; and worst of all, he recalled, in this connection, a certain dream he had had in the past, to be specific in the days when he was called Pyotr and had become a partisan in the Castelli. It was towards the end of that period, when food was scarce, and one night he was standing his turn of guard-duty at the base, outside the hut. What with the fatigue of staying awake, and his weakness due to scant nourishment, at a certain hour of that night he had been overcome by a terrible drowsiness. And to master it, he did nothing but pace up and down, never stopping or, still less, sitting down; but all the same, at one point, he had irresistibly dozed off against a wall, on his feet, like a horse. Although surely very brief, his sleep had sufficed to bring him a dream. And this was the dream:

he is in a white cell, barely a man's width, but with a dizzyingly high ceiling, so high it vanishes from sight. And his eyes peer upwards, waiting, because certainly, in a short while, from that invisible ceiling, an extraterrestrial Being is going to descend to him with a Revelation. It will be (and this is already known) a single, short sentence: which, however, will contain the sum of universal truths, the sole definitive solution that will free the human intellect from all seeking . . . The dreamer doesn't have to wait long. The Being is not slow to descend, almost to his level. He is a superhuman figure, in a tunic, with a white beard, majestic-looking like the prophets of Jerusalem or the sages of Athens. He stops, in mid-air, facing the dreamer, and says to him in a resounding voice: *to make a hot soup, you can also boil old shoe-leather!* Then he vanishes.

Now the memory of this dream, in fact, was accompanied by an immediate suspicion: *perhaps I believe I'm saying all sorts of important things, and instead, ever since I opened my mouth, I've done nothing but bawl ridiculous banalities, without any connection or logic* . . . this, however, was only a fleeting obfuscation for him, beyond which he found, lucid, his today's fixation: he had to untangle a certain skein, as in legends, to arrive he really didn't know where . . . perhaps to save someone, or at least something . . . But save whom? The people in the tavern? Or what? A testimony? A ring? A letter? Unless it was, on the contrary, a question of striking down . . . executing . . . He had no idea. He knew only that today was the day. As if he had to get across a bridge which would afterwards be forbidden to traffic.

He then flung himself, with new energy, into the continuation, after the last obstacle had been leaped over: "What I mean, in other words," he declared in a voice still louder than before (at least so it seemed to him), "is that only a pure man can drive out the money-changers and say: *the earth was the temple of total consciousness, and you have made it a den of thieves!*"

He had uttered this sentence with firm confidence, pronouncing it syllable by syllable, as if reading something written on the wall. But an ironic interjection by the Superego led him to translate it into simpler terms, to assure its clarity. "Right. Only a clown," he clarified, raving, "can say to another man: *executioner*, when he, as his turn comes, is ready to operate the same machine . . . of slaughter . . . There. This is a clear definition!" The weariness of his muscles was so great it could be seen even in the physical movement of his lips.

Still, though it was clear enough, his *definition* aroused no appreciable echo from his audience. "The fact is," he reproached himself secretly, "I'm a lousy demagogue. To the crowd, you have to speak of parties . . . flags . . . I bore them. You need the knack of entertaining them . . . amusing them . . ." Here he had a brilliant idea, which made him laugh in advance, with an innocent, trusting sweetness: "I don't remember in what book," he narrated, "I read the story of a writer who goes to visit an insane asylum. A patient comes over to him and, pointing to another patient, whispers: *Watch out for that one. He's crazy. He thinks he's a button. But believe me: if he really was, I'd be the first to know it, because I'm a buttonhole!!*"

This gag of Davide's likewise failed to produce the hoped-for effect, also because, I believe, it reached his public in a very confused form. The only one who laughed at it, in fact, was Useppe, who, for that matter, was Davide's sole attentive listener in that room; and it didn't matter, really, that Useppe understood almost nothing of those speeches, because for that very reason they sounded to him more venerable, like oracles. All the same, he sensed from the beginning something disturbing in his friend's behavior, worse than sadness or a sickness, and so he was often tempted to say to him, "Davide, why don't we go?", but he didn't dare. Meanwhile, another old acquaintance of his had come into the tavern, the news-vendor friend of the Marroccos, whom he recognized at once, although he could see the man had changed. But though the man had always been cordial to him in the past, he now answered Useppe's festive greeting with a vague gesture of rejection. A few months before, he had been stricken by a thrombosis, which had confined him a long time in the hospital, leaving him half-paralyzed. He leaned on a cane, all tilting, and in his face, dejected and swollen, you could read a constant fear of dying. He could no longer peddle papers or drink wine. From the hospital, he had moved into the home of a daughter-in-law, a second-floor apartment, noisy and confined, overpopulated with young grandchildren. And at present he considered all living children a disaster. It is quite probable, moreover, that he didn't even recognize that kid waving at him from the other side of the table. And as for Davide, the man apparently hadn't seen him again after that first meeting in the Marrocco home. The two didn't greet each other, in any event, or show signs of recognition; nor could Davide, for his part, have indulged in greetings or such formalities, now overwhelmed by his verbal flood like certain sick people forgotten in wards.

Every now and then, true, his eyes roamed around the table, questioning and bewildered, lingering a moment on this face or that, as if begging for a reply; but the only interlocutor (if such he could be called) who remained still at his disposal was Clemente Black Hand. He, latterly, had not stopped looking at Davide, a bit obliquely, only from the lower part of his eye, always with the same irked expression of boredom and sarcasm. He seemed to have condemned, in advance, as stale and nonsensical chatter, everything the other might say.

At the moment of telling his joke, Davide had made another attempt to stand on his feet, but he had soon slumped down again, overwhelmed by the exhaustion that almost made him faint, and at the same time drove him to speak, as in unhealthy states of insomnia. His voice was becoming more and more dim and hoarse; while he kept feeling the frequent but discontinuous sensation that he was shouting, as if at a rally. This exaggerated and involuntary volume of his voice now embarrassed him, also because the tortuous thread he was trying to unravel, as he displayed it now, was bleeding in his hands like a bared nerve:

"I," he muttered, sweating, "am a murderer! In war, some can kill heedlessly, like going hunting. But not me. Every time, I was murdering! One day, I murdered a German: a hateful, repulsive being! And while he was dying, I gave myself the pleasure of finishing him off, kicking him, stamping on his face with my boots. Then, in that very act, I was overcome with the thought: *Here I have become just like him: an SS slaughtering another SS* . . . And I went on stamping on him . . ."

From the other side of the table, Black Hand's lungs emitted their usual hollow notes, which Davide perceived as mocking laughter. And he suddenly felt singled out in that room, an object of overpowering indecency. Like someone in the confessional who suddenly realizes he has raised his voice so that his secrets are echoing through the vaults and along the naves, crammed with people. It seemed to him, in fact, in his familiar delusion, that he had shouted these last sentences in an excessively loud voice: "All of us," he then blurted desperately, in his own defense or salvation, "carry an SS hidden inside us! And a bourgeois! and a capitalist! and maybe even a Monsignor! and . . . and . . . a Generalissimo all decked with fringe and medals like Mardi Gras! All of us! bourgeois and proletarians and . . . anarchists and communists! All of us . . . That's why our struggle is always a hamstrung action . . . a misunderstanding . . . an alibi . . . false revolutions, to evade the true revolution, and to preserve the reactionary inside us! *Lead us not into temptation* means: *help us eliminate the Fascist inside us!"*

He was addressing Black Hand, as if expecting from him a plenary indulgence or, at least, a partial absolution. But Clemente Black Hand had drawn back again to cough into his lapel, into the little overcoat of his poverty, with the attitude of a man deliberately turning his back on the talk. So, at least, it seemed to Davide. Who, all the same, staring at him, was sure he could read within him, as if through an x-ray, the following tacit reply: "Keep your moral maxims for yourself. If you have a General-issimo inside you, that's your business. Who gives a damn? For myself, as the naked eye can see, I carry nothing inside me but a simple infantry private of the ex-ARMIR, with a permanent discharge, unemployed, muti-lated, with rotten lungs." This was enough to make Davide blush, like a schoolboy being punished. Inopportunely, at this point, the old man with the medal raised one eye towards him from the cards:

"After all is said and done," he asked, "are you a Christian?"

". . . me?! . . . What christ are you talking about? The Galilean, who was crucified . . ."

". . . died and was buried . . ." the old man with the medal recited, in a tone of good-humored teasing. His neighbors laughed, also good-humoredly.

"There's no argument about him: he was a real christ, if he's the one you're talking about," Davide declared, confused and blushing. He used the *voi* form, out of respect, addressing the old man with the medal. And meanwhile he moved closer to the man's face (since the player still kept his eye on his cards) in the eager concern of a kid explaining his motives to an adult: "We have to get this clear," he insisted, filled with anxiety, *"that one* mustn't be confused with the ghost of the same name that History puts on altars, and on platforms, and thrones . . . and . . . and pastes on signs advertising its usual frauds . . . slaughterhouses . . . and thieves' stands . . . always using him to conceal its one real idol: the puppet of Power! Christ isn't a ghost; he is the only real substance in movement . . . And that christ, historically speaking, was a real Christ: that is, a man (ANARCHIST!) who never denied total consciousness, for any reason! Obviously, then, there can be no argument: anybody who looked at him, saw heaven! And anybody who heard him, heard God! GOD isn't a word! it's THE word!!" More people were coming into the tavern. It was that hour, towards sunset, when many inhabitants of the neighborhood, returning from the movies or an excursion, dropped by a moment before going home, where their wives had preceded them, mean-while, to fix supper. I remember with particular exactness the song broad-cast by the radio (it was one, in fact, I already had in my head, perhaps because it had come out just after the war, or at least in time to be sung by Ninnuzzu; it was from him, I think, that I learned it). I still know a few lines by heart . . .

> Boogie woogie, how they dance,
> They could make a buffalo prance . . .
> Seven whiskies here, and twenty sheriffs there
> And okay-okay everywhere . . .

Davide's hands and knees were seen to sway for a moment, to an absent rhythm, futile and meaningless, accompanying the tune of the song. However, he undoubtedly perceived its notes unaware, through a subliminal hearing, all intent, as he was, on proceeding with labored breath along the spinning track of his obstacle race: "the term *christ*," he informed those present, forcing his voice: "is not a personal name or surname: it's a common title, to designate the man who transmits to others the word of God, or the total consciousness which means exactly the same thing. *That* Christ was named, according to the documents, Jesus of Nazareth, but on other occasions, in various times, the christ has presented himself under different names, male, or female—he pays no attention to gender—and with light skin or dark—he puts on whatever color comes along—and in the east and the west and in all climes—and he has spoken in all the languages of Babel—always repeating the same word! In fact, that is how you recognize christ: from the word! which is always one and the same: *that one!* And he has said it and repeated it and said it again, orally and in writing, and from the mountaintop and in the jails and . . . and from insane asylums . . . and *departút*, everywhere . . . Christ pays no attention to places, or to the historic hour, or to the techniques of slaughter . . . That's right. Since the scandal was necessary, he had himself slaughtered obscenely, with every available means—when it's a question of slaughtering christs, nobody economizes . . . But the supreme offense against him was the parody of mourning! Generations of *Christians* and of *revolutionaries*—all accomplices!—have gone on whining over his body— and meanwhile, they took his word and turned it into shit!"

Davide's crucial problem in this late phase of his race was physical strain; his breath almost failed him. But he still exerted himself all along his course, as if between the exhausting track and his broken and drugged limbs—flung there on a seat—there was only an unreal relationship: "And so, from now on," he stumbled on, clearing his throat at every phrase, "if he comes back, he won't say words any more, because anyway, the ones he had to say, he's already shouted to the four winds. When he appeared in Judaea, the people didn't believe he was the true speaking God, because he presented himself as a poor man, not in the uniform of authority. But if he comes back, he'll present himself even more miserably, in the person of a leper, a poor misshapen beggar-woman, a deaf-mute, an idiot child. He is hidden inside an old whore—*find me!*—and you, after using the old whore for a screw, leave her there, and when you're out in the open air, you seek in the sky: *'ah, Christ, for two thousand years we've been awaiting your return!'* 'I,' he answers from his refuges, *'have NEVER left you. You're the ones who lynch me every day, or worse still, walk by without seeing me, as if I were the shadow of a corpse rotted underground. Every day I pass close to you a thousand times, I multiply myself in every one of you, my signs fill every inch of the universe, and you don't recognize them, you claim to be waiting for who knows what other vulgar signs . . .'* They tell of a christ (it doesn't matter which; he was a christ) who once was walking along a country road and he was hungry, so he went to pick a fig from a tree. But since it wasn't the right season, the tree had no fruit: only inedible leaves . . . And then Christ cursed it, damning it to perpetual sterility . . . The meaning is clear: for anyone who recognizes Christ as he passes, the season is always right. And he who doesn't recognize him denies him his own fruit with the excuse of the time and the season, and is cursed. There's no arguing. There's no excuse to postpone, because Christ isn't going to descend from the stars, or from a past and future God knows where; he's here, now, inside us. This is no news; it's well known, shouted to the four winds: that there's a Christ inside each one of us. So what's needed then, for the total Revolution? Nothing. An elementary movement, two seconds, like laughing or stretching when you first wake up. It would be enough to recognize the Christ in everybody: me, you, the others . . . Yes, the news is so elementary it's sickening to have to repeat it. It would be enough . . . And then the fruit of the revolution would be born, beautiful and spontaneous, on all the trees, we would all exchange it happily; no more hunger exists then, no wealth, or power, or difference . . . All past History is discovered for what it was: a grotesque Grand Guignol, lunatic, a store of filth in which we've stubbornly infected ourselves for centuries, rummaging with dirty fingernails . . . And then the folly of certain questions would be obvious: *are you a revolutionary? do you believe in God?* like asking somebody if he was born!! Are you a revolutionary? . . . do you believe in God? are you a revolutionary . . . do you believe . . .''

In a sing-song tone, snickering, Davide went on repeating these two questions, several times, until they were a kind of meaningless tongue-twister. But by now his speech had necessarily become a monologue, because his voice had sunk so low that not even his nearest neighbors, had they wanted to, could have made out his words. He had taken on a sullen look, as if threatening or accusing someone or other, and he stared into his glass, just like Clemente, without drinking a drop, as if overcome with disgust: "I must still make a rectification," he was mumbling, "about that German, at that crossroads at the Castelli: I, who was murdering him, had become an SS, all right. But he, who was dying, was no longer an SS or a soldier of any army! He had a look in his eyes: *where am I? what are they doing to me? why?*; his eyes were very pale and stupid, as if they were just opening, as if he were being born, not dying. Me, an SS: but he had become a baby again . . ."

"Let's say: a brat," at this point, whispering into his ear like a little mocking lash, the Superego made himself heard once more. Davide laughed:

"That's right! Better: a brat," he corrected, obediently. And this, as I recall, was the last point scored in their match by the Superego, who at that very moment, with a kind of victorious spin, left him, vanishing definitively, abandoning him to his disastrous weakness.

"He was a baby!" Davide shouted after him. His face, now, had a spoiled-child's expression, a look that came over him at times when he was absolutely exhausted. But he exerted himself still, with incredible obstinacy, in the final dash . . . even if the prize was now revealed to him, irremediably, for what it might be: nothing but a little paper flag at most, very worn, and ripped as well . . . "A man who kills somebody else, always kills a baby!" he insisted, breathless, wringing his hands. "And now," filled with bewilderment, he confided to his own glass, "I see him again, that one, flung there in the pile. In the pile!" he repeated, frightened, "in the same heap with the *veci*, and the *putèla* . . . Together, not Germans or Italians, not pagans or Jews, not bourgeois or proletariat: all the same, all naked christs, with no difference . . . and no guilt, as they were born . . . I," he stated, with one of those strained, curtailed breaths, characteristic of children in the midst of a tantrum, "I can no longer divide the world into black and white, fascists and communists, rich and poor, Germans and Americans . . . This porno—porno— . . . this lurid . . . farce has been going on too long . . . enough! . . . I . . . am . . . fed . . . up . . ."

Not even Clemente Black Hand bothered, anymore, to pay attention to Davide Segre, who in fact seemed fatally lost now, in a drunken raving. He meandered on, I don't know how long, in his obsessive chatter with a thick and stammering voice, alluding to various objects and events, with no connection among them. He said that before Galileo people believed the sun revolved; afterwards they believed that the earth revolved, and later it turned out the movements are relative to each other, so you can say the earth and sun both revolve, or both are still, it doesn't make any difference.

Then he repeated that he was the cursed tree, and that he had insulted Christ after having murdered him. And if his family was dead, the fault was his, since he had had no charity for them, who were basically simple children, inexperienced and deceived. And if his girl had ended like that, the fault was his, since in pursuing his fictitious politics he had neglected his only love. And if his dearest friend was dead, the fault again was his, because the boy was actually a child seeking a father—he was an orphan, without knowing it—and without knowing it, he was asking Davide to act as his father. And if the old whore was dead, the fault was again his, because she was a child with a pure heart, born for pure love . . . And the guilt of all the deaths was his . . . And in reality the bourgeois was himself . . . and the whore was him . . . and the pimp was him . . . and the origin of all obscenity was him . . . It must be said that Davide was surely not the only one, in the tavern, who was babbling . . . By this hour, the empty wine jugs on the tables were beyond counting. The holiday break was about to end. And all around, the voices of the yammering old men could be heard, meaningless, boasting obscenities, coughing and hacking. The radio meanwhile had broadcast I don't know what papal messages from the Vatican . . . now it was repeating a summary of the afternoon sports news. Again some young men clustered around the radio, while the proprietor, who knew the day's sports results by now, was yawning, or else giving orders to his wife, on hand to serve the tables. In the midst of all this, Davide appeared a case of normal drunkenness; whereas, in reality, he felt all too clear-headed. His lucidity throbbed in his brain like so many glistening splinters. Suddenly he said, smiling, in a more resonant voice:

"I read somewhere, I don't know where, that a man visiting a Lager glimpsed something living, moving in a pile of dead bodies. And he saw a little girl come out. 'Why are you here in the midst of the dead?' And she answered him: 'I can't stay with the living any more.' "

"That actually happened!" he guaranteed, in conclusion, with a strange, forced, didactic hauteur; and in saying this, he sank down with his arms on the table, sobbing. Actually, you couldn't tell if they were sobs or laughter. "This is it, all right, you drank yourself a skinful," the old man with the medal said to him, giving him a paternal slap on the shoulder. It was here that Useppe, shy, frightened, came closer and said to him, tugging at his shirt:

"Let's go, Vàvide . . . come on, let's go 'way . . ."

For some while, namely since the moment Davide had sat down again, speaking more and more deliriously and in a lower voice, Useppe had slipped from his own chair, crouching beside Bella on the floor. He didn't dare interrupt his big friend, afraid of making him mad; but he felt a growing fear of some unknown danger being prepared against him. Even the word GOD that constantly returned to his lips was becoming, for Useppe, a source of fear: as if this famous God might come forward suddenly, engaging Davide in a hand-to-hand fight. Among them all, Useppe was the only one who didn't consider Davide drunk: he suspected, instead, that he was sick, perhaps because he didn't eat enough. And he was wondering if, afterwards, he couldn't convince him to come home to supper with them in Via Bodoni . . . Meanwhile, in an attempt to drive away fear, he played with Bella. Without noise they played paws and hands, or else she tickled him, licking his ears and throat, until she provoked little laughs, promptly stifled out of respect for the place.

". . . Come on, come on, Vàvide!! Let's go 'way!"

Useppe's face was pale, and he was trembling, scared; but he also had a comical, indomitable manner, as if he intended, personally, to protect Davide from some numerous onslaught. "The kid's right," the old man with the medal said, also urging Davide, "go on home. You'll feel better." Davide stood up: he wasn't weeping and he wasn't laughing; he had, instead, an opaque stiffness in his features, and glassy eyes. He didn't go towards the door, but, staggering, headed for the toilet. Useppe followed him with his eyes, afraid of seeing him fall; and he didn't notice that meanwhile Annita Marrocco had looked in at the door for a moment. She didn't see Useppe either; his smallness hid him amid the adults' height. She greeted the proprietress from the distance with a brief, melancholy smile, her little black head bent languidly to one shoulder, as if her hair were weighing it down; and seeing the place too crowded, she withdrew. "That one," Clemente commented, chuckling, "is still waiting for her bridegroom to come home from Russia . . ." And he went on snickering, as if he had told a little ghost story, the kind that, at night, keeps the guests of the castle awake. But actually the only one who heard him was the former news-vendor, who grumbled something incomprehensible in reply.

When Davide came back from the toilet, he no longer seemed the same person; or rather, he had passed to a new stage of his exaltation. Useppe was the only one who noticed a little dot of blood on his shirt; and in his ignorance, he supposed simply that the wound in his arm had started bleeding again. I, for myself, don't know what other *medicine* he had injected into his body during his brief absence; I know that lately he had not only been using the ones preferred in the past months, but was also trying out all sorts of substances, often of opposing effect, mixing or alternating stimulants and narcotics in a breathless succession. Especially during the last week, you might say this had become his chief nourishment: perhaps also because the season's first warm days stirred again in his blood his innate instincts of life and of health, those energies that, in him, were then inexorably converted into forms of sorrow. Nothing frightened him so much as the return of certain states of his, absolute awareness or total wretchedness, at times accompanied by dreams, at times by too-lucid wakefulness. And rather than be caught off guard by them, he never failed to carry with him a supply of his remedies when he left the house . . . In those days, such cases went unnoticed, especially in poor neighborhoods.

He crossed the noisy room again, walking unsteadily, but merry, like certain crack-brained animals driven in circuses by the whip. His unnatural pallor betrayed him. But worse than the pallor was the strangeness of his eyes; there had suddenly reappeared in them that kind of depravation which had disfigured him on his arrival at Pietralata after his capture and flight from the Germans, and which for some time had seemed expunged. Even in his brief journey from the radio to the table, he found a way of performing some numbers worthy of a vaudeville show: although, in his surprising lack of inhibition, he didn't lose that special clumsiness, a shy and sullen child's, incurably part of his nature. Moreover, anyone could notice that, beneath the artificial excitement, his physique was exhausted from God knows what excesses and malnutrition. Useppe, however, was not sorry to see his friend revived and jolly.

In the space around the radio, Davide attempted first a parody of dance, though the set at present was not broadcasting a musical program, but a very serious talk, of quasi-official or perhaps ecclesiastical nature. Then he burst into singing the anarchist anthem:

"There will be the revolution,
and the black flag will fly . . ."

interrupting it with a raspberry: a sound, this, so unnatural on his lips, that little Useppe (who, alone among all the others, laughed at his friend's performance in childish solidarity) felt an instinctive sadness. Arriving at the table, he started slapping the backs of the various people there, calling them all *comrade*; at which, the man in the messenger's uniform, who was an outspoken anti-Communist, was roughly outraged. The players, having put aside their cards by now, were preparing to leave; the old man with the medal had already gone, and the peddler was putting his box around his neck again. But Davide stubbornly wanted to make them stay; and with a millionaire's gestures, he purchased the peddler's total stock, scattering cakes and fritters and little paper cones of peanuts to everyone, insistently offering drinks all round. He himself filled his glass, then, presenting himself before Clemente, gave him a military salute, with the invitation, among other blasphemies: "Let's drink to that pig God," and he drank, in fact, a sip on his own, but spat it out again immediately, nauseated. He shifted around, shoving and taking clumsy steps like a sailor on deck in a rolling sea, amusing himself by blabbering (if anyone was listening) certain private affairs of his, now loudly, now confidentially, but alway in a tone of cheap gossip. He informed them, for example, that he was a steady customer of brothels (and in fact, in these first weeks of June, rather than go back to pacing those sad bridges, he had lapsed a couple of times: bringing home from them a fury of indecency and remorse, since he considered brothels a social abjection, almost as bad as Lagers) . . . Or else, mockingly, he resuscitated his famous voluntary experience as a worker, ending each day in fits of vomiting . . . And he insisted on revealing to all, as if it were a very important secret, that he was the principal murderer, he was the pimp, he was the Fascist . . . He talked of corpses and beauty contests, of Betty Grable and the massacre of peasants at Portella della Ginestra in Sicily, and of cold war and hot, and of banquets and of bombs, etc., mixing, in his chatter, tragic and comic and indecent references, but always with unseemly laughter, as if everything he said were funny. And in these various *numbers* of his, he was accompanied every now and then by the fresh and uneasy laughter of Useppe, who understood nothing of what was said, but felt encouraged to enjoy this clowning. Not to mention Bella, who could finally let herself go, jumping, wriggling, and wagging her tail, as if it were Carnival. At the height of the party, Davide had chanted a vulgar little song from the days of his grandmother:

> Seneghin seneghin
> Stick your shirt-tail in again

inviting all present to a kind of chorus. But those present, really, paid no attention, only slightly and absently amused by him and his showing off, in fact, half fed-up, as at a drunk's normal spectacle. The tavern, for that matter, was emptying. Clemente too had gone off all alone, dragging his mutilated body, which shuddered in the warm breeze, in his unseasonal overcoat. Davide left without saying goodbye to anyone. Useppe and Bella hastened after him.

.   .   .

These were the longest days of the year. The sun was not yet setting, although it was already time for the Evening News on the radio. Along the street, from the windows, odds and ends of the latest news arrived:

> . . . *a police ordinance, issued in the name of the Minister of the Interior, has ordered all Chiefs of Police to forbid political rallies or assemblies in factories* . . .
> . . . *the Red army is advancing towards Sinkiang* . . .

. . . the Greek government has ordered a large-scale round-up of . . .
. . . In Washington, the House of Representatives . . .
. . . Prime Minister Pella announces that the government . . . special taxes . . . indirect taxation of . . .

"Shall we have a race? See who gets across the bridge first?" Davide proposed, when they reached the beginning of Ponte Sublicio.

The challenge was accepted. Bella won. Davide, breathless as he was, came second, with his long legs; and Useppe, though good at running, was left behind, because of his small size. At the finish line, however, both were received with equal celebration by Bella. Useppe, giddy from the game, though the loser, arrived laughing like a madman; and Davide, leaning against the railing, gasping, also laughed, totally carefree. It is a fact that, after having started across the bridge in jest, he suddenly, without meaning to, began to race seriously (especially striving against Bella), like a kid who in some contest forgets his homework and every other earthly concern. And a gust of that illogical wind swelled his lungs for perhaps ten seconds. Then he went on laughing for a long time, but already a piercing incredulity, in nervous shocks, was punctuating his thoughtless laughter.

"How about playing Chinese Morra?" he suggested to Useppe.

"Essssss!"

To tell the truth, Useppe didn't know this game; and Davide took the time to explain it to him. However, Useppe, when they actually got into it, did nothing but get confused, his hands moving happily, confusing the sign for *paper* with that for *stone*, or extending three fingers instead of two for *scissors* . . . This stupidity of his sent him into gales of laughter, revealing his twenty teeth, like grains of rice . . . Davide also laughed, and his face, as he looked at Useppe, reopened in that luminous relief, filled with friendship, with which he had hailed the child's entrance into the tavern. Suddenly he grabbed his hand and, gazing at it, gave it a little kiss, with the simplicity and childish innocence of someone kissing a holy picture. And Useppe promptly kissed him, too; but as Davide moved, this kiss landed on his nose. The trivial incident was enough to arouse the hilarity of all, Bella included. The first to become serious again was Davide: "You," he said to Useppe, with an almost bitter gravity, "are so pretty that the very fact you exist makes me happy at times. You could make me believe in . . . in everything! EVERYTHING! You're too pretty for this world."

Useppe, however, rather than appreciate Davide's compliment, had noticed the shift in his humor, which from merry, suddenly, had turned grim. "Now what game'll we play?" he urged.

"That's enough now."

". . . No . . . More!" Useppe protested, in a tone between pleading and complaining. Davide meanwhile was moving away from the railing. "Here," he declared, "is where we separate. I go one way, and you two, another."

Useppe swayed. "Wy," he proposed boldly, "don't you come and eat supper at our house, with us? Mamma's made meatballs for supper . . . and . . . and there's wine, too!"

"No, no, another time. I'm not hungry this evening."

"Where're you going now? To sleep?"

"Yes, to sleep." Davide started off, with his lanky and now exhausted gait. An inexpressive dullness had spread over his eyes.

"We'll walk you to your door," Useppe decided. The sheepdog, though puzzled, didn't object. And Davide, more out of laziness than for any other reason, let them come. For the two vagabonds, actually, the supper hour was now striking and, indeed, behind Davide's steps, a kind of debate was going on between the couple, which reached him only in the form of canine whining. Bella, in fact, also out of her respect for punctuality, still insisted on inviting him to supper; and among the other arguments, she wanted to inform him that at their house, besides the meat dish already promised, with vegetable, etc., there was also soup. She was referring, specifically, to her own evening mush (composed of leftover spaghetti, cheese rinds, water, bits of tomato and other ingredients). But in the end Useppe, with eloquent if mute signals, discouraged her from insisting. What kind of attraction, for a great guest like Davide, could a dog's bowl of mush be?

Such a weariness had come over Davide that his house, perhaps another fifty yards away, seemed to him a remote and somehow yearned-for destination. But at the same time, he was gnawed by a kind of nostalgia: like a boy (the same one who, a little earlier, had become involved in the bridge race?) forced to come home when the daylight, outside, wasn't yet gone. But who was forcing him? He could find no answer to such questions except a threatening, irreparable negation.

Also from the familiar tavern this side of the hovels, the radio's voice was emerging as usual. Now it was broadcasting some names of cities, and some numbers: I suppose they were the lottery drawings. Of the inhabitants of the hovels, the majority had not yet come home; there was only a little group of women with three or four tiny babies; and from some point, to greet Bella, two dogs came running, a pair. One, already encountered previously, was the dog that resembled a monkey; and the other, a newcomer, seemed a composite of various animals, with a generally agreeable result. (To Useppe's considerable relief, the famous Wolf was again absent: he was obviously on an outing with his master.) Bella returned the pair's greeting, though in great haste, moving off to study the evening odors of the area; but soon, with a solicitous mien, she came back to Useppe, dragging her leash after her in the dust.

Davide's inner restlessness, combatting his exhausted body, kept him in that unnerving state produced by certain poisonings or, at times, by hunger: a kind of low no-man's-land, between the outskirts of reason and those of dreaming, where you are tormented in a wretched confinement. In sight of the first hovels, he happened to close his eyes, with the wish to see nothing but black; then, reopening them, he didn't at first recognize the usual landscape, and he asked himself: "Where have I got to?" He was assailed by certain stupid popular tunes, alternating with a sentimental poem written by himself in his schooldays, which began with the verse: "I love you, Happiness!" And mixed with these torments were film titles or other random phrases, at present empty, for him, as burst balloons: *The Maginot Line, Gilda, The Bargain Center, Simun the wind of the desert, a Fascist of the first days* . . . In the last stretch towards the room, he mechanically began to walk faster, though the idea of shutting himself up in there now revolted him. Useppe, his eyes raised towards him, hurried after him.

"Wy are you going to sleep so early?"

"Because I'm sick," Davide explained laughing. And worn out, as he hunted in his pocket for the key, he sat down on the ground, his back against the door.

"You're sick . . ." Useppe said, pensive, but asking no explanation. He was on the point, rather, of telling him (as if to boast of being a colleague) that he too was *sick*, but he restrained himself in time. He was, in fact, suddenly afraid that Davide, too, if he had learned of this bad sickness, would perhaps avoid him like other people.

He decided, instead, to ask him:

"What did you do to your arm?"

"A mosquito bit me."

With difficulty, Davide had fished the key from the pocket of his pants; but an extreme heaviness of his muscles kept him sprawled there on the ground, lingering outside his own door, like a beggar. And still unable to bring himself to stand, he started banging his fist on the closed door. Then, assuming a deep bass voice, like someone speaking from inside, he said: *Who's there?*—immediately answering, in his normal voice, announcing himself: it's me!—*Me, who?*—Davide Segre. And who are you?—*Me!! Segre Davide!*—And what are you doing in there?—*Sleeping* . . .

Useppe laughed at this new game, though observing the opening of the door with some anxiety. In the deserted little room, the panes of the little window were also closed: so there was a stagnant odor of sleep, as if somebody had really been lying there for several hours. Otherwise, the filth and the disorder seemed even more tumultuous than the other time, like the aftermath of an invasion. Davide sat down, slumping on the unmade cot: "Now," he announced to Useppe, "it's time for us to say goodnight."

"It's still day . . ." Useppe pointed out, hesitating on the threshold of the little room. He had picked Bella's leash up from the ground, while she had sat down outside, near the open door, patiently waiting. Only, every now and then, she gave the leash a little tug, to insist: *It's late. We have to be going*, and Useppe, dissatisfied, would tug the leash from his end, in reply. He couldn't bring himself to leave Davide here alone, sick, and with no supper; but he didn't know what to say to him, and he swayed on his legs.

Davide meanwhile had stretched out full length on the bed, all dressed, not even taking off his shoes. In his ears, he heard roars and buzzing, which didn't bother him, however, but rather seemed to cradle him like a fabulous story. But still, inside his brain, a point of steady wakefulness lasted, almost horrifying, which made him foresee a difficult night. For some time, in fact, an unpredictable chemistry had been taking place in his body, thanks to which his drugs didn't always affect him according to their proper nature; they functioned at random, in a kind of wager with his nerves: so even sleeping pills, at times, stimulated him further, instead of calming him. And this ambiguous wager frightened him this evening, like a whim of fate. For the moment, he had even forgotten the presence of the child and the dog; but a whiff of wild and caressing freshness, almost joking, from that point of the little room reminded him the two were still there.

"What are you doing here? It's late!" he exclaimed towards them, raising his head slightly, without turning his eyes. "We're going, we're going," Useppe mumbled, "it's not night yet."

"In the lands of the white nights," Davide began saying, in a musical and disoriented voice, "in some seasons it's always day. And elsewhere it's always night. As you prefer. Too many forms, too many colors. And so many meridians and parallels! On one parallel the houses are made of snow, and towers and palaces of ice, huge, walking on the waves, and they dissolve. On another, cement and glass, marble, cathedrals, mosques, pagodas . . . And forests and forests! Rain forests, *nebulas*, no, nebular . . . and half-submerged, with airy roots . . . I used to like geography, in school, thinking of journeys in the future. And now that the future has come, once in a while I say to myself: why not? But then, if I imagine ME walking, any street or town of the earth seems like a shithole to me, neither better nor worse than this room. Nothing, anywhere, but a lousy, dirty room, where it's always day and always night, as soon as I see myself going past . . ."

From Useppe's direction there came a vague murmur. His real answer (if he had known how to formulate it) would have been that to him the opposite effect happened; namely, that any place at all, even the lowest den, became a splendor for him if Davide was there, or a friend of his. "This room isn't lousy . . ." he mumbled, almost offended.

"That's right, it's enchanted!" Davide laughed. "On some occasions, visions take place here . . . No, not really visions! That would be too great an honor! Only some transformations, exaggerations . . . You, for example," he twisted slightly to look at Useppe, "now I see you as if through a telescope: great big, too huge to get through the door. And now I see you tiny, tiny, tiny, as through the wrong end of a spyglass. And with lots and lots of little blue eyes, looking from every part of the room."

"And now? How do you see me now?" Useppe asked, coming forward hesitantly.

Davide laughed: "You look little to me. Very very little . . ."

Useppe remembered the doctors' answers:

"I'm not growing much," he confessed.

"Well, we'll say goodbye now. Goodnight," Davide determined, laughing. However, he added:

"You want me to tell you a story?"

He had recalled, unexpectedly, a childhood memory of his sister, who, like all children, often didn't want to go to sleep at night. From the crack beneath the door, she could see the light still burning in the adjoining little room of her brother (who read until late, in bed), and then she would gently turn the knob, and appear at the door, in her nightie, asking him to tell her a story or a fairy tale, before she went to sleep. Everyone in the family knew, in fact, that Davide had great imagination, indeed, he had almost decided to become a writer when he was grown up; and his sister, too little to be able to read, exploited his imaginings. Normally, her brother became angry at these evening intrusions; but at his sister's tenacity, to get rid of her, he would finally launch into some sort of beginning, as a tease: "Once upon a time there was a cabbage . . ." "Once upon a time there was a broken pot . . ." "Once upon a time there was a drum . . .", however, from this point, immediately and irresistibly, he was led to improvise the rest. So in conclusion, almost against his will and with a kind of resignation, he finally contented his sister with a story born by chance, but complete in itself, and satisfying to her. One evening, for example, determined to refuse, to end the matter quickly, he had shouted at the suppliant, almost as an insult: "Once upon a time there was a chicken's shit!!" But he was immediately inspired to add that this hen laid golden eggs. And it naturally followed that the eggs were unbreakable, since they were gold: until a cock, full of courage, split them with a peck.

Then some golden chicks came out, who proved to be so many young princes in disguise, all sons of the cock and the hen and endowed with the magic formula to destroy the evil spell. In fact, hen and cock were really the king and queen of India, victims of an enchantment of their enemy, the king of somewhere or other . . . Nothing exceptional, as you can see, in little Davide's stories; however, stories they were, with a beginning, a plot, and an end, according to the ordinary rule.

In that same way, that evening, promising Useppe a story, Davide had no idea in his head, only a hollow confusion. To begin, he uttered at random the first words that came to his lips: *"Once upon a time there was an SS . . ."* and from this beginning, almost automatically, a little story sprang forth. Not, surely, a great creation, even in this case; but still a proper story, indeed a kind of fairy tale or parable, with an inner logic of its own and a conclusive meaning.

". . . there was an SS, who, because of his horrible crimes, one day at dawn, was being led to the gallows. He was only about fifty paces from the place of execution, which was being held in the courtyard of his prison. And as he walked forward, his eye happened to light on the crumbling wall of the yard, where one of those flowers sown by the wind had grown, those flowers that bloom wherever they fall and apparently live on air and rubble. It was a miserable little flower, of four purplish petals and a couple of pale leaves; but in that dawning first light, the SS saw in it, to his amazement, all the beauty and happiness of the universe. And he thought: *If I could go back, and could stop time, I would be willing to spend my whole life adoring that little flower.* Then, as if he had become two persons, he heard inside himself his own voice, but joyful and clear, though distant, coming from some unknown place, shouting at him: *Verily I say unto you: for this last thought you have had on the point of death, you shall be saved from hell!* Telling you all this has taken me a certain amount of time; but there, it lasted only half a second. Between the SS, walking in the midst of the guards, and the flower blooming on the wall, there was still, more or less, the same distance as before: barely a step. 'No!' the SS shouted, inside himself, turning back furiously, 'you can't fool me, not again, with those old tricks!' And since his hands were bound, he tore away that little flower with his teeth. Then he dropped it on the ground and trampled it under his feet. And he spat on it. There, that's the end of the story."

"But there isn't really any hell!" Useppe commented firmly, at the story's end. *Isn't any*, in his language, half Roman dialect, meant *doesn't exist*. As if amused, Davide turned his pupils towards that minuscule figure, emanating, at that moment, a comical audacity.

"Hell doesn't exist?" he asked, in reply.

Useppe repeated his personal opinion, declared, not orally this time, but with a Sicilian-style *no*, thrusting his chin up and making his lips protrude: a movement inherited from his brother Ninnuzzu, who in turn had inherited it from his own father, Alfio, of Messina.

"And *why* do you think it doesn't exist?"

"Because . . ." Useppe said, not knowing what to answer. From Bella he received a little bark of encouragement. And finally his answer was:

"Because people fly away . . ."

This explanation, to tell the truth, came out somewhat dubiously, barely a whisper. But to make up for it, the pronunciation came out very well, correct. "And horses, too," he hastened to add, "fly away . . . and dogs . . . and cats . . . and grasshoppers . . . everybody, I mean!"

"Do you know what an SS is?"

Useppe had known this for a long time: at least since the days of The Thousand. Indeed, in his prompt reply, he used the terms perhaps previously learned from Carulina herself, or perhaps from some other member of that numerous tribe:

"*Germanian police!*"

"Bravo!" Davide said to him, laughing. "And now, goodnight. Go on, run along; I want to sleep . . ." In fact, his eyes were closing on their own, and his voice already sounded thick, and low.

"Goodnight . . ." Useppe answered, docile. But still an uncertainty made him linger:

"When will I see you?" he asked.

"Soon . . ."

"When?!"

"Soon, soon . . ."

"Tomorrow?"

"Yes, yes, tomorrow."

"Tomorrow you want us to come here, to your house, like that other time? After lunch, like that other time?!"

"Yes . . ."

"That's it, then, eh? We have a date!"

". . . yyes . . ."

"I'll bring the wine!" Useppe announced, turning to leave. But at this point, having let go of Bella's leash for a moment, he ran back. And, as if in a fraternal ritual now permitted, indeed consecrated, he gave Davide a little goodbye kiss, which this time landed on one ear. In his drowsy haze, Davide was left wondering if that kiss were real, or the fragment of a dream. Nor did he hear the little click of the door, closed with great respect after the two visitors.

By now dusk was falling, and the belated pair marched in great haste towards home, already plotting, however, en route, a complete plan for the next day. The appointment with Davide, in fact, hadn't made Useppe forget his other friend, Scimó. So it was established, between him and Bella, that they would go to the river in the morning to visit Scimó (getting up earlier than usual tomorrow), and would dedicate, instead, the afternoon to Davide. In Useppe's little head, now, there stirred such a festive air that it dispelled any suspicion of disappointment; while at that very moment, with Bella, he was walking along the side of the Porta Portese square dominated, at the end, by the Reformatory building. Neither of the pair knew Scimó was now shut up right in there, behind those walls; but Bella—who knows why?—at the sight of the square, flattened her ears, and turned away, almost stealthily, towards the bridge.

7 During that whole night, the repose that had seemed promised to Davide since dusk was instead denied him. To tell the truth, he was already sleeping when Useppe went out of the room; and as Useppe had left him—fully dressed, his shoes on his feet—he continued to sleep till morning. But his was a kind of false sleep, morbid and broken, more tiring than insomnia. That wakeful point which had remained fast in his brain since yesterday, now resisting drugs and free of his body's lethargic inertia, seemed alert there, ready to thrash him, like a whip assigned to guard him, to prevent escape. If he barely began to sink towards the depths of unconsciousness, he was suddenly roused by imaginary lightning-flashes or alarm bells in the dead of night. And waking and dozing, he found himself constantly involved in a ridiculous little theater, like a mocking surrogate of the visions he had just recently sought from drugs, and which he no longer expected. In fact, by now he had said farewell forever to the hope of seeing—at least in the form of obvious hallucinations—his family cured of the leprosy of the Lagers of Ninnuzzu unharmed, or of witnessing an array of celestial apparitions that might deceive him, temporarily, with who knows what revelations or special grace. He received, instead, inferior products, which irked him with their evident fakeness and their stupidity. Tonight, however, these falsifications weren't limited to the usual accessory distortions of the furniture or the shadows, which he had only to turn off the light to dispel, nor to the usual soap-colors which flashed to him, fairly innocuous, in the dark room, vanishing as he dozed off. In light or in darkness, the machine which since evening had been set in his brain never stopped, sometimes in neutral, sometimes driven, you would have said, by a precise intention, even if obscure. For a long stretch of the night, it insisted on manufacturing an

assembly-line of jokes, so cheap that he himself couldn't understand why they should torture him so much. For example, as soon as he turned off the lamp, he was awaited in the void by a one-dimensional invasion of common geometrical abstractions: rhombs, triangles, squares, multiplied in myriads, in a tumult of absurd colors. And if he turned on the lamp again, he found the familiar room, on the contrary, ravaged by abnormal concrete things: the floor was a flabby, agitated substance, and the walls swelled, covered with scabs and tumors, or else they split in cracks. Now he succumbed (and this was the bizarre part) to such jokes, recognizing their silliness at the same time. He saw how in themselves they were gratuitous and meaningless little tricks, but meanwhile he looked on them as nameless horrors: not even the worst monsters of the apocalypse could have been more repulsive to him. Not knowing whom to call, in his panic he murmured "God God," like a child, covering his eyes with his hands . . . And God appeared to him as in the oleographs of the Sacred Heart and the Holy Bishop, which he, rather than offend Santina's memory, had left hanging over the bed, merely covering them with some newspaper. At his call, the two oleographs jumped from their places. And that was God: a stupid, pink young man with a little blond beard, and a half-pound of beef-heart in his hands; and a dumb old man, with all the trappings of established power and authority. "If you really were a saint," Davide addresses the latter, "you wouldn't get yourself up like a high priest, you wouldn't wear chevrons and carry a baton . . ." And now, for the twentieth time that night, he falls to sleep again. And he dreams: however, in his dream he remains aware, as usual, that he is lying on his bed in his own little room. He has set out, meanwhile, to fulfill a schoolboy wish of his, towards a marvelous city he has learned of in his history and geography and art books. In the dream, this city has an indefinite name, and it would seem to be an emblem for him: a kind of social and egalitarian synthesis of labor, brotherhood, poetry . . . He already knows its image, pored over in his texts . . . But as he walks on and on, in the place of those famous architectures he finds only enormous and sordid blocks of apartments massed together to the horizon, still not finished but already marked with zigzagging cracks, like electric shocks . . . In this jumble, the streets are a honeycomb, cluttered with flotsam and stones, and filled with interminable lines of windowless freight cars, like reptile carcasses. He forces his way through the main streets, looking for the king. It is hard for him to get his bearings, also because of the thick blackish smoke that comes from the cars and the buildings, accompanied by the constant scream of sirens. Obviously the city's buildings are all workshops and brothels. In fact, from the street you can see their interiors, illuminated by spotlights; but the spectacle is monotonous, the same everywhere. On one side, there are long

lines of men in whitish uniforms, chained to one another, and busy solder-
ing into more chains some heavy iron rings with their bloodstained hands;
and on the other, some half-naked women, who make obscene movements,
and all have bloodstains on their legs: "Only the sight of blood can arouse
the customers," someone explains to him, laughing. And he immediately
recognizes the king, who, as he now seems to have known, is none other
than the accursed tree. Davide finds himself facing him: a little character
in an officer's uniform, wriggling on a cement platform (a kind of dancefloor) and laughing continuously. Davide would like to ask him various
questions: "What have you done with the revolution? Why have you
degraded labor? Why did you choose ugliness?" etc., etc., but filled with
embarrassment, he realizes he has become a schoolboy again, in short
pants, so the questions are truncated, and he can only manage to say
"Why? . . ." in an excessive shout. "Because," the other man answers,
nevertheless, laughing, "beauty was a fraud, to make us believe in paradise,
when it's well known that we are all condemned at birth. We won't fall for
certain tricks any more. Awareness is man's honor." And he continues
laughing in Davide's face and still wriggling hysterically: "This," he explains to him, "is the Upa-upa, the flat dance." And, with this, in fact, he
flattens himself, until he has disappeared. Davide is now grown up again,
as in real life, with long pants and a summer sports shirt; and around him
there is a colonnade of stupendous architecture. In the place of the dancefloor, below him there is a cool meadow, and right in its center, directly in
front of him, stands a tree, damp with dew, covered with fruit and leaves.
Not far off the sound of water can be heard, a bird's voice. "There,"
Davide says to himself, "all the rest was a dream. But this is real." And, in
proof, he decides to leave one of his shoes beneath the tree; so when he
wakes, finding one foot bare, he will have the certitude that, here, he
wasn't dreaming. At this point, he heard some bright familiar voices of
little boys or girls, in chorus, calling from beyond the wondrous colonnade:
Davide! Davide! and he woke with a start. The voices were imaginary; in
reality no one was calling him. The lamp had remained on, and he found
himself lying in the rumpled bed, as before. Both his shoes were on his
feet. It was still late at night, but he couldn't know exactly what time it
was, having forgotten to wind his watch that evening. Actually, while his
dream adventure, as he remembered it, seemed rather long and spacious,
this interval of sleep had lasted no more than three minutes.

Here begins another phase of that endless night of his. He no longer
saw abstractions or concrete things, his senses lay idle; but his brain was
working constantly, feverishly, in certain elucubrations or complicated discussions. He didn't know whether he was waking or sleeping, or whether
the two states alternated in him. He seemed to be reasoning about univer-

sal problems of advanced philosophy, and suddenly he realized that, instead, they were shopping bills, laundry lists, calculations of dates or distances, etc. He regretted not having answered the king of the city, and his answer came to him, belatedly, clearly: "What you say is false. The truth is the exact contrary. God is the real essence of all existing things, which confide their secret to us through beauty. Beauty is God's modesty . . ." when suddenly, to illustrate this principle, his brain began an elaborate disquisition on the octanes of gasoline and the proof of alcoholic beverages . . . The question now before him was human *superiority*, consisting in the intellect; and he had to demonstrate to his comrade Ninnuzzu the various species of violence, and that the worst violence against man was the *degradation* of the intellect. From there, he passed to the distinction between intellect and substance, or rather God and nature, which Davide's brain, tonight, attributed to Hegel and Marx, declaring it a manichean distinction, that is to say wicked; as science now confirms, for that matter. And at this point, from God knows where, Bakunin spoke up, to say (so Davide's brain asserted) that atomic weapons would also disintegrate the intellect . . . Whereupon the debate with Ninnuzzu resumed, except that it now concerned the various types of automatic guns and revolvers, and questions of caliber and firing-range. Suddenly Davide reproached Ninnuzzu for having hastened his own death: *Anyway,* Ninnuzzu seemed to rebut, *if you don't die fast, you die slow. And, if you ask me, slow is shit.* The English word *slow* prompted a confused dispute about popular dances, with a quantity of American terms, and Spanish, Portuguese, Afro-Cuban . . . mingled with gossip about the sex of Creoles . . . Similar subjects and others of every kind crowded and clashed incessantly in Davide's brain, in an involved and jumbled activity, sometimes spinning like wheels, sometimes exploding like bubbles. And this foolish bustle, which he couldn't elude, seemed a shocking humiliation to him. He remembered having read somewhere that in the future, scientists will succeed in keeping a human brain alive indefinitely, separated from the rest of the body . . . And he imagined the toil of this nerve-matter, isolated, with no possible relationships; it would have to resemble a feverish grinding of leftovers and rubbish, illuminated briefly from time to time by some reminiscence, which would shine all the more painfully because it would promptly be ground up with the rest. The worst anguish of such a sentence, he felt, was humiliation. And he recalled having heard that in a Turin institution they keep alive a female *creature,* all of whose organs and limbs are in the embryonic state, except the lower part of the trunk and the sexual system . . . The word *humiliation* suddenly reminded him of the most horrible sound he had ever heard: the young German's weeping as he had stamped on his face with his boot. That sound returned often to

517

persecute him day and night: a wretched, feminine voice, like the imploring paroxysm of dissolving matter. *The worst violence against man is the degradation of the intellect* . . . Now in his brain, in a shaft of light, G. has appeared, her hair shaved; she is in her working smock, pulled up to her thighs, as she writhes on the ground with her legs spread. Then, a new picture, a rickety wheelbarrow is seen passing, heaped with plaster arms and legs, like ex-votos, of a livid, repulsive whiteness; and this is followed by the old man with the medal, two horns on his head like Moses, who flings down a card and says: *There's nothing to be done here, my boy. There is no act which, once performed, does not revolt your conscience.* Now Comrade Ninnuzzu pops up again, laughing and shooting in all directions . . . But a little later, unexpected, the photograph of Aunt Tildina appears and is distorted to assume the face of Clemente . . . *I want to sleep I want to sleep,* Davide says. The impossibility of true sleep, empty, refreshing, torments him like a new law, promulgated today against him by special decree. Signs and billboards flash into his mind: *Coca-Cola—The Pause That Refreshes;* or else *Beautyrest—Sleep Like an Angel.* He realizes he is invoking all known divinities: Christ, Brahma, Buddha, and even Jehovah, whom he finds disagreeable. And in his raving the usual bazaar of helter-skelter words and phrases is always intruding: *I don't want to think, I want to sleep, the accursed tree, goodnight, the syringe, the urinal, the curfew, intravenous or oral,* and more and more often the word ORDEAL. It seems impossible, but in this wandering of his brain, Davide has spent at least a quarter of the earth's rotation. And at the end he has sunk into another of those inescapable dreams of his, which entangle him like a birdlime, just as he passes the first threshold of unconsciousness. In this dream, the accursed tree (which this time is clearly himself, Davide) is not only a betrayer of the true revolution, a born murderer, a man of violence, but also a rapist. In his bed there is a girl, a virgin, very thin, as if consumptive, with pubescent breasts just emerging, and long hair, already white, with little white childish legs and thick plebeian feet, and a fat behind; and he rapes her. Then, when he is paying her, he realizes he has only useless money, probably Moroccan coins. She doesn't reproach him, but only observes him with a meek smile: "These are no good . . ." and then he cheats her, saying they're collector's pieces, of great value on the market. And he flings them at her, and the coins make a sound like a machine gun.

At their unreal clatter he wakes (the light of day is already appearing) and masturbates repeatedly, till blood comes. He hopes this at least will help him sleep; but instead, though totally exhausted, he remains still half-awake, in a state of stupor and searing guilt. In his brain, God knows why, the isolated word ORDEAL starts ticking again like a clock. He makes an effort to recall its meaning: and it seems to him that it is a kind of divine judgment, revealed through a test. At this point he thinks he understands that his *ordeal* would be to give up drugs of every kind, including alcohol, accepting the terrible privilege of rationality. To ply any trade: worker, farm-laborer, writer, explorer . . . gaining in his own flesh the experience that matter and intellect are a single thing, which is God . . . Then he sees himself walking on the earth again: no longer with Comrade Ninnuzzu, or G., or relatives, or friends. And all the earth, from the Caribbean to Siberia, to India, to America, appears to him like the landscape of his first dream tonight: bloodied chains, and himself inquiring about the revolution, and people laughing in his face ("Here there is no longer any act, among all you could perform, that must not repel your conscience"). He decides, in any event, that his definitive ORDEAL begins today (*Never put off till tomorrow!*), but all the same he stands up, staggering and goes to the little suitcase where he keeps a certain supply of drugs. There are the capsules of red and black sleeping pills which have been betraying him for some time (giving him at most a sudden, abnormal sleep like a delirium and leaving a nasty, indecent taste in his mouth). There are powders, or stimulant tablets to inject in the vein after having pounded them to dust (this is presumably the operation performed in the tavern latrine which gave him new drive). There is some kif left, bought from a Moroccan, who also supplied him with a special little pipe. There is, from the same source, a sample of crude opium, of a dark amber color, the size of a walnut, etc., etc. In these last times, truly, he had capriciously transformed himself into a kind of human guinea pig; and now he laughs, bending over the case, thinking that, to justify himself somehow, he had perhaps presumed these experiments, in his *vile body*, were his ORDEAL.

In the case there is also a little copybook with some fairly recent poems of his, discovered in his house in Mantua. He tries to reread them, but the letters dance before his eyes, the sentences twist, stretch, contract, fragmenting in his brain, meaningless. "There," he says to himself, "*the degradation of the intellect*. Maybe I'm already crazy, I reduce myself, on my own, to the condition of insanity . . . TO UNDERSTAND, on the contrary! It's necessary TO UNDERSTAND! The vital end of man is: to understand. The straight way of the revolution is: to understand." Davide girds himself for a supreme act of bravado. He will make ready on the usual chair beside the bed all the familiar array of his favorite *medicine* (his true friend, the one of his Naples initiation: peace, the fantastic night), and he will begin an endurance contest: it is there, waiting, and he will not touch it. Only seeing it, actually, he feels an impatient hunger for it, like a puppy at the bitch's teat. But this, precisely, is the ORDEAL.

On the chair, with trembling hands, he has arranged everything:

medicine, cotton, matches, syringe, strap for his arm. And he will not touch them. The contest has begun. "We will write poems, we will write more poems, we will print, we will publish. Now there is freedom of the press (even if bourgeois 'freedom' perhaps . . .) and even the Jews are *citizens equal to the others*" . . . Suddenly he has decided that, later, he will go out and eat; but at the mere thought, he feels at once a nausea, which rises from his stomach to his throat. He has stretched out again, and the mattress seems to be crawling with insects. In reality, there are no insects in the room, despite the disorder and the filth: he defends himself against them, in fact, with a daily, downright savage profusion of DDT, the powerful insecticide brought by the Allied troops with the end of the war . . . But you would say that his senses and his brain are inventing every kind of joke to prevent his repose. The sun is already high, the day is very hot, and he is all covered with sweat, but the sweat freezes on his skin, making him shudder and, at the imaginary teeming of insects, he is filled with revulsion. His brain's working has slowed down, but at the first glimpse of the open threshold of awareness, he draws back, full of suspicion and anguish and he does nothing but roll and toss and yawn, in alarm at the new day invading the world. In his little room, the electric bulb remains burning; nor is there, truly, much daylight penetrating the dirty panes of the window, covered by the curtain. But even that scant light from outside, the signal of full day, is too much for him and exasperates him. Now he regrets the night, which, at least, suspends all traffic and empties the streets: any night. And the familiar sounds of every morning, from outdoors, hammer at his temples like an anonymous threat: "*Màma mia, màma mia . . .*" he begins to say: but even those two primordial syllables *ma-ma* have been ruined for him by destiny, in such an aberrant wrench that no oracle, ever, could have foreseen the like, at any man's birth. Suddenly raging, delirious news runs through the room, as if by now all the world's childhood had been devastated for eternity, and all infants raped in their nests, because of what was done to Davide's mother. He, orphaned, would like at least a ghost to rock him, to make him sleep, while his raving, childishly, has become fixed on a precise memory of more than a decade ago.

At thirteen, Davide was already tall, taller than other boys his age, so he had earned the right, in advance, to dress *like a man*. And on this occasion, his mother proudly came back from shopping, bringing him as a present a special purchase: a necktie! She had chosen it herself in the most elegant shop in Mantua, where the young men of the highest society bought their clothes . . . And for his part, Davide at that time had not yet repudiated the bourgeois use of the necktie (later, indeed, he had a number of them, bought on his own, which we wore as a bold symbol . . .) But this particular one didn't suit his taste at all; so he gave it a cross look, and despising it, said brusquely to his mother: "Give it to somebody else! Anybody you like!" Her eyelashes trembled, she forced a smile, and took it back.

That was all! But today, from some unknown crevice of his memory, that tasteless tie is resuscitated before him. He recognizes it: a pale blue ground, with some whimsical paisley pattern . . . And he sees it unfurled over the whole globe, among Fasces and Swastikas! From every part of the earth, sharp lines converge towards one point: the murder of his mother. And one of those countless lines comes from the ill-fated necktie. Who knows what happened to it? And how to rub it out of space and time? If he could sleep, have a long real sleep of at least ten hours, it seems to him this perverse little banner would also be erased, with the other nightmares, and he would feel able to face a new day.

But sleep no longer comes to him now, in any form. He blames the daylight and the others' voices, and he relieves himself in curses and banalities that fall unheard in the room, and he beats the side of the bed with weakened fists. All the world's population is fascist, all have murdered his mother, and he is one of them. Finally, in himself Davide hates all, and this is a new sickness he has never felt before. His deepest feeling towards others has always been compassion (it was this, really, that made him so sulky, in his shame), but today, suddenly a vindictive aversion towards everyone grows in him. The voices outside belong to fascists and enemies, and they have shut him up in a bunker: any moment they may kick the door open and burst into his lair, to load him onto their trucks. He knows very well this is a delirium, that the voices and racket outside are only the usual kids with their football games, the dragging steps of the landlady, the slam of blinds and of garbage cans . . . But it's as if he didn't know; he would like no window or door, he would like to break off all communication . . . There might still be a possible means, there, ready, on the seat of the chair: just this once, at least . . . Davide casts a glance in that direction and turns away at once, refusing the cowardly surrender. But obviously, the ORDEAL the boy had insisted on imposing upon himself was too difficult.

So, after the outburst of the new solar day, another quarter of the terrestrial rotation passed. It was two o'clock on Monday afternoon, and Davide's condition was growing worse. As for the appointment with Useppe, he retained no trace of it in his memory, if ever he had known anything of it (he was, in fact, already as if absent in the moment when he said: yes, tomorrow). It may also be that in the course of the night two little blue eyes had sometimes flashed here or there in his room; but they were too small to count for anything.

That Monday, from early in the morning, was very busy for Useppe and Bella. According to the plan established the previous day, they got up before the usual hour, and had promptly undertaken their familiar walk towards the river, in their eagerness to meet Scimó. Among other things, Useppe wanted to propose the idea of inviting a friend of his (Davide) to the little beach, making him an exclusive participant in their common secret: with the guarantee that Davide, surely, would not betray them!

On entering the hut, they found it in exactly the same state as yesterday. The alarm was still stopped, at two. And the briefs were still flung on the same place on the mattress, suggesting that Scimó was not at present there in the neighborhood having a swim (for example). Indeed, it was fairly obvious, now, that he hadn't come to sleep in the hut last night or the night before. But Useppe, in a defensive reflex, denied even the suspicion of his possible capture; and he preferred to believe the fugitive had lingered in the evening in some wondrous movie house or phantasmagorical pizzeria, taking refuge for the night in other hidden quarters . . . and that, without fail, this very day, or tomorrow, he would return to the hut.

Bella declared herself of the same opinion. After having sniffed about the area a bit, she sat on the ground, with a grave and resigned look, which clearly said: "No use searching. He's not in these parts." Today, again, she gave up her swim, rather than leave Useppe alone. The day was sultry, and the fields were already beginning to turn yellow; but beneath the tree tent the grass remained still fresh, as in spring. Many little birds went by, but Bella, made sleepy by the heat, paid no attention to them. Late in the morning, up in the trees, a chirping began: yesterday's first cicada was already accompanied by others, new ones, making up a little consort. The imminent arrival of a great orchestra could be foreseen.

After waiting almost two hours, they gave up any thought of seeing Scimó today, deciding to come back tomorrow and look for him. And at the noon bells, they started back towards home. Along the calm expanse of the river banks, windless, a few scattered voices could be heard: on Monday (and with the schools not yet closed) the river-boys were few, and almost all little kids.

At two in the afternoon, when Ida was lying down on the bed to rest as usual, Useppe set off again with Bella for the *appointment* with Davide. He had taken with him the famous flask of wine (which, every now and then, along the way, he set on the ground a moment, to rest from his burden). And in addition, with the usual change that Ida gave him daily, he thought to buy his friend something to eat, along with the wine. So he purchased some thick, dark cakes, which are still sold today, if I'm not mistaken, with the name of *ugly-but-good*. Unfortunately, those cakes, of an economical variety, and carelessly wrapped by the shopkeeper, were dropped halfway to Davide's and scattered over the ground, so they were not only *ugly* but also broken: "still *good*, however," Bella promptly barked, to console Useppe, who was collecting them, with some anxiety.

It was almost the solstice; but the summer, fairly mild till yesterday, seemed to have exploded suddenly in its full ripeness, and this was the most torrid hour of the day. The siesta's lethargic vapors had drained the streets, all the windows showed closed shutters and lowered blinds, even the radios were silent. And the narrow cluster of huts, near Davide's house, looked like a deserted African village. The scant grass that sprouted there in spring, among the rocks and the rubbish, was now burned and consumed by the dust; and from the garbage rose the sweetish odor of decomposition. The only voice to be heard, already from a certain distance, was the ferine, solitary barking of the famous Wolf, who, today, perhaps in his owner's absence, was tied to the fence of his hut, with no comfort save the slender shadow of the pales.

Useppe was all sweating and breathless, but gripped by such animation that this time, despite his load, he preceded Bella towards the room. Immediately, at the first knocks on the door, Davide was heard inside, exclaiming: "Who is it?!" in a hoarse and threatening voice, almost frightened. "It's us!" Useppe was quick to reply. But to this, there was no answer, except a kind of feverish grumble, so hollow and uncertain Useppe wasn't sure he had really heard it.

"It's me! Useppe! Useppe and Bella!" No answer. Useppe ventured another little knock.

"Vvàvide . . . ? you asleep? We came . . . the appointment . . ."

"Who is it?! who is it?! who is it?!!!"

"It's us, Vàvide . . . We brought you the wine . . ."

This time from the little room a kind of exclamation was heard, confused, interrupted by a spasm of coughing. Davide, perhaps, was very sick . . . leaving the flask of wine in front of the door, Useppe went around to the window, followed by Bella, who was panting with the heat, her head down.

"Vvàvide . . . ? you asleep? We came . . . the appointment . . ."

From inside a movement was heard and a clatter of objects upset in passing. The window was flung open. Behind the grille Davide appeared, an unrecognizable sight. He was grim, distraught, his hair over his eyes, his face livid, pallid, with red patches at the cheekbones. He gave Useppe a lusterless glance, in a blind fury, and shouted at him with a brutal voice, alien, absolutely transfigured:

"Clear out, you ugly fool, you and your lousy dog!"

Useppe heard no more. The window had been closed again. Certainly, at that moment, the earth didn't tremble; but Useppe had exactly the same sensation as if an earthquake had been released from the center of the universe. The *ugly-but-good* cakes dropped from his fist and began to spin around him, in a cyclone of black dust, along with the rubbish, the collapsed fences, and the walls, in a thunder of barks that pursued one another endlessly. A moment later he started running, seeking escape along the path home. "Careful!" Bella pleaded with him, galloping at his side, dragging her leash, "wait before crossing! Can't you see the tram? A truck's coming!! Watch out! There are beams here! You'll run into a wall there . . ." Reaching the top of the stairs at home, the little boy was dripping from head to foot, as if he had stepped from a flooded stream; and unable to pull himself up to the doorbell, he began to whine and call: "Hey, mà . . . mà . . ." with a voice so faint it resembled a whimper. Bella came to his aid, emitting loud summonses; and when Ida rushed to the door in alarm, Useppe took refuge against her breast, still lamenting: "Mà . . . mà . . ." but without giving her any explanation, unable to find an answer to her anxious questions. He avoided looking over his shoulder, and his uneasy and dazed eyes saw nothing. At her caresses, however, he was somewhat reassured, and Ida preferred not to insist with too many questions. For a good part of the afternoon, the child clung to her skirts, starting if there was a louder noise from the street or the courtyards. Finally, with extreme gentleness, Ida asked him once more the cause of his fright, and he first mumbled some convulsive excuses about a certain truck "that big" that ran over a little boy, and "catches fire" and some water, "big and black"; but then all at once he blurted angrily: "You know, mà . . . you know . . ." and he hit her with his fist, bursting into tormented sobs.

Around five, the western breeze brought some relief. Useppe had huddled on the kitchen floor against Bella, and Ida heard him laugh because the dog was tickling his ears and neck with her tongue. The sound of his familiar little laughs considerably alleviated Ida's anxiety; but this evening was unlike the other, usual evenings of this fine weather, when Useppe would come back from his great excursions with Bella, filled with hunger and chatter, boasting of his famous *forest* down on the river, and certain friends of his . . . This evening he said nothing, alienated or stupefied, and every now and then he turned his eyes from his mother to Bella, as if seeking help or asking forgiveness for some unknown shameful deed . . . With effort, feeding him like a little baby, Ida managed to make him swallow some crackers soaked in milk. But all of a sudden, with a furious gesture, he overturned the bowl of food on the table.

With the darkness, the sultry heat had returned. During the night, Useppe had an attack. Waked by some faint footsteps in the room, Ida found the bed beside her empty, and in the light of the lamp she saw the child walking, spellbound and aghast, towards the wall. A moment before his cry, Bella (whom Ida, in her old domestic prejudices, sometimes banished from the room for the night) burst in, almost breaking down the door with the weight of her body. And as if crazed she started licking Useppe's naked little legs, stretched out, motionless, after the convulsion. This time the attack lasted much longer than usual. Several minutes went by (and it is known that every fraction of time, in certain instances, is stretched to immeasurable enormities), before the little, celestial smile of his return opened in Useppe's face. And the sleep, which always followed his fits, this time also lasted longer than the norm. Except for some brief intervals, Useppe slept through the remaining night of that ferocious Monday and also the following day and night, until Wednesday morning. Meanwhile, over at the Portuense, David Segre's destiny was fulfilled.

In reality, when Useppe had seen him appear at the window on Monday afternoon, Davide, you might say, had already entered his death-agony. Now, in fact, his presumed *ordeal* was about to conclude in final, shameful surrender. Towards evening, somebody heard moans in the room, but paid little attention, because it was no novelty to hear that sullen boy in there shouting curses or maybe laughing, even when he was alone. The first suspicions began the next morning, when it was noticed that the light, inside, had remained burning, and that he didn't answer anyone's call, while a flask of wine, undoubtedly his property, was still on the ground outside the closed door, where it had already been remarked yesterday (indeed, a kid of the local gang had considered taking it, but had been restrained by fright, since Davide, among his neighbors there, was deemed a tough character). After a while, the landlady's son was led to force the lock of the window with a crowbar, from outside: an easy task. And then, when the curtain was pushed aside, Davide could be seen sleeping on the bed, hugging a pillow, and half-sprawled in a defenseless position, which strangely made him seem more fragile, and even physically smaller. His face was invisible. And when, after they called him, he gave no answer, they decided to break open the door.

He was still breathing, though imperceptibly, when they found him. But as soon as they tried to raise him up, he emitted a little childish sigh, almost tender, and his breathing stopped.

He had obviously been killed by an *overdose*; but perhaps in injecting it, his desire had not been actually to die. The boy had suffered too much fear and too much cold; and he wanted only some sleep, to heal him. A deep, deep sleep beneath the lowest threshold of the cold and the fear and of every remorse or shame, like a hedgehog's hibernation or a baby's pre-natal slumber inside its mother's womb . . . Beyond such a wish for sleep there may also have been a wish to wake up again, perhaps later. But waking, in these cases, is a matter of chance and whim: a hypothetical, stellar point which meanwhile in perspective moves away from the earth in a distance of light-centuries . . .

My opinion would be that Davide Segre, by nature, loved life too much to rid himself of it knowingly from one day to the next. In any case, he "left no explanation of his act."

8 Of this final enterprise of Davide's, neither Useppe, nor Ida, nor Bella ever had any word. After waking from his Monday-night attack, Useppe, as usual in these cases, never mentioned Davide's name again (except perhaps once to Bella?) and Ida respected that silence, though she had no idea of its motive. She didn't even notice that the famous flask of wine, formerly kept in reserve for the great Davide, had disappeared at that time from the cupboard.

After the severe heat of the previous days, the sky had clouded over, and from Wednesday to Sunday the weather remained grim and rainy; but Useppe, for that matter, showed no desire to go out. After this last attack, he no longer seemed the same. Even his eyes were clouded, behind a sort of mist that seemed to be all wrapped around him, confusing time and space for him: so he called tomorrow *yesterday*, and vice versa, and he wandered around the house's little rooms as if he were crossing a great plain without walls, or were walking on water. Perhaps, at least in part, these were the consequences of the Gardenal that Ida, during the past few days, had secretly resumed giving him. For some months, in fact, Useppe, who in the past had been so docile about medicines, had begun to reject them furiously, and Ida had to use treachery to make him swallow them, dis-guised and mixed with sweets and with nice drinks. But every time, she felt that with this deceit she was offending her son and maiming him, no less than when she used to incarcerate him in the house. And since, after his excursions with Bella, Useppe almost always enjoyed a fine natural sleep at night and woke up alert and lively, she—again deceived—had relaxed and almost stopped the cure: so she now blamed herself for his relapse, for not having followed the Professor's orders.

The idea of going back to him at the hospital frightened her too much; indeed, at the very thought, she was filled with superstitious repug-nance. But that same Thursday, as soon as Useppe seemed able to move, they went to see the lady doctor again. As was to be expected, she scolded Ida for not having obeyed Prof. Marchionni's instructions to the letter. But noting that Useppe, so vivacious the other times, today was motionless, answering her questions irrelevantly, as if under the effect of a stupefying philter, she frowned worse than before. And she advised Ida to give him Gardenal regularly, to be sure, but reducing the dose, to avoid the dangers of asthenia and depression: later, then, it might be a good idea to have another EEG . . . These letters, uttered by the doctor, made mother and child start, together; and the woman, looking at the two of them, shook her head with an almost grim expression. "For that matter," she remarked in a skeptical tone, "an EEG, in the 'intercritical period,' actually explains little or nothing . . ." In reality, she thought that perhaps no science could help Useppe's illness, and she almost had the feeling of deceiving mother and child with her therapeutic suggestions. What disturbed her most, in the child, was the expression of the eyes.

At this point, seeing him fairly suntanned beneath his pallor, she asked the mother if she had sent the child to the sea; and then Ida, blushing all over, confided to her in secret that she was preparing a surprise for him this year: for some time, in fact, she had been laying money aside, to take him to the sea or to the country, in the coming months of July and August. The doctor advised her to choose the country, the hills, in fact, because the sea might make the boy more nervous, in his condition. Then, suddenly, she too for some reason turned all red, like Ida, and began saying that perhaps Useppe's present upsets were probably due to his second teeth . . . When this period was past, the child would naturally be normal again . . . etc., etc.

In conclusion, despite the doctor's usual shrewish manners, Ida came away from the examination with her heart opened to hope. As they were going down in the elevator, she already became animated and couldn't restrain herself from revealing to Useppe the surprise she was preparing for him for full summer; but Useppe, who had also dreamed of "holidays" as a fantastic myth reserved for others, looked at her with his boundless eyes, saying nothing, as if he hadn't even understood her words. Nevertheless, Ida thought she could feel his little hand throb in hers, and this was enough to give her confidence.

Meanwhile, the doctor, looking down from her office window, saw the little couple coming out of the door below. And the sight of that trembling, almost hopping little woman, who looked twenty years older than her age, and of that little child who, on the contrary, at about six, looked less than four, made her suddenly think, with a sort of cruel certitude: "There go two creatures who don't have much longer to live . . ." But, in the case of one of the two, actually, she was mistaken.

. . .

On Saturday, our lady doctor received another phone call from Ida. In her shy, old-woman's voice, always seeming afraid of being a nuisance, the mother informed her that, since yesterday, even the reduced dose of the usual medicine, instead of calming the child, seemed oddly to make him more restless. Shortly after taking it, the boy began to grow nervous, and also at night his sleep had been rather agitated, often interrupted, and sensitive to the slightest sound. It seemed to Ida that the doctor's voice, answering her, sounded upset, and rather hesitant. She advised the mother to reduce the necessary daily dose still further, to the minimum; and to report back to her by Monday. Indeed, here the doctor curtly suggested to Ida they could go together to the Professor if the situation warranted; she herself would take mother and child to the hospital, as soon as the Professor was free to see them . . . but as soon as possible, the beginning of the week . . . This suggestion was received by Ida with incredible gratitude. For some unknown reason, it seemed to her that the old maid's presence would be enough to divest the Professor of the official, shifty hauteur that clothed him, in her eyes, like a uniform, and which so frightened her . . . But at the same time, as the doctor was proposing this urgent visit to her, Ida suddenly had the physical sensation of seeing her at the other end of the phone: in her white jacket, not completely buttoned up, her smooth hair in the untidy, crooked knot, and her big, hollow eyes, frank and impetuous, which now seemed to conceal some obscure diagnosis . . . Ida didn't dare ask any explanation on this point, but she felt the doctor, for her part, was remaining silent out of pity. And even more strangely, Ida thought to recognize in her—who knows why?—a double kinship, with her mother Nora and also with Rossella the cat. She would have liked to hug that old maid tight, like her own mother or grandmother, and say to her: "Help! I'm all alone!" Instead she stammered: "Thank you . . . thank you . . ." "Not at all! That's settled then!" the doctor dismissed her angrily. And the rapid conversation was concluded.

Now the doctor herself, to tell the truth, couldn't have explained what she had seen, that Thursday, in Useppe's gaze. It had been like the reading of an exotic word, which still meant something, irreparable and already distant. The fact is that those little eyes (aware, without knowing it) were saying to everyone, simply, *goodbye*.

. . .

So some may think it is now useless to narrate the rest of Useppe's life, which lasted a little over two days more, since the end is already known. But it doesn't seem useless to me. All lives, really, have the same end: and two days, in the brief passion of a kid like Useppe, are not worth less than years. Allow me, then, to stay a bit longer in the company of my little kid, before coming back alone to the secular life of the others.

The school year was ending, but the teachers had various tasks to perform even after classes were over. And Ida, always tormented by the suspicion she might lose her post for inefficiency, went to school punctually every morning even those days, after she had done her shopping the moment the stores opened. As a rule, the seasonal reduction of her work left her free earlier than usual (so at her return Useppe had just wakened); otherwise, she would rush to the telephone in the secretary's office, at least to hear his voice say: "Hello, who's that?"

On those mornings, she was almost grateful for the bad weather, which, with Useppe's listlessness, relieved her of the odious necessity of double-locking the door. It was clear that, in Useppe's present state, he couldn't be granted his usual freedom to go out; still, she didn't dare put such a prohibition into words: to him it would surely sound like a punishment. Thus, between the two of them, in those days, a tacit understanding existed; and for that matter, Useppe seemed actually frightened to look out of the door; so in the not long journey to the doctor's office, she had had to hold him tight and had felt him tremble.

About three times a day, Bella went out by herself, to deposit her corporal wastes in the street. And Useppe would anxiously stand guard at the kitchen window, to wait for her. Now his waiting didn't last long, because the shepherdess would tend to things dutifully, resisting the street's various temptations; but the moment he saw her reappear down in the courtyard, he would run to the door, pale with emotion, as if she were coming back from some immense expedition.

Starting already on the Friday, after Ida had reduced the doses of the sedative, his little body had regained some of its color and movement, freeing itself from the fog that had oppressed it until the day before. Indeed, in his features and in his skin a constant sensitivity now throbbed, like a minuscule zone of disturbed air. His features and colors were tenderly shaded by it, and his voice sounded more fragile because of it, but more silvery. Now and then he had joyful smiles, full of wonder, like a convalescent after a very long illness. And he had become far more desirous of caresses than usual, staying always close to Ida, acting like a kitten or even like an enamored seducer. He would take her hand and rub it over his face, or else he would kiss her dress, repeating to her: "You love me, mà?" Ida began speaking to him again about their imminent departure for the country. She had asked information of a colleague, who had recommended a stay at Vico, a village not too far from Rome, cool and rich in beautiful woods. There were rooms to be rented reasonably, and there was a lake not far away and a farm that raised horses. "But Bella's coming, too, though!"

Useppe said, worried. "Of course," Ida hastened to assure him, "all three of us are going, on the bus that the hunters take!" He brightened. Then, with the confusion of time that had come over him these days, a little later he began to speak of Vico in the past tense, as of a holiday already finished: "When we were at Vico," he said, with a certain wise animation, "Bella played with the sheep, and ran after the horses and the sea!" (he couldn't be persuaded that at Vico, with everything else, there wasn't also the sea: such a "holiday" without the sea seemed an impossibility to him). "There weren't any wolves there!" he stated. And he laughed, content; however, in his contentment there was already a flavor of legend. It seemed that suddenly in his confused forebodings, Vico had become an unattainable harbor, beyond the seven oceans and the seven mountains.

What the view in his memory was, in these hours, is hard to say. Perhaps it was of the last events before the attack; and of Davide, and of Scimó, and of their fates, he had a vague notion, barely initiated, protected by the semi-darkness. Sunday morning (it was the last Sunday of June) he took his papers and his colored pencils and began to draw. He declared that he wanted to draw snow, and he was upset because the pencils' colors weren't enough for him. "You remember when there was the snow?" Ida said to him, "and everything was white . . ." But he actually became indignant at Ida's ignorance. "Snow," he said, "has lots of colors! lots lots lots lots . . ." he kept repeating again and again, in a sing-song tone. Then, abandoning the subject of snow, he became involved in drawing a scene which, to his eyes, obviously, seemed bustling and varied, because his face accompanied his work with the most diverse expressions: smiling, or frowning and menacing, or biting his tongue. This drawing of his then remained there in the kitchen, but to a profane eye it would seem a tangle of unrecognizable forms.

At that point, the striking of noon, followed by the usual great pealing of bells, upset Useppe excessively and incomprehensibly. Paying no further heed to the drawing, he ran to his mother and, clinging to her, said in an uncertain tone: ". . . is today Sunday?" "Yes, it's Sunday," Ida answered, pleased to hear that he again recognized the days of the week, "you see? I didn't go to school, and for lunch I also bought you some cream puffs . . ." "But I'm not going out, not out, eh, mà?" he almost shouted, in alarm. "No," Ida reassured him, "I'll keep you with me, don't be afraid . . ."

It was immediately after dinner that the weather, cloudy now for several days, broke, with a joyous turbulence. As usual, Ida had gone to lie down on the bed, and from her room, in her first doze, she heard some sound in the entrance hall. "Who is it?" she asked, almost in a dream. "It's Bella," Useppe answered, "she wants to go out." In fact, Bella, as she generally did more or less at this hour, had given the signal of her second obligatory exit, scratching at the front door with some expressive whimpers. The scene, in these past few days, had become habitual, and Useppe seemed to take pride in seeing Bella out and awaiting her return . . . Here Ida, without suspicion, plunged into her heavy afternoon sleep; while Useppe, there in the hall, hesitated at the opened door, unable to decide to close it behind Bella. He had the sensation, in fact, of having overlooked something, or of awaiting something, he didn't know what. Dreamily, then, he went out on the landing and shut the door after him. In his hands he was carrying Bella's leash, which on passing through the hall he had automatically taken from the peg where it normally hung.

From the small window on the landing of the stairs the cool sky-blue wind burst in, chasing the clouds as if it were a little horse frisking. Useppe was seized by a sudden palpitation: not because of the infraction (which he didn't realize at all) but because of the pleasure of living! His sleeping memory promptly emerged again to greet him in the air, but directed backwards, like a flag against the wind. It was unquestionably Sunday: however, not precisely *this* Sunday, another, previous one, perhaps last week's . . . In the afternoon, with the sun, it was just the time to go with Bella to the tree tent . . . Bella had run ahead of him, and he, murmuring confused little words, started off in turn down the stairs. So Useppe set out on his next-to-last enterprise (of the last, which came the next day, I dare not imagine what the departure was like).

The old concierge was napping in her little lodge, sitting with her head on her arms. Bella and Useppe met immediately outside the main door, where Useppe hooked the leash to her collar, according to their familiar rule. Bella, we know, often became a puppy again; and moreover, while she kept a clock in her head, she surely kept no calendar there. She welcomed Useppe with a festive and natural dance, finding herself in immediate agreement with him that this was the time to go to the tree tent; and that in those parts there was a tacit appointment, perhaps since yesterday or the day before, with their friend Scimó. You would have said that Bella, too, in her fervent happiness, counted absolutely on Scimó's presence today in the usual place! But it is further known that, in her, bumpkin ignorance often alternated with a great wisdom: and who knows that today this wisdom wasn't advising her to encourage Useppe in the defensive games of his memory . . . ? In any case, for both of them the grim week just ended seemed temporarily erased from time.

The broken, pursued clouds ran derelict in the advance of a refreshing wind that seemed to fling streets and avenues wide. It was as if, at its passing, immense doors slammed open, all through space, and even beyond the sky. Clouds do not always dim the sky; at times they illuminate it: it depends on their movement and their weight. The sun's zone was totally free, and its glow dug precipices in the nearest clouds and caverns of light, which then broke up, struck by new gusts, of which Useppe heard the splendid din. Then the rays were redoubled, or shattered into so many fragments; and at the clashes, as the erratic masses kindled, they allowed dark tunnels to appear, or galleries decked with strings of lights, little inner rooms aflame with candles, or blue windows which opened and shut. As always at this hour the streets were half-empty, and the passing of the few vehicles and the people's footsteps seemed puffs of breath. It isn't rare for weakened and enervated people to receive from sedatives, especially small doses, a stimulating effect, like that of alcohol. And little Useppe was in a state of vivid and thirst-quenching intoxication, like a torn twig that receives a wetting. His awareness and his memories, along the way, were coming to life again, but only in part. Nature seemed to arrange their order for him in time and space not at random, but according to an intention. So the last week still remained shielded by a screen of shadow; and the memory of Davide, which returned fleetingly to visit him, brought back a Davide *before* last Monday. This memory, still, gave him an obscure sense of laceration; but immediately nature took care to heal this wound. Chatting with Bella along the street, at least a couple of times he tentatively mentioned an appointment they had made with Vàvide . . . But Bella, in agreement with nature, promptly said to him: "No! no! we don't have any appointment with him!" It seems that once, frowning and examining her with suspicion, he insisted stubbornly: "Yes, yes! Don't you know? We have an appointment!" But then Bella started dancing and singing to him, in every possible tone: "Now we're going to see Scimó! To see Scimó!" like a wet-nurse when distracting a baby by saying: "Look, look! There's a cat flying!" and then exploiting the moment to make her charge swallow another nourishing spoonful.

When they reached the bank of the river, the clouds were gathering at the end of the horizon, like a long chain of mountains around the limpid, radiant sky. The ground still hadn't had time to dry out after the rain of the last few days, and even the water of the river was muddied by it, and the whole bank was deserted. At the sight of the water, Useppe instinctively drew back towards the hill; then walking, he heard again in his memory Scimó's promise to teach him how to swim, and, at the same time, the warning that on Sunday the first show at the movies began at three. Perhaps they were already too late to meet Scimó; and Bella confirmed this suspicion of his: it was definitely past three . . . As they were nearing the hut, Useppe had already lost any hope of finding his friend there today.

At their first glance inside the hut, they saw somebody must have visited it in Scimó's absence, looting it and leaving it in disorder. "The

Pirates!" Useppe cried, with extreme agitation. The contents of the mattress, including the camouflaged tunic, were scattered on the ground, near the collapsed sack; and both the alarm and the flashlight had vanished. The candle stub, instead, was still in its place on the stone; and it was further ascertained that the chief treasures, also kept in the mattress, were fortunately safe! Above all, the famous medal of the Giro, in good condition, though without its double wrapping which, anyway, Useppe soon found in the midst of the rags. And also the buckle with the diamonds, and even the colored comb! Useppe retained in his memory a precise count of these possessions. The only one missing, goodness knows why, was the (half) windshield-wiper. The cans of meat, etc., were also gone, but these could easily have been eaten in the meanwhile by Scimó himself.

Sniffing around, with her first-rate detective sense of smell, Bella firmly dismissed the Pirate hypothesis. To judge by the smell, here they were dealing with a single person, perhaps having come in to get out of the rain because, among other things, the place stank of dampness. Other recognizable stinks were: sheep and old age. It must then have been an old shepherd: and obviously a bald one, since he had neglected to take the comb.

Though cross, Useppe smiled with futile relief: such an old man didn't seem too dangerous. And for that matter, the famous band of Pirates would surely not have been content with mere theft, in its terrible attacks! Useppe had never forgotten the list of their misdeeds, as Scimó had enumerated them to him! He carefully started tidying up Scimó's property, flung at random on the ground: he wrapped the medal in its double protection, after having shined it as best he could with the hem of his shirt, and he replaced it with the camouflage tunic and the various objects inside the mattress-cover. Among other things, he came upon the briefs, still wet and stiffened by the dampness. And here, suddenly a suspicion (previously rejected by his thoughts) went through him, like a bitter taste: this hut was now uninhabited. Scimó didn't sleep here any more . . . But at that instant, Bella, busily sniffing the mattress, declared with the self-important tone of a Chief Inspector:

"Very recent odor of Scimó! No more than three hours old! Our friend slept here until noon!!"

Here the reality, alas, was different: so then, either the distraught Bella's scent was deceiving her (something that can happen to any detective, even the most illustrious) or else she was bluffing, or lying outrageously, having guessed Useppe's suspicions. This time, too, the surmise is not impossible: animals, like all outcasts, are occasionally inspired by an almost divine genuis . . . In any event, her pronouncement was enough to reassure Useppe, who immediately laughed, consoled.

It was decided that today Bella would remain on the alert, like an antitheft guard, against any possible attempt on Scimó's property. Meanwhile, when the hut was neat again, the two went off together to the tree tent. The ceiling of air had now become all radiant and clear to the farthest horizon; and Useppe, after hoisting himself effortlessly to his usual branch, had the surprise of hearing many little bird-voices singing the well-known song: "It's a joke a joke all a joke" . . . etc. The strange thing was that the singers' bodies couldn't be seen; and even their voices, though in chorus, sounded almost imperceptible, so they seemed to be whistling the song in his ear, meaning only him to hear it. Confused, Useppe explored the terrain with his eyes lowered: the field, the trunks; then he stared upwards. But down below there was only Bella sniffing the air, and above only flights of swallows could be seen, fleeing in silence. In the end, as happens on occasion when you stare at a sight for a long time, his gaze saw the sky reflect the earth: something like his dream of the previous Saturday, only in reverse. And since he had now forgotten that dream, the sight produced in him a double wonder: of the presence now, and of the unconscious reminiscence. I think there was also a play of certain scientific terms, mysterious to him, which he had heard from Davide the Sunday before: "rain forests, and . . . *nebulas,* no, nebular, and half-submerged . . ." because, reflected in the sky, the earth seemed all a marvelous aquatic vegetation, peopled with wild animals who cavorted everywhere, swimming or hopping among the branches. In the distance, those animals seemed so small they looked like the minnows and the almost microscopic birds sold at fairs in cages or glass bowls; but as his pupils gradually became accustomed to them, Useppe represented in their persons many species of little Ninuccias and nephews of Scimó, more or less as in his forgotten dream. And all of them, truly, made no sounds, or at least the distance prevented him from hearing them; however, like Oriental mimes, they spoke with the movements of their bodies, and their language was not difficult. It isn't actually sure they said: "it's a joke, a joke, all a joke." But undoubtedly the meaning was the same.

The spectacle amused Useppe like a divine tickling; and at the very moment it was vanishing, he invented the following poem:

"The sun is like a big tree
that has nests inside.
And it sounds like a male cicada and like the sea
and it plays with the shadow like a little cat."

At the word *cat* Bella pricked up her ears and gave a humorous bark, interrupting the poem. This, as far as I know, was Useppe's last poem.

After a vision or a mirage, the real dimensions of phenomena may take time to reassert themselves. For an interval, the senses, especially sight and hearing, may expand external effects to an abnormal extent. Suddenly, a terrible explosion of voices reechoed from the shore to Useppe's ears; and his eyes saw a company of giants descend from an enormous ship on the shore.

"The Pirates!" he cried, precipitously hurrying down from his branch, while Bella, in alarm, was already flying ahead of him out of the tree tent towards the hut. Having arrived there, the two stopped, taking positions behind the edge of the hollow, as if in a trench. Bella, eager for the assault, was already emitting some low and menacing growls; but Useppe silenced her with a hiss, remembering that those Pirates, among other things, "killed animals," according to Scimó's report.

It's rather unlikely this was really the famous river gang. From the boat (a kind of old raft with two oars), now tied up among the reeds, about seven or eight males had disembarked, all under fourteen, at least to look at them; and a couple (the most enthusiastic, indeed) were little first-grade kids. None of them seemed to answer the description of the terrible chieftain Agusto; nor was this name heard among the many with which they called one another, shouting. If there was a chief among them, he could perhaps be identified in a skinny half-adolescent, with a grumpy face, named Raf, who seemed, however, to take pride in keeping them all under control, rather than urging them on. He treated them with condescension as if he thought them a bunch of snotnoses. In short, this didn't seem a real band, but only a Sunday boatload of little urchins, beginners: still capable, most of them, of crying if their mothers whacked them!

But for Useppe and Bella, their identity remained certain: they were the notorious Pirates, killers and looters, enemies of Scimó! On guard, with her ears half-erect and her tail taut at the line of her back, Bella felt she had returned to her ancestral origins, when from the far edge of the steppe, towards sunset, the hordes of wolves were awaited!

The sun was now blazing; and the first act of those characters, as soon as they landed, was to undress and take a swim. To the trench, from below, came the racket of their fights, dives, and shouts, which in Useppe's ears were enlarged infinitely. "Stay here!" he kept ordering Bella, his whole body trembling, though he remained standing straight, ready for the signal of the siege, like a barricadiero. It must have been about half past four, when the signal went off, and for him it was as if a great black smoke invaded the little hollows and the wood. The Pirates' voices were coming nearer: "Hey, Piero! Hey, Mariuccio!!" they called one another along the hill, "come here, dammit! Raf! Raaf!" There is no knowing what their intentions were then: perhaps it was the first time they had come swimming in this place, and they simply wanted to explore inland, running around here and there . . . Suddenly, Useppe saw their GIGANTIC forms advancing towards the trench.

"Stay here!" he repeated to Bella, agitated. And at the same time, he ran to a heap of stones Scimó kept near the hut, as a doorstop. "I don't want! I don't want!" he grumbled, arming himself, his face flushed by an access of terrible wrath. And having run up to the top of the hollow, he shouted to the advancing forces, with fury:

"Go 'way! Go 'way!" Then, imitating their own language (which, for that matter, he had long since acquired in his various neighborhoods) he supported his threat, adding with the same ferocious emphasis:

"Bastards! Sonsabitches! Fuckoff!!"

In reality, the effect of that tiny pygmy must have been rather comical, with his red and enraged face, and the two pebbles in his hands, as he presumed to drive a whole band from the scene. And in fact, they really didn't take him seriously; only the youngest of all (about his own age) said to him, snickering, with a superior manner, "What's wrong with you, kid?", while the other little one, who made a pair with him, imitated his sneer. But at that same moment Raf intervened, stopping them halfway across the field:

"Hey, watch out for the dog!"

Coming around, from the bottom of the hollow, Bella had instantaneously appeared to reinforce Useppe; but to tell the truth, it would have been hard to recognize her in the terrifying monster now confronting the band and making it draw back. With her jaws wide and her fierce teeth bared, her big eyes resembling two pieces of volcanic glass, her ears taut in triangles that broadened her brow, she was letting out a low snarl, more fearsome than a howl. And climbing to Useppe's side, there on the trench, she seemed a colossal bulk, such was the violence that swelled the muscles from her chest to her withers to her ready fetlocks, in a fever to attack. "Hey, that animal bites! He's mad!!" voices were heard to exclaim in the troop of tough kids; and one of them, at this point, picked a stone from the ground, or so at least it seemed to Useppe, and advanced threateningly towards Bella. Useppe's face was distraught: "I don't want! I don't want!" he burst out. And furiously he hurled his stones towards the clump of enemies, failing, I believe, to hit anyone.

It's difficult to describe the brawl that followed immediately afterwards, its duration was so brief: actually only a few seconds. We must suppose Bella flung herself forward, and Useppe followed her to defend her; and the *Pirates*, having caught that daring kid in their midst, slammed him around a bit to punish him, maybe hitting him a couple of times. But the strange expression that meanwhile had appeared on his face made one

of them say: "Aw, leave him alone! Can't you see he's simple-minded?!"
And here, suddenly, in the midst of the tumult, an incident took place,
dismaying the little band, which didn't understand its nature. At the point
when the kid, flung around in the gang, opened his eyes wide and let his
jaws sag like an idiot, the dog became miraculously sweet. She seemed to
beseech them all; and she ran towards the kid like a ewe towards the lamb,
transforming her earlier growl into a very soft whimper. Among those
present, she alone, as far as we can understand, was able to recognize the
cry that came from the child's contracted throat, while his body, falling
backwards, rolled down the inside slope of the trench. For the others,
who had no practical experience of certain fits, the obscure event took on
the appearance of a catastrophe. They stood there a moment, looking at
each other, dumbfounded, without the courage to peer over the edge of
the hollow, from which a kind of breathless rattle was heard. A moment
later, when Raf and another of his buddies took a look down, the child,
now that the convulsion stage had passed, was lying immobile, with a dead
face. The dog was circling around him, trying to call him with her little
animal moan. A thread of bloody foam escaped his clenched lips.

They surely must have thought they had killed him. "Let's get out of
here!" Raf said, turning to the others, all white in the face, "we better clear
out fast. Come on, don't act like dopes! Out!" The patter of their flight
towards the landing-place could be heard, and the murmur of their con-
fabulations (Me, what did I do to him? You were the one who hit him
. . . sshhh . . . let's pretend we didn't see . . . don't say a word to
anybody . . .) as they embarked, with the first rustle of the oars. This
time, only Bella was present when Useppe reopened his eyes, without
memory, with his usual faint, spellbound smile. Gradually, from little
changes in his face, you coud observe his passage across the various *thresholds of vigilance,* as the doctors say. Suddenly, he turned his head slightly,
looking to either side with suspicion.

"They're all gone!" Bella announced to him without delay, "there's
nobody here . . ."

"All gone . . ." Useppe repeated, more serene. But in the space of a
breath, quite a different expression appeared on his face. He forced a smile,
which turned out rather a wretched grimace, and said, turning his eyes
away, not looking at Bella:

"I . . . *fell down* . . . didn't I?"

In reply, Bella attempted to distract him with some hasty licks. But he
rejected her, withdrawing himself, and he hid his face behind his arm:

"And now," he moaned, with a sob, "they saw me . . . them too
. . . now . . . they know . . ."

537

He moved, uneasily. Among other things, he realized he had wet himself (a usual effect, common in such convulsive fits). And he was worried by the shameful idea that the Pirates had noticed.

But already his little eyes were blinking, overcome by the drowsiness that always followed the attack. In the little hollow a westerly breeze was blowing, gentle as the breath of a fan, and the afternoon was so limpid that even the lengthened shadow of the hut mirrored the sky's color. On the river, the rustle of the Pirate oars had disappeared into the void; and it was here that Bella let herself go in an exhibitionistic release, celebrating with a great bark the enterprise of the trench, according to her own personal version. To Useppe, who was falling asleep meanwhile, that solitary canine anthem arrived confused, as the violet-blue of the air was confused among the threads of his lashes. And perhaps to him it seemed that a legendary blare was running over the field amid an unfurling of flags.

The ignorance of dogs, truly, is often foolish to the point of mania; and the shepherdess, according to her visionary psychology, was giving, of today's events, the following interpretation:

THE DEFEATED WOLVES HAVE RETREATED IN FLIGHT, ABANDONING THE SIEGE OF THE HUT AND THE ENGAGEMENT ENDED WITH THE SENSATIONAL VICTORY OF USEPPE AND BELLA.

After having barked this news to the four winds, Bella, sated and spent by her emotions, fell asleep in turn, next to Useppe. When she stirred, alerted by her usual natural clock, the sun was much lower in the west. Useppe was sleeping profoundly, as if in the heart of the night, his mouth half-open in a regular respiration, and his pale little face colored with pink towards the cheekbones. "Wake up! It's time to go!" Bella called him; but Useppe barely raised his lids, showing his eyes veiled with sleepiness and rejection, then promptly closed them again.

Bella returned to her urging, though with some remorse. And she insisted, trying also to shake him with her paw, and to tug at his shirt with her teeth. But after having turned over two or three times with an expression of repugnance, in the end he pushed her away, kicking almost frantically: "I don't want! I don't want!" he exclaimed. Then he sank back to sleep.

Bella remained seated there a little while, then she stood on her four paws, torn by a dilemma. On the one hand, a peremptory instinct ordered her to stay here beside Useppe, while, on the other, a no less irremissible determination obliged her to go back home to Ida on time, as she did every evening. It was during this very interval that back in Via Bodoni Ida woke at last from her prolonged sleep.

What had happened to her today was incongruous and unusual: to take such a long afternoon nap. Perhaps it had been the accumulated insomnia of these last nights that had betrayed her. Her sleep had been very profound and, surprisingly, calm, uninterrupted, like a girl's. Only in the last stage did she have a brief dream.

She finds herself in the company of a little kid, outside the gate of a big dock. A large, solitary ship is about to sail, and beyond it spreads an open ocean, absolutely calm and cool, of the charged blue color of morning. Guarding the gate is a man in uniform, very authoritarian, and with a jailer's manner. The kid could be Useppe, and could also not be he; however, it is certainly someone resembling Useppe. She is holding his hand, hesitating at the gate. They are a poor couple, in beggar's clothes, and the guard drives them off because they have no ticket. But then the kid, with his dirty, clumsy little hand, rummages in his pocket and digs out a minuscule gold object, whose nature she can't identify: maybe a small key, or a pebble, or a shell. It must, in any case, be an authentic pass, because the guard, after barely glancing at the kid's hand, promptly, though reluctantly, opens the gate. And then she and the kid, delighted, board the ship together.

This was the end of the dream and here Ida woke. She sensed at once the house's abnormal silence; and finding the rooms deserted, she was overcome by an incoherent panic and rushed down to the door of the building, dressed as she was. As usual, for her afternoon rest, she had stretched out on the bed in her clothes. She was wearing her little housedress, worn and greasy, with sweat-stains under the arms, and she hadn't even combed her hair. On her feet she had hastily slipped her clogs, which made her gait more awkward than usual, and in her pocket she had her change-purse with her keys.

The concierge said she had seen no one go by: true, it being Sunday, she hadn't spent the whole time on duty in her cubbyhole . . . But Ida didn't stop to hear her out, flinging herself at random into the street, and calling Useppe loudly through the neighboring streets, like a wild woman. If anyone questioned her, she answered, with fevered tone and gaze, that she was looking for a little boy who had gone out with a dog; but she rejected all advice or help, resuming her search alone. She had the sure sensation that, in some part of Rome, Useppe was lying in the grip of an attack, perhaps even hurt, perhaps among strangers . . . In reality, for some time now, all Ida's fears were coagulated in a sole terror, situated in the center of her nerves and her reason: that Useppe might *fall*. Every day, in leaving his cage open, she fought an exhausting battle against the *grand mal*: that it might keep far from him, at least in these happy summer flights of his, and not humiliate him among his great honors of a young male at liberty . . . And today, here, Iduzza's extreme fear was coming true: the evil had taken advantage of her sleep, to insult Useppe treacherously.

Outside the neighborhood of the house, the first itinerary that instinctively occurred to her was the route towards the famous *forest* on the river, of which Useppe had so often boasted to her. According to the child's infatuated explanation, it seemed to her that, from Via Marmorata, the path continued along Viale Ostiense, as far as the square of the Basilica . . . And she set off along Via Marmorata with the febrile insensitivity of someone running in a pursuit: so intent on her impulsive direction that the city's movement whistled around her, invisible. She had covered about two-thirds of this street, when, from the end, boisterous and fervent barking greeted her.

Tortured by her own dilemma, Bella had resolved suddenly to make a dash home to call Ida; but in galloping towards Via Bodoni, she felt as if cut in two: for meanwhile she had been forced to leave the little sleeping Useppe all alone in the hollow. Now, this meeting with Ida in the street seemed a downright magical event to her.

Between them there was no explanation. Ida picked up from the ground the leash Bella had dragged after her, and she allowed herself to be led by the dog, in the certainty they were going to Useppe. Naturally, with her crazy, hopping gait, hindered further by the clogs, she was a torment for Bella, and every so often, the dog, in her natural impetuosity, gave her some impatient tugs, as if pulling a cart. Finally, when they reached the uneven terrain along the river, Ida dropped the leash, and Bella began to trot ahead, stopping now and then to wait for her to catch up. Though anxious to arrive, Bella didn't seem sad, but rather lively and encouraging, and so Ida's apprehensions about Useppe's condition were somewhat calmed. Too dazed to distinguish her surroundings, Ida sensed, nevertheless, as she passed them, a kind of luminous spoor, with the prints everywhere of her little son, who had so boasted of these places to her. The hours he had spent here animated the surroundings feverishly, like a flood of colored mirages. And his little laughter and chatter returned to greet her, thanking her, in chorus, for the beautiful days of freedom and trust enjoyed down here . . .

The question: "what will I find, in a little while?" pressed urgently on her nerve centers, weakening her to the point that when the dog urged her to hurry with a bark that clearly meant, "He's here!" she was almost about to fall. After disappearing from her sight for a moment, the dog had climbed back up to summon her from a dip in the ground, and this call, really, sounded triumphant. Leaning over the hole, in her turn, Ida felt her heart open again, because Useppe was standing there, at the entrance of a hut, hailing her appearance with a little smile.

In Bella's absence, in fact, he had waked up, and on finding himself there alone, he had perhaps believed everyone had abandoned him, because you could still sense a certain anxious trepidation in his smile. Moreover, to defend himself against possible invaders or enemies, he had armed himself with a reed, which he grasped firmly in his fist, refusing to let go of it at any price. He seemed more dreamy and unremembering than ever; but a little later (in the present whims of his memory) the Pirates' assault came back to him. He then made a hesitant little search of the hut, and laughed with satisfaction, seeing all was safe: there had been no fires or devastations. Coming home that evening after the cinema and the pizzeria, Scimó would find his little bed ready and waiting for him as usual (the old bald shepherd's thefts could be replaced, later, through the munificence of the arcane Faggots).

With confused and delighted chatter, Useppe displayed his personal satisfactions to his mother. "Don't say anything to anybody, eh, mà!" was all she managed to understand. In the sunset light, the child had rosy-tinged cheeks and blissful, transparent eyes. But on the point of heading home, he displayed a sudden repulsion. "Let's sleep here tonight!" he proposed to his mother, tempting her with that special new seducer's smile of his. And he gave way, resigned, only after Ida's horrified beseeching. It was obvious, however, that in his exhaustion and sleepiness, he couldn't stand on his feet. He was unable to walk by himself, nor did Ida have the muscles to carry him in her arms. In the little purse she was carrying, with her keys, luckily she also kept some change, enough for tram tickets home from San Paolo; but meanwhile they had to reach San Paolo. And here Bella came to their aid, offering the support of her own back to the family.

They walked together, huddled close to one another: Useppe astride Bella as if on a pony, his head leaning against Ida's hip, as she held her arm around him to keep him erect. When they had gone only a few steps, as they were passing the outside of the tree tent, Useppe was already nodding, half-asleep; and it was only here, finally, that he relaxed his grip on the reed and dropped it. The sun was setting, and a company of birds had assembled by appointment up there over the tent, in the top branches. I presume they belonged to the starling family, which has in fact the habit of gathering in family groups towards evening, to hold concerts together. Useppe had never been on the scene at such a late hour, and this great concert was a novelty for him. What he heard of it, in his drowsiness, I can't say; but the surprise must have pleased him, because he uttered a fleeting laugh of amusement. And this evening's concert was, in fact, comical in character: one of the choristers whistled, one warbled, one trilled, one pecked at the air, and then they imitated one another, repeating each other's notes, or else mocking other classes of birds, even the voices of cocks or baby chicks. Such, precisely, is the special virtuosity of starlings. And the Bella-Ida-Useppe group proceeded so slowly that this evening concert followed them a good part of the way, accompanied by the subdued sounds (from grass or river) of early evening.

At San Paolo, Ida and Useppe, with some outside assistance, were hoisted onto the tram, while Bella, with great commitment, ran after the vehicle on foot. Seated amid the crowd, in the twilight, Ida had the impression that Useppe's body, asleep on her lap, had become even more tiny, minute. And suddenly she remembered the first tram journey she had made with him, bringing him home, a newborn infant, from the San Giovanni quarter, residence of the midwife Ezekiel.

Later, also the San Giovanni quarter, like San Lorenzo and the fashionable neighborhoods around Via Veneto, had become a place of fear for her. The universe had become more and more restricted, around Iduzza Ramundo, since the days when her father used to sing *Celeste Aida* to her.

From San Paolo to Testaccio the distance was not long. At every stop, Bella, from outside, assured Ida of her own presence, making some leaps towards the window, almost touching it with her nose. Seeing that nose, the passengers inside, around Ida, laughed. In her race with the tram, Bella won. Ida found her already waiting, festive, at their stop.

The most toilsome journey was the climb up the stairs, floor after floor, until they reached home. The concierge must have been at supper in her back room down below. With her usual shyness, Ida asked no one's help. They proceeded in their ascent, the three of them, clinging together, as they had before along the bank of the Tiber. Useppe asleep, his locks falling in his eyes, allowed himself to be carried, unawares, only uttering a little mumble from time to time. The news broadcast was already over. Through the windows open onto the courtyard a program of popular songs echoed from the radios.

After her long afternoon sleep, Ida remained awake much of the night. The next morning, and also the following day, she was obliged to go to school; then, at last, the real closing-day would come. Meanwhile, however, tomorrow morning it was necessary to consult the doctor again, as agreed, and perhaps to face an examination by Professor Marchionni. Ida knew such an examination repelled little Useppe as much as it did her, and she already felt a double fear of it. She saw herself and Useppe again crossing the hospital corridors, which now became for her a livid and tortuous trail, amid a lunatic bawling; then, like reversing binoculars, she observed in the distance, small as the eye's pupil, the green view of their holiday at Vico; and then again Useppe and herself, hand in hand, confused among the subterranean automata of the EEG . . . But a little later, the uncertain tomorrow was detached from her, like ballast. She found herself suspended in the present, as if this calm night, filled with sweetness, was never to end.

Useppe was sleeping, apparently serene and placid, and so was the dog, lying a pace from him, on the floor. But Ida, not sleepy, delayed going to bed. She was as if spellbound in the position assumed in the early evening, on her knees by the bed, where she rested her head on her arms. And there she remained, her eyes open, watching Useppe breathing in his sleep. There was no moon; in that top floor room, however, the stars' glow was enough to make the sleeper visible, as he rested on his back, his fists relaxed on the pillow, his mouth slightly open. His body, in the bluish-gilded penumbra, still seemed shrunken, doll's size, making almost no outline under the sheet, as in the time of hunger in Via Mastro Giorgio. But tonight, as long as the doll was hers, here in the safety of their room, Ida believed she heard in his breathing the pulse of a time that could not be consumed.

When all the radios were silenced, and the belated midnight traffic had also stopped, you could hear, at intervals, only the clang of the last trams, heading for the car-barn, or the soliloquy of some drunk passing by on the sidewalks. It seemed to Ida, in a kind of reverse vertigo, that these poor sounds became tangled in the thick and silent net of the stars. At a certain point, the night had released our little room in a blind flight, without navigation instruments. And this could be a night of the previous summer, when Useppe didn't yet "fall," and in the next room Ninnarieddu was sleeping.

The darkness was still deep when a city cock, from some roof in the area, raised his precocious cry. A little later, Bella grumbled in her sleep: was she perhaps dreaming of the Pirate-wolves' attack? At the very first glow of dawn, she suddenly sprang up on her paws. And hastily leaving her place in the bedroom, she went to lie down in the hall in front of the door, as if she meant to guard the house against the invasion of some thief or alien. Ida meanwhile had dozed off on the bed for a little while. The first bells could be heard, from the church of Santa Maria Liberatrice.

The day was clear and windless, and it was very hot from early morning. When Ida prepared to leave the house, around eight, Useppe was still sunk in sleep. His hot cheeks, in the calm light of the shutters, seemed to have regained the pink color of health; and his respiration was calm, but his eyes were circled by a little dark halo. Ida delicately moved aside the locks moist with sweat on his forehead, and whispered in a very low voice: "Useppe . . ." The child barely blinked, in a trembling, to show a minimum strip of his blue eyes, and answered:

"mà . . ."

"I'm going out, but I'll be back very soon . . . you wait at home for me, eh? Don't move . . . I'll be right back."

"Ess."

Useppe closed his eyelids again and went back to sleep. Ida tiptoed away. Bella, who meanwhile was flying back and forth from bedroom to entrance to kitchen, silently accompanied her to the door. Ida hesitated an instant, uncertain whether or not to double-lock it from outside, but then she didn't, ashamed to insult Useppe in the dog's presence. Instead, trusting her, she said to her softly: "Wait for me in the house, both of you, eh? Don't go off. I'll be back soon." As she went out, downstairs, she asked the concierge to go up around eleven, to take a look at the boy, if by chance she herself wasn't home by that time.

But little more than an hour had gone by (it must have been about half-past nine) when she was overcome by a kind of unbearable sickness. She was in the Headmistress's office, in a meeting with other teachers, and at first, since certain nervous phenomena were not new to her, she forced herself nevertheless to follow the discussion in progress (it was about summer camps, family certificates, questions of merit and students' rights . . .) until she was convinced, with an almost blinding certitude, that none of this concerned her any longer. She heard the sound of voices around her, and she also heard the words, but in a topsy-turvy dimension, as if those voices were a memory which meanwhile were jumbled with other memories. It seemed to her that outside, under the burning sun, the city was invaded by panic, and people were running for their doorways, at an insistent warning: "it's curfew hour!" and she no longer understood whether it was day or night. Suddenly she had the cruel sensation that, from inside, scratching fingers were clutching at her throat, to strangle her, and in an enormous isolation, she listened to a little distant cry. The strange thing was she didn't recognize that cry. Then the great fog dissolved, and the present scene reappeared to her normally, with the Headmistress at her desk and the teachers seated around her, discussing. They, meanwhile, had noticed nothing: in fact, Ida had simply turned pale.

A few minutes later, the same sensation, already experienced, came over her again, identical: once more the scratching nails, strangling her, the absence, and the cry. It seemed to her that this cry, really, belonged only to herself: a hollow moan of her lungs. In passing, it left in her a mark of physical offense, like a mutilation. And in her clouded consciousness, tattered shreds of memory flapped together: the young German soldier in Via dei Volsci, stretched out upon her, in orgasm . . . herself a child, in the country with her grandparents, in the courtyard where a nanny-goat's throat was being cut, for Sunday dinner . . . Then all was scattered in disorder, as the fog faded. In the course of perhaps a quarter of an hour, the thing was repeated twice more. Suddenly Ida rose from her chair, and stammering some incoherent excuse, she ran to the secretary's little office, deserted today, and called home.

This was not the first time that, at her call, for one reason or another, the familiar little voice of Via Bodoni delayed replying. But today, the futile rings at the other end of the wire came to her as a signal of rebellion and invasion, ordering her to rush home urgently. She let the receiver fall from her hands, not thinking to hang up. And without even looking into the head's office, she started down the steps towards the door below. Again, halfway down the steps, she was overtaken by that strange repeated spasm, but the interior cry that accompanied it, this time, was more like an echo: and it brought her an obscure hint of its own source which it answered, stark, retarded. The fog, too, which had stopped her halfway down the stairs, this time dissolved immediately, clearing her path.

In the entrance, the school porter shouted something after her: in fact, as usual, Ida had left in his care her bag with the shopping, already done before working hours. She saw him shift and move his lips, but she didn't hear his voice. In reply, she waved her hand in a vague gesture, which seemed a kind of greeting. She made the same gesture to the old concierge of Via Bodoni, who laughed and nodded as she went by, pleased to see her coming home so soon.

In the brief distance from school to home, Ida had been excluded, really, from external sounds, because she was listening to another sound, like something she hadn't heard since her last walk in the Ghetto. It was, again, a kind of cadenced dirge which called from below, and summed up, in its tempting sweetness, something bloody and terrible, as if it were calling towards scattered points of misery and toil, summoning the flocks inside for the evening. Then, as soon as she came into the second courtyard, the real voices of the morning assailed her again, with radio sounds from the windows. She avoided looking up at her own kitchen window, where Useppe, in the days of his domestic imprisonment, usually waited for her, behind the pane. In fact, almost absurdly, she was still hoping she would see, if she looked up today, that familiar little form. And she was also trying to elude the certainty that, instead, today the window was empty.

While she started up the stairs, from the top floor, she heard the sound of her own telephone, which had gone on ringing since she herself had called the number a few minutes earlier in the school office, without hanging up. But when she arrived at the last landing, the stupid signal fell silent.

Then, beyond the door, she heard a painful weak voice, like a little girl crying. It was Bella's whimper; in her own solitary lament, she didn't even react at hearing the familiar footsteps coming up the last flight. Here Ida started, seeing a grim figure facing her, menacingly, but in reality, it was only a stain on the stairway wall, flaking and damp because of the water-tanks nearby. That stain had been there ever since they had lived in the building; but till today Ida had never even noticed such a terrible presence.

In the dark little entrance hall, Useppe's body was lying, arms flung out, as always in his falls. He was fully dressed, except for his sandals, which, unfastened, had dropped from his feet. Had he perhaps, seeing the fine sunny morning, insisted on going again today with Bella to their *forest?* He was still warm, and just beginning to grow rigid; Ida, however, absolutely refused to comprehend the truth. Denying the earlier premonitions received by her senses, now, in the face of the impossible, her will withdrew, making her believe he had only *fallen* (during this last hour of his incredible battle with the *grand mal*, there in the hall, Useppe had really fallen again and again, in one attack after the other, almost without respite . . .). And after having carried him to the bed, she stayed there, bent over him, waiting for him to raise his eyelids in that usual, special smile of his. Only belatedly, when her eyes met Bella's, did she understand. The dog, in fact, was there looking at her with a mourning melancholy, filled with animal compassion and also with superhuman commiseration: saying to the woman: "What are you waiting for, you wretched creature? Don't you realize we have nothing now to wait for?"

Ida tried the stimulus of shouting; but she fell mute, thinking immediately: "If I shout, they'll hear me, and they'll come to take him away from me . . ." She bent threateningly towards the dog: "ssh . . ." she whispered to her, "hush, we mustn't let them hear us . . ." And after having drawn the chain in the entrance, she began to run about the rooms in silence, bumping against the furniture and the walls with such violence that there were bruises all over her body. It is said that in certain crucial states people see all the scenes of their life pass before them at incredible speed. Now in the dull and immature mind of that little woman, as she ran wildly around her small home, the scenes of the human story (History) also revolved, which she perceived as the multiple coils of an interminable murder. And today the last to be murdered was her little bastard Useppe. All History and all the nations of the earth had agreed on this end: the slaughter of the child Useppe Ramundo. She landed in the bedroom again and sat on the chair by the bed, in Bella's company, to look at the kid. Now, beneath his clenched lids, his eyes seemed to dig into his head, deeper and deeper with every passing moment; but still, among his tousled locks, his single, central tuft could be recognized, the one that would never lie flat with the others and stood there in the middle, erect . . . Ida began moaning in a very low, bestial voice: she no longer wanted to belong to the human race. And meanwhile she was surprised by a new auditory hallucination: tick tick tick was heard all over the floor of the house. Tick tick tick, Useppe's footsteps, the past autumn, when he was constantly walking up and down, all through the place, in his little boots, after the death of Ninnuzzu . . . Ida began silently swaying her whitened head; and here the miracle occurred to her. The smile, which she had awaited uselessly in Useppe's face, appeared to her on her own. It wasn't very different, to see it, from the smile of calm and of wondrous ingenuousness, which came to her in her infancy after her hysterical attacks. But today it wasn't hysteria: her reason, which had always had to struggle to maintain its hold in her inept and frightened brain, had finally let go.

The next day the news report appeared in the papers: *Pathetic drama in the Testaccio quarter—Crazed mother watching over little son's corpse.* And at the end you could read: *It was necessary to destroy the dog.* This last detail—easy to understand—referred to our shepherdess. In fact, as could have been foreseen, Bella displayed a bloody ferocity, capable of anything, against the strangers who, having forced the door, came into the little Via Bodoni home to perform their legal duties. She absolutely refused to allow them to take Useppe and Ida from the house. We may note at this point that sterilized animals, according to what people say, usually lose their aggressiveness; but Bella, obviously, at least for the moment, contradicted this physiological law. Her defense yesterday against the river pirates was nothing compared to her war today against the new intruders. Alone, she managed to frighten a squad of enemies, at least two of whom were armed with ordnance weapons. No one had the courage to face her directly. And so she kept her word, given Useppe the day of her return home: "They'll never be able to separate us, in this world."

At the shot which killed the dog, Ida's head gave a brief jerk: and this, apparently, was the last stimulus to which the woman reacted as long as she remained alive. Her existence was to last more than nine years afterwards. In the ledgers of the hospital, where she was taken that same day, never to leave it till the end, her decease is dated 11 December 1956. She apparently died of pulmonary complications after an ordinary attack of fever. She was fifty-three years old.

From the information I have been able to gather, it seems she remained frozen in the same attitude from the first day to the last of those nine and more years: the same pose in which they had found her when, breaking down the door, they had taken her by surprise that late June day in Via Bodoni. She was seated, her hands clasped in her lap, moving them every now and then, entwining her fingers as if to play; and in her face there was the luminous and bewildered stupor of someone who has just waked and doesn't yet recognize the things he is seeing. If you spoke to her, she had an innocent and meek smile, full of serenity and almost of gratitude; but it was useless to expect any answer from her. Indeed, she seemed hardly to perceive voices, understanding no language, perhaps distinguishing no words. At times, in a dreamy murmur, she would repeat some vague syllables to herself, which seemed to belong to a forgotten language, or the language of a dream. With the blind, with deaf-mutes, it is possible to communicate; but with her, who was not blind or deaf or dumb, there was no possible communication.

I believe, really, that the little senile figure, whose peaceful smile is still remembered by some in the raving wards of the Asylum, survived those nine years and more only for the others, that is, according to others' time. Like the advance of a reflection, which, from its ridiculous, small point, is multiplied in more and more mirrors, over a distance, the duration of nine of our years was barely the space of a heartbeat for her. She too, like the famous Lesser Panda of legend, was suspended at the top of a tree where temporal charters were no longer in effect. She, in reality, had died with her little Useppe (like his other mother, the Maremma shepherdess). With that Monday in June 1947, the poor history of Iduzza Ramundo was ended.

Muerto niño, muerto mio.
Nadie nos siente en la tierra
donde haces caliente el frio.
MIGUEL HERNANDEZ

19 - -

In Italy, the series of crimes organized by landowners in the South against peasants and farm-workers and their associations continues (in two years, 36 union organizers are killed).—In Rome, attempted assassination of Togliatti.—Martial law and violent repressions in Greece (152 guerrillas executed).—Mahatma Gandhi assassinated in New Delhi by a right-wing extremist.—In Palestine, the Jews found the republic of Israel and defeat the Arab League.—In South Africa, the National Front controls the government and initiates the policy of racial segregation of the blacks.—The cold war between the Powers of the two blocs is exacerbated. The dispute over the fate of Germany continues. Accesses to West Berlin blocked by the USSR, thus preventing supplies reaching the Allied sectors of the capital. Airlift established by the Allies to continue flow of supplies. Intensive mobilization in the USSR.—The armament race goes on, incessant, and so does underground activity surrounding the nuclear secret. The technology of ballistic missiles is perfected.

About twenty years after the beginning of the civil war in China, definitive victory of the Red army. Mao Tse-tung and the other Communist leaders enter Peking. The Nationalist leaders flee to Formosa.—The Western Powers with the nations of their bloc (including Italy) sign a military alliance known as the Atlantic Pact (NATO).—First Soviet atomic experiment.—With the breaking of the American atomic secret, a new stage in the armament race begins. The Major Powers, with the total and progressive employment of their sciences and their industries, dedicate themselves mainly to the increase of their stockpile of bombs (proliferation of nuclear weapons). This competition will take the name of balance of deterrents or of terror. In it, the two leading possessors of Power in the world (United States and USSR) will spend a great part of their enormous resources of wealth and labor.—It is calculated that in the poor countries of the globe the number of deaths from starvation is 40 million annually.

Beginning of the Korean war between the people's forces in the North and the government forces in the South, supported by the United States. President Truman declares a state of national emergency.—In Vietnam the conflict continues between the French and the Vietminh partisans, led by General Giap.

General mobilization in Vietnam.—Development of strategic atomic artillery in the United States . . . . .

On the Korean front, American air raid at Pyongyang, with the death of six thousand civilians.—Reciprocal commitment of France and the United States against Communism in Indochina.—On the island of Cuba

(Central America) the Batista dictatorship is established, with the support of the USA.—Violent anti-Semitic campaign in the USSR with the elimination of many Jews, mostly intellectuals. The entire Soviet population held by Stalin under a paroxysmic regime of persecution and terror.—Experimental explosion of the first British atomic bomb and the first American hydrogen bomb (H-bomb).

In USA debate concerning the possible use of the atomic bomb in Korea.—In USSR death of Generalissimo Stalin.—Conflict in Egypt between British and Egyptians, who demand the evacuation of the Suez Canal zone.—With an armistice, sanctioning the division of the country, the end of the war in Korea, which cost the two sides a total of about three million lives.—In the USSR, leaders of the Stalin period sentenced to death. First testing of the Soviet H-bomb.

French capitulation in Vietnam.—In Guatemala, with US support, a dictatorship is established, with the assassination of five thousand leaders of the people and the return of the lands to landowners.—In the United States production of the latest type of H-bomb, which releases 15 megatons of energy (equaling fifteen million tons of TNT), 750 times more powerful than the bomb dropped on Hiroshima.—Repression by French colonialists in Tunisia and Algeria, in revolt.

State of emergency in Algeria.—USSR declares the end of the war with Germany, now divided into two Republics: the German Federal Republic (Western bloc) and the German Democratic Republic (Eastern bloc). Still no solution to the question of Berlin, situated physically inside the Eastern territory, and politically divided between the two opposing blocs. Constant flight of Berliners from the Eastern sector to the Western.—The army of the German Federal Republic is officially formed.—In opposition to the military Pact of the Western bloc (NATO), the countries of the Eastern bloc sign a military alliance of their own (Warsaw Pact).—USA tests the first underwater atomic bomb.—USSR carries out the first experimental dropping of an H-bomb from a plane . . . . .

. . . . . *1956–1957–1958–1959–1960–1961*

The battle of Algiers against the French begins.—At the Twentieth Party Congress in the USSR, Khrushchev denounces the late Stalin's reign of terror. Destalinization begins.—Revolt in Hungary, put down by Soviet military intervention.—Suez crisis. Egypt closes the Canal, blocking the flow of emigrants and Jewish refugees from every part of the world towards Israel. Victorious attack of Israel against Egypt. Military action of the French and British who try to occupy the Canal, bombing Egyptian territory. Threats of Soviet intervention and withdrawal of the Franco-British forces.—In Cuba, guerrilla war led by Fidel Castro against the Batista dictatorship.

In Indochina, finally evacuated by the French, the struggle for liberation begins, with the Communist partisans, followers of Ho Chi Minh (president of North Vietnam) against a dictatorial government established in South Vietnam under American protection.—Experimental explosion of the first British H-bomb.—USA and USSR produce intercontinental ballistic missiles with nuclear warheads, capable of reaching any part of the globe.

No agreement among the Powers on the city of Berlin.—In Cuba, triumphant victory of Fidel Castro's revolutionaries and flight of the dictator Batista.—Political and ideological differences begin to be evident between the two major Communist Powers (Soviet Union and People's Republic of China).—Clashes on the China-India frontier.—Insurrection movements in the Belgian Congo, under the leadership of Patrice Lumumba. The Belgians abandon the colony. Fighting and disorder throughout the country.

Demonstrations in Italy against the recently established government, neo-Fascist in tendency. Police attack demonstrators; dead and wounded in the whole country. Resignation of the government.—First French atomic bomb tested.—Heightening of the dissension between Communist China and Soviet Union.—In Germany, a process is invented (State secret) for the production of atomic weapons also by countries without means.—Chaos in the Congo. Lumumba assassinated.—In Algeria the struggle for independence continues, with fierce repression from the French colonialists. —Anti-Castro attack on Cuba, with the landing of an expeditionary force at the Bay of Pigs and bombing of the capital. The attack is repelled.—In Moscow, the Chinese delegates, in protest, abandon the USSR Party Congress.—In East Berlin (Soviet sector) construction of a fortified wall along the border with West Berlin. Eastern sector closed to West Berliners. Commuting forbidden to East Berlin residents employed in the Western sector. East Berliners prohibited from going to the West. Orders to shoot on sight at any attempt at infraction.—In Vietnam, opposition to the dictatorship continues. Useless methods of repression adopted by the Government (the peasant population, habitual accomplice of the partisans, is segregated in fortified villages, etc.).—In the advanced nations, the progressive and colossal development of industry expands, devouring the best energies and concentrating all powers in itself. Instead of serving man, machines enslave him. Working for industries and buying their products become the essential functions of the human community. The proliferation of arms is accompanied by the proliferation of ridiculous consumer goods, promptly outdated because of the market's requirements. Artificial products (plastic) alien to

553

the biological cycle transform land and sea into a deposit of indestructible refuse. In the world's countries, more and more, the industrial cancer spreads, poisoning air, water, and organisms, besieging and devastating built-up areas, as it deforms and destroys the men condemned to the assembly-lines inside the factories. For the systematic indoctrination of maneuverable masses in the service of the industrial powers, popular media of communication (newspapers, magazines, radio, television) are used to spread and propagandize an inferior "culture," servile and degrading, which corrupts human judgment and creativity, blocking all real motivation of existence, and unleashing morbid collective phenomena (violence, mental illness, drugs).—With the exclusive fever of earning and consuming a temporary period of economic boom in various nations, Italy among them.—Economic-industrial competition with America on the part of the rival USSR, where heavy industry is still favored.—After political differences, the USSR withdraws its technical advisers from China, suspending 178 industrial projects in that country.—Further Soviet experiments with nuclear weapons: explosion of a super-bomb, its energy equal to about 100 million tons of TNT (five thousand times more powerful than the Hiroshima bomb).—According to the latest calculations, expenditures for armaments throughout the world amount to about 330 million dollars a day . . . . .

. 1962–1963–1964–1965–1966–1967

Victory of the forces of liberation in Algeria.—Conflict between Catholics and Protestants in Ireland.—Installation of Soviet missile bases in Cuba and consequent blockade of the Soviet fleet by the United States (Cuba crisis). Dismantling of the bases by the USSR.—Encyclical "Pacem in terris" by Pope John XXIII.—Death of John XXIII.—In Vietnam, partisan offensives and Government repression continue. In protest against the dictatorship, some Buddhists burn themselves alive.—Border skirmishes between Algeria and Morocco.—In Dallas, John Kennedy, President of the United States, assassinated.—Open break between Communist China and the Soviet Communist Party.—Military coup d'état in Vietnam, with the support of the United States, which intervenes with massive bombing in North Vietnam.—China tests its first atomic bomb.—The United States proceeds with its escalation against Vietnam, in which the strategy of total war is followed, with the three alls (kill all, burn all, destroy all). New scientific technologies for the anti-personnel bombs (capable of freeing in a single explosion millions of steel pellets with mortal effect), herbicides and chemical defoliants for the total destruction of vegetation and nature, etc.—Military coup in Algeria.—Military coup in Indonesia. Communism outlawed. Half a million Communists killed.—Subterranean atomic experiments in USA and USSR.—Intensive industrialization continues and expands, promoted by Eastern and Western Powers.—Whole populations killed by famine in the countries of the Third World.—American escalation goes on. Three thousand six hundred twenty one aerial bombardments in Vietnam in a six months' period, the United States declares.—In Greece, army officers seize power and suspend the constitution. Mass deportations and arrests . . . . .

. . . . . and History continues . . . . .

All the seeds failed, except one.
I don't know what it is, but it is
probably a flower and not a weed.

(Prisoner no. 7047 in the Penitentiary of Turi)

THE END

NOTES

AUTHOR'S NOTES

page v. The verse, placed here as dedication, is from a poem by César Vallejo.

page 125. Pitchipoi: this name was apparently invented in the camp of Drancy by Jewish children awaiting deportation, to signify the mysterious land towards which the trains of deportees set out. (cf. Poliakov, *Nazism and the Extermination of the Jews.*)

page 125. water for death: part of the funeral rites of the Jewish faith.

page 209. Reschut means: *run away.*

page 327. macère: in Ciociaria this is the name given to the terraces where flax is cultivated.

page 334. "a page of glory in our History": this is Himmler's definition of the "final solution" in an address to the SS generals at Poznan, 4 October 1943.

page 494. ZYKLON B: for those who do not know, this is a chemical compound used by the Nazis for extermination in the gas chambers.

As far as the bibliography of the Second World War is concerned, since it is obviously vast, I can only refer readers to some of the many accounts everywhere available on the subject. Here I must limit myself to mentioning—also by way of thanks—the following authors who, with their documentation and testimony, have given me some (real) suggestions for some (invented) individual episodes in the novel: Giacomo Debenedetti (*16 ottobre 1943*, II Saggiatore, Milan, 1959); Robert Katz (*Black Sabbath*, Macmillan, Toronto 1969); Pino Levi Cavaglione (*Guerriglia nei Castelli Romani*, Einaudi, Rome, 1945); Bruno Piazza (*Perché gli altri dimenticano*, Feltrinelli, Milan, 1956); Nuto Revelli (*La strada del Davai*, Einaudi, Turin, 1966, and *L'Ultimo fronte*, Einaudi, Turin, 1971).

TRANSLATOR'S NOTES

page 114. Lazio and *Roma* are the two professional football (soccer) teams of Rome. They are bitter rivals, and their fans have always been prone to heated, even violent argument.

page 130. Negus was a term well-known also in the US at the time. Here it is an insult because it refers to Nino's outlandish getup.

page 141. Morra. A game for two or more players in which each participant throws a number of fingers in his right hand while simultaneously calling out a number. The player to call the correct number of total fingers wins.

page 174 ff. The reversed name order, placing the surname before the first name (as here in Vivaldi Carlo), is a European usage that generally means the tone is either official or working-class or peasant. Thus when Eppetondo presents himself as Cucchiarelli Giuseppe it shows he is working-class. The author uses the form frequently—especially in the case of Vivaldi Carlo—to indicate how others think of the person in question.

page 180. Castelli. The Castelli Romani are a group of towns scattered over the Alban hills south of Rome. As the name suggests, they were the sites of castles of Popes and Roman patrician families. There are more than a dozen Castelli, including Frascati, Albano, Castel Gandolfo, Nemi, etc.

page 225. PAI. Polizia Africa Italiana. A military police force set up by the Fascists originally for their African territories, but functioning also later in Rome, where its members collaborated actively with the Nazis. See also pages 286–87.

page 304. Segnorine. GI's in Italy in 1943–4 used to accost young women, saying "Segnorina" (mispronouncing "Signorina"). Among Italians the mispronunciation soon came to mean prostitute or, more specifically, a girl who went with the Allied soldiers.

page 506. Seneghin seneghin: a disparaging term for Jew in the dialect of the region of Emilia, used at the turn of the century.

A NOTE ON THE TYPE

*This book was set in Electra, a type face
designed by W(illiam) A(ddison) Dwiggins for
the Mergenthaler Linotype Company and first
made available in 1935. Electra cannot be
classified as either "modern" or "old-style." It
is not based on any historical model, and
hence does not echo any particular period or
style of type design. It avoids the extreme
contrast between thick and thin elements that
marks most modern faces, and is without
eccentricities that catch the eye and interfere
with reading. In general, Electra is a simple,
readable type face that attempts to give a feeling
of fluidity, power, and speed.*

*W. A. Dwiggins (1880–1956) began an
association with the Mergenthaler Linotype
Company in 1929 and over the next twenty-
seven years designed a number of book types,
which include the Metro series, Electra,
Caledonia, Eldorado, and Falcon.*

*The book was composed, printed, and
bound by American Book–Stratford Press,
Saddle Brook, New Jersey.
Typography and binding design
by Cynthia Krupat.*